Windfall

Also by Penny Vincenzi

Old Sins
Wicked Pleasures
An Outrageous Affair
Another Woman
Forbidden Places
The Dilemma
The Glimpses (short stories)

Windfall

Penny
Vincenzi

ORION

Copyright © Penny Vincenzi 1997
All rights reserved

First published in Great Britain in 1997 by
Orion
An imprint of Orion Books Ltd
Orion House, 5 Upper St Martin's Lane, London WC2H 9EA

A CIP catalogue record for this book is available
from the British Library

ISBN 0 75280 086 8 (hardcover)

Typeset by Deltatype Limited, Birkenhead, Merseyside

Printed in Great Britain by
Clays Ltd, St Ives plc.

For Emily and Claudia with much love.

And gratitude for everything, especially
for their inspiration over the coffee . . .

ACKNOWLEDGMENTS

Windfall has been a particular joy to write; but I am very aware that I do owe many thanks (as always) to a great many people for the help, guidance information and quite often inspirational advice that has been given (as always) so generously; and it is not an exaggeration to say that without the following, the book could quite literally not have been written.

Peter Townend; Felicity Green; Adrienne Spanier; Pierre Barillet; Ursula Lloyd; Noni and Roger Holland; Sir Peter Bristow; Dr Oliver Scott; Sue Stapely; John Lovatt; Peggy Doughty. Some particularly tumultuous applause for Gwendolyn Sparkes, Athena Crosse and Angela Fox for bringing the twenties and thirties, in all their gossipy glamour, most wonderfully alive; for Dr Joan Waters for a unique and extraordinary insight into the life of the medical student and young doctor at that time; and John Granger of the Brooklands Museum for his encyclopaedic knowledge and tireless enthusiasm. I have found several books quite invaluable: most notably *Edward VIII: The Road to Abdication* by Frances Donaldson, and *Elizabeth's Britain* by Philip Ziegler.

And at home, huge and heartfelt thanks to Carol Osborne for continuing to create calm and cheerful order out of frequently dreadful chaos.

I have also been – as always – wonderfully published by Orion; I'd like to thank particularly Rosie Cheetham, editor extraordinaire, for many inspiring things, but perhaps most importantly for that most crucial quality in an editor, appreciativeness, and of course a steely self-control in never, ever mentioning the l (for late) – word; Susan Lamb for unfailing emotional and practical support; Claire Hegarty for yet another glorious cover; Louise Page for yet more splendid publicity; Richard Hussey for supervising the production with tireless calm; Dallas Manderson, Jo Carpenter, and the rest of the sales team for getting the book Out There. And of course Desmond Elliott, so much more than agent, rather wise and witty companion and friend.

And finally, as always, my family, and in particular my husband Paul, so tirelessly and soothingly supportive through yet another long year.

Penny Vincenzi
London, August 1997

CHAPTER I

JUNE 1935

Cassia Fallon was scrubbing the altar steps when she heard that she had inherited half a million pounds. She often thought afterwards, given the storybook nature of the whole thing, that it could not have been more auspicious; had she been doing one of the other things that typically filled her life – like bathing her children, or tending to her garden, or presiding over her dinner table, or seeing to the rota for the Women's Institute, or taking one of the hundreds of phone calls that came into her house every week, requesting her husband's presence at some sickbed or other – then it would not have made nearly so poignant a story. However, the juxtaposition of those two events, being down on her knees, scrubbing stone steps, for heaven's sake, and hearing that she had suddenly become extremely rich: that was really very intriguing indeed, worthy of the highest drama.

Of course it hadn't been quite as dramatic as she afterwards remembered it: Edward had simply arrived at the church with her godmother's solicitor, Mr Brewster, who had been very agitated to find her not at the house, given the importance of the news he had to impart. She had in fact arranged for him to come, only she had forgotten, or rather had got the wrong day, and Edward, irritated by her inefficiency as usual, had brought Mr Brewster down to see her.

'Mr Brewster said it was vital he spoke to you himself, showed you the will, in fact. He's come all the way from London. I do think it's too bad of you to have forgotten,' Edward said.

Cassia stopped her work and apologised, and went to sit in the church porch with Edward and Mr Brewster. He was an extraordinarily dull-looking caricature of a solicitor, dressed in a dark grey suit, dark grey tie, black bowler, and carrying a rather battered black briefcase. His voice was equally dull, monotonous and slightly whining, but Cassia listened to it attentively while he read her the relevant section of the will, and explained it to her carefully – aloud. And when he had finished, when she had heard the extraordinary words, when she had told him that yes, she did understand, and asked him if there was anything she should do immediately, and he had said there was not, she asked if he would mind if she just finished washing the steps. Mr Brewster, who had clearly long ceased to be amazed by any human behaviour, however eccentric, said that of course he would not, but Edward followed her down the aisle and stood over her as she started wringing out the cloth again.

'You did realise what he said, didn't you?' Edward said. Cassia sat back on her heels and studied him, the wet cloth oozing soapily out on to the cold steps. 'I mean the amount. You did hear him?'

'Yes. Yes, of course I did. Thank you.'

'Right. I just wondered. Your reaction does seem a little … odd.'

'I'm sorry, Edward. What did you think I should do?' she said, smiling at him. 'Burst into song, or perhaps utter a fervent prayer of thanks?'

'No, of course not,' Edward said irritably. 'You just seem so calm. I … well, I don't feel very calm, I must say.'

'Sorry,' Cassia said, not quite sure for what.

'And I do think you should come back to the house.'

'Is there any huge hurry? I mean I ought to finish this. Really. If you take Mr Brewster back and ask Peggy to give him a cup of tea, I'll be back very soon.'

Edward stared at her in silence again, then pulled out his handkerchief and blew his nose. He always did that when he didn't know how to react. 'Cassia,' he said, 'I really do wonder if you've actually grasped—'

'Edward, I've grasped it perfectly. Thank you. As perfectly as I could be expected to. I've been left half a million pounds. By my godmother. But it's not going to go away, I don't suppose, and Mrs Venables will be furious if I leave this all messy and unfinished now. There's a wedding tomorrow. And as Mr Brewster's come all this way anyway, I'm sure he won't mind waiting another ten minutes or so.'

'Yes,' Edward said, staring at her, as if he wasn't quite sure who she was any more – rather accurately as it happened. 'Yes, all right.' Then he turned his back on her and walked rather quickly back to the porch. She heard him talking to Mr Brewster, and then their footsteps slowly fading away as they walked down the path.

Cassia squeezed out the cloth, and wiped the steps very carefully, making sure there were no streaks left on them, then she carried the dirty soapy water out into the vestry and tipped it down the sink.

Mr Ball, the verger, was there, tidying up the choirboys' cassocks. He nodded at her. 'Afternoon, Mrs Fallon. Lovely day. Oh, they are naughty, these lads. Know perfectly well they've got a wedding tomorrow, made no effort at all to put these away tidy. I blame the mothers, of course. They've got no discipline these days, have they? All this modern nonsense, let them do what they want, whenever they want to—'

'Well, Mr Ball,' Cassia said, 'it's quite hard, making little boys do what they're told. Especially if you're not there with them all the time. I should know.'

'Well, we did, when we were lads, that's all I can say. Terrified of our mother, we were—'

'Good for her,' said Cassia, 'she was obviously a fine woman. Now look, Mr Ball, I'm off now. I've done the steps and the porch, and Mrs Venables will be in shortly to do the flowers. Can you tell her we've got absolutely masses of roses in our garden if she wants some more for tomorrow? I'm going back there now.'

It was a lovely day; an appropriately lovely day, she thought, as she walked slowly back to the house, and then thought how silly that she should expect the weather to fit in with her extraordinary news. If it had been an unseasonably horrible day – or seasonally perhaps, given that this was June and England – wet and windy, that might have seemed quite appropriate too, for she could tell herself they could all go somewhere warm and sunny for a holiday, to the south of France for instance, and that might even be rather better.

Cassia wondered why she didn't feel more odd; she was sure she ought to. Maybe she was in shock; shock did strange things to people. When she had worked in Casualty, she had seen people quite literally with their fingers or toes cut off, sitting calmly waiting for the doctor to do something, discussing the weather with whoever was sitting on the next chair. On the other hand, she didn't feel as if it had been a shock, and nor did she feel it couldn't be true, or that there had been a mistake.

The nearest she could get to defining how she felt, finding something to compare it with, was ... what? When she heard she had passed her finals with exceptionally high marks? No, because that had been down to her, a result of her own work and cleverness. When Edward had asked her to marry him? Or rather told his father she was going to marry him? No, because that had been a rather more complex state of affairs. When Bertie was born? Or even William? No, that had been a pure wild happiness, nothing to do with this rather calm, warm acceptance. Perhaps, though, when they had told her Delia was a girl. A nice quiet little girl, she had thought, smiling up at them through the clearing pain, a contrast to the awful, noisy, lovable little boys. That had been a sense of simple straightforward pleasure (not knowing, of course, that Delia was to be the noisest of the lot). That was nearer, more like it, but it did seem rather awful to compare the arrival of a much longed for daughter with that of a large sum of money.

Cassia gave up. This wasn't like anything she had ever known, and how could it be? She didn't feel anything really, anything at all. Not yet.

It was a very nice walk from St Mary's to their house: Monks Ridge House it was called, being built high on the ridge above the village of Monks Heath, with its view right over the small valley, of the winding river, the tight complex of houses round the picture-book green, the church set at the back of it. Square, redbrick early Victorian, it was a classic West Sussex country house, with a very dark slate roof and an exceptionally pretty fanlight over the front door. However tired Cassia was, however discouraged by her failure to perform as the perfect doctor's wife, however cross or anxious over her unruly children, her heart lifted as she turned the last corner in the lane and looked at Monks Ridge. It was like seeing a friend standing there, waiting for her, uncritical, undemanding, pleased to see her. There was so much that was critical and demanding in her life, she found the house extraordinarily soothing.

Cassia had loved it from the first moment she had set eyes on it. Edward had been less certain, had said they should look at others, further afield, but she had known this was the house she wanted. You move in here, it seemed to say, and you won't get any trouble. And they hadn't. It was warm in winter, cool in summer; its pipes never froze, its fires lit and burnt beautifully; its rooms were neither too large nor too small, its garden good tempered and undemanding.

There was a large extension at the side, not beautiful, but not ugly either, added in the last year of the old queen's reign, which made a perfect surgery for Edward, and at the back, beyond the dining room, a small conservatory with black and white tiled floor and arched windows, where Cassia had managed to grow and train a vine, and where on summer nights when she couldn't sleep (usually because she was trying to soothe a crying baby) she would sit in her rocking chair, watching the stars.

Cassia had always loved the stars: one of her very early memories was of standing in the garden at night, holding her father's hand and gazing up at the sky while he showed her the constellation after which she had been named. She could never actually distinguish it, work out the shape of a lady sitting in a chair, holding out her arms, but she pretended she could to please him. She liked too the story he often told her of how Cassiopeia had been sent to the heavens for boasting about the beauty of her daughter Andromeda.

She liked her name (while recognising that it was a little cumbersome for every day) and told her father on her fifth birthday that she had decided that when she was grown up she would do something very important, to suit it. Her father, greatly to his credit, smiled at her approvingly and told her he was delighted to hear it. Quite often these days she wondered how he would feel if he could see what she was actually doing, and whether he would consider it important at all. She rather thought he would although she was very much afraid her mother wouldn't.

Cassia loved the conservatory – it was known as her room – although Edward hated it and said it wasted heat and space. She could see his point about the heat, but the other objection was clearly nonsense: there was at least half an acre of garden beyond it, mostly grass, studded with shrubs and fruit trees and sloping gently down to the valley.

Oddly (significantly even, she thought), as she walked into the house, she found Edward sitting in the conservatory now, with Mr Brewster.

'Hallo. Sorry I was so long. Is Peggy making tea?'

'Yes, and I really should be on my way. Lot of calls this afternoon. Can you manage now?' Edward said.

'Yes, of course. We can manage, can't we, Mr Brewster? I don't suppose there's a lot to manage. You can tell me a bit more, I expect, and I can listen.'

'Yes, indeed,' said Mr Brewster.

As Edward left them, Peggy came in with the tea tray, looking flustered. She didn't like strangers in the house; they unsettled her, made her nervous.

'Thank you, Peggy. Mr Brewster, would you like a piece of cake?'

'That would be delightful. Thank you.'

The cake wasn't delightful at all, of course, as Cassia had made it. It had sunk in the middle and the icing had streaked down the sides, but Mr Brewster ate it uncritically and indeed accepted a second piece.

'Now then, perhaps we should go over this again. So that you are quite clear about it all.'

'Yes, I'd like to look at it properly. Was anyone else left anything?'

'Only a few small bequests to servants and so on. Lady Beatty obviously felt you were the most worthy recipient.'

'Yes. I'm sure I wasn't, though.'

'Well, clearly she made up her own mind on that matter. And of course having no children, and being estranged from Sir Richard ...'

'Yes, but he had married again, of course. Does he know about this?'

'Not yet. Naturally I will be informing him, as a courtesy, as they were married for many years.'

'Yes. I wrote to him when Leonora – Lady Beatty – died,' Cassia said.

'You were notified of her death by her brother, I imagine?'

'Yes. Well, actually by her brother's wife. Cecily Harrington. We have remained quite close. Nothing for any of them in the will?'

'Only a small bracelet for the eldest child. Here, see.'

'Oh, yes, Fanny. Dear little thing, she is. Well, not so little now, she's nearly ten. I'm sorry, Mr Brewster, not very interesting for you.'

Mr Brewster smiled at her. 'Fortunately, I do find other people's families of endless fascination.'

Cassia stared at the will, at the words: 'I exercise my power of appointment in relation to the Maple Trust, in favour of my goddaughter, Cassiopeia Blanche Fallon ...'

'It doesn't say how much money it is, though,' Cassia said.

'No. That is because the money was invested by the trustees, and at the time the will was drawn up, it was not possible to say how much it would be worth. As it happens, it is worth a little more than five hundred thousand now, five hundred and eleven to be precise.'

'Goodness,' said Cassia. 'It grows, doesn't it, money?'

'Well invested, yes. Of course it can also shrink.'

'Yes, I suppose so. It seems very complicated. Why didn't she just leave it to me? I mean, why the trust and everything?'

Mr Brewster cleared his throat. 'I believe Lady Beatty was a little ... extravagant. She explained to me that it was thought best to put the money in trust for you.'

'Yes, well, that's certainly true. I see. And the Harringtons, they don't know about this either?'

'No indeed. I visited your godmother in Paris last March, at her request, to draw up the document. You are naturally the only person to have had sight of it. You and your husband, that is.'

'That was at the apartment in Passy, I suppose?'

'Indeed so. Very beautiful it was, I must say.'

'Yes, I heard it was very nice. She must have been quite ill then?'

'She certainly did not appear to be in robust health, no,' said Mr Brewster, 'although she was clearly being very well taken care of.'

'Was she alone?'

'Yes, I saw her quite alone. Apart from the staff in the apartment, of course, and I understood there was a resident nurse.'

'I see.' So at least it had been quite true, and Leonora had lived out her last days in comfort. Cassia had wondered – wondered and feared. 'Well, what happens now, Mr Brewster?'

'Naturally, there are certain formalities. The money is not available for your use quite yet. As the executor for your godmother's estate, I have to obtain grant of probate, but you need have no concerns about it. Oh, and here is a letter, also lodged with me, from your godmother.'

Cassia took the slightly worn-looking envelope from him, opened it very carefully. It felt odd, almost as if Leonora had come suddenly into the room, and was holding it out to her. Reading the extravagant writing, slanting loopily across the thick cream paper, was like hearing her voice, her husky, amused, voice.

'My darling Sweet Pea ...' Oh, that stupid name, Cassia thought, that ridiculous name, and suddenly she was back there, on the terrace at the Ritz, twelve years old, led in by Benedict ...

Cassia had come to London for the Peace March, invited to stay with Leonora, her rich and glamorous godmother. She had only met Leonora a few times at that stage, and not at all for the last three years. Although she was very excited, she was also extremely nervous as she stood on the platform at Euston station trying to spot Leonora in the crowds of people, all arrived for this great national celebration.

In the end, after almost a very long hour, it had been Benedict Harrington, Leonora's brother, who had suddenly appeared beside her, charmingly apologetic for his lateness: 'Leonora has been held up, God knows how. She phoned me out of the blue and asked me to come and fetch you, she really is the absolute limit. I came the minute I could, but it must have seemed a very long wait, I'm so sorry.'

Benedict was tall and slim, golden haired and rather unusually brown eyed, really very handsome, Cassia thought, and most beautifully dressed in a dove-grey suit and very soft leather shoes – she had never seen shoes like that on a man. She had smiled at him, and assured him she had been perfectly all right. He said she must, in that case, be extremely brave, that he would have been terrified at being all alone in London at her age, but that he hoped they could now make it up to her. He had been instructed to take her to meet Leonora at the Ritz hotel, where she was having tea with some friends. 'She thought that would be more fun for you than just going back to the house.'

Cassia had said politely that it did sound great fun, although she was beginning to feel increasingly shy and would actually have preferred tea at home with Leonora, and followed him to the taxi rank.

As they travelled through the streets of London, turned red, white and blue, Benedict took out a gold cigarette case with a slightly shaking hand, and proceeded to smoke all the way to the Ritz, while pointing out to her the various London attractions they were passing on the way. She wondered why he should be nervous, and decided it must be the thought of the march the next day, in which she knew he was to lead his regiment. Anyway, she decided, nervous or not, she liked him very much indeed: he handed her out of the taxi when it stopped, as if she was an adult, picked up her shabby brown leather case and ushered her through the swing doors into the Ritz.

Inside, Cassia stopped and gasped aloud; she couldn't help it. Nothing she had ever seen could have prepared her for this place, with its tall, tall ceilings, it gilt chairs, its chandeliers, the unbelievably smart people everywhere.

'Come along, through here,' Benedict said. 'Oh now, there she is, look,' and there indeed Leonora was, coming towards them, smiling and holding out her arms.

'My darling!' she said, giving Cassia a kiss. 'How incredibly lovely to see you, come with me.' She led her up a couple of steps on to a wide terrace, set with tea tables and a lot of rather large palms, to a table where several other ladies were sitting. They were all dressed most wonderfully, Cassia thought, in pastel-coloured afternoon dresses with elaborate hats. Leonora's dress was apricot silk, and her hat a most wonderful confection of roses and feathers. But it was the ladies' stockings that Cassia noticed first, for they were not black or even dark brown but very very light beige. She had never seen stockings like that, had not even known they existed.

Leonora put her arm round her as they reached the table, and looked down at her. She was tall like her brother, with the same golden hair and brown eyes. 'How pretty you are!' she said. 'And very tall for your age. Now what am I to call you? Cassiopeia is a bit of a mouthful.'

'Most people call me Cassia,' said Cassia, smiling at her, 'but—'

'I don't like to do what most people do. Cassia sounds very dull to me. I shall call you – let me see – Sweet Pea. How will that do? A little bit of your name, and that is how you look: one of those flowers, very curly and colourful and delicate. Everyone, I want you to meet my goddaughter, Cassiopeia Berridge, but we shall all call her Sweet Pea. Benedict, darling, sit down and have some tea with us, won't you?'

'No, Leonora, thank you, I have to go. I have a great deal to do before tomorrow.'

'Oh, very well. Sweet Pea, go and sit down there, darling, next to the lady in yellow.'

Benedict smiled at Cassia, bowed briefly over her hand. 'Goodbye,' he said. 'I leave you in safe hands, I trust. I shall see you tomorrow after the march.'

'Goodbye and thank you,' she said, 'and good luck tomorrow.'

'So divinely handsome, your brother,' said one of the ladies.

'Still not engaged, then?' said another.

'No, not yet,' said Leonora quickly – very quickly, Cassia thought. 'Now, Sweet Pea, have a cup of tea, and would you like a cake or some sandwiches?' and she waved at a waiter.

And then, to Cassia's absolute horror, Leonora rummaged in her small bag and drew out a very pretty cigarette case and picked out a cigarette. The waiter was hurrying anxiously towards them, and Cassia felt quite sure he was going to ask her to put it away at once, or even to tell her to leave the restaurant. Smoking in public was the most terrible thing a lady could do, she knew that. However, he did nothing of the sort, but produced a book of matches from his pocket and proceeded to light Leonora's cigarette for her.

In the corner of the terrace a pianist was playing 'If You Were the Only Girl in the World'. Cassia sat listening to it and gazing at these ladies in their light stockings smoking their cigarettes, and knew she had indeed entered an utterly and most wonderfully different world.

Cassia wrenched her mind back from her memories, forced it on to her letter.

My darling Sweet Pea,

By the time you read this, I shall no longer be with you. Nasty thing that I've got, there is no hope at all, the doctors say. I just hope it carries me off quickly.

You are to have the money and to spend it not wisely – heaven forbid, darling – but well. Do anything at all you like with it – even what I might have done, although that would probably be a waste – but have fun with it. Lots of fun. You were my dearest child, the one I never had. I've missed you horribly, more than any other person or thing since leaving England. Watching you grow up, having you to live with us, presenting you at Court, all those things made me terribly terribly happy. This is to say thank you.

Bless you, darling.

Best love, Leonora.

The letter swam, blurred as she read it, read it again.

'Are you all right, Mrs Fallon?' Mr Brewster's voice was concerned, almost anxious.

'Oh, yes. Yes, thank you,' she said, fumbling for her handkerchief, wiping her eyes. 'It was just a bit of a shock, that's all. Reading the letter. It brought her alive again. I did love her very much.'

'Of course.' There was a silence, then he said, 'She was a friend of your mother's, I believe?'

'Yes. She was much younger than my mother, but their mothers were great friends, and my mother used to treat Leonora like a doll – push her around in her dolls' pram, carry her about, dress her, bath her. Leonora adored her.' She really couldn't imagine Mr Brewster would be interested in this, but she wanted to explain just the same. It seemed important, to set Leonora in context in her life. 'Right to the end, they were friends – well, till my mother died – although their lives were so different. Leonora married twice, both times to terribly rich men in London; my mother to a very modestly paid librarian in Leeds. Of course they drifted apart, but ...'

'You were the link, I imagine?'

'Yes. Yes, I was. I lived with Leonora and Sir Richard for many years, all the time I was doing my medical training. She gave a dance for me, presented me at Court, oh, all sorts of wonderful things, but I first went to stay with Leonora in 1919, for the Peace March, you know. She invited me down. I thought I'd landed up in Wonderland. I was just a little girl from the provinces, very unsophisticated, only twelve years old, and there I was, in this great, grand house, with servants, meeting all these wonderful exotic people ... More tea, Mr Brewster?'

'Yes, please. Do go on. Tell me about the Peace March. My father was involved in that, but I didn't see it.'

'Oh, it was amazing. How sad you missed it. I shouted and shouted until I was completely hoarse. It went on for hours, all the noise and colour and pageantry. The King marched, of course, and the princes, and all the Heads of State, Haig, Admiral Beatty, Sir Roger Keyes, Field Marshal Smuts, the Old Contemptibles, all the bands, and horses, great groups of men, all marching down Whitehall, past the temporary Cenotaph, saluting it, saluting the glorious dead. And I thought, we all did that day, that to have died for your country was truly the next best thing to living. I'd lost three uncles in that war, and just for that day I felt it was somehow worth it. Only of course it wasn't ...'

'My father lost both his legs,' said Mr Brewster quietly. 'Fortunately for him, for all of us, he had a small private income. But so many of those wretches have spent the next ten or fifteen years selling matches. It's a disgrace.'

After another silence he smiled at Cassia again, then said, 'Well, this won't do any good, will it? I mustn't take up too much of your time.'

'It's me taking up the time, Mr Brewster. I'm sorry. It just seemed ... appropriate somehow. To talk about Leonora, and those days.'

'Of course.' He patted her hand. He really was a very nice man, Cassia thought, not nearly as forbidding and dreary as she had first thought. 'Now if you have any more questions, do ask me. As soon as the money becomes properly available to you, then I will notify you. Otherwise, I should be getting back to London. I wonder if I could telephone for a taxi to the station?'

'Yes, please do. I'm sorry I can't take you, but Edward needs the car for his rounds.'

'Naturally. No, a taxi will do splendidly.' His lugubrious face eased suddenly into something approaching a smile, a conspiratorial smile even, as he put his papers back in his briefcase. 'You might consider buying a little car of your own now. Just a suggestion of course.'

'Goodness,' Cassia said, 'yes, I suppose I might. We'll have to see. Anyway, I'll just go and phone.'

As she stood in the hall, waiting for the local taxi service to answer its phone, she thought how very odd it would be to be able to consider buying anything, anything at all for herself, of her own volition, without asking Edward, without having interminable discussions first.

It did seem a rather agreeable prospect.

After Mr Brewster had gone, Cassia went out to the kitchen and did a bit of clearing up. She never managed to get the kitchen properly clear, because it was like the Forth Bridge, and as soon as one end was tidy, the mess spread to the other side, but she did like to keep trying. Actually, she didn't like it, she loathed it, as she loathed any kind of domestic work, mostly because she was so bad at it, but she knew it had to be done. Monks Ridge was much too big really for her to look after with only Peggy's rather incompetent help, especially with three small children. 'How you manage without a nanny, Cassia, I can't imagine,' Cecily had said once, and Cassia had replied quite briskly that she managed somehow, like everyone else who couldn't afford one.

She looked at the clock: almost two. Delia had been asleep for much too long. It had been wonderful, but she'd never sleep tonight – or rather she'd sleep even less tonight. She'd have to wake her up and perhaps take her for a walk – that might be a good idea, because then she could think. Cassia wasn't quite sure what she was going to think about, but she was beginning to feel it was necessary. Bertie wouldn't be back from his little school until four, and William had gone to play at the vicarage, so she and Delia could have the afternoon to themselves. Delia was always better when the boys weren't there.

She went to find Peggy, who was ironing Edward's shirts. Peggy liked doing that: she didn't do them nearly as well as Mrs Briggs, the daily, but it made her feel important.

'Peggy,' Cassia said tactfully, 'Peggy, do leave those, I'd much rather you got on with the supper. I thought we could have fish pie and I won't have the time to make it. I've got to collect William and—'

'It's all right, Mrs Fallon, I can do both,' said Peggy, smiling at her and pushing her straggly mouse-coloured hair back from her face, 'and I know the doctor's particular about his shirts.'

'Er ... yes, he is, but—'

'Don't you worry, Mrs Fallon. Is everything all right? That wasn't bad news from that man, was it?'

'No, Peggy, I don't think you could have called it bad news. Just a bit of ... well, family administration.'

Cassia walked slowly up the stairs and into the nursery. Delia was still very firmly alseep, her small bottom stuck into the air, her thumb stuck into her rosebud mouth, her fair curls coiled damply on to her head. A great mountain of teddies, dolls, books and a slate filled two thirds of the cot; Delia was squeezed down into the far end of it. She was so lovely when she was asleep, it seemed a terrible shame to wake her. More than a shame, a crime – like Macbeth, murdering sleep – but it had to be done. Cassia moved about the room, carefully noisy, pulling back the curtains, humming to herself. Delia squirmed, moved, opened her large dark blue eyes – her mother's eyes – and promptly started to grizzle.

'Darling!' said Cassia, deliberately cheerful. 'Hallo. Want a cuddle?'

Delia shook her head, buried herself deeper into her corner and grizzled more loudly.

'Come on. Time to get up. I thought we'd go for a walk.'

She shook her head again.

'Well, I'm going,' Cassia said, feeling already the rising irritation,

12

trying to fight it down, 'and you'll have to come with me. We can go to the woods, might see a bunny ...'

She picked Delia out of the cot.

'Right, darling, come on then. Down we go. Shall we take Buffy?'

Cassia carried Delia downstairs, gave her a drink, then strapped her in the battered old pram which stood in the porch. She told Peggy to take any calls very carefully, and that she wouldn't be more than an hour, then called Buffy, a basset hound of quite extraordinarily sweet temper set off down the lane, thinking about Leonora. She sang 'One Man Went to Mow' loudly, trying to drown the sound of Delia's wails. She didn't feel very much like a half-millionairess.

Cassia was twenty-eight. She was arresting to look at, rather than conventionally pretty, with rich corn-coloured hair, very dark blue eyes, and a sensuously full mouth that could have looked sulky had it not curved upwards at the corners. She was slim and very tall, five foot ten in fact, a factor which she claimed had had a great effect on her personality, leading people to assume from her earliest years that she was older than she really was.

She had been born in 1907, exactly nine months after her parents' marriage. Duncan Berridge and Blanche Hampton had fallen passionately in love over an overdue library book, and been married only eighteen months later, a rather hasty courtship by the standards of the time. It was a love affair that had never faltered or abated in any way: each adored and admired the other equally, and despite some rather dark prognostications by Blanche's father, who felt – and did not keep his feelings to himself – that the only daughter of a prosperous solicitor could have done rather better for herself than marrying someone he persisted in labelling a clerk. However, he was anxious to get her settled, and since Blanche was rather serious and didn't appear to have a capacity for attracting large numbers of young men, and he had very little money to settle upon her, he agreed to Duncan's request for her hand.

Serious Blanche might have been, but she was beautiful in a quite unconventional way, with heavy dark hair drawn back from a pale, oval face, and the startlingly dark blue eyes she had passed on to her daughter. Repressed by her four brothers and an oppressively dictatorial mother, she blossomed in her happy marriage and became, besides a supportive wife and talented housekeeper, something of a champion of women's rights. Some of Cassia's earliest memories were of her mother reading to her father reports from the paper of the Suffragettes and their battles, and expressing her admiration for them – an admiration which, most unusually for a man of his generation, he shared.

Cassia's birth, so soon after their marriage, had led Duncan and Blanche to expect a large family, but in fact for many years there were no more babies. This had a profound effect on Cassia: the absence of brothers led her to assume that there was nothing remotely superior about the male sex, and the absence of any rivals for her parents' affection gave her a serene self-confidence. Her parents were proud of her, but did not spoil her. She was also, as a result of spending a great deal of her time in their company, very mature for her age.

It was inevitable, perhaps, given all these factors, that her determination to do something important should continue and indeed increase.

She was educated initially at boarding school. It was fairly unusual for a small girl in 1916 to be sent away to school, and it was in some ways Cassia's misfortune that her parents, who both loved her dearly, were so anxious to see her well educated. Her father had had to leave school at the age of fourteen, on the death of his own father, and although he was well read and musically accomplished, frequently performing on both the piano and the clarinet, he had no professional qualifications of any kind, and felt painfully and helplessly disadvantaged in the company of those who did. Blanche, who had been the only member of her family deprived of a decent education, purely on account of her sex, felt her own daughter deserved better, so when Cassia was only nine and there was no good prep school of any kind in their neighbourhood a solution was found in a small boarding school thirty miles away. A few decades later she would have been transported there and home again each day by a rota of parental chauffeurs, but in 1916 only the very rich had cars, and the Berridges were not very rich. Boarding school fees of twenty pounds a term seemed more affordable.

And so Cassia became a pupil, on the first day of the autumn term halfway through the war to end all wars, of Hammond House, a large rather forbidding Victorian house on the outskirts of Leeds, filled with a lot of other generally friendly and jolly little girls. Miss Hammond, the headmistress, was an enlightened and warmhearted woman, educated under the wonderful aegis of Miss Beale and Miss Buss at Cheltenham Ladies' College. She held a passionate belief that girls were not only as clever as boys, but could and should do as well in their chosen careers, and indeed many of her students went on to the excellent Leeds Girls' High, Cassia among them. She also loved her girls and wanted them to be happy, and held tea parties every Sunday afternoon in her study, where the children sat on the floor in front of the fire toasting teacakes on long forks and drinking hot cocoa and were allowed to talk to her about anything at all. In Cassia's case, this was very frequently of her absolute and unswerving determination to become a doctor.

When Cassia was ten, Blanche had enlisted as a VAD and worked as a nurse in a hospital just outside Finchfield. She had always wanted to nurse, but had been forbidden by her own parents, and laughed at by her brothers. She wouldn't say she was exactly grateful to Kaiser Bill for giving her the opportunity, because that would have been unpatriotic, but in some ways she had never been happier than she was then, setting off early in the morning on her bicycle for the three-and-a-half-mile ride, and returning late at night, her back aching, her legs throbbing, to tell Duncan over the supper they always ate together, of the sometimes rewarding but more frequently dreadful events of her day. There was nothing she was unwilling to do, and the most unpleasant tasks – emptying bedpans, washing bandages, fumigating louse-ridden clothes – always fell to the VADs. To her relief, Blanche found herself totally unsqueamish, and with a genuine talent for her new task: she could change a dressing, soothe a fretful patient, distinguish between a genuine need for pain-relieving medication and an irritable demand for it, and anticipate a deteriorating condition more easily and swiftly than many more experienced and fully trained nurses. She saw things which horrified her, heard things which broke her heart; but overall she was happy, felt properly fulfilled for the first time in her life and, most important of all, knew she was doing her bit for her country – which, as everyone knew from the famous poster, needed her.

The war had not really entered Cassia's consciousness very strongly. Of course she knew it was going on: the history lessons at school were full of it, and their prayers every day, and in church every Sunday, were for its satisfactory conduct and the welfare of the men at the Front. Every so often a girl would be called out of a lesson and into Miss Hammond's office, and would emerge weeping at the news that a brother or uncle or, most dreadfully, a father, had been killed or injured.

Cassia knew also that the fighting was very terrible, but that our men were very brave and were winning the war steadily and indisputably under the superb direction of their generals. She knew also that bombs called Zeppelins were dropped over London and the big dockland cities like Hull, but that there was very little likelihood of that happening anywhere near in Leeds. Three of her mother's brothers were at the Front: one had been wounded, although not severely, and was in a field hospital, and the other two had miraculously escaped.

She was deeply grateful that her father was not fit enough to have to go to France, and glad too that he looked quite old, as it meant he wouldn't be handed a white feather in the street for being a coward, a terrible fate that had befallen several men in the town. Most of them were physically unfit, but two of them were pacifists, and although they worked very hard at the same hospital as Blanche, they were still considered outcasts. It must have been very hard, Cassia thought, for them to continue with their views. She did not really approve of them herself, but her father went to some trouble to explain that pacifism was a noble and indeed a very constructive philosophy and required as much courage at that time as enlisting and marching off to the Front.

One afternoon in the summer holidays in 1917, Blanche asked Cassia if she would like to come to one of the hospital concerts and sing for the men. 'Poor things, they have very little to live for, some of them, and these concerts cheer them up so much. I've asked Matron and she is more than happy for you to do so. Your father will play for you.'

Cassia was more than happy too. She had a very pretty, quite strong voice, and had performed in several concerts at Hammond House which had always been a great success. She practised a few of the favourite war songs, like 'It's a Long Way to Tipperary' and 'Pack Up Your Troubles In Your Old Kit Bag', and a couple of more romantic favourites, like 'If You Were the Only Girl in the World' and 'Daisy, Daisy'.

Blanche told Cassia to wear her new white muslin dress with the frills and white stockings and shoes, and tied a white ribbon in her dark gold hair. The three of them set off together in the governess cart that one of Blanche's brothers had lent them, along with a rather lazy pony, for the duration of the war.

The concert was to take place in the early evening, and Cassia, who had never seen the hospital, felt suddenly nervous as they drew up outside its great, grim walls. Nervous and swiftly saddened by what she saw: the grounds were full of men, some of them in wheelchairs, others sitting with their eyes bandaged, or walking slowly about on sticks or crutches, all dressed in the dark blue flannel suits of the wounded. Most of them looked at the cart and its occupants and smiled, and even waved at Blanche whom they recognised, but a few remained motionless, staring blankly in front of them with white, gaunt faces. Cassia knew they were suffering from shellshock. Blanche had explained it to her, and how its sufferers lived partly or totally withdrawn in a dreadful, haunted, half-real world, unable to communicate with anybody much of the time: 'In time, it is hoped, with good nursing and the love of their families, they will return to a proper life and rediscover themselves, but meanwhile, poor things, they are in a terrible way.'

Far worse, Cassia thought, were the men sitting in wheelchairs, with both legs amputated; and she was amazed to hear two of the blind men laughing raucously. It seemed almost impossible to her that anyone should ever smile, let alone laugh, with so much to endure. She knew she would rather have died. But she smiled and waved back to them all, and followed her mother over to a few of them and said 'how do you do?' and shook their hands; 'bless her' she heard several times and 'pretty little angel', and she stopped being nervous and when it came to her turn in the concert, she greatly enjoyed standing on the stage in the big hall of the hospital and singing her songs, and when they were all cheering and shouting 'encore, encore' and Duncan beamed at her and nodded and started to play 'Are There Any More At Home Like You?' and they clapped even before she had sung the first note, she really felt she had done something properly useful for the first time in her life.

Afterwards, Blanche left Cassia with Duncan while she had a discussion about her duties the next day with Matron. They were standing in a corridor, waiting for Blanche to return, when they heard a dreadful groaning coming from a small side room. Cassia, drawn to it, she felt, quite against her will, and ignoring her father's command to stay at his side, pulled free from his hand and ran over to the room and opened the door.

A man lay there in a high-sided bed, so that he could not fall out, clearly in agony. He was writhing about, tossing his head like a terrified horse. His eyes were bandaged, his breath rasping, but as he heard the door open, he turned towards her. 'Please,' he said, 'please, I can't stand it. Please, for God's sake, help me.'

Cassia looked at him for a moment, then said, 'Wait, I'll come back, I promise,' and turned and collided with her mother who was standing in the doorway, looking distraught.

'Mama, Mama,' Cassia said, clasping both her mother's hands, pulling her back into the room, 'this poor man, you must help him, he is in the most dreadful pain. Give him something for it, please, please.'

'Cassia, I can't possibly give him anything,' said Blanche. 'That is not for me to do.'

'But you're a nurse and he needs it. You must, you've got to, please, listen, he's crying—'

The man uttered a strange mixture of groan and sob, calling out again for help.

Cassia burst into tears. 'What is it? What's happened to him? Why won't you help?'

'Cassie, he has gas poisoning. It's a dreadful thing. He's only just been brought here and—'

'But he is here, and you must be able to help him. That's what this place is for.'

Blanche looked at the man's notes, hanging at the foot of his bed, then drew Cassia outside the room, and closed the door on the man. His cries were stronger, could still be heard as loudly.

'Mama, please. You're cruel, it's horrible. Why won't you—'

'Cassia, listen. It is not for me to decide what drugs he has. Only the doctors can do that. They know best, and they have decided he cannot have anything more until the morning.'

Cassia looked at her for a moment, trying to ignore the dreadful sound of the man's pain, and then turned and walked very determinedly towards her father who was standing talking to the matron: a tall, imposing woman, rather beautiful, with dark red hair and a very long, elegant neck. 'Ah, Cassia! What a pleasure your singing was. I was just telling your father how much you must have pleased the men—'

'Please,' said Cassia, 'please go and help that man. That man in there.' She pointed towards the door. 'He's in such pain, and my mother says—' She stopped, tears spilling over her lashes, rolling slowly down her cheeks, frightened horrified tears.

'Yes? Your mother says what?'

'That only the doctors can do anything, decide what he can have.'

'That is quite right. Of course. A doctor saw him only an hour or so ago, and prescribed what he must have. He has had it, and is much better for it.'

Cassia stared at her. 'He's not better for it at all. He's suffering terribly, you know he is, and you won't help him any more.'

'Cassia!' said Blanche, her voice faint, shocked. She clearly expected a thunderbolt to descend on both her and Cassia.

'Cassia,' said Matron, however, kneeling down and taking her hand, 'I know how it must seem to you. And it's not that I won't help. I can't. We are doing all we can for that poor man. I'm sorry you should have had to see him.'

'It doesn't matter that I've seen him,' said Cassia, pulling her hand free, 'just that he's in such a lot of pain. Surely you could give him some more? The doctor must have got it wrong, not realised how bad he was. I think you should tell him—' She brushed the tears from her eyes again.

'I'm afraid that's not how it works,' said Matron. She was beginning to look a little less patient. 'We all work together here, as I'm sure your mother will have told you, and it is not for us to question the doctors' decisions.'

'Well, I think you should,' said Cassia staunchly.

'Cassia, be quiet immediately!' said Blanche.

'Cassia,' said Matron, 'you are obviously a very kind, caring person. I admire your courage in all sorts of ways, but you really do not understand this situation. Perhaps one day you can come back here and learn for yourself. And put your courage and your kindness to good use. As a nurse.'

Cassia looked at her. 'No,' she said, 'not a nurse. I really don't want to be a nurse. I want to be able to decide things for myself. I'm going to be a doctor.'

Only, in spite of that moment of vision, a passionate determination to succeed, and her graduation from one of the finest medical schools in the country with the highest possible marks, the nearest she had come to medical practice was acting as unpaid secretary to her husband, giving unofficial advice to pregnant and recently delivered young women, and making up cough mixture and bandaging the occasional knee as its owner sat wailing in the surgery. And that hurt, hurt very badly, every day of her life.

CHAPTER 2

'This is very good fish pie, Peggy.' Edward smiled at Peggy over his empty plate. 'Is there any more?'

'A bit, Dr Fallon. I'm glad you like it.' Peggy blushed. She was very devoted to Edward, and his praise was not easily won. 'Mrs Fallon said you were very busy, and I thought the fish pie would help. Brain food, my mother always said it was, fish.'

'Goodness,' said Cassia quickly, seeing that this statement was not going to get a very good response from the pedantic Edward, 'I had no idea.'

'Oh yes,' said Peggy, 'most definitely. I'll go and see if there's a bit more.'

She disappeared. She wasn't actually a very good housekeeper – which was what she liked to be called, although Cassia, with clear memories of proper housekeepers and real staff, found it very hard to think of her as such – but she was devoted to the Fallons. She didn't mind what she did, not even the most menial tasks, like cleaning or washing nappies – although Mrs Briggs did most of the heavy work – and that, Cassia supposed, made up for a lot of her deficiencies. Peggy came back in now with the dish and ladled some more pie on to Edward's plate.

'Daddy doesn't need to feed his brains. They're absolutely huge already, aren't they, Daddy?'

'I hope so,' said Edward, smiling at Bertie, 'but I'm not over-confident about their size.'

'They must be, otherwise you couldn't be a doctor. Could he, Mummy?'

'No, of course not,' said Cassia. She smiled determinedly at the pair of them, her husband and her elder son, so staggeringly alike, with their straight brown hair, their brown eyes, their long faces, their thin bodies. Bertie already had hands that were too big for his body, fixed to the end of skinny wrists, and bony ankles and big feet. He had a tendency to stoop, and was already the tallest boy in his class, already clumsy. William on the other hand was still slightly chubby, blond and blue eyed like his mother and baby sister.

'Oh God, there's the phone. Not another baby, please! Not tonight,' said Edward with a sigh.

'Are any due?'

'Maxine Foster is. Almost. And she's very big, she might well be early. Yes, Peggy?'

'It's Mr Harrington for Mrs Fallon.'

'Oh, tell him I'll call him back, could you? Explain we're having supper. And find out if he's in Devon or London.'

'Yes, Mrs Fallon.'

'What's he calling about?' said Edward.

'I've no idea,' said Cassia shortly. She wondered if Benedict had phoned about the will – he was Leonora's brother after all. They had been terribly close, he must have known about it.

She was beginning to feel extremely strange; obviously, as for her patients in Casualty, sensation was returning. Her prime emotion, she realised, was not excitement, not even surprise, but a great sadness. She had not known how ill Leonora had been, that she was dying, and so had not been to see her. She had missed the funeral in Paris, quiet, hastily arranged, and had consequently felt an appalling remorse as well as grief at the time. Somehow the day, the bequest, above all Leonora's letter, had made her freshly aware of it. She sat there quietly, watching them eat, thinking of Leonora, of her courage, her silliness, her beauty, her capacity for fun – and realised afresh that she was gone, quite quite gone, and that none of them would ever see her again.

She lifted her head and saw Edward looking at her, sympathetic, concerned, and half smiled at him.

He smiled back, and said, 'Why don't you go and sit down? Have a rest.'

Sometimes, just sometimes, she remembered why she had married him.

As she sat by the fire, flicking through the *Telegraph*, Delia's wails trailed down the stairs. It was no use, no one else could calm her. She'd have to go to her.

She went and made Delia a bottle, gave it to her, settled her down again, then walked down the stairs. Edward was in the hall.

'I'm just going to phone Benedict back,' she said.

'Oh, all right. Don't talk too long, will you?'

'No,' she said, unreasonably irritated, 'but it is important. To me.'

'I know, but I'm half expecting a call about that baby, and anyway, trunk calls are—'

'Expensive?' she said, amused, looking at him very levelly. 'Don't worry, Edward. Maybe I can help with the bill.' She always regarded that afterwards as an absolutely definitive moment.

Cecily answered the phone. 'Cassia. How nice. How are you?'

'I'm fine, Cecily, thank you. And you?'

'Oh, pretty well. Awfully busy, of course. It's Ascot next week and we're taking a house down there, and then soon after that we're off to the South of France, with the children and some chums. Actually, Cassia, why don't you all come and join us? It would be such fun.'

'Cecily, I really don't think we could. Much as I'd love to. Edward doesn't get what you might call holidays, and—'

'Well, come on your own. Without him, I mean. Just for a few days. It would do you good. You looked so tired last time I saw you.'

Yes, I probably did, thought Cassia, I always do. I always feel tired, my life is totally, unrelentingly tiring. She had a sudden vision of a fortnight, a week, a few days even, just lying by a pool in the South of France, somewhere near Nice probably. Benedict and Cecily took a villa there every July, filled it with friends, with amusing, good-looking people. Cassia had gone once, the year before she had got married, the year of her finals, just for three days. She had lain there in the sun, sipping cocktails, talking and listening to nonsense, playing bezique and backgammon, dancing at night by the pool to the gramophone, or going down to Nice to some nightclub or other, and once to the casino. Leonora had been there, had arrived on Cassia's last day, full of gossip about Paris and Le Touquet, demanding gossip about London. It had been a magical, hedonistic, enchanted time and, like so much of her past life, seemed now an unbelievable, impossible dream.

'I don't think so,' she said finally. 'Edward does like to have me here, he works so hard, but thank you for asking me. Um, could I speak to Benedict? He phoned me earlier.'

'Yes, of course. Just hold on a minute. And do think about coming to France. I'd love to have you there. It's going to be such fun.'

Dear Cecily: she was so genuinely affectionate, so irresistibly optimistic. She needed to be, of course: she might have a lot of life's goodies, but she certainly earned them.

'Cassia, hallo. It's Benedict. Thank you for ringing back. Baby all right?'

'As all right as she ever is. Little beast. Anyway, what can I do for you?'

'I just wanted to let you know we're having a memorial service for Leonora.'

'Oh, what a nice idea.'

'Yes, it was Cecily's initially. So many people missed the funeral, after all, and it seems so shabby somehow, not to do what we can for her. We thought the end of this month. How would the twenty-eighth sound to you?'

'Fine.'

'Good. It seems to suit most of the key people. I'm organising some speakers, and I thought you might have an idea about music.'

'Yes, I might, I suppose. Where will it be?'

'St George's, Hanover Square. It's a lovely church and the vicar is a friend of mine. I'm afraid it won't be a very comfortable occasion – I don't suppose Richard will come, although naturally I shall ask him, and so many of Leonora's old friends have somehow disappeared – but a lot of the old crowd will be there, and Harry of course. In fact I've asked him to speak. He said he would.'

'Oh good,' she said carefully, 'and what about Rollo Gresham?'

'I don't know,' said Benedict, almost too quickly. 'He's very elusive these days. Since Leonora died.'

'But he was her ...' What was he? How did you describe exactly Rollo Gresham's role in Leonora's life? Her lover, yes, but more than that: she had lived with him for years, and although they had parted, it had been on amicable terms, Leonora always said. He had left her very well provided for ... very well indeed, it seemed. 'I just thought he'd want to be there,' Cassia finished lamely.

'We shall see. Naturally I shall make every attempt to notify him.' Benedict sounded irritable. 'And then I thought it would be nice if Rupert Cameron came. Leonora was awfully fond of him. Only I don't have an address or phone number for him, So if you could—'

'Yes, of course. It's a Brighton number, 4270.'

'Marvellous. Do you think he'd speak? Or read something? That marvellous voice of his, it would be wonderful. What do you think?'

'It's a very good idea. And he'd like it, he was very fond of her too. He's resting at the moment, as they say in his profession, so I'm pretty sure he'd be able to be there.'

She smiled at the thought: Rupert would indeed like it. He had adored Leonora as she had him. And it would be lovely to have him there – she would feel very much alone otherwise, as Edward would inevitably make some excuse, as he always did on such occasions.

Benedict cut into her rather rambling thoughts. 'Good. Well, I think that's all for now. Keep the date, and I'll get on to Cameron. Oh, and I heard Cecily asking you down to France. It's a nice idea, we'd love to have you.'

'I'll think about it, but I really can't see how—'

How what, Cassia? she thought. How to get away, afford the fare, buy some clothes, leave Edward without his support system? But she could. At least consider it: it was all suddenly so much less difficult, so much less impossible. Just for a few days. Not for the first time since Mr Brewster's arrival she experienced the heady, almost shocking realisation that she could, actually now, do what she liked. She crushed it firmly: it wasn't fair, nothing had changed, not her relationship with, her loyalty to, Edward. Just because she had some money. That wasn't going to change anything important. She wouldn't allow it.

She went back into the drawing room where Edward was sitting, listening to a concert on the wireless. He reached out, turned the volume down. 'What did Benedict want?'

'They're going to have a memorial service for Leonora. He wanted to talk to me about it.'

'That's a nice idea.'

'Yes. You'll come, won't you?'

'Of course, if I can get cover that day. Not that it would matter much if I didn't.'

'It would matter to me.'

'Would it?' he said and smiled at her, the slow sweet smile that was there less and less frequently these days. 'Well, I'm pleased to hear it. But all those people – her friends, that lot. I won't be a very valuable addition, will I?'

'Oh, Edward, don't be silly. Please. Such a cracked record, that one.'

'I'll come if I can. All right?' There was a silence, then he said, 'Did Benedict know about you? And the money?'

'He didn't mention it, and I didn't feel it was appropriate to. Under the circumstances.'

'Why on earth not?'

'Oh, Edward, I don't know. I just didn't. Anyway, what was I going to say? Guess what, Leonora's left me half a million pounds?'

'Half a million pounds,' Edward said. 'It is an awful lot of money. I hope it'll be all right.'

'Edward, of course it'll be all right,' she said, half amused, half irritated. 'Why shouldn't it?'

She sat in an armchair, and thought about Leonora, wondering against the background of the music what happened to people that they could take a life, a lovely, loved and joyful life, and fill it with fear and greed and distress? What had driven Leonora to do that? To throw everything away, in that dreadful madness? And it had been a madness. A sickness.

It's an addiction,' Benedict had said to Cassia, on the dreadful day when Leonora had finally run away to France, away from Sir Richard, who had changed from loving husband to bitter jailer, away from safety and security, and into her new, empty, wretched life.

Cassia had never forgotten that day. She had been living with them, in the middle of her medical studies, and had come home to find the house silent, dead, Sir Richard locked in his study. She had gone round to Benedict and Cecily for comfort, had sat crying, staring at Benedict as he struggled to explain. 'She's an addicted gambler. It's as much a sickness as cocaine or alcohol addiction; she can scarcely help it.' He had known all along, had tried to help: first by trying to stop Leonora, to warn her against the associates who saw her and her wealth coming; then by bailing her out endlessly as she got into debt, giving her money, paying off casinos, private gambling clubs, all her debtors; then finally when he could do no more, when Richard discovered what she was doing, standing by her as she faced her husband and struggled to redeem herself.

The final showdown had come when an antiquarian friend of Sir Richard's had come to dinner and asked if he might borrow a tiara that had belonged to Richard's grandmother, worked in India and worn at the maharaja's court. 'I've never forgotten it, it really is the most perfect example of worked gold, and the settings of those rubies, quite extraordinary.'

'Of course we'll lend it to you,' said Sir Richard. 'Why ever not? Leonora has it now, but it would be an honour, wouldn't it, my dear?'

'Yes, but ... that is ... when did you say ...'

'Not until November, only I would like to have sight of it a little before then, so that it can be catalogued, and so on.'

'Well, no time like the present,' said Sir Richard. 'We'll get it and—'

With a loud crash, the chair Leonora was leaning on slipped from under her and she fell to the floor in a dead faint, catching her head on the edge of the table on the way.

It had all come out: slowly and painfully. The tiara had been sold; all Leonora's jewellery had been sold, much of it heirlooms belonging to Sir Richard's mother. She had had very good copies made, and worn those, and paid her debts with the proceeds. It had been a dreadful, wretched time, and Cassia had never quite got over it.

Sir Richard had moved Miss Monkton into the house, to keep an eye on Leonora. Nominally a companion, actually a spy, Miss Monkton, with her thin wispy hair and her halitosis, was paid to watch her charge, to listen to her conversations, to go everywhere she went. Cassia had watched Leonora disintegrate under her misery, grow quiet, colourless, fat as she ate too much, her only remaining self-indulgence. Deserted by her friends — for who, after all, would wish to be associated with such very open disgrace? — Cassia had had to endure living in a house that had become silent, miserable, full of hostility and harsh words. And to be denied an understanding of the reason, for Leonora would not speak of it, and Sir Richard could not. Finally, almost two years later, she had come home to find Harris, Leonora's maid, weeping, Richard locked in his study, and Leonora gone.

Cassia had been to visit Leonora in Paris several times. She lived in a very grand penthouse apartment on the Avenue Foch — 'We can almost reach out and touch the Arc de Triomphe, look,' she had said, leading Cassia out on to the balcony — with Rollo Gresham, a dreadful great slob of a man whom Cassia loathed. How could she? Cassia had wondered, before she came to recognise that Leonora needed money more than anything in the world, money from a source that understood her addiction — and Gresham had a very great deal. For five years they had lived together, while Sir Richard divorced her and remarried the blessed Margaret, as Rupert irreverently christened her. Although finally Rollo Gresham left Leonora, she had been extraordinarily well provided for, and he had gone to enormous lengths, it seemed, to see that she had the best possible medical care. He had clearly been a much kinder, better man than she had given him credit for, Cassia thought now, thinking of Leonora: poor Leonora, so brave, so lovely, so generous — so very, very generous ...

The concert ended; she was relieved. It was a Mozart violin concerto and its throbbing poignancy didn't serve to lift her mood.

Edward switched off the radio, and said, 'Let's go up, shall we? Come on you look exhausted.'

'I'm not in the least exhausted,' she said, irritable herself.

'Well, it would be nice anyway.'

The smile again; the sweet smile. She knew what it meant, that smile, in conjunction with bed; that he wanted to make love to her. Well, that was all right. It happened less and less these days, and it was seldom more than just nice any more; but she still enjoyed it, still felt closer to him, more loving, more forgiving. Forgiving: why, for heaven's sake, did she need to feel forgiving? It was nonsense. It wasn't Edward's fault that he was a doctor and she wasn't; not his fault that she was a lousy housekeeper and only a tolerable wife; not his fault that she was deeply, uncomfortably, rawly discontented. If it was anyone's, it was hers.

'Yes,' she said, smiling back. 'Yes, it would be nice.'

She lay in bed watching him as he undressed, folded his clothes neatly (as he always did in case he needed them quickly, urgently in the night, for a birth, or a death), brushed his hair and his teeth, got into bed naked, turned out the light. She was naked too; acknowledging, by the nightdress still in its case on the bed, that she was ready for him, wanted him. She was ready, very ready: she could feel herself reaching out to him, from hungry, unsatisfied depths, hoping, yearning that tonight, as there had not been for a while, there would be time, that he would wait for her, let her climb, soar, come. Often now, Edward's needs, suddenly, urgently felt, did not allow for patience, for her. She felt wrongly used in bed, as she was in the rest of their marriage: necessary, an important, a crucial requirement even, but not a recipient of proper consideration or care.

He turned to her now, took her in his arms, began to kiss her, slowly, carefully, as he did everything. Her emotions intensified by the events of her day, by the memories it had almost physically stirred, she suddenly wanted him very much. She responded, with her mouth, her hands, her voice, telling him she loved him, wanted him. He didn't like that usually, was embarrassed, half afraid someone would hear, but tonight he seemed pleased, told her he loved her too.

He began to stroke, to smooth her body with his hands, slowly, rhythmically, caressing her breasts, her stomach, her thighs. She rose within herself to meet him, feeling herself clenching, tautening, releasing in a smooth, mounting delight. It would be good this time, she told herself, it would be good, the long, sweet unfolding, her body would take its due from him. Even as she began to know within her the brilliance, the high peaks of pleasure, began to reach for them, to feel for them, to ride, she felt him change, tense, and knew he wouldn't wait, wouldn't take her with him, that yet again he would go on alone, leaving her behind, calling out to him, that it would be over for him, and she would be left there, disappointed, still hungry, and terribly, horribly alone.

Well, she said to herself later, sitting in the kitchen drinking a cup of tea (having left him snoring, smiling beatifically, full of grunted gratitude and protestations of love), perhaps that was what marriage was. That was what became of it, became of passion, became of the bright, brilliant thing that once was there; and then she thought (because such thoughts turned her to honesty) that there had never been any bright brilliance with Edward. It had always been sensible, warm, affectionate reason.

She had met Edward when she was still at the university, had not even moved over to the medical school. He was two years ahead of her, doing his clinical studies, actually working in the hospital. It was such a huge step up from the three years of theory that preceded it. She could still remember seeing some of the students on ward rounds on her first day, distinguished from the real doctors by their short white coats, talking to patients, allowed to examine them even, under the watchful eye of their Honoraries. She remembered thinking how unimaginably far away even so modest an achievement seemed. That first day had been the most terrifying, as well as the most wonderful of her life, she thought now with a smile, as she sipped her tea. She remembered her seventeen-year-old self, standing in a vast room stretching into what seemed to be infinity, filled with large glass-topped tables, and on them, rows and rows of white-swathed objects.

The Dean had been standing in the doorway, directing Cassia and the other new medical students inside. 'Ah, Miss Berridge,' he had said, when she reached him, 'you go to table number twenty-four and take the left leg.'

The sense of nightmare had grown: these were the corpses, the cadavers, the Dean had just urged them to respect. Dead bodies, once people: and she had been given the left leg of one of them. She advanced to table twenty-four, looked at her body. The smell was awful, formaldehyde, she supposed. More awful still, the veins stood out, dark and red. For a ghastly moment, she thought she was going to be sick. She took a deep breath, then another.

Everyone around her had looked perfectly normal, cheerful even. A couple had already picked up their scalpels and were cutting into their corpses: Cassia had stood there, helpless, unable to move, wondering if it would be braver to run, to leave then, to go home, or to stay and do what she was told.

'It's only dye,' an amused but kindly voice said. 'Don't worry. Come on, I'll show you what to do.'

Cassia looked up and saw another girl standing in front of her, smiling. She was short and slightly plump, with a riot of red curly hair. 'I'm Jenny Porter. You all right? You look terrible.'

'I feel terrible,' said Cassia.

'This is the worst bit, apparently. My father told me about it. He was— '

'Don't tell me, a student here. I must have the only father who wasn't. I'm Cassia Berridge. Okay then, let's get it over with,' said Cassia, picking up her scalpel. She wondered if it was possible to cut into a vein successfully with your eyes shut.

Some time later, she was sitting in Casualty with a badly sprained ankle, sustained from slipping on a piece of liver, hurled by one of her fellow students across the lab at another.

'Cassia, are you all right?' Jenny Porter had held out a hand to haul her up.

'Yes, I think so,' Cassia had said, trying out her ankle cautiously. A knife-edge of pain had shot through it. 'Jolly painful, though.'

'Let me look,' Jenny had said. 'Golly, it's swelling up. We'd better take you over to Casualty. Come on, Tom, you can help me. Cassia, put your arms round our shoulders. God, you boys are a menace.'

Casualty wasn't too crowded, it being a weekday afternoon. Jenny and Tom Cavanagh, a particularly irreverent student and another of Cassia's best friends, had left her to find themselves a cup of tea. The nurse in charge had a look at Cassia's ankle, prodded and twisted it a bit and then pronounced it a sprain.

'It'll need strapping up. Here, you.' She waved imperiously at someone Cassia recognised from his short white coat as a student. 'Come here and strap up this ankle.'

The owner of the short white coat came over. Cassia was bent over her foot, rubbing it to try and relieve the pain, and the first glimpse therefore that she got of Edward Fallon was of a pair of very nice hands. Hands mattered to Cassia. Edward Fallon's hands were very nice indeed, large but slender, with very long fingers. He had bony wrists, and wore a rather battered gold watch on a shabby leather strap, and she noticed that his shirt cuffs were frayed. Not a rich student, then: maybe on a scholarship, like herself.

'Hallo,' he said. His voice was very nice too, quite light, slightly diffident. 'I'm—'

'I can see,' she said, looking at his badge. 'Mr E. Fallon. How do you do? Cassia Berridge. First year.'

'Fourth. What have you done to your foot?'

'I slipped in the lab.'

'Oh dear. Liver or frog?' He grinned at her. He had nice teeth too, Cassia thought (why was she noticing all this?), a bit crooked, but very white. She took in the rest of him – slightly long face, wavy brown hair, hazel eyes, freckles, nice, smily expression – then pulled herself back to reality with an effort.

'Liver.'

'Dear, oh dear, these medical students,' he said. 'Right, then, let's get this on.' He started winding on the bandage, his head bent over her foot.

Cassia thanked whatever deity thanks were due to, for seeing that she had cut her toenails the night before, and said, 'So is it fun, doing Clinical?'

'Yes, it's wonderful. I'm really enjoying myself.'

'Was your father here?' she said.

'No, although my grandfather was. Was yours?'

'No. This must be a first, two students meeting, neither of them with fathers here.'

'Mine's a teacher,' said Edward Fallon, expertly tucking in the end of the bandage and putting the safety pin into place. 'Prep school in Sussex. Yours?'

'Librarian. In Leeds.'

'Ah. So where do you live, in one of the hostels?'

'No, with my godmother and her husband.'

'Oh. Nice for you, that. Bit of homeliness. Digs are awful.'

'Yes,' said Cassia, thinking of the vast house in Grosvenor Gardens where she lived, the servants, the lavish meals; homely was hardly the right word for it.

'You don't sound very sure. Well, there you are, that's done. How does it feel, if you put your weight on it?'

'Fine. Much better. Thank you. Now I have to wait for my friends.'

'Right-oh. Would you like me to get you a cup of tea? I can say you're suffering from shock, if you like.' He grinned at her again.

'Oh, no. Honestly, it's fine. I'll just sit out there and watch. See what it's like really to be a Casualty doctor.'

'It's okay,' he said. His voice was considered, careful. Cassia thought if you asked him if it was going to rain, he would give the matter a great deal of attention before answering. 'As I said, I'm enjoying it all very much.'

'What branch do you intend going into?'

'Oh, surgery, I think,' Edward said.

'Me too! I—'

'Mr Fallon! Over here, please. *If* you have a moment ...' Sister's voice was terse, sarcastic.

Edward Fallon gave Cassia a last, quick smile and hurried off. She sat looking after him thoughtfully. He seemed an awful lot nicer and an awful lot less arrogant than most of the male students.

She had almost forgotten about him when the sergeant on the reception desk at the university building called her over as she left one evening. 'Miss Berridge! I have a note for you. Left by a young gentleman.'

'Thank you.' Cassia smiled at the sergeant, who took it upon himself to know everything about all of them. He was holding the note out to her with his one hand – he had lost an arm at Ypres.

'Very nice young gentleman, he was. Student at the hospital. Aren't you going to open it?'

The message was written in a well-formed, neat hand: an invitation to the medical students' Christmas ball from Edward Fallon. Cassia wondered if her coming-out dress, almost two years old now, would appear seriously out of date. She decided Edward Fallon would be most unlikely to notice even if it did.

'You look absolutely beautiful,' said Edward Fallon and blushed. He blushed a lot, and Cassia rather liked it. She had never had dealings with a diffident male. She liked everything about him: his rather untidy good looks (greatly enhanced by his dinner jacket), his slow, gentle voice, the slightly serious interest he showed in everything she had to say, his lack of arrogance, his passion for his medical career, his extremely old-fashioned good manners.

Edward had insisted on collecting her from the house on the evening of the ball, and had a taxi cab waiting outside; it was only much later that she discovered he had walked all the way to Grosvenor Gardens from Camden Town, where his digs were, that being the only way he could possibly afford a cab to take her home again.

He was very respectful, without being obsequious, to Sir Richard, who had insisted on meeting him, and charmingly courteous to Leonora. He was clearly taken aback by the house and establishment in Grosvenor Gardens, while remaining rather sweetly dignified, she thought, not tongue-tied at all.

The dance was held at the Students' Union, a classically showy, early Victorian building with neoclassical overtones. The organisers, who included Edward, he told her proudly, had worked extremely hard, dressing it up in the Christmas spirit with great branches of holly and yew, and an extravagance of red ribbons in garlands and bows. Vast bunches of red and white balloons hung from the ceiling. The tables were decorated with holly and Christmas roses, and at suppertime (against the advice of some of the more sober members of the committee) the central lights were turned down and candles lit on the tables. Happily, the more sober members were proved wrong.

Edward introduced Cassia rather formally to some of his friends, and then set her down at a table with some of them and went to fetch her a drink. He asked her very seriously if she would like to dance.

'Of course I would!' said Cassia. 'Isn't that why we're here?'

He was not – inevitably, she supposed – a good dancer, which she did mind a bit, because she was very good herself. However, he was extraordinarily generous about allowing her to dance with his friends, although when she and one of them gave what amounted to an exhibition of the Black Bottom, and everyone stopped to watch, he stood on the edge of the floor looking rather lost, and she promptly felt rather mean.

He made her stay at the table while he fetched supper for her, saw that her glass was carefully topped up, his own remaining at a steady level (again, she discovered later, because he could not afford more than one additional bottle of wine, the ball ticket covering the price of one half), and asked her several times if she was warm enough.

'I'm very very warm, Edward, thank you. Even in this rather revealing dress. It was my … well, that is, I first wore it in the summer. Not this summer either,' she added hastily, for she had a terror of him thinking her rich, 'last.' Which was when he had told her she looked beautiful.

'Thank you,' said Cassia lightly, and smiled into his hazel eyes.

He did not smile back, but looked at her intently for a moment and then said, 'I mean it, you are, I'm not just saying it. I don't just say things.'

'No,' she said, serious herself now, 'I can see you don't.' It was an oddly potent moment.

After supper they danced some more. It seemed mean now to do the showy numbers with his friends, so she sat them out and took to the floor only with Edward and only for the safe dances – the waltz and the occasional quickstep.

'You've obviously done a lot of dancing,' he said, as they sat back at the table for a while, watching some rather irritatingly theatrical tangoing.

'Oh, well, I learnt at school, and I went to a few dances last year.'

'So where do your parents live?'

'My father lives in Leeds. My mother died a long time ago,' she added quickly, before it became awkward, thinking at the same time how much Blanche would have liked Edward.

'And is your father as rich as your godfather?' Edward said, suddenly awkward.

'Goodness, no, he's very hard up.'

'I find that difficult to believe.'

'It's true. If you want proof, I'm on a scholarship. It was just that my mother and Leonora were friends as children. Father is not rich at all, I assure you. And he was happier about me being in London if I was safely under Richard and Leonora's roof.'

'My father isn't rich either,' Edward said, after a long, careful pause.

'No,' she said lightly, 'I can tell,' and could have bitten her tongue out, for he flushed and looked down, taking a rather large sip from his almost empty glass.

'I'm sorry,' Cassia said, for it was too big a gaffe to ignore, and put her hand on his. He pulled it away and cleared his throat, and began fiddling with his cufflinks. 'Edward,' she said, 'please forgive me. You misunderstood what I meant.'

'I hardly think so,' he said, with a sigh, and after one of his longer pauses. 'You meant it was extremely obvious that I was hard up. I'm sorry, I'm not what you're used to, I'm sure.'

'Of course it's what I'm used to,' said Cassia, in exasperation. 'Just because I stay in that … that silly house in term time doesn't mean our house is like that. Our house is a very ordinary one in Leeds and my father lives in fear and trembling of losing his job, and I went to the local girls' high school, where my very best friend lived over her father's greengrocer shop.'

He turned to her then, and smiled his slow, careful smile, and after another pause said, 'I know it's silly of me to be so sensitive about it, but—'

'Very silly,' said Cassia, 'when it couldn't matter less and nothing bores me more than rich people and their silly nonsense and—'

And then it happened, absurdly, melodramatically on cue.

'Cassia! Darling! How lovely to see you. I thought it was you, and in your coming-out dress too, how too sweet.'

She looked up, recognising the voice, of course, half wondering even then if she could ignore it, but of course she couldn't. It was Edwina Fox-Ashley, dazzling in a silver dress and silver shoes, a tall silver feather in her gleaming dark hair, hanging on to the arm of a red-faced boy who was clutching a bottle of champagne in his other hand. 'Why are you here, darling, who brought you?'

'Edwina, can I introduce Edward Fallon, a fellow medical student. I'm doing my first year here, I thought you knew.'

'Good Lord, are you really? I do remember you were rather serious, but I didn't think it was going to come to anything. Archie Symington, by the way, he's a student here too. Hates it, don't you, Archie? Only doing it to keep his pa happy. Listen, darling, we have to go now, but I'll catch up with you later. Kiss kiss. And you, Edward. Lovely to meet you.'

Cassia turned back to Edward Fallon and saw, as she had known she would, an expression very close to distaste in his eyes.

'Your coming-out dress?' he said. 'Did you do all that?'

'Well, yes, I did,' said Cassia reluctantly, 'but only to—'

'Keep your pa happy?' said Edward. His voice was very cold. Cassia knew there was nothing she could say or do to restore the evening to its earlier happiness: absolutely nothing at all.

Months had passed, and Cassia had put Edward out of her head, worked hard, had fun. And then her father had died – a dreadful, unexpected, unforeseen shock – of lung cancer. Only it wasn't really lung cancer, or so Cassia had always felt. It was the result of the long, lonely years, struggling to bring her up and keep his job without the help and support of his beloved Blanche, to manage the distinctly substandard domestic staff he had been able to afford – to manage without the help Cassia could, and she felt should, have given him.

She had been at dinner with Cecily and Benedict when the news came, listening to a lot of silly gossip about the Prince of Wales, of all absurd things. Adams had called Cecily to the telephone. Cecily had come back very quietly and put her arms round Cassia and led her out to the hall, where she told her that she must go home at once, that night.

The worst thing had been the shame: the shame and the guilt. Shame that she hadn't noticed how ill he was – or had she been careful not to notice? – guilt that she had left him when he was so patently frail.

'How could I have done that?' she said to Leonora, who had come up to Leeds with her. 'How could I have just gone off, back to my stupid, beastly, selfish life, not noticed how ill he was?' Her voice rose with each word, she stood there, shaking with misery.

'Because, my darling – come over here, sit down, come on, have a cuddle, that's right, that's better – because that was what he wanted.'

'But he didn't, he didn't want it. He wanted me to stay at home and be a companion to him, and I just turned my back on him, and didn't even write very often. I was impatient with him at Christmas – he was getting deaf, you know, and you had to say everything quite loudly, or else

34

twice, and in the end I didn't say anything much because it was so irritating. And he was getting more and more long-winded, and I avoided him for that reason as well, and even on my last evening I promised to sit with him and listen to a concert on the wireless and he was so looking forward to it, and then some of the girls from school turned up and asked me to go out with them for a meal, and he said go on, off you go, I'll be fine. And I did. My last evening with him. Ever. And when I left that last morning, I knew he was ill, he was coughing and coughing and I should have stayed, I should, Leonora, and I—'

'Sweet Pea, stop it. Listen. He had cancer. Lung cancer. He would have died whether you'd been here or not. And of course he didn't want you to stay at home with him, he would have hated it. And he was lucky, given that he had it anyway: he died suddenly and really quite painlessly. Very often it's months, months of terrible pain—'

'Leonora, don't try and make me feel better,' said Cassia, pulling away from her in a flash of anger. 'I don't deserve it and it's impossible. Do you really think he wasn't in terrible pain anyway? I could have helped him, given him so much care and love, and made him comfortable. Do you think Phyllis and Molly were any use? But I was down in London, doing exactly what I wanted and— Oh God! I hate myself.'

She got through the funeral somehow. Afterwards it became the most clichéd of nightmares, with touches, at times, of farce: it rained relentlessly; Cassia slipped on the mud and almost fell into the grave, only saved by Rupert's restraining hand; her grandmother, dressed in black from head to foot, had a cold and coughed endlessly throughout the whole thing, a ghastly ghostly reminder of Duncan's illness.

There was a small gathering at the house afterwards. Cassia looked round the drawing room, over-neatened for the occasion, and thought it would never again seem like home, and thought too that she had never felt so alone. Only Rupert, standing at her side throughout, holding her hand, seemed to be properly with her, as he always was; the rest, even Leonora and Sir Richard, were distant, almost unfamiliar figures.

Her father's death did one thing for her: it reunited her with Edward. He had seen Cassia standing in the reception area of the hospital, waiting for Tom Cavanagh who had come to find his houseman elder brother. Edward told her how sorry he had been to hear of her loss. 'It must be terrible.'

'Yes,' she said simply, 'it is. But one just has to come to terms with it.'

'Yes, of course. Well, that's all, really. I'm glad I was able to speak to you. I thought of writing, but ...'

'It was very nice of you to speak to me about it,' said Cassia. 'Most people are too embarrassed. They pretend nothing's happened, or that I've had a cold or something.'

'Really?' He looked genuinely surprised. 'Oh, dear, that sounds rather odd to me.'

'People are odd, aren't they?'

'I suppose they are. Well, goodbye, anyway. It was very ...' There was a long pause. He's as bad as Father, thought Cassia. 'Very nice to see you again.'

'And you, Edward.' He turned away, and she was still looking after him, smiling, when he stopped, obviously thinking for a moment, then turned again and came back to her. 'There's something else,' he said.

'Yes?'

'I ...' Another long, agonising pause, then, 'I was perhaps a bit foolish that night. At the ball. About your family.'

'Oh, I don't know,' said Cassia, carefully. 'I could quite see how you felt. How it seemed.'

'Could you?' he said, blushing again. 'I do hope so. Anyway – ' the words were rushing out now – 'anyway, I thought maybe you'd like to go to the cinema one night. Or don't you like the cinema? If you don't, we could have a meal or—'

'I love the cinema,' said Cassia. 'Thank you.'

'That's all right. Saturday, then? I'll pick you up. It would be nice to see your godparents again. I liked your godfather particularly. He seemed a jolly nice chap.'

'He is,' said Cassia, 'jolly nice.'

Cassia had been in love before, with Rupert Cameron, so she knew what she felt for Edward Fallon was not that. It wasn't painful, it didn't leave her heart thudding and her stomach churning, and so far, at least, he had had no real effect on her senses. But then the nearest they had come to sexual contact had been a few rather hesitant, tentative kisses after visits to the cinema or Lyons Corner House when he had bought her supper, and, as summer wore on, after the picnics they had in Hyde Park by the Serpentine, or in Kensington Gardens. What she did feel in his company, however, was a clear, easy happiness, for the first time in her life she was close, properly close, to someone who felt about life as she did, with the same concerns, interests, ambitions and hopes. They shared political views too, being gently socialist in their views, behind the miners, against

36

the more rigorous manifestations of the English class system, anxious to see the poor and disadvantaged taken better care of. They were both determined that when they were practising as doctors they would support any scheme for bringing medical help to those who at the present time feared to seek it because of its cost. Edward (unlike many of his colleagues at the medical school) was even fiercely supportive of the infiltration of women into the medical profession.

'I think you'll make a marvellous doctor,' he said earnestly to Cassia one lovely summer's evening, as they walked beside the Round Pond in Kensington Gardens, 'really marvellous, and whether you're male or female is neither here nor there. Why should it be?'

'No reason at all,' said Cassia, 'but tell me, Edward, how would you feel if you actually had to work for a woman? I mean, have her telling you what to do?'

'That would be different,' he said.

'Why?'

'Well, because I feel ...'

'Men really are the more important sex?' she said, smiling up at him.

'Not more important, but perhaps more naturally in command. I mean that is nature, isn't it? The male of every species is dominant.'

'That's mostly for physical reasons,' said Cassia. 'You don't think they're dominant because they're cleverer, I hope?'

'No, of course not, but more – well – authoritative.'

'I see. So in twenty years' time, when I'm an Honorary and I have medical students following me on my rounds, and I'm instructing them what to do, should I only take the female ones? Because I couldn't be authoritative enough for the males?'

'No, but—'

Cassia laughed suddenly. 'It's all right, Edward. I'm only trying to catch you out. I do happen to think there will be lots of women Honoraries, and they will be very authoritative, but we can wait and see.'

'Tell me,' Edward said, looking at her slightly awkwardly, 'if you were married ...'

'Yes? This isn't a proposal, is it, Edward?'

'No. No, of course not,' he said, blushing furiously.

'Sorry, just teasing. If I was married ...'

'Would you go on practising?'

'Yes, of course,' she said, genuinely astonished by the question.

'What, even if you had children?'

'Yes. I hope you're not telling me, Edward, that if you were married to a doctor and she had children, you'd expect her to give it all up. Why should she? And what a waste.'

'Yes,' he said, slightly doubtfully, 'yes, I suppose so. It would be a bit hard on the children, though, wouldn't it?'

'Oh, I don't know. Obviously I'd have help. But a miserable, frustrated mother isn't going to be any good to anyone, is she?'

'Why should she be miserable and frustrated?'

'Because she's not doing what she wants to do,' said Cassia impatiently.

'Surely looking after children is more important, more fulfilling, than anything else?'

'I don't agree with you at all, I'm afraid. No, I'd be a doctor first and a mother second. My husband would just have to recognise that.'

Edward wasn't conventionally romantic – he never bought her flowers or paid her lavish compliments, or wrote her silly little notes like some people's boyfriends did – but he was very thoughtful and sweet and always remembered things she said. When he discovered she had a rather unlikely fondness for fashion magazines, for instance, he delivered a large envelope to the sergeant the week after she had made this confession, marked for her attention; it was the previous month's copy of *Vogue*. 'My aunt takes it, so I've asked her to send each one when she's finished with it for you.'

Cassia was so touched by this that she stood looking at the cover and, indeed, his note through a blur of tears, and wondered at the same time that he could be so unsophisticated that it did not occur to him that Leonora would automatically order such a thing.

'You're sweet and I adore you,' she said, kissing him lightly on the lips when they next met. He looked rather startled and she realised she must have sounded more like Edwina Fox-Ashley than herself, and to redress the balance hastily told him about a fascinating physics experiment she had done that day.

Flicking through the magazine later in bed, she saw a photograph of Edwina Fox-Ashley at a party, looking ravishing in a long gold lamé dress and a mink stole, partnered by Harry Moreton, equally ravishing in his white tie and tails. For some reason it made her extremely irritable and she had to have a second cup of cocoa before she could go to sleep.

She and Edward were, by the end of June, accepted as a couple. Cassia herself was slightly surprised to find this, so informally and easily had it happened.

The occasional letter from Rupert, who had gone to Hollywood to seek his fortune and had found only a succession of starlets with whom he was having a succession of apparently disastrous affairs, reminded her what passion actually felt like, but served to make her grateful that its discomfort was no longer a constant companion. She was very fond of Edward, and since she was hardly looking for a husband or even a lover, he suited her and her life admirably; indeed, she sometimes wondered if he was capable of becoming a lover at all, so gentle and passionless did he seem. And then something happened which changed everything.

'I've failed. I've failed my finals.'

Cassia sat there, looking at him, looking up at Edward – at his head drooping between his bony shoulders; at his white face, disbelieving that this thing could have happened; at his hands, clasped together in some kind of supplication – and could think of nothing that she could say to comfort him.

'I told my father,' he said. 'I telephoned him straight away, and he was very nice about it. He said he'd get Grandpa to have a word with the Dean, just to find out how bad it had been. It's so hard on him, on both of my parents – they've made such sacrifices to keep me here. My mother was sweet, really sweet, as mothers are, not understanding properly, just worried I'd be so upset. She said I must go home and see them, and I will, I think, straight away, as soon as I can get packed, and I have to sort things out, decide what to do, and ...'

She had never heard Edward talk so much. It was as if he couldn't stop, as if he was afraid of stopping because then he would have to do something else, take his first steps into the terrible unknown that lay outside the world of the hospital and the operating theatre and indeed everything he cared about.

'Edward,' she said, 'Edward, come here. Come and sit down here. Please.'

She was sitting on his bed, in the small room where he lived. She had spent a lot of time in that room over the past year. She was now a fully fledged medical student herself (having passed her Second MB top of her year), and it had become a kind of second home to her, with the encouragement of his rather liberal landlady who liked her and took a most motherly interest in Edward, and said she could see there would not be any hanky panky going on in his room. Cassia had studied there with him, read, chatted, listened to concerts on Edward's tinny radio there; eaten mountains of sandwiches, drunk gallons of tea; welcomed Edward back, grey with exhaustion, from forty-eight-, sixty-, seventy-two-hour stints in Casualty, Obstetrics, Surgical; helped him with his notes, his thesis, his revision; learnt to be silent when he required it, to talk when he did not. She often thought (without, of course, saying anything of the sort) that they were more like an old married couple than a young courting one.

Edward came over to her and she held out her arms. He sat down on the bed beside her and buried his head on her shoulder, and then suddenly got up and started punching the door with his fist. She was so startled by this most unusual display of aggression from the normally gentle Edward, and so afraid he would hurt his hands, that she told him quite sharply to stop. He sat down again and stayed there in total silence for quite a long time.

'I worked so hard,' he said suddenly, sitting up, 'so terribly, terribly hard. It's so unfair; lots of people who didn't work passed. I suppose I must just be very stupid. Is that the explanation, do you think? Just not clever enough, as simple as that.'

'Edward,' Cassia said, 'of course you're clever, you're terribly clever, everybody says so. You're just bad at exams. You get these dreadful awful nerves, it can't be helped—'

'No,' he said, 'it can't be helped, and look what's happened, as a result of that: I've failed, and I'll go on failing.' He was growing angry again now, his voice rising, angry with her. 'It's all right for you,' he said. 'You're good at exams, you thrive on them. You don't know what it's like, sitting there with your brain like bloody scrambled egg, trying to make sense just of the questions. You have no idea, and you ought to have. It's easy for you and—'

Cassia stood up. 'I'm sorry, Edward, but I don't think there's much future in this conversation. Not now. I'll come back later. When you're feeling calmer.'

'No,' he said, panic in his voice, 'don't go, Cassia, please. I'm sorry, don't go. I need you here, I really do. I love you so much and—'

There was a silence, an absolute silence, and the room was very still. Cassia stood there, not moving, just staring at him.

Edward stared back at her. 'Did I say that? Did I really say that?'

'Yes, you did,' she said quietly. 'You really did.'

'Good Lord,' he said, and his slow smile began to break. 'I can't believe it. I've been wanting to say it for so long, and I couldn't. Every time I saw you I would screw myself up and tell myself that this time I would, and then I couldn't, and all the time in between I'd be cursing myself and promising I would next time.'

'Oh,' she said. 'Oh, I see.'

There was another silence, then he smiled, for the first time that day.

'Well, anyway, I do. I love you.' He seemed to be exploring the thought. 'I love you very much. Very, very much. Oh God. Now I've embarrassed you, haven't I?'

'No,' she said, 'not at all. It's lovely.'

'So do you … Oh, good Lord, Cassia, what do you think? What I mean is, you don't think, do you, that you might love me too?'

'Yes, Edward,' she said, realising with something of a shock that she might think that, think that she did love him. 'Yes, I really think I might.'

And then because she wanted to comfort him and make him feel better, she lay down on the bed and held out her arms to him. Everything became very confused after that: he was kissing her, kissing her and caressing her, and telling her how very much he loved her, and then he turned away from her on to his back with a great sigh and said, 'No, no, this is wrong, I can't do this.'

'Oh Edward, but you know what I think about it,' she said, for they had had several conversations, and even at times fierce arguments, in which she had outlined her view that sex was about love and not marriage.

He said that whatever she thought, it didn't change what he thought, how he felt, which was precisely the opposite; and they lay there for a long time quietly, just holding hands, and then finally he said, 'I think I should ask you to go. I don't want you to, but I have so much to do.'

Cassia stood up and straightened her clothes and put on her coat and then bent and kissed him. Edward said, quite simply, 'You've made it so much better. Thank you.' As she reached the door, he added, 'I really do love you.'

Cassia turned and he was lying down again, smiling at her with an expression of perfect happiness on his face, and just for a moment she felt frightened, scared by the intensity of what and how he felt. She blew him a kiss and left.

They had become engaged entirely by accident. Had anyone told Cassia beforehand that such a thing could happen, especially to such a person as she – strong minded, independent, clear sighted – she would have been scornful, incredulous. Nevertheless it did.

The Dean said Edward could resit the exams in a year. 'I told you so,' Cassia said, 'especially as your grandfather was here.'

'Yes, but it's so hard on Father, another year of keeping me, and he was hoping to retire soon, he's overage already. He's taken it very hard, very hard indeed, he's desperately disappointed. I have to pass next time, and really well; I have to.'

'You will. Of course you will.'

His father was hoping Edward would take over the local practice. The GP, a great friend, was retiring shortly; it was a point of issue, Edward said.

'He just doesn't understand how much I want to do surgery. But after this, perhaps I should give in, do what he wants.'

'On something as important as that,' said Cassia firmly, 'you must do what you yourself want.'

Edward was going home for a couple of months: he couldn't start again until September, and his parents had expressed a desire to see something of him.

'And I can spend some time with David Martin, that's the GP, accompany him on his rounds, help in the dispensary. It'll be good experience. I shall miss you terribly,' he said.

'I'll miss you too,' Cassia said and meant it.

Halfway through August, she got a letter from Edward: his parents had asked to meet her ('I've told them so much about you') and had invited her down for the coming weekend. 'It's lovely here, I so want to show it all to you. The weather is perfect, bring a tennis racket – we can use the school courts, as of course the school is empty at the moment – and a bathing suit, just in case we get to the seaside. I could meet you on Friday night at Haywards Heath. Do come. I love you. Edward.' Cassia wrote back that she would love to.

The Fallons were at once nicer and less impressive than she had somehow expected. They lived in a rather forbidding small house, just on the edge of the school. Every wall was covered with photographs of small boys, in groups, with Desmond Fallon. There was a large painting of him, in his cap and gown, hanging in the hall, and a painted shield bearing the school motto (*Ad Astra Per Labor*) hung above the front door. 'That means "to the stars, through work," ' Edward explained as he ushered her into the hall. Cassia just slightly tactlessly said that yes, she had worked that out for herself.

Desmond Fallon was a deeply serious man, pompous in the way of schoolteachers, openly proud of his son, although clearly embarrassed by his temporary failure. Mrs Fallon was quiet and shy, welcoming to Cassia, and seemed almost nervous of her. They gave her a small glass of sherry and talked awkwardly of her journey and the weather.

'We had hoped so very much,' Desmond Fallon said, on the very first evening, at the very first meal, 'hoped that Edward would have qualified by now, and that I could have retired at Christmas. But it was not to be, and I feel I must support him until he wins through, which I trust he will.'

'Of course he will,' said Cassia firmly, smiling at Edward across the table, thinking that if this was the kind of thing he had to contend with, it was not surprising his self-esteem was so shaky, that he found exams an almost unimaginable ordeal. 'He's going to pass next time. He does so well generally, he's extremely highly thought of—'

'Is that so, Miss Berridge?' Barbara Fallon leaned forward, her pale blue eyes anxious. 'So it really is only a temporary problem, you think?'

'Of course it is, Mrs Fallon, and please call me Cassia. You must realise the Dean wouldn't have allowed him back otherwise. Everyone is convinced he's going to be a marvellous surgeon.'

'That's very nice to hear,' said Barbara, 'isn't it, Desmond?'

'Yes, although we are actually not quite so keen for Edward to be a surgeon, Cassia. We were very much hoping that he might consider going into general practice, here in the village. It's such a marvellous way to serve the community, in my view. The present doctor is a close friend of ours and it would be very good to feel that Edward was the link between the past and the future.'

'General practice is excellent,' said Cassia carefully, 'but surgery is much more exciting.'

'I did not realise one went into medicine for excitement,' said Desmond Fallon drily.

Cassia managed to smile at him. 'Oh, Mr Fallon, it is the most exciting thing in the world. Getting a diagnosis right, solving a problem, saving a patient ...'

'Indeed? I had certainly not seen it quite like that. Edward is not quite as articulate as you are.'

Edward smiled slightly awkwardly at his father, then at her.

'Cassia is extremely articulate,' he said. 'I wish I shared that gift. But yes, that is why I want to go into surgery, for the drama, the—'

'Good gracious,' said Barbara Fallon, 'you make it sound all very different suddenly, both of you. I had always thought the whole point about medicine, family medicine at any rate, is a lack of drama, simply a good, solid contribution to the community.' She looked at Cassia rather piercingly. 'And you, Cassia, surely you don't see yourself as a surgeon? Not the sort of field a woman would want to enter, I would have imagined.'

'I do, actually,' said Cassia, smiling at her. 'I would very much like to do surgery. Probably obstetrics.'

'Indeed! How very admirable. It must be quite unusual, even these days, for a woman to be at medical school and with such ambitions.'

'Very. Only six in my year. Seven in the following one. Of course it's getting better all the time.'

'Whether better is the word is a matter open to discussion, I would have thought,' said Desmond Fallon. He spoke mildly, but his eyes were probing as he looked at Cassia. 'I happen to think this new desire among women to have careers, rather than regarding marriage as their vocation, could be a little destructive. Society is built on the family, as I'm sure you would agree, and the woman, as wife and mother, is the lynch pin that holds it together. Too many women neglecting that role, and we shall be in very serious trouble.'

'I think we can do both,' said Cassia carefully. 'Work and support the family.'

'Oh, now there I would have to disagree with you,' he said. 'Marriage is a full-time job, and it cannot work any other way.'

'We mustn't get Cassia on to this subject,' said Edward, unexpectedly and smoothly firm. 'She is inclined to become very excited.'

Cassia stared at Edward, faintly shocked, not wishing to be rude, but feeling an absolute compulsion to continue to state her case. 'The thing is,' she said finally, 'the world is changing. I think we have to be open minded about these things. Don't you?'

'Yes, of course,' said Barbara carefully, and then visibly seeking to change the subject, 'I believe your own background has been quite unusual, Cassia. That you lost your own mother when you were very young. So sad.'

'Yes, it was. She died in childbirth when I was thirteen. She was a wonderful woman,' she added staunchly. 'She managed to instil in me a belief that women should lead their own lives, follow their own hearts.'

Cassia felt disproportionately upset suddenly, the memory suddenly vivid, of being there in the tiny room at the hospital looking at her mother's body, trying to relate this still, silent being, so remote and so peaceful, to the vibrantly busy, indefatigable person who had loved, disciplined, inspired and supported her; who had walked and bicycled and played and talked with her so tirelessly; who had been a companion and friend as well as a mother; who had shared jokes and fun with her; who had never been shocked, answered all her questions, and above all made her feel there was nothing she could not do, nothing at all, if she wanted it enough. And then she remembered her father coming in, oddly insubstantial, white, drawn with grief, saying. 'Well, Cassia, we only have one another now, and we must be brave for her.' She remembered trying to understand, to come to terms not only with the terrible cruelty of what had happened, but with her father's remorse, feeling as he did partly to blame, and that had the tiny sister, who had lived only an hour, never been born, her mother would have been alive and well and with them still.

'Much of what I've achieved, I feel I've achieved for her,' Cassia explained rather lamely into the slightly awkward silence, and blew her nose hard.

'Indeed?' said Barbara Fallon. 'How very nice.'

Silly, buttoned-up woman, thought Cassia.

'And your father, he had to bring you up on his own. That must have been difficult.'

'Very difficult, yes. And then of course he died, in my first year at medical school.'

'Dreadful. Very, very sad.'

Another silence, during which Cassia began to feel like a character in a Victorian melodrama, and then Desmond Fallon said, 'You live in London with your godmother and her husband. Quite well-off people, as I understand?' His eyes were suddenly sharper. Ah, thought Cassia, he likes the thought that his son has found someone with rich connections. 'Yes,' she said carefully, 'yes, my godfather has a large industrial company.'

'He was knighted, I believe?'

Now why on earth would Edward have told them that? 'Yes. For services during the war, manufacturing munitions and so on.'

Edward said suddenly, 'I thought perhaps, as it is such a nice evening, Cassia and I could go for a walk. I'd like to show her the village.'

'Very good,' said Mrs Fallon. 'Show her the surgery while you're about it. Perhaps one day it will be yours. It's the heart of the village life,' she said to Cassia, 'that and this school, of course.'

Edward was interestingly unapologetic about his parents. 'I can tell they like you,' he said, taking her hand as they walked down the hill.

'I hope so. I don't think I'm quite the sort of girl they'd like you to be involved with.'

'Oh, not at all. They're rather impressed by you actually. Especially with the Beattys and so on. A bit snobbish, I'm afraid. It's running this school, you see, trying to impress parents all the time.'

'Yes,' she said, although she was still surprised he had even told his parents about her background.

'I know they might seem a bit heavy,' he said, 'going on about my future all the time, but they've made so many sacrifices for me, sending me to Malvern and so on. They want so much for me to succeed. It's very touching, don't you think?'

'Very,' said Cassia carefully.

Next day, Cassia and Edward went on a picnic. She listened as Edward talked again for a long time about his parents, about their life at the school, their position in the local community, about how important it was to them that he should live up to what they saw as their own high standards.

Finally she said, 'Edward, this is very interesting, but let's stop talking for a bit, shall we?' and lay down on the bracken carpet of the woods while he kissed her for a long time, with his long, slow, careful kisses.

'I love you,' he said, 'very much. You do love me too, don't you?'

'Edward, you know I do,' said Cassia warily. She was beginning to understand how deep his insecurity must be, why he minded so much about such things as her background, her life with Leonora and Sir Richard, people like Edwina Fox-Ashley. And Harry Moreton.

The Fallons went out that evening – 'to a party at the Manor House,' said Barbara Fallon, clearly anxious that Cassia should understand that they did indeed mix with the very best people in the neighbourhood. 'Edward, Doris has prepared a meal for you and Cassia. Only cold, I'm afraid, but—'

'I'm sure it will be delicious,' said Cassia.' 'Thank you.'

The cold meal was very cold and not at all delicious: slices of lamb, salad, and bread, followed by extremely small portions of trifle, and then biscuits and cheese. School food, thought Cassia, recognising the type suddenly – adequate, sustaining, dull. The memory came to her, unbidden, halfway through the trifle, of the wonderful meals at Grosvenor Gardens, and at the Harringtons' house in Eaton Place: course after course, five or six even, on formal occasions, and was horrified to hear herself sigh.

'Are you all right?' said Edward, and yes, she said, of course, just a bit tired. And then he said what was he thinking of, he hadn't even offered her a glass of wine. He would get a bottle from the cellar. 'Father won't mind, he's very generous like that.'

Cassia found it hard to imagine Desmond Fallon being generous about anything, but she smiled at him over the table and said how very nice.

The wine was all right – a nondescript red – but it had the desired effect, cheering her up and relaxing her, and after a while, when they had cleared away and washed up, she asked if they could go and play some gramophone records.

There were a few rather old-fashioned dance records amongst them ('Mother and Father used to enjoy dancing,' he told her) and they danced. After another couple of glasses of wine, they started kissing rather enthusiastically on the sofa, but after a few minutes Edward sat back, clearly feeling awkward.

'I'm sorry. It's just that I think they might be back quite soon.'

'Well, let's go upstairs. To your room. Or mine.'

Edward flushed. 'Oh, well, I don't know. I mean—'

'Mummy wouldn't like it. Edward, for heaven's sake. You're a grown-up. Anyway, she won't know we're both in there. She'll just think we've gone to bed early – which we might ...' She was rather drunk, she realised. She smiled at him, leaned forward, kissed him very hard on the mouth, her tongue searching for his.

He pulled back from her. 'Cassia, you know—'

She felt a stab of irritation. 'Oh, Edward. Yes, I do know, and sometimes I wonder if you really want me at all.'

'You know I do,' he said.

'I don't. I don't know anything of the sort. Actually. Prove it to me.'

'Yes, all right,' he said, and his face changed suddenly. 'Yes, I will.'

And thus it was that somehow they were lying on Edward's bed, and he was kissing her, and she was returning the kisses, and great shards of desire were moving through her, and she was feeling for him, feeling into his trousers, feeling his erection, hard, trembling, and she wanted it, very badly, wanted it in her, and she told him so, and no he said, no it was wrong. 'It's not wrong, Edward,' she cried out in a passion of frustration, and pulled him down on to her again, kissing him hard, frantically, and then he was kissing her back, one hand up her skirt, searching, feeling for her, the other on her breast, caressing it, working at it, and then just as he raised his head, looked into her eyes, said, 'Oh, God, I love you,' the door of the bedroom opened, and over Edward's shoulder, she saw Desmond Fallon's face staring at her in a mixture of disbelief and distaste. And then heard, incredulous, Edward's voice as he rolled off her, struggled into a sitting position, Edward's voice saying, 'Father, I'm sorry, sorry if you're upset, but – well, we are going to be married.'

She would have thought, had she been asked, that she would have denied it herself, then and there, said no we're not, that has nothing to do with it, but she was so taken aback, so humiliated, so absolutely diminished in herself by what had happened, that she went along with it. She smiled meekly at Desmond Fallon, and sat silently while Edward said quite firmly that of course he was sorry, desperately sorry, but times had changed since his parents were young, that many engaged couples had a physical relationship these days, that it was no longer the near crime it had seemed to the generation before them.

Desmond was not instantly mollified, he said he was shocked that a son of his could behave in such a way, that he would like to see him downstairs, and left them.

Edward looked at Cassia awkwardly, sheepishly, and said nothing while she looked back at him, wanting to argue, to ask him why he had made his announcement, why he had not asked her first, wanting to say that they were not going to be married, it was not true, but not liking to in the face of his embarrassment and distress.

Finally he said, 'Perhaps we should tidy up and go downstairs.'

'No, Edward,' she said, 'I am not going downstairs. I'm sorry to leave you to face them, but I feel upset. I am going to bed. Please explain.'

He said he would and left the room, looking utterly dejected. Cassia heard him in the bathroom and went herself along to her own room, where she crawled rather miserably under the covers. Greatly to her surprise, she slept.

In the morning she awoke to a very nasty headache; a headache and a strong sense of remorse, mingled with panic. Things had to be resolved.

She got up and had a bath, dressed and then packed her case. The best thing, she felt, would be to leave the Fallon household as soon as possible, first making clear that Edward's announcement of the night before had been in error. She went downstairs cautiously and into the dining room. Desmond and Barbara were not there but Edward was standing at the sideboard helping himself to bacon. He turned and smiled at her.

'Cassia. Good morning! Did you sleep well?'

'Yes. Thank you. Surprisingly so. Edward—'

He interrupted her. 'I had a very good conversation with my parents last night. I had hoped you would come down, but your door was shut and your light was out, and presumably you were asleep.'

'Yes,' she said, 'I was. Edward—'

'They've been marvellous,' he said, 'quite marvellous. Very broad-minded, even my mother. I think they think – well – ' he smiled, slightly bashfully – 'that I'm just a red-blooded young man. Doing what comes naturally.'

'But we weren't doing anything.'

'I know, but we were alone in my room, lying on the bed with the door closed. It was obvious what might have happened.'

'I see,' she said, her voice sounding cool. 'And me, what am I if you're a red-blooded young man? A trollop?'

'No, of course not. They said, once they'd calmed down, they liked you very much. I told you, they are very impressed by you.'

'How nice,' she said.

'Yes,' he said, clearly missing the irony in her voice, 'and they said long engagements did put young people under a lot of strain. That they could remember what it was like to be young.'

'But there hasn't been a long engagement.'

'I know, but it helped to imply that there had. Unofficially, of course. And they seem quite happy about it.'

'Edward, there isn't anything to be happy about. We're not—'

The door opened, and Desmond Fallon came in. He nodded at her briefly, said good morning and that he and Barbara were going to church. 'It would be nice if you would join us.'

'I will, of course,' said Edward. 'Cassia? Will you?'

He looked so desperate, so pleading, that she said she would. When they got back, she could sort things out.

The church was packed. After the service various friends came up to the Fallons. To her surprise they introduced her to all of them, very courteously, and in Barbara's case quite proudly; told them she was at the hospital studying with Edward.

'A couple of years behind him, of course,' Barbara added carefully each time, as if it was unthinkable that they should be at the same stage.

Desmond said each time, 'Very unusual for a woman to be studying medicine, of course.'

It began to occur to her that in the intellectually snobbish world in which the Fallons moved, a woman medical student, and moreover a woman medical student who was their son's girlfriend, was something rather impressive.

When they got back to the house, Desmond and Barbara disappeared.

'Edward,' Cassia said urgently, 'we must talk and then I want to go.'

'Go! Go where?'

'Back to London. I really can't stay here. It's too difficult for me, and besides—'

49

'Ah, there you are.' Desmond Fallon was almost smiling. 'Come into the drawing room, we'd like to say a few words.'

Again the panic rose. She looked desperately at Edward, but he was smiling encouragingly, had taken her arm, was ushering her into the room. Barbara stood by a side table; there was a bottle of champagne on it, and four glasses. Desmond went over and opened it with a flourish, poured it out, handed her one. It was warm, and very sweet; she tried to look enthusiastic.

'Well,' Desmond said, still looking at Edward, 'congratulations. To both of you. Of course we have our reservations. You're very young, but you're obviously very serious about each other.'

'Mr Fallon—' Cassia began.

'No, don't say another word,' Desmond said. 'Of course you have a long wait ahead of you. There can be no question of marriage until Edward is fully qualified. And – ' he gave her a look that was almost conspiratorial – 'I dare say your views on working women and marriage will change. So here's a toast. To the two of you. And the future.'

'The future,' said Barbara, and flushed.

It seemed impossibly cruel to say there wasn't going to be a future. Or not of the kind they envisaged.

Edward took Cassia to the station later that day; she said she had to get back. Desmond lent him the car. They were early and sat waiting for the train.

Cassia took a deep breath. 'Edward, we're not engaged, and you know we're not. You should never have—'

'But we could be. We should be. All I've done is bring it forward a bit. I love you. Very much. And you love me.'

'Edward ...'

'You do, don't you?' he said, and he looked so hurt, so anxious, that she was frightened. 'You said you did, anyway. You said you loved me.'

'I do love you, but—'

'Well, then. What could be more wonderful and more natural than getting married? Cassia, if I have you, I can do anything, I know I can. I love you so much, and I'm so happy.' He smiled down at her. 'You know, it was just as well it happened like it did. I'd never have plucked up the courage to ask you in cold blood, so to speak. Oh, look, here's the train now. Let's find you a seat. Come on.'

There was a friend of his parents on the platform, a bluff, noisy man Cassia had met outside the church. He said he'd join her if she didn't mind. Cassia said of course she didn't, and gave up all hope of explaining to Edward until she saw him again in London.

And that had been the fatal, irrevocable mistake.

CHAPTER 3

'My darling, you look simply wonderful.'

Cassia smiled rather feebly up at Rupert, thought how untrue it was; thought how he on the other hand did look rather wonderful, and how unfair that men, even when they were in their mid-fifties, as Rupert most definitely was, could still be so extremely attractive while women at the same age were old, past it, finished.

And oh God, he was attractive. The silvery blond hair was as thick as ever, the blue eyes as brilliant, the wonderful, chiselled features as sharp, the tall body as slim. He was dressed so well too. Somehow he always managed, even though he had never had very much money, almost none at all indeed, to look as if he was in the hands of a good valet and a fine tailor. It was all part of his gift, part of his charm: the actor's charm. Just as he bestowed upon any gathering pleasure and humour, so he bestowed upon his surroundings an interest and a kind of grace. Today, he was wearing a dark grey pinstripe suit, which would have looked very ordinary without the striped black and pink silk tie – tied in the Prince of Wales knot, of course – the black hat with its just slightly overwide brim, the antique gold watch chain fixed across his waistcoat.

Cassia stood there, drinking him in, thinking how much she still loved and missed him. She reached up and kissed him gently on the cheek. 'Oh, Rupert,' she said simply, 'it's so lovely to see you.'

'And you, my darling. And I mean it, you look quite marvellous. I love that hat.'

'Do you? I bought it early this morning. I was a bit frightened, I haven't bought anything to wear for so long, but I thought I couldn't let Leonora down, so I went to Harvey Nichols as a sort of memorial gesture to her. Is it really all right?'

'It's perfect. It looks expensive.'

'It was. Very,' she said, and smiled at him. It was a reckless smile. She had felt reckless as she wrote the cheque, glancing constantly at the hat as it lay, still untissued, in its box: black straw, shallow crowned and huge brimmed, with a wide red ribbon, tied in a most outrageously theatrical bow. The rest of her outfit – a narrow, black silk dress and coat – did not quite match up to it, she knew, but that didn't matter. The hat was for Leonora; her tribute to her.

'Where's Edward?'

'He couldn't come. Emergency after emergency yesterday and then a breech baby this morning. He only delivered it at seven, after a very long night; he was exhausted. He really didn't want to come anyway, and he didn't know Leonora very well after all.'

'No, but it would have been nice for you to have him here.'

'Yes, I suppose so,' she said quickly.

'Well,' Rupert said, bending to kiss her, 'I shall play the role of husband-by-proxy. With the greatest of pleasure, I might add. Not to mention pride. How would that be?'

'It would be lovely, Rupert, thank you.'

'Right, then. Take my arm. Now shall we go inside, or are you waiting for Benedict and Cecily? I am very nervous about my reading, I can tell you. Far worse than a first night.'

'Rupert, you don't know what nerves are,' said Cassia, laughing, 'but it's lovely that you are going to do it. What have you chosen? Or did Benedict do it for you?'

'No, he was surprisingly deferential about it. Asked if I had any suggestions. I chose the lovely thing from Revelations, you know?'

Cassia shook her head. 'No. I'm not very godly, I'm afraid.'

'Well, it will be a nice surprise for you, I hope. Ah, here is Benedict now. And Cecily. Will you excuse me a moment, darling, I just want to have a final look at my reading. I'll join you inside. Keep a place for me.'

'Cassia, my dear,' said Benedict Harrington, kissing her. 'How nice you look. Doesn't she, Cecily?'

'Marvellous,' said Cecily. 'Lovely hat, Cassia.'

'Do you like it? I thought it might be a bit frivolous.'

'Well, if it was, which it isn't, no matter. This is a memorial service, not a funeral,' said Cecily firmly, 'and Leonora's life was dedicated to frivolity.'

Cassia smiled at her, bent to kiss her. Cecily was at least six inches shorter than Cassia, deliciously, voluptuously pretty, her capacity for prattle a dazzling disguise for a sharp, clear intelligence. She was wearing a very fine hat herself, in brilliant yellow straw, an interesting adjunct to a dove-grey crêpe dress.

'No Edward, then?' said Benedict.

'No, he …' Cassia embarked on the explanation about the breech birth, thinking that even now, Benedict was a most vivid evocation of Leonora: same fair hair, same brown eyes, same fine features. They were – well, had been – almost Shakespearean in their brother-and-sister alikeness. And it wasn't just their features: Leonora had been tall and imposing, Benedict slight for a man. As she looked at him, Cassia drew back, shut out the associations, the memory of Harry Moreton at her coming-out dance, telling her the unspeakable, the shocking, spoiling what had until then been so perfect, so magical an occasion. She smiled at Benedict now, determinedly blotting out the memory. 'This is a wonderful occasion, Benedict. I'm so glad you thought of it.'

'She deserved it,' he said simply. He looked very sad suddenly.

'Yes, she did,' said Cassia, and surprised herself by kissing him again. She tended to forget, they all did, how much he had loved Leonora.

Benedict smiled down at her, recognising the sympathy, then turned as he heard his name.

It was the Fox-Ashleys. Cassia was pleased to see them: they were such a splendid pair, almost a pastiche of themselves, Sir Marcus tall and elegant in his morning suit, perfectly and gently mannered, his wife dangerously chic, utterly self-confident, her voice rising above the rest of the rather subdued chatter that was going on.

'Benedict, dear, what a turn-out. Of course people never can resist this sort of thing, can they?'

'Can't they?' said Benedict, smiling at her with his unfailing courtesy. 'Well, I'm very pleased you couldn't, Sylvia. How lovely you look.'

'Don't flatter me, Benedict, please.' Sylvia Fox-Ashley glared at him. 'I look at least a hundred, as one of my dear little great-nieces told me yesterday. Feel it too.'

'Of course you don't,' said Benedict. 'You look hardly older than your daughter. Where is Edwina, by the way?'

'Oh, somewhere over there,' said Sylvia, 'and don't say that to her, for heaven's sake: nothing makes her more annoyed, and she's in a frightful bait already. I believe she and Harry are going to stay with you in France?'

'I hope so,' said Benedict, 'but what's put her in a bait?'

'Oh, Harry of course. He insisted on riding this morning. Edwina was simply furious with him, but don't worry, he'll be here, won't miss an opportunity of showing off. He's frightfully tickled about being asked to read, sweet of you.'

'He was Leonora's cousin, after all.'

'Yes, I suppose. So complex, your family. Oh, Cassia, I didn't see you. Lovely hat, dear.'

'Thank you,' said Cassia. 'Benedict, shall we go in?' She had only one wish in that moment: to be in her place, safely settled with the Harringtons, before Harry Moreton arrived.

The church was packed. She was surprised, as was Benedict; 'I didn't think so many would come. It's marvellous. Look, the Parson-Johnsons, and the Steeds and – oh, Cassia, good heavens, it's Richard.'

Cassia felt tears, the first of the day, sting behind her eyes. 'I'm so glad,' she said, staring at Sir Richard, with his new wife, Margaret, so unlike Leonora, so uncompromisingly sensible and clever, so staunchly behind him in everything he did.

Sir Richard saw her, came over to the pew, bent down and kissed her. 'Good morning, my dear. Lovely to see you.'

'Lovely to see you too, Godpa. I'm so pleased you're here.'

'Did you think I might not be?' he said, and looked so surprised and hurt that she felt ashamed of herself. The organ began to play suddenly, the wonderful lyrical ripples of 'Jesu, Joy of Man's Desiring'. He patted her hand. 'See you afterwards.'

She smiled at him rather weakly, and settled back into her seat.

'Thank God,' said Benedict suddenly in her ear. 'Harry's arrived.'

With an extraordinary effort of will, she didn't look round.

Benedict had planned the service very skilfully: it was both moving and impressive. Cassia kept thinking how much Leonora would have loved it, wishing absurdly she could have been there. Perhaps she was, she thought, gazing up at the vaulted roof, perhaps somehow she was with them all, enjoying the celebration of her difficult, interesting, amusing life.

There were prayers, hymns, the twenty-third psalm, then Rupert stood at the lectern and began, in his low, resonant actor's voice, the lovely lines from Revelations: 'And behold, I saw a new heaven and a new earth.'

As he finished, reading, 'There shall be no more death, neither sorrow nor crying,' Cassia felt her grief suddenly, physically, felt it fill her, wound her. She bit her lip until it almost bled, to silence the rising sobs, grasped Cecily's hand, scarcely realising she did so, and she watched Harry Moreton walk to the nave, and turn to look at the congregation, through a great veil of tears. His dark eyes fell on Cassia; recognised but did not acknowledge her, did not look away either. He stood there completely still, for a long time, and then finally opened the book he was holding, and began to read.

'Ecclesiastes,' he said, 'chapter three,' and paused for another long while. 'To every thing there is a season and a time to every purpose under the heavens. A time to be born and a time to die ...'

His deep heavy voice, not lyrical, not musical like Rupert's, was nevertheless immensely moving. Cassia sat, her eyes closed now, listening to it, wishing the years away, wishing Leonora back with her, and not only Leonora, but Leonora's time, the happy, wonderful time when she and Harry had been children and Leonora had been young and beautiful and fun, when her only concerns had been clothes, and parties and cocktails and her friends, when the house had been filled always with people, when Sir Richard had adored her and everyone had loved her and the nightmare had scarcely begun.

Looking at Harry now as he stood at the lectern reading, she remembered too when their strange, dangerous, difficult relationship had begun; thinking of that tall, sulky boy brought to have tea and to play with her on her first visit to Leonora.

'Harry is my second cousin,' Leonora had said that morning, 'a dear boy. You'll get on with him awfully well, I know. He'll be company for you. I have to go out this evening to a reception with Richard. Harry's almost the same age as you, so you should have lots of fun.'

It didn't seem very likely, Cassia thought, looking at Harry as he stood there in the doorway of the morning room, dressed so oddly, she had thought, in a silk shirt and short trousers, when he was clearly much too old for such things, his dark curls too long, almost girly, his brown eyes heavy with distaste both for her and the occasion. He was tall, almost exactly the same height as Cassia.

She had dressed carefully, for she had been looking forward to meeting Harry, had put on one of the new dresses Leonora had bought her, in tartan wool, low waisted with a wide collar, skimming over the bosom which was just beginning to develop. She wore black stockings on her long legs, and new shoes too, black patent with silver buckles, and her hair was drawn back with a tartan ribbon. She had gone forward to Harry smiling, holding out her hand, and said, 'Hallo, I'm Cassia'.

Harry had shaken her hand, but not returned the smile. He merely nodded at her and then turned to the uniformed nanny who stood behind him and said, 'You may go now. I shall send for you when I wish to leave here.' He sat down in a chair in the window and stared out into the garden.

'What would you like to do?' Cassia said, intrigued as much as anything by this strange creature.

'I really don't care,' he said, pulling up his stockings, not looking at her.

'We could play Ludo. Or a card game. If you like.'

'I hate games,' he said, picking up a copy of the *Illustrated London News* and flicking through it.

'What about a jigsaw puzzle?' she said, refusing to be beaten, but he said he hated jigsaw puzzles too. 'Or we could go for a walk in the garden.'

'It's raining, isn't it?'

She had given up at that, become cross. She sat down herself at the jigsaw-puzzle table and started to do one. After a while Jarvis, Leonora's maid, had come in and said would they like tea. Sitting at the table in silence, watching Harry eat his way silently through a pile of sandwiches, she tried again. Perhaps he was shy, or not feeling very well.

'This is very nice cake, isn't it?' she said through a mouthful.

'It's all right.'

'Are you on holiday from school, like me? Where do you go to school?'

'I don't go to school,' he said, his voice making it plain that he considered this a question of extreme foolishness. 'I have a tutor. Until I go to Eton, of course.'

'Isn't that a bit dull? Lonely?'

'Not at all. I enjoy my tutor's company. I prefer adult company in any case.'

Cassia glared at him: she had had enough. 'Aren't you a little old,' she said, 'to have a nurse?'

'No,' he said. 'Someone has to take care of me.'

'What about your mother?'

'I don't have a mother. She died when I was born.'

Compassion filled Cassia. She was shocked both at his situation and at herself and what must have seemed like gross insensitivity. 'I'm so sorry, Harry,' she said, 'how dreadful for you.'

Harry Moreton looked at her, his expression more hostile still. 'Not at all,' he said. 'I never knew her, after all.'

'No, but what about your father? I suppose you spend a lot of time with him.'

'I don't have a father. He was killed at the Battle of the Marne. When I was eight.'

This was too much for Cassia. She looked at him in silent horror for a moment, then stood up and walked out of the room.

'I just couldn't bear it,' she was to explain to Harry, years later, 'that

57

you had to endure this awful thing, live in this awful way, and nobody had thought, bothered to tell me something so important.'

When Leonora came to find her on her return much later that night, Cassia was lying on her bed, fully dressed, deeply upset.

Leonora was extremely angry. 'Cassiopeia –' and that was a measure of her anger, using her full name – 'how dare you treat Harry so rudely? I understand you left him at the tea table, never to return.'

'He was very rude to me,' said Cassia staunchly, 'very rude and unfriendly.'

'I find that very hard to believe. And however he behaved, he was a guest in this house, where you have received considerable hospitality, I might add, and it was your duty to be courteous. I am very shocked at you, Cassiopeia, very shocked indeed.'

'Well, I'm sorry,' she said. 'I did try. Honestly, Leonora, I tried and tried. And why didn't you tell me that he has no parents?'

'I didn't think it would matter to you,' said Leonora, 'one way or the other.'

'Of course it matters,' said Cassia, indignant herself now. 'It matters terribly, that someone of my age should have no parents, no one to love them and care for them. It explains such a lot. Who does look after him anyway?'

'Oh, servants,' said Leonora. 'There are plenty of people in the house.'

'No grandparents even?'

'No. Well, there is the old man, Harry's maternal grandfather, but he's quite dreadful. He does live there, but he has nothing to do with Harry. He has never forgiven Harry for killing his daughter, as he sees it. I believe he visits the nursery very occasionally, but as soon as Harry goes to school, his grandfather will move back into his own house.'

'And he'll live alone? Just with servants?'

'He does more or less already.'

'Oh,' said Cassia. Her mind was whirling at the horror of it, of Harry's wretched, lonely, unloved life. 'Leonora, I'm sorry if I was rude. If I'd known, I would have made allowances, really I would. I'll – I'll write to him, if you like, make my apologies.'

'It might help, I suppose,' said Leonora, slightly mollified by this, 'but just the same, I expect courtesy at all times in my house.'

Cassia had written to Harry, a stumbling, awkward note, which she had started and restarted a dozen times. He had not replied, and she had not seen him again for two years.

'A time to be born and a time to die.' Harry had read the words again at the end of his text, to make it the more poignant; he closed the Bible now, stood looking at them again, and then walked slowly back to his place by Edwina, his heavy, imposing body seeming somehow to fill the nave as he did so. As he passed Cassia, he looked at her thoughtfully, as if he did not know quite what to make of her. She met his eyes, those deep dark eyes, steadily, and did not look away.

Some prayers and a final hymn – 'God be at my end' – and it was over. They filed out into the sunshine. People released from the strain of solemnity became themselves again, greeting one another, waving, laughing. Rupert as always was the centre of a lot of attention, people drawn to him not only by what was a very modest fame, but also by his charm and, on this occasion, his wonderfully moving reading. Cassia stood waiting for him and the Harringtons (who were to take them back in their car to the house in Eaton Place), unwilling to join in the chatter, feeling lost, wishing, longing that Edward was with her.

'Cassia, darling, how too lovely to see you. Marvellous hat.'

'Hallo, Edwina.' She wondered what people would have said to her if she had not bought the hat.

'Harry's disappeared, God knows where to. I was so angry with him, making us late, just because he wanted to ride. He is such a selfish pig, but I must say I was quite proud of him in the church. He read awfully well, didn't he?'

'Yes,' said Cassia, 'awfully well.'

'And how is the brilliant doctor?'

'Very well, thank you.'

'Don't you sometimes—' Edwina stopped, stared at her. 'Oh, no, sorry, too rude.'

'Don't I what, Edwina? You can be as rude as you like to me.'

'Well, wish you'd stayed on, become a doctor yourself? Not for me, of course, no brains at all I've got, everyone knows that, but you were doing so well. It seems such a waste somehow.'

'Not at all,' said Cassia carefully. 'I think what I'm doing is just as important.' It felt like biting on an abscessed tooth.

A buffet luncheon was set out in the dining room at Eaton Place, the french windows open to the warm golden air. The garden was studded with small tables, which were filling now with groups of people, all chattering, laughing, kissing. Staff moved through the hundred-strong crowd with trays of canapés, filling and refilling glasses with champagne. Vintage, thought Cassia, studying the labels with open curiosity, marvelling at the extravagance, the sheer, absurd generosity of it all, contrasting it, despite herself, with her modest, careful life in Monks Health.

'Cassia, are you all right?' It was Cecily, her dark eyes concerned.

'I'm fine, thank you. This has been so marvellously organised, Cecily, you're so clever.'

'Not a bit. Anyway, I don't have anything else to do, not like you. Now look, could you possibly, do you think, go and talk to Richard? He looks a bit set apart.'

'Yes, of course. I wanted to anyway. It was so good of him to come, don't you think? Where's the Blessed Margaret?'

'Gone to do something virtuous, I think,' said Cecily, laughing. 'Cassia, that sounded like the old you, just for a moment.'

'What do you mean, the old me?'

'You know. Funny.'

Oh dear, thought Cassia, I must have become so dull.

'Godpa, hallo.'

'My darling child, how lovely to see you. And how well you look. Although a little thin. Margaret has had to leave, one of her charity committees, you know. I would have preferred to go home, but I didn't want to appear unfriendly. I was quite saddened, you know,' he said, his fierce old face softened suddenly, 'by Leonora's death. I had been so very fond of her, and I felt perhaps I handled it all badly. I don't know.'

'You did what you thought best,' said Cassia.

'Indeed, but what we think the best can be actually the worst. Anyway. Nothing to be done about it now. I think I was the wrong husband for her all along. Sadly.'

'Godpa, you weren't. She loved you very much. I know she did.'

'She did? I hope so. Not as much as she loved you, though. You really were the light of her life. The child she never had. Poor Leonora. Very sad, all that. Losing that baby, in her first marriage, tragic, tragic. That's why I was so keen for her to be allowed to present you at Court and so on. Lot of bloody nonsense, of course, but it made her happy. And I don't suppose it did you any actual harm.'

'No. It was a wonderful summer, and I shall never forget it.'

'And how's that clever young husband of yours?' he said after a silence.

'Oh, fine. Working very hard.'

'Well, that never did anyone any harm. Children all right?'

'Yes, yes, they're fine.'

'Nice to see Rupert,' Sir Richard said suddenly. 'What a voice.

Harry's reading, that was all right, but Rupert's – beautiful. Where is he, not here?'

'He's here somewhere. In the garden, maybe.'

'Perhaps I'll find him on my way out. I must be going now. Come and see me some time, won't you? Margaret was awfully impressed by you. Sorry you didn't carry on with your medicine, of course, but I suppose the children and so on ...'

'Yes. Um, Godpa?'

'Yes, my dear?'

'Leonora ... well, that is, I expect you know, she left me some money. In her will.' She felt she ought to tell him, that it would be somehow wrong not to; and then she looked at him, as she told him, and was disconcerted by what she saw: an expression of – what? Shock? No. Surprise? Yes. Disbelief? Almost. And then a careful ironing-out, a smooth, bland smile.

'How very nice. I'm delighted. I told you, you were the child she never had. Well, don't waste it, my dear. And spend it on yourself. Put it towards a holiday, or some clothes, or a little car of your own perhaps. That's what she would have wanted.'

She felt awkward now, unwilling, unable to go on, to say no, that he didn't understand, it had been a lot of money, not the sort to put towards anything, but that felt tasteless, somehow impertinent. Ridiculous, but there it was. She reached up to kiss him. 'It's been really lovely to see you. Give my regards to Margaret. Oh, look, Rupert's over there, you can have a quick word before you leave.'

She stood watching Sir Richard's tall, beautifully dressed figure moving across the buzzing room, between all the other beautifully dressed figures, thinking again how very different this was from her life now; from what she had come to expect, to see as normal. She felt at one and the same time that she had no place there, and as if one had been somehow kept for her, should have been kept for her even. She might not belong in this world any more, but she understood it, she knew how it worked, knew how the people in it thought and felt. It was familiar to her, in a way; she could not, did not wish to even, quite shake it off.

'Cassia?' It was Harry Moreton's voice behind her.

She turned round slowly, reluctantly, knowing that she couldn't put it off any longer, that she had to face him, talk to him, answer his questions, respond to him.

'How are you?'

'I'm very well, thank you, Harry. And you? I liked your reading very much.'

'Good,' he said carelessly. His expression was very solemn. Then slowly, his eyes took in hers, and then the rest of her face, moved down to her mouth, her throat and back again, She felt, unwillingly, trying unsuccessfully to ignore it, the tug, hard, harsh, deep within herself, towards him and his sexuality; tried and failed also to avoid his eyes. He smiled, recognising it, clearly savouring it.

'It's extremely good to see you,' he said after a charged silence. 'I was so pleased you could come.'

'Of course I came. And I thought the service was wonderful.'

'Wasn't it?' He sighed, his eyes heavy again. 'It brought her back – for a little while at least.'

'Yes. Dear Leonora. I do miss her.'

'I too. The world is a drabber place without her.'

'I thought perhaps,' Cassia said, 'that Rollo Gresham might have been here.'

'Well, you were wrong,' Harry said shortly. He was hostile to Gresham, as well as Benedict, and Cassia wondered why – perhaps because Gresham should have been there and wasn't. 'Is the doctor not here?' he said suddenly. He always referred to Edward as the doctor.

'No, he had a baby to deliver,' she said shortly.

'How very exemplary. Well, now, tell me how it's all going: life in the country, the family, all of it.'

'It's all going very well,' she said, 'and the family's fine.'

'I'm delighted to hear it. And what are you doing with yourself? Any medicine?'

'Oh, there's no time for that,' she said, quickly. 'I have the house to run, and then I'm very involved with village life, of course, the various committees and so on.'

'Oh, dear,' he said, 'that sounds a little worthy.'

'Harry,' she said, hoping, praying she didn't sound sanctimonious, 'there is nothing wrong with worthiness.'

'I think I would disagree with you there,' he said, smiling, his eyes malicious, settling his large frame against the wall, as if to indicate a long conversation was about to take place. 'I think there is a great deal wrong with worthiness. Worthiness is tedious, dull, self-congratulatory. And unattractive.'

'And I suppose,' she said, 'that unworthiness has great virtues in your eyes, does it?'

'Oh, indeed it does. It's amusing for a start. Its practitioners have a certain charm. It could even be called challenging. And it certainly isn't self-congratulatory.'

'Is isn't of much value either,' she said.

'I would disagree again. There is great value in amusement. And charm.'

'This is a ridiculous conversation,' she said; and then looked at him and saw he was grinning at her.

'Oh, I'd forgotten,' he said, reaching out his hand, patting her arm, 'I'd forgotten how wonderful it was to tease you.'

'It's nice to see you,' she said suddenly, forgetting to be careful, surprised at herself.

'It's nice to see you too. Well, I'm glad you're happy now with the good doctor.'

'Yes, I am. We have a wonderful life down there.'

'I'm sure. And you have no regrets about anything? Like your lost career, or—'

'No, of course not.'

'Oh, Lord. Edwina's coming for me. We have to go. I'm in dreadful disgrace, you know. What a pity, when you've finally been allowed out for a day.'

'Of course I'm allowed out,' she said irritably. 'I just don't have that sort of time. Life in a country practice is very busy.'

'I see. Well, we had better part, I suppose. As always, such a pity.' He took her hand, and bent and kissed her cheek, then stood back studying her. 'That is a most wonderful hat,' he said finally, 'and it looks quite horribly expensive. I'm surprised a doctor's salary can run to such a thing.'

CHAPTER 4

'Cecily and Benedict have asked us to go and stay with them,' said Cassia. She had been rehearsing this in her head since she had woken up, but now that she actually got the words out, her voice sounded false, silly.

'What, in London? Bertie, don't fidget like that,' said Edward.

'No, of course not in London. In the South of France.'

'France?' said Bertie. 'Can we go? I'd love to go to France. We just started French at school and—'

'Bertie, don't be silly, of course we can't go. Any of us. Least of all you.'

'Yes, he could,' said Cassia quickly. 'He's invited. We all are.'

Edward flushed, looked uncomfortable. Then he said, 'Clearly it's out of the question. Nice of them to ask us, but—'

'Why is it out of the question?'

'Cassia, please! I can't possibly leave the practice, I'm terribly busy. I can't afford a locum, and anyway, the fare to France for all of us would be very expensive. I—' And then he looked at her, and she knew what he was thinking: that actually, should she choose, she could pay for them, could pay for anything now. She had this strange sudden freedom to do what she wanted. Only you don't want to, that look said, you wouldn't, couldn't want to ...

'Yes,' she said quickly, 'you're right, I should have thought.'

'We could go, Mummy, just with you,' said Bertie. 'It'd be so fun. Daddy wouldn't mind, he's always saying oh for a bit of peace and quiet.' He smiled seraphically at Cassia, his brown eyes wistful. 'He'd have lots without us. Specially without Delia.'

Cassia hesitated, her mind drawn irresistibly towards the idea, trying to ignore it, ignore the temptation.

Delia picked up her cue and started to wail from her highchair, hurling pieces of sticky bread mingled with orange juice on to the floor.

Edward looked at Delia with something close to distaste and said, 'I

64

must go. I have the real world to contend with. Surgery's already filling up. I'll see you later.' He left the room without a glance at any of them.

Bertie looked at Cassia. 'Please, Mummy?' he said.

Later that morning, surprising herself, she phoned Mr Brewster.

'I just wondered how long it might be before I could have access to the money. A bit of it, that is.'

'A couple of months, I should have thought. These trusts are a bit complicated, but I think probate should be through by then. Why, did you have something particular in mind? That car, for instance?' She could hear him smiling down the phone.

'Oh no. I just wondered, that's all. I mean, we might be doing some work on the house and—'

'In that case, Mrs Fallon, you should know that any bank would make you a loan on the basis of the will. You have only to put them in touch with me, no need to wait. Really. Not if it's urgent.'

'It isn't urgent, honestly. I just wondered. As I said.'

'Yes, well, think of two months. I'll notify you, naturally, of any progress. All right?'

'Yes. Thank you.'

Edward came in at lunchtime in a bad temper. 'Cassia, I would be grateful if you could be more available when I'm doing a big surgery like that. I know you can't be sitting in there constantly, but twice I wanted something made up and you weren't around. It can't be so difficult to spend your mornings in the house, surely.'

'Edward, I had a lot to do this morning,' said Cassia.

'I can't see why any of that could not have waited,' said Edward. 'It's just a matter of organisation, surely. You used to be so good with your time, I can't understand— Oh God, there's the phone. If that's Mrs Cook, tell her I'll be round this afternoon to look at her husband's leg.'

Cassia took a deep breath, and went out to the phone. It wasn't Mrs Cook: it was Mary Foster, who was going to start giving Bertie piano lessons in September. Would he like to come over one day so she could assess him?

By the time she had returned to the dining room, Edward was pushing his napkin into its ring with a face like thunder. 'I do wish you wouldn't tie the phone up like that, for hours on end. You know patients are always trying to get through.'

Cassia counted up to ten and said she was sorry, and then, feeling it was best got out of the way as soon as possible, added that she wouldn't be in the house the following morning either because of the dentist.

'For God's sake,' said Edward, 'is it really beyond the bounds of possibility for you to arrange such things in the afternoons? It doesn't seem so much to ask. I cannot run this practice without your help – I would have thought you would be able to see that very clearly. You know everything's that's involved and— Look, I have to go, I'll see you later.'

'Temper, temper,' said Bertie, looking after him, shaking his head, and then looked at Cassia and grinned.

'Don't be cheeky, Bertie,' she said, trying not to smile back.

'How lovely,' said Cecily. 'Cassia has agreed to come to France.'

'Good,' said Benedict.

'With the children. And without Edward.'

'Better and better.'

'Yes. I'm delighted. She looked so tired, I thought, last week. A bit of sunshine will do her good. Sunshine and fun. 'I'm afraid that little one is a bit of a trial, but we'll have Nanny, after all. I sometimes think that's all Delia needs: a few weeks with a good nanny. Such a pity they can't afford one.'

'Mrs Venables, I won't be able to do the flowers next week, I'm afraid. I'm going away.'

'Away, Mrs Fallon? Where to?'

'France.'

'Good gracious. The doctor didn't mention it when I saw him last night.'

'The doctor isn't coming.'

'Oh, I see,' said Mrs Venables.

You don't, you don't see at all, thought Cassia, putting down the phone and gazing at the threadbare carpet. She seemed to have spent a lot of time looking at that carpet over the past few days, concentrating on it rather hard as she had made all her phone calls: to Cecily, to Mr Brewster, to the travel agent, to Harrods – Harrods for heaven's sake, ordering holiday clothes for the children. It was easier than taking them all shopping, dreadfully easy in fact. She had just opened an account, and given their sizes, and asked for a selection of shirts and shorts and swimsuits and sunhats, which had all arrived four days later. Then she had gone up to London for a dizzy day, feeling sick with guilt and excitement, to buy things for herself: a couple of linen dresses, some of the new wide slacks and loose knitted silk jersey tops, sandals, a new bathing suit, a huge-brimmed sunhat and a long pale pink crêpe dress for the evening, just in case they went into Nice. They were only going for six days; it seemed an awful lot of clothes for six days, more than she had bought in six years.

Mrs Venables couldn't possibly see, couldn't know what those six days represented, and indeed Cassia was trying very hard not to see it for herself: not just the taking of a well-earned rest, not even just a bid for independence, but a blow, a harsh, swift blow at the soft underbelly of her marriage, the first time in its six-year history that she had defied Edward, done what she wanted and what he did not want her to do. It was nothing, really, to do with the money: she could have managed it anyway, if she'd really wanted to; could have travelled down with Benedict and Cecily in their car – Nanny and the children always went by train, so much better for them, Cecily said – and she had had no real need for the clothes. It was simply to do with becoming herself again, just for a few days, with seeing quite clearly that there was no reason at all for her not to go. Edward would be fine: he would still have Peggy to look after him, and Mrs Briggs, and the whole village would rally round, invite him for meals and so on; there was even a strong possibility that any of his patients who felt they could wait until she got back would do so, just to be helpful.

However, that was wrong, she knew. Of course it was to do with the money. That was what the row had been about: not that she was going, not that Edward would be left on his own, not that he had accused her of wanting to get away from him; not even, in his words, that he did not know why she should want to go without him. It was to do with the money. And Edward, sitting quietly, anxious to be conciliatory after his initial hostile outburst, at last said that he thought she did actually deserve a break, agreeing that yes, it was a good idea, had also known that it was to do with the money.

'Isn't it lovely?' said Cecily. She was standing by the pool with Cassia and Fanny.

Fanny, who had been diving into it all day, was sunburnt, her little face flushed, freckles appearing on her small retroussé nose. She was enchantingly pretty, with her mother's dark hair and liquid eyes, but tall and slender like her father, her long legs and arms already turning a pale gold.

'It's beautiful,' said Cassia, smiling, 'quite, quite perfect. Like a fairy story.'

The pool was built into a white-tiled terrace edged with olive trees and trailing bougainvillaea about a hundred yards below the house. The staff were preparing the area for the evening, lighting lanterns, setting small tables, carrying out glasses, cocktail shakers, a gramophone, records. Below the pool terrace a lawn reached out towards the sea, edged with tall pines and oleanders; the air was thick with the heavy scent of flowers, mingled with the lighter one of herbs.

'We usually have drinks here,' said Cecily. 'Our neighbours from the next villa are joining us this evening, terribly nice. Nothing formal, Cassia. If you're feeling tired you can just sit and doze off. Then we have dinner up there.' Cassia looked up: more staff were setting a long table with linen, silver, glasses, ice buckets, on a second wide terrace. The house was ravishing: palest pink, built in the deco style, with curving balconies and an almost flat tiled roof.

Bertie appeared on one of the top balconies and waved. 'Mummy! Come up here, it's like a boat.'

'I'd better go back to them,' said Cassia. 'Delia's probably screaming her head off and—'

'Nanny will deal with Delia,' said Cecily. 'Fanny darling, you go and bring Bertie and William down here. They'd probably like a swim to cool off before they go to bed. Now, Cassia, sit down here and have a drink. Cocktail, champagne ... you say.'

'Oh goodness. Champagne, please. If you'll join me.'

'Of course I will, although I mustn't drink too much. Doctor's orders.'

'Really? Why?'

'I haven't told anyone else yet, but I'm in the club again.'

'Oh Cecily.' Cassia leaned forward and kissed her. 'How lovely. I'm so pleased. How do you feel?'

'Oh, you know. Bit sick. Not too bad. I just hope that this time it's a boy. Keep Benedict happy.' And there's a piece of irony, Cecily thought, sipping her champagne just a little cautiously – for quite often it did start the nausea – and reaching for her cigarette case and lighter. What a thing to say. How horribly, hideously appropriate.

She was lucky, Cecily knew, to have conceived again. The opportunities were few enough, God knew. Mostly she was very patient, never tried to force it, to force him, but one night, a few months ago, she had become very upset. She hadn't said anything, of course, for she never did, but she had heard him on the phone, having what seemed a rather odd conversation. As it turned out, it was perfectly innocent, but he had known why she was upset, had come to her room, had tried, silently, to comfort her, and she had suddenly wanted him very much and he had responded to her, greatly to her surprise. He had lain beside her afterwards, holding her in his arms, telling her how much he loved her, how lucky he knew he was. Which, of course, he was.

When she had told him a few weeks later she was pregnant, he had been, as always, wonderfully, overwhelmingly happy. Of course there was more than one reason for his happiness: it wasn't just because he loved his children, loved fatherhood – it was the fact that he could prove to the world yet again that here he was, a happily married, family man.

Oh God, thought Cecily, throwing back her head, smiling carefully at Cassia, a suddenly slightly blurred Cassia, how hard she earned all this: the beautiful houses, the servants, the luxurious background to her difficult, dangerous life. Not many women would be able to manage it. Not many women at all.

Benedict joined them, their friends arrived, and everyone drank too much. Benedict put the gramophone on, and they danced in the soft dusk, the children too, Fanny teaching a bashful Bertie how to tango, William whirling his mother round in a breathless polka. Through the darkness the cicadas called endlessly; faintly through the pine trees they could hear the music from other villas, other parties.

'Look,' said Cecily to Cassia, calling her to the edge of the terrace, 'look at the moon on the sea. Isn't that lovely?' And there it was, far below them, looking exactly like a stage set.

'It's divine,' said Cassia, and then laughed at herself for using that silly, extravagant word, one that she would never have even thought of in Monks Heath. 'Oh, Cecily, you're going to have to be very firm with me on Tuesday. When it's time to go home.'

'I shall do my absolute best to keep you for longer,' said Cecily. 'Come on, let's go and have dinner. Fanny, darling, take the little ones up to Nanny, will you? Tell her we will be up to kiss them later.'

'May I—'

'Yes, my angel, you may. Only change into something pretty.'

'She's so sweet,' said Cassia, smiling after Fanny as she led the children up the steps.

'Isn't she? She is the most important thing in my life, you know. From the moment she was born she made me feel quite different, cleverer somehow, less hopeless.'

'Cecily!' said Cassia. 'You were never hopeless.'

'I was. Not clever like you, not witty and sparkling like Leonora, not a good housekeeper like Mother, not up on current affairs like Sylvia Fox-Ashley. All the time I was pregnant and all the time I was having her, I was just determined that this was something I was going to do well, from the very beginning. Even when it was really hurting, you know, I thought I'm not going to yell, I'm not going to scream. I'm going to just shut up and get on with it, make her proud of me. Dr Waters said that I was one of the bravest mothers he'd ever delivered, and the calmest.' She smiled. 'Well, I don't know about that. You've seen lots of babies born, lots of mothers being brave. Probably I wasn't so good.'

'Not many are,' said Cassia. 'It does hurt so horribly. I remember feeling so awful, when I had Bertie, thinking of all the women I'd told to pull themselves together, stop yelling, and I was yelling my head off.'

'Really? I can't believe that. Anyway, here she is, nearly ten years old, and still so important to me.' Cecily held out her glass to be refilled. She was rather drunk, thought Cassia, too drunk really for a pregnant woman. 'It's not easy, you know,' she said suddenly, 'what I have to live with. Always worried, always afraid. And thinking people know – well, of course they must know—'

'Cecily, I'm sure they don't.'

'There was gossip, I do know that. I just hope that—' She visibly shook herself, smiled at Cassia. 'That it really is all over. That he's all right now.'

'You can't talk about it to him?'

'What? Oh, good heavens, no. It's always been my cardinal rule. Ignore it, pretend it was never there. That's the only way he – we – can be safe. And I think it's all right. I think he's happy, don't you?'

'I think he's very happy,' said Cassia, 'thanks to you.'

'And you, Cassia, are you happy?'

Cassia was startled, almost shocked by the question and its unexpectedness; called her face, her voice under careful, steely control. 'Of course I am. Terribly happy. How could I not be?'

'Oh, you know. I just wondered. Not everyone is. And you do have quite a difficult life,' said Cecily quickly.

'Nonsense, it's not difficult at all. Oh, I know we don't have lots of money, and ...' she paused, wondering if this was the moment to tell Cecily, or at least to find out if she knew, then changed her mind '... money and help and things, but that doesn't bother me. I didn't grow up to it, as you did, and it's all just the best fun. I'm very lucky and very happy,' she finished, hoping the speech didn't sound too carefully written, over rehearsed.

'Good,' said Cecily lightly, 'that's marvellous. What I hoped you'd say. Now look, let's go up and join the others, shall we? I'm starving, and I have to eat, if only so there's something there to throw up in the morning. I always forget how utterly miserable all that is.' She stood up and slipped her arm through Cassia's. 'It's lovely to have you here. Thank you for coming.'

'I'm loving it. Thank you for asking me.'

The days slid past: golden, idyllic, hedonistic days, greedy, self-indulgent. Three were gone before Cassia had begun to grow idle, early rising and a constant compulsion to be busy having become ingrained in her. However, she woke on the Sunday to find it already eleven, and the villa strangely quiet. She got up and went out to her balcony. The children were not in the pool, seemed to be nowhere indeed, the adults not on the terrace, the only sound endless church bells filling the hills. It was a perfect day. She put on her bathing suit under her robe and went down to the first terrace.

Smith, one of the maids from the London house, smiled at her. 'Good morning, madam. Mrs Harrington asked me to tell you they have gone to meet friends from the railway station, down in Nice. And Nanny has taken all the children for a walk. There is a small playground down the road, apparently. Would you like some breakfast, madam?'

'No, thank you, Smith. Just some coffee. And perhaps some orange juice.'

She sat sipping it, her face raised to the already hot sun. God, how was she going to face real life after this? Even Delia was responding to the magic – or to Nanny – and had hardly grizzled once in the last forty-eight hours. They only had forty-eight left: in less than two days they had to leave, make their way home to England. Monks Heath. And Edward. Oh God. To Edward.

'I, Cassiopeia Blanche, take thee, Edward Harold, to be my lawful husband ...' What was she saying, how had this happened? Panic gripped her. She thought even then of running away, out of the church. Stop it, Cassia, stop it. You love Edward, you're having his child, he loves you, this is going to be a good, wonderful marriage. For richer for poorer, for better for worse ...

She had waited that autumn for Edward to come back to London, so that she could clear things up once and for all. She was now in her second year of clinical medicine; her own life was clear, purposeful. She could not allow into it any confusion, anything she felt not absolutely right. She could still hardly believe that she was a medical student proper, with a white coat, working on the wards, assigned her own Honoraries – the specialists, so called because they were not paid, but worked at the hospitals in return for recommendations from past students, now distinguished colleagues. This year she would do Casualty and Surgery or Obstetrics. She sat in her room at Grosvenor Gardens, ticking off the words, the magical words, over and over again, as if she was saying some kind of prayer, rather as Phyllis, her father's maid in Leeds, who had been a devout Catholic, muttered over her rosary.

The night Edward came back she went to see him. He was already tense, nervous: he had an interview with the Dean next day. 'A lot hangs on that. I have to impress him, make him believe I can do it.'

It didn't seem fair to have The Conversation, to worry him, make him more nervous.

The next day Edward was allotted a place in Casualty. He had to move into the hospital so that he could be permanently on call. He was on duty for seventy-two hours, without a break. When he came off he was grey, ashen with fatigue. She couldn't have The Conversation then either.

The pattern continued: opportunities came and then went again, always with a reason not to speak, not to upset Edward. A man came into Casualty one night with raging septicaemia; Edward sat with him and watched him die. A young woman who had clearly been to an abortionist was brought in haemorrhaging; Edward stopped the bleeding, set up a transfusion and then found her dead from shock. A child arrived, beaten about the head so badly he was scarcely recognisable as human; his parents swore he had fallen down the stairs. When he died of his injuries, the father beat Edward up for allowing it to happen.

Edward, constantly exhausted, with a clear need to study at the same time, was in no condition to discuss the future. When this stint was over, when he was doing something slightly less stressful, then they could talk. There was no rush; nothing had changed. She still loved him, was very happy with him. It was just that she didn't want to be engaged to him.

She got three days off at Christmas; Edward was on duty the entire time. The department was permanently packed, mostly with road accidents or women beaten up by their drunken husbands. They spent Christmas evening together, in his small room in Casualty, eating turkey sandwiches.

'I couldn't get through this without you,' he said, leaning forward, kissing her. 'I really couldn't. I love you so much.'

She couldn't spoil what pleasure there was for him in his Christmas.

Shortly after Christmas Cassia was moved on to a surgical ward. Her Honorary was Horace Amstruther, one of the most distinguished surgeons of his day, famously eccentric, with a high, piercing voice and a very long nose which he would poke into the faces of his terrifed patients as he asked them questions about their conditions.

Cassia was extremely lucky, she knew, to have been allotted to him; nevertheless it was a considerable and terrifying ordeal, entailing long hours in the operating theatre, observing the great man at work, turning her observations into a written report, and frequently being subjected to a public humiliation across the table. Mr Amstruther's antics in theatre were well known: passed a knife that did not suit him, he would hurl it over his shoulder and demand another; he would sing loudly, usually from Gilbert and Sullivan, as he worked, and when he had finished to his satisfaction, he would wrench off his cap and gown and throw them over the nearest nurse before stalking out.

It was extremely difficult to see what was happening on the table, surrounded as it was by the anaesthetist, a theatre sister, at least two other nurses and the house surgeon, as well as the great man himself. Writing down a detailed description of what was going on inside the patient's body, from your position of humble observer on the edge of this crowd, was almost impossible. If you were lucky the sister would help, but sisters were notoriously hostile to female students.

In only her second operation – an appendicectomy – Cassia gave up altogether and stood gazing miserably at the bottom of the table, to be jerked to attention by Mr Amstruther's voice: 'You seem to be rather more interested in carpentry, Miss Berridge, than what is going on on the surface of the table. You haven't written anything down for some time now.'

Miserably she had begun to write something, anything, and as she trailed out of the theatre after everybody else, Sister fixed her with a grim glare and said, 'If you can't cope with an operation as simple as this, Miss Berridge, the outlook for you is pretty dim. I would advise you to pay closer attention in future. You are occupying a much sought-after place, you know.'

What she meant was a place much sought after by a man, Cassia knew, as she forced a meek apology. This was the root of the nurses' hostility: resistance to the female of the species doing a job that belonged, by unarguable right, to the male.

Nevertheless, Cassia loved the theatre, and had done from the first moment: the intensity of the atmosphere, the fierce concentration, the ongoing danger, the crises of falling blood pressure, failing heartbeat, the terrifying discoveries of extended infection, of tumours larger than anticipated. She had minded none of the sounds, the smells, the sights that she had been warned might make her faint: indeed she found she could stand for many hours, and not even realise she was tired until she finally fell into her bed, or her seat in the doctors' canteen. Her personal life seemed of very little importance.

In the spring, Edward was moved on to Obstetrics. His finals were looming, and he was in an appalling state. He would stagger off the ward, after sometimes ninety-six hours on duty, and struggle to study. One night she found him weeping in his room: a baby had died, and he blamed himself.

'I made a hash of it, didn't get it out fast enough, it was blue. If I hadn't been so bloody tired …'

'Edward, don't blame yourself. You know these things happen, we've been told that a hundred times. You mustn't take it personally.'

'The thing is,' he said, staring at her hollow eyed, wiping away his tears, 'the thing is, I can't concentrate on anything. Not my studies, not my work on the wards. I feel … oh, I don't know. Despair is the nearest thing.'

'Edward, don't. You'll get through it. It'll be over soon, then you can settle down and start being a good doctor, a good surgeon.'

'Christ,' he said, 'I hope so. Oh, Cassia, just go on telling me that, go on being there, won't you?'

'Yes, of course I will.'

Edward did pass his finals, but only just. Not well enough to win him a place as a houseman at St Christopher's, not well enough therefore for him to go on and do surgery, become an Honorary. The best he could hope for was a post at a general hospital, rather than a teaching one, and from there, general practice. He sat staring at Cassia, a horror carved into his face that she had never forgotten, silent; facing the implications, the dreadful disappointment of his future. That night, they made love for the first time; she felt it was the only thing she could do to comfort him. That too was a disappointment – to her. He lay in her arms, and alternately castigated himself and told her he loved her and that she was wonderful.

He got a job as houseman at a hospital in Harrow. He hated it, but it was the only way. Cassia didn't see him very often, every third weekend at the most. It was a relief: partly because he was so unhappy; partly because she was so wonderfully, ecstatically absorbed, working in Obstetrics. When they did meet, briefly, usually in his digs near the hospital, they talked little, and certainly not of the future, his being too uncertain, hers too threatening.

They made love whenever possible; that at least began to be good. Cassia, discovering her body, its hungers, its capacity for pleasure, could be uninhibited and demanding in bed at least. Edward was more tentative, still instinctively guilty, but became slowly skilful, his cautious, careful approach to everything extending, inevitably, to sex.

And then it had happened. The thing that had changed nothing, that could have changed everything, that should have changed everything. Cassia stirred now, lying there in the hot sun, the memory so vivid, so strong that her body clenched, softened to it, and then she turned her mind away from it. She could not bear, even now, to acknowledge it; it was too dangerous, too horribly, hideously menacing. She kept it locked away, far from her. As long as she did that, it could not harm her.

She discovered she was pregnant the week she began her finals. She was disbelieving, sure it was the stress, the anxiety, keeping her period from coming, causing the nausea. She had always been so careful, had seen to birth control herself, consulted a woman doctor who had fitted her with a cap and instructed her in the use of it. There had only been the one time when she had failed to use it: she and Edward had been to a party, had too much to drink; she had been particularly hungry for him, he unusually responsive. She had left her cap at home, but did a swift calculation and told Edward conception defied biological possibility. Her calculations were wrong and biology did the impossible.

'I'm pregnant,' she said, staring at him across his small room, wondering even as she did so why he was smiling, looked so happy.

'I think I've got a practice,' he said, seeming not to have heard her. 'Not in our village, but near there. Father is lending me the money to buy it. It's not expensive, I can pay him back in a couple of years.'

'Good,' she said, 'I'm so glad,' and then, 'Edward, I'm pregnant.'

'That's all right,' he said, as if she had said she wanted a cup of tea. 'That's perfectly all right. We can get married now. It doesn't matter – in fact it's wonderful.'

And she had stood there, staring at him, wondering at his blindness, his stupidity, and much too unhappy for both of them to tell him she had passed her finals with outstandingly high marks and been offered a house job at St Christopher's.

★

75

And so the nightmare had really begun. She struggled, wrestled with demons. She had thought, initially, she would have a termination – she could arrange it quickly and quietly, and then be free to return to her life – but the child was not just hers to do with what she would: it was Edward's, and she knew she must consult him. Edward, who had endured and indeed lost so much from his own life, was deeply, horribly distressed at the prospect.

'It's alive,' he kept saying, staring at her in disbelief, 'alive in there, our child. You can't do that, Cassia, you can't just kill it. I cannot believe you could even think of such a thing.'

He kept saying over and over again that he could see no need for it: they loved one another, they had planned to be married, he was in a position, or about to be, to support a family.

'But,' she cried out in agony, still not brave or cruel enough to say she didn't want to marry him, 'but there's my life, my career. I want to do surgery, you know I do, and I can, I—'

'Yes, I know you can,' he said, looking at her, his eyes full of terrible pain. 'You can do what I can't. I know that.'

'Edward, it isn't like that.' God, how could she put this right, make him feel better, less diminished, less humiliated?

'Yes, it is,' he said, 'and you can't make it any different. You are cleverer than me, you can do better than me, you can do anything you want, and I can't. Well, how very nice for you, Cassia, how very, very nice.'

It went on for hours, until he said, finally, 'Do it if you must. Have your own way. Get rid of our child. Do what you want. That's what matters, isn't it, Cassia? What you want.'

She left him so that she could think, talk to people. Termination suddenly seemed impossible. Would it be possible, then, to work, as a doctor, with a child?

'In general practice, possibly,' said her mentor, Caroline Martin, a fine woman obstetrician at the hospital, 'but not as a surgeon. No hospital would give you a job, a hearing even. Enough prejudice against women as there is: against a single, pregnant one ... well, just think, Cassia.'

She thought. It was frightening.

Edward's misery was shocking. 'You said you loved me,' he said, over and over again. 'What has happened? What did I do?'

'I do love you,' Cassia said, consumed by guilt, 'I do. I just don't know that I can marry you.'

'But why not? What's changed? You said you would.'

'No,' she said, 'I never did. Actually.'

'You never said you wouldn't.' That was true. 'All I've done, all I've endured, this past three years has been for you. Loving you has kept me going, kept me sane. You've no idea how often I nearly cracked, gave in. And then I just kept on thinking, no, one day it will be worth it.'

'Don't, Edward, please.'

'You can't shut me up,' he said, angry suddenly, 'keep me quiet, just because it suits you. You have to know.'

She went to see Rupert, to discuss it with him, as she did everything in her life. She had expected him to be on her side, and was amazed when he wasn't.

'You can't just do what you want,' he said simply. 'Life isn't like that. You have responsibilities: the child, Edward's happiness and ultimate success, your own. Go your own way now and you will wreck three lives.'

'It's all right for you,' she said. 'You're free, you can do what you want. You've never seen your career threatened.'

'Cassia, you're talking like a child,' he said, his face sterner than she could ever remember. 'You have to give in to life sometimes, you can't drive it all your own way. Edward loves you, and I think you love him. You have everything in common, your lives would work. That is what matters, that is what you must hang on to.'

Time was running out on her, and Edward, amazingly, was still ready to forgive, ready to marry her. Her pregnancy was advancing, and it wasn't fair on him to start his life in his new practice with a scandal. If she was going to do it, she must do it quickly.

She confided in Jenny Porter, her friend at the hospital. Jenny stared at her, her round face puzzled. 'But you're going to marry him anyway, surely,' she said. 'What does it matter? Edward's sweet. I think you ought to marry him.'

'Jenny, I – oh, I expect you're right. Everyone thinks I ought to marry him.' The words 'except me' hung in her head; she kept them at bay.

The one person she could, should, have consulted – Harry Moreton – she didn't. She knew it was because she was afraid of what he would say.

In the end, worn out with guilt, self-distaste, physical sickness and a longing to have it settled, she said she would marry Edward. She was mad not to, she told herself: Edward loved her, and of course she loved him. There was their child to consider. They were compatible in every single possible way; there was no reason not to marry him. And she was a qualified doctor, Edward told her, she told herself; in a few years, she could perhaps begin again, not as a surgeon, but in general practice, perhaps, specialising even in obstetrics. All was not lost; it was simply delayed.

She was doing absolutely the right thing.

She was married, perversely, from her grandmother's house in Halifax. It was the only way she could see to keeping it small, controlled. A handful of guests: none of the London people, just Rupert, a tiny group from the medical school, Benedict and Cecily. Leonora refused to come: she said she would be the spectre at the feast. Cassia begged, argued, pleaded, to no avail.

Sir Richard gave her away and a month later, they moved to Monks Heath, where she was known simply as the doctor's wife.

'Well, well, well, it's the doctor's wife.'

Cassia opened her eyes. The voice was instantly recognisable, the face, with the blazing sun behind it, a dark blur.

'You really shouldn't be lying there, in this sun, in that rather revealing bathing suit,' said Harry Moreton. 'Very pretty incidentally, lovely colour, but you're getting burnt.'

'I went to sleep,' she said, trying not to sound sulky, knowing he was right.

'Let me get you a sun umbrella, and perhaps you should put a robe on. Here, is this yours?'

'Yes. Thank you. I didn't know you were coming today,' she said, taking it, pulling it on, wincing slightly, for her shoulders were indeed burnt and sore. She was cross with Cecily for keeping his arrival from her.

'I didn't know either. We had planned to come next week. Edwina had some very serious shopping to do, but then July really isn't the best time for that. We saw some friends yesterday for lunch, and they are coming out here tomorrow, to their villa, and suddenly we thought we'd come today. London is deadly, terribly hot, nobody there. Got the Golden Arrow all the way. Marvellous trip.'

'Yes, I know. I came that way too,' said Cassia.

'Oh really?'

'Yes. Are you surprised?'

'No, of course not. Nothing you did would surprise me, Cassia.'

'I just might see that as a challenge,' she said lightly. 'Edwina, hallo.'

Edwina Moreton was striding down the steps from the house. She looked tired and irritable, and her white linen suit was creased. 'God, it's hot. I hope this was a good idea, Harry. Hallo, Cassia. You are terribly burnt.'

'Yes, I know,' said Cassia.

'I can't find anyone to unpack for us, and I want a drink, and—'

'Perhaps you could unpack for yourself. At least, as far into your luggage as your bathing things.' Harry's expression as he looked at Edwina was interesting, Cassia thought: absolute detachment.

'Harry, I haven't travelled for almost twenty-four hours to act as my own maid. I wish we'd brought Mildred now.'

'And I'm extremely glad we didn't. I'm perfectly happy to act as my own valet. I'll see you later.'

'Arrogant pig,' said Edwina. She sounded surprisingly upset. 'I'd like to see him looking after himself for so much as one day.' She sat down, pulled out an emerald-studded gold cigarette case and matching lighter, and offered the case to Cassia, who shook her head. 'Well, we're here, for better or worse. It seems pretty nice, I must say.'

'It's lovely,' said Cassia. 'I'm already dreading going home.'

'Really? How sad. I would have thought you'd have been dying to get back to your sweet, lovely husband.'

'Of course I miss him,' said Cassia hastily, 'but it's been such a marvellous rest, and I do love the sun, and as for having Nanny—'

'You mean you don't have one? How extraordinary. Some progressive new idea, or something?'

'No,' said Cassia, 'we can't afford it,' and then thought, as she seemed to keep thinking these days, that actually now she could. She stopped concentrating on Edwina and what she was saying and started wondering instead if she might consider having a nanny, and how on earth a nanny might fit into the rather humdrum household at Monks Ridge, and whether Edward would agree and—

'Cassia, do listen. I said, what time is lunch usually?'

'Oh, sorry. About one thirty. We have it down by the pool, very informal.'

'I think I might go and have a zizz. I really am frightfully tired. Oh Lord, here's Harry coming back. I'm going to nip up the other side before he gets down. See you later.'

Harry reappeared, dressed in a black towelling robe. 'I'm going to swim. Want to join me?'

Cassia shook her head, and put on her sunglasses. She lay back in her deckchair and tried not to watch him. She felt edgy, her easy pleasure quite gone. If she had known Harry was going to be here, she would not have come. It was as simple as that. Why on earth hadn't Cecily told her, warned her? She knew how Cassia felt about Harry. Well, she knew something of how she felt about him. The ongoing antagonism between them was famous.

She found herself watching him. He had taken off the robe, and was wearing a black bathing suit beneath it. His arms and legs were heavily muscled; he looked as always extremely fit, not an ounce of fat on his broad, powerful frame. His stomach was flat, and – Cassia averted her eyes from him again and picked up her book. There was a loud splash as he dived in. She stared at the pages of her book, turning them over, having no idea what she read.

After a while he appeared again in front of her, towelling himself down. The bathing suit clung to him; she fixed her eyes on his face with an immense effort.

'Good book?'

'Yes, thank you.'

'What is it?'

'It's called the *Constant Nymph.*'

'Love story?'

'Of a sort,' she said coolly.

He sat down on the terrace beside her, grinned up into her face. 'You really are burnt. Let me rub some oil into you. It'll help.'

'No,' she said sharply.

'Don't be so bloody ridiculous,' he said. He shook some oil into the palm of his hand, and began to smooth it gently but very firmly into the skin on her shoulders. She could only run away or give in, so she gave in. The pleasure was uncomfortably intense.

That night, six more people joined them for dinner. 'I feel we have to amuse Edwina,' said Cecily, 'she's so very demanding. I'm sorry they're here at the same time as you, darling. I know how you feel about Harry, but I really couldn't stop them.'

'It doesn't matter,' said Cassia.

'It does, but they just phoned early this morning to say they were in Nice. Jolly cheeky, actually. Apparently Harry phoned Benedict earlier in the week to see if it would matter if they came early, and Benedict said no. Not a word to me, of course.' She was flushed, clearly put out. 'You know what Benedict's like about Harry. Leonora was the same: both of them absurdly indulgent. Think the sun shines out of his muscular bottom.'

'Cecily, that doesn't sound like you,' said Cassia, amused.

'Well, I'm sorry. I feel cross about it.'

'Look, if it's me you're worried about, it doesn't matter. I can cope with Harry quite well these days.'

'I know. Anyway, we should have a good evening. I must go and have another word with Cook, she's just slightly edgy today. Says she doesn't like doing four courses on a Sunday. I mean why on earth not, how absurd ...'

Cassia smiled at Cecily's bustling back.

The four courses were superb: iced tomato soup, red Mediterranean mullet, boeuf stroganoff, peaches stewed in brandy, and then wonderful cheeses, piles of grapes, strawberries, melons. And of course an endless progression of wines. Cassia, dressed in her pink crêpe dress, sat between two extremely good-looking men – Cecily had carefully placed her as far from Harry as it was possible to be – her senses growing slowly and sweetly confused in the soft, scented darkness. The talk was amusing, self-indulgent gossip: about friends, parties, who was where.

'Marvellous spot, this, Benedict,' said one of the good-looking men, whose name was Max. 'Best spot on the whole coast.'

'Yes, we like it,' said Benedict, modestly, rather as if he had created it himself.

'Isn't that Gresham's place down there?' said Cassia's other neighbour, pointing out some lights shining far out on the promontory. 'Gorgeous, we dined there one night a few years ago.'

'Was,' said Max. 'He's sold it now, apparently. Probably wanted to be nearer the casino.'

Everyone laughed. Except, Cassia noticed, Harry, whose expression was morose, almost angry. She had never realised how antagonistic he was towards Gresham; his attitude towards him in the early days had been of tolerant near amusement that he had taken Leonora on. And they had raced their cars and gambled together as well. Something must have happened between them.

The conversation turned to the Prince of Wales and Mrs Simpson, currently holidaying together (although of course with a large party), about the progression of their affair, the old Queen's absolute hostility to her, about what Thelma Furness and Emerald Cunard and the Prince's old flame Mrs Dudley Ward had to say about it, about the chic of Wallis – 'Too dazzling,' said one woman. 'She makes every other female in the room look dowdy.'

'But hard, don't you think?' said another. 'I always thought the prince liked pretty ladies.'

'Ah, but this one has very special skills, I'm told,' said Edwina Moreton.

'Oh, you don't believe all that nonsense, Edwina, surely?'

'Well, of course I do. Everyone knows he has a tiny problem and—'

'Tiny being the word,' said one of the men, laughing.

'Then how did he keep Freda with him all that time?'

'Oh, Mamie, really, who wouldn't stay with him, problem or not? I certainly would. Anyway, maybe *she* has the special skills too,' said Edwina, and then laughingly refused to disclose any more.

Harry was looking at Edwina, Cassia noticed, with the same expression of absolute detachment he had shown that morning. She was certainly looking marvellous, in white silk wide-legged pyjamas, matching gold and emerald slave bangles on her thin arms, emerald clips in her dark hair. She was also extremely drunk.

'Well, I would like to see him become king soon,' said one of the handsome men. 'The country needs him; he will do a great deal for it.'

'I really don't see why,' said Benedict. 'He has shown no talent for anything at all, so far as I can see, except dancing and playing golf.'

'Not true,' said Harry mildly. 'He is marvellous with people. He seems to understand them, to be able to see what an ordinary life is like, to communicate ...'

'The present King gets by without any nonsense like that,' said Cecily. 'He's simply a splendid figurehead. As is the Queen.'

'Yes, and the days for that are passing very quickly,' said Harry. He had just lit a large cigar, and was leaning back in his chair, his face slightly obscured by the smoke. 'The world, society everywhere, is changing.'

Cassia watched him from her position at the other end of the table. You could never be sure with Harry what he meant and what he didn't: he was immensely contrary, would voice the establishment view in the presence of the liberal, propose some revolutionary notion to outrage the old guard.

'Yes, and he seems genuinely concerned about the miners and the unemployed generally,' she said. 'I think he feels very strongly for his people: all of them.'

'Do I detect the voice of socialism here?' said her neighbour.

She turned and met his eyes, smiled her sweetest smile. 'Yes, I suppose you do, if socialism is caring about ordinary people with no wealth, no voice of their own to make heard.'

'They seemed to make their voices pretty clearly felt in the General Strike,' he said. 'I can't quite go along with that view, I'm afraid. And then all these absurd marches, virtually riots, in Sheffield.'

82

'Yes, but with good reason,' said Cassia. 'Those people are desperate, hungry, and the government were threatening to cut what little help they were being given.'

'Yes, and they got their way, didn't they? The Minister of Labour, what's his name, Stanley, had to give in to them. The man on the Clapham Omnibus, or whatever you like to call him, seems to be doing pretty well to me.'

'Oh, Max, what a very simplistic view,' said Harry drily, 'and how easy for you to voice it, sitting here, drinking Benedict's Premier Cru. I don't think you would like to change places with that man at all. And I tell you it's one of the reasons Baldwin doesn't like the Prince, the fact that he has so many of the people's hearts. He's jealous. I wouldn't be at all surprised if Baldwin blocked this relationship, if it came to any kind of a crunch, forced a constitutional crisis.'

'What nonsense, Harry, it won't come to that,' said Cecily. 'He's just enjoying himself, having fun with Wallis while he can. Anyway, this is all getting terribly serious. Shall we dance? Benedict, get the records, would you, and we'll go down to the poolside.'

Cassia stood up; her head swam slightly. She picked up her bag and climbed the steps into the house. She went up to her room, poured herself a large glass of water, drank it and then another; then brushed her hair, renewed her lipstick, sprayed on some perfume. It was for the benefit of the handsome men, of course. And she wanted to dance. Music was drifting up from the poolside, all her favourites: 'Just the Way You Look Tonight', 'Let's Face the Music and Dance', 'Let's do it' ...

She found the table deserted, except for Harry; he was drinking a brandy, pulling on his cigar. He looked at her and smiled, indicated the chair next to him. She hesitated briefly, then sat down.

'Nice to find you on my side, for once,' he said.

'What? Oh, you mean, about the Prince of Wales. Well, I did agree with you. I think he does have that gift.'

'But Wallis doesn't,' he said. 'The people won't have it, they won't like her. Anyway, thank you for taking my side.'

'I wasn't exactly taking your side,' she said, laughing. 'I honestly think that, as you very well know.'

'Yes, I do,' he said, suddenly serious. 'Tell me, Cassia, do you regret giving up your career, giving up helping those people?'

'Oh, no,' she said quickly. 'Besides, I'm helping Edward to help them. It's one of the things we share.'

'I see,' he said. 'That's very commendable.' His eyes were amused as he looked at her. 'Tell me, have you enjoyed your evening? You certainly look very nice.'

'Thank you. Yes, I have.'

'And forgiven me for arriving?'

'Harry, there was nothing to forgive, don't be ridiculous.'

'I'm not being ridiculous,' he said, 'as you very well know.' His eyes studied her, moved over her, slowly in the way he had, as if it was in some way important to miss no detail. 'How are the shoulders?'

'They're fine. Thank you.'

He put out his hand and touched one of them very gently, grazing it with his thumb. 'Sure?'

'Yes, thank you,' she said stiffly, and then because it suddenly, surprisingly, seemed important that he should know, she said, the words coming out rather hurriedly, 'Leonora left me some money, Harry.'

'Oh, really?' His voice was politely interested. He reached out, poured himself a cup of coffee. 'How nice for you. This coffee is filthy. I really wouldn't advise you to have any. Extraordinary how people will spoil a good meal with bad coffee.'

'I wasn't going to have any, thank you, Harry. Yes. Yes, it is very nice. About the money.'

'Well, she was extremely fond of you. But you know that.'

'Yes, and I was of her. I wish I'd seen more of her those last few months. I feel so guilty about it.'

'You didn't know,' he said, 'how ill she was. None of us did, really.'

'Not even you?'

'Not really,' he said, his voice, his eyes, absolutely devoid of emotion. 'Not until the very end.'

'But she was all right? I mean, she wasn't alone? I couldn't bear to think—'

'Cassia, she wasn't alone. She was very well cared for. I promise you that.'

'So you saw her?'

'Yes, I saw her,' he said abruptly. He seemed upset: he and Leonora had been very fond of each other.

'You must miss her,' she said carefully.

'Yes, of course I do.' He sounded impatient, pulled on his cigar, then said, his voice lighter, 'And what are you going to spend it on, this money? More hats?'

'Harry, I don't know,' she said, and added, surprising herself again, 'It was quite a lot of money.'

'All the more reason,' he said, his voice still light, 'to know what you are going to spend it on. Well, I'm delighted for you. I hope you have fun with it.'

'That's exactly what Leonora said. In her letter to me about it.'

An almost imperceptible pause. 'Well, that's what money's for,' he said.

She laughed. 'Harry, you really are ridiculous.'

'I'm sorry,' he said, and, as so often, Cassia wasn't sure if he was being serious or not. 'I'm afraid I can't help it.'

There was a silence; then he said, clearly wishing to change the subject, the mood, 'Well, no doubt you would like to go down and dance. You like dancing, don't you, Cassia? Rather good at it, as I recall.'

'Not any more, I'm afraid,' she said.

'Does the doctor not enjoy dancing?'

'Not much.'

'What does he enjoy, then? Food? Wine? His work?'

'All those things,' she said briskly.

'And you, I hope. Does he appreciate you, Cassia, as he should?' The voice was light, carefully so.

'Of course he does.'

'Good. You are lucky, then. I don't think Edwina appreciates me.'

'I'm sure she does.'

'I'm afraid she doesn't,' he said, and his voice was harsh suddenly. 'Let us not have any foolish platitudes here. But then what could I expect, eh, Cassia?'

'I don't know,' she said. She was beginning to feel panicky; afraid of the direction the conversation was taking.

'Well, you should,' he said. 'Now, come along, let us go down to the pool. I'm sure you will have plenty of partners, but save a dance for me, will you?'

She would have danced with him; they might have talked more, grown closer in the next two golden, Mediterranean days. However, a message arrived from Edward, brought to her by the butler even as they walked down the steps to the terrace below, asking her to telephone Edward immediately. She felt ashamed that he would not even pay to hold on for just a few minutes. She was told, as she stood there, gazing out at the moon on the sea, the red oleander flowers disappeared now into the darkness, the white ones still shining, that his mother had died, and that Edward wanted her to come home immediately.

CHAPTER 5

'I'm afraid I find that very offensive,' said Edward. He looked at Cassia with something close to distaste.

She sighed, struggled for patience. She was finding it very difficult, finding everything at home difficult, unsettled by her South of France idyll. 'I'm sorry, Edward, I certainly didn't mean to be that. I only said—'

'I heard what you said. Thank you. Bringing everything back to yourself, as you so often do. Cassia, my mother has died. I am extremely upset. I resent your implication that—'

'Edward, I wasn't implying anything. And I know you're upset. All I said was that losing your mother as a child was worse. You can't imagine what it's like to lose your mother at the age of thirteen.'

'So you've often told me,' he said coldly.

She looked at him, trying to be generous, biting back further words, and said quietly, 'Would your father like to come and stay for a few weeks, do you think?'

'I don't think so, but I will ask him. He might stay briefly after the funeral, but he is very busy, sorting out all the new boys for next term, all that kind of thing. Work is a wonderful therapy, you know.'

'Yes,' she said, carefully, 'I do realise it must be,' and left the room quickly before she said something else that would make him angry.

Life was extremely difficult over the next few weeks. Edward was morose, and Desmond, having refused the invitation to stay, proceeded to do so; for almost three weeks he was there, a depressive shadow hanging about the house. He had a stomach ulcer which required a special diet, and he liked walking, he told her, which meant he accompanied her each day when she took Buffy and the children, which would have provided her with an escape from his heavy presence. The children took advantage of everyone's distraction to be difficult, and this provided Desmond with an opportunity for airing his views on discipline to her at great length.

There were the usual dismal after-death tasks to be accomplished: sorting out Barbara's things; disposing of her clothes; helping Desmond to write letters, and to field endless offers of support, none of which he wanted, preferring to deal with his grief silently and stoically alone. Only once did she see him break down, bury his head in his arms and weep: he had been in the sitting room and she had passed and gone in, and instinctively put her arms round him, tried to comfort him, but he had been horrified that she should have seen him displaying such weakness. He pretended that he had merely developed a bad cold, and sent her away, gruffly embarrassed. It was so exactly how she knew Edward would have behaved that she was quite shocked.

It was also impossible for her to do the right thing. Edward snapped at her, complaining about the children, the state of the house, his own crushing workload. When she pointed out, quite mildly she felt, given her fierce feelings on the matter, that she could help a great deal with the workload at least if he would only allow her, he told her she had no idea what she was talking about and stormed out of the room, slamming the door. She knew it was only because he was upset, that he had genuinely loved his mother, but it was still hard to bear.

When Edward came back to say that he was getting very tired of her harping on about her own career instead of supporting him in his, she lost her temper and did what she always did when life got on top of her: went off to Brighton to see Rupert.

'And I've got something to tell you,' she said to Rupert, when she phoned to arrange it, 'as well as being in need of cheering up. Something important.'

'What a complex meeting we shall have. This sounds serious.'

'It's not really,' she said and laughed. 'It's actually quite fun. Well, the news part of it.'

'Then why do you need cheering up? Darling, of course you must come. I'd love it. Bring the little 'uns.'

'No, I want to come alone. The news is sort of private.'

'Private *and* fun! Sounds good. Are you going to seduce me at last?'

'Oh, Rupert. As if I could. Dowdy old matron like me.'

'Nothing dowdy about you, my darling. Anyway, yes, come over, and I'll take you out to lunch. How about that?'

'No, Rupert,' she said, 'I'll take you.'

How often had she dreamed of such a thing, she thought, as she sat on the train chugging along the Brighton line from Haywards Heath: dreamed of being grown up and glamorous and buying Rupert Cameron lunch. Or dinner. And then dreamed of what might happen next, of Rupert declaring passionate, desperate love for her and begging her to run away with him, and her saying, yes of course, and them finding themselves in some wonderful suite in some amazing hotel somewhere and ...

She told Rupert about it, laughing, as they sat eating enormous prawns and drinking some extremely good white Burgundy: 'I want to take you somewhere expensive,' she had said. 'This is not Lyons Corner House news.'

'I loved you so much,' she said, 'so terribly much.'

'Does that mean you don't love me any more?'

'No, of course not, but it's different. Obviously.'

'Why so obviously? Aren't I attractive any more, have I lost my sex appeal?'

'No,' she said, laughing, 'but I'm married and we're both older.'

'Marriage never stopped a really good seduction,' he said, his blue eyes smiling in that wonderfully intent way into hers. 'In fact all the very best ones take place within its confines. By definition, I'd say.'

'I know that,' she said, flustered, 'but I'm happily married.'

'I hope so,' he said, reaching out, suddenly serious, stroking her cheek. 'I hope you are.'

'It's only these past few weeks that have got me down. And Desmond is leaving next week, he absolutely has to, so it's nearly over. You were right, telling me to marry Edward. It was an ideal marriage, I did what you said and—'

'Was that decision really based so much on my advice?' His face was solemn as he looked at her, his eyes concerned.

'You did have a very big influence on it. On me. You always have. You know that. I suppose it tipped the balance.'

'But it wasn't the only reason? Surely?'

'No, of course it wasn't,' she said, feeling suddenly it was important to reassure him. 'Don't be silly. I just needed you to point it all out. You knew that we were so perfectly suited, that there was more to life than just doing what I wanted, that there was the responsibility of the child—'

'Oh God,' he said, 'you seem to remember every word of the bloody script.'

There was a long silence, then he said, 'Well, I hope he's nice to you. Appreciates you.'

'Funny. That's what—' She stopped.

'Yes?'

'Oh, that's what Harry said. The other day.'

'You were talking amicably to Harry? Good heavens!'

'Rupert, we're quite good friends now. Well, we're polite to each other at least.'

'And where did this polite conversation take place?'

'In France.'

'In France! Whatever took you both to France?'

'Cecily. And Benedict. You know they always take that lovely villa down there, near Nice. I went to stay with them.'

'How very decadent. I'm surprised at Edward.'

'Edward didn't come,' she said quickly.

'Oh, I see.'

'No, you don't see,' she said, 'and that's to do with my news. I'm sorry I haven't told you before, but a lot of things have happened, there's never seemed a good time.'

She told him. He was first surprised, amazed even, then delighted, then thoughtful for her, exactly as she had known he would be.

'How did Edward take it?'

'He was pleased,' she said quickly.

'It's a lot of money,' Rupert said soberly. 'You'll need investment advice.'

'Yes, I'm getting some. From Benedict.'

'Good.' He looked at her carefully, then said, 'Good for Leonora, then. Knowing you were the person to need it most.'

'Yes, it was amazing. I had no idea she had that sort of money still. It was tied up in some kind of trust, I suppose to stop her getting at it, gambling it away, you know. I didn't like to ask, obviously.'

'You told Richard?'

'Yes. He was sweet. Although he kind of assumed it was a much smaller amount, from what he said. I didn't think it was very tasteful to go into it.'

'Quite right. Very vulgar, talk of money. As your grandmother would certainly have said. And poor Mrs Fallon.'

'Yes,' she said, laughing. 'She always lowered her voice when it was mentioned. A sort of lavatory subject.'

'Much worse than lavatories.'

Cassia laughed. Her difficult few weeks, Edward's bad moods, suddenly didn't matter any more. 'You always make me so happy,' she said and reached across the table to kiss him.

Their main course arrived: grilled lobster. They chatted about the children, Rupert's latest girlfriend – a redheaded dancer called Adele –

and then Rupert said, 'And what are your plans for yourself, with this money? Long term, I mean?'

'I don't know,' she said, carefully careless.

'You could go back to your medicine, couldn't you?'

'Rupert, I couldn't,' she said, shocked by him saying it, the unsayable, the unthinkable, unthinkable even to herself. She had shunned that thought, shot it out of her head, horrified, when it had dared to enter, refused to give it a moment's consideration.

'Darling, why? Or rather why on earth not? Surely that's exactly what Leonora would have wanted to have given you, the freedom to go back, to do what you always wanted.'

She stared at him. The argument sounded somehow prepared, well planned. 'She didn't talk to you about it, did she, Rupert?'

'No,' he said, 'I had no idea what she was going to do. It just seems so obvious somehow. There you are, with all that money, such a lot of money, the wherewithal to have your dream, and you're turning your back on it. I mean, what are you going to do, for God's sake, spend it on frocks or something?'

'No. No, of course not.' She felt rather emotional, suddenly threatened by his mood.

'I'm sorry, poppet. I've said too much. It's just that I care about you so much, and what happens to you. I always did.'

'Yes, I know you did,' she said, and she was back there again, back in that wonderful, magical, romantic time when he had first stayed with them, in the house in Leeds.

He had insisted on taking them out to dinner, that first evening. He had come to the Leeds Playhouse with a repertory company and had looked her father up. Cassia had been just fifteen years old, and she had changed into one of the outfits Leonora had bought her on her most recent visit, a navy dress in fine wool, trimmed with cream ribbons. Although slightly too short for her now, it was still very flattering and quite grown-up looking.

Rupert had insisted on pouring her a glass of wine – 'It will do you good' – and she learnt that he and Duncan had met at school; that Rupert had been rescued from some bullies by a much older Duncan, and been friends for years; that he had been one of the ushers at Blanche's and Duncan's wedding, and then lost touch with them as he pursued what he swore was an unsuccessful career, but which sounded to Cassia wonderfully glamorous. He was to appear for three weeks at the Leeds Playhouse, opening with *Justice*, the 'social' drama by Galsworthy, about a clerk who forges a cheque for love, and then goes to prison. He was to play the lead.

'Of course I'm a little old for it,' he said, smiling ruefully at Cassia, 'and you must think I am quite an old man, but for some reason I have got the part.'

'I don't think you look at all old,' she said, smiling at him, emboldened by a second glass of wine, poured at Rupert's insistence and rather against her father's will. 'I think you look very young. Actually.'

'What an extremely charming girl your daughter is, Duncan,' he said. 'You must be very proud of her.'

'I am,' said Duncan, 'very proud,' and they both sat smiling at her, admiring her. She thought that for the rest of her life she would remember that moment, looking at them, enjoying their admiration, her father and this wonderful, handsome stranger, sitting there in the warm, golden candlelight of the restaurant, just slightly confused with the wine, but able just the same and for the very first time to recognise the flicker of sexual attraction within herself and to see it echoed in the eyes of a man.

'Can we come and see you in your play?' she said later.

'I shall be deeply upset if you don't,' Rupert said, 'each one, each week. We are doing three: *Pygmalion* is my favourite—'

'Are you really doing *Pygmalion!* cried Cassia, in genuine excitement. 'My favourite play of all. I suppose you are to be Freddy."

'My dear Cassia, you flatter me dreadfully,' said Rupert. 'Of course not Freddy. I am to be Professor Higgins. Which I am very excited about, I must tell you. I hope you have a kindly theatre critic up here, who might give me a nice notice.'

'I'm quite sure he will,' said Duncan, 'and if he does not, we shall write him poison pen letters. And where are you staying?'

'Ah, now that is not quite such good news. The most terrible, terrible landlady is probably on the doorstep waiting for me with a rolling pin even now. Why she is taking in such folks as us I cannot imagine. The list of house rules in my room is so long it practically covers the entire wall. No smoking, no drinking, no entertaining in the room, and breakfast is at seven thirty – can you imagine anything more dreadful? High tea is at six, but if we are even five minutes late we must go without. Baths can only be taken between the hours of eight and nine at night, and that by prior arrangement.'

Cassia was smiling at him, and thinking how in some ways he was a bit like Benedict, charming and able somehow to make everything sound amusing, when she heard her father speaking the wonderful words.

'Well, you must come and stay with us. No, no,' he went on, 'don't even begin to argue, there is plenty of room. Please do come, the house lacks adult company. We'd love to have you, wouldn't we, Cassia?'

'Yes,' she said, 'we'd simply love it.'

There followed three weeks of pure happiness. Rupert Cameron was, she swiftly discovered, not merely charming, but possessed of a genuinely delightful nature, tirelessly good tempered, funny and fun. When she came down in the morning to breakfast he was always there. He would greet her most courteously, always standing up, his blue eyes smiling into hers, and would ask her if she had finished her work the night before to her satisfaction (for she had confided in him how hard she was finding combining it with looking after her father). He always had some funny story from the night before, about the audience or the other actors, a cue missed, a laugh mistimed, a latecomer interrupting some crucial dramatic moment. And when she came home from school (earlier than she had done for months, hurrying up the street rather than dragging wearily along it) he was usually there, and would make her a cup of tea, wanting to know about her day.

They had been to see him in *Justice*, and Cassia had thought him quite wonderfully good; the local paper had pronounced him 'lightweight', which she had thought outrageous, but the second week the company did Chekhov's *Cherry Orchard*. Rupert played Lopakhin to rather smaller audiences, but to a better review.

She never usually saw him when he came home at night, for it was late, and she was in bed, but one night when she couldn't sleep and went down to make herself a cup of cocoa he arrived home and came into the kitchen.

'Well met by moonlight, Proud Cassia,' he said. 'Make me one of those too, would you?'

Warm with pleasure, she made him a big mug and sat down with him while he drank it and chatted to her.

Finally he said sadly, 'I could sit here all night most happily talking to you, but I suppose your father would not like it.'

He got up and walked over to the kitchen door, then turned and studied her as she sat there, in her lumpy old dressing gown – if only she had known, she would have put on the beautiful silk one Leonora had given her. He blew her a kiss and then came towards her, bent over and kissed her again, very gently on the lips.

'How pretty you are. And what a lovely ending to my day,' he said.

Cassia sat there for over an hour, savouring that moment, reliving every phrase, every word they had exchanged, remembering each smile, re-creating each time that his eyes, thoughtful, gentle, appreciative, had explored hers, exploring the thud of pleasure that was half emotional, half physical, felt deep within her body as he had kissed her. Then she crept upstairs, past his room and lay in her own, sleepless with pleasure for hours.

Rupert had left soon after that. He wrote occasionally, once with the news that he had gone to call on Leonora, as Cassia had suggested, and she had been wonderfully welcoming, had invited him for cocktails. He had met her brother, and liked him very much, and of course Sir Richard as well. Then many months later, he wrote again to say he was to appear in the *Merchant of Venice* at the Manchester Playhouse and he very much hoped that Duncan and Cassia would come to see him.

The tickets had been bought, even a hotel room booked for the night – for it was too far to travel back to Leeds late – and then on the morning of the performance, Duncan had awoken with a severe migraine, and was pronounced by the doctor as completely unfit to do anything but stay in bed.

'So I just came on my own,' she said to Rupert calmly, over dinner in Manchester, after the play.

'But won't they be terribly worried?'

'No, not at all. Father has been given a sleeping draught and won't wake till morning, and Molly and Phyllis think I am staying with a friend.'

'I'm not sure I should be a party to the deception, but I am deeply touched that you should have risked so much to see the play.'

'You,' she said firmly, 'not the play. And it was wonderful, you were wonderful, and it was absolutely worth it.'

'You're quite a determined person, aren't you?' he said. 'And how are the studies, and the plans for your future?'

'Not good,' said Cassia, and found herself, to her own huge exasperation, bursting into tears, and trying to explain through them the appalling difficulties of being a very ambitious schoolgirl while being expected to look after a rather tetchily demanding father who could not see at all why she should not cook his supper each night and supervise the running of the household.

'Of course it is difficult,' Rupert said, tenderly, reaching over and passing her a handkerchief, 'and I can see you need help. Perhaps I should try to explain to your father about your difficulties.'

'He wouldn't listen,' she said briefly, 'and anyway, he doesn't really want me to do medicine. He thinks I should leave school now and learn to be a secretary.'

'Well,' he said, laughing, 'if it came to a battle between your irresistible force against his immoveable object, I know which side I'd stand on. In fifteen years' time, when I am really old and have all kinds of unpleasant diseases, I shall say, "Send for Dr Berridge, she will cure me," and I shall hope not to be disappointed.'

'Don't patronise me,' she said, angry suddenly. 'I'm an adult and I'm going to do what I want with my life, and nobody is going to stop me.'

'Tell me, Cassia,' he said suddenly, 'do you see me as very old?'

'No,' she said, quickly, 'not at all. I certainly don't think of you as Father's age. And what does age matter anyway when two people—'

'Yes?' he said, his voice very gentle. 'When two people what?'

She felt the wretched uncontrollable blush of colour rising again, and took a gulp of wine. 'Nothing, nothing at all.'

There was a long silence, and then 'Look,' he said, clearly anxious to get the conversation back on to a more lighthearted, easy note, 'it's very late. I have a duty to get you back to your hotel, and I am still scared silly as to what your father is going to have to say to me about all this anyway. If he does find out—'

'What could he say?'

'Oh, my darling,' he said, half laughing, half deadly serious, 'if you don't know that, then you really are a child.'

'Oh,' she said, very quietly, and she knew then what he meant, and knowing was deeply and mysteriously exciting. She stared at him across the table, across the candlelit space between them, and could see her feelings for him, the warm, leaping, disturbing feelings, mirrored in his eyes. 'I do know,' she said quietly, 'and I don't care. I wouldn't care even if—' she hesitated, then said the brave, the unthinkable thing 'even if what he might think were true.' For a moment she knew he was thinking, contemplating, that same thing, and she was ready for it, recklessly wonderfully ready. Then: 'Cassia, my darling,' he said very firmly, 'you do, you would care. Or you would tomorrow.'

'No,' she said, 'no, I don't. I wouldn't.'

'Well, I do,' he said firmly, trying again to smile, 'and I am going to take you back now, and see you to your room, and in the morning I think I should personally escort you to Leeds and brave the old lion in his den and assure him that nothing in the least unseemly took place.' He stood up, held out his hand. 'Come along, and we can discuss your future on the way.'

Humiliation filled Cassia. She felt hot, sick with shame. She had been horribly, terribly wrong, had thrown herself at him, and he was embarrassed and miserable. She stood up, very quickly, and met his eyes quite steadily. 'Yes, all right. What a good idea.'

He arrived at her hotel just as she was paying her bill (from her savings; her medical student fund, she called it). 'Ah,' he said brightly. 'Sleep well?'

'Yes, thank you,' she said, carefully not meeting his eyes, keeping her voice cool, steady with an immense effort. 'Very well.'

'Good. Come along, then, we can catch the eight o'clock train.'

'I really don't see there is any need for you to come with me,' she said, cooler still.

'Well, I do. And anyway, I have to talk to you, there are things I must say to you. I have been awake most of the night thinking about you.'

'How very tedious for you,' she said.

'Not at all. But a little ... worrying. Look, there's a taxi now. Let me take your bag.'

'Now then,' he said, as they were finally settled in an empty compartment, 'you are to listen to me very carefully, and not interrupt. We don't have very long and it's important you should understand.' He leant forward and kissed her gently on the forehead. 'Don't look so frightened, it's none of it very serious. Except in so far as it affects myself.'

Cassia sat back, clasped her hands very tightly in her lap and fixed her eyes on them.

'I want to begin by saying how much I admire you,' he said. 'I think you're very mature, and very brave. And quite extraordinarily attractive. Which is why I am having to talk to you like this now. I have behaved appallingly, with the daughter of a very dear old friend. I have taken advantage of you horribly. I've flirted with you, and treated you as if you were a great deal older than you are, simply because I do find you so attractive. I think you're absolutely glorious, Cassia. I could ... well, never mind what I could do. I'm sure you can imagine. Perhaps you can't. I never know how much young girls know these days.'

Cassia dared a look at him. His eyes were fixed on her, and the expression on his face was so painstakingly honest, so helplessly remorseful that she almost laughed. 'Oh, quite a lot,' she said carefully, turning her attention back to her hands. 'You must remember, I am a science student. We have studied a great deal of biology, I have no misapprehensions in my head about gooseberry bushes or storks.'

'Thank God for that at least,' said Rupert, with a heavy sigh. 'But in any case, my behaviour has been disgraceful. Having said all that, you see, I do want you to understand how much I was attracted to you. I don't want you feeling spurned and humiliated. It took every ounce of self-control I had last night to reject you. I have no doubt it was very good for me and went some way towards being a penance for my dreadful behaviour earlier. Kissing you, leading you on, when you are only fifteen years old, and a lonely, unhappy fifteen years old at that – I should be shot. I have the morals of an alley cat, and the only reason I got the better of them last night was because I like and respect you so much. You do understand, don't you?'

'I think so,' said Cassia.

'I just want you to see me as the rotter I am. And to know that, rotter or not, I can't help admiring you. Very much. Is that terrible, have I made things even worse?'

Cassia felt quite different suddenly, no longer a foolish, embarrassing virgin, but a desirable, self-confident woman. Even her voice sounded steadier, slightly deeper. 'You've made them absolutely better,' she said, 'thank you. And I suppose I shall grow older, and then you will feel less guilty, and then who knows what may happen.'

He took her hand then and sat staring at it, his thumb massaging her palm, and then, as he had done once before, in the park in Leeds, he raised it to his lips and kissed it, only for longer, lingering on it with his mouth, turning it over then and kissing the palm for a long long moment, working on it. She sat and looked down at him, looked at his bent head, concentrating on the moment, thinking that she must remember it, every tiny detail of it, for ever, and then he lifted his head and looked at her and his face was very solemn, very intense, and he said, 'Oh Cassia.'

Suddenly a leaping courage seemed to be taking her over, telling her what to do, a sense that she could take more yet from this wonderful moment, that it was not yet quite finished with, and she leant forward and took his head in her two hands, and pulled him towards her very gently, kissing him on the mouth.

She felt his surprise, his shock, felt an initial gentle attempt to withdraw, but she resisted it, continued to hold him there, and then she felt a change in him, felt him pulling her towards him, very gently, felt his mouth on hers change, become harder than before, felt his lips move, his tongue beginning to explore hers, and it was wonderful, marvellous, and she felt a response to him, not just in her mouth, but a warm leaping, deep within herself, and as she pressed towards him, eager, longing for more, he set her back from him quickly, urgently almost, as if it must be done quickly, met her eyes with his own rueful, brilliant blue ones.

'I do deserve to be shot,' he said. 'No, not shot, that would be too painless, not horrible enough – to be strung up, hung, drawn and quartered. Cassia, Cassia, you must forgive me, I—'

'Rupert,' said Cassia, half laughing now, 'stop being so very absurd. It was me, I made you do it and— oh God ...'

The train had pulled into Leeds station, and standing in the corridor, staring into their compartment, clearly quite transfixed, and having seen every tiny detail of what had been going on, was Mr Devenish, her father's boss and manager of the Leeds Public Library.

There was the most appalling series of scenes. She said nothing to Mr Devenish, beyond 'Good Morning' (a greeting which he failed to return), and Rupert hailed a taxi cab and took her home to Arthur Terrace.

Her father, still shaky from his illness, turned first white, then grey with horror at the story. Looking back from the perspective of several years' experience and increased wisdom, Cassia could see that the chief source of horror was that it had been Mr Devenish who had seen her (and who would without doubt spread his report all over Leeds before the end of the day). Second in this order was what Leeds would have to say about it; third, that it was his own, oldest friend who had been involved in this dreadful thing; fourth, that Cassia could so thoroughly have deceived him; and very much last, what might or might not have happened to her during the night she had been away from him and in the company of the oldest friend.

Duncan was indeed assured – temporarily at any rate – comparatively easily on this last point, Rupert having thrown himself into a display of dramatic remorse and painstaking detail as to what had actually taken place. More powerfully, Cassia told her father that if he did not believe them, he could take her down to the doctor's surgery and have her virginity confirmed there. He was clearly shocked at the frankness of this speech and indeed the extent of the knowledge that made its delivery possible, but it served its purpose. However, the horror of having his daughter branded a trollop all over Leeds, the loss of the family's respectability, the dread that he himself might lose his job, was almost unbearable. Rupert was told to leave the house and the city at once and not to return. It was not the instruction itself, but Cassia's cool insistence that he obeyed it, that sent Rupert walking dejectedly to the station at midday: 'You'll just make him worse if you stay, more upset. Just go. He'll get over it in time, I know he will.'

Cassia's grandmother was sent for. She listened to the story, her lips folded tightly, her eyes hard with distaste, and then said she should clearly move into the house permanently herself, to make sure that Cassia was properly supervised and chaperoned at all times in the future. She added that Cassia should leave school at once, be made to stay at home and do her duty as a daughter, as she should have been in any case for the past year.

Cassia listened to Duncan agreeing to both these measures, thought very fast and then said that of course if her grandmother wished to come and live with them, that was entirely her affair. However, if they tried to force her to leave school, then she would see to it that the rumours about her behaviour and what had happened overnight in Manchester were greatly elaborated to extend to a full seduction and even a possible pregnancy—

Her father sent her to her room, but she knew she had won. He sent for her an hour later and said that after giving the matter a great deal of thought, he had decided she could stay at school, providing they would have her. 'It seems to me you may find yourself expelled if they come to hear of this, in any case.'

She was not, of course, expelled; indeed, news of her extremely modest misdemeanour never reached the headmistress. What did astonish and please her was how much the arrival of her grandmother in the household actually helped her. The old lady took over all her domestic duties, freeing her for her studies. She recovered a lost place at the top of her year and the headmistress sent for her and told her she was delighted with her progress and thought she should set her sights very high indeed: 'Possibly a scholarship even, to medical school. Well done.'

The night with Rupert, as she always thought of it thereafter, had been a turning point in more ways than one.

And so he took his place in her life as chief advisor, mentor and lover-like friend; always there when she needed him, with his clear-sighted, hard-headed advice – although inevitably expressed in his wonderful, poetic way. He argued, first quietly, then with increasing passion, with her father and her grandmother when they tried to block her application to medical school, and when Leonora had written to her father to propose that she should present Cassia at Court and pay for her to do a London Season – a prospect which pleased her father far more than the most brilliant medical career – Rupert talked her into that as well.

'I know you don't want to do it, but I think you should. It will not only please Leonora and make her happy, when she has been so kind to you, it will delight your father, make him more receptive to your plans,

98

and it will do you no harm either, meeting all those rich and influential people who can become your patients one day. And I dare say you will even enjoy it,' he added, laughing at her furious, disbelieving face. 'Most young girls would give their teeth for such an opportunity.'

He had even managed to persuade her headmistress that the few weeks she would need to be away from school to do the Season could be quite easily made up later in the year, an extraordinary feat, partly accomplished by his deliberately playing on the fact that Miss Cartwright had seen him on the stage several times and admired him as an actor, and partly by some heavy emotional blackmail as to Cassia's motherless state. And in the fullness of time, for he was by then quite close to Leonora and Sir Richard, who liked him enormously, he enlisted their help in persuading Duncan that, providing she was living with them, she would be perfectly safe living in London and attending medical school.

Looking back, she could see how skilfully he had guided her out of her early schoolgirl crush, into the loving, flirtatious friendship they had shared ever since. This had been finally accomplished by an experience so painful she was still unable to laugh about it.

When she was almost seventeen, still dazzled by him, still haunted by the memory of that first kiss, her first experience of any kind of sexual feeling, he had invited her to come and see him in a musical in Manchester, and to have dinner with him afterwards. Excited, thinking that perhaps now, at last, he was actually going to declare his love for her, perhaps even consummate their relationship, she rushed round to his dressing room after the show (wearing yet another very grown-up dress bought for her by Leonora, daringly short in blush-pink silk, her hair bobbed to the new length) and threw herself into his arms.

'You were wonderful, wonderful,' she said.

'You *look* wonderful, wonderful,' he said, smiling down into her eyes, 'and so grown up, oh, dear Cassia, yet more temptation for me to resist.'

She had said, very serious suddenly, 'Stop resisting it, Rupert, please,' and pulled his face down to hers, as she had done on the train. She began kissing him rather intently on the mouth, so intently indeed that she did not hear the door open.

It was only a voice, sounding half amused, half irritable, saying, 'Rupert, darling, I had no idea you were two-timing me,' that made her turn her head and see the leading lady, a glorious creature with raven-black hair, dramatic dark eyes, and a pair of incredible breasts which were extremely visible since her silk robe was hanging open.

She had stared in horror for a long moment, absorbing the obvious intimacy between them, the equally obvious familiarity of the scene, and that Rupert's face was a caricature of discomfort; and then she pulled herself away from him and ran as fast as she could down the corridor and to the safety of her hotel, where she lay sleepless almost all night, in a state of utter misery and humiliation.

He came to find her next morning, as he had the time before, and sat holding her hand as he tried to explain, so skilfully that at the end of the hour she was no longer angry, no longer embarrassed even, and had accepted the fact, albeit sadly, that however much he loved her, she must remain to him a very dear and precious friend.

'You are divinely attractive,' he said, 'but I am a dreadful old rake, as you have seen. I look to you for reform, not encouragement.'

Reluctantly, she had accepted it, and had come quite swiftly to enjoy what she could see was a unique place in his life, for he paid her the compliment of confiding in her as she did in him. She learnt swiftly too to regard the ceaseless procession of young women through his bedroom and his life with a lofty amusement, and to recognise that had she joined them, she would have lost him for ever.

He was still, to her, in many ways, the ideal man: she supposed a psychiatrist would have had a field day over it, have said he was another father figure, that she already played surrogate wife to her own father. But she would have told that psychiatrist that he was quite quite wrong, that she had always loved Rupert and always would because he was charming, easy and handsome, somehow roguish, that he made life colourful and amusing and fun and she owed him a great deal, since he had been the man who had first made her aware of the strength of her own sexuality. She might also have told him that whoever she had loved and desired since, whoever she had married, to whomever she had borne children, Rupert still possessed the capacity to disturb, if not excite her, and that he was arguably still the most important man in her life.

'Anyway,' she said now over lunch in Brighton, leaning back, smiling at him, aware that she was flushed with too much Burgundy, aware also that she was looking very pretty in a new navy crêpe dress she had bought for the occasion, 'I feel I can thank you properly now at last, for all that you did for me all those years ago. Making my father see sense about my career and all that. It meant everything at the time and I vowed I would do something splendid for you when I could. And now I can.'

'Darling ...'

'No, Rupert, don't try and talk me out of it. It would make me so happy. You once said you'd give anything to be able to put a play on yourself, that if only you could find someone to invest in it, it would make all the difference. Well, maybe I could do that now. You saved my career, now perhaps I can save yours.'

'Oh, my darling,' he said, and his blue eyes were very brilliant suddenly, 'how sweet you are. How much I love you. I do appreciate it so very much, and the thought alone is quite enough—'

'No, Rupert,' she said firmly, 'the thought is not enough. I want to do it. Or something like it. Now promise me you'll think about it. Or doesn't it interest you at all any more? Because I could always buy you a yacht instead—'

'I'd quite like that,' he said, then leant forward, took her hand, raised it to his lips. 'You're marvellous,' he said, 'and thank you. It's very sweet of you to offer, to remember my ramblings. It could be marvellous. May I get back to you? And while we're talking careers, can I ask you to at least think about getting back to medicine?'

'I'll think about it,' she said, smiling, 'but I really can't see it's possible. For all sorts of reasons. Not least what my husband would have to say about it.'

'Oh, Cassia,' said Rupert. He sat back in his chair, looking at her, and shook his head. 'Whatever happened to the person who was going to do what she wanted with her life and nothing was going to stop her?'

'You know what happened to that person. And you of all people shouldn't reproach her for it.'

'No,' he said, very quietly, 'I know. I just wonder if I should reproach myself. That's all.'

'Cecily,' said Cassia, 'there's something I have to tell you.'

Cecily was doing some flowers. She turned her face to Cassia, her large brown eyes politely, carefully interested.

She knows what I'm going to say, thought Cassia, she knows – well, she would, Benedict would have told her – and felt silly, and then told Cecily just the same.

Cecily said she had heard, of course, but she hadn't liked to say anything before. She kissed Cassia and embraced her and said how thrilling she thought it was, and what on earth was she going to do with it, and Benedict should advise her on investment, and how much Leonora must have loved her and …

'Silly of me not to have told you before, I suppose. It's all a bit embarrassing somehow. Don't ask me why. Anyway, it's clearly got to start coming out now.'

'What does Edward have to say about it?' said Cecily slowly.

'Not a lot. It's difficult. We haven't talked about it, not properly at least. He feels ... I don't know, threatened, I suppose.'

'Yes, that's what I thought. I mean, I could see he might. Well, there's plenty of time, isn't there? For him to get used to the idea.'

'I suppose so, yes. We haven't begun to think what to do with it. I've bought a few clothes, and there it's stopped. It frightens me a bit. The only really exciting idea so far is that I might put some money into a play for Rupert.'

'Really? My goodness, that would be glamorous. What are they called, people who do that? Angels?'

'I don't know,' said Cassia, 'but I would love to do it for him. He's been so marvellous to me all my life, and it could make all the difference to him. Why are you looking at me like that?'

'Well ...' Cecily hesitated. 'I do think it's a lovely idea, of course I do, but I just wonder what Edward might think about it, that's all. I mean, he's always been a bit jealous of Rupert, and—'

Cassia looked at Cecily and heard, to her immense astonishment, her own voice, very cool, saying for the first time the unthinkable, unspeakable thing. 'I don't think it has anything to do with Edward,' she said. 'The money is mine, after all, isn't it?'

'It is,' said Cecily, after a fractional pause. 'Yes, of course it is.'

The day after Desmond went home, Edward looked at Cassia across the breakfast table and smiled at her, rather shamefaced. 'Cassia, I'm sorry I've been difficult.'

'That's all right, Edward. I understand.'

'I hope so. You've been very patient. Now look, I've been thinking. This house is in a bit of a mess, isn't it?'

'I thought we liked it like that. You always said you wanted to live in a proper home, not all over-tidy like your mother's house.'

'No, I mean it could do with some money spending on it. Painting it and so on. Maybe put in some central heating. It does need a new roof, and I'd really like to rebuild the surgery. Extend it. So I thought that's what we should do. As soon as possible, really.'

'Good idea. With my – that is, with Leonora's money,' she said, unable quite to analyse how she felt.

'I had thought of it,' Edward said, 'as our money.'

'Yes,' she said quickly, realising with horror that what she felt had been possessiveness over the money, her money, as she couldn't help thinking of it. How awful, how dreadful that she could be so mean, so ungenerous about it, to Edward of all people, who had always given her, shared with her, everything he had. And then, to try to make amends, anxious to appear as generous as she could possibly be, she said, 'Edward, you wouldn't like to buy a different practice, would you? A bigger one, perhaps?'

'Why on earth should I?' he said, astonished.

'I just thought perhaps a London practice, or—'

'Cassia, my medical career is my own. Something I've worked for, earned by my own efforts and merit. I don't want any fancy rooms in London.'

'That's not fair,' she said. 'I didn't mean fancy rooms. You know I didn't. But we always used to talk about the problems of people living in the cities, underprivileged people, wanting to help them.'

'No,' he said, his voice cold, 'I'm extremely happy here. It might seem a very modest practice to you, Cassia, but it affords me a great deal of satisfaction. And I think I give the same to my patients. Or perhaps you have reason to think otherwise.'

'Edward, you're choosing to completely misunderstand me. I never suggested the practice was in any way deficient. It's marvellous, you've done a lot with it, and your patients all think you're wonderful. I only wondered—'

'If I might like something better.'

'No!'

'Well, I don't see how else your remark might have been interpreted. And I don't, and I certainly don't want you offering to procure it for me. Now you must excuse me, I have work to do.'

She looked after him, feeling suddenly panicky, without being quite sure why.

'I've had a few estimates done,' he said a week later, a slightly uncomfortable, strained week, 'for the house.'

'Oh really?' She struggled to sound, to feel, calm, happy. 'I would have done that.'

'Well, you seemed a bit lukewarm, and what with getting the boys back to school and so on ...'

He had never made those sorts of allowances for her before. She smiled at him uncertainly, knowing what it meant, that he was sorry for his outburst but didn't want to say so.

'So—' he reached for a file, pulled out some pieces of paper – 'for about two hundred, we can have a new roof. Then painting the whole house, inside and out, three hundred. And to rebuild and enlarge the surgery, five hundred. Very good, don't you think?'

'Yes. Very good.'

'Mr Cartwright's was the best estimate, and we know him, so I've told him to go ahead. He says the roof should be done very soon, before the winter sets in.'

'You've told him to go ahead?'

'Yes. And meanwhile, Mr Morris is going to get to work on the surgery. It means I'll have to move into the dining room, but it won't take long. By Christmas, with a bit of luck, I'll have a spanking new place to work.'

Cassia sat and stared at him.

'What's the matter?'

'Nothing. Nothing at all. It's just that … well, maybe we could have talked about it a bit more first.' Cassia, don't, this is wrong, this is awful, what does it matter?

'But we have, frequently. Last week specifically. About the roof, about the terrible state of the surgery.'

'Yes, I know, but I mean about doing the work. I'd have liked to think about it a bit.'

'But why? What on earth is there to think about?'

'Oh, I don't know. You just seem to have gone ahead and taken decisions and—'

'Cassia,' he said, his voice infinitely patient, 'I just explained, you've been very busy and I really did want to progress it and— Dear God.' He stopped suddenly, staring at her, and said, 'This is about the money, isn't it?'

'No, of course it isn't.'

'About it being your money.'

'Don't be absurd. It's just that we've always discussed everything very carefully before. Before deciding on it.'

'You didn't discuss your going to France with me,' he said.

Careful, Cassia, be very careful; it's true, you didn't. 'That was different.'

'Why?'

'Well,' she said, smiling, trying to make it sound funny, lighthearted, 'we'd had a row, hadn't we? I said I was sorry. Said I was wrong.'

'Yes,' he said lightly, but his eyes were hard as he looked at her. 'It was wrong. Quite wrong. So let's get it right with this work on the house. Our money, our house.'

She was sorry and she tried to make him make love to her that night, so that she could show him, but he wouldn't. He lay far from her, distantly thoughtful, even while he held her in his arms.

Three weeks later the house was in chaos: scaffolding all over it, full of dust, patients trooping through the hall into the dining room, which had become the surgery, using the cloakroom, those who knew her popping into the kitchen to say hallo.

'It must be very exciting,' said Mrs Venables, pushing her aged mother down the passage in her wheelchair, 'getting all this work done. The house is going to look wonderful.'

'It is,' said Cassia, 'very exciting.'

'Such an expense, having work done these days, too.'

'Well, I was left some money by my godmother, you see, and that—'

'Really? Oh, I see.' Mrs Venables looked uneasy suddenly, finding herself in unfamiliar, unworked territory. 'I hadn't realised that.'

Now why did you have to tell her, Cassia? Why not let her think Edward was doing so well he could afford to pay for it? Why tell her it was your money, within your gift to do all these wonderful things to the house? It was mean, petty.

But she knew why. It had become very clear to her one night after he had been dismissive of something she had said about a breech birth, of the dangers, of the arguable need for Caesareans in all such cases. She had looked at her new freedom, her new power and felt better. It was her revenge for all the years of being the doctor's wife. Cleverer than the doctor, more highly qualified, but only his wife, with no acknowledgment from the doctor of that fact, ever. And now, richer than the doctor, able to pay for things herself, that the doctor couldn't actually afford. The revenge might be inappropriate, but it was something at least.

CHAPTER 6

The money was there now, sitting in her bank account. Her own bank account. Her new bank account. It had been Mr Brewster's suggestion that she should have a special account for it: a high-interest bearing deposit account. She was going to see Benedict shortly, to discuss investment.

'It would clearly be very foolish,' Mr Brewster had said, 'to leave the money just sitting there in the bank, however much interest it might be earning. Money has to be put to work: you should buy stock, shares, and if I might suggest it perhaps, set up trust funds for your children. With your husband's agreement, obviously.'

'Yes, obviously,' she said, wondering why a husband had to agree to such a thing, why he should not in any case.

'And if I wanted to buy something, I can just make a transfer to my – our current account.'

'You mean something like a car?' he said, and his mournful eyes twinkled at her suddenly. 'Yes of course. Not bought it yet, then?'

'I haven't bought anything very much yet. Only a new roof and a few clothes and things. And I might invest in a friend's play – only my husband doesn't know about that,' she had added hastily, 'just in case you see him.'

'Mrs Fallon, lawyers and doctors are, like priests, not given to divulging the details of their clients' lives. May I say how rare and refreshing it is to see such common sense, such a grasp on reality.'

'Thank you,' said Cassia, wondering if he realised how terrified she was of even starting to spend the money on anything, anything she really wanted, because of its implications on her life, on her marriage, on herself . . .

That evening, she did broach the subject of the car. She started by suggesting they bought a new family car: their own was three years old, and mostly used by Edward. What about a Daimler? she said. Nothing too expensive, that would take all the family easily, but would also be suitable for Edward and his house calls.

She was interested in cars, quite knowledgable about them indeed. Sir Richard had been the first private car owner she had known, had taken her for a ride in it around London on her very first visit. A wonderful dashing thing it had been, an open cream-coloured Buick with wooden spoked wheels. Benedict had owned a Bentley, much more sedate, but very beautiful. Harry, of course, had had endless cars, wonderful glamorous things, their names forming a roll call of motoring glamour: a Delage, a Bugatti and a Maserati – all of which he raced – a gorgeous Rolls, the Hispano Suiza which he had claimed did seventy miles an hour ... Cassia wrenched her mind away from Harry's cars and waited while Edward pronounced on his own purchase.

It would be very nice, he said, to have a new one, and a Daimler was a good idea, but on the other hand, it was hardly necessary, and they had spent a lot of money recently on the house. She sat politely, listening to him for a while, and then said if he didn't want a new car, she did.

'Well, then,' he said, slightly impatiently, 'let's get one, then. A Daimler, yes, that's a thought. I'll take a look at the market, see what's around.'

'Yes, but what I also meant was I'd like to have one. Of my own,' she said, listening to her voice falling into the silence, the very still silence. Edward looked at her, his face blank, but his eyes sharp, and said finally that he really couldn't see that was at all necessary.

'Edward, of course it's not necessary, but it would be lovely. It would make my life much easier, and anyway, I love cars, you know I do.'

'Well,' he said finally, 'I suppose if that's what you really want. But for heaven's sake, get something small and easy to handle. You haven't driven much and the roads are so crowded these days. Get an Austin Seven, that's my advice, you can't come to much harm in that, and don't expect me to look after it for you when it breaks down.'

She had been so angry she went straight to London and bought a Jaguar SS 100. It was an enchantingly pretty sunshine-yellow convertible, with chrome wheels and trim, and a particularly pretty running board, curving up over the front wheels. 'It suits you, it's like a really nice hat,' Cecily exclaimed happily when she drove it round to the Boltons to show it off. It did at least sixty, the salesman told her, and it did indeed, she found, flying down the A24 towards Monks Heath that golden October day. When she arrived in the drive at Monks Ridge it made such a noise that everyone in the house came rushing out to see it.

'Cripes!' Bertie had said, and 'Goodness gracious!' William had screamed.

'Oh, my Lord,' Peggy said, her hand on her plump bosom.

Edward was out, but Cassia was in the kitchen making some pastry when he got back, and his face thunderous with rage was enough, as Peggy had remarked to Mrs Briggs next day, to turn the milk sour.

'What in the name of heaven is that thing sitting out there in the drive?'

'It's my car,' she said, smiling sweetly, continuing to roll her pastry. 'I bought it today. Do you like it?'

'It's ridiculous,' he said. 'You can't possibly keep it. I can't believe you've done such a thing. I told you to get an Austin Seven.'

'Perhaps,' she said carefully, conscious of Peggy's round eyes, Bertie's even rounder, 'we should go into your study. Talk about it there.'

He glared at her, then stalked out of the kitchen into his study. She followed him. He stood with his back to her, staring out of the window. 'What the hell are you playing at, Cassia?'

'Edward, I'm not playing at anything. I wanted a car, I've bought a car. It wasn't very expensive, a few hundred pounds—'

'A few hundred pounds!' he said. 'Not very expensive! And you dared to argue with me about the roof. God help me, what is happening to us?'

'I didn't argue about the roof.'

'Of course you did. And why in the name of heaven didn't you get something sensible, like the Austin or a Morris Minor?'

'It's perfectly sensible. There's a back seat for the children and ...'

There was a long silence, then Edward said, 'I think you should take it back, Cassia. I want you to take it back. Tomorrow.'

If he hadn't added that 'tomorrow' she might just have done so, but it was too much, too peremptory, too arrogant. She met his eyes very steadily. 'I'm not taking it back, Edward. Sorry. I got what I wanted. I know about cars, I like cars, I wanted this one.'

'Yes,' he said, 'I know you know about cars,' and stalked out of the room.

Almost three years ago it had been, she thought, looking after him, looking out of the window at her car, that Saturday that ended so painfully, so angrily, began so innocently – or so she had managed to tell herself. Bertie had been three, William almost two.

Cecily had telephoned her a couple of days earlier, asked her to join them for a picnic. 'It'll be such fun, Cassia. We're going to Brooklands, to watch the car racing. It was Benedict's idea, and he suggested you came too. Of course Edward's invited as well. It's lovely there, and it's so exciting to watch. We have lunch in the club house, take a picnic tea …'

'Oh Cecily,' she said, 'I'd love to come, really love it, but what would I do with the children? They're too little to bring.'

'Ours will be coming down just for the picnic tea, Nanny will bring them. Why don't you bring yours here, and Nanny can look after them. If you come up on Friday, you can stay the night. Oh, go on, Cassia, neglect your duties just for once.'

'I'll ask Edward, and ring you back.'

Edward said he could think of nothing worse than sitting by a noisy racetrack for hours on end, and that anyway, he was much too busy, couldn't possibly get away.

'What would you feel about me going on my own? Cecily said Nanny would look after the children, and I would really love it. I've always wanted to go.'

'I can't imagine why,' he said, 'but if you really want to, then of course you must.'

And so she had gone. What Cecily hadn't mentioned was that Harry Moreton was going to be there, racing his Bugatti.

She had seen photographs of Brooklands, but nothing could have prepared her for the reality: the snaking track, the steep banked curve which the cars rode at terrifying speeds and angles, the relentless ebb and flow of noise, the smell of the exhausts, the sense of energy and excitement.

'It's wonderful,' she said, smiling from the top of the grassy bank near the entrance, already covered in picnickers. 'I'm so glad I came.'

'Thought you'd like it,' said Benedict. 'Now look, come along, we can go down to the pits, see them getting the cars ready. Harry said he'd look out for us.'

'Harry?' she said, containing her voice with a great effort. 'I didn't know he was going to be here.'

'Oh, yes, it's a club day, and he's racing. Does it quite a lot.'

'Oh, I see,' she said, wishing suddenly, and hating herself for it, that she looked a bit smarter. Cecily was dressed in a wonderful red silk dress and a very rakish red and white straw hat, and all the women were dressed extremely well. Her own blue cotton floral dress seemed very commonplace and dowdy by comparison, and she hadn't even thought to wear a hat. It hadn't really seemed to matter very much before but—

'Come on, Cassia, buck up,' said Cecily, pulling at her arm. 'It's great fun in the pits, honestly …'

It was: like something in a film, men in white overalls working furiously, often three to a car, people rushing about, shouting, engines revving, tyres being whipped off, replacements being wheeled across the area at a run like great children's hoops.

'There's Harry, look,' said Benedict, and there he was, dressed in white overalls and a brown leather helmet, walking towards them, waving, smiling, a cigarette in his mouth, his goggles hanging from his hand, absolutely relaxed, as if he was going to do no more than stroll up to the club house with them, rather than take his car round the track at a hundred miles an hour.

'Good morning!' he said. 'And Cassia, what a lovely surprise. How pretty you look, blue always did suit you.'

'Thank you,' she said. Why was it, how was it, that everything he ever said managed to imply a shared past, tugging her back to it, disturbing her hard-won tranquillity.

'So when is your race, Harry?' said Cecily.

'Not till three o'clock, so I'll be able to join you for lunch. Apparently Gresham's over from France, flying his plane into the aero village over there, right on the other side of the track. He's got a Maserati here, and I've told him a dozen times the Bugatti's the better car, so we shall see this afternoon.'

'Leonora's not coming, I suppose?' said Cassia hopefully.

'No, sadly. Too busy enjoying life, I expect. Well, you must excuse me, I'll see you at lunchtime. Save a chair for me.'

'That should be interesting,' said Benedict as they walked away. 'There's a huge ongoing rivalry between those two where horsepower's concerned. I'd have thought the Maserati was the faster car myself, but we shall see.'

'Goodness,' said Cecily, 'a race within a race, how exciting. Shall we go and place our bets?'

The club house served a very good lunch, but Cassia was finding it hard to swallow. She was sitting next to Harry, who had arrived late, and a place had been laid hastily for him. Edwina had arrived now, and the table wasn't really big enough for five, and Harry was pressed rather close up against her.

Edwina was looking dazzling in a white linen suit and a wide-brimmed black straw hat with a huge white bow set on the front. She smiled graciously at Cassia and told her she looked tired. 'I'd have thought the country air would have been good for you,' she said, shaking out her napkin. 'It's obviously very over-rated.'

'So where is the doctor?' said Harry, picking up his glass. 'This is very good claret, Benedict. Just what I need to steady my nerves.'

'You haven't got any nerves,' said Edwina, 'and I'm sure you shouldn't drink before a race, Harry.'

'Oh, nonsense. Helps on the bends. Yes, where is your husband, Cassia? Wouldn't he enjoy this sort of thing?'

'Yes, I'm sure, but he's working,' she said hastily.

'Really? Well, you know what they say, all work and no play ... Although I'm sure you don't find him dull.'

'Of course I don't,' said Cassia irritably. She moved her right leg, which was pressed very hard against his left one, away from him; he moved his slowly but very deliberately after it. Cassia picked up her glass, took a large mouthful of wine, and discovered her hand was shaking. She put it down hastily, and realised he was looking at her, his eyes very intent on hers.

'Are you all right?' he said suddenly. She felt his leg move again, felt the dreadful, treacherous stirrings deep within her, frowned at him.

'Don't you start telling me I look tired,' she said.

'I was only going to tell you that you look a little sad.'

'I'm not in the least sad,' she said, trying to smile as brilliantly as Edwina, as Cecily, and failing.

'I'd hate you to be sad. Even if—' He stopped suddenly, obviously reconsidering what he might have been going to say, then smiled, and said, 'Well, tell me what exciting things you've been getting up to out there in the wilds. I want every tiny detail. Oh, Kay, hallo! How are you? See you later.'

'Is that Kay Petre?' said Benedict.

'Yes. Pretty, isn't she? Doesn't look like a racing driver. Bloody good, she's beaten me twice.'

'Goodness,' said Cassia, relieved at the change of subject, 'I didn't realise women raced cars.'

'Good Lord, yes, they brighten our lives no end. There's another, Doreen Evans, also very good. She and her two brothers all race here at the same time. Oh look, there's Gresham's plane coming in now. Nice little thing, isn't it? Leopard Moth. I'm thinking of getting one myself.'

'Don't you dare,' said Edwina.

The cars lined up at the start at two forty-five, an extraordinary assortment of sizes and shapes. They were handicapped, the tiny Austins and Morrises moving off first, at the wave of the black and white flag, then the Rileys – one driven by Kay Petre in her trademark blue overalls – and the MGs. Finally the big boys, Harry's Bugatti, gleaming silver-blue in the sunshine, and Rollo Gresham's black Maserati, somehow threatening, left almost together, Rollo a second ahead.

They were all standing watching on the girder bridge, over the great banked curve; Cassia felt very odd, the sexual disturbance of lunchtime somehow confused in her senses with the exhaust fumes and the vibration and the sense of vertigo that came from looking down on the cars.

'I don't think I can stand much of this,' said Edwina. 'I think I might go and wait in the club house.'

'Don't do that!' said Benedict. 'You can't deprive Harry of your support at a moment like this.'

'He doesn't need it,' said Edwina. 'His ego is so huge it provides quite enough support for the whole— Oh my God.'

There was a sudden roar as the two cars swept under the bridge, the Bugatti fractionally ahead; it was at the very top of the bank, only just within the safety line, clinging to the track at its seemingly impossible angle. They swung round the curve, lower down.

'Why do they have that ghastly slope?' said Edwina irritably. 'What's the point? And why don't they fall off?'

'Braking device, in essence,' said Benedict, 'and centrifugal force. Holding them on, I mean. Anyway, two more laps, then it'll be over. Hold my hand, Edwina.'

'I don't need my hand held,' said Edwina. 'I'm cross, not frightened.'

Kay Petre's Riley and a couple of Rovers came under the bridge first on the second lap, and then hard behind her the Bugatti and the Maserati, lower down this time, Rollo ahead by what could only have been feet, seeming to glide upwards as he approached the curve, pulling away from Harry.

'I hope to God Rollo doesn't win,' said Edwina. 'I shall have an appalling weekend if he does.'

The smaller cars were coming through now, people shouting, urging them on; it was very like a horserace meeting, Cassia said.

'In the early days, the drivers wore coloured silk overalls,' said Benedict, 'rather like jockeys. The whole thing was like a glorified flat race. Christ almighty, here they come again.'

The Maserati came through under the bridge, ahead by half a length; Harry's Bugatti, above it on the bank, suddenly moved higher still, right to the rim, and then like a horse that has been kept in check, pushed apparently effortlessly forward, gravity helping him on the downhill stretch. Gresham, obviously seeing a last chance, shot very sharply into the bend, skidded slightly and for a moment looked as if he would crash hard into Harry. He righted his wheels and for several terrifying moments they were exactly parallel, not more than six inches apart. Their wheels apparently locked, sliding crazily together round the bend, then they were lost to view again, in a scream of tyres.

'Jesus,' said Benedict, 'I think they've—'

'What?' said Edwina. 'They've what, Benedict? Not crashed? God, of all the stupid—'

'I'm not sure. Let me through, can I get through, please ...'

Rollo Gresham won by a whisker: it was a photo finish. The two of them climbed out of their cars, grinning, stood posing for photographs for the cine-camera enthusiasts who lined the track.

Cassia and the others had run down from their vantage point to join them, Cassia absolutely behind Benedict on legs that were now suddenly weak, the panic that had risen slowly subsiding, Edwina and Cecily several yards behind.

'Jolly good race,' Gresham was saying, 'and you're buying me dinner, I think.'

'Dinner? What dinner?' said Edwina.

'We said the loser would buy the other one dinner,' said Gresham. 'Coming, Edwina?' He was sweating, breathing heavily, grinning at her in his strangely insolent way. Cassia thought how much she disliked him and wondered, as she always did, how Leonora could possibly have chosen to live with him.

'Of course,' said Edwina, 'that's the least you can do for me, after practically killing my husband. Where shall we go?'

'Le Touquet. That was the idea.'

'Le Touquet! No fear! I hate those little planes. Harry, you can go alone, if you're going to Le Touquet. Why can't we have dinner in London somewhere?'

'Because I like Le Touquet,' said Gresham, 'and I won the race. Cassia, you're very pale. Are you all right?' He pulled out his cigarette case, took out a cigarette with a surprisingly shaky hand.

'Yes. I'm fine, thank you,' she said slightly irritably, aware that everyone was looking at her, afraid they might know why. 'Is Leonora going to be in Le Touquet?'

'What? Oh, no. She's in Paris. She said to give you a kiss if I saw you, so may I?' He leant forward; he was very hot, and he smelt of sweat. He was a large man heavily built with wavy dark hair, and light blue eyes, and good looking, she supposed, in a rather coarse way.

She had to brace herself to receive the kiss, to return it. As she pulled back, she saw Harry's eyes on her, thoughtful, concerned.

'You *are* pale,' he said. 'Are you sure you're all right?' I don't want you passing out on us.'

'Don't be ridiculous.' She managed to smile at him. 'Is she well?' she said, turning back to Gresham. 'Leonora, I mean.'

'Very well. Full of life. And looking marvellous. You must come and stay with us in Paris. Very soon.'

'Yes, I'd like to. Thank you. And please give Leonora my love, won't you?'

'Look,' said Harry, 'I'm going to change. When do you want to leave, Gresham?'

'Not yet. I'd like to see a few more races, have a few drinks. Edwina, are you sure you won't come? It'd be much more fun if you did. And Cassia, what about you? I've got room for four.'

'No thanks,' said Edwina.

Cassia shook her head. 'No, really, thank you, I have to get home. My children are arriving in a minute, and then as soon as we've had tea, we'll have to be on our way.'

And there it might have ended, innocently, virtuously, harmlessly; only as the Harrington Daimler pulled into the car park, a cloud of steam shot out of the radiator and Preston got out, looking worried. 'She's been overheating all the way, Mr Harrington. Needs a bit of work done on her, I'm afraid.'

'Well, we're in the right place for that,' said Benedict. 'I'll go and find Harry, ask if we can borrow a mechanic.'

Nanny got out of the car, followed by the older children, and lifted William out. He was crying. 'He's not very happy, Mrs Fallon, I'm afraid. He's got a tummy ache, he says, and he's a bit hot.'

'Oh dear,' said Cassia. 'Come here, darling, let me— goodness, yes, he is. We'd better leave at once, I think, if Preston could—'

'What's the matter?' Harry had appeared with his mechanic.

'I need to get home rather quickly, William isn't very well. If the Daimler's out of action, maybe Benedict could take us, but—'

There was a pause so brief, so imperceptible no one else would have noticed it but she did.

'I'll take you,' said Harry, 'I'll take you now. If that's what you really want.'

'Oh, Harry, no, you've got your French dinner and I don't want to spoil your day.'

'It wouldn't spoil my day,' said Harry. 'How extraordinary that you should think it would. And don't worry about the dinner, I can be back in plenty of time.'

Cassia looked at him. His face was grimy and streaked with sweat, his hair even wilder than usual, released from its helmet. She was still disturbed by the race and her fear that he had crashed, and felt suddenly a surge of violent sexual excitement, careless, dangerous. She knew that she should refuse at once, or there would be most undesirable – or did she mean desirable – consequences.

'That would be marvellous,' she said.

He had come in his Bentley, a huge cream thing, with a brown soft top which Harry opened to the lovely afternoon air. She settled the goggle-eyed boys in the back, and said goodbye to the rest of the party.

'You're sure about this, Harry?' said Cecily. 'Because Benedict could easily—'

'No, it's perfectly all right, and Benedict wants to see the last race. I'll be back by six thirty, Gresham, seven at the latest. Bye, Edwina, I'll see you later.'

'No, you won't,' said Edwina. 'I'm going home. I've had quite enough of this beastly place. And don't wake me up when you come in.'

'He won't be back tonight,' said Rollo Gresham, grinning at her, 'I promise you that.'

After half an hour the boys both fell asleep. Cassia fixed her eyes carefully on the road, trying not to look at Harry, horribly aware of what she had done, aware that he knew too.

'Are you all right?' he said suddenly, abruptly.

'Yes, I'm fine. It's wonderfully comfortable, this car.'

'I didn't mean the car, as you know very well. I meant are *you* all right? You really did look dreadful for a while back at the course.'

'No, I'm fine. I was just—' She stopped, just in time.

'Cassia, you know how much I hate this sort of conversation. Just what?'

'Well, I was scared. I thought you'd crashed.'

'Really? You minded that much? How sweet.' He smiled at her, but his eyes were soft; she felt the emotion and looked determinedly in front of her. There was a silence.

'How is that ridiculous marriage of yours?' he said suddenly.

'Harry, it's not ridiculous,' she said, laughing in spite of herself.

'Of course it is. Jesus, Cassia, I wish—'

'Harry, don't. Please don't.'

'Why not?' he said, and there was an underlying rage in his voice.

'Because there's no point, that's why not. It's too—'

'Too what? Too late, you were going to say, weren't you?'

'Yes,' she said simply.

'Bloody nonsense. Bloody criminal stupidity,' he said, glaring at the road. 'Marrying him like that, when we—' And then he stopped, turned his head and looked at her, very steadily. She met his eyes, just for a moment too long, felt the excitement again, smiled at him. She couldn't help it. 'Oh, Christ,' he said.

They were driving down the A24 now; it was busy with weekend motorists. A car coming the other way hooted loudly. Harry swore, swerved to avoid it. 'You're very bad for me,' he said. 'You'll kill us at this rate.'

'*I'll* kill *you!*' she said, laughing. 'I like that.'

'Yes. Let's get off this bloody road.'

Half a mile further down the road, they passed a lane. He turned sharply into it, so sharply that the tyres screamed.

'You're not on the racetrack now,' she said.

'Sorry. Did you enjoy the racing?'

'I absolutely loved it. I thought it was terribly exciting.'

'I thought you did,' he said. 'It's exactly like sex, the whole thing, I find,' and then turned the car again, down a track.

'Where are we going?' she said slightly weakly.

He looked at her and his face was absolutely intent on her, his expression almost hostile. 'Somewhere I can kiss you,' he said, 'somewhere I can get close to you for once.'

'What! Harry, the boys are—'

'Asleep. Shut up, or you'll wake them.' He slammed on the brakes, the car lurched violently, stopped.

'Harry, I can't.'

'Of course you can.'

And then she was in his arms, and his mouth, lazy, slow, confident, on hers, and she didn't resist, didn't protest, just kissed him, kissed him back, on and on, in a sweet, urgent darkness. It was more than a kiss, more than an embrace: it was a long-kept promise, a long-planned rediscovery, timeless, endless. She felt his hands in her hair, on her neck, then moving to her breasts, felt herself responding, swiftly, violently, knew what she wanted, knew she had to have it. It was as if the excitement of the day, the ferocity of the speed and the noise, had somehow entered her, become part of her, and even as she recognised the danger, her fear, she would have ignored it, helpless in the face of such blinding, violent temptation.

She would have got out of the car and lain down on the ground, and taken him into her, there and then, but 'Mummy,' said Bertie, 'Mummy, where have we come to?'

He hadn't seen, she kept telling herself, as they drove hard, silently on to Monks Heath, he hadn't seen anything, and if William had, he was too little to tell; but fear, blind, hot fear filled her. Harry, angry at what had happened, hostile at her anxiety, her insistence that they left at once, did not even look at her. It was very hot, and the sun beat down on them, and the lurching round bends made her feel sick. The boys loved it, squealing with delight as the tyres screamed on corners or the car shuddered to a halt at crossroads, William seemingly quite recovered again. When finally they pulled into the drive at Monks Ridge, they leapt out, ran into the house calling for Edward. Harry sat, still staring straight ahead, and said, 'When will I see you again?'

'You won't,' Cassia said, restored to sanity by the sobering, domestic events. 'You mustn't,' and got out of the car herself. 'Goodbye, Harry, thank you, I won't ask you in,' she said loudly, and looked at her house in all its dullness and its frustrations, and at Edward, walking out of the door now, his face set in disapproval. She mentally set her shoulders and walked up to him and kissed him briefly. She waved Harry off as he nodded at Edward in silence and then pulled, very hard, too hard, out of the drive again.

She was about to ask Edward how his day had been when Bertie's small voice said, 'He's nice. He kissed Mummy.'

'Edward, you are being ridiculous,' she said, as he faced her in the drive. 'Of course he kissed me: he kissed me goodbye, that's all.'

'I hope that's true,' he said. 'I hope that was all.'

The fact that she was lying, combined with her frustration and the turbulence of her day, made her more indignant, not less.

'How dare you!' she said. 'How dare you imply such a thing. I've spent a day with friends, a happy day which you were not prepared to join me in, however much I might have wished it.'

'I cannot stand those friends,' he said, 'any of them, you know I can't. How dare he drive away like that without even speaking to me, patronising me, in that ridiculous car.'

'He raced another car,' said Bertie, 'a big blue one, with another man in a black one.'

'Raced? He raced?'

'Yes,' she said, foolishly still hoping, still trying to soothe him, placate him. 'Harry was driving a Bugatti, and Rollo Gresham a Maserati. It was very exciting and—'

'And he had a plane,' said Bertie. 'The other man had a plane.'

'A plane. A Bugatti. A Maserati. And of course a Bentley. Occupying at least half our rather modest drive. I see. How very fortunate for them all. Clearly, Cassia, you must find it very dull here—'

'Oh, shut up,' she cried, 'stop it. Your bloody jealousy spoils everything. What have I done, except enjoy myself for once—'

'For once. Well, I'm sorry your life here should be so unenjoyable, Cassia. It seems rather sad. I'm afraid I have to leave you now, I have work to do. Perhaps you should get the boys to bed, they look very tired.'

She followed him into the house, silent with rage, with misery, and did what he said, for the sake of peace, and because she had no option and was in any case to an extent remorseful. She said she was sorry if he had been upset, and an uneasy truce was formed, but from that day on talk of cars was dangerous between them.

It caused a great stir in the village, her car. It changed the way people saw her. Well, she thought, cars did that. The women were openly disapproving, rarely mentioning it, looking what she could only describe as irritably at it as it stood outside a shop or the church; the men patronisingly impressed, alternately offering condescending advice and flirtatious comment.

She loved her car: for it didn't only provide her with freedom, it symbolised it as well.

Benedict took her out to lunch to discuss investments. They went to the Savoy. 'Goodness,' she said, looking round, 'do you remember the first time we came here together, Benedict? You and me and Harry and Leonora, for tea it was. You and Leonora danced the Black Bottom wonderfully, and Harry sat and sulked.'

'He did a lot of sulking in those days,' said Benedict with a smile.

'I know, although he was better then than the very first time I'd met him. Once he'd been at Eton for a year or so, he seemed a bit more normal. At least he was in long trousers. That first time he was in shorts, and looked very strange indeed: he was already huge. He'd written me a note when my mother died, which really surprised me. When I thanked him, he said he could imagine it must be rather sad. Poor Harry.'

'Poor Harry. What a nightmare of a childhood that was. No wonder he's so …'

'Difficult?' said Cassia briskly.

'You certainly always seemed to find him so, although I believe you are better friends now. You seemed to be getting on rather nicely in France.'

'Well,' she said briskly, 'quite nicely.'

'That's a pretty hat,' he said, looking at it, 'and the suit, very chic.'

'Thank you.' She had bought them both the week before, on a shopping expedition – disguised from Edward as a visit to Mr Brewster – the suit dark brown wool, with the new long, narrow jacket, the hat a slouch-brimmed trilby in camel with a dark brown trim.

'You mustn't spend it all on clothes,' Benedict said, smiling, signalling for the waiter to refill her glass.

'That's exactly what Rupert said. Have you two been in cahoots over it?'

'No, of course not,' he said, and there was something in the way he said it, just fractionally too fast, too firmly, that for a moment seemed significant; then he smiled again, his charming, easy smile, and the moment was gone. 'I expect we all feel the same. That's all. It's such a lot of money, you need to look after it carefully.'

'I thought Leonora might have told you,' she said, 'that she was going to leave me this money?'

He was lighting a cigarette; he didn't look at her. 'No, I had no idea.'

'Oh, I see.' She was taken aback, had somehow assumed he must know. 'I just thought – well, I knew you'd been to see her, those last few weeks. When she was dying. Benedict, was she all right?'

'As all right as she could have been,' he said mildly.

'I'm sorry. I know it sounds stupid. I meant, was she being cared for really well, medically? It's worried me so much.'

'Cassia,' said Benedict, 'Leonora was superbly cared for medically. She had twenty-four-hour nursing, and any pain was being kept well under control. She was peaceful.'

'I'm sorry,' Cassia said again. 'I wish I could have seen her.'

'I know, but she didn't want that, she wanted everyone to remember her as she was. She didn't want you in particular worried and upset. And in the end she died much more swiftly and easily than any of us expected.' His voice shook. He looked at her, smiled apologetically, drew on his cigarette.

'I'm sorry, Benedict. You must miss her so much.'

'Yes,' he said, 'I do.' He smiled, a rather lopsided smile. 'I miss her quite dreadfully.'

There was a silence, then he said, clearly anxious to change the subject, to bring them on to safer emotional ground, 'Well, what about this windfall of yours, then? Dangerous things, windfalls.'

'Yes, but I'm being careful with the money. I'm quite a sensible person really, you know.'

'I do know. Now, I've drawn up a list here of suggested investments, look. It's a pretty wide spread, very safe, very gilt-edged, with just a few wild cards if you wanted a bit of a flutter. For instance, I think you might consider buying into the aviation business – flight really is the travel of the future – and I really would urge you to think hard about the building trade. All these suburbs shooting up everywhere, rows and rows of houses, really big potential there. I'm putting a fair bit of my own money into it, as a matter of fact. Then there are some government stocks, and so on. I'd suggest a trust fund for each of the children—'

'Yes, Edward and I have discussed that.' They had: it had been awkward, difficult, and the discussion had never actually been completed. He had plainly seen her suggestion as arrogant, overbearing, a takeover of her children's financial future, however much she used the words 'we' and 'our'.

'I'd like to make a bequest,' she said suddenly, 'if that's the right word.'

'Explain a bit more.'

'I'd like to give a scholarship to be awarded annually at the hospital, at St Christopher's. Can I do that?'

'Of course you can, providing they're willing. Which I imagine they would be. Or a research chair, something like that. It's a very nice idea. I would have thought the best person to talk to would be the Dean. He could advise you. I should go and call on him, he'd be pleased to see you.'

'Do you think? He was so angry when I told him what I was going to do, shouted at me for ages, told me I was wasting myself and the hospital's money. I was very upset,' she said, remembering with hideous vividness the awful scene, the way she had cried afterwards for hours in her old room at Grosvenor Gardens, misery taking an absolute hold on her, thinking this was the day her real life, the one she really cared about, had ended.

'I expect he'll have forgiven you by now,' said Benedict cheerfully, 'especially if you're waving a cheque book at him. Wonderful what money can do. You write and tell him what you want to do, and he'll have the red carpet out for you, mark my words.' He hesitated for a moment, then said, 'You haven't thought of going back into medicine yourself? Now that you could.'

'Rupert said that as well. Are you sure you haven't been talking about this? No, it's all right, I'm only teasing you. I don't see *why* I could suddenly. What's changed? I'm still married to Edward, still living in the country, still have three small children ...'

'True, but you could buy yourself some freedom, pay for a good nanny, I don't know, you qualified well enough, God knows.'

'Yes, I know but five years is a long time in medicine, things change, and who would be interested in a woman who'd never done her house job? Wonderful as the thought is,' she added with a sigh.

'I think you should talk to the Dean about that as well,' said Benedict, 'before you quite put it out of your mind.'

She looked at him; his face was very serious. She was surprised and touched he should care so much. 'Benedict, I can't. You don't understand. There's Edward to consider. He would find it – unbearable.'

'I don't see why.'

'I'm afraid you have to take my word for it. And actually I think if you put yourself in his position for one moment, you'd see quite clearly.'

'You really do love him, don't you?' he said.

'Yes, I do,' she said quickly. 'Now look, can I order something off that wonderful trolley and then I must go. I have to catch the three thirty from Victoria, or I shall be in terrible trouble.'

'Any progress?' said Cecily when he got home.

'Not a great deal. She's bought some more clothes. And she wants to set up a scholarship at the hospital.'

'Does she? Well, that's at least a step in the right direction. Good.'

'But she seems very set against going back into medicine herself. Says it wouldn't be possible, and very hard on Edward. I don't see why.'

'Oh, Benedict, really! How would you feel if it was me? If I was a much better stockbroker than you were, and I was setting up in a rival firm.'

'Is she really a better doctor than he is?'

'She would have been, as I understand it. Much better.'

'Yes, I suppose I'd forgotten that. Poor Cassia. Very tough.' He looked at her. 'How *do* you feel, Cecily?'

'All right. A bit tired. Why?'

'I thought we might discuss Christmas. This party you've been talking about, the guest list and so on. I've drawn up mine. Here.'

She looked at it, and recognised most of the names. 'Who's Dominic Foster?'

He wasn't looking at her, was pouring himself a drink. There was a pause, just fractionally too long, and his voice as he answered her was just slightly too casual. 'Architect I met. Working on one of these garden city developments I've invested in. Nice chap. You'd like him. Very clever. I was telling Cassia, she ought to put some money into that field. Huge potential.'

'Oh,' she said. 'Yes, well, do let's invite him.'

He looked at her then and she could see that he had, as always, understood, that he knew what she was thinking. Whether she was right or wrong, she knew she was right to go on enquiring, being careful, making sure – and making sure he knew what she was doing. She had to: for both their sakes.

CHAPTER 7

Cassia wrote to the Dean, and got a charming letter back. He would be delighted to see her. Would she not join him for coffee one morning the following week to discuss her proposal? He would like to know how she was getting on, how her husband was getting on. Would her husband be with her?

Cassia phoned his secretary – who remembered her well – and arranged to go in the following Wednesday. She said her husband would not be with her.

She told Edward that she had to see her dentist in London, that she was having trouble with a wisdom tooth, and when he was in the surgery went and changed into the dark brown suit and camel-coloured hat and drove to the station in the Jaguar, thinking how well the yellow went with the brown of her outfit.

Peggy, who had been watching her as she hurried out of the front door and climbed into the car, said to Mrs Briggs, 'She's changing, Mrs Fallon is. Every day, she's changing a little bit more. It's that money she's come into, that's what's changing her.'

Cassia was early for her appointment with the Dean. She walked slowly through the medical school, down the long corridors, past the lecture theatre, past the labs; the smells, the noises, even the colours, the endless green and cream, taking her back, rendering her seventeen again, seventeen and terrified. She smiled at the vividness of the memory, forcing down the inevitable regrets, and knocked firmly on the Dean's door.

'You were very happy here, weren't you?' he said, his thick eyebrows meeting over his piercing dark eyes. 'Did well too, which is more to the point. Damn shame.'

'It couldn't be helped.'

'So you said at the time. I held a different view. I'm afraid you damaged the female cause here for a few years. The board kept quoting you whenever I wanted to admit a woman. Oh, I know, you did what you felt you had to. More's the pity. How's that husband of yours?'

'He's very well. Doing well too.'

'In general practice, isn't he? You didn't want that, did you? As I recall?'

'No, I wanted to do obstetrics.' It hurt, even to say it.

'Instead of which, you had to have brats of your own. Dreadful waste. Dreadful. Well, there you are. You've made your bed and I suppose you have to lie on it. Now then, what's all this about a scholarship or a fellowship or something? Come into some money, have you?'

It was decided a research chair in obstetrics should be set up, with an annual donation of ten thousand pounds.

'Jolly fine idea, this,' said the Dean, 'most generous. What shall we call it? The Fallon Chair?'

'No,' Cassia said quickly, 'not Fallon. I thought perhaps Beatty. That was my godmother's name, the one who left me the money. But I should have to ask her husband. He's still alive, he might not be happy with it.'

'Well, that's up to you. Husband know about this, does he?'

She met his eyes steadily. 'No. Actually, he doesn't. Not yet. Of course I'm going to tell him.'

'Probably best. Not very bright, as I recall, your husband. Failed first time round, didn't he?' The eyes were more piercing still.

'He's very bright,' said Cassia, defensively. 'He just suffered horribly from exam nerves.'

'Funny how the really brilliant chaps always manage to overcome those. Sorry, speaking out of turn. How does he feel about you having all this money, then?'

'Oh, all right.'

'Good. Funny thing, money. And I dare say he was touchy, you doing better than him. Probably just as well for him that you decided to get out, if you really had to marry him. Not for you though.'

'Yes,' she said, and then because he seemed so kind, so approachable suddenly, so genuinely sorry that she had left medicine, she took a deep breath and said it, said what she had sworn she would never say, never ask, never think even: what chance would there be of her returning now?

'Well, to come back here, absolutely none, I'm afraid. You had your chance and blew it. I suppose you might persuade a general hospital to take you on, as a houseman. It'd be very tough, though. And you couldn't do that, could you? Couldn't move into a hospital, leave those children?'

'No, I couldn't possibly.'

'Well, you could go into general practice. Not the same thing, but still, better than wasting everything. Have you thought of that?'

'Not really,' she said, thinking how impossible it would be to explain to him about why not general practice, about Edward's jealousy. She stared at him and tried to smile. Her heart seemed to have become a leaden weight in her stomach. 'I just haven't got that sort of time.'

'Tell you what you might do,' he said suddenly, 'if you're really serious. These birth control clinics setting up all over the place now – more power to their elbows, I'm sure you'd agree. There might be a chance you could work at one of those. They want women doctors. It's pretty mundane work, not the sort of thing some keen young medic wants to do. Glorified nursing, really.' He sat back in his chair and looked at her. 'If you're serious, if you think you might like that, get in touch. I know a few people in that field. In fact a friend of my wife's runs one in Highgate. God knows quite how it would work out, how you'd get yourself back into training, so to speak, but if you wanted to talk to this woman at least, I could arrange it.'

'Thank you,' she said, and realised that the weight had lifted just a bit, that the coldness was easier. 'Thank you, yes, and if I do, I'll let you know. It's probably out of the question, and my husband would have to agree and—'

'For God's sake,' said the Dean. He slammed his fist down on the desk and she jumped. 'I thought you women had got the vote these days. What was I doing, giving a valuable place to you, just to hear that your husband will have to agree to your doing a bit of work? You of all people, you were so strong. Amstruther thought a lot of you. Said you had the makings of a real surgeon. He was furious, you know, when you left.'

'Yes, I know,' said Cassia humbly.

'Well, I mustn't upset you, or you might change your mind about the Chair. Let me know about the name, won't you, in due course. And thank you for that. Thank you a hundred times. Give my regards to that husband of yours.'

'Yes, I will. Thank you.'

'Nice hat,' he said suddenly. 'I like to see a nice hat on a pretty woman.'

She was still smiling when she reached the street.

London was looking very Christmassy, lights everywhere, windows decorated lavishly. She wandered down Bond Street, enjoying it, and then started worrying about Christmas itself, about how she was going to get it right. She had started thinking she wouldn't spend a lot of money, that she would only buy everyone the sort of present she and Edward could afford together, nothing expensive, nothing that he would find threatening. And then, as she had sat in her car, her ridiculous, lovely, rich-girl's car in the High Street in Haywards Heath and looked in the window of the bicycle shop and seen a gleaming red and chrome Raleigh bike with a three-speed and lamps, and thought of how much Bertie longed for such a thing, and thought also of the Meccano set (size 3) she had actually bought him, it all seemed extremely silly, if not downright mean. So she had bought the bike, a trike of comparable splendour for William (for whom she had already purchased another Meccano set) and a wonderfully frilly dolls' crib for Delia.

She hid them all in the loft and looked at them – and thought, extravagant as they might seem to Edward, they were hardly absurdly extravagant, not the kind of presents really rich people bought at all.

She had bought expensive presents for Peggy and Mrs Briggs too (knowing that they knew, that they were talking about it all, the money, knowing they would simply find her mean if she did not): a soft lambswool shawl for Mrs Briggs and a pretty woollen blouse and skirt for Peggy, and hampers from Fortnum's for both their families. And then, while she was on the phone to Fortnum's, she had ordered one for themselves too. Edward could hardly expect them all to sit down to a modest meal and a bottle of Burgundy while down the road his servants' families were downing the champagne and foie gras that his wife had provided.

She had no idea what she was going to buy Edward ...

Just the same, she realised, gazing into Asprey's vulgar windows, wondering whether she shouldn't buy a present for the house, a pair of candlesticks perhaps, or a silver jug, and then telling herself that really would be dangerous, she was increasingly nervous. Perhaps she should leave all the expensive presents in the loft, and get out the Meccano sets and the rag doll she had bought in the first place. But that really did seem silly.

She wrote to Sir Richard about the research Chair at St Christopher's, telling him that she had agreed with the Dean that one should be set up, explaining that she would like it to bear the Beatty name, 'because I thought Leonora would like that. But of course if you have any objections, let me know.'

He wrote back, saying that of course he would be delighted, and it was most generous of her to give it Leonora's name, 'and most generous of you also to make what is clearly a so very considerable gift to the hospital. I do hope you are being at least a little selfish with the money.' He still obviously had no idea how large the bequest had been, Cassia thought, smiling at his overneat handwriting. He signed it 'Yr affectionate Godpa' and added a postscript suggesting she came to luncheon with him and Margaret next time she was in London.

Cecily was enjoying her party; she always did. Apart from anything else, she liked just standing and observing it as it reached its peak, studying it, this creation of hers, this carefully choreographed company. The women were dressed, most of them, in narrow black dresses, many elaborately beaded or embroidered, often bare-backed; a few were in the latest rage, white rayon jersey, draped and hung in the Grecian style; the men in their perfectly tailored doubled-breasted, wide-lapelled suits; a marvellous, good-looking, interesting roomful.

She was a natural hostess: generous, thoughtful, socially imaginative. Nobody at her parties ever had an empty glass, stood alone on the edge of a group, found him- or herself rooted for more than a few minutes in uncongenial company. She moved around her guests tirelessly, smiling, chattering, enquiring, exclaiming, transferring people from group to group, anticipating who they would like to meet, what they would like to talk about. People always left happily, pleased with themselves as well as her, having not only seen many of their own friends and acquaintances, but made new ones with new interests as well.

She gave this party every Christmas, a cocktail party, still very much the vogue, the great drawing room in the house in Eaton Place absorbing over a hundred people with ease. It was never quite a predictable mix: the major part was inevitably made up of glossy London society, with even the occasional minor royal – she had twice entertained the Duke of Gloucester and his pretty duchess, and once the Princess Royal and Lord Lascelles – but she also liked to include members of the international set, women like Natalie Paley, daughter of the Grand Duke of Russia, Mme Martinez de Hoz, even once Diana Vreeland, her guest list a glittering roll call of the smart and interesting.

After the party, a couple of dozen – carefully, tactfully briefed – would stay for supper. When they had gone, the family and perhaps one or two very close friends would be left, settled usually in the smaller drawing room, the staff dismissed, Benedict wandering round cigar in one hand, bottle of Armagnac in the other, Cecily relaxed into a sofa, sipping a restorative glass of champagne, smiling, pleased at her night's work.

Tonight the family representation was small: Harry and Edwina

Moreton, Cecily's parents, and Cassia Fallon. Edward had been unable to come, due to an influenza epidemic sweeping the Home Counties. The close friends included Rupert Cameron and the high-profile architect Dominic Foster and his wife Nicola, thin, dark haired, almost impossibly chic. Foster, tall, dark, languidly good-looking, was reputedly single-handedly responsible for converting a very large stretch of green countryside around the south-eastern edge of London into suburban streets.

Nicola Foster had been talking for some time to Edwina Moreton: Cecily watched her, thinking how much she would like to look like that, with a boyish figure, a neatly cropped head, wondering if after this baby she should put herself on a starvation diet, go to M. Rene to have her glossy curls clipped off, her dark eyebrows plucked away. Well, even if she tried it, it was a long way off, thanks to her burgeoning bump; and the cost to herself would be enormous. Cecily didn't care how often people told her that thin people didn't eat as much as fat people: she had sat, miserably, watching Cassia and Edwina, the two women she knew best, spoonful by spoonful and observed that over a period of, say, twenty-four hours, they ate far more than she did and weighed a great deal less. She felt quite sure that Nicola Foster devoured four square meals a day.

Nicola was coming over to her now, smiling. 'Thank you so much, we've had a marvellous time, but we must go now. Where is Dominic? Ah, Dominic, there you are. I must just go and powder my nose, and then we must move off.'

Dominic stood looking down at Cecily. He really was very good-looking, she thought, with those rather gaunt, high-cheekboned features, those burning dark eyes. He was beautifully dressed too, in a very dark grey suit, perfectly tailored, nothing remotely flamboyant; and his charm was undeniable.

'Cecily, goodnight. It's been the most wonderful evening. I have enjoyed it, thank you so much for inviting us.'

'Well,' she said, standing up, offering her face as he bent from his considerable height to kiss her, 'you should thank Benedict. It was his idea initially. I'm so glad you were able to accept. You and your wife must come and dine with us one evening, after Christmas.'

'We should be delighted. Thank you. And a happy Christmas to you.'

He half bowed, smiled at her, then turned away, went over to Benedict, who was sitting down, talking to her mother.

Cecily watched them closely: Benedict looked up at Dominic, smiled, stood up, shook his hand, and then, clapping the other arm on his shoulder, ushered him gently out of the room. It was nothing, nothing but the most urbane of gestures, and Benedict was back very soon. Within less than sixty seconds, he came over to her, sat down beside her, kissed her hand, told her how clever she was, what a wonderful evening it had been. Nevertheless, she knew. She always knew. And some dark, fearful instinct told her, reflecting upon Foster's absolute and very stylish self-assurance, that this time she might very well not be able to do anything about it.

Cassia was sitting on the sofa with Rupert; thinking how much she loved him still (while no longer being in love with him), watching the room, chatting idly about this person and that, envying and trying to analyse Edwina's chic. Tonight she was in emerald green, looked herself like a glittering jewel with her sleek dark hair, her brilliant brown eyes, her perfectly shaped glossy mouth.

'You look infinitely beautiful tonight, my darling,' said Rupert, smiling at her, and she smiled back, startled as always by his apparent ability to read her thoughts. 'Edward is very foolish to let you out on your own.'

'Rupert, I'm a hick matron of twenty-eight with three small children. Don't be so silly.'

'Twenty-eight I have to allow you, immense age that it is, but hick you are not. You look extremely stylish. That is a wonderful dress, black always did become you. No one would ever believe one baby had disrupted that waistline, never mind three. God, I wish I was twenty-eight again.'

'What were you doing when you were twenty-eight?' she said curiously.

'Very much the same as I am doing now,' he said lightly, 'being an unsuccessful two-star actor, touring in various two-star companies, with a long string of disastrous love affairs already behind me. Only then I knew I was going to be successful one day – now I don't.'

She stared at him, shocked by the genuine sadness in his voice. 'Rupert, I've never heard you talk like this before.'

'I don't very often. I don't mind very often. Mostly I know I'm lucky to be working at all, to have survived the war, to be happy, to have friends like you, but turning fifty-five hurts a bit. Makes you think.'

Dazzled as she always had been by him, by his looks, his charm, his wonderful voice, she had never paused to consider the actual standard of his success. Rupert was an actor, he appeared on the stage all over the country, a couple of films, his name was on placards in front of any theatre she had seen him in, near the top of any cast list on any programme; that seemed to her immensely glamorous. She smiled at him slightly awkwardly; she didn't know quite what to say.

He patted her hand, smiled back. 'Sorry, darling. Not quite the time to embark on an attack of self-pity.'

'But there's no need for it, Rupert. You've done films—'

'B-movies they're called. And only in supporting roles.'

'And the wireless plays ...'

'Yes, at least two. Or was it three? And as for the things I've auditioned for, well ... No, what I mind is never playing the West End. Not once. And never will now, I fear.'

'You might.'

'I don't think so. It would take a miracle to manage that.'

'What sort of a miracle?'

'A multi-parted miracle: a producer I knew, an inexhaustible team of angels – I know you've offered, but I can't take it – a director who really wanted me, a part that was perfect for me, a light comedy, probably, nothing too difficult, a famous leading lady who was madly in love with me and made my playing opposite her a condition of accepting the role ...'

'Who could do that?'

'Gertrude Lawrence, perhaps.'

'Is she in love with you?'

'Sadly not. If she is, she doesn't know it. Or me, for that matter.'

Cassia laughed. 'Well, here's to all that. And remember my offer does stand. To miracles.' She raised her glass.

'To miracles. Cecily looks wonderful, doesn't she? So serene. It suits her, pregnancy.'

'Yes, it does. Although ...'

'I know. I saw it too. Nothing to worry about there, I'd say. He's much too ambitious, that young man. Extremely clever but pretty harmless in this context, I would say. I shall go and tell Cecily so right away.'

'Rupert, be careful. She doesn't like ... well, you know, anyone knowing.'

'Of course she doesn't. When was I anything but the soul of tact?'

'Never,' said Cassia, laughing.

He kissed her lightly and got up. She watched him move over to the sofa, perch on its arm, start chatting to Cecily, obviously telling her some joke, then gossiping. And saw Cecily suddenly look up at him, startled, then smile, and visibly relax.

Later, much later, Cassia asked him what he had said.

'Oh, not much,' he said, 'just that there was only one thing Dominic Foster really wanted and would stop at nothing to get, and that was a knighthood, and that his every action was directed at that.'

'Is that true?' she said.

Rupert hesitated. 'Not *quite*, but, my darling, the end result will be exactly the same. He certainly won't do anything remotely risky. It was shorthand for that. And it made Cecily feel much better.'

'You're wonderful,' said Cassia, reaching up to kiss him, 'and I love you.'

Christmas passed with surprising ease. Cassia had, with infinite care, put her case to Edward, had said how Scrooge-like it seemed not to buy everyone nice presents, had explained about the bicycles in the windows, and the dolls' cot and about Peggy and Mrs Briggs and the hampers and indeed their own, and he had accepted it all with a very good grace. On Christmas Eve, in spite of her tiredness, after she had taken the children to the blessing of the crib in the church and served up Christmas Eve supper to everyone, including, of course, Desmond, and finally got the children to bed and made the stuffing for the turkey and glazed the ham and filled the stockings, she had given him his present – it was nothing too spectacular, just a very plain gold watch, which he was plainly delighted with.

Afterwards she persuaded him to make love to her. It hadn't happened for a long time: he had been distant towards her, not unaffectionate, just seeming to be – what? Not afraid exactly, but cautious of any closeness. Lying with him now, afterwards, her body fallen sweetly into peace – for it had been good, the lovemaking, the first time for months that she had flown, soared with pleasure – she said, 'Edward, I do love you very much.'

'I know you do,' he said. It was an unexpected response; she was disconcerted by it.

'And I presume you still love me?' She was half nervous, smiling into the darkness, her hands still moving tenderly over him.

'Of course I do.' He leaned towards her and kissed her, then turned over into his sleeping position, his back towards her.

And she felt, in spite of the sudden closeness, his cautiousness was back, and knew she couldn't do anything about it, anything at all.

Edward gave her a wonderful present: it made her cry. He had had a photograph taken of the children, and somehow sworn them to secrecy.

It had been hand coloured, most beautifully, and there they were, the three of them – Bertie and William in sailor suits, Delia in a riot of white frills – smiling out at her from a heavily worked silver frame. She sat and looked at it and thought of the organisation, the care, the trouble that he must have gone to, to find the time and the opportunity, and to have bought their silence, especially William's, and the enormous ease with which she had acquired his present, and felt a great weight of guilt and gratitude and love descend on her.

'It's wonderful,' she said, kissing him. 'So wonderful. You couldn't have given me anything I could like more.'

He looked at her rather oddly. 'It seemed the only thing I could give you,' he said. 'The only thing that would mean anything.'

Somehow, that spoilt it just a bit – that he had to spell it out.

On 20 January, 1936 King George V died at Sandringham. The Prince of Wales, informed by Queen Mary of his father's approaching end, flew in his own plane from London. The old king had scarcely drawn his last breath before Queen Mary kissed her eldest son's hand and said, 'The King is dead, long live the King.' The new reign had begun, and the new king was said to be possessed by a frantic grief. There was immediately across the country not only sadness, an echo indeed of that grief, but a sense of excitement at the accession of this new, young, charismatic king.

Next day Edward VIII travelled to London, to present himself before the Accession Privy Council and broadcast to his people, and the following day the Accession was proclaimed at four different points in London, the first being St James's Palace. A photographer caught sight of the king standing in the window just before he left the palace, talking to a slender, pale, dark-haired woman, still unknown to most of his subjects, to the man in the street. Next day almost every newspaper carried that picture of the King and the unknown woman. She was not unknown for very long.

'I'm going to London on Thursday,' said Cassia at supper one night early in February.

'Oh really? And what for this time? More shopping?' Edward smiled at her, but his eyes were wary. 'I'm sure it will be very dreary up there, the capital must still be in mourning. Absurd, the whole thing,' he added.

'What, that everyone should be sad the King has died? I don't agree with you.'

'Oh, I forgot you had met him,' said Edward, his voice heavy with irony.

'Mummy! You met the King!' said Bertie, his brown eyes wide with excitement.

'Bertie, of course I didn't meet him.'

'Daddy said you did.'

'I – well, I ...'

'How, where?'

'At Buckingham Palace,' said Cassia quickly. 'It was just a big sort of party thing.' She smiled quickly, looked nervously at Edward. He was scowling at the newspaper.

'Golly! Mummy! What was it like?'

'Quite exciting,' she said, risking the scowl being directed at her, resentful at it suddenly.

'Did they have their crowns on?'

There was a scrape as Edward pushed his chair back. 'I have to go,' he said. 'I have work to do. Why are you going to London, if it's not to join in the mood of national mourning?'

'I'm going to have lunch with Godpa and Margaret.'

'Whatever for?'

'No particular reason,' she said, trying not to sound irritated. 'Do I have to have one?'

'Of course not,' he said, making it plain she did.

'They invited me ages ago, at the memorial service, you know. And I've put it off and off and now it seemed a nice idea. Is that all right?'

'Yes, if you can spare the time.'

'Of course I can spare it,' she said. 'I haven't exactly got a full-time job.'

'Well, things have changed rather,' he said.

'What do you mean?'

'I mean that you used to find it difficult to arrange to be here with me in the mornings even, because you were so busy with the church and the WI and so on, and now you seem to be able to dash off up to London at a moment's notice.'

'Boys, off you go,' she said, seeing Bertie's eyes watchful suddenly, less starry. 'Go and find Peggy, ask her to wash your faces.' And then as they left the room she closed the door and said, 'Edward, that's not fair. I haven't been near London since before Christmas. I've chosen Thursday because you don't have a morning surgery, and Bertie's at school, and Peggy's happy to look after Delia and William.'

'I don't like her being in charge of them too much,' he said. 'She's very conscientious, of course, but she's very limited and it means she gets behind with her other work.'

'Edward, I don't call one day in a month too much.'

'I think it's rather more than that. Actually,' he said.

Cassia suddenly felt a spin of anger. 'It isn't. Actually. I'll go through my diary if you like and prove it to you. Anyway, if you're so bothered, maybe we should think about getting someone less limited for them.'

'What on earth do you mean?'

'I mean a nanny.'

'A nanny! I don't want a nanny in this house, it would be ridiculous.'

'You might not, Edward. I might. And sometimes I think I want it very much. I have three children under six, one a very demanding baby.' Delia obligingly chose this moment to empty her bowl of uneaten cereal on to the floor. 'It's a lot of work. Most women in my situation have a lot more help than I do.'

'Most women! Is that really the case? I don't seem to recall that many of my patients' doors are opened to me by a nanny, even if there are six children under six inside.'

'Oh, Edward, stop it. You know perfectly well what I mean.'

'Yes,' he said, 'I do know perfectly well what you mean. And I have to say I find it rather offensive. The implication is that I have never been able to afford to provide the sort of help you have a right to expect.'

'You are being childish,' she said, starting to unstrap Delia from the chair harness. 'Childish and – oh, never mind.'

'But I do mind,' he said, 'I mind very much. I find your attitude insensitive, to put it mildly. Anyway, you go off and have your lunch with your rich relations. I'm sure it will be a lot more enjoyable than cold meat and salad here with me.'

'Oh, for God's sake,' she said, and left the room, slamming the door behind her.

He had still hardly spoken to her when she left for London on Thursday morning.

She actually caught a far earlier train than was strictly necessary: she just didn't want to be hanging around the house. Having consequently got to London far earlier than was necessary, she decided to go and do a little shopping.

London was very quiet; the death of the King was very much felt still. All the shop windows were draped with black, and many of the men wore black bands round their sleeves, but inside the stores it was more cheerful.

She went to Harrods (so convenient, so much easier than anywhere else) and began to enjoy herself. Delia needed some new dresses (it was so wonderful to have a girl to dress, at last), and then while she was in the children's department at Harrods she bought a few things for the boys as well. She wandered down to the fashion floor and bought a couple of dresses for herself, one a day dress, in fine navy jersey which would be very useful, and the other a cocktail dress which certainly wouldn't, in black silk crêpe, ankle length, with long narrow sleeves, scooped out at the back and with a long fall of the same fabric, reminiscent of a train, almost as long as the dress. Heaven knew when she'd be wearing it, probably not until Cecily's next Christmas party. And then because she had no shoes to go with it, she bought a pair of black suede shoes, elegantly narrow with slender heels, and a bag to match with a rhinestone clasp, and then found herself looking at hats, and trying on and finding it impossible not to buy a wonderful, ridiculous hat, broad brimmed and shallow crowned, with a huge osprey feather set right across it.

She felt quite differently when she had finished her shopping. It was alarming how it could do that for her, shopping, she had discovered, comparable to lying in a very hot, expensively perfumed bath, or drinking a glass of very cold, dry champagne. She was able to think about Edward more tolerantly: so tolerantly indeed that she bought him a new red and blue silk tie in a rather dashing pattern before visiting the flower shop and acquiring an armful of lilies for Margaret.

She went out of the back door of Harrods with a view to hailing a taxi and directing it to Grosvenor Gardens. There weren't a great many taxis about, and as she stood there waiting, she realised that she was standing opposite an estate agent, and really for no reason at all, simply idle curiosity, she crossed the street, leaving her shopping in the charge of the Harrods doorman, and studied the houses on offer in the window. They were for the most part absurdly expensive, but there was one that caught her eye, not for sale, but to rent, an enchanting little dolls' house of a thing, it looked, in Walton Street. 'Long summer let, drawing room, dining room, three bedrooms, staff quarters in basement, pretty garden. £250 per calendar month.' And because Walton Street was so extremely near, and because she was still going to be a little early for her lunch, she walked the five minutes or so down the street and stood looking at it. Purely out of curiosity, of course.

It was at the Harrods end of Walton Street, a tall, narrow little house, built in stucco and London stock brick, with steps with iron railings running up to the red front door. Cassia looked at it and smiled, for the house had charm and a certain aura of happiness about it. Which was ridiculous, of course, for any pretty house would have looked delightful that morning: the sun had recently come out and was dancing on the windows, making the stucco brilliantly white, and the smoke spiralling out of the chimney was being tossed every which way in the blue air.

She went back to Harrods, checked her parcels were still safe with the doorman and went into the estate agents, only really to confirm that the house was actually let.

No, indeed, it was not, said the rather middle-aged young man at the desk. It was available from March until September, a most delightful property, and ideal if madam was for instance thinking of taking a house for the London Season. The owner was moving to New York for six months, and if she was interested he could arrange a viewing.

Cassia had no thoughts of taking a London house for the Season, or indeed for anything else, and heard herself saying, to her own considerable surprise, that no, she needed a house for more than six months, unfortunately. Then, because the young man was so nice and so clearly disappointed, she allowed him to take her name and address so that he could inform her of any other properties which might suit her. She finally retrieved her parcels from the long-suffering doorman and allowed him to hail her a taxi which she directed to Grosvenor Gardens.

And then partly because sitting in a taxi on her way to Grosvenor Gardens, surrounded with bags and boxes of clothes, suddenly brought it rather forcefully back to her, and partly because of the conversation at breakfast, she found herself suddenly reliving, vividly, as she had not for years, that summer of 1924, when she had done the Season, been a debutante, presented at Court by Leonora; when despite her misgivings, her reluctance even, she had had such a wonderful time ...

Cassia had been actually shocked to find how much she had enjoyed it, almost from the beginning. She had not wanted to do it in the least, had resented the time taken away from her studies in the last precious year before she needed to qualify for medical school, had seen herself going through it in a spirit of something approaching self-sacrifice to please all the adults in her life who so absurdly wanted it, had imagined each day almost an ordeal to be ticked off that she might return to her studies and the real world as quickly as possible. The reality was rather different.

Of course a lot of the girls had been silly, and a great many more of their mothers, whom they met at the early luncheon parties in April, were terrible, but many of them were friendly. She did rather have the feeling they all belonged to a club that she was not actually a member of, but since she didn't greatly care, that didn't matter very much. Leonora was immensely popular, which had helped to make Cassia more so, and in insisting on giving her a cocktail party in April as well as her dance in

June, had sent her status up, establishing her as one of the more important girls, one to be courted.

She managed to tell herself (albeit with increasing infrequency) that it was all extremely silly, but just the same, she would hardly have been human if she hadn't liked, at the age of seventeen, the experience of being bought literally dozens of lovely dresses, of going to wonderful houses all over London, and in the country at weekends, and dancing night after night away, of finding herself clearly, and to her great surprise, attractive to young men – pretty silly some of them too, but some were all right and some were actually quite good-looking and amusing – of finding her dance programme filled up quite early in each evening, of eating a lot of wonderful food and drinking a great deal of extremely nice champagne – too much, very often, but who cared how you felt in the morning, when you could lie in bed late, have breakfast there and wait to feel better.

It had been very exciting too, and considerably more interesting, to go to things like the Chelsea Flower Show, and the private view at the Royal Academy, and they had had a most marvellous evening at Glyndebourne, when they saw the *Marriage of Figaro*.

Sir Richard had taken them, with Benedict and Cecily. Leonora had wanted to make up a bigger party, but Sir Richard said he wasn't going to Glyndebourne to have it spoilt by a lot of silly social chit-chat, the opera was what counted. It was a marvellously lyrical milky-mild evening, the sky slowly fading to a deep dark blue, and the sun setting in a blaze of theatrical glory as they picnicked on the lovely lawns of Glyndebourne House. It was quite a grand dinner, not a picnic at all, really: smoked salmon and cold beef Wellington and strawberries and cream and of course champagne. Sir Richard told her she looked more beautiful than he would have imagined possible, and Benedict agreed, although Cecily got just a bit jumpy at that point, and they all had to make a fuss of her instead.

It was the first opera Cassia had ever seen, and she was spellbound, clutched in a fierce emotion that startled her, and frequently close to tears. She told Sir Richard she was glad that no one else had been with them as she would have been unable to concentrate if they had, and he told her she was clever and sensible as well as beautiful.

The presentation at Court, which she had been particularly scornful of, had in fact been (she admitted to her diary) quite amazingly wonderful. From the moment she had stood in the drawing room in the house at Grosvenor Gardens beside Leonora, both of them in their white Court dresses with long trains, and the three white osprey feathers – the Prince of Wales feathers – in their hair, and seen Sir Richard's face tender with admiration as he raised yet another glass of champagne to them both, she had felt as if she were living some strange, enchanted dream. They had gone out to the car and driven towards the palace.

It was early evening when they reached the Mall, and joined the long, long queue of cars and taxis, and by the time they pulled into the courtyard a blue dusk was settling over St James's Park. There were crowds of people, all peering into the cars, wishing them luck and waving to them: 'Too sweet, aren't they?' said Leonora absently. Cassia thought it was ridiculous. It wasn't as if they had done anything to deserve such wellwishing, they weren't even getting married, but it was very nice in a way, and she supposed a bit like being a film star.

There were over three hundred girls being presented that night, and there was a very long wait in the anteroom. She felt nervous now and longed for the lavatory, but there wasn't one, merely a chamber pot in another small room, behind a screen, for those in the direst need. Cassia decided her need wasn't that dire, and distracted herself by reciting her Latin declensions. She felt quite sure none of the other girls would have even known what a declension was: she had been much struck by the fact that for most of them and their mothers, education was something almost entirely wasted on girls. Education and employment of any kind were a purely male concern for the upper classes: the females were reared and prepared for a life of marriage, motherhood, and housekeeping at its loftiest level, and had no thoughts or ambitions beyond it.

She was just thinking that the most humble of her classmates at Leeds Girls' High, the ones on scholarships, were worth ten of each of these foolish, vapid, spoilt creatures, and wondering not for the first time in the past six weeks what on earth she was actually doing here, when she and Leonora were ushered into the throne room, and more appropriate thoughts immediately entered her head.

The throne room was vast and almost impossibly grand, all huge gilt mirrors and fine paintings and red velvet hangings and incredibly elaborate crystal chandeliers. There was a string orchestra playing in the gallery, and at the end of the room, under a gilt and velvet canopy, were set the two thrones. It was all more like a stage set than a stage set.

Their Majesties were both smaller than she had expected, but immensely, glitteringly imposing, Queen Mary's famously statuesque stance accentuated by her piled-up hair and impossibly deep pearl necklace. As Cassia made her deep, deep curtsy to Her Majesty, her head bowed (terrified her feathers would somehow escape their moorings and fall off), she suddenly remembered Rupert studying a picture of her and saying he thought the Queen was probably not real at all, but stuffed, and felt a wild and inappropriate desire to giggle.

Later, much later, when they were having supper at the house, she repeated this story to Sir Richard. She had thought he would laugh, but he looked rather stern and said the King and Queen were of priceless importance not only to Britain but the Empire.

'Oh, really, Richard,' said Leonora, who was quite drunk, 'what an old bore you are. I think that's the most lovely story, Sweet Pea, and I shall tell it all over London tomorrow.'

'Well, I trust London will not be amused,' said Sir Richard, and left them, but not before he had kissed Cassia again to show he wasn't really shocked, and told her again how proud of her he was.

Cassia's own dance had been held in the second week of June – 'Before Ascot and Henley. People are beginning to get just a little jaded after that,' Leonora had said when the date was first discussed. There was to be a dinner party for twenty beforehand, in the dining room, and then the dance would begin at ten in the marquee. Four hundred people had been invited; it was to be one of what the papers called the Season's most important balls. Every time she thought about it, Cassia felt a mixture of nerves and total disbelief. Her dress was gloriously simple, not a debutante confection at all, in palest blush-pink silk crêpe – 'It should be white, but let's cheat a little, and make you stand out,' Leonora had said blithely as they looked at endless toiles and fabrics. It was long-waisted, skimming over her slender body, hinting at, rather than outlining her small high breasts, with a softly tiered skirt falling almost to the floor and dipping into a slight train behind her. On her golden-blonde hair, carved now into a perfect, jawline bob, she wore a diamante bandeau, and her only other jewellery was her present from Leonora and Sir Richard for the occasion, a double string of pearls.

She had gone down the stairs – thinking again this was more like one of Rupert's shows than real life – and they had been waiting for her at the bottom, Leonora and Richard, and as she reached them, saw them looking at her in something more than admiration, she glanced in the great gilt mirror that hung in the hall and saw herself afresh, differently from how she had appeared in her bedroom mirror. It was as if, on her journey from the top to the bottom of the stairs, she had undergone a change, and was no longer a pretty schoolgirl on leave from her studies, playing games at being a debutante, but a young woman, not only beautiful but sensuously aware of the fact.

And then Harry had arrived. She had not seen him for years and had scarcely recognised him, had looked down at him, observing him in the simple act of handing his cloak to Jarvis, acutely and arrogantly aware of the sheer force of his own presence, and remembered afresh how much she disliked him.

He looked up and saw her, and bowed just slightly, and as she reached the bottom of the stairs, he took her hand and kissed it. 'Well, well,' he said, 'how grown up you are. I would not have known you.'

'Nor I you,' she said coolly, and then she looked up at him and saw something at the back of his eyes, something reluctant, something she could see he found difficult.

He had said, almost as if against his will, 'You look lovely, Cassia. Really very lovely indeed,' and she had remembered that moment for the rest of her life: the one in which Harry Moreton became no longer convinced of his total superiority over her, and the situation between them shifted just a little.

'Well,' he had said again, clearly slightly lost for words, 'you do look very grown up. I'm impressed.'

'I am grown up. Almost. And you too have changed, Harry. Up to Oxford in October, I hear. I may join you there next year.'

'You!' he said, and the expression in the dark eyes changed, became at once amused and sceptical. 'You at Oxford! Surely not.'

'Yes, me at Oxford. Just possibly. Only more likely, I am going to London, to St Christopher's medical school.' She smiled at him, making it plain that she would like the conversation to be over. 'Shall we go into the drawing room?' she said.

Harry had spent much of the evening standing on the sidelines watching, his expression brooding and slightly disdainful. He clearly wished to make it plain that debs' dances, even one as grand as this, and given by his second cousin, were not his choice as an evening's entertainment. He danced a few times with some of the more sophisticated girls, and once Leonora laughingly asked him to dance. Cassia watched amused and impressed as the two of them gave what amounted to an exhibition of the Charleston. The entire floor cleared and everybody watched. Harry danced extremely well, and she had been surprised: in her experience it was small slight men who danced well, not six-footers who looked like rugby fullbacks.

She had had a wonderful time: everyone told her she was beautiful, that evening, everyone wanted to dance with her, everyone admired her dress. It was a perfect night: warm, brilliantly moonlit, the air thick with the scent of roses. She felt wonderfully, perfectly happy, as if some kind of seal had been set on her life: her charmed life.

And then Harry had come over to her, bowed briefly, said, 'May I have this dance?'

It was a waltz. She had moved, slightly awkward, into his arms. She had never been close to him before; he was very warm, and he held her very firmly. It was not an unpleasant sensation, and dancing with him was oddly sensual: he moved surely, easily, rythmically. For the first time in a year she felt the strange deep stirrings in her that Rupert had once inspired, and resented them. Those were for Rupert, he was the love of her life, she didn't want to feel anything for any other man, and certainly not for Harry Moreton, Harry whom she disliked.

'Shall we slip away?' said Harry suddenly.

'I'm sorry?' She was so astonished that she stopped dancing and stared at him.

'Go to a nightclub. Maybe the KitKat. It's terrifically smart there.'

'Harry, I can't believe what you're saying. You're suggesting I should leave my own dance and go to a nightclub?'

'Just for an hour or so. No one'll know. The chaperones are all upstairs playing bridge, and Leonora is far too drunk even to notice. Surely you've done that before? I can't believe you've stayed dutifully right through every single dance. I was just chatting to Edwina Fox-Ashley and she told me she hadn't spent more than an hour at any party this year.'

Cassia was silent, then she said, 'Harry, I don't think I want to dance with you for a single moment more. I'd like to go and sit down now. Perhaps you'd get me a drink. Before you leave.'

'Oh, for God's sake.' He looked irritated. 'It was only a suggestion. Yes, all right, I'll get you a drink. If that's what you want.'

She went outside the marquee and stood breathing in the cool, soothing air, trying to calm herself, not to mind so much what he had said, reminding herself he was a stupid, spoilt, childish youth, however much he might resemble an adult, that he had had an isolated, miserable life, had never had a chance to learn any social graces, that it was not his fault. When he found her he was carrying two glasses and a bottle of champagne, and was looking slightly uncomfortable.

'I'm sorry. If I upset you. Didn't mean to.'

'Well, you did. It was horribly rude. You'd better go if you want to, I should think. It's getting late. I'd hate to keep you.'

'Oh, no hurry,' he said. 'These places all stay open till dawn.'

He seemed genuinely unaware of how much he had hurt her, and against her will she smiled at him.

'You're appalling, Harry.'

He shrugged. 'If you think so. Sorry again.' He poured himself another glass of champagne, and drained it and then another. She realised suddenly that he was very drunk. 'You do look very nice,' he said, and bent suddenly and tried to kiss her on the lips.

Cassia turned her head away, but he pulled it round sharply and kissed her again, holding her face still. His breath smelt of alcohol; she pulled away from him. 'Harry, don't. You're drunk.'

'Of course I'm not drunk. I haven't had enough to get drunk. Come on, Cassia, let's go to the KitKat. I'd really like to take you there.'

'Oh, for heaven's sake,' said Cassia, 'stop it. I'm not going to the KitKat. You go, it'll be a relief to get rid of you.'

'Thank you for that,' he said, and grinned at her, a lazy, sensuous grin. 'I'll remember that.'

'I'm afraid you won't. Look, I have to get back.'

'Little Miss Goody Two Shoes,' he said. 'How sweet. Just an innocent little girl from the backwoods, aren't you, Cassia? Dressed up as something quite different.'

'Don't talk to me like that,' said Cassia sharply.

'Why not? It's true, isn't it? You really don't know how the world works at all. Or maybe you do.'

'Harry, would you please stop patronising me. I resent that, very much.'

'Well, let's see. Put you to the test.' He looked at her, an odd expression in his eyes, malicious, almost mean. 'Let's see how much you know about real life, shall we?'

That was when he told her about Benedict.

She had been horribly, hideously upset, had felt sick, physically shaken. She put out a hand to steady herself on the side of the marquee and it swayed, increasing her sense of disorientation.

'You all right?' he said peering at her. 'You don't look it. I think I'd better get Leonora. Stay there.'

'Just go away,' she said, half shouting now. 'Go away, get out of here, out of my dance. You've spoilt it, you spoil everything. You're foul and vile and I wish I'd never met you. Get out, get out of this garden, this house. Go, go go.'

Harry opened his mouth, as if he was going to say something, then shut it again. He looked, for the first time since she had known him, unsure of himself.

'I said go!' she shouted again.

★

She had no idea how long she stayed out there, trying to compose herself, trying to come to terms with what she had heard, trying to make sense of it. Finally she heard Leonora calling her.

'Cassia! Sweet Pea, are you out here?'

'Here, Leonora,' she said, taking a deep breath, going over to her. 'Sorry, I felt a bit dizzy.'

'Oh, dearest! What a shame. We've all been looking for you. Benedict wants to dance with you. He says you're the loveliest debutante he's ever seen. Cecily apart, that is.' She kissed her, then looked at her sharply. 'Have you been crying?'

'No, not really. I'm fine. Everything's fine. Honestly.'

'Where's Harry? Didn't I see you talking to him?'

'Oh, he's gone,' said Cassia. Her voice sounded bitter, even to herself. 'He wanted to go to the KitKat club.'

'How very charming of him. Well, it is awfully good fun there. But he does lack a certain finesse, that boy. Handsome though, these days, wouldn't you say?'

'Not really,' said Cassia. 'I think he's ghastly.' She smiled at Leonora, and with a great effort of will, took her arm. 'Let's go back inside. I've missed quite enough of my lovely dance already.'

'I'm glad you've enjoyed it, darling. It's certainly seemed quite perfect to me.'

'It has been,' said Cassia, 'quite, quite perfect.'

It had been – until Harry had done that to her: made the evening ugly, threatening, thrown something into it she was not ready for, could not quite understand.

For years she had been puzzled by it, by why he had done it; when finally she saw, that he had found her rejection of him unbearable, had sought for revenge and found it in a piece of wanton cruelty, she saw also why he had felt her rejection so strongly. Only of course by the time she understood, it was too late. Much too late.

She had piled most of her parcels and boxes up on to the pavement, and was rummaging in her purse for money, juggling with the lilies and the hatbox as she did so, when she heard a voice, amused, that she knew very well indeed saying, 'An expensive morning, Mrs Fallon, I presume?'

She lifted her head, and because she had been thinking about him, or rather trying not to think about him, she found herself filled with all the old emotions, rather than the new, nudging towards friendship, and looked very coolly at Harry Moreton. 'No, not really, just a few things for the children.'

'Really?'

'Yes,' she said, bending to pick up the bags, and promptly dropping the hatbox, which he recovered for her – only not before the lid had slithered off and revealed the contents in all its absurd extravagance.

'An unusual hat for a child,' he said, 'but perhaps life in the country is more interesting than I had imagined.'

She looked at him, trying to summon up the carefully nurtured hostility, and then, because the situation was so extremely silly, smiled. 'I did think I deserved one thing for myself,' she said.

'I'm sure you do. And it is a very fine hat indeed,' he said, 'and I'm sure it will look much better on you than your children. I do hope you can find some suitable occasions for it. Not too many down in a Sussex village, I imagine.'

'I do occasionally leave the Sussex village,' said Cassia.

'As I see. With a slightly increased frequency, too, I fancy. Now let me help you in with those and— Do put the hat on, give Richard a treat. Margaret has many virtues, but she's not God's gift to the couturiers. I hear you are lunching with them. Sadly, I can't join you, I have a dreary assignation at the Reform Club. I've been discussing the new Waterloo Bridge project with Richard.'

'What are you doing to Waterloo Bridge?'

He stood staring at her, his face first surprised, then thoughtful. 'I'd forgotten what an unfeminine interest you take in such things,' he said slowly. 'It's rather nice.'

'Harry, really, that's a monstrously old-fashioned remark. Women do have much more in their heads these days than – well, than hats and the staff shortage.'

'Do they?' he said. 'I hadn't noticed. Anyway, Richard is involved in the construction of the bridge and I am investing in it. That is, my company is investing in it.'

'I didn't know you had a company.'

'There is a great deal you don't know about me, Cassia,' he said lightly, 'to my regret. And I have several companies. Anyway, let me help you carry all those clothes for your children.'

She was still laughing when Jarvis opened the door.

Harry was persuaded to join them for a drink before lunch, and then departed with huge expressions of regret 'I might even come back and help you to Victoria.'

'That will be absolutely unnecessary,' said Cassia firmly.

Sir Richard was touchingly delighted to see her; Margaret in her undemonstrative, rather severe way was also welcoming. She really could not have been a greater contrast to Leonora, Cassia thought, with her long, rather fierce face, her solid figure, her severely drawn-back grey hair.

'I'm afraid I have to leave you shortly after luncheon,' Sir Richard said. 'I have a crisis at the factory, and it really does demand my attention. Will you forgive me?'

'Of course. Besides, I'm very used to your crises. I cut my teeth on them, don't forget.'

'I don't, my darling, believe me.'

She hoped Sir Richard wouldn't think she was referring to any crisis of an emotional nature.

Lunch was delicious: clear soup, lamb cutlets, apple tart. It was, indeed, she thought with a suppressed sigh, smiling up at Jarvis as he filled her wineglass for the second time with some excellent claret, much nicer than cold meat and salad. Afterwards they moved into the drawing room.

Over coffee, Sir Richard said, 'Well now, tell me more about this Chair you are planning to set up at that hospital of yours.'

She told him that it was to be a Chair of obstetric research, that she desperately wanted to do it, that it was the nearest she was going to get to doing obstetric research of her own now.

'Very sad, that,' Margaret interjected.

'Yes, well,' Cassia said, smiling, a little over-bright, 'I try not to think about it too much. And I just might be able to do something else, it seems, something at least a bit medical.'

'Really?' said Sir Richard. 'But not at the moment, surely, not while your children are so young? I really don't like the idea of that.'

'Godpa, you mustn't be so old-fashioned,' she said, laughing. 'Motherhood isn't the be-all and end-all of women's lives any more, you know. It can be combined with other things, other ambitions.'

'To the great detriment of their families, in my view,' he said firmly, 'and yours is such a lovely one. I would hate to think of them neglected.'

'I promise I won't neglect them,' she said, and then, anxious not to pursue what was obviously a difficult subject, 'Anyway, back to the Chair. I want it to bear the Beatty name, in Leonora's memory, as I said.'

'Well, darling, it's very sweet of you, and exceedingly generous. I think you deserve to spend the money on yourself.'

'There's plenty left for me,' she said, laughing, her inhibitions about approaching the amount of the legacy released by the second glass of claret.

'Oh really?' he said carelessly; then, after a pause, while he made a great performance of cutting and lighting the cigar Jarvis had brought him, 'Enough to get the car I thought would be nice for you, for instance? I hope so.'

'Godpa, of course. It was a lot of money.'

'A lot?' She couldn't see his eyes through the smoke.

'Oh, dear, I sort of thought you'd know. Had seen the will.'

'No, no. I'm not a beneficiary obviously, and I felt – well, doesn't matter what I felt. Nothing to do with me, anyway.' His voice was carefully jovial.

Margaret suddenly stood up. 'If you'll excuse me, Cassia, I have to make a phone call. I'll be back shortly.'

Left alone with Richard, Cassia looked at him rather awkwardly. 'I hope she didn't feel she had to go.'

'No, she has a very healthy attitude towards my past. Only interested in the present.'

There was a long silence. Cassia knew how much he hated talking about anything difficult, how he had found it almost impossible to acknowledge to her that there had been any kind of problem with Leonora, even after she had left.

'You mustn't feel guilty about Leonora,' she said finally.

'I don't. Not exactly guilty, but I sometimes think I should have dealt with matters differently.'

This was so huge a concession she was astonished; sat waiting.

'What do *you* think?' he said, surprising her more.

'I don't know. I was very young at the time.'

'I think perhaps I drove her away. And—' His voice, reluctant, quiet, stopped. He cleared his throat loudly. 'But what's done's done. Isn't it?'

She looked at him and knew that now, now that it was so far in the past, there was no point in doing anything but reassuring him, trying to make him feel better. 'Of course it is. And I think she was perfectly happy.'

'Do you? Do you really?'

'Yes,' She said staunchly, crushing the memory of Leonora sitting alone, brave, brittle, just after Rollo had left her, telling Cassia how much she loved Paris, how happy she was still, how wonderful her new friends were being.

'I hope to God you're right,' Sir Richard said. 'Well, I'm very pleased about the money. You certainly deserve it. It was quite a bit, you say?'

And then because it seemed almost hostile not to tell him, she said, 'It was half a million pounds,' very quickly, and then took a large draft from the glass of red wine she had carried in with her from the dining room.

There was a very long silence, during which she carefully didn't look at him, and then she did look at him, and almost at once he was smiling at her.

He stood up and came over to her, and bent and kissed her and said, 'My darling, how wonderful, I'm so very delighted for you,' but not before she had seen in his eyes an expression of such absolute and unmistakable shock that she was seriously shaken herself.

CHAPTER 8

'Right, Mrs Moreton. Do get dressed and come back into the consulting room.' The nurse turned away tactfully as Edwina stood up, took off the starched cotton wrap and pulled on her own silk camiknickers and stockings. She then handed her her cashmere sweater and narrow skirt, and watched her as she put them on and stepped into her lizard-skin shoes. Then she said very gently, as she did at this point to all Mr Fortescue's ladies, 'Can I offer you a cup of tea, Mrs Moreton?'

'No,' said Edwina, 'no, thank you.' She managed a wry smile. 'A gin would be more like it.' She meant it. She picked up her lizard handbag – which matched the shoes – and walked through to Mr Fortescue's consulting room, thinking that she now knew precisely what the word heavyhearted meant.

Mr Fortescue was sitting behind his large desk. He was a large man, and his face was round above his multiple chins. He had assumed an expression of careful sympathy. Edwina thought rather irrelevantly that he looked like an overweight bloodhound.

'Well now, Mrs Moreton,' he said, 'yes, do sit down. I'm afraid, as I know you suspected, that there is no sign of a pregnancy. Other than the amenorrhoea. That is to say, the failure to menstruate.'

She supposed she knew he had been going to say that, but it still hurt. Two missed periods: it would have been reasonable, at least, to assume that meant a pregnancy. She smiled; she could feel the brittleness of that smile, the speed with which it left her face again.

'Now,' he said, 'of course nothing is certain, and the human body and its reproductive capacity is not an exact science. All sorts of things affect it, in particular state of mind. However—'

'I'm not ever going to be able to have children?' she said, forcing the words out, each one a struggle.

'It seems unlikely, from the investigations I have done. It would appear that you are simply not ovulating, and unfortunately the progesterone injections have not worked either. Which means—'

'I know what it means,' she said. 'No eggs. For the jolly little sperm to meet.' Another brittle smile.

'Yes. Correct.'

'And there's no treatment for that?'

'I'm afraid not, no. We don't even know why this should happen. Or rather not happen. We've been through this before, of course, but I would like to recap. You are quite sure you haven't had any infections, as far as you know? Of the uterus, or ... well, of a gynaecological nature?'

'No,' said Edwina firmly. 'I haven't.'

'Well, of course, where there's life there's hope.'

'Or rather where there's hope, there might be a life.'

'Er, yes.' He looked at her rather uncertainly. He was a very nice man, he had been very kind to her, but he did lack humour. 'But it would be wrong of me to encourage you to think there was really any reasonable hope of your conceiving. I'm sorry.'

'So why do you think I've missed two periods when they're usually so painful and heavy?'

'I would say almost certainly for psychological reasons. The power of the mind over the body is immense. You wanted to be pregnant so much you managed to persuade your body that you were.'

'Yes, I see.' She pulled out her cigarette case, lit one, smiled at him through the smoke.

'It's a pity your husband couldn't come with you today,' said Mr Fortescue. 'I would have liked to talk to you both anyway.'

'He's out of London this week,' said Edwina quickly.

'I see. How does he feel about your failure to conceive?'

'I don't think he minds. Very much.' That was a lie: she knew Harry was beginning to mind very much indeed.

'But you have talked about it? He knows you've been seeing me?'

'Oh, yes. Of course.'

'Well, do tell him that if he has any questions, if I can give him any information, he is most welcome to come and see me.'

'Yes. Yes, I will.' As if he would; as if Harry, who would not tolerate failure in any area, and in anyone, would agree to discuss his wife's infertility with a complete stranger. Even an expert on the subject.

'You mustn't blame yourself, you know,' said Mr Fortescue. 'This is just one of those things, one of those cruel tricks played by Mother Nature. I know it's hard not to feel you are not quite a complete woman, but that is not the case. And this is actually a much more common problem than you might imagine. Many, many people are sterile.'

'You could have fooled me,' said Edwina bitterly. Thinking of all her friends, most of them filling nurseries at a great rate, even Bunty Savage now, after a few years of difficulty. It had been Bunty who had suggested she saw Mr Fortescue: 'Honestly, Edwina, he's a magician, he'll have you in the club in no time.'

Mr Fortescue was talking again. 'And of course having children is not the be-all and end-all of a marriage. Some of the happiest marriages I know are childless. Couples often grow much closer to one another without the distraction – and indeed extremely hard work – of raising a family.'

'Really?' He'd obviously been through this script a few times.

'Yes. Really. Of course it will take time to adjust to the idea, and for your husband, but I'm quite sure it will happen.'

'Right. Well, thank you for being so honest with me. I'm very grateful.' She hesitated. 'And there's no chance of it being my husband's fault?'

'Not really, no. The problem, you see, is your own failure to ovulate. Of course, if you would like to pursue this avenue as well, there are tests we can do—'

'Oh, no!' Edwina was horrified. She knew about those tests: she knew about them all; she had spent quite a lot of time studying the subject. Harry submitting himself to a sperm test, of fantasising sexually over a test tube or whatever, was so absolutely unthinkable it didn't justify a moment's discussion. 'No, that's not a good idea,' she finished lamely.

'Well ...' He was clearly winding the conversation up, felt they had spent long enough on it. He had more patients waiting, patients who might be more rewarding than she was.

She stood up, held out her hand. 'Thank you very much, Mr Fortescue.'

She turned and left the room, knowing he was going to pursue the subject of her talking to Harry, discussing it, and she didn't want him to. There was no way she was going to tell Harry; she would get through it somehow.

It was growing dark when she emerged into Welbeck Street and there was a raw wind blowing up it; she felt tired and very depressed. She didn't want to go home, she couldn't face Harry yet. They were going out to dinner later, that would cheer her up. She walked down towards Oxford Street, and Marshall and Snelgrove; she would have tea and try to pull herself together.

The restaurant was full of women who had clearly come up to London for the day, well dressed but not really smart. She could see they were studying her, her hard-edged chic clothes, her expensive shoes and bag, envying her even, and wondering what she was doing there, all alone. Probably thought she had no friends, or was even divorced.

So many people were getting divorced these days. If Harry knew about this, about her infertility, he would probably want to divorce her. Perhaps it would be a good idea anyway; they had so little in common, were hardly happy. She should never have married him, really; she had known at the time, deep down, it was a mistake, but everyone had been so excited about it when she had told them, her mother acting as if she were having one long orgasm, her father beamingly delighted, her friends envious, all the papers writing about them, the wedding tipped as the wedding of the year – every day had made it more impossible. And, besides, he had been the most amazing catch: good-looking, sexy, charming, clever – and rich. So extremely rich ...

So that when he had asked her, when he had said ... and how could she ever forget what he had actually said ...

'Edwina, I'd like you to marry me.'

She had been sitting beside him at a table at a ball. She had thought at first he was joking, had looked at him and laughed (thinking at the same time she wouldn't have minded if he was not, he looked so absurdly handsome in his tails), and then seen that the expression in his eyes was very serious. Not exactly warm, not exactly lover-like, but serious. Almost desperate.

So she had sat back in her chair, put a cigarette into her holder and asked him for a light (playing for time), and looked at him, and said, 'I presume you don't actually mean that, Harry. Or do you?'

'Of course I bloody well mean it,' he said, his voice raw with irritation; and then clearly realising this was hardly lover-like behaviour, pulled himself up almost visibly and said, 'I want you to marry me very much. I think you're beautiful and extremely interesting and very very sexy and I'm sure we'd be happy.'

It was the word 'interesting' that did it: she had always tried to be interesting, and thought she had failed, that she was too empty headed, too concerned with trivia to qualify as such.

Beauty, she knew she possessed; she observed it every morning and indeed at many other times during the day as well – her oval face, her creamy skin, her brown eyes and her gleaming dark hair – and she knew she was sexy too.

She loved sex, and indeed had discovered her body and the pleasure it could afford her when she was only fifteen and sharing a bed with a friend at an overcrowded country house party where her parents were guests. The girl, a tall, rather statuesque creature of sixteen who had been making a great play of reading a story by Virginia Woolf in bed, had begun almost at once making advances towards Edwina, stroking her breasts and her thighs, and then when Edwina had (to her own great surprise) plainly liked it, had not withdrawn, but started kissing her. Edwina, who had never been kissed by a boy at that stage, who had indeed only known kisses of the most sexless variety, had found the soft mouth on hers, its tongue seeking out her own, wildly exciting, and responded. Her delight when the girl began to feel between her legs, and thence further, seeking out an area of almost unimaginable sensation, sensation and pleasure, surprised but did not in any way repel her. She had grown up in the company of an outrageous mother: Sylvia Fox-Ashley had innumerable lovers, a fact accepted, if not welcomed, by her husband Sir Marcus, and had talked to her openly about sex, in all its manifestations and pleasures, from her earliest years. Lesbian and homosexual sex of all kinds had always interested rather than shocked Edwina.

She and the statuesque girl had enjoyed several experiences before the house party was over. Edwina left her with regret, eager for more, and a little anxious, she supposed, that she might be entirely lesbian. An introduction to heterosexual sex a year later, with a sweaty Etonian after a New Year's Eve party in Scotland, disappointed her and increased her anxiety: there was none of the sweet, swooping pleasure she could remember so vividly. But she persevered, and several more experienced lovers later she was happy to accept that her true sexuality was of the more conventional kind; although she had continued over the years to enjoy the occasional lesbian encounter.

She had not slept with Harry Moreton until the night he had proposed to her so unexpectedly, and completely overwhelmed by him and the intoxicating prospect of marrying him, she had gone home with him to his great house in Lowndes Square very shortly after that and found herself experiencing such extraordinary and ferocious pleasure in his bed that for days afterwards her body continued to stir and throb at the memory.

She finally fell asleep to find him leaning over her, looking at her with a mixture of desire and a strange impatience; she smiled and he said, without smiling back, 'You haven't yet said if you'll marry me.'

She said she would, of course she would, that she would love to, that it was what she thought she would most like, and then (greedy for more of him) pulled him down on to her and into her, and they did not talk any more.

It was days later, after a great many bottles of champagne had been drunk and congratulations received, that she realised that not only had the proposal been extraordinarily sudden, that he had never hinted that he was thinking of such a thing before – despite their having been closely associated ever since her coming-out six years earlier – but that he had never said he loved her. Nor had he asked her if she loved him.

She buried the thought deep under a welter of plans and did not allow it to surface until long after the wedding.

When it had been hopelessly too late.

For some reason, after she had finished her tea, Edwina decided to go and see Cecily. It was, she knew, in some ways an unfortunate idea, as Cecily was now seven months pregnant, and looked like a symbol of fertility, but Edwina was very fond of her. She was so kind and gentle and such good company, in her rather simplistic way – a strange wife for the complex, clever Benedict, Edwina had always thought – and extremely easy to talk to. She had had no intention of telling Cecily about her afternoon and indeed any of the preceding afternoons with Mr Fortescue, but sitting drinking yet another cup of tea with Cecily, listening to her talking happily about Fanny and Stephanie and how they felt about the new baby, she suddenly burst into tears and then found herself telling her all about it.

'Oh, darling,' Cecily said, getting up awkwardly, coming over to her, putting her arms round her. 'I'm so, so sorry. I can't think of anything worse. Oh, dear, that's not very tactful, is it?'

'Don't be silly,' said Edwina impatiently. 'I can't imagine anything worse either. I know I'm not exactly anyone's idea of the maternal type, well, neither is Mummy and she's absolutely terrific at the whole thing, but I did see having children as part of marriage, and so did – does Harry. And now – well, I don't know.'

'What does Harry think about it all?' said Cecily.

'He doesn't know,' said Edwina sharply, 'and he's not to.'

'Edwina, you can't keep it from him. I mean, it's obvious, and—'

'Yes, yes, I know he can see there aren't any yet,' said Edwina impatiently, 'and anyway, we took huge precautions the first two years or so, didn't want them for ages, so it's not too long – but I don't want him to know there's no hope at all. He'd hate it. I know he would. Much better to let him go on thinking it might happen. And besides,' she said, distorting Mr Fortescue's actual words on the subject slightly, 'he did say there was some hope. Just that it was very unlikely.'

'I think you ought to tell him,' said Cecily firmly.

'I can't, and I'm not going to. And you are not to.'

'Edwina, of course I won't. Don't be absurd. But think, you could adopt or—'

'No, we couldn't. Can you imagine Harry, with all that male arrogance of his, taking some other person's child into his life and thinking of it as his own?'

'He doesn't have to think of it as his own,' said Cecily, 'just love it and bring it up, give it a home. There are enough of them out there, poor little things, heaven knows.'

'Yes, well, he wouldn't. He'd much rather stay without. Look, don't start worrying about Harry,' said Edwina fretfully, 'it's me who needs the sympathy. Harry has lots of other things in his life: his work, his paintings – God, the money he spends on those things, bought a Modigliani last week for thousands – his horses … at least he hasn't got a mistress. Yet. At least I don't think so.' She lit another cigarette.

'Oh, Edwina, of course he hasn't. Don't be absurd.'

'It's not absurd. And of course sooner or later he will have. It's inevitable.'

'I don't see why.'

'Well, I do. Harry is rich, very attractive and getting bored with me. I know he is. I irritate him, I can see it. We get on quite well, and I make him laugh, but it just doesn't work any more. So it would be extremely naive of me not to expect it. I can't quite make out why it hasn't happened already, as a matter of fact. Or maybe it has and I just haven't heard.' She smiled, a quick, bright little smile. 'Anyway, when he does, of course, then I shall take a lover. Which is something to look forward to, I suppose.'

'Is that really and truly what you'd do?'

'Immediately. It's the only way. Much better than making a fuss, don't you think? And much more fun as well. I suppose I might take one first, that's the only thing, forestall him.'

'Do you have anyone in mind?' said Cecily, laughing.

'There are lots of people I'd be happy to jump into bed with, if that's what you mean, but no one who's actually asked me. Seriously, that is.'

'Well, I hope they don't,' said Cecily, 'and I'm sure Harry isn't about to have an affair. I'm sure he loves you very much.'

'Cecily, he doesn't love me at all. Never has. Don't look like that. Harry only loves himself. And I'm not sure I love him. We just suit one another, that's all. Or did. Oh God.' And the tears began again. 'What I need,' she said, wiping her eyes, blowing her nose, 'is something to do. I can't really devote the rest of my life to buying myself frocks and giving parties.'

'I'll try and think of something,' said Cecily. 'There's always charities, of course.'

'I don't really like charity work. I want more of a career. God, I wish I'd been a bit better educated. Like Cassia.'

'A lot of good it's done Cassia,' said Cecily briskly. 'Completely wasted, thanks to that prig of a husband of hers.'

'Well, she should stand up to him more,' said Edwina, 'do what she wants for once. I've no sympathy with her, actually, none at all.'

'Mummy! William's been sick. All in his bed and then on mine.'

'Oh God.' Cassia dragged herself out of sleep, and wondered why she was so reluctant, why reality, even the hideous reality of a vomiting child, should be so especially unwelcome, and then remembered the sweet, rather charming dream she had been having, about driving Rupert into London in her yellow car, wearing nothing but the new hat. 'I'm coming, Bertie, tell William to go to the lavatory.'

'He's in there already. He's crying.'

She pulled on her dressing gown, and went to find William, shutting the bedroom door carefully behind her. It was three o'clock. Poor Edward had only been in bed for an hour, after delivering a very reluctant baby.

She found William sitting shivering on the lavatory. He was crying, clutching his stomach. 'I feel sick again,' he said, the colour draining dramatically from his face. She grabbed the potty just in time.

An hour later she had changed his bed twice more, and was sitting wearily beside him, waiting for the next event, when there was a loud scream from Delia's room. She rushed in, to find Delia throwing up copiously all over her cot and the floor. By the time she had sorted her out, William had been sick again. And then Bertie started. It was a very long night …

By seven o'clock they were all three asleep, glassy pale, but the worst over. She crept in beside Edward. He groaned, looked at the clock, said he had to get up.

'They've all three got d and v,' she said. 'I've had a terrible night.'

'It was that mince they had for supper,' he said. 'I thought it smelt off.'

'Well, why on earth didn't you say something?'

'I thought you'd make your own judgement,' he said.

'Clearly I did. I thought it was off and I thought, oh, good, they'll all be sick. Thanks for your help, Edward.'

'You stay there for a bit. Get some rest. I'll see you later. Did you give them plenty to drink? It's very important to keep up their fluids.'

'Edward,' she said, trying not to shout, 'I do know about the treatment of d and v. Thank you. I just want you to know that everything, every-thing they had, including water, came right back up again. All right?'

'Yes, all right,' he said. 'I just thought I'd mention it.'

She hoped she could get some sleep; she felt slightly queasy herself. Obviously psychological: she hadn't had any of the wretched mince. A couple of hours and she'd be fine. She heard the sounds of the household moving into action below her: Peggy clattering in the kitchen, a smash and some swearing as she dropped something (a daily occurrence – replacing Peggy's breakages cost almost more than her wages); Edward shouting at her from the dining room for his bacon – God, he was arrogant in his quiet way, as arrogant as Harry Moreton; Mrs Briggs arriving, giving Peggy a rousing account of a row she'd had with Mr Briggs the night before; Buffy barking at the milkman; Edward shouting at Buffy to be quiet. Then more barking, and the front door bell ringing; Mrs Venables' voice at the door – oh no, she thought, not the flowers, not today; and then Edward's footsteps on the stairs, the door opening carefully.

'You asleep?'

'I was,' she said untruthfully.

'Sorry, but Mrs Venables wants to know if you can talk to the Young Wives in Haywards Heath tonight. Apparently they've been on to her, crisis, their speaker's let them down. She thought you could talk about being a medical student in the twenties, the same one you did here.'

'Edward, I can't. I'm done for.'

'Well, what shall I tell her?'

'Tell her I'm ill. How about that?'

He looked at her reproachfully. 'I think you should if you can. Honestly.'

'Oh, for God's sake, all right. Just leave me in peace for a bit now, will you?'

He left, giving her a pained look, and she tried to get comfortable.

Silence. Peace. Her mind began to spin woozily. Then, 'Mummy! I've been sick again.'

*

She was dragging the sheets off Bertie's bed when Edward came in holding some letters.

''Fraid Mrs Briggs isn't feeling too good, I've told her to go home. Maybe it wasn't the mince did for these three. So I'll have to haul you into the surgery later. Peggy said she had too much to do to help this morning. You all right?'

'Oh, everything's absolutely fine, Edward. I've still had no sleep, Bertie's just been sick again, and now you tell me Mrs Briggs is going home and you want me in the surgery. Why don't you tell Peggy to go to bed as well, just in case she feels ill later?'

'Don't be ridiculous. You all right, old chap? Try to drink some water. Anyway, I brought you your post up.' He stopped, looking at her; there was a certain wariness in that look. 'There's something from St Christopher's for you,' he said, carefully casual. 'Any idea what it is?'

'Er, no. Reunion, I expect.' Damn, she should have told the Dean to write to her care of Cecily, but normally she managed to intercept letters.

'*I* haven't had anything from them.'

'Perhaps it's for both of us.'

'They wouldn't send it just to you, surely? Mind if I look?'

'Well, I—'

'Mummy! Sorry. Oh, sorry. All over your nightie.'

When she had had a bath and washed her hair, she walked wearily into their bedroom.

Edward was sitting on the bed; he looked very odd. 'What the devil is this about?' he said.

'What?' But she knew.

'This letter. From the Dean. About a research Chair.'

'Oh,' she said, 'that.'

'Yes. That.' There was a silence, then he said, 'Cassia, what the bloody hell are you playing at?' He never swore: she knew it meant he was very upset.

'I'm not playing at anything.'

'Of course you are. Does this mean what I think it means, that you've been to see the Dean behind my back, asked him to set up a research Chair at St Christopher's, at my hospital—'

'Mine too.'

'Don't play games, please. My hospital, without even discussing it with me. Have you any idea what sort of humiliation this represents to me, what the Dean must be thinking?'

'Edward, don't be ridiculous. Why should he be thinking anything? Except that he's grateful for the money.'

'The money,' he said. 'Oh yes, that. The damn money.'

There was a ring at the bell. Peggy called up the stairs, 'Doctor! First patient's here.'

He stood up. His face was drawn, grey. He looked at her with absolute distaste. 'Please come down as soon as you can. I need your help. We'll talk about this over lunch. It has to be cleared up. And what's this nonsense about a family planning clinic?'

'I don't know. You haven't let me read the letter yet.'

She picked it up. The Dean had scrawled a postscript by hand: 'Spoken to my colleague about the family planning clinics. She'd be pleased to see you, discuss things. Her name is ...'

She put the letter down. She felt very sick herself.

It was a very long morning. Delia was also sick again, and Peggy came into the dispensary, where Cassia was mixing a bottle of tonic, and said she couldn't manage.

'I don't like sickness, Mrs Fallon, never could, it turns me up myself.'

'Well, it's lucky the rest of us like it so much, Peggy,' she said tartly.

'Pardon?'

'Oh, nothing. You'll have to tell the doctor why you're here instead of me for a bit. Can you read to Delia or something if I clean her up?'

'Only if you're sure she won't be sick again.'

Cassia went out of the room and slammed the door.

By lunchtime her head was throbbing. The children were all asleep. She walked rather warily into the dining room. Edward was already at the table. He looked at her with a weary hostility.

'I just have to ring Mrs Venables,' she said. 'I really can't do this talk tonight.'

'I've already told you,' he said, 'I think you should. You seem to manage to find the time to do everything else. Like visit the Dean with absurd schemes, have lunch with your London relatives—'

'Oh, Edward, for God's sake. I can't do it. Not tonight.'

'And I am telling you that you are to do it.'

If he hadn't said she had to, if he had said no, of course, I can see that you can't, even if he'd said he felt very sympathetic but he really felt she ought to if she possibly could, the rest of the conversation might have been different. But he didn't; and it wasn't.

'I'm going to get a nanny,' said Cassia. 'I've decided.' She was sitting in her chair, on the opposite side of the fire from Edward, she doing some tapestry, he the crossword: a picture of domestic harmony, she thought. Who would think what a bitter battlefield their marriage had become in so short a space of time?

'Oh, really? And do I have any say in this? Since it is my children who are to be handed over? It seems not.'

'Obviously I wouldn't hire anyone without your approving her. I've alerted several agencies. I'll do some interviewing, and when I've got a shortlist I'll obviously ask you to see them.'

'I mean,' he said, 'do I have any say in the fact that you are intending to engage a nanny at all? I have to tell you I'm most unhappy about it. You are their mother. You should be looking after them.'

'You never minded Peggy looking after them. Peggy who is scarcely fit to look after herself.'

'You were never far away.'

'No, I wasn't, and as I intend to be at least a little away, some time in the future, I want someone more responsible to take care of them.'

'How extremely conscientious of you.'

'Oh, go to hell,' said Cassia.

'That's clearly one of the places you'd wish me,' he said, and walked out of the room. She heard him going into his study and shutting the door, and tried to analyse what she felt. It seemed to be horribly little.

'That must have been very very hard,' said Dr Pamela Richards; her rather severe face as she looked at Cassia was full of sympathy. 'To have come thus far, done so well, and then had to give it all up.'

'Well,' said Cassia carefully, 'I was pregnant. And my husband had bought the practice in Monks Heath. I felt I had to yield to those responsibilities.'

'I don't imagine the Dean was very pleased. Or Mr Amstruther. I gather you were something of a pet of his.'

'Well, I don't know about that. He was furiously angry. Shouted at me for about half an hour.'

'That means you were his pet.' Pamela Richards smiled. 'He wouldn't have wasted half an hour otherwise. Anyway, as a wife and a mother myself I can sympathise. Although it is a terrible pity you couldn't at least have done your house job. Then you'd have had a base to move forward from.' She looked just slightly reproving for the first time. Cassia felt as if she was back at Leeds Girls' High, in the presence of one of her teachers there. 'Anyway, you want to do something now, I understand,' she said.

'Yes. So much.'

'Well, the Dean was right, we do need women doctors. You'll have to do a course, but you won't find it very arduous. Can you manage that, get the children taken care of and so on?'

'Oh yes.'

'Good. And, of course, you'll be looking for a clinic down in Sussex, I suppose.'

'Ideally, yes. Monks Heath is near Haywards Heath. That sort of area. But I have a car, I could easily drive to Brighton. It's only about fifteen miles.'

'I'll see. What about towards London, Croydon area? More clinics that way.'

'Yes. Anything, really.'

'I'll do my best, but I can't promise anything. Meanwhile I'll put you down for the next course. It'll be in about a month, I think.'

'Wonderful.'

'I have to warn you,' said Dr Richards, 'this is not the most exciting work. Not for someone with ambitions in obstetric surgery, but it would be immensely worthwhile.'

'I don't mind. I really don't mind. It will be a lot more exciting than manning the surgery and the pharmacy for my husband and doing the flowers in the church.'

Pamela Richards laughed. 'Yes, I dare say.' There was a pause. 'He's happy about it, is he?'

'Oh yes. Of course. Absolutely.' She almost believed it herself.

CHAPTER 9

'Cecily's had a little boy,' said Cassia. She smiled at Edward, who looked at her blankly, then managed a faint shadow of a smile back.

'How nice,' he said after a pause. 'If you'll excuse me, I must go now. I have a particularly large surgery this morning. You'll be able to help later, will you?'

'Yes, today, but you know I won't be here tomorrow? Or the rest of the week?'

'I was hardly likely to forget,' he said.

'But Janet can help you, can't you, Janet?'

'Of course. I'm looking forward to it.' Janet Fraser beamed at her – she did a lot of beaming. She had been with the family for a month now and was generally a great success. She was quite young, twenty-nine, small and slim, with neat dark hair, very large sparkling dark eyes and a wonderful wide beam of a smile. She exuded not only that most invaluable of nanny qualities – calm – but a great cheerfulness. Nothing fazed her or seemed capable of even temporarily lowering her spririts, not Delia's tantrums or William's almost unbelievable messiness or the general chaos of the household. Her father had been a fairly senior civil servant in the Foreign Office and Janet was both well travelled and highly educated.

'I especially don't want an old dragon,' Cassia had said to her confidingly when she was interviewing her. 'Just someone who can be part of the family.'

'That's what I want too,' Janet Fraser had said, 'and yours is such a lovely family. I've always thought it would be very special to work for a working mother. There aren't that many of of you,' she said carefully, 'so if you did feel I would suit you, it would be really very nice indeed.' That was the first time Cassia saw the beam.

Janet Fraser was Princess Christian trained, and although she wore the brown uniform and looked very efficient – as indeed she was – and certain adjustments had been made to live up to her, she had proved remarkably easy to live with. The spare bedroom had been turned into a bedsitting room for her, with a new carpet and curtains and a pair of very nice chairs. A new pushchair had been bought for Delia to replace the rickety old pram, the nursery bathroom painted and some new lino fitted in the place of the torn and split piece that had been there before, so the house as well as the family had benefited from her arrival.

Peggy had been instructed with immense tact – 'I need you to help me make her feel part of our family' – to serve Janet's supper in her room, but she ate all her other meals with the family. Peggy had rather surprisingly taken to her (although Mrs Briggs remained resistant) and the children loved her.

Delia's behaviour had improved 'one hundred and fifty per cent', as Cassia told Cecily, half amused, half rueful, and the boys both said she was a jolly good sort. Although she was firm with them, she played all sorts of games with them, taught them card tricks, took them for long walks exploring the countryside (and had even been known to climb trees), and had managed to accomplish what no one else in the family had, namely teaching Bertie to ride his new two-wheeler bike. She didn't even mind Buffy, his muddy feet and and his increasingly odoriferous presence; she had grown up in a house in the wilds of Scotland, she said, and animal smells and mess were part of family life to her.

Best of all, in Cassia's view, she could drive, and when Cassia didn't need her car, could fetch and deliver the children to and from school, parties, the dentist and extra lessons.

Only Edward was resistant, grudgingly and finally agreeing to see her when she came for her second interview, asking her virtually no questions, refusing to respond to the beam, and looking at her blankly when Cassia told him, smiling with particular brightness, that Miss Fraser had studied first aid at college and had matriculated with honours in chemistry and would therefore be able to help in the surgery if he needed it.

'I don't actually need anyone with much knowledge – I obviously have that – just someone sensible,' he said.

'Yes, but Miss Fraser is more, better than sensible,' said Cassia, counting up to ten under her breath, wondering how she was going to resist the temptation to point out how rude he had been when Miss Fraser had gone.

There was a long silence, broken mercifully by Peggy, who came in to say there was a call from Mrs Parker over at Monks Hollow, whose little boy had fallen off the garage roof and been very sick, was it concussion? Edward excused himself (with minimal courtesy), and Cassia and Janet Fraser watched him go.

'I'm sorry,' said Cassia. 'He's terribly tired and overworked. And shy,' she added. 'When he gets to know you he'll relax.'

'Well, men are all difficult, aren't they?' said Janet Fraser with a particularly bright beam. 'It doesn't bother me, Mrs Fallon, it's the mummies and the children I really need to get along with.'

Cassia agreed that all men were indeed difficult and said she thought that was all for now, and she would drive Janet back to the station. 'I'll let you know tomorrow. Is that all right?'

'Of course. But I can tell you, if you do offer me the job, I shall certainly accept.'

Edward said, under pressure that night, that he supposed Janet was the best of the three he had been asked to see, if that was sufficient for Cassia to base her decision on.

Cassia couldn't remember him smiling at Janet once in the month she had been there. 'I do wish,' she said at the end of the third week, 'you would be a little more polite to Janet. It's so very obvious, your rudeness, and it must be difficult for her.'

'Cassia,' he said, 'I didn't want her to come, I don't like her being here. I'm prepared to tolerate it, but don't ask me to make a bosom friend of her.'

'Don't be ridiculous, Edward, no one's asking you to be her bosom friend. Just a courteous employer.'

'Well, I'm not her employer, am I?' he said with the cold, hard look she had come to dread. 'You are. And I don't want her driving my car. I don't actually like her driving yours.'

'She's not going to drive your car. And I can do what I like with mine.'

'As you do with everything else in your life.'

After a long silence Cassia said, 'Edward, this is so silly. Can't we be friends again? What's changed, what's different, except that life has become a bit easier for me?'

'You are changed, you are different,' he said, 'and life has become much more difficult for me. I can tolerate it. Just. But don't expect me to like it.'

She went out of the room and slammed the door. In the kitchen Peggy looked at Mrs Briggs and raised her eyebrows.

★

'Cecily is a very old friend,' Cassia explained now to Janet. 'Her husband is my godmother's brother.'

Janet frowned briefly, then said, 'I think I understand.'

'She's fat,' said William.

'Not any more,' said Cassia. 'That was the baby in her tummy, and it's been born now. Janet, if I could just run over the arrangements for the rest of the week ...'

Janet Fraser had already grasped all the arrangements for the rest of the week; there was really no need to run over it at all. Cassia had known that really; she just felt she should, that it was irresponsible not to. But when Janet actually said, 'I expect you'd like to visit your friend and her new baby after you finish your course tomorrow, so if you're not back by seven I'll make sure Mr Fallon's supper is served,' Cassia had great difficulty in not leaning forward to hug her.

'Mrs Moreton?'

'Yes, that's me.' Edwina pulled off one of her heavy Chanel pearl earrings as she answered the telephone, and sat down on the chair by her desk.

'You don't know me. Mary Whittaker's the name. I was given your number by Cecily Harrington. Such good news about her baby, isn't it?'

'Yes. Very good,' said Edwina politely.

'She said you were looking for something to do. Said you had some time and were prepared to do a bit of work. I'm on the management committee of St Christopher's Hospital. One of our other members has just left, and we need someone to help on the flag day sub-committee. How would that sound to you?'

'Well, I'm not sure,' said Edwina, to whom it sounded perfectly dreadful. 'I mean, it sounds very interesting, of course, but I do have another – another thing in prospect, which I'm not sure about yet. Er, what exactly would be involved?'

'Well, organisation,' said Mary Whittaker, sounding mildly put out. 'I was told that was your forte. This is a countrywide event, in June, you know, and we need all our operators, collectors and so on, primed, briefed, deliveries of their flags monitored, that sort of thing. It really is most important work, and naturally we would give you some help. Lady Southgate is in overall charge, I expect you know her, everyone does, but, of course, if you're not interested—'

'It's not that I'm not interested,' said Edwina, 'just that I might not have the time. After all.'

'Oh, I see. Well, in that case I've been misinformed. Most unfortunate. How is your mother, by the way?'

'She's very well. Thank you.'

'I know her, of course,' said Mary Whittaker, as if an acquaintance with Sylvia Fox-Ashley was an obligatory requirement for any normal person. 'In fact, I shall be seeing her this evening. At a dinner party. Perhaps she will know someone with genuine time to spare.'

She was obviously very much put out that Edwina hadn't jumped at the opportunity she had offered, that she had other claims (however fictional) on her time. Perhaps it was a great honour to work on one of these things, Edwina thought, maybe she should have been more grateful and gracious.

Anyway, one thing was quite certain: her mother would hear about it that evening, about her ingratitude, and would moreover be on the phone in the morning. If not that night. Damn.

'Edwina?' Sylvia Fox-Ashley's voice was heavy. Edwina knew that tone, and sighed.

'Yes, Mummy.'

'Darling, black mark. You've offended Mary Whittaker, and therefore Sir Simeon, who's an important client of your father's.'

'Mummy, I'm sorry. I didn't know. I thought it sounded a bit—'

'Edwina, just for me, do it, will you? It needn't take up too much time, and anyway it's a very good cause. About time you did something with your life, if you're not going to start a family yet. No news on that front, I suppose?'

'No, Mummy. None at all. I told you, we're just not in a hurry, that's all.'

'That's what I thought you'd say. Honestly, darling, much better have the children straight away, get it over with, and then get on with your lives. Good staff and you need hardly know you've got them. Take my advice, Edwina, and tell Harry you want a child as soon as possible. Or is he being difficult about it? Because if he is, then perhaps I should have a word—'

'No, Mummy, he's not and I forbid you to have any kind of a word about it. Absolutely forbid it. You're on very dangerous ground. I warn you.'

'All right, all right, darling, keep your wig on. I wouldn't dream of interfering in anything so personal.'

'Good,' said Edwina coolly.

'Just the same, it would be very helpful if you could do this thing for me. For us. Daddy hasn't had such an easy time since the crash. It's taken time to get his business right back on a firm footing and Simeon Whittaker is important to him. Besides, those committees are a hoot, you know: lots of ladies playing God. It would amuse you. And if you cared about such things, which sometimes I really fear you don't, you could do some good as well. All right, darling?'

'Well—'

'Good. Will you ring her, or shall I?'

'I'm going to do some voluntary work,' said Edwina to Harry, settling down opposite him at the breakfast table.

'Oh really? How exemplary of you. In what area?'

'Hospitals.'

'Very exemplary. Which one?'

'St Christopher's. That was Cassia's hospital, wasn't it? I've only just put two and two together.'

'Yes, it was.' His voice, as always when he was talking to her these days, was courteously disinterested.

'Someone called Mary Whittaker. Do you know her?'

'Thankfully not.'

'She's asked me to be on the management committee. To help run the flag day.'

'How very impressive.'

'Well, it's nice to know I have your support,' she said. His power to still hurt her was always surprising.

'Sorry. Do tell me more. When does this begin?'

'I don't know. Next week, I think.'

'You'll find it quite time-consuming,' he said, 'I warn you.'

'What on earth do you know about flag days, Harry?'

'One of my companies runs a contributory scheme for hospital care. Big business, the whole thing is, although St Christopher's has quite a struggle to make ends meet. It's not rich like Tommy's and Bart's and Guy's. Nothing like the amount of property.'

She stared at him. 'What a lot of pies your fingers are in, to be sure.'

'Yes, well, if you took even the remotest interest in my business affairs, you might find it less surprising.' He stood up, looked down at her with the familiar mixture of affection and disapproval. Sometimes, she thought, she'd rather it was actual dislike. It would be easier to live with. Then she could just dislike him back.

Cassia sat in a taxi on her way to Cecily's and Benedict's house in Eaton

Place in a strange state, an amalgam of excitement, exhaustion and severe self-doubt. Mostly self-doubt. She wondered how wise she had been to have embarked on this. On a return to the dangerous, potentially deadly world of medicine. She simply didn't feel equipped for it any more. Which was ridiculous, really; all that she would be required to do in the immediate future was to take a woman's gynaecological history, examine her, fit her with a contraceptive device and instruct her in its use: and she already found the prospect terrifying. Well, not terrifying, but certainly daunting. The contraceptives would fail, the women become immediately pregnant, some would seek abortions, unwanted babies would be born, marriages fail, lives thrown into disarray – and it would all be her fault.

Oh, for heaven's sake, Cassia, she thought, staring out of the window fretfully, what has happened to you? What had happened to the self-assured young woman, who had assisted in the operating theatre, delivered babies, sutured wounds, made diagnoses (admittedly all under rigid supervision) and never wondered for a moment if she might be in any way failing her patients? Or at least not doing the very best for them that she and modern medicine could? Gone for ever, she supposed, her identity blurred by years of marriage, of motherhood, of housewifery, of struggling endlessly to do something she was not very good at.

That was what had wrecked her confidence: failing, endlessly, depressingly, falling short of her own high standards, while knowing her real skills were being wasted, falling away – and minding so very much that they were.

Impossible to recapture those skills suddenly, that confidence; it was like lying in bed for weeks, when she had had a very bad attack of measles as a child, longing to get up, gazing greedily down out of the window at the garden; and then finally allowed to get up, and walking unsteadily down the stairs on legs that had grown weak and spindly, and instead of running out into the sunshine, climbing a tree, playing on her swing, finding herself still unable to do more than sit on a chair and look out of another window with just a slightly different view.

But her legs had grown stronger and she had climbed the tree and played on the swing in time; and in time now (she told herself firmly) she would grow stronger herself, trust herself, trust her judgement, deal with her patients. She must just have faith in herself, somehow. The trouble was there was no one else who did ...

'What a lovely baby,' she said, smiling into the blue-trimmed crib, at the squashed, ruddy, indignant features of Laurence Harrington, smiling

167

across the room at Cecily, at Fanny and Stephanie lolling on their mother's bed, filled with quasi-maternal pride themselves. She tried to believe that Bertie and William had ever been this ugly, feeling quite sure they had not.

'Isn't he? And so good. The monthly nurse is brilliant, of course, but even she says he's particularly well behaved, that he'd sleep over the four hours if she let him – which naturally she wouldn't.'

'No, of course not,' said Cassia carefully. She had found the four-hour rigid scheduling of feeds impossible herself, never having had the benefit of a monthly nurse, and had fed all her children when they cried, which was sometimes after three hours and sometimes after five; she had also, very unfashionably, breastfed them all. She and Edward had agreed before Bertie was born that this would be better for their children (having observed a great many babies in poorer homes nurtured in this way and the benefit in terms of quiet and serenity it had seemed to bring to both babies and mothers) and it seemed to have worked. Suddenly, sharply, she thought of the happiness, the tenderness in spite of everything that had existed between them, herself and Edward, at that time, his delight and excitement about the baby, the intense love and pride he felt for her, their shared conviction that their family should be happy and secure – and found it almost impossible to believe, so totally it seemed lost to them now. She dragged her mind firmly back to Cecily and Laurence.

'And how do you feel?'

'I feel marvellous,' said Cecily, 'really quite well enough to get out of bed, but of course I can't. Ten days to go at least.'

'I did,' said Cassia.

'Really? How soon?'

'Oh, about three days after. Two, I think, with Delia.'

'What, actually out of bed?' Cecily looked as shocked as if Cassia had announced she had joined a circus two days after her confinement.

'Yes, of course. Well, there was so much to do. I didn't have much help, you know. And women in primitive communities don't lie about for a fortnight after they've had their children, and nor do animals – they get up the minute they can.'

'But you don't know that that's good for them.'

'I can't see why it shouldn't be,' said Cassia, 'and nor does Edward, actually.'

'Does he advise it, though? To the women he delivers?'

'Well, so many of them are very poor, they don't have much option. They have to get up as soon as possible, look after the other half dozen or so children. It doesn't seem to do them any harm. But, yes, he does encourage it. After about a week, anyway.'

'Good gracious,' said Cecily, 'how very revolutionary. Well, my maternity nurse Davis certainly wouldn't allow it, nor Dr Rushton. Girls, run along now and have your supper, it's well past the time. And then come back and I'll read to you before you have your baths.' The girls clambered obediently off the bed, kissed her, kissed Cassia and disappeared.

'I wish my children were that well behaved,' said Cassia. 'We have half an hour's argument after any orders I give any of them.'

'Well, mine have been raised by Nanny Hawkins,' said Cecily. 'Nobody argues with Nanny Hawkins. How's your new nanny, by the way? Good decision?'

'Marvellous decision. And she's absolutely wonderful. I adore her, the children adore her, even Peggy likes her.'

'Edward?'

'Oh, yes,' she said quickly, 'he's getting to really like her too. And Benedict, is he pleased with his son?'

'Thrilled. Frightfully pleased with himself as well. There really is something about boys, isn't there? I hate to admit it, but—'

'I do too, but, yes,' said Cassia. 'You feel you've got a real stake in immortality, don't you? The name continuing and so on.'

'How is Edward, Cassia?' said Cecily suddenly. 'Really, I mean. Does he mind what you're doing?'

'What, working? Thinking about working, anyway? After today – I've been doing a sort of course, you know – I'm not sure if I'll dare. Goodness, I've forgtten a lot. Anyway, yes, he's quite happy about it.'

'Really?' said Cecily. Her brown eyes were thoughtful as she looked at Cassia. There was a silence.

Cassia said, 'No, not really. He's being ghastly. Hostile. Cold. I don't know what to do. Short of giving up before I begin.'

'Which you mustn't. You really mustn't. He'll come round.'

'I don't know why you should be so sure,' said Cassia, 'or why he should.'

'I'm certainly sure he should. I think you've been self-sacrificing for quite long enough. I can't personally imagine why you want to do any sort of work, of course, when you can just stay at home with your lovely children, especially now, and enjoy yourself, but I know how much you do want it, and how good at it you were going to be, and I think you deserve it.'

'Oh, I don't know,' said Cassia fretfully. Her course and the demands it had made on her fragile self-confidence had made her generally wretched. 'I think maybe I've been wrong. All I'm doing is making Edward miserable, driving a great wedge between us. Maybe I should give up again, do what you say.'

'No,' said Cecily, 'no, Cassia, don't.'

'But you don't understand, it's so miserable, so hard, a battle every inch of the way. There's a horrible atmosphere in the house, he hardly speaks to me, won't touch me even. I suppose I have been rather tactless over it, over the money and everything, but I did want this so terribly much and I can't see why he couldn't be more generous ...' She heard her voice shake, felt her eyes fill with tears, brushed them away impatiently. 'Sorry.'

'Darling Cassia, you cry if you want to. I feel terribly sad for you, if it's really that bad. It seems so unfair, after all you gave up for him. He could spare you a little generosity, I'd have thought. And of course you must give up if you really want to, but I don't think you do. Not really. I think you deserve it, deserve a chance. Edward is very sweet, and I'm very fond of him, but he shouldn't sit on your ambitions as he has. You haven't seemed happy for quite a long time.'

'Haven't I?' Cassia said.

'No. You haven't. And it's sad. Very sad.'

'Well,' she said, with a sigh, 'I don't know that I'm making myself any happier now, but I'll go on a bit longer. See how things work out.'

'Good.' Cecily lay back on her pillows, smiled at her. 'I think that's the right decision.'

'You seem very concerned.'

'Cassia, I'm very fond of you. I mind that you're not happy. I mean, tell me I'm wrong and I'll be delighted to change my mind.'

Cassia was silent, then she said, 'Well, not completely, no. But who is? Are you?'

'Oh, you know.'

'Yes, I do know. So what's so different?'

'A lot, I think,' said Cecily firmly. 'I can't do anything about my situation. Well, no more than I already have. You can.'

'Would you leave Benedict?' She was aware even as she asked it what a challenging question it was.

Cecily flushed, stared at her in silence, then said, 'No. No, I wouldn't. I love him. You know I do.'

'I'm sorry, Cecily. I shouldn't have said that.'

'It was reasonable, under the circumstances. Let me ask you. Would you leave Edward?'

'No, of course not.'

'Do you love him?'

Another silence, then Cassia said, 'I think so. I hope so.' And burst into tears, real tears this time, aching, rising tears that hurt, were not a relief to shed.

Cecily held out her arms, as if she was little Fanny. Cassia went and sat on the bed, lay on the pillows beside her. 'This is ridiculous,' she said.

'No, it isn't. Poor Cassia. I'm so sorry. I do so want things to be right for you. I owe you such a lot.'

'Oh, Cecily, don't be silly.'

'It was so wonderful,' she went on, looking at her, her face very serious suddenly, 'what you did, all those years ago. I've never forgotten it and I never will. I still owe you a huge debt.'

'Well, I certainly don't see it like that and I don't want you even to think of paying it,' said Cassia, blowing her nose. 'It was a pleasure. In a warped sort of way. Now look, I have to go, it's awfully late, and if I'm not home for supper Edward really will blow a gasket. I think your little Laurence is heaven. Absolute heaven.'

'Would you be his godmother? I've been meaning to ask you.'

'Cecily,' said Cassia, the tears starting again, but easier, sweeter ones this time, 'I'd love it. What an honour. Thank you for asking me.'

CHAPTER 10

Six months in Obstetrics and six months in Casualty had prepared Cassia for much of what she saw at the family planning clinic: women of thirty who looked fifty, pregnant with a tenth, or twelfth child, girls of eighteen pregnant with a third or fourth, girls of thirteen of fourteen just ... pregnant. In Obstetrics they would be bearing the child, in Casualty losing it, often bleeding to death as a result of a backstreet abortion. She was not even shocked by the signs of violence inflicted on these women, the bruising, the cuts, sometimes even broken bones. It was distressing, but she had grown used to that.

What she had not seen before was the crowds of small children, runny nosed, scrawny, with the greyish pallor of poverty that surrounded their mothers, the poverty which was the ongoing legacy of the Depression, the poverty whose existence was denied round the middle- and upper-class dinner tables of England; and what she had not heard were the women's stories. Stories of hopelessness, until now, of grinding poverty, of crushing hard work, of perpetual poor health, all accentuated by the ongoing terror of yet another pregnancy.

She sat in her small room, and a seemingly endless procession of these women, women who might have lived in another age, another country from herself and her circle, trailed through it; her sessions began at two and were frequently still running at eight, for it was a point of pride with the Association that all who came were seen. They waited, patiently, the women, through the long afternoons, while their children whined and played and fought, and their babies were fed, sometimes twice or even three times, and while they waited they exchanged stories, sometimes sad, often bitterly humorous, of their husbands and the treatment they endured at their hands.

She glimpsed in those long afternoons the kind of careless brutality she liked to think no longer existed; imagined what it must be like to be one of those women, lying in bed, hearing heavy footsteps on the stairs, smelling drunken breath, waiting, dreading what was yet again going to happen – and its inevitable consequence. Time and time again she was told, often quite cheerfully, "'E's fine when 'e's not drunk, Doctor,' and, 'He won't take precautions, says it spoils things,' this followed by the equally cheerful, 'Then of course he gets mad when I tell 'im I've fallen again.'

She went home sobered by those experiences, ashamed of herself for complaining about her lot, for thinking Edward – always so kind, so considerate, so careful in bed at least – anything other than perfect.

She tried to tell him about it one evening, not just about the women but her gratitude, her remorse (thinking this at least might soften his hostility, might open the paths of communication between them), but he listened politely for a while, then said, 'I saw plenty of that sort of thing in Harrow, of course. I'm sure I told you about it.'

'No, Edward you didn't,' she said (knowing all they talked about in the few hours they had was his work, his struggles, his exhaustion, and very occasionally her own), but he looked at her rather distantly and said perhaps, then, she had not been listening and would she excuse him now.

'Oh, for God's sake,' she said, 'no, I won't excuse you. I need to talk to you. I can't stand this, it's awful, we can't go on like this.'

'I'm surprised to hear you say that,' he said. 'The whole thing, all the changes in our lives, have been at your instigation, and if you don't like it—'

'What I don't like,' she cried in a passion, 'is your attitude, your hostility, when all I am doing is just a little of what I have longed for ever since we got married. It doesn't affect you so very much. You should be glad for me, glad I am getting my chance—'

'I am very sorry,' he said, 'that you have been so unhappy in our marriage until now.'

'I didn't say I was unhappy, and you know I didn't. I said I was longing to work. As a doctor. As I have since I was a little girl.'

'Ah,' he said, and his voice was icy, 'that old story.'

'What do you mean?'

'You're very fond of that bit of your history, aren't you, Cassia? The hard-working ambitious child, struggling against all those odds. We hear less about all the help you had, the input from your relations, your London Season, your rich friends. Just the sad little motherless soul up there in Leeds.'

'That is monstrous,' she said, standing up, physical violence rising in her, wondering if she should perhaps not resist it, hit him, whether that might bring home to him the strength of her feelings. 'Why are you doing this? Why are you so bitter, so angry?'

'I'm angry,' he said, 'because you continually imply that up to now you have had nothing, and I have had everything, when the reverse is a great deal nearer the truth. Now I trust I've answered your questions satisfactorily because, as I said, I do have work to do.'

He walked out of the room and into his study, and she heard the door slam. She sat staring into the fire, and wondered, not for the first time in those extraordinary months, that the money had not only empowered her finally to do what she wanted, but had also rendered her helpless to be the wife Edward wanted any more.

She didn't often think very much about the money at all; she did not allow herself to, knew if she did it would become an obsession. The small extravagances, self-indulgences, life changes that she had brought about for herself, were sufficient to satisfy her, to make her feel it was not being quite wasted. When she did contemplate it, as she was now, it was as something oddly abstract, a huge force, somehow threatening, irresistible if actually unleashed. Its power frightened her: she tried to keep it at bay, dammed up behind the wall of intense willpower and steely common sense that she had built up over the past few years, but she could feel it growing stronger now, forcing its way in small but inexorable forays into every corner of her life.

Contemplation about what she might do, could do, also became increasingly irresistible: the knowledge that she could accomplish so much was frightening in itself. She moved from the professional – from wild thoughts of founding her own hospital, of setting up a medical foundation – to the personal – to taking her children and travelling the world, seeing its wonders, possibly for years.

And then there was what she had labelled the desire element, the least obviously hazardous, the easiest to fulfil: and thus the most dangerous. She thought of great houses, of fine furnishings, of beautiful pictures; she dreamed of exquisite clothes, of fine jewellery; she fantasised over yachts, racehorses, aeroplanes.

All these things – or certainly many of them – she could have; but not within her marriage, not as Mrs Edward Fallon, not as the doctor's wife. Were she to use the money, the great wealth that had become so absurdly hers, then she could see quite clearly her marriage must end, the marriage to the man she did not love, had never loved – but who was the father of her children, central to all their lives and for whom and whose happiness she felt an almost unbearable responsiblity. It would end not only in bitterness and hostility, but intense pain and humiliation on his behalf. It was impossible, given the condition of their relationship, that it could continue against the background of the money, her money. And so she waited, waited with her wealth walled up, to see what would happen, where it would end: and without quite even realising it, prayed that that end would come, somehow miraculously, through no fault or even action of her own.

She wasn't working the next day. It was a lovely morning, lush with spring and its excesses, and she put Delia in her smart new pushchair and pushed her down into the village to get some things from the shop.

'Good morning, Mrs Fallon,' said Mr Wallace, who had run Monks Stores ever since he came home from the war in 1917, minus a leg.

'Good morning, Mr Wallace. How are you?'

'Oh, can't grumble. Haven't seen much of you lately. I heard you gone to do some doctoring of your own.'

'Yes, I have. Only a little, of course, just two afternoons a week.'

'Is that all? Seems like more than that. As I was saying to Mrs Wallace, the doctor must miss you, I said. Still, it's the modern way, I suppose.'

'Yes, it is, Mr Wallace. And I'm enjoying it. Those two afternoons,' she added firmly.

'That's good. Well, the children seem happy enough. A very nice person she seems, that nanny of yours.'

'I'm glad you like her. *They* certainly do. Now can I have some sugar, please, a pound, and a large bag of flour, and some eggs. Oh, yes, and half a pound of butter. And a bottle of orange squash. I think that's all. Thank you.'

She was waiting for him to get the things together, smiling out of the window at Delia in the pram and at Buffy, sitting patiently beside it, when the door opened and Mrs Venables came in.

'Hallo, Mrs Venables. I was on my way to see you.'

'Oh, really?' Mrs Venables' tone was not exactly cold, but it wasn't warm either.

'Yes, I was thinking it was only ten days till Easter and you must need to get the flower rota organised. I'm free on—'

'That's quite all right, Mrs Fallon. It is all settled. Thank you.'

'Oh, but—'

'I had assumed you must be too busy for that sort of thing these days.'

'Mrs Venables, that isn't quite fair,' said Cassia. 'I've never suggested for a moment that I couldn't do the flowers, or help with the cleaning or whatever.'

'We can't expect you to do that sort of thing any more,' said Mrs Venables, flushing slightly.

Cassia stared at her. 'Why ever not?'

'Well, I just thought that – we thought …'

She decided to meet this head on. 'Mrs Venables, just because I've come into a bit of money, it hasn't changed me in any way. Of course I still want to help with village life. I'd be very sad not to.'

Mrs Venables looked at her awkwardly. 'I see. It's just that – well, the doctor said—'

'The doctor! What did the doctor say?'

'He said you were very busy these days, and simply wouldn't have the time. To help.'

'Oh, he did!' Deep breaths, Cassia, stay calm. 'Well, that was a misunderstanding. Now will you promise to tell me the very next time you want the church cleaned and I'll do it? All right?'

'Yes, Mrs Fallon, of course.' Mrs Venables sounded almost subdued.

Cassia paid for her shopping, said good morning to Mr Wallace and pushed Delia very fast back up the hill.

As the door closed behind her, Mr Wallace shook his head.

'Poor doctor,' he said. 'He really doesn't look himself at all these days.'

Mrs Venables smiled, but simply gave him her order; it didn't do to gossip with tradespeople. Not in a village like Monks Heath, anyway. But there was no doubt that 'poor doctor' was the phrase on most people's lips these days.

When the last patient left, Cassia put her head round the surgery door. 'Edward, can I have a word with you?'

'Couldn't it be over lunch? I've got a lot of calls this afternoon.'

'No, it couldn't. What do you mean, telling Mrs Venables I don't have time to help in the village any more, with the flowers and so on?'

'It seems fairly obvious to me. She phoned, you weren't here, she wanted an answer—'

'I see. Well, in future perhaps you'd consult with me before you make pronouncements on what I can and can't do. All right?'

'I'm afraid there isn't always an opportunity to consult with you, Cassia. You surely won't deny that very often these days you aren't here. It's as simple as that.'

She didn't even answer: there was no point.

In a dingy rehearsal room in Croydon, Rupert Cameron was being told that if he didn't bloody well pull himself together and learn his lines, he would find himself without his part. And would he care? he thought miserably (while smiling charmingly, earnestly at the director, assuring him that of course he would know them perfectly by the very next rehearsal – he'd thought he did, it was just this ghastly cold he was developing that had fuddled his memory). It was a rotten lousy part, second lead in a very inferior drawing-room comedy, which clearly the author saw as being rather better than all the works of Noël Coward put together. But he would care because he needed the money; he was in a bit of a financial fix just at the moment. It would have to be another cruise ship at this rate, and that really would be a humiliation, playing cabaret again.

God, he was too old for all this: much too old. What on earth was going to happen to him? What happened to all washed-up unsuccessful actors, he supposed. A steady slither into the odd bit of teaching, extra work at the film studios, and finally, if you were really lucky, a job as stage hand. It was all very depressing.

He decided to go to the pub for a drink.

He was just putting on his raincoat when a very pretty girl arrived at the door: fair haired, blue eyed, with a Cupid's-bow mouth. She was clearly nervous.

'Hallo,' she said, 'I've come for the reading. I'm late, I'm afraid. I got lost, I couldn't find this place. But I'm only the maid, so I don't suppose it will matter terribly.'

'We hadn't got to your bit,' said Rupert, 'but you're wrong, it's quite an important part, the maid. In this play.' He held out his hand. 'Rupert Cameron, playing the hero's best friend. Frightful twit. The best friend, not me.'

She giggled. 'I'm Amanda de Lisle.' Oh yes, thought Rupert. De Lisle! Lyons, more like it. But she really was very pretty. 'I'm just going for a drink,' he said. 'It's the lunchbreak. Would you like to come with me?'

Amanda de Lisle smiled up at him, fluttering her long curly eyelashes. She had very deep, very delicious dimples. 'I'd like it very much,' she said.

Rupert suddenly felt a lot less depressed.

Cassia looked at her watch. Almost five, but only three women left, Jane the secretary had said, so she should be away in about half an hour, and that would mean she could make the Savoy by six after all. She wasn't at her usual clinic, but doing an emergency cover at one near the Elephant and Castle. She supposed she ought to go tonight. She had said she would if she could, that she'd be there unless Edwina heard otherwise. And it was to help St Christopher's, or so she had been told. But Edwina, of all people …

177

She forced her attention back on to the young woman sitting in front of her. 'Go on,' she said gently.

'You see, the thing is, Doctor, I really do need the help. I've had four babies now in five years. My husband doesn't like using things, you know, and the last little baby died.'

'Oh, I'm so sorry,' said Cassia. The girl didn't look more than twenty; she had said she was twenty-two. She somehow doubted that. 'What was it? Diphtheria, or—'

'No, she died at birth. They said it was partly due to her coming so soon after the other. Just ten months, there was, between them.'

'Yes, that is very close,' said Cassia. It was actually an unlikely reason for the baby's death, but ten months! She thought of that baby's conception, the father who didn't like using condoms, and thought it was just as well for him that he wasn't there too.

'Of course you must have help. We can certainly prevent that happening again. Now I'm just going to examine you, and then I can fit you with a contraceptive, and explain how to use it. When was that baby … born?' It was so difficult sometimes, finding the right words to fit these sad, difficult lives. When was the baby born? When had it died?

'Only about six weeks ago.'

Poor little thing. 'That is a little soon. Your body will still be adjusting, returning to its normal shape. Internally as well. So we might have to do something temporary, ask you to come back.'

'Oh dear. But not – not the—'

'No, not the condoms. Not much use if he won't use them, anyway.' She smiled at her. 'Possibly what we call a pessary. Then a cap later on. I'll explain. Now if you get undressed, and on to that couch over there …'

The girl was still tender from her baby's birth, shrank from the examination. Cassia's heart ached for her.

'Right,' she said, ten minutes later, handing the girl a neat packet and a leaflet, 'come back in three months. And good luck.'

'Yes, Doctor. Thank you so much.' Her eyes suddenly filled with tears, and she wiped them with the back of her hand. 'I'm sorry. I didn't mean to cry. It brought it back, you know, talking about it.'

'I know. You cry, I don't mind. Talk some more, it might help.'

'Oh, no, it's all right. And I've got the others, I'm lucky. But it's a terrible thing, going through it, all the pain and that, and then seeing your baby, just … well, not alive.'

'I understand. Was your husband good about that? Sympathetic?'

'Oh yes, he's very good really. He just – well, you know what men are like.' She managed a watery smile.

'I certainly do,' said Cassia.

She caught the omnibus from the Elephant to the Strand; it jolted along quite fast, and she sat looking out of the window, hearing the girl's voice, remembering another baby that had died, remembering her distress, her guilt, remembering what had happened afterwards … Don't, Cassia, don't think about it now, not today, not this evening, for heaven's sake …

'Cassia, hallo. Sweet of you to come.' Edwina was looking dauntingly chic as always, in a black suit and a red hat, set dashingly over one eye. 'You must be exhausted after your work. I've ordered two martinis. I hope that's all right. I seem to remember you like them. This is rather fun, isn't it, meeting here, without any men? Love the coat, darling, whose is it? Stiebel?'

'No, I got it in Selfridges,' said Cassia, 'and yes, it's great fun here. A martini would be lovely.' She felt heavyhearted, out of sorts, found it difficult to detach herself from the afternoon, acutely aware of the absurd contrast of poverty and martinis, stillbirths and couture.

'Good. Well, the thing is, I just need a bit of help. I've been asked to do some charity work for St Christopher's, to help with their flag day in June, and I just thought you could prime me a bit. I've got my first meeting tomorrow and I don't want to look a complete idiot.'

'Edwina, I'm sorry, but I can't help you very much,' said Cassia. 'I had absolutely no contact with the management side of the hospital at all. I know the chairman of the board of governors was very important and very powerful, and everyone had to do what he said – if he was coming round the hospital you had to be ready almost to curtsy. That's about all I can tell you.'

'That's not much help at all, I'm afraid,' said Edwina. She looked mildly outraged, as if Cassia was keeping information from her deliberately. 'I was hoping for some background information. You know.'

'What, about the comittee?'

'I think I know what they'll be like: perfectly ghastly. Mummy's warned me about them. No, I thought you'd be able to tell me about the hospital, you know. How long it's been going, how many wards, all that sort of stuff. And do you think I'll be expected to know anything about its medical work?'

'No, of course not,' said Cassia, laughing. 'I don't think you'd be

179

expected to know how many wards there were either. But let me see, the hospital was founded in fourteen hundred and forty-two, can't remember how many times I was told that, it used to be near Smithfield, but got moved out towards Victoria in the early nineteenth century because there were Guy's and Bart's already in the City. They're not as rich as Thomas's, but—'

'No, that's what Harry said.'

'Harry? What on earth does he know about it?'

'Harry knows a lot about everything,' said Edwina vaguely. 'It always surprises me. He runs some medical insurance scheme or something. I don't quite know.'

'Good Lord,' said Cassia. 'Anyway, although they do get quite a lot of legacies and so on, and from donations and investments, I do know it's an increasing struggle. So things like your flag days are vital. Oh, and they just might be impressed that you knew they were one of the very first hospitals to offer anaesthesia in childbirth. Let me see ... oh, yes, the sisters are called after their wards, not their own names, and they're doing a lot of research into TB at the moment. Hoping to find a breakthrough. How's that?'

'That's marvellous,' said Edwina. 'I knew you'd be able to help. You're just too modest, Cassia, that's your problem. How's Edward?' she added dutifully. Edwina and Edward were not fond of one another, but Edwina did at least make an effort on the few occasions they met. Edward did not.

'He's fine. Very busy.'

'And how's the work? Are you enjoying it?'

'Yes, very much. Of course it's pretty mundane, but it's a start.'

'What is it, something to do with women?'

'Something, yes. Birth control clinics. It's a growing movement and—'

'It must be fascinating,' said Edwina, putting down her glass, examining her very long red fingernails. 'Do you want another drink?'

'No, really, I ought to get back.'

'Oh, come on. It'll cheer you on the long journey. Do you enjoy country life? It always seems all right for a weekend, but I get desperate if we stay for longer.'

'Yes, it's lovely,' said Cassia, thinking of Edwina's country life, the enormous and beautiful house in Wiltshire, home to absurdly lavish house parties, and then left empty again, often for weeks at a time, occupied only by servants and horses; and of her own, real country life: the church, the shop, the village nursery school which she and Edward had agreed they should support, Mrs Venables, the Women's Institute.

Any kind of comparison was not only impossible but absurd. 'And of course it's so good for the children, living in the country, they—'

'Oh God,' said Edwina, 'here's Harry. He threatened to come. I told him not to, but he obviously decided to ignore me. Hallo, darling.' She raised her face to be kissed. Harry bent over her, kissed her briefly, then looked at Cassia, paused and kissed her too. 'Hallo, Cassia.'

'Hallo, Harry. I'm just going, actually.'

'Charming as always,' he said lightly. 'Why not make a huge effort, stay for one drink?'

'Of course she will,' said Edwina. 'Harry, order them, will you? Martinis, we were drinking. I'm going to the cloakroom. Back in a tick.'

He sat down beside Cassia, studied her. 'How are you?'

'I'm very well, thank you, Harry,' she said, feeling the inevitable tug of sexual tension, situated so uncomfortably somewhere between her head and her heart.

'You look tired.'

'Well, thank you for that,' she said, hearing her voice sound defensive, wishing it didn't.

'Cassia, there's nothing wrong with being tired. Working too hard?'

'Not really.'

'But you are working? At your medicine?'

'Yes.'

'Good,' he said, sitting back into his chair, an expression of great satisfaction on his face. 'I heard you were. High time you went back to it.'

'Not you as well,' she said. 'Everybody says that, all the time, it's like some sort of conspiracy.' And then looked at him, and at the back of his dark eyes saw something she couldn't quite understand, wasn't even sure about, a sort of wariness; then it was gone.

'And are you enjoying it?'

'Oh yes, very much.'

'Good. And can you help Edwina? With this new project of hers? I have to tell you I really don't see it lasting.'

'That seems a little unfair,' said Cassia. 'She's hardly begun and she's certainly making a great effort.'

'Well, I have a great capacity for being unfair. As you know.'

The waiter arrived. 'Three martinis, please,' said Harry.

'No, really. Not for me.'

'Why ever not? It'll do you good. And what's the rush?'

'I have to get home. I don't want to be late.'

'Three martinis,' he said again to the waiter, and smiled at her.

'How fortunate your husband is, to have a wife so anxious to get home to him. Do you work every day?'

'No, only two afternoons. Quite long afternoons. Sometimes till about eight o'clock at night.'

'In London?'

'Not what you'd regard as London,' she said, 'but yes, on the outskirts of Brixton. Although today I was at the Elephant and Castle.'

'And then you have to do the long journey home. I'm surprised you don't get yourself a little house in town. Stay there on those late evenings. And then travel down in the morning.'

'What a ridiculous idea,' she said, laughing. 'How could I possibly do that?'

'Quite easily, I would have thought. Now that you are a woman of independent means. Think of what it would save you: the clockwatching, the tension ...'

'And what do you think Edward would have to say about that? Not to mention the children?'

'Edward could surely spare you a couple of nights a week. He's usually out delivering babies anyway, as far as I can make out. And I understand you have a nanny now, so the children would be perfectly all right.'

'Harry,' she said firmly, 'I'm afraid you don't understand me and my marriage at all.'

'No,' he said, looking at her very intently, his eyes thoughtful, 'I'm afraid I don't.'

She couldn't help it in the end. She sat on the train, staring out into the growing dusk, her head spinning slightly with the martinis, thinking, remembering, reliving it. That day. It was the girl who had done it. The girl at the clinic that afternoon and her baby. Her dead baby ...

She had heard you never quite got over it, your first death, that it haunted you for the rest of your career. She could believe it: she would never forget, she knew, the sight of that little baby, dragged finally from its mother, poor, exhausted, terrified girl, only fifteen or so, and it was so clearly dead, an awful bluish-white colour.

Cassia had been on the obstetric ward for two months, had found it and all its attendant drama – the pain, the tension, the stoicism and courage, the fear and despair – everything she could have hoped for. This was where she felt she belonged; this was where she wanted to work for the rest of her days, where life began, was coaxed, eased, bullied out of struggling bodies, where every time, at every first cry, the joy was a tangible, vital force. Until then. Until that day. When that baby died. It was a boy; Cassia looked at it, its little face tranquil, almost smiling, its limbs limp and somehow heavy, and burst into tears.

'Now then, now then.' The midwife looked at her sternly. 'You're not going to get far as a doctor if you get emotional over everything. It's the poor young woman here who should be crying, not you. Turn on your side, dear, let me give you an injection, help with the afterbirth. Miss Berridge, you take this baby along to the sluice for now. I'll be with you shortly. Do stop screaming, dear,' she said to the mother, 'it's all over now.'

It was all over, thought Cassia, very much so; nothing to show for all those hours of pain but the tiny blue corpse. Suddenly she felt very sick. She laid the baby gently on a slab in the sluice, and although it was foolish, wrapped it in a towel and then threw up into the sink.

One of the student nurses who was in there looked at her sympathetically. 'It's awful, isn't it? Happened to me last week. Poor little chap.' She went over, looked down at the baby. 'They're so bloody callous, these midwives, won't give the mothers anything to help the pain, seem to think they've a mission to make them suffer.'

'Last week,' said Cassia, smiling rather feebly, 'we delivered a baby to a midwife. I've never heard anyone scream like she did, and afterwards she said she'd never felt so ashamed in her life, remembering all the mothers she'd told to shut up. I tell you, I've developed a great admiration for women since I've been here. Well, all women who've had children, anyway.'

She went home shortly after that. It was Friday night and she had been looking forward to the break. During the week now, while she was on Obstetrics she lived in the hospital, in a tiny room next to the obstetric house surgeon's, but he had given her the weekend off. 'Get some studying done. It's been a tough week for you. I do know.'

It seemed a very long ride home on her bike; it was a hot evening, the streets were noisy and seemed particularly filthy. Grosvenor Gardens had never looked more beautifully welcome.

Harris let her in. 'You look terrible, miss. Shall I run you a bath? Then I'm going out, it's my evening off. If that's all right. And Sir Richard's gone off to Norfolk. He told me to tell you.'

'Yes, Harris, of course it's all right. And I think I can manage to run myself a bath.'

'All right, miss.'

'Are you from a large family, Harris?'

'Oh yes, miss. Quite large. Eleven of us, there were. Well, fourteen born, but three died, of course.'

Of course. Three out of fourteen would. Actually that wasn't bad then. Things were much better now, hygiene improved and everything. She thought of Harris's mother, enduring childbirth fourteen times, enduring having seen three of her babies die, and wondered how she, how any of these women, ever got over that, went on, with their unshakable courage, to try again.

She pulled off her jacket, straightened her aching back. 'How sad. I'm not going to have any children, I don't think.' She felt disillusioned, wretched.

'Mother says that's what they all say, miss.'

'I expect they do, but at least we can do something about it now.'

'Yes, miss.' Harris was obviously embarrassed. 'Well, I'll be off.'

'Yes, please do. Have a good evening.'

'Cook's gone to the pictures, as well, miss. Said to tell you she left your supper out.'

'Thank you.'

She went upstairs, very slowly; ran a very deep bath, lay in it, soaking away her exhaustion, trying to forget the poor little blue corpse. She couldn't. She wished she could have talked to Edward about it; he would have understood, have comforted her. But he was working right through the weekend at the hospital, in Casualty, sleeping at the hospital; she couldn't possibly contact him except in the direst emergency. Which this certainly wasn't.

She climbed out of the bath, pulled on a light cotton frock and went downstairs to the dining room. She wasn't really hungry: she felt too tired and too upset to eat. She picked at the salad, then pushed it aside and walked through into the drawing room; that seemed large and gloomily dark in spite of the heat outside, so she went instead into the morning room. God, this was a huge depressing house without Leonora. She hadn't heard from her for ages; she hoped she was all right.

The bell rang sharply; Jarvis would get it. But he didn't. It rang again, and then again. Damn. She would leave it. They'd go away, whoever they were. Why wouldn't Jarvis answer? Then she remembered: Jarvis was on holiday. It was his annual week, he had gone to stay with his mother in Frinton. One more peal and then hopefully whoever it was would go. One more peal came. And then another.

Cassia sighed, got up, went across the hall, opened the door. Harry Moreton stood there, wearing only a white shirt and cream linen trousers, with tall brown leather boots. His dark hair was more ruffled than she had ever seen it. He had a leather helmet under his arms, and some goggles swung from his wrist. He was smiling; he looked quite extraordinarily happy.

'Hallo, Cassia.'

'Oh, hallo.'

'I took a leaf out of your book, came on a bike. Well, not exactly a bike, a motorbike. Look, there she is. I just bought her. Isn't she gorgeous?'

She looked. The motorbike stood against the railings, not terribly big, but gleaming and impressive. 'Yes. Very gorgeous.'

'I'll take you for a ride later. If you like. Can I come in?'

'Well, I'm awfully—' Tired, she had been about to say, make an excuse, tell him to go away again, but then she thought how mean she always was to him, how pinched and miserable she must seem to him, and made a huge effort. 'Yes. Please do. I'm afraid everyone's out.'

'How very compromising for you.' God, she hated his voice, that awful Etonian drawl.

'Oh, I don't know.' She managed to smile at him. 'You said yourself we were practically related, that last time we met.'

'Did I? Oh, yes. Well, anyway, I wanted to tell you something. Two things, actually. I have a present for you. From Leonora. I just went to see her in Paris.'

'Oh, Harry, I wish I'd known. How is she? Is she well? And I've got a book I know she'd love, I was going to send it, and— Oh, God, I'd love to see her, I miss her so much.'

'Yes, I expect you do,' he said, just slightly impatient. 'She's fine. She said to tell you to go and visit her. And then I have some news.'

'Yes?'

'I got a First,' he said. 'I just heard.'

She was about to say something flippant, thinking how typical, how arrogant of him to come and tell her *that*, of all things, when she looked at him, at his eyes, searching hers, at his face, oddly uncertain. She realised it wasn't really arrogant at all, rather the reverse, quite engaging really, that he felt it worth coming personally especially to tell her; and thinking too that he had no one else to tell, no parents, no brothers or sisters, Benedict and Cecily were away in France, she really was the only person he could tell, who was in any way connected to him. She said, with genuine warmth, 'Harry, that's marvellous. Really marvellous. Well done. You must be very pleased.'

'Well, you know. Pretty pleased, yes. I hate to admit it, but I did work quite hard in the end. After all that messing about, you know.'

'Yes,' she said, 'I do know.' His Oxford career had started two years late, after him suddenly declaring, a week before he was due to go up, a desire to spend more time travelling, to see the world. He wanted to go to India and South America, of which he had only got a tantalising glimpse. There had been, not surprisingly, a most enormous row about it, threats that he would lose his place, intervention from the highest authority. Two things had finally saved him: his considerable size and (linked to this) his prowess on the river at Eton, which had clearly marked him out as a potential blue.

'Even my tutor seemed a bit surprised,' he said, and grinned again.

'I expect he did,' she said, and grinned back. 'Look, this is worth a drink. Jarvis is away, but I'll go and fetch some champagne from the cellar.'

'No, I'll go,' he said. 'I know where it is. If you're sure that's all right. I mean, you're not too tired.'

'No. No, really. I'm not.'

He returned with a bottle of Krug and two champagne glasses; opened it with a great flourish, poured her a glass.

'Here's to you,' she said.

'And to you. To success.'

'Success.'

That reminded her rather sharply of Edward, who was not a success, who had passed his exams so conspicuously badly (having needed to pass them so well and so much more than Harry did), thought how much this would anger him, be seen as yet another example of injustice, the towering injustice of the rich and privileged. She sighed.

Harry looked at her. 'You do look all in,' he said, 'really rotten, in fact.'

'Thank you,' she said, the old tartness in her voice, wishing suddenly and rather surprisingly she had something just slightly more attractive on than a washed-out cotton dress, aware that her legs and feet were bare, that she had no make-up on, that her hair needed cutting.

'Now don't get defensive,' he said. 'I suppose you've been overdoing it, working too hard?'

'Yes, I suppose I have. Well, not too hard, but very hard.'

'And what thrilling things have you been doing today? Who have you been snatching from the jaws of death?'

'No one,' she said, 'no one at all,' and thought of the little baby, lying very much in the jaws of death. It was a most apt description, and her eyes filled with sudden, hot tears.

She fumbled for a handkerchief, blew her nose, not looking at him, thinking how stupid he would think her, how she was going to look plainer than ever, but, 'Cassia,' he said, and his voice was very gentle, gentler than she had ever heard it, 'Cassia, what is it? What's wrong, what happened?'

'Oh,' she said, 'a baby died today. A newborn baby. It was born dead, you know, and the midwife gave it to me and told me to take it to the sluice, the sluice of all places, as if it was a – well, as if it was waste. And I—'

'Cassia,' he said, and she looked up and he was looking at her with the most extraordinary expression on his face: concern, and horror and a sort of wonder. 'Cassia, do you mean to tell me you have to do such things? That you're actually there, with women giving birth, that you have to handle a dead child?'

'Yes, of course I do,' she said, half amused by his naivety about what she did. 'How else would we learn, what else would we do?'

'I don't know,' he said, still looking very shocked. 'I suppose I thought you'd just learn about it. Not have to do it, be confronted by it. It can't be right, someone like you. How old are you? Just twenty-one. It's appalling.'

'Harry, the mother of this baby was fifteen. Now that really is appalling. No, we do all that: deliver babies, observe operations, dress hideous wounds …'

'How brave you are,' he said, still in the same gentle voice, 'how very brave.'

'But I'm not,' she said, 'not brave at all. I wasn't very brave today, but it was my first, you see, my first death, and – oh, dear. I'm sorry, Harry.'

She sat down on the sofa, sobbing helplessly; he'd probably leave in a minute, he'd be horribly embarrassed, and she was being such a total idiot, but: 'Come here,' he said, and sat down beside her and opened his arms. Too distressed, too exhausted even to think about it, she did what she most wanted at that moment and moved into them.

His white shirt was very crisp cotton and she could feel her tears soaking it, turning it limp; he smelt slightly of sweat, but it was fresh sweat, and of the Turkish cigarettes he smoked. It was a surprisingly agreeable mixture; it was a surprisingly agreeable place to be. Slowly the tears ceased.

'Here.' He fumbled in his pocket for his handkerchief, dried her eyes, smiled down at her. 'That's better.'

187

'I must look awful,' she said, sitting back from him, sniffing, rubbing her hand across her nose.

'Cassia, you look perfectly ... all right. But I do draw the line at sniffing. It's disgusting.'

'Oh, sorry.' She blew her nose on his handkerchief, managed to smile at him. 'That was a bit more like you.'

'What do you mean? Like me?'

'Well, critical.'

'Oh. What else is like me?' He was smiling at her.

'I don't want to say now. Not when you're being so nice.'

'Aren't I always nice?' he said, handing her her glass of champagne. 'Here, finish this, it'll do you good.'

'Thank you. And no,' she said, smiling again, 'you're not always nice.'

'Since this conversation seems to be cheering you up, shall I tell you what you're like?'

'Yes,' she said, quite distracted by this thought, 'I'd like very much to know what I'm like. How I seem to you.'

'Fierce,' he said. 'Very fierce. And cross, quite a lot of the time.'

'Cross! That's not fair. Most people say I'm very good tempered.'

'Well, most people must be luckier than me. That's what I see. Self-opinionated. Tough. Awkward. Defensive. And incredibly sexy.'

'Thanks a—' she started, and then thought she must have misheard the last. 'What did you say then?'

'God, Cassia, perhaps you should get that hospital of yours to test your hearing. I said you were self-opinionated and tough and awkward and defensive and incredibly sexy.'

'Oh,' she said. 'Oh, yes, I see.' She sat back and looked at him. She felt very odd: confused, shocked, absolutely vulnerable, and—

'You're blushing,' he said gently, and reached out and wiped a last tear away with his finger; then put the finger in his mouth and licked it.

She went on staring at him, and although he was not even touching her, not even sitting close to her, she felt a stabbing deep within her, a harsh, strong movement that she knew was desire. A desire stronger, more powerful, more invading than anything she had ever felt before. He didn't move; just studied her, his eyes moving over her, very slowly, her hair, her eyes, her mouth, then down, down to her breasts.

And then he moved near her; and without touching her began to kiss her, very tenderly at first, his mouth, his tongue, exploring her upper lip, then within her mouth, very slow, very careful, and as it moved, the desire moved too, travelled deep within her, great sprawling tendrils of it, reaching, probing at her, and she moved with it, shifted, became closer to him. He pulled back then and smiled, just briefly, and then put his hands on her shoulders and began to smooth, to stroke them, and then, gradually, moved to her breasts, and all the time working at her mouth with his, and as his hands began to fold round her breasts, to hold them, his thumbs outlining her nipples through her thin dress, she couldn't help it, she moaned, aloud, pushed her own tongue under his and she could feel his response to that moan. He smiled, she could feel the smile, and she smiled herself in return, and he unbuttoned her dress then, and bent to kiss her breasts, licking the nipples, his tongue slow, terribly slow and lingering.

She looked down at his head and tried to think that this was Harry, her enemy, Harry whom she had hated since she had been a child, Harry who was everything she disliked, and tried to think of Edward, Edward whom she was supposed to love, and more than anything in the world she wanted to be in bed with Harry, with him naked beside her and around her and inside her, and then she thought, with one last despairing and detached look at him and at herself, that she could not, must not do this thing and then somehow, just in time, she sat back and held Harry's face in her hands and told him he must go away.

It took a long time to persuade him. He said, first amused and indignant, then disbelieving, then hurt, then finally angry, that he could not, would not go, that there was no reason for it, then again, finally, that she was a foolish, prudish virgin. She clung with something approaching terror to her decision, came close to giving in to him, to her own desire for him, several times, felt literally sick with distress, with misery; only that last, furious insult saved her, made her angry, convinced her she was doing the right thing.

'How dare you,' she said, dashing away the tears that had begun again in this extraordinary, complex amalgam of passions, 'how dare you say that to me, when—'

'Well, is it not true?'

'No,' she cried, and that was her great, her terrible mistake, 'no, it is not true.'

There was a very long, still silence. He was across the room from her now, white faced, exhausted himself. It was beginning to grow dusk, and, confused, she thought that she must turn on some lights. As if it mattered.

'Ah,' he said, 'so there we have it. The doctor, I presume. The whey-faced medic. Well, I doubt he is very skilful. Whether you have experienced much pleasure at his hands. No wonder you don't wish to—'

Rage swept over her then: rage and outrage. 'You are disgusting,' she said, 'to talk like that, of such things.'

'Such things!' he said. 'What an expression. You sound like your own mother. Such things! How ladylike, how unlusty. Fucking, that's what I'm talking about, Cassia, fucking. You do know that word, do you? Fucking, fucking, fucking. You fucking the doctor. How very uncarnal that must be. Do you lie there, under him, as he plunges up and down, do you lie there, waiting for it to end, thinking of England? I would have given you other things to think of, Cassia, I do assure you. But I dare say—'

'Harry!' she shouted, and it was almost a scream now, the tears pouring down her face, her breath coming in hard, struggling bursts, like a labouring woman, sweat breaking out not just on her forehead but in her armpits, her back. 'You are disgusting. Totally digusting. Get out. Get out of this house. And never, ever come near me again.'

'I won't,' he said, turning to the door. 'You can be sure of that.'

But he did: the night before she left for Leeds, for her wedding. He appeared, pale, grim, at the door, asked if he might see her just for five minutes. She said he might, and led him into the drawing room. He was clearly going somewhere, to some social function, was wearing tails – she remembered, abruptly and irrelevantly, Rupert's comment that Harry always looked dressed more for a part on stage than real life – but he had lost weight, seemed somehow hollow, slightly less substantial. He did not even sit down, merely looked at her and said, 'I told myself I wouldn't, couldn't come, but I had to. I can't believe you're doing this, Cassia. It's not too late, don't, please don't. I—'

She looked at him, and knew she must stop him saying whatever it was, fearing, knowing, she would hear the one thing she could not bear. 'Harry,' she said, 'I have to. I have to do it. I am—'

'Yes?' he said 'You are what?'

'I am pregnant.'

There was a silence. He stood there, studying her, his eyes moving over her, lingering first on her breasts, then her stomach, staying there for a long time, then moving up again to her face, to her eyes.

'Is that all?' he said. 'Is that the only reason?'

'No,' she said, quickly, too quickly, 'not the only reason, but—'

'Do you love him?' he said. 'Because that's the only reason. The only real reason. If you tell me you love him, I shall leave you alone. Now and for ever.'

'I ...' There was an endless pause while he stood there, his eyes probing hers, seeming to break into her, and somehow she said, and it was as if she was saying the words against a great physical force, 'I do … love … him.'

'Good,' he said quite briskly and matter-of-factly, and turned on his heel and walked out of the door and her life. For several years.

CHAPTER II

The eyes boring into Edwina's were cold, disapproving, filled with something close to dislike. She met them for as long as she could, then looked down nervously at her hands, thinking irrelevantly that the new darker red that Babette had suggested last time she had had her nails done really had been a very good idea, much smarter than the scarlet, made her hands look whiter, and then said, 'I'm sorry. Really. I've just been rather busy lately.'

'Mrs Moreton, we're all busy. I understood when you took this work that you weren't busy enough, that you were looking for something useful to do.'

'Yes, I know. I mean I am.'

'And now here we are, almost into April, and you tell me you haven't sent the letters out yet to the regional organisers. It's very disappointing.'

'I can see that. But I've almost finished writing them, I can get them out in a couple of days. Is that soon enough?'

'It will have to be. I think perhaps you need someone to help you. I'll ring Jennifer Barling, see if there's something she can do. Dear, oh dear. This is very serious.' Her voice was genuinely angry.

Edwina felt a stab of panic. This was worse than if she'd never started. She could see that. Certainly worse, from the point of view of helping her father with Sir Simeon. Damn. But it really was so tedious, and they were all so awful, the old bats, and writing a hundred letters did take an awfully long time, and—

Mary Whittaker was talking again. 'In fact,' she said, her nose seeming to grow longer by the minute, 'I think perhaps I should ask Jennifer to take over from you altogether. If she has the time. She's very good at making it, when it matters. We simply cannot afford to have people not pulling their weight.'

The panic grew; if news of this got back to her mother, she really would fly off the handle. 'Oh, no,' she said, quickly, 'I promise I want to do it, want to help. It's just that this isn't quite my thing. Not really.'

'I can see that, Mrs Moreton.'

And then out of the ether, inspiration came: blinding, brilliant. 'Lady Whittaker, there was something else I did want to talk to you about.'

'Yes?' The voice was brusque, impatient.

'You see, I was thinking there was something I could do, something much more ... me, if you like.'

Mary Whittaker's expression implied that anything that was more Edwina was highly unfortunate.

'I thought I could put on a fashion show for you. I mean, for the hospital. A charity one, you know? I have a lot of contacts in the fashion business, a great chum works on *Vogue*, and masses of my friends would model, I do know that. We could put it on in one of the big hotels, the Dorchester would be terrific, that new ballroom where the ice-rink used to be, and it would raise a lot of money. Another friend, Venetia Hardwicke, I expect you know her—' Mary Whittaker shook her head coldly. 'Well, she did one for St Thomas's, and it was a huge success. I'm really, really sorry about the flag day, Lady Whittaker, and I will see it through, but it's just all so strange to me, outside my orbit. Whereas the fashion show ...'

Mary Whittaker looked at her, then she said, with extreme reluctance, 'I did hear that the fashion show for St Thomas's raised a lot of money. We did discuss it, as a matter of fact, the possibility of having one for St Christopher's, but we have no one on the committee with the necessary knowledge.'

That was painfully obvious, Edwina thought. She smiled encouragingly at Mary Whittaker. 'Well, now you do. And I really would throw my heart into this one, Lady Whittaker. Give it my all. I swear.'

'I shall have to put it to the committee, of course. And naturally the flag day would have to be your prime concern for now. But it does have a certain attraction as an idea, I must admit. When would you see it happening?'

'Oh, not till the autumn. They're quite complicated to organise, Venetia says. Early autumn would be perfect, and then we could have all the divine new clothes. I do always prefer winter clothes, don't you? So much more ...' She paused; she could see this was not a line of conversation Mary Whittaker would be interested in pursuing.

'Well, as I say, I shall speak to the committee and come back to you. Meanwhile, will you *please* get on with those letters.'

'Yes, Lady Whittaker. Of course.'

She drove home still shaking slightly. Stupid old bat. Still, she had been naughty. She'd only written about ten of the beastly letters; she really must get on with them now. But first ...

'Venetia? It's Edwina Moreton. Darling, are you free for lunch today or tomorrow? Tomorrow? Good. Would you like to come over here? I need to pick your brains very, very hard. About one, then? Marvellous. I'm terribly grateful.'

Cassia had woken up that same morning feeling rather cheerful. Things seemed to be settling down. Her clinics were going well; the children were happy; Janet continued to be a joy, and even Edward had admitted, grudgingly, that she was very good with the children. Best of all, his attitude towards Cassia had suddenly eased. He had been more friendly, less critical, had made no reference to the money or to any change in her for some time; had even talked to her a little about her work, and in fact last night, for the first time since Christmas, he had made love to her.

She had lain there in the darkness, expecting the usual brief, scarcely warm kiss, and his hand had come out for hers, and then he had moved towards her and said, 'Cassia?' in the particular tone of voice he used when he wanted her. She had said, scarcely daring to hope even, 'Yes, Edward?'

'Oh Cassia,' he had said, and leant over and kissed her. And then started stroking her breasts, and kissing her mouth, and her body had gratefully, joyfully, gone to meet him. He had been particularly careful, especially considerate; she was almost more surprised by that than anything, care and consideration for her having been the last things he had shown lately.

It hadn't been a total success; she hadn't quite managed to come, but it had been very lovely, to be wanted, to be with him again; and afterwards she lay in his arms quietly as he drifted rather noisily off to sleep, and lay thinking about herself and their marriage, wondering why she was so pathetically grateful for his changed attitude towards her, for his seeming to want her again.

Guilt, she supposed; she could see, if she was really honest, that she had been less than tactful, less than careful, had flung the money in his face. It must have been horribly difficult for him, very hurtful. It was just that – Cassia hastily crushed the rather complex rationale of what it just was, and started to drift off to sleep, thinking that perhaps, after all, their marriage might be restored, in time, to its former self. Whatever that might be: good, she told herself firmly, turning over, settling against Edward's back, very good.

★

It was early when she woke. She got up quietly, and lay in the bath for a while, smiling out of the window, at the bright day, the scudding clouds. It would be so nice to be living with a friend again, rather than a cold, hard enemy.

She heard the children getting up, heard Janet talking to them, getting them dressed. God, it was wonderful to have her. She got dressed, ran downstairs singing.

The postman had just arrived. There were several letters for Edward, which was quite usual, as he got a lot of mail from official bodies, representatives of the pharmaceutical companies – although three of these were handwritten – and two letters for her: one typed with an SW3 postmark, one in Rupert's florid hand. She started to open Rupert's then found her knees being tackled in a bear hug.

'Mummy, guess who?'

'I can't. Delia.'

'No.'

'Bertie?'

'No.'

'Um … not William!'

'Yes.' He laughed she looked down at him, thought how much she loved him. He was much more of a Berridge than a Fallon, blond, blue eyed, less gangly than Bertie. 'Mummy, when can I go to Bertie's school? I hate that silly village one.'

'Not till you're five. Or four and a half.'

'I'm nearly four.'

'I know you are. But that's not—'

'Bertie says his school is really excellent.'

'Does he now?'

'Yes, and they play football. I wish I could play football.'

She was silent for a moment, a shadow over her happy morning. Bertie only had one more year at the school in Haywards Heath, then he would be off to prep school. Off, on his own, into the world, no longer hers. And he was looking forward to it: that was the worst thing. He had no idea what horrors lay within it; and she knew they did – the homesickness, the tears, the bullying, the loneliness. No one escaped. Not entirely. She had tried, tried again and again, to dissuade Edward from this seemingly extraordinary determination: all in vain.

'Of course he must go,' he said, telling her yet again that it hadn't done him any harm, and had been to see the school, taken Bertie with them, watched his face: excited in the playing fields and the gym; doubtful in the classrooms, and occasionally scared, such as in the

195

dormitory, the big communal bathroom, the lavatories without doors. He had shaken hands with the headmaster, who said how much he would look forward to 'having you with us, Fallon. Make a young man of you, eh?'

Horrible, hideous. Her baby, being made a young man. She couldn't even smile at the head before getting into the car.

'Come on, William,' she said now, 'you're learning lots of useful things at Mrs Rigby's school, and if you want to get into St John's then you'll need to learn still more.'

Nanny came down the stairs smiling, with an also smiling Delia, and Bertie slid down the banisters, hugged her.

Edward appeared, looking flustered. 'It's late. Any post? Ah, yes. Thank you. Good morning, children.' He didn't look at the letters, she noticed, just stuffed them into his jacket pocket; that was odd.

They went in to breakfast.

The letter from SW3 was from the estate agents near Harrods. Several particulars of houses fell out, including those of her house, as she thought of it, in Walton Street, and a note from the earnest young man.

'Dear Mrs Fallon,' it said, 'With reference to your enquiry about the house in Walton Street, this is still available and we are now able to offer it for a longer let than six months; I wonder if this might be of interest. I also enclose details of several other properties. I remain at your service, for D. S. Pritchard, E. Throgmore.'

Nice Mr Throgmore, she thought, remembering his earnest face, his intently pleasant manner; he deserved to do well. She didn't think, however, that Edward would appreciate Mr Throgmore or her enquiries, and placed the letter in her bag, which was hanging on the back of her chair.

The second letter, from Rupert, was more interesting. 'Darling,' it said, 'Only just a silly thought, but if you still fancy joining the angels, I have a tiny project. Give me a ring if you want to talk. Best love, Rupert.'

Angels, what was he talking about? Then she remembered: the people who invested in plays. Well, she would certainly talk to him about it. The money sat there, in various banks and insurance companies, growing bigger all the time, overwhelming almost, waiting for her to use it, use it properly. It might as well do something useful. If it sounded like a good idea, obviously. She would have to ask Benedict.

She looked across at Edward. He was reading his letters now, rather intently, frowning. She thought of asking him what they were, then thought he might ask her about hers, and that wouldn't do.

'Goodness,' she said, suddenly, looking at her watch. 'Nearly half past eight. Janet, I'll take the boys. You might take Delia down to feed the ducks.'

'Yes, of course, Mrs Fallon. What a nice idea.'

They drove into Haywards Heath quite fast. It was such a lovely day that she agreed to the boys' request to have the roof down. As they left the village, she saw Mrs Venables coming out of her rather ugly house, and they all waved. Mrs Venables smiled stiffly back at them, then turned and said something to her husband. Cassia could imagine what it was.

When she finally got home it was after ten: Edward was not in the surgery, his car was gone.

'Peggy, what's happened? Where's Mr Fallon?'

'It was Mrs Clark. Her husband phoned in a panic, just after you left. She's gone into labour early. Doesn't look too good. Sent the patients home, the doctor has.'

'Oh dear, poor Mrs Clark. Well, I'll be in the dining room. I've got lots of letters to write.'

She went into the dining room, sat down at the table, and then caught sight of Edward's letters, put by Peggy on the sideboard. She was curious about them: there had been something about his face, the intensity with which he had been reading them, which had bothered her. She resisted the temptation for about ten minutes, then went over and picked one up.

It was in a neat hand, the postmark Brixton. Brixton! Maybe it had been for her, this one, from one of her patients or something; making that her rationale, she picked it up, turned it over and with slightly shaking fingers, pulled it out ...

'Dear Dr Fallon,' it said, 'With reference to your advertisement for an assistant ...'

It was a long hour and a half before Edward came back. He came into the hall and called her name. She went out to see him. He looked drawn, but rather pleased with himself.

'Hallo, Edward. How was Mrs Clark?'

'Oh, fine. Baby's fine too. A month early, but perfectly all right. Five pounds, doesn't even need to go to hospital. Now, I wonder what to do about surgery. I had to cancel it, you know ... Silly situation, isn't it? Not having any kind of back-up.'

'Yes, Edward, very silly. Is that why you're advertising for an assistant?'

197

He flushed: a deep, dark red. 'What? How do you know about that? Have you been—'

'Reading your letters? Yes, I have. I'm sorry. A bit underhand, I know, but they were lying there on the sideboard. Not as underhand, though, I'd say, as your doing this behind my back.'

'Don't be so ridiculous.' His voice was louder than usual. 'It was not behind your back. It has nothing to do with you.'

'Nothing to do with me!' She heard the anger throb in her own voice, low, almost frightening. 'Edward, how can you say such a thing? Your practice, in this house ...'

He looked at her, awkward now. 'Well, of course I was going to talk to you about it. Lots of times. But you're always so busy.'

'Busy! For God's sake. When I sit in that damn room every night, after supper, trying to resist the temptation to do my own work, so that I'm available for you—'

He did look shamefaced briefly, then said, 'Very good of you.'

'Edward, spare me that, please. Why the hell didn't you talk to me about this? How do you think it makes me feel, knowing you were planning this, had already gone to these lengths to get an assistant when—'

'I'm sorry,' he said. 'I can see I should have talked to you, but I don't know why you're quite so upset. What difference is it going to make to you?'

'What difference!' Her voice rose now, more angry. 'What difference, when you know I'd give my soul to do that job myself? You know that, Edward, we used to talk about it. One day, you said, one day ...'

He looked at her awkwardly. 'Did I? I really don't remember. And it hardly seems practical, Cassia, does it? Besides, I thought general practice was something you regarded as very second rate. I thought you would only settle for surgery—'

'Ah, yes, but I seem to remember giving that up, for some reason – what was it now? Oh, yes, to get married.'

He brushed that aside. 'And then you have the children, your own work—'

'As if I wouldn't give that up, my two pathetic birth control clinics, to work here with you. I'm little better than a glorified nurse. Why didn't you ask me, Edward, why didn't you talk to me about it?'

'I was going to,' he said, looking more awkward still, 'I really did intend to tell you what I had decided.'

'Oh, I see. Not even a discussion. Just a decision.'

'You've done a few things without discussion,' he said, 'over the past six months.'

'That's not fair.'

'It's perfectly fair. The nanny, your car—'

'Those are hardly comparable.'

'The Chair ...'

'Ah,' she said, 'now we come to it. I'd forgotten that. The Chair. That really hurt, didn't it, Edward? Really, really hurt.'

'It made me angry,' he said. 'I wouldn't say it hurt. Exactly.'

'Well, this has made me angry. Very, very angry. Are they any good?'

'What?'

'The applicants. Are they any good?'

'I haven't had time to study them yet. You can help me make that judgement if you like. Having read the letters.'

She ignored that. 'Well, I'm very glad the practice can support an assistant. What will you have to pay him, five hundred a year?'

'About that. But – well, with your money, certain worries have ... eased, haven't they? Like Bertie's school fees, the work on the house, the new surgery.'

'So I am to subsidise this appointment.'

His face turned very white. 'That was a foul thing to say,' he said.

She flushed, horrified, amazed at herself that she could have said such a thing. 'I'm sorry. It's none the less true. It would have made it all the more reasonable for you to have discussed it with me, don't you think?'

'Not really. No.'

She felt sharply, horribly guilty; tried to lighten the mood, be more conciliatory. 'Let me ask you something, Edward. Now that you know how I feel, would you not consider taking me on as your assistant? Or at least—' she managed a smile now – 'at least giving me an interview?'

Another long silence, then he said, 'No, I'm sorry. I don't think it would work. Not in the village, not here.'

'Why not in the village, for God's sake? Where better, where everyone knows me? I could take on the women, maybe, and the children's clinic—'

'Oh no,' he said sharply, 'that would never do, not taking things on, taking them over—' and stopped, realising he had made another mistake.

'God, you're pathetic,' she said. 'You can't bear to lose the tiniest little bit of your position here, can you? The doctor, the wonderful, all-powerful doctor, whom the whole village doffs its cap to, that's what it's really about, isn't it? You want a new, lowly assistant, who can be seen as such, stamped as such, not any kind of an equal.'

She stopped again, thinking, thinking over the past few weeks, understanding them suddenly: his anxiety to be more friendly, not to complain about her own work, not to make any reference to the money, to appear more loving, more—and then remembered the previous night, the sudden desire to make love to her after so long a time.

'Dear God,' she said, 'you've even dragged our sex life into this, haven't you?'

'Be quiet,' he said. 'Peggy might hear—'

'I don't care who hears. Is that why you fucked me last night, Edward? It was, wasn't it? To please me, make me happy, feel better towards you, so that you could broach the subject of this – this ... Oh, you're disgusting. Horrible. I don't want to talk to you about it any more. Or indeed anything else.'

She walked out of the door and slammed it, went out into the drive, and got into her car. As she drove viciously out of the gate, she looked back and saw him, still standing there in the dining-room window, staring blankly in front of him.

'I think it's monstrous,' said Rupert, handing her a handkerchief. They were sitting in the kitchen of his small house in Brighton, drinking coffee. 'You've been so loyal, so good—'

'Not in the past year I haven't,' she said, sniffing, smiling at him tearily.

'Oh really? Have you been taking lovers or something?'

'No, of course not, but I haven't been very tactful. About the money, you know? A bit wilful. You know what I'm like.'

'I'd begun to forget,' he said, and smiled at her. 'It's been rather nice to see it again. Anyway, it's hardly comparable, buying a car, taking on a nanny. Hardly big spending. Well, what can I do?'

'You can't do anything. I just wanted to tell you. Like I always do. You know. See what you thought.'

'Oh, poppet. I'm sorry.' He reached out, stroked her cheek. 'We're not a very nice species, I'm afraid, we men.'

'Rupert, you are a wonderful example of your species. What are you talking about?'

He sighed. 'I've been making a bit of a fool of myself recently.'

'Oh, Rupert. Who with this time?'

'Pretty little thing called Amanda who was in this play I've just done which has closed so quickly. I thought she liked me and – well, she was found in the arms, or rather on the casting couch in the director's office.'

'Oh dear,' she said, shaking her head, 'will you never learn?'

'Probably not. Anyway, it was fun while it lasted. Now how can we distract you? Can I take you for a walk, to the pictures?'

'I know what you can do,' she said slowly. 'You can tell me about this show that you want angels for. I've only just remembered, your letter came this morning. Only Edward's came in the same post. That would distract me.'

'Oh, darling, I couldn't bother you with that now.'

'Of course you could. Nothing could be nicer than to think about something that had nothing to do with medicine or birth control or legacies even. Go on.'

'Well, it has a bit to do with legacies. I suppose ...!'

A friend in the business had approached him. 'It was that miracle I was talking to you about. A producer actually wants to put on a show that would suit me. Very low-key, not Shakespeare or Gershwin. Or one of these ghastly comedies I seem to be saddled with. Just a very simple thing, a play by some young chap, consisting entirely of letters between two old people, well, old by the end of the play. The letters are found by a granddaughter when one of them dies, tracing a love story over fifty years, of meetings and partings, the war comes into it, of course, and the Depression, all the things that will touch people's hearts. They sit on either side of the stage, reading them to one another; very simple. Very cheap to produce.' He smiled at her rather nervously. 'How does it sound to you? So far?'

'It sounds wonderful. I haven't been to the theatre in London for years, but I hear a bit from Edwina and Cecily, and it just seems to be one huge musical. Some people must want a change occasionally. Something simpler. I know I would.'

'I think so. So does my producer. And there doesn't always have to be a cast of thousands – there are only four people in *Private Lives*, after all. And we have a director who's dying to get to grips with it.'

'And your co-star?'

'Haven't thought of anyone yet. It shouldn't be too difficult, though, because although we want a name, we don't want a star. She'd eclipse me for a start.'

'No one could eclipse you, Rupert.'

'Oh, my darling, just keep saying that. Not true though, I'm afraid. Anyway, neither should she be too young. And there are an awful lot of wonderful middle-aged actresses – by which I mean perhaps in their late thirties – who have never quite made it, but have all the necessary experience. And modest names.'

'Where would it be? Drury Lane?'

'That's the first time I've seen you really smile all day. Either Drury Lane or, if we thought we couldn't *quite* fill it, there's a charming little theatre in Victoria, called the Second House – get it? – near the river, earning quite a nice intellectual reputation at the moment, and we could get that.'

'And how much would be required from the heavenly host, Rupert?' she said.

'Well, we already have a couple of other interested backers, each prepared to put in— oh dear, it sounds rather a lot.'

'Rupert, at this moment I would empty my bank account for you.'

'Don't say that sort of thing, darling. Anyway, each putting in ten thousand. Of course, there's other money available: my producer's company has access to some funds, and—'

'Rupert, you can have ten thousand. Of course you can. When do you want it?'

She drove home, feeling initially better, then gradually, as she drew nearer to Monks Heath, worse again, her mood darkening with the day. She parked her car about a mile from the house, wondering how she could face them, all of them: Edward's mood, whatever it might be; face family supper; face Janet's cheerful interest, then realised she had never told her she was going out. 'Oh dear,' she said simply, resting her head against the window of her car, and burst into tears again.

After a bit she stopped, rummaged in her handbag for the sodden handkerchief Rupert had told her to keep. A letter came out with it. Her letter, received that morning, this morning all those years ago, from the estate agent. She sat there, staring at it through blurred eyes, first distractedly, then slowly focusing on it, remembering it, that dear little house, so pretty, seemingly so happy, and remembering too, suddenly, dangerously, Harry's voice that evening in the Savoy, saying, 'You should get yourself a little house in town.' The evening he had said he didn't understand her marriage. She didn't understand it either, not any more.

For just a moment it became reality. She could, she thought sitting there, her head singing with the possibility and the power; she could get herself that little house, and stay in it – just very occasionally, of course – after her clinics, as Harry had said. Be herself again, clear thinking, hopeful, clever; away – just very, very occasionally – from Edward and this new, wretched situation. If she wanted that, she could have it; no one could stop her. She had only to write the cheque. No permission need be sought, no enquiries made, no discussion held. She could take possession of the house now, today, or almost today; put and keep part of her life in it, a life that was all her own. She could. It was very, very simple. And, of course, she thought, real life reasserting itself uncompromisingly, absolutely out of the question.

Cassia arrived back at Monks Ridge just after six. The children greeted her noisily; Janet smiled just a little too brightly; Edward said hallo awkwardly, almost warmly. She realised they must have been worried, realised, too, what an alarming sight she must be, tear stained, swollen eyed. She didn't care.

She went into the kitchen, sat down at the table. Peggy made her a cup of tea and William climbed on to her lap. Bertie still wasn't back from his party. Edward sat down opposite her, asked Peggy to answer the phone, which was ringing, to say he would call back unless it was an emergency. Janet tactfully withdrew, taking a plaintive William with her.

'We were worried about you,' Edward said.

'Well, I'm very sorry about that,' she said briskly.

'Are you all right?'

'I'm absolutely fine. What about you?'

'Fine, yes. Er, about this assistant business ...'

'Yes?' She thought for a moment he was going to say he had changed his mind, he would like her to work with him; if he had, she would have forgiven him everything, even then.

'I really do need someone,' he said. 'I'm sorry if it's upset you, if I was tactless. But someone really full time, absolutely committed, that's the point. That's why it couldn't have worked out with you. You do understand, don't you?'

'Yes, of course.'

He seemed relieved that she wasn't fighting it any more. 'Good, marvellous. I'm so glad you don't feel too bad about it after all,' he said, and then all in a rush, 'By the way, the best candidate so far seems to be a woman. Which would be ideal, in lots of ways, I think. Don't you?'

'Oh, yes,' she said, 'absolutely ideal.'

She went up to bed quite soon after that, and pretended to be asleep when Edward came up half an hour later.

However, she was still awake when the grandfather clock in the hall struck three and then four, wondering how she could bear it, and deciding, as dawn finally broke, what she was going to do.

'Cassia's taking a house in London,' said Edwina. 'What do you think about that?'

'Is she?' said Harry. His voice was light, but there was an underlying note of self-satisfaction in it. 'Well, I suggested that to her. The other night.'

'Really? It seems rather odd to me. I mean I'm delighted, of course, but I can't think what she's going to do with it.'

'Live in it perhaps? That's what people usually do with houses.'

'Oh Harry, don't be tiresome. You know perfectly well what I mean. What do you think Edward will have to say about it?'

'I have absolutely no idea. Whatever it is, I am sure it will scarcely bear listening to. He is the epitome of dullness.'

'Yes, he is. Harry, could you do this up for me? The clasp is so stiff.' She held out a marcasite bracelet to Harry. He fixed it on to her wrist and then kissed her hand casually, his eyes moving over her. 'You look very nice,' he said.

He didn't often compliment her; his praise was hard earned, and when it did come, it was always minimal. It had disconcerted her in the early stages of their relationship, accustomed as she was to the extravagant language of the social set in which she moved, but she had come to appreciate it. If Harry said she looked nice, she knew she looked extremely chic; if he said a hat or even a dress did not really suit her, she would more often than not discard it. His taste was impeccable and for the most part coincided exactly with her own. She looked at herself in the mirror now in her black beaded dinner dress, diamanté clips in her dark hair, the twin bracelets on her slender wrists, and she could see she did indeed look very nice. As Harry did; as he always did.

Harry's looks and style were important to Edwina, a large factor in their relationship. She found it incomprehensible how some women seemed not to care in the least what their husbands looked like. She played no part in the selection of Harry's clothes, and he would not have wished her to; he and his valet, and his tailor and shirtmaker and shoemaker, saw to it all, and he spent an interesting amount of time with them.

It intrigued many of Edwina's friends that Harry Moreton should be unarguably a dandy. His courage on horseback and in the hunting field, his recklessness on the racetrack, his astuteness in the business world, even his large, heavy frame, his rather wild good looks, did not seem to suit so urbane a quality. It seemed somehow illogical, out of order. Nevertheless, he paid his appearance an enormous amount of attention; and looking at him now, in his dinner jacket, midnight blue rather than black (a fashion instigated by the Prince of Wales a decade earlier), his lawn shirt, the front finely pleated also in the new style, the double French cuffs fastened with the heavy gold links that had belonged to his father, she smiled quite literally with satisfaction and pleasure.

They were taking a party of friends to the White City for the greyhound racing, a form of sport spectatorship Edwina always enjoyed. Horse racing was often cold and wet, and the car track noisy and alarming; enjoying an excellent meal, and fine wine, while watching, or pretending to watch, a series of extremely short races was much more pleasant.

'Well,' she said, 'it will be odd to have Cassia in London again. Not that we ever saw a great deal of her, I suppose. She was always so busy with her wretched studying. Such a waste of time.'

'Presumably she didn't see it quite like that,' said Harry drily. 'Now come along, Edwina, we are going to be late. And I want you to pay particular attention to Binkie Norton tonight and his tedious wife. I'm trying to persuade him to join one of my boards. Bloody clever, and very good connections.'

'Yes, all right,' said Edwina. She would have preferred to go on talking about Cassia and her new house for a little longer – it really did intrigue her – but Harry always avoided the subject of Cassia; the old animosity between them had continued down the years. She had never properly understood it: chemistry, she supposed.

'I'm dining with Dominic Foster tonight,' said Benedict, walking towards the door. His tone was light, casual – too casual. Cecily looked at him sharply. She was feeding Laurence in bed; Benedict had come up to say goodbye.

'Benedict …'

'Yes?' he said, and then turning, saw her face and flushed deeply. 'Cecily,' he said, 'for God's sake. Dominic Foster is married.'

'So are you,' she said briefly. He went out and slammed the door.

Cecily sat there, concentrating very hard on Laurence's little head, until he had finished; then she rang for Nanny, told her to take him and change him, and went to have her bath, concentrating on thinking about the dinner party she was giving at the weekend, wondering whether to change the menu.

She went downstairs to discuss the puddings with Cook and then into the morning room where her dressmaker was waiting with some fabrics and patterns, and was able to concentrate very hard on them. Next, she made some telephone calls asking people if they would like to make up a table at a charity ball in May, and had to concentrate very hard indeed on that, since several of them already had prior engagements –

another charity ball, the same night, someone had slipped up, thank goodness it wasn't her – and then found it was still not quite lunchtime and there was nothing left to concentrate on, and she was forced, out of sheer necessity, to think about Benedict, Benedict and the long, worrying, difficult years.

She had been very young when they had been married, not quite twenty. He had been thirty-five, getting on for twice her age, and considered a great catch: immensely rich, charming, amusing, sophisticated. He was tall and very slim, and always beautifully dressed. Cecily had fallen in love with him straight away, the very first time they had met, at a party given by one of her friends' mothers: he had paid her a great deal of attention, seemed to find her attractive and interesting; two nights later he asked her to cocktails at his sister's house – 'And then we could go out to supper, if you would like that.' She said she would like that very much.

In the event, they stayed to dine at Leonora's house. She liked Leonora very much indeed, Cecily's only problem being a certain streak of jealousy that quickly crept into her relationship with Benedict. He and Leonora were phenomenally close: met almost every day, frequently lunched together. In those days Benedict had not had a job, and 'I must talk to Leonora' was the phrase most frequently on his lips. She also couldn't help noticing that Sir Richard, Leonora's husband, was clearly rather less enamoured of Benedict, but decided that he must feel rather as Cecily did: hostile to the closeness that was almost like that of a married couple.

She was amazed when Benedict asked her to marry him. She had thought, hoped indeed, that he more than liked her, and he had kissed her a few times, told her how beautiful she was, how attractive he found her, but she had had no idea that his feelings were sufficiently strong to inspire thoughts of marriage. Nevertheless, when he had turned up at her parents' house in Sloane Street late one afternoon, bearing a box with an exquisite ring in it which had belonged to his grandmother, and told her he loved her and would be most honoured if she would consider marrying him, she did not pause for a moment, merely flung her arms round his neck and said that she didn't need to consider it, she would love to.

Her parents were delighted, particularly her mother. The wedding date was set for three months hence, and it was agreed that they should move into Benedict's house in Eaton Square, rather than finding somewhere else.

Benedict also had a magnificent house and several hundred acres in

Devon, near Dartmouth, which he was very fond of; he liked to spend the winter months there, hunting. Cecily was perfectly happy with this; her entire being was concentrated on her wedding day. The thought of doing something as grown up and difficult as finding and furnishing a house, simply because it would, under most circumstances, have been the thing to do, was extremely daunting. Benedict told her she could occupy herself looking for a different house, if she liked, after they were married. But she never even considered it, contented herself simply with redecoration and refurnishing, both of which were badly needed. Looking back, she often wondered if moving into his life, rather than establishing one that they could share, had been her most crucial mistake.

The wedding was a huge success, proclaimed one of the finest of 1923. For their honeymoon they went to Egypt, took a cruise up the Nile. It was extremely romantic, and the thing that had been worrying her considerably, sex, largely due to her mother's rather cryptic and doomy prognostications, proved to be at least not as bad as she had feared. It wasn't very good either, she had to admit; tolerable was the nearest she would have come to describing it. But her main anxiety had been that she would be hopelessly inadequate, not know what to do – which, of course, she didn't – and that Benedict would be exasperated by her. In fact Benedict, surprisingly for someone of his age, she thought, did not seem very confident in bed; indeed, on their wedding night she had the absurd thought that he was as nervous as she. But at least it had happened, she thought next day, sitting on the deck of the boat, watching the banks of the Nile, enjoying the heat on her face, the strange lovely sounds and smells; she was no longer a virgin, and everyone knew it took time to get it right.

It did take time, and after a while she became bitterly disappointed, having gathered from her more racy girlfriends that it was all the best fun, not at all the dreary business their mothers had led them to believe. She had also read in the book everyone was talking about, entitled *Married Love* by the infamous Marie Stopes, that she could expect unimaginable pleasures in the marriage bed.

She had experienced no pleasures at all, even after several months. She assumed this must be her own fault: Benedict was so much older than she was, and must after all know what he was doing. He was terribly sweet and kind, comforting her when she apologised in the early days for not being more responsive, remaining tactfully silent later when she turned from him in tears after some increasingly unrewarding episode, even when it should have surely been getting better. It was just that it was always over so quickly: she had imagined wonderfully long-drawn-out closeness, holding and kissing and caressing, before anything actually happened.

On the nights when Benedict seemed to want her, he would turn to her, almost impatient, with his thing – she hated the technical term – already hard, and it was as if he had to get it into her really quickly. And she wasn't ever ready, not really, she felt sort of dry and horrid, and he would plunge away for a bit, up and down into her, and she would try, so hard, to feel something, and there was nothing, nothing at all, certainly not the rhythms, the ebb and flow spoken of so lyrically by Dr Stopes, and then she would feel his thing shuddering into her, and he would kiss her and tell her he loved her and quite often just fall asleep and snore. She would lie there, feeling sore and miserable, and wonder what she ought to be doing to make it better – for both of them.

Worse were the nights when she really felt she might be able to feel something, a sort of softness, an urging, it was so hard to explain. She would put out her hand and feel for him, and say, 'Benedict,' hopefully.

He would either pretend to be asleep, or he would make a bit of a joke of it and say, 'Not tonight, darling, I'm a bit tired, can't keep up with my passionate young bride,' and then she would turn over and pretend to be asleep and quite often cry, very quietly, and would hear him get up and sigh and creep out of their room and go into his dressing room and not return until the morning.

And then she had become pregnant, and everything had changed. Benedict was pleased, unbelievably pleased, more even than she'd thought, and not complaining about anything, not that she had to spend most of every morning in bed because she was horribly, dreadfully sick, and was rather failing in her domestic duties, and if it wasn't for Mrs Jenkins being so superbly competent a housekeeper, she really didn't know what she would do – the larders would be empty, and the staff totally unsupervised. And he had cancelled so many social engagements without a word of reproach because she simply didn't feel up to going anywhere, and kept telling her he was only concerned that she should rest and take care of herself and consequently their baby.

He had taken a job now, at a large firm of stockbrokers. He told Cecily it was no longer acceptable for men to do nothing but nurture their own financial interests and gamble and hunt. She had seen this as a sign of his increasing sense of responsibility and was delighted. Besides, it was very nice to have the house to herself for a regular few hours each day.

Fanny was born in September, a large, healthy child, after a long tough labour which Cecily had endured with great courage. Benedict, coming in an hour or so after it was all over, kissed her tenderly and told he had never loved her more or been so proud of her. She said nervously she hoped he didn't mind the baby being a girl, and he had kissed her again and said he had always thought girls were much much nicer than boys.

She adored motherhood; took to it with ease and delight. Her relationship with Benedict had shifted from its slightly uneven nature: she no longer felt a foolish child living with a sophisticated man, but a woman, a grown-up, competent woman. She was very happy.

Shortly after that, Norman Duvant had entered her life.

He had written to her first, such a nice charming letter; she had been touched by it, had shown it to Benedict.

'Do look, Benedict, this is so sad.'

'What is it?' he said irritably. He was deep in *The Times*, hated to be interrupted.

'It's a begging letter, I suppose. From a Mr Duvant.'

'Let me see it, please. Please.' He sounded very odd, she thought, quiet, but very strained, and his voice had a tremor in it. She handed it to him, watching him as he read the letter. 'Have you had any others? From this man?'

'No.'

'Are you sure?'

'Benedict, of course I'm sure. I've never had a letter like this before, from anyone. I would have remembered if I had. It's such a sad story, his mother dying and him losing his job. There's so much of that these days. How do you think he got my name?'

'Oh, out of the society pages, I expect. These people feed off those.'

'Do they? Well, what do you want me to do about it? I mean, should I—'

'I will deal with it Cecily, and any others like it. You must inform me immediately if there are any more, do you understand?'

'Yes, Benedict, of course.'

'Or if this person tries to contact you in any way.'

'Yes, Benedict. I'm sure he won't.'

'I hope not,' he said, and stuffed the letter into his pocket and walked out of the room.

She had felt bad about poor Mr Duvant for a few days, and then forgotten about him. She had more important things to think about. Benedict was working too hard and was tired and edgy; he was also asking her to do quite a lot of business entertaining. She didn't mind in the least, in fact she enjoyed it, but it was complicated, quite a different thing altogether from normal social entertaining.

Benedict was also out a lot, often unexpectedly, returning very late, drunk and short tempered. He had also more or less stopped wanting to share her bed – this was the only thing that really worried her. Apart from anything else, she didn't want Fanny to be an only child; and besides, once or twice when he had begun to make love to her, he had failed, and retired, wretchedly ignominious, to his dressing room. She told herself it was a temporary thing and certainly didn't press him on the subject; everyone knew that made matters worse. He also seemed to be spending an inordinate amount of time with Leonora; she did ask him about that, and he told her shortly that Leonora had investment problems and he was helping her with them.

One late autumn day, soon after Fanny's first birthday, when she was having tea in the drawing room, waiting for Fanny's return from a party, Susan came in, looking slightly awkward and flushed. 'It's a gentleman, madam, says you'll know his name, wants to see you. I said you were busy, so no need if you don't want to.'

'Well, what is his name, Susan?'

'Duvant, madam, Norman Duvant.'

'No, I don't think— Oh, yes, of course. How odd.'

'He said he had something he'd like to talk to you about, madam. What shall I do?'

Cecily felt very uncertain. Benedict had been so clear that she was never to see or communicate with Norman Duvant, that she was to tell him immediately should she ever hear anything of or from him again; but then, he was busy, very busy indeed, she could hardly bother him at the office. And she had liked Mr Duvant's letter very much last time, had been rather shocked that Benedict had refused to consider helping him, when he had been in his regiment and everything; and here they all were, so happy and so fortunate, and what harm could it do just to see him and perhaps offer some advice, suggest a name perhaps that he could write to?

'Show him in, Susan. Tell him I have fifteen minutes or so. Bring another cup and a plate. And be sure to come immediately if I ring.'

She liked Mr Duvant immediately: he was polite and well spoken, surprisingly well dressed and very deferential. He was in his early thirties, she supposed, rather good-looking, with light brown hair and grey eyes. It seemed impossible to imagine he could mean anyone any harm.

'What a lovely room,' he said, looking round, after shaking her hand.

'I am most grateful to you, Mrs Harrington. You'd be surprised how few people welcome us.'

Cecily looked doubtful. 'Oh, I'm sorry, I should have explained. I am forming an association of unemployed ex-soldiers from my own regiment, which was your husband's own, of course. I don't know if he ever mentioned me ...'

'No,' she said, feeling embarrassed, upset that Benedict had not, when Norman Duvant's letter had come. It seemed to make her silence all the more callous. 'I'm sorry.'

'Well, why should he? Anyway, this association is more of a social thing than anything else. Time hangs heavy on our hands, you know, especially those of us who are young and active, and that is a bad thing.'

'Indeed it is,' said Cecily.

'I have found a hall, in Paddington, where we can meet every day, where anyone can come. Just for a cup of tea and a chat. Nothing ambitious, but you'd be surprised how it keeps people's spirits up.'

'Of course it does. What a wonderful idea!' said Cecily.

'Indeed. But even that costs money. The rent, heat, lighting, and then although someone supplied us with tables, I have had to buy a few secondhand chairs and rugs. And of course cups and saucers and so on. I'm not asking for a gift, but some of the men have carved some small wooden toys – look, I have some samples here – and I thought you might be interested in buying a couple. I know you have a child and—'

'How do you know that?' said Cecily, slightly sharply.

'I saw the announcement in the regimental newsletter,' said Duvant.

'Oh, yes, of course.' She felt ashamed of her suspicions. 'Yes, naturally I'll buy some toys, and tell some of my friends about them, they're charming. Why not let me give you a subscription as well? To put towards your expenses. It's so wonderful, I think, what you're doing.' Benedict surely, surely, couldn't disapprove of this: it wasn't as if the man was begging. In any case, there might be no need to tell him. She could take the money out of her own bank account.

'That is extremely kind of you, Mrs Harrington. I am most grateful. I wonder if I might leave this letter for your husband? It's simply a copy of our own newsletter. I thought he might be interested in what an ex-comrade-at-arms might be doing with his life.'

'I'm sure he will be,' said Cecily.

He left quite shortly after that, and then Nanny arrived back with Fanny, over-excited from her party, and she went up to watch her have her bath; showing off her new prowess at jumping up and down, Fanny slipped suddenly and fell, hitting her head on the side of the bath. It was nothing more than a nasty bump, but a large ugly bruise appeared, and it was very hard to calm her. Cecily took her downstairs to her sitting room to give her some milk and a cuddle.

The letter from Norman Duvant lay on her small table still; she wasn't quite sure what she should do about it. Clearly Benedict had to see it: he would be very cross if he knew she'd kept it from him. On the other hand, he'd be furious if he knew she'd entertained Norman Duvant in his house.

Well, she thought, looking down at Fanny's small face, with its huge egg-shaped bruise, peaceful now, sleepy and smiling, it wasn't really very important. She would put it away safely somewhere for a day or so; it could keep.

'Rock-a-bye baby,' she sang very quietly, rocking Fanny in her arms. Fanny reached up a small hand and touched her face. Cecily felt a sudden and very intense happiness. She was so very lucky, really.

The phone rang suddenly. She reached out to answer it, knocked the letter without realising it on to the floor.

It was Benedict. 'Everything all right?'

'Yes, thank you. Fine.' No point worrying him with Fanny's accident; there was nothing he could do and it wasn't serious.

'I wondered if you'd mind organising a dinner party tomorrow or the next night for a couple of these Americans. I realise it's short notice, but I'd like to offer them some hospitality. They're such a hospitable race themselves.'

'Yes, of course I will. Look, if you can hold on, I'll have a quick word with Cook now, see which night would be better. Thursday, I should think.'

'Fine. Thank you, darling.'

She went down to the kitchen with Fanny: Cook said Thursday, and she went back to the drawing room to report to Benedict. Fanny, getting bored with the course of events, wriggled off her mother's lap and started crawling round the room. She saw the letter under the table and smiled; she liked letters, liked trying to get things out of envelopes. It was a bit difficult at first, but a tug from her sharp little teeth ripped off a corner of the envelope, and then it was easy to get a finger inside and pull the contents out. By the time Cecily had finished talking to Benedict, the letter was in three large pieces on the floor.

'But, Benedict, this is blackmail. Can't you get that into your head?'

'Of course I can get it into my head. Don't speak to me as if I were a child.'

'You're behaving as if you were a child. And a very stupid one.'

'Oh, for God's sake,' said Benedict wearily. 'Just stop it.'

'*I* stop it! I make this horrifying discovery about my own husband, in no way through any fault of mine—'

'I told you,' he said heavily, 'never to have anything to do with that man.'

'Yes, well, if you'd explained why—' She stopped, realising how impossible such an explanation would have appeared.

'You should take notice of me, anyway,' he said.

'And why, may I ask? Because I'm your wife? In some way subservient to you? I'm sorry, Benedict, but that just doesn't seem quite right. Under the circumstances.'

'I don't know what you mean,' he said.

'Let me explain. I discover that you have been having some kind of a relationship with a man. Which, whatever form it took, clearly has served to convince him he has some hold over you. A man, moreover, you have known for years. Whose presence in your life has given you cause for great anxiety – and which you have handled extremely ineptly, if I may say so.'

'Cecily, please be careful what you say to me.'

'I will say what I like to you,' said Cecily, 'and if you don't like it, you are at liberty to leave. Although if you do I shall go straight to the police.'

'The police!'

'Yes, of course. That's what you do with blackmailers. You tell the police. It's a crime. And it's what you must do.'

'So is what Norman Duvant is accusing me of,' said Benedict quietly.

'I realise that. Thank you.'

'Should we perhaps … talk about that?' he said.

Cecily looked at him, at the husband she had loved and thought she knew, whose child she had borne, whom she had promised to love and cherish and obey, and knew they had to talk about it.

'Yes, perhaps we should,' she said after a long silence.

He talked about it. He spared himself – and her – nothing; at the end of an hour, she had heard it all. Norman Duvant had been not merely in his regiment, but his batman. Their affair had not begun until after the war, when Benedict had helped him to get a job in a bank, taken an interest in him, helped him along.

'Because you … were attracted to him.'

'Yes,' he said, very quietly.

She sat and tried to understand. Her knowledge of homosexuality was extremely hazy, but of course she understood it: it was a condition, an illness, that afflicted some men, usually rather weak ones – she had heard it could be cured – and it was absolutely illegal. In the light of that, Benedict had been doing some extremely reckless things; she listened in horror to stories of letters, dinners, then weekends in Devon, expensive gifts. He had even bought Duvant a house in the suburbs.

'A house, Benedict, a house – how could you?' she said, looking at him in horror. 'I know, I know,' he said, burying his head in his hands, 'but it was when he had begun to blackmail me. I thought it would finally shut him up.'

Only of course it hadn't, and Duvant had pursued him, ever more relentlessly, with letters, phone calls, threats.

'And now I don't know what to do, I simply don't.'

'So that was why you married me? To shake this spectre off?' She hadn't thought anything could ever hurt so much.

'It was one of the reasons,' he said, after a long silence, harrowingly honest.

'Oh! So there were others. I suppose you thought I was naive enough, stupid enough, for you to get away with it. For me not to guess, not to work it out.' He didn't look at her. So something *could* hurt as much, hurt more even. Cecily closed her eyes, sat there with her head bowed, wondering how she could bear it.

'Didn't you love me at all?'

'Yes, of course I did. I do!' said Benedict. 'You have to believe that. I love you very dearly. I think you are beautiful and sweet and a wonderful mother to our daughter and—'

'Well,' she said, 'that all sounds very satisfactory, I must say. What a fool everyone must think me.'

'Cecily, of course everyone doesn't think you a fool. Everyone doesn't know.'

'But some people do?'

'There was gossip, at one time, but since our marriage it has entirely ceased. You have to believe that.'

She was silent. Then, 'How was it I never heard anything of it?'

'It was not the kind of gossip that would have reached you. It only permeated a particular seam of society. Which does not contain your friends, I am happy to say.'

'But you were afraid it would spread?'

'I suppose so. Yes.'

Another silence. The pain deepened, ground into her. 'Does Leonora know?'

'Yes, she does,' he said, very quietly. 'She has tried to help. In various ways.'

'And Richard?'

'I think not.'

'And have there been others?'

'Occasionally. Not for a very long time. I have struggled for so long, Cecily, tried so hard ...'

'Well,' she said, 'at least a few mysteries are cleared up.'

'Such as?'

'Your unwillingness to visit my bedroom.'

He said nothing, looked at his hands.

'Look at me, Benedict!' The words roared across the room, startled, almost frightened her: He looked up at her. 'Have you ever, ever desired me?'

Another long silence, then, 'I have loved you,' he said.

That answered her question. She stood up suddenly, unable to bear any of it any longer. 'I'm going to bed,' she said. 'I have to think. About all of it. But there is one thing you have to do, Benedict, and that is go to the police. That creature cannot be allowed to get away with this. It will just go on, getting more and more horrible, more and more dangerous. And if you don't go, I will. I have this letter, and it is evidence enough. Goodnight.'

She looked back as she left the room. He was staring at her, his face filled with a terrible remorse, and something else: an appalling, naked fear.

'I mean it,' she said. 'It is for the best. I am not going to change my mind on this, Benedict. It has to be done. For all our sakes, not just yours. Mine and Fanny's too. You have to be brave. For us.'

He did not go to the police, he said he couldn't risk it; but he did go to Maurice Castle, a lawyer whom Leonora had put him in touch with, an interview with whom he reported back very fully to Cecily. A certain calm had filled her, and she found herself able to listen to the most unsavoury details with surprising detachment.

Castle had been soothing, competent, thorough: how much evidence could Duvant actually produce? Were there letters, copies of cheques, anything like that? Benedict had said yes, there were letters – although not, as far as he could recall, anything really explicit. Castle was concerned that Duvant had been taken to the country house, asked if the servants had seen anything, witnessed a sharing of a bed. Benedict had said he thought almost certainly not.

'Surely,' said Cecily, 'surely the servants would not be disloyal?'

'I trust not,' said Benedict, 'but one can never be sure. Money can change hands, and servants can often be bought. Apparently—' He stopped.

'What?'

'You don't want to hear.'

'I want to hear. Everything.'

'Well, apparently, stained sheets were produced by the servants in the Oscar Wilde case.'

Still the strange calm; she said only, 'Go on.'

'Well, Castle said he thought it was most unlikely that Duvant would go to my business associates, which was his main threat. Or to anyone, really. He said, and I have to trust him on this, that these fellows never seem to grasp that they are guilty of the crime as well. Or rather more to the point, perhaps, they bank on their victims not grasping it. He too would be tried and, if found guilty, imprisoned. It is all a bluff, and he said I should call it. And if he did talk, then I should deny it. It would be my word against his. He also said that if there was no real evidence – you must remember, the burden of proof falls on the prosecutor, there has to be no reasonable doubt – then Duvant would really have lost in every way. The source of money would have dried up and he himself would be under investigation. And in the worst case, if I were to be sent to prison, that would do Duvant no good either. Where would his money come from then?'

'Indeed.'

'And then he said—' He looked at Cecily rather warily, then for the first time there was a flash of humour in his voice. 'He said that if he were Lord Chancellor, he'd make the whole thing legal.'

'Legal!' said Cecily. 'What, homosexuality?'

'Yes. Think about it. Of course, I don't expect you to agree, but he says the current situation simply leads to more, to further crime. If it was legal, that would inevitably stop.'

Cecily was silent, then she said, 'That would never happen. The British public would never accept it. Not in a thousand years. Nor should they.'

Benedict said nothing, just looked at her, helpless.

'And what,' she said, a tremor in her voice, 'and what sentence might there be? If you were tried and found guilty?'

'Oh, life imprisonment, I'm afraid. Still. No doubt about that.' He sighed, then looked at her again, the shadow of amusement back in his eyes. 'It was a hanging offence, you know, until the middle of the last century. At least I won't be—'

'Benedict, please. It isn't amusing.'

'I know,' he said quietly, 'I'm sorry.'

She had fretted, sleepless, for what seemed like weeks, still convinced he should go to the police, still unable to persuade him, frightened, heartsore, the numbness wearing off; then one day in late November, she had been sitting, trying to read, when Cassia had arrived unexpectedly. She was in her second year at medical school and was radiantly happy; Cecily had always been fond, but slightly in awe of Cassia, of her fierce ambition, her clearly brilliant mind. She wasn't sure if she could cope with her at this particular point in her life. She smiled at her rather weakly.

'Sorry not to warn you,' Cassia said, kissing Cecily, pushing back her untidy fair hair, 'but I was passing on my bike, and I realised I got my timetable wrong, didn't have a lecture till eleven, and I thought I might just see Fanny for a minute. Do you mind?' She had been a frequent visitor since Fanny's birth, adored her, loved to come and play with her.

'I'm sorry,' said Cecily, 'Fanny's fast asleep. She's got a bit of a cold.'

'Oh, I'm sorry. Well, I'll just go away again.'

'No, don't,' said Cecily with a great effort. 'Stay and have a cup of tea or something. What would you like?'

'Hot chocolate, please. It's awfully cold out there.' She looked at Cecily sharply. 'Cecily, are you all right? You look awfully pale. Not having another one, are you? Oh, sorry, how awful of me, I shouldn't have said that, how rude. Cecily, don't cry. What is it? What's the matter?'

And astonished that she was able to do such a thing, Cecily managed, somehow, to get the dreadful words out, to tell Cassia what Benedict was. She had always had such respect for Cassia, in spite of the awe: she was so clear sighted, so honest, and it was a lot safer to talk to her than any of her friends, and although she always seemed very young, being a student, she was actually only three years younger than herself. And she also thought that maybe, because of what Cassia did, what she was studying, she might be less likely to be shocked, might even know something about it, indeed about any cures there might be.

Cassia was not in the least shocked; she seemed not even surprised. That worried Cecily for a while: maybe she really had been the only person in London who hadn't known, like a deceived wife. Which, of course, she was.

'Do a lot of people know, do you think?' she said, her voice small and frightened.

'No,' said Cassia quickly (too quickly, Cecily thought). 'I have never heard a word spoken of it, ever.' She came over to Cecily and put her arms round her and gave her a hug. 'How sad. How very sad for both of you. I'm so sorry.'

'Is that how you see it?' said Cecily. 'Just sad?'

'Yes, of course,' said Cassia, clearly surprised by the question, 'and only sad because of the attitudes of everybody. Making it a crime and all that nonsense.'

'So you don't see it as one?' said Cecily.

'No. How could it be? Do you?'

'I don't know. No, I don't think so. But I just— Oh, I don't know about anything at all any more.'

'Why don't you just talk about it?' said Cassia, pouring her another coffee. 'All of it. And remember I'm a scientist and thus completely unshockable.'

And suddenly she had been able to talk about it, not her own sadness so much, her own humiliation, but the nightmare situation – the blackmailing, Benedict's refusal to go to police, Maurice Castle's advice, her own instinct in the matter. 'What can I do, Cassia?' she had said, grasping Cassia's hands in her own. 'What on earth can I do?'

And that was when Cassia had made her offer.

'Can you drive us to his house?' Cassia said. 'I don't think this is a meeting the servants should know about, do you? We don't want Preston driving us.'

'Yes, of course I'll drive. Should we go now, do you think? Suppose he's not there, what should we do? Sit outside the house all day? Oh, maybe this isn't such a good idea, maybe we should—'

'I know it's a good idea,' said Cassia firmly, 'and the sooner we go the better. If he's not there, we'll leave a note, and ask him to let you know when you can come back. He won't have the first idea, he'll think it's about his Association, I expect. Anyway, I expect he will be there. He's out of work, after all. Do you think that's the address, that one in Ruislip?'

'I asked Benedict. He said it was.'

'Where is Benedict?'

'He's gone to the office,' said Cecily briefly, and then in a rush of courage, 'Yes, all right, let's get it over with. What should I wear, do you think? I've got a very nice new blue suit which might be quite suitable, but— Why are you laughing?'

'Oh Cecily,' said Cassia, who was clearly finding this very funny, 'what on earth does it matter what you wear to confront your husband's blackmailer?'

'I think it always matters what you wear,' said Cecily, with dignity.

Norman Duvant's house was halfway down a small, neat street in Ruislip; they found it quite easily. Cecily parked her Morris, and they sat looking at it: at its pretty, flower-filled front garden, its bright red front door, its muslin curtains blowing in the breeze.

'I know what you're thinking,' said Cassia finally.

'What?'

'That it doesn't look like a blackmailer's house.'

'No, it doesn't, does it? It looks like a happy little family house. If it was horrible and dingy, I might feel a bit braver.'

'I'm feeling very brave,' said Cassia, getting out and slamming the door. 'Come on. Let's get it over with.'

'Oh dear,' said Cecily, 'I'm beginning to—'

'Well, I'm not. Look, you start the conversation and I'll just back you up. All right? And if you feel your courage waning, just think of Fanny. None of it's her fault.'

'No. No, all right. Do I look frightened?'

'You look magnificent,' said Cassia firmly.

It was actually quite easy. Cecily was surprised to find a very strong, firm little speech had formed itself in her mind, which, confronted by Norman Duvant's complacently patronising face, made itself very clearly felt.

He came to the door, smiling. They invited themselves in, and Cassia asked for a cup of coffee for them both. 'I thought we might as well put him to a bit of trouble,' she said afterwards.

The front room was pin-neat, oddly impersonal, furnished with a three-piece suite, covered in chintz, and a pale blue carpet. There were several vases of flowers, some rather bad watercolours, and a few photographs which Cecily was too frightened to look at, in case they featured Benedict. Cassia told her afterwards they were all of Norman Duvant as a small child with his parents.

'Well now,' Norman Duvant said, sitting down, his hands folded, 'to what do I owe the honour of this visit? No little one with you today, Mrs Harrington?'

'No,' said Cecily, 'I wouldn't have brought her here.'

'Indeed? But the air out here is so nice.'

'I find the air quite horrible,' said Cecily, and then the speech came out, almost without a pause. She told Norman Duvant exactly what she thought of him, and of what he was doing; that she knew all about his relationship with her husband; that she also knew that he had been blackmailing him.

'Which puzzles me,' she said, 'since you must realise that if he were arrested, so would you be. I can't believe you are quite that stupid, Mr Duvant, or that you think my husband should be so. I have taken legal advice and I am assured that there is no way you would avoid criminal charges, should any be brought against my husband. If, in the extremely unlikely event of my husband being sent to prison, and your remaining outside, any money you might have been extracting from him would stop immediately. Which really wouldn't do you any good at all, either. So I think the best thing you can do is leave him alone, forthwith. Neither of us has any intention of ever seeing or speaking to you again. If you value your own security you will remove yourself from our lives. If you continue to pester us, we shall take further legal measures against you.' ('I have no idea if I could do that or not,' she said to Cassia as they drove home, 'but it seemed worth a try. He was looking a bit less sure of himself by then.')

Norman Duvant was silent for a while, then he said, 'I wonder how your husband's employers at the Stock Exchange would view any of the information I might give them.'

At this point Cecily's courage, suddenly and horribly, failed her: the prospect not only of Duvant writing to Benedict's firm, but of her having more or less invited him to do so without consulting Benedict, made her feel physically faint. She felt herself slump in her chair, saw the room spin; saw Cassia realise what had happened, and then saw her, wonderfully, taking over.

'Mr Duvant,' Cassia said, very cool, crossing one long leg over the other, 'I really very much doubt if they would give you the time of day, never mind long enough to acquaint them with any information of any kind whatsoever. Mr Harrington is an extremely valuable partner in his firm, with a fine record. I do assure you that is of more importance to them than anything you might try to tell them.'

'Well, we shall see about that,' said Norman Duvant. 'I shall write to them with a very full report this evening.'

'Of course you are at liberty to do so, but I would remind you again of the blackmail laws in this country. And that Mr Harrington is already in consultation with an extremely prominent lawyer on the subject. Now you must excuse us. Come along, Cecily, we have other, more important claims on our time.'

Cecily felt quite suddenly strong again. She stood up, smiled radiantly at Cassia. 'Indeed yes,' she said, pulling on her gloves. 'I have shopping to do for a start. Good morning, Mr Duvant. I hope we shall not meet again.'

Cecily was astonished at herself; in that moment the entire thing seemed worthwhile. Enjoyment was slightly too strong a word, but she felt at the same time that she could, had the requirement been expressed, have flown through the air, walked on water, or done any other number of hitherto unimaginable things.

They left him then, walked out of the front door, down the front path, out into the car; Cecily started the car, put it into gear, drove it very fast and competently to the end of the street. There she stopped suddenly, leant out of the door and was violently sick.

'Sorry,' she said, 'sorry, Cassia.'

'That's all right. Here, take my hanky. You were magnificent. I was so impressed.'

'Were you? You were wonderful too. I'd never have done it without you. I hope it works, that's all. I can't believe it'll be that simple.'

'I think it will be,' said Cassia. 'It was the point about blackmail that really got through to him. Didn't you see his face? So, as long as Benedict doesn't give in to him, I don't think we'll hear any more from him. You must tell Benedict what you've done.'

Cecily leant back in her seat, wiped her eyes, taking deep breaths. She still felt very sick. 'Do you really think I should?'

'Of course. Otherwise he may do something off his own bat.'

'Well, if you think so. Oh dear. I feel absolutely terrible suddenly.'

'I expect you do. Would some fresh air help? Look, there's a little park down there. We could sit on the bench till you feel better.'

'Yes, good idea. As long as Mr Duvant doesn't decide to take a constitutional.'

'If he does,' said Cassia cheerfully, 'I shall take great pleasure in personally kicking him in the balls. Sorry, Cecily. Coarse medical student talk. Come on, lean on my arm.'

They sat for a while. There were some children playing on the swings; Cecily watched them, thinking of Fanny, thinking of the nightmare that hung over that small life also, through no possible fault of her own.

'I hope it works,' she said.

'It'll work. You were magnificent. I kept wanting to jump up and down and cheer.'

'I couldn't have done it without you, Cassia.'

'Of course you could. I didn't do much. Except come along.'

'Oh, but you did. It was your idea for a start. Thank you. For everything. I'll never forget it. Ever. Most of all not minding about it, you know?'

'Yes. Yes, I think I know.'

'And of course you won't ever—'

'Cecily! Of course I won't.'

'Sorry. I shouldn't even have said that.'

There was a silence. A little boy had hit a cricket ball near them; Cassia stood up and threw it back to him, then she said, very casually, 'What do you think you might do next?'

Cecily knew what she meant. 'I shall just go home and continue. Unless something very dreadful happens.'

'With everything just the same?'

'Why ever not?'

'Well, I don't know. I just thought perhaps—'

'Cassia,' said Cecily firmly, 'if you were thinking I might divorce Benedict or leave him or something, you couldn't be more wrong. He needs me. He needs me more than ever. I'm going to make our marriage work. I know I have to and I know I can.'

'So you still do love Benedict?'

'Yes, of course I do. I love him more than ever. And he needs help to overcome this ... this problem, and I'm going to give it to him. I'm not going to fail him now.'

'That's ... wonderful,' said Cassia. She smiled at Cecily: a quick, slightly awkward smile.

Cecily could tell she wasn't entirely convinced, but she knew she could do it. What Benedict needed was a great deal of help and sympathy and understanding, and she could, in time, see him through this whole awful thing. It was, after all, only an illness of a sort – a psychological illness – and people did get over illnesses. It was just a question of the right approach. Above all, he must be made to see that she wasn't shocked or repelled by it, that she was prepared to forgive him – and that, most important of all, she still wanted him.

She would learn to be more what he wanted in bed, less inhibited; that must have made things more difficult for him. They could rebuild their marriage and have more children, and in a few years the whole thing would seem like a terrible nightmare. She just had to show him, that was all, show him how much she loved him and that she understood him and ... it. Together they could face all the problems. That was what marriage was all about. For better and worse. The worse was over now, hopefully, and they could put it behind them.

However, in a way it had not been over, and for the rest of her life she knew she must live in fear of it starting all over again.

CHAPTER 12

'The man's gone mad,' said Harry. Edwina looked at him; he was stirring his boiled egg with his teaspoon, in the clear belief that it was his coffee, so engrossed was he in a report in *The Times*.

'Harry, don't try to drink that, will you?' she said. 'Who's gone mad?'

'What? Oh. The King. Completely and utterly mad. He gave an official dinner party last night at St James's Palace, it's reported here; entertained the Mountbattens, the Baldwins, Diana and Duff Cooper, and the Simpsons, for God's sake.'

'What's wrong with that?'

'Oh, Edwina, really! Can't you see what he's doing? Trying to inveigle that woman into his official life by the back door. Smuggling her, literally, into Court society, hoping we'll all just come to accept the whole thing, just because she's got her elegant feet under the same table as the Prime Minister.'

'But she's married to Ernest.'

'At the moment. I'd put a lot of money on that changing soon.'

'Do you really believe all this gossip?'

'I do now.'

'Oh, I don't,' said Edwina, putting down her coffee cup. 'I think he'll get tired of her like he does of everyone else, in time. And even if he doesn't, he can't marry a divorced woman, he really can't. He's the King of England, Defender of the Faith and all that.'

'And terribly in love. Diana Cooper told me herself last week, he really seems to feel he can't face life and his royal duties without her. Edwina, this is horrible coffee. I can't believe this is freshly ground. I don't ask much from you, but—'

'You ask a great deal, and I'm sure it is fresh. I'll check with Cook, don't go on about it. Anyway, the King doesn't have to face life without

224

Wallis. She can stay there in the background, playing hostess at Fort Belvedere, waiting for him to get back from the royal duties.'

'I'm telling you, he's going to want more than that. And this dinner party proves it.'

'Well, we shall see,' said Edwina. 'I must go, I'm terribly busy today.'

'With which branch of your life? The medical? The pseudo theatrical? I'm getting quite dizzy with it all, Edwina.'

'Oh, go to hell,' said Edwina goodnaturedly. 'The fashion show, actually, if that's what you mean by theatrical. I have a meeting with Leon de Rosay this morning, and then after lunch I'm seeing Venetia and Rose at Victor Stiebel's to discuss the possibility of him supplying some evening gowns for the show. And then—'

'You must forgive me, I'm finding this all a little too complex, fascinating as it is. I'll be late tonight myself, dinner at the Sporting Club. With your pa, amongst others. So I'll see you this time tomorrow, probably. Goodbye. Don't work too hard.' He got up, bent briefly to kiss her.

She smiled at him absently, and then picked up the post which had just been brought in. Oh God: she recognised that rather rigid writing. Mary Whittaker. Well, she wasn't going to be distracted by it now. She would read it tonight. While she dined alone. Again.

'Leon, that is the most marvellous coat. Could I order one for me while we're about it? And that suit, please, in wine. I just adore the padded shoulders. Only maybe just a little longer. And—'

'Mrs Moreton, I thought this was your business meeting. If you want me to summon a vendeuse, of course I will, but I cannot concentrate on two things at once.'

'Leon, don't be tedious. And of course you can. You're going to sell hundreds of extra things through this show of mine. De Rosay is going to be as big a name as Stiebel and Lachasse in six months' time. But I do want the suit. Please. Don't forget. There's no need to get some stuffy vendeuse in.'

'But—'

'Leon, concentrate. Now, let me see. Where were we? Oh, yes, you'll do six suits, four cocktail dresses and a few evening gowns. If you have the time. Well, of course you will. Which is all wonderful. And you need to have the girls in as soon as possible for fittings. That's no problem. And you can get Maria Guy to do some hats, you say?'

'I think so. Certainly I'll speak with her.'

'Let me know. You're an angel. Goodness, this is exciting. I'm loving it. Are you hungry? Because I could eat a horse.'

'Perhaps a tiny foal,' said Leon de Rosay, smiling at her. 'Shall we go and find one? And you can tell me about this race meeting you are going to in Deauville. How I envy you. What are you going to wear?'

'I think I have something for that. Not quite sure about the hat, though. Anyway, we can talk about that over lunch as well. So yes, let's go.'

She stood up, thinking how much she enjoyed the company of homosexuals: so amusing, so interested in one, so undemanding. And Leon was so good-looking too, with his chestnut hair and his wonderful aquiline nose. Leon de Rosay, indeed! He had come a long way from Leonard Rosewall, born and bred in Clapham. She had known him for over two years now, been introduced to him by her friend Venetia Hardwicke, who worked on *Vogue*: 'You'll adore him, Edwina, and his clothes are exactly you. I want to help him along a bit, we're featuring one of his suits in the August issue. Buy something of his and wear it around a bit, darling, just for me. Get people noticing.'

'Are you in love with him?' Edwina had said, and Alicia had laughed and said absolutely not, beautiful as he was. 'Boys only, darling, but he is fun. And I've persuaded Hugh to put some money behind him, so it'll be a double benefit.'

She had bought one of Leon's dresses. He was a designer in the Worth mode, a brilliant tailor besides having a penchant for showy evening gowns. Harry had liked it; she had bought more, taken her friends to the next collection. Leon owed her a lot and they both knew it. He was being generous with her fashion show: it was a lot of work for him, and would cost him money, but it was no more than her due.

'Where shall we go?' she said.

'Oh, not one of the big places, please. You know how I hate to be seen.'

'So shy and retiring, aren't you? You choose, I'll simply follow. With my appetite.'

He took her to a small French restaurant, round the corner from his salon in Sloane Street; it was small, dark, intimate, smelt of rich food, every table a tiny, dimly lit island.

'Leon, this is marvellous, so romantic. What a pity we're not having an affair.'

'Mrs Moreton, if that is what you want—'

'You tart!' said Edwina affectionately. 'You'd even do that, wouldn't you, if you thought it would make your name even bigger?'

'I would try,' he said, and kissed her hand.

'Well, you don't have to. I adore you as you are. Now look, let's order and then I want to hear all about the Surrealist exhibition. I was so terribly angry we had to miss it, but Harry— Leon, what's through there?'

'Another, smaller dining room. For even more private affairs than our own. Why?'

'Oh, nothing.'

But it wasn't nothing. Or perhaps she hoped it was. A man had just walked quickly through the main restaurant into the small, inner room, and had been greeted with a warm handshake by another man, rising half from the table. She recognised very well the man sitting down. It was Benedict Harrington.

She would have left, quickly, before he had seen her, but Leon was in the middle of a long funny story at two thirty, when the first man left, alone. She recognised him at once, now: it was Dominic Foster, the high-profile architect. He had been at Cecily's Christmas party, with his wife. He didn't see her.

Leon recognised him too: he was very strong on gossip. 'Now there's a man of the moment,' he said, looking after Foster. 'Everyone's talking about him. He even got a write-up in *Vogue* last month.'

'Well!' said Edwina briskly. 'What an accolade for an architect.'

This was wasted on Leon; he smiled at her. 'Yes. He designed an amazing set of studios in Pimlico. A friend of mine is taking one. Quite gorgeous they are, almost entirely glass – walls, roofs. Only problem, which no one thought of, is the pigeons ...'

'Oh, yes?' said Edwina abstractedly.

Benedict had just emerged from the inner room. He looked distracted, anxious. He saw her, was clearly shocked, then recovered, came over and kissed her. She could feel the tension in his body. 'Edwina! How nice!'

'Hallo, Benedict. Have you met Leon de Rosay? The most brilliant couturier in London at the moment. Leon, Benedict Harrington. My husband's cousin.'

'How do you do, Mr Harrington.' Leon stood up, held out his hand.

She could see him taking Benedict in, reacting: not sexually, of course, but emotionally. They always knew one another straight away. Or rather about one another. The famous coded question they were supposed to ask – 'Are you a friend of Dorothy's?' – was so terribly unnecessary. Only for someone like Benedict, maybe it wasn't. Poor Benedict.

She smiled at him, her heart aching at his patent misery; she was very fond of him. 'Leon is helping me with a fashion show I'm organising, in aid of St Christopher's, aren't you, Leon?'

'Mrs Moreton,' said Leon, with a sigh, 'if you will excuse me, I simply must go. I have a client arriving in three minutes, a difficult client, not in the least like you.'

'My goodness, I wonder who she is. You wouldn't tell me, I suppose?'

'Discretion is my most outstanding quality.'

'Yes, I've noticed. Of course you must go. I'll ring you about the hats in a day or two. If that's all right. Thank you for a wonderful lunch and all your help.'

'My pleasure, Mrs Moreton. Thank you. Goodbye, Mr Harrington.' He half bowed to them both, walked out, signing the bill at the desk on the way.

Benedict looked at Edwina, seemed about to say something, then stopped again. He was clearly miserably anxious.

'Benedict,' she said firmly, 'sit down a minute. Let's have a glass of wine. Or are you in a frightful rush?'

'No, not at all. That is …'

He sat down, and she signalled for the waiter. 'Two glasses of champagne,' she said briskly, and then, 'I always think champagne is the best thing after lunch. After anything really, of course. Or before it. Don't you?'

'Oh, yes. Thank you.' The champagne had arrived. 'To you, Edwina,' he said, and raised his glass, then virtually drained it.

'Benedict,' she said, laughing, 'didn't you have anything to drink with your lunch?'

'Yes, of course I did,' he said, slightly irritably, 'but you're right, it is a lovely way to end a meal. It wakes one up so beautifully.'

'And do you need waking up? Difficult afternoon?'

'It could be. Edwina—'

'Benedict,' she said, 'Benedict, I promise I won't say a word to Cecily. Or anyone. About you being here. Don't worry.'

'Oh, it's perfectly all right,' he said. 'I wasn't going to—' and then met her eyes with his own and looked first resigned, then amused. 'Yes, I was. Well, I was going to try. To ask you that. So thank you. It's just that – well, Cecily doesn't like Dominic Foster very much. I can't think why.'

'Benedict, please!' she said, the exasperation so clear in her voice that he looked startled. 'That's a tiny bit offensive, I have to say. I might find myself having to tell Cecily after all if you're going to treat me like some sort of constipated idiot. I'll never, ever, say a word to anyone, you know I won't, but of course I know why Cecily doesn't like Dominic. And why you're here with him. As you very well know. Let's at least be honest with each other, there's no one else here.'

He looked at her, his eyes absolutely and carefully blank for a moment, then he said, 'Thank you. I didn't mean to offend you.'

'Well, you did. Benedict, you know I don't care. Have you really forgotten that evening?'

'No,' he said, 'no, of course not. And you were wonderful then. But—'

'Well then. Just relax.'

'Thank you,' he said again, and smiled at her.

She was silent a moment, remembering the evening: she had left a nightclub in a rage, stalked off into the night, having had a row with Harry, who was still inside, drunk and belligerent. She had found herself in a tiny street in the maze behind Park Lane, and as she walked down it looking for a taxi, she had seen Benedict suddenly leaving a house a few doors in front of her, taking his leave of a man.

They were not in any kind of physical contact, but it was so clear, simply from the expression on Benedict's face, and the way he was looking up and down the street, checking it for witnesses, what he had been doing there.

He saw her, of course, and it was almost funny, so appalled, so absolutely defeated did he look. Then he managed to smile, came over to her, and said, 'Hallo, Edwina.'

She said, 'Hallo, Benedict. I'm trying to find a taxi. Would you like to help?' – more to give him something to do, to ease his wretchedness, than anything else.

'Yes, of course, I'll go and get one. You wait here.'

She had slipped her arm through his and said, 'No, don't be silly, we'll walk together.' They had walked along, and into the agonising silence she had said, 'Benedict, it's all right. Please, please don't worry about it.'

'What? What are you talking about?'

'You know what I'm talking about.'

After a very long silence, finally he had said, 'Did you know ... before?' and she had said, yes, she had, and it was fine by her and she could be as silent as the grave when required, only nobody would ever believe it. 'Where's Harry?' he said, and she had explained that Harry was probably even now under a table in the nightclub and needn't ever know they had met at all.

'Of course he knows,' Benedict had said abruptly. 'He's always been marvellous about it.'

Edwina had said there was nothing to be marvellous about, in her opinion. 'And now look, there's a cab, I'm going to jump into it. Goodnight, Benedict, thank you for your help.'

And they had never mentioned it again, until now.

'I'm sorry,' he said again, 'I really didn't mean to offend you. I always forget how ... oh, you know. How different you are.'

'Well, that's one way of looking at it,' she said, draining her glass, waving at the waiter for another. 'Do you want another one?'

'I'd better not. I really do have to go and do some work. Sadly.'

'You should have more fun, Benedict,' she said, looking at him thoughtfully. 'You're always working. Or doing good works.'

'Fun is a little dangerous,' he said, smiling, avoiding her eyes, 'for me.'

'Well, you can have fun with me. No danger there. So have another glass. Go on. You're not going to tell me you have a boss somewhere, watching the time you get back from lunch. You must be able to buy that firm of yours several times over.'

'Not quite the point,' he said, 'but yes, all right.'

They had another glass, and then another. She talked to him about her fashion show, saw him slowly relax. At half past four they were still there, into their second bottle, and he was doing a wonderful imitation of his secretary looking first at the office clock, then her watch as he came in late from lunch.

'I'm sure she's the only person who cares,' said Edwina.

'Yes, but Cecily might phone.'

'Are you so frightened of Cecily?'

'Not frightened of her, but I am afraid of troubling her.'

'It's such a shame,' she said suddenly, 'that she can't accept it. Just a little.'

'Edwina! How could she?'

'Oh, I don't know. But a little less ... rigidness would help, make you both happier. You've loved her and stayed with her for a very long time, after all.'

'Yes, but she worries about me being caught. The disgrace.'

'But why should you be? And what disgrace, anyway? London is so tolerant these days, nobody minds a bit. Look at Noël Coward, and Syrie Maugham.'

'Nobody minds a bit in theory, and in that tiny, theatrical segment,' said Benedict soberly. 'If our friends, our charming, conventional, well-bred friends were to get a real whiff of it, it would be very different. Look at poor old Stuart Southport, had to leave the country for good a couple of years ago, or face charges. It's still a crime, Edwina, you really mustn't forget that.'

'It's so ridiculous, it makes me livid,' said Edwina. 'My own first sexual experience was a lesbian one. It was wonderful. I shall never forget it, ever.'

'Is that really true?' he said. His expression was odd, she thought: not shocked, not surprised even, but intently, almost fervently relieved.

'Of course it's true. And it wasn't just once either. Took me a while to adjust to the other way, I can tell you. I still sometimes see a woman and think ooh, yes, she'd be interesting. Chemistry, you know. But of course you do know,' she added, laughing. 'Anyway, I haven't for years. Not since Harry, anyway. Now then, this is all getting a bit disgraceful. Another glass and I'll be jumping on you. That'd be interesting. Don't look so frightened, Benedict, I'm only joking. Oh, God, look at the time, I should have been at Stiebel's half an hour ago. I must dash. Bye, Benedict, darling, and please don't worry, I swear I won't say a word. To anyone.'

Poor Benedict, she thought, as the taxi bore her through the streets towards Stiebel's showroom: what a nightmare of a life. And poor Cecily too, with her ongoing mission to cure him of his affliction, as she saw it. Well, that was how Harry said she saw it, and he was clearly right. One thing you could say for Harry: he was wonderfully liberal and tolerant.

Cassia kept telling herself that nothing had really happened, nothing at all. It didn't mean a thing, any of it, not really; she might have taken a house – a very small house – in London for a year, but it wasn't in any way significant. It might have been a little bit extravagant, just to sleep in for two nights a week, in fact it would probably have been cheaper to have stayed in a hotel, but it was easier, simpler this way. Hotel rooms had to be found, booked, weren't always what you wanted.

She didn't have to worry about extravagance, thanks to Leonora, and Leonora would certainly have approved of this manifestation of it. She would very much have disapproved of Cassia doing the late drive home from Brixton – first through the dark crowded streets, then the endless stretches of developing suburbs and then the even more endless dark country roads. It was just so much more sensible, every Tuesday and Thursday, simply to get into her car and be in her – the – house in less than half an hour. That was all it was, sensible: an extraordinarily good, workable plan, which was going to make her working life a lot easier. And every Wednesday and Friday morning, she would leave Walton Street at six and be home by half past eight and be able to take the boys to school. It wasn't going to make the slightest difference to them: all three children were fast asleep when she got home after the clinic, and she never saw them until the morning, anyway.

They were all rather excited about her taking the house, quite unmoved by the news that she would be away for two nights a week.

'We're in bed, anyway,' said William. 'London! Can we all go and stay?' said Bertie. 'Go to the zoo?'

'Yes, of course.'

'And Big Ben?'

'Yes, and Big Ben.'

They were all going to come up for Saturday, this very week, to see the house and stay the night if they wanted. There was room, which had been another reason for getting the house, rather than staying in a hotel. She didn't want the children to feel her life in London was somehow removed from theirs, had nothing to do with them. Being connected as it was with her work, which was so important to her, it therefore should matter to them. It was part of her life as a doctor, the house, she explained to Bertie, who was the only one old enough to understand. It wasn't for her, to live in by herself; it was somewhere she could stay, so she could do her work at the clinic more easily, without worrying about getting home.

Bertie had obviously understood this, although he had asked why she couldn't work at a clinic nearer home, even in the village. She had explained there wasn't one, and he had said she should start one. Maybe one day, she had said very carefully. Maybe she would.

Janet had said she thought it was a splendid idea, getting the house. She worried about Cassia doing that drive late, she said, and so did the doctor, although he had never actually said so, but she could tell, he was always edgy until he heard the car in the drive. Now they would all be able to relax those evenings. Cassia smiled at her and told her, not for the first time, that she had no idea how she had ever managed without her.

And of course Edward had seemed to understand about the house: what it represented. Which had been very important too. He certainly didn't see it as a threat. He'd just nodded when she'd told him, explained about it, said, 'good idea,' and gone back to studying an article in the *Lancet* on post-operative infection, hardly listened as she explained about getting back before breakfast and taking the boys to school. He hadn't expressed any interest in coming to see it, he was terribly busy, but there was plenty of time for that. 'You do whatever you think best,' he'd said. Very rational. The whole thing was very rational.

Only of course that wasn't why she'd taken the house at all.

★

Maureen Johnson had come for her interview two days after her letter of application had arrived. Edward asked Cassia to meet her from the station; incredulous at his insensitivity (and hoping it was only that, and not malevolence), she sent Janet instead and greeted Maureen with immense graciousness on the doorstep, dressed in a new and very expensive dress from Harvey Nichols. She had no idea why, it just made her feel better.

Maureen was pleasant looking with neat brown hair, scrubbed skin and rather small blue eyes; she also, Cassia noticed with some satisfaction, had very thick ankles. It was completely irrelevant to the situation, but again it made her feel better. Maureen was well qualified, clearly efficient, with a particular interest in paediatrics. She treated Cassia with a mixture of the deference due to a prospective employer's wife and the superiority of the professional woman over the housewife. She was, she explained to Cassia while they waited for Edward to return from a house call, fresh from a two-year house job at Kingston hospital in Surrey; she had actually trained at University College Hospital. Cassia didn't mention her own training at this point; she smiled as sweetly as she could and asked Maureen why she was going into general practice rather than taking up a hospital position. Maureen told her she thought there was more scope in general practice for a woman. 'But were you not invited to stay at UCH?' said Cassia, and knew from Maureen's flush that she had not qualified for that particular honour and, moreover, that Maureen knew she knew.

Edward had interviewed her for over an hour and then taken her out with him on a call to a child with suspected diphtheria. They came back engrossed in a discussion about inoculation which continued through lunch. Cassia sat and first tried to smile, then flicked through the latest copy of *Vogue*, and finally asked them to excuse her as she had to collect William from school.

When she got back, Edward was in the surgery with Maureen. The door opened abruptly and he said, 'Could you possibly see your way to taking Maureen back to Haywards Heath?'

The sun had come out and Cassia wound down the hood of the Jaguar, explaining that the boys loved it that way. It was, despite the brilliance of the day, very cold and windy, and she watched Maureen Johnson's neat hair grow tangled and her slightly ruddy face turn white, with some satisfaction.

'Goodbye,' she said graciously, as they reached the station, 'it's been lovely to meet you. I still think you should have stayed on at UCH, done paediatrics there. I was asked to stay on to do obstetrics at St

Christopher's after my finals, and I found it absolutely irresistible. Only, of course, Bertie came along and I had to say no in the end.'

The expression of confusion and dislike on Maureen's face stayed in her memory for weeks and helped her through Edward's fulsome praise of Maureen, his decision to take her on, his request that Cassia should look for rooms for her in the village, and his enthusiasm at Maureen's suggestion for a regular children's clinic every Wednesday afternoon in the surgery. He actually greeted this suggestion as something wonderfully revolutionary. Cassia tried to remind him pleasantly that she had mooted it several times herself, heard the venom in her own voice and gave up.

'And I do hope,' Edward said, 'you'll be able to help Dr Johnson to settle down, introduce her to everybody in the village, perhaps even be available in the background for a few of her early surgeries, so you can tell her who people are, give her a bit of background. Only don't get involved in anything medical, obviously.'

'Obviously,' said Cassia.

That was the day she phoned the estate agents and asked to see round the house in Walton Street. And had stood there, in the pretty first-floor drawing room, looking down on to the street below, feeling dangerously, powerfully independent, and said that she would take it.

It was a month before she had actually moved in, a long, painful month during which Maureen Johnson settled into life as Edward's assistant. As well as helping him with the surgery, and initially accompanying him on his rounds and then taking on the more basic cases herself, she had already delivered several babies (under the watchful eye of the local midwife), and even handled a couple of real emergencies when Edward had been out on call – one when Daphne Simpson had phoned in a panic to say her five-year-old was screaming with stomach pain and she just knew it was the appendicitis. Maureen had examined him and, with some courage (appendicitis being very popular in the village at the time), diagnosed acute constipation and administered an enema, thus affording the child immediate and dramatic relief, to his mother's very slight chagrin.

And another day old Joe Phillips had cut three quarters of his finger off, chopping wood. Maureen had stitched it back on by the light of the guttering oil lamp (the Phillipses not having the electric) with a cool competence that had impressed not only Joe himself, but Mrs Joe, who had been extremely doubtful as to Maureen's ability to handle the case at all, and had had half a mind to insist on waiting for the proper doctor, as she called him.

There was no doubt that Edward had made a wise choice. Maureen had already been accepted in the village, despite an initial resistance on the grounds of her sex. Cassia tried and failed to feel that her own position was not being eroded, and it was the thought of her house, her very own house, that sustained her.

The clinic finished particularly late her first evening there, and it was almost nine thirty when she left Brixton; it helped with the justification of taking the house at all. She pulled up outside and sat looking up at the windows; she had hired a woman to clean it and keep an eye on it, and come in at tea time on her working days, light the fire and switch the lights on. The house looked warm, welcoming, pretty; she smiled up at it, pleased, as if it were a new and very charming friend.

She felt rather odder when she got inside, as if she was acting a part, not living real life at all; she seemed to be watching herself as she took off her coat and hat, and laid them down on the hall chair, and walked upstairs to the drawing room. It was a very pretty drawing room: she supposed if it was really her own, she might have done it differently, but given that it was a stage set, it was a very nice one, all shades of cream and blue – blue carpet, cream walls, blue curtains, blue and cream patterned upholstery, a button-back sofa, two button-back chairs, and three very nice upright drawing-room chairs as well. The fireplace was carved wood, with a pretty cast-iron grate and some hand-painted tiles, and on either side of it, floor-to-ceiling bookshelves set in alcoves. The shelves were bare, and so were the walls; she would have to fill both, but that would be fun. She could go out and buy boxes of books, in secondhand bookshops, and as for pictures, she could collect them gradually. She would bring some photographs of the children up – that would help make it more hers.

She tried not to think of the children, on their own for the very first night without her, but they were perfectly all right, of course. Janet had phoned and said they were all fine, and she had spoken to Bertie and William earlier from the clinic, and promised them that on Saturday they could all come and spend the night there; and she would see them in the morning, after all, at breakfast.

She got up and went down to another part of her stage set, the little kitchen, and made herself a cup of coffee. It was very odd to be able to do that: just make it without having a long conversation with whoever might be in there, probably make a couple more, get involved in a discussion with Bertie about his homework, or Peggy about the next day's meals, or Edward about the next day's surgery. Not that that particular conversation took place much any more: it was held with Dr Johnson instead. Every time she felt even slightly wobbly at being here on her own, Cassia thought of Maureen Johnson and her nerve steadied.

Mrs Horrocks, the daily woman, had left her a fruit cake and a tin of biscuits. She was hungry, she realised, having had no supper, and sat at the small kitchen table, eating biscuit after biscuit. She was just going upstairs again to see if Mrs Horrocks had turned down her bed as instructed, when the phone rang. It was Edwina.

'Darling, how thrilling to have you in London. What a marvellous idea, I do envy you. I'd simply adore to have a little house all to myself, get a bit of peace and quiet.'

As Edwina had her own very large house to herself a great deal of the time, this seemed to Cassia a rather extraordinary comment, but she didn't say so. 'That's not the idea at all, Edwina,' she said. 'It's just that my clinics finish so late and then it's such a long drive home. This seemed more sensible.'

'Oh, I see,' said Edwina. 'Well, if that's your story, Cassia, I certainly won't tell anyone any different. But presumably you'll use it other times as well.'

'Oh, yes, the children are really excited, they're coming up this—'

'Well, look, I'm giving a dinner party a week next Wednesday, and I want you to come to that.'

'Edwina, I can't, you don't understand, I've no intention of—'

'Of course you can. There'll be lots of interesting people for you, including Leon de Rosay, he's a couturier, up and coming – oh, you know, do you? Sorry, I always forget you're not quite the bumpkin you were. Anyway, I'm putting on a fashion show in aid of your hospital – did I mention that?'

'No,' said Cassia, genuinely interested.

'Well, I am. So you see, you ought to come. Mummy and Daddy will be there because she's helping with tickets, and you know how Daddy adores you, and then I wondered if we could ask Rupert. He could help with the actual staging, I thought. What do you think?'

'I don't know,' said Cassia. Her sense of being on stage herself was growing. 'Fashion shows aren't really his bag.'

'Surely a show is a show. Could you ask him, darling, please?'

'Well—'

'Good. That's settled, then. Let me know about Rupert, won't you? Now I must go, and congratulations again about the house. I think it's marvellous. But you might have told us.'

Cassia went back upstairs to the drawing room again, switched on the wireless. There was a concert on: a Bach organ recital. Edward didn't like Bach, always asked her if she would turn it down. Not off, of course, down. She loved Bach; she turned it up. God, this was wonderful.

She sat down on the sofa and put her feet up, and looked about her, savouring the peace, the Bach, the guilty happiness. Of course she'd much rather be at home, only even now, she thought, looking at her watch, she wouldn't be home, she'd still be driving anxiously fast, through the winding lanes. So it was all right; and she shouldn't feel guilty. The Bach and the peace were a bonus.

The walls were very bare; she would have to fill them quickly. Only you couldn't buy pictures quickly – it took time, and care. Suddenly she remembered her room at Grosvenor Gardens; she had several pictures there that Leonora had given her. There were two in particular that she loved, a pair of watercolours, early Victorian landscapes; and a pair of eighteenth-century prints of Vauxhall Gardens, she remembered, they were pretty too. She wondered if Sir Richard would mind her taking them. She went over to the telephone and dialled his number. Jarvis answered the phone; yes, Sir Richard was in.

'Godpa! It's me.'

'Darling girl, how nice. How are you, where are you?'

God, more explanations. She made them quickly, smoothly, not giving him time to interrupt. 'You must come and see it very soon. Maybe on Saturday, I'm bringing the boys up. Come to tea, bring Margaret.' (This was fun too.) 'The thing is, I have some very bare walls. And I wondered – well, would you mind terribly if I at least borrowed a few of the ones from my room there? They were mine, I think.'

'Darling, of course you can. Any time. Saturday would be fun, yes. Thank you.' There was a pause. Then, 'It sounds a splendid idea, your little house. Very sensible.' She could tell he didn't think anything of the sort. 'But what a surprise. You might have told us.'

She might, thought Cassia, as she settled into her new pink and grey bedroom, worrying already about the amount of time she might after all be spending in London. She might indeed have told them all. But she hadn't. She hadn't because she couldn't face the fuss. The fuss and the explaining. And she had to do that now anyway. It was going to be quite difficult, making people understand. They would all think it was quite different from the truth, would think the money was finally going to her head, that she was going off the rails, setting up a new life for herself, a new, shinily independent life, where she could do what she wanted, what indeed she had always wanted. As Leonora had, perhaps intended ...

Well, they might think that, but it was quite quite wrong.

CHAPTER 13

Edwina had planned with enormous care the dinner party which would launch her fashion show. It was one of the things she was best at, entertaining. She loved it: it satisfied in some small way her creative instincts, and her managerial ones too. She loved drawing up a guest list, pulling together disparate yet somehow compatible people, doing the *placement*, working out menus, ordering the flowers, planning what she should wear. And this one was particularly important, even the guest list had proved challenging, adjusting the balance of the fashion, business and social element. She looked at Harry at breakfast on the day slightly nervously.

'Harry, you won't be late tonight, will you?' she said.

He looked at her, his face blank. 'I'm afraid I can't guarantee being back before nine,' he said, 'if then.'

'But Harry, it's such an important evening for me, please.'

'Edwina, I'm extremely sorry but I do have slightly more important things to do than fill my allotted position in your table plans.' He stood up, sighed, walked towards the door.

Edwina looked at his back with acute distaste. 'I can't believe you could let me down like this,' she said.

'I haven't let you down – yet,' he said. 'I simply said I couldn't guarantee being here.'

'So I have to worry all day about it. Harry, you are the absolute limit. I really—'

He turned round. She looked at him and realised he was smiling at her. 'Edwina, of course I'll be here. I'm impressed by this new entrepreneurial spirit of yours. What time is curtain-up?'

'Well, they're asked for seven thirty,' she said, not sure if relief or irritation was stronger, 'but if you could be ready by seven I'd be grateful.

You see, it's all a bit delicate: I've got Leon de Rosay coming, he's doing a lot for the show, and I'm not quite sure if the Whittakers would quite appreciate his style, and if they got here before the rest—'

'Edwina, I'm afraid I have to tear myself away from this absolutely riveting discussion. I have a building or two to buy. But I'll be on parade at seven. All right? Well, providing ...' He paused.

'Providing what?'

'That the Bank of England doesn't crash, or my car doesn't run out of petrol or—'

'God, you're a nightmare,' said Edwina. 'Yes, Bishop?'

'Telephone, madam. Lady Bushnell.'

'Oh God,' said Edwina, hurrying out of the room. She came back looking cross. 'Bloody woman can't come. My perfect seating plan, all to pot. Harry, do stop laughing, it's not funny. Why can't you, just for once, do something to help me with my life?'

'I pay for it,' he said. 'Surely that's a start?'

He phoned her an hour later. 'I've done something to help. Replaced the Bushnells. Benedict just rang me about something, he and Cecily are free, and prepared to fill a chair. Or rather two. I hope you're pleased.'

'Oh, Harry, no! Not them, not tonight.'

'Why on earth not? Not many people can come at such short notice, and Benedict's always good value. Not to mention a few hundred quid. And Cecily will sell tickets.'

'Harry, you don't understand. It's – well, it could be very difficult. Disastrous even. Oh God, why couldn't you have asked me?'

'Edwina,' said Harry, 'you asked me to help, and I have. I tell you, it's certainly the last time.'

'Good,' said Edwina, 'now get off the line. I have to ring Leon de Rosay.'

But Leon de Rosay was not in his salon; he was out of town, the directrice told her, and not expected back until after four.

'Then get him to ring me, will you, please?' said Edwina. 'It's really very, very urgent indeed. Don't forget.'

'Well, that didn't take long,' Edward had said.

'What?' she had said, knowing quite well.

'Using your little place in town for your social life. Not merely somewhere to lay your head at the end of a hectic afternoon.' He had smiled at her as he spoke, but his voice had been cool.

'Don't be silly, Edward. It's hardly a social occasion, more a – well, almost a meeting. About this fashion show Edwina's putting on for the hospital. I really ought to go, you must see that.'

'I don't, actually,' he said, 'but I can see you want to. And why not?'

Why not, indeed? No reason why not at all. Foolish not to accept Edwina's invitation to an evening she would enjoy, had a reason to be involved in, would have attended anyway; and clearly quite absurd to struggle back to Sussex after it.

Nobody minded: Janet said it would be quite all right; the children hardly listened to her explanations, only wanted to know when they could go again to stay in London, spend another day at the zoo. It was absolutely absurd of her to feel anything but pleasure at the prospect.

She woke on the day of the dinner party with a headache, and a strong sense of foreboding.

She decided to spend the morning at Grosvenor Gardens, sorting out her pictures. Sir Richard and Margaret were both going out, Margaret had told her, but Jarvis was expecting her and she was to make herself at home.

'Richard said to tell you there were a couple of pictures of Leonora's own that you might like,' said Margaret. 'I'll put them in your room as well. Just leave them if you don't want them.'

It was still referred to as her room: Cassia found it very touching.

It was very strange to be there, alone in the house, in the great hall. Leonora haunted it, an oddly vivid ghost; she somehow expected her to appear at the top of the stairs or out of one of the rooms and fall upon her ecstatically, hugging her, telling her how lovely it was to see her, offering her tea, lunch, a drink. She could hear her voice, her pretty, musical voice, saying, 'Sweet Pea, darling, how lovely to see you,' breathe in her warm, fragrant scent. But she wouldn't, she couldn't: poor Leonora, she was gone, not only from this house, this city, but from the world and the lives of all those who had loved her.

'Oh, Leonora,' she said aloud, hearing the catch in her own voice, 'I do miss you.'

'Would you like some tea, miss? Or some coffee?'

It was Harris. Cassia was always 'miss' to Harris; it was rather nice. She smiled at her and said tea would be lovely, and could she have it in her room.

'Of course, miss. I'll bring it up. You must miss Lady Beatty,' she added, looking at Cassia's face. (Damn, now she was crying.)

'I do, Harris, yes.' She rummaged in her bag for a handkerchief, half amused by Harris's clear view that it was Leonora who was Lady Beatty still, wondering how she saw Margaret. 'Anyway, it's nice to be here.'

'How are the children, miss?'

'All very well. Thank you.'

'I do miss having young people in the house. It's not the same at all. They were happy days, when you and Mr Moreton were children – what a funny child he was, so serious, like a little old man.'

'Yes, he was rather. Well, he seems younger now.'

'Oh, he's a lovely gentleman, so thoughtful. Always sends me and Jarvis a Christmas present.'

'Does he?' She was amazed that Harry should show such consideration.

'Oh yes, miss, always. And when I was ill in hospital, he sent me some lovely flowers.'

'Good heavens. That is very nice. I'd better go on up, Harris.'

'Yes, of course, miss. I'll bring the tea up.'

She walked upstairs, wondering at a Harry Moreton who could be so rude, so difficult, so absolutely ruthless, and yet who sent presents and flowers to elderly servants; a Harry Moreton who still, clearly, she hardly knew.

It was exactly the same, her room: even her nightdress case on the bed, some of her books on the bedside table. She might take them too: *The Citadel* by A. J. Cronin (signed 'with best love, Rupert' on the fly leaf), *If Winter Comes* by A. S. M. Hutchinson, and *The Water Babies*. That was Leonora's, a beautiful edition; she flicked through it, found an old note from Leonora: 'Darling Sweet Pea, I've gone to see Benedict and Cecily, your supper's left out for you in the dining room.' It must have been on the hall table when she had come in one night, and she'd used it as a bookmark; dear Leonora, always so thoughtful, in spite of everything. Her unhappiness had been the only shadow over her student years. Well – the early student years ...

The pictures were still hanging on the wall, and the two which Sir Richard had thought she'd like propped against the bed. They were very pretty: slightly sentimental early Victorian portraits, exactly what Leonora would have liked, but perfect for her new drawing room. One was of a small boy and a very large dog, the other a little girl sitting in a dog cart: they would sit very happily on either side of the window or on the staircase. They were in very nice maple frames, although one of those was very battered. It would need fixing. She turned it over; the backing was very loose, completely unfixed on one side. Maybe she could just stick it down, but it was bulging a bit. There seemed to be something inside. Cassia pushed her fingers in carefully, and a sheaf of papers fell out.

They were pawnbrokers' tickets: dozens of them. It was very sad. Leonora had obviously seen the frame as a safe hiding place. Much better than a drawer or a wallet. They were mostly for jewellery, but there was also one for a 'mother-o'-pearl picture frame', another for some hat pins – God, Leonora must have been desperate – a cigarette case, 'gold with ruby'.

Cassia sat looking at these relics, this desperately sad evidence of Leonora's addiction, and wondered how it happened, how she had come to this. She had never understood; she supposed she never would. Strange, too, that she and Benedict should both have been misfits, in their very different ways: what manner of childhood, or combination of genes, she wondered, could produce two such sadly hungry characters?

She looked at the tickets: they were all dated from very long ago, some as early as 1920. Never redeemed, of course: and everything long sold, no doubt. She knew Benedict had tried to trace some of the jewellery, in vain. Well, pawnbrokers had a living to earn, they sold everything after six months, or was it a year? She looked at the addresses: all over London, places like Paddington, Croydon, Golders Green. And one in Leather Lane, 'just off [it said] Hatton Garden'; that was the photograph frame.

The frame sounded very pretty. She couldn't actually remember it, but could imagine it: it would be small and elaborately worked and probably a bit battered. Leonora had loved such things, was always bringing them home from antique shops, having paid far too much for them. Obviously there was no point in even trying to get it, but she wasn't far from Hatton Garden. She still had a lot of day to fill. And the date on the ticket was only 1928. Well, it was ridiculous. That was eight years ago. Of course it wouldn't be there. But something tugged at her. She would just check. It could do no harm. It might have been hard to sell such a thing.

She took the pictures back to Walton Street, stood them round the drawing room, made herself a sandwich and then took a cab to Hatton Garden. She walked down a small alley to Leather Lane, half expecting the pawnbroker's itself to be gone: but no, there it was, with the statutory three brass balls outside. She went in.

There was a young man at the counter, impatiently half polite; well, she supposed courtesy was not an essential quality in a pawnbroker. She started, rather haltingly, to explain her mission. When he saw the dates on the ticket he smiled, a rather condescending smile.

'We wouldn't keep anything that long,' he said, 'especially not something like that, valueless, you know.'

'Yes. Well, I just wondered—'

'It costs to store things, you know. We don't just have unlimited space. So ...' He was obviously anxious to be rid of her. She sighed, said, 'Then I won't waste your time.'

'Got a problem, Mr Taylor?' A much older man had appeared from the back of the shop. He looked as if he never set foot outside it, his skin parchment coloured, his hair in need of cutting, even his nails too long.

'No, no problem,' said the young man. 'This lady seemed to think we might keep things for nine years or more.'

'Well,' said the old man, smiling at her, the papery skin crinkling round his eyes, 'it's been known. What is it you've got?'

'Just this ticket. Practically an antique in itself, actually.' She smiled at him; she liked him. 'It was my godmother's.'

'Let me see.' He took it. 'Oh, yes, I see. Mother-of-pearl frame, eh? Unusual. Well, I'll have a look. Hard to sell, I'm surprised I bought it. She must have been a very regular customer. What did she look like?'

'Very pretty. Fair, blue eyes. Very well dressed. Loved hats. And big fur collars with the foxes' heads. About forty. She probably brought you lots of things.'

'Oh! Mrs Jarvis.' So she had used the butler's name, Cassia thought, touched yet further by this illustration of Leonora's dangerously secret life. 'Yes, I do remember her. She was a very regular customer. Brought in the most lovely cigarette case once, modern it was, Cartier. Broke my heart, taking that from her. How is she? Haven't seen her for a little while.'

'No, I'm sure you haven't,' said Cassia. 'Very sadly she's died. She died last year.'

'I am very sorry to hear that. She was a great lady. Always gave me a little gift for Christmas. I wondered why not last year—'

'Last year? But ...' Leonora had been in Paris for years; how extraordinary to remember her pawnbroker.

'Yes, that was the first time she forgot. Well, of course she didn't forget, poor lady. Now you wait there, and I'll just go and see if I can find that frame.' He disappeared upstairs. Cassia sat on a hard chair and waited.

After ten minutes he came down, shaking his head.

'No frame, sadly. But there is this.' He held out a gold filigree bracelet. 'This was hers, she was very upset at parting with it. Her mother's, she said. Well, I could afford to keep it, I thought she might just be able to

244

redeem it one day.' He shook his head, looked at the bracelet. 'Lovely, isn't it? Beautiful piece of work, done in India, she said.'

'Yes, it is lovely.' She didn't remember the bracelet, but then Leonora had had so much jewellery. Most of it faked. 'Could I buy it now? Redeem it, I mean. I'd like to.'

'Of course. It's quite expensive though. Let's see … a hundred pounds. That's less than I gave her, but I was sorry for her. Sorry to see her come back.'

'Back? What do you mean?'

'Well, it was after she'd gone abroad. She did go abroad, didn't she? I haven't got it wrong?' Cassia nodded. 'Yes, I thought so. I thought with the new life she'd be all right.'

'Oh, but she was.' It seemed important that he should understand, should not see Leonora as some broken-down fallen woman. 'She was living in some style, in Paris. Honestly.'

'Really?' He looked at her doubtfully. 'Well, if you say so. But she was desperate for the money for this, I can tell you that. Desperate. That's why I gave her so much.'

'And when was this?' said Cassia. She felt rather odd suddenly, slightly scared, she had no idea of what.

'Not long ago. Look, the ticket's on it. November 'thirty-four. That's when she gave me my Christmas present. "I'm sorry its so late, Mr Fisher," she said, "but better late than never," and gave me a little box of truffles. I felt bad, because she clearly couldn't afford it, if she was selling her mother's bracelet, but she insisted. Are you all right, madam? You look a little pale.'

'Yes. Yes, I'm fine, really.' She managed to smile at him. 'You must let me give you the full amount, what you paid her. What was it?'

'A hundred and twenty. But you don't have to do that.'

'Yes, I do. To say thank you. And that was the last time you saw her?'

'Yes, that's right.'

'I see.' She wanted to get out of the shop now, get back to the house, sit down quietly and think. 'Well, thank you again, many times. And for your kindness to her. Goodbye, Mr Fisher. Thank you.'

Outside, she hailed a cab, sat in it, looking at the bracelet. Trying to work out some kind of explanation. Because if Leonora was still desperately pawning things six months before her death, how in heaven's name could she have had half a million pounds to leave to Cassia? However carefully it had been put in trust? And surely, in any case, the interest earned on that sort of money would be very considerable indeed?

It simply didn't make any sort of sense. Any sort at all.

By four o'clock, Leon de Rosay still hadn't phoned Edwina. She was very anxious. 'It's terribly important I speak to him,' she said to the directrice, 'really desperate. You will give him the message the minute he gets in, won't you?'

'I will, of course, Mrs Moreton, yes,' said the directrice. Her voice was cool; she obviously didn't approve of Edwina chasing her employer in this rather unseemly way.

'When do you leave the salon?'

'When my work is done,' said the directrice, more coolly still. 'I have no official hour of departure.'

'So you're sure to see him?'

'Yes, Mrs Moreton. Quite sure.'

Edwina decided to ring Benedict to warn him that Leon was coming, but he wasn't in his office. 'He's gone home early, Mrs Moreton,' said Mildred Waters. 'Stephanie is singing in a school concert, and he has gone to hear her.'

'Will he be back?'

'I think not.'

She tried the house; neither Benedict nor Cecily was there. She left a message asking for Benedict to phone her, and went up to her room to try and decide which of the two dresses she had just bought from Leon de Rosay she should wear that night.

Cassia phoned Mr Brewster when she got back to Walton Street. He wasn't there, but his secretary said he would be back at five and she would ask him to ring her then. 'Is it urgent, Mrs Fallon?'

'No,' said Cassia, 'not exactly. But I would like to talk to him very much indeed.'

'Mrs Moreton, I've just had a call from Mr de Rosay. I'm afraid he won't be back in the salon this evening. He asked me to tell you he will come to your house straight from the silk suppliers at St Albans.'

'So did you ask him to ring me?'

'I did, yes, Mrs Moreton, and he said he would if it was at all possible.'

'Oh well, thank you anyway. Good afternoon.' Then when the line had been cut, 'Silly bitch,' she said viciously to the telephone.

It rang again almost at once. It was Cecily. 'Edwina, did you want me?'

'Oh, yes. Well, no, not really, it was Benedict, about some … stock I'm interested in.'

'He's playing with Laurence at the moment. Shall I get him to ring you?'

'Yes please. If he's got time.'

'Edwina wants you to ring her,' said Cecily. 'It's about some stock she's thinking of buying.'

'Oh Lord,' said Benedict, 'surely it can wait. I've promised Fan I'll play the piano with her in a minute. I'll see Edwina tonight. Did you think it seemed urgent?'

'No. Not urgent at all.'

Mr Brewster phoned Cassia at a quarter past five; he said he was sorry not to have done so before, but he had been in court all day. 'Is there a problem, Mrs Fallon?'

'No,' she said, looking at Leonora's bracelet, sitting now on her own wrist: she liked it being there, something so personal; it brought Leonora back to her just a little. 'Well, not really. I just wanted to discuss something with you. That's all.'

'Do you want to come into the office?'

'Yes, please. If that would be all right.'

'Of course. Tomorrow morning? Half past ten?'

'Fine. I shall be in London. You have got a copy of the will there, haven't you?'

'I have, indeed. Well, until tomorrow, then. Good evening, Mrs Fallon.'

Cassia put the phone down and sat staring at it. He had seen Leonora, just after she had made the will; he would surely have got some idea of her circumstances. There must be some kind of an explanation for it all; and if he didn't have it, maybe he would know where to find it.

'Edwina, that dress looks quite ghastly on you, absolutely the wrong colour. Why don't you go and change it quickly before anyone else arrives?'

'I don't want to change it, Mummy,' said Edwina firmly, 'and I think it's absolutely the right colour. It's called shocking pink, surely you know, Schiaparelli invented it.'

'You can't invent a colour, Edwina.'

'Well, Schiaparelli did. Anyway, it's Leon's version of it.'

'Who's Leon?'

'Oh, Mummy! I do wish you'd listen when I tell you things. Leon de Rosay, he's *the* new name in couture, he's coming tonight and he's making a huge contribution to the fashion show.'

'Oh, I see. Well, I shall certainly make sure not to go to him for anything. Marcus, do go and find me a drink, and where's Harry, Edwina?'

'Late,' said Edwina briefly, 'getting here about eight, he says.'

She had hardly been able to speak to Harry when he phoned to say that, after all he had said, he would be late. 'I'm sorry, Edwina, I really cannot help it' he had said. 'I have a huge deal going through, and the chap who's organising the finance has been held up at the Bank of England.'

'He really is the limit. Do you think he's got a mistress?'

'I don't know, Mummy, it's really not the sort of thing I'd want to discuss with him, is it? Daddy, can I have a drink too? Just ring for Bishop. There's champagne on ice, of course, and everything else. I'll have champagne. What about you, Mummy?'

'No, dry martini for me. Vodka, Marcus, don't forget, not gin. Who else is coming to this dinner, Edwina?'

'Mummy, I told you. The Whittakers, obviously, which is why I've asked you and Daddy, and Venetia and Paul Hardwicke, and Cassia, and—'

'Oh God, not that terrible husband of hers. Tedious little man.'

'No. But Rupert Cameron.'

'I like Rupert. He's so charming, always so interested in one.'

'Yes. And Benedict and Cecily, and Leon de Rosay, as I said. But the main thing is to keep Mary Whittaker happy, and impress on her how hard I'm working on the fashion show, so she won't be too terribly cross about my flag day.'

'How is your flag day, darling?'

'Flying at half mast. I never got all the letters out even, someone else has taken over.'

'Edwina, that is very naughty,' said Sylvia Fox-Ashley severely. 'Oh, now here is Rupert, and Cassia too. How lovely to see you, Rupert. Come and tell me all about your madly glamorous life. I always look for reviews about you in the paper, but I don't often find any, I can't think why ...'

Edwina was getting rather drunk. She had invited everyone for seven thirty, with a view to serving dinner at eight; at eight fifteen Harry had still not arrived. God, she could kill him; she was sure he did it on purpose.

He walked in, outrageously cool, at eight twenty, still in his suit, kissed her, kissed her mother, bowed to everyone else and asked them to excuse him while he changed into his dinner jacket. 'Five minutes, I swear. Why don't you all go and sit down? Really, I won't mind a bit.'

'Do let's, Edwina,' said Sylvia. 'I'm simply starving and your father will fall over in a minute, he's so tight.'

'All right,' said Edwina, 'let's go in.' Leon de Rosay had not arrived either. Her evening seemed doomed.

She had placed herself on the opposite side of the table from the door, next to Sir John Whittaker; it would be doubly difficult to jump up and intercept Leon when he came in. She'd put him as far as possible from Cecily, in between Cassia and Venetia; he would enjoy them both, and hopefully become so engrossed in conversation about the fashion show that he wouldn't say anything to Benedict. There was nothing more now that she could do except pray.

Harry came in, looking sleek and slightly complacent in his dinner jacket; he sat down, smiled at everyone. 'Sorry again. Edwina will have me flogged later.'

'Sounds fun,' murmured Venetia. 'Harry, have you heard the latest on the little man and Wallis?'

'Depends which latest.'

'He's taken legal advice from Walter Monckton. About Wallis's divorce.'

'Yes, I had heard that,' said Harry. 'Lord Beaverbrook told me.'

'Extraordinary, isn't it?' said Sylvia Fox-Ashley. 'I simply do not understand it. Why can't he just live with the woman quietly, instead of going in for all this nonsense?'

'He's supposedly in love with her,' said Venetia.

'And what does that have to do with it? He can still be with her, whenever he's out of the public eye. I've no patience with him, none at all.'

'How very unusual,' muttered Edwina.

Harry turned to Cassia, who was sitting next to him. 'And what do you think about our beloved King and his behaviour?' he said quietly, smiling at her, his eyes dangerously brilliant.

'I don't have many views on the matter,' she said.

'Really? I'm surprised. The conflict between love and duty: I would have thought that would have been right up your street.'

'Harry, please—'

'You look so very charming when you blush. Anyway, this is a nice surprise. I didn't think we'd get you swept up into our modest little parties quite so quickly after your return to London. I was extremely flattered, by the way, that you took up my suggestion.'

'Harry, I haven't returned to London, as you put it. I'm simply spending two nights a week here after my clinics. And what suggestion, anyway?'

'That you should get a little house up here. I knew you'd see it was a good idea once you'd thought it over. Surely you remember, we were in the Savoy, and—'

'Harry, it was my idea to get the house. As I said, so I didn't have the long drive home after my clinics.'

'Did you have one today? A clinic?'

'Well, no, but—'

'There you are, then,' he said, sitting back, an expression of great satisfaction on his face, 'not just for the clinics. For you as well. And why not? You look very nice, by the way. Lovely dress. Vionnet?'

'Yes, actually,' said Cassia, slightly unwillingly.

'New? I imagine you can't wear anything quite that stylish in the country.'

'Not very,' said Cassia, who had bought the dress the day before with the dinner party absolutely in mind (telling herself it was not for that at all, but to wear all summer, being in cream silk), 'and of course I could wear it in the country. We don't actually walk round with straw in our hair, you know.'

'You don't? You surprise me. Incidentally, you realise what a huge responsibility you have, sitting there, don't you? Next to our guest of honour. Who doesn't seem to have had the courtesy to turn up.'

'He's been held up, apparently, buying silk or something. And I do realise the responsibility. I'm sure I shall enjoy it.'

'Well, you look a lot nicer than Edwina does, I must say. She's wearing something of his. I don't greatly admire his style myself, it's too hard.'

'You're very interested in clothes, aren't you?' said Cassia curiously, confident that this was a safe topic. 'What is it you like about them?'

'I'm very interested in women,' said Harry, leaning back, his eyes moving over her face. 'That's what I like about clothes. What they do for women. How they work. How women choose them and for what reasons. To make themselves look sexy, or chic, or whatever, to show themselves off or to hide behind – it's a very fascinating psychological game. Take you, for instance. What you use your clothes for.'

'Harry, I don't use them, I wear them,' said Cassia irritably.

'Ah, but you're wrong there, you see. I know exactly what you use them for.'

'Oh, you do?'

'I do. To disguise yourself.'

'Disguise myself! That is really ridiculous.'

'The woman we see, these days anyway, is chic, stylish, very cool, very in control. Which, of course, is nonsense.' He grinned at her, picked up his glass. 'You're not drinking; this is excellent wine.'

'Why is it nonsense?'

'Because chic and stylish though you may be, you aren't in control at all.'

'Is that really so?' she said, forcing herself to smile at him, praying her voice would stay steady.

'Absolutely so. You're positively careering along, driven by the most fearsome passions. Much more interesting.' He smiled back at her.

'How nice it must be for you to be able to read everyone so expertly, Harry,' she said. 'Do you never make mistakes?'

'Very, very seldom. And certainly not about you, I know you much too well.'

Sensing the danger, she decided to change the subject, to a matter at once safer and more deadly still. 'Harry, I want to ask you something. It's about—' She had been going to say Leonora, but at that moment the door opened.

'Leon!' Edwina got up, walked round the table, kissed Leon de Rosay where he stood in the doorway, ushered in by Bishop. 'How wonderful of you to come after your dreadful day. Do come in and meet everyone.' The introductions went round the table, Leon smiling, bowing, shaking hands, kissing cheeks.

Cassia watched him, thinking how handsome he was, that he was probably, almost certainly, a homosexual (although most soberly and carefully dressed and most modestly behaved), observing people reacting to him, admiring Edwina's élan as a hostess that she should invite him to her dinner table with people like the Whittakers. But of course, in his role as couturier, that was somehow all right: he was simply a turn, the star of the evening, served up for everyone's amusement.

She watched Rupert greeting him, so easily charming, Cecily smiling, but oddly watchful, and then, oh God, then heard him say, into what seemed a very big silence, as he was introduced to Benedict, 'Yes, of course, we met the other day, did we not, at lunch?'

'Really?' said Cecily, smiling more sweetly than ever. 'Benedict, you didn't tell me.'

'Yes,' said Benedict, and he was just very slightly flushed, Cassia noticed, but immensely, intensely casual. 'That's right, so we did, at – oh, now where was it?' He paused, waiting, probably praying, she thought, but his prayers were not answered.

'It was at Chez Victoire,' said Leon de Rosay. 'So amusing there, isn't it? And such wonderful food. I was with Mrs Moreton, and you were with Dominic Foster. Such a very clever man, isn't he? An artist friend of mine has bought one of those wonderful studios in Pimlico, really quite extraordinary they are. Such great style he has. Not quite le Corbusier, perhaps, but still ... Now, please, do all sit down and continue with your meal.'

'What a nightmare,' said Edwina. She was sitting at her dressing table, brushing her hair viciously.

'Oh, I don't know,' said Harry. He was lounging in a chair, smoking, drinking a last brandy, watching her closely. 'I thought it was rather fun.'

'Yes, well, it might have seemed fun to you. And your being late didn't exactly help. Dinner being served an hour after everyone arrived. Apart from anything else, it makes Mrs Barclay so cross, when she's timed everything so carefully. The partridge were hopelessly overdone. And then Cecily sitting there, hardly talking, looking as if she had a golf ball up her backside, after Leon's little announcement.'

'You could have warned your friend Leon, for God's sake. Told him not to say anything. I really didn't like him, by the way. I'd rather you didn't ask him again.'

'Harry, I was trying to get hold of him all day to warn him. I couldn't. And I told you, he's doing an incredible amount for my fashion show. And whether you like him or not is immaterial.'

'It's not immaterial when he's sitting at my dining table,' said Harry. His voice was hard.

Edwina changed the subject. 'And then Benedict getting so drunk and practically climbing inside Venetia's dress, I suppose to show us all how normal he is, and Mary Whittaker giving us all a moment by moment account of last year's flag day. It's the last time I try and help anyone, that's all I can say.'

'Let's go to bed,' said Harry. 'It wasn't really that bad, and you carried it off extremely well. As usual. You really are extraordinarily competent, Edwina. So very good at taking control. Of everything.' He stood up suddenly, came over to her, put his hands on her shoulders, moved them down towards her breasts, kissed her hair.

Edwina looked at him warily in the mirror. 'Harry, please don't. I've got the curse and—'

'Again?' said Harry lightly. He moved away from her. 'It seems to happen with great frequency these days.'

'Yes, well, it is a regular occurrence, Harry, in case you didn't realise.'

There was a silence. Then: 'Edwina, I've been thinking. It's about time, I would say, that we had a child. What would you say?'

'I don't know. I haven't really thought about it very much at all.'

'No? Well, perhaps you could begin. Thinking about it. I find I rather like the idea of a son and heir. Suddenly.'

'And what if I don't?'

'I'd see that as rather unfair. Actually. We've been married quite a long time. Five years. I've been very patient. Now I find I'm getting rather impatient. All right?'

Edwina was silent.

'So perhaps you'd stop using whatever it is you do use, and start keeping at least one of your marriage vows. Goodnight, Edwina. I'll see you in the morning.' He picked up his brandy glass and walked out of the room, closing the door rather firmly behind him.

Edwina looked after him and sighed: a heavy, almost tearful sigh. She felt a bit sick. It really hadn't been a good evening – in any way at all.

CHAPTER 14

Cassia had just turned her light out when the phone rang. She picked it up, her heart beating very fast, terrified it was Janet, or even Edward, to say that one of the children was ill, missing, the house was on fire, Edward himself had had a car crash ...

'Cassia? It's Rupert. Darling, I've missed my last train. Could you give a poor vagrant a bed for the night?'

'This is lovely,' he said, looking round the drawing room. 'What fun, Cassia, I do envy you.'

'Isn't it? I feel awfully guilty about it, but ...'

'Why on earth should you feel guilty? Silly girl. You've got all that lovely money, and Leonora wanted you to enjoy it. You must do that, for her.'

'You're right, I am being silly. Anyway, it's only to help me do my work.'

'What does Edward think about it?' said Rupert casually. 'Was he very cross?'

'No, not really. He's treading a bit warily at the moment, what with Maureen Johnson and everything. Incidentally, Rupert, what do you think about this? It's really worrying me.'

She told him about the pawn tickets, about Leonora, about her own bafflement. 'She'd pawned this bracelet. Look, I bought it back today. From this place in Hatton Garden. It was her mother's, apparently. Her mother's! Who would pawn something of their mother's unless they were desperate?'

'I shouldn't worry, darling. You have to remember it was a sickness she had. It's not like you or me pawning something of our mother's. She'd obviously got herself into a mess, didn't want to tell Rollo.'

'Yes, but how could you be in a mess if you had the sort of money she was leaving me?'

'It was in trust, wasn't it? That was the whole point, I thought. She couldn't get at it.'

She was silent, too tired to begin to make sense of it. 'It just worries me, that's all. It doesn't feel right. Did you see Leonora at all, during the last year or so?'

'Once, yes,' he said.

'Where did you see her, though? In London?'

'Yes. She came over to see a doctor here. Thought he might be able give her better, different news.'

'Oh God, I wish I'd known. Why didn't anyone tell me?'

'She made us all promise not to—'

'All? Who's all?'

'Oh,' he said easily, 'me, Harry, Benedict. She thought you had enough to cope with. If the news had been good, then she'd have rung you up, asked you to lunch, taken you shopping, I expect. As it wasn't ...'

'You all still seem to think I'm a child,' she said sulkily. 'It's so unfair.'

'Cassia, we don't. But you were – well, your life wasn't easy.'

'Don't make it sound as if I was living in some kind of a workhouse,' she said, angrily, 'I was –' she corrected herself – 'I *am* perfectly all right. I'm very happy. I have a good marriage, I have three lovely children, we have a nice house – of course I could cope with Leonora being ill. It's ridiculous. I could have comforted her, been with her, helped her. There are all sorts of new ideas about cancer treatment, anyway. I might even have been able to help.'

'She had the very best treatment,' he said firmly, 'that money could buy. The best doctors, the latest drugs.'

'Organised by Rollo?'

'I suppose.'

'Even though he'd left her?'

'He was most concerned that she should be properly cared for. He visited her, right up to the end.'

'How do you know that?' she said curiously. 'He was so ghastly, I just find it hard to believe.'

'Harry told me. And I believe Harry saw him too. He did a lot for Leonora, you know, Harry. He was ...' He hesitated. 'He was with her when she died.'

'I didn't know.' She was almost shocked; somehow it seemed so unlike Harry. It took a particular kind of courage, that, a willingness to confront pain; and he had never told her, never sought to impress her with it. Yet again her view of him shifted; yet again that was uncomfortable.

'So you see, she was as well looked after as she could possibly be,' said Rupert.

'Yes. Yes, I do see,' she said. It all seemed to make sense: perfect sense. She just didn't feel quite easy about it, that was all.

'Talk to your solicitor chappie again about it.'

'Yes, I'm going to. Thank you for listening. As always.'

'My pleasure, darling. Funny evening, wasn't it? A bit tense.'

'Just a bit. Clearly Cecily was very unhappy about the lunch.'

'Well, we saw it coming, didn't we? At Christmas. And she can't fight it. Neither of them can. Oh, dear. What a mess. Poor Benedict.'

'Poor Cecily too. The thing is, Rupert, she just doesn't understand it at all. She sees his homosexuality as a mixture of a crime and an illness. She's forced him to have some awful treatment.'

'Really? What sort of treatment?'

'Oh, it's hideous. I read about it when I was studying genito-urinary medicine. They show these poor chaps pictures of pretty boys and then give them an electric shock. Or sometimes an emetic. It's supposed to cure them.'

'Jesus,' said Rupert.

'I know. Hideous. But I suppose it is so hard for her. Poor Cecily.'

'Yes.' There was a silence; then he said, 'Harry was very good, I thought. Smoothing things over quite brilliantly, changing subjects like mad. I was very impressed, I'd never seen him as a social lubricant before.'

'No. Nor had I.' She could hear her own voice, cool, half hostile.

Rupert looked at her, half amused. 'You still feel very ambivalent about him, don't you?'

'Who, Harry? No, Rupert, I don't feel in the least ambivalent. I still find him rude and difficult. In fact, I quite dislike him, most of the time.'

'All right, darling. Have it your own way. I must say I'll never forget your performance at the Embassy. It was very dramatic.'

'Oh, don't,' said Cassia. 'I've worked very hard on forgetting that.'

'You shouldn't forget about it, you were magnificent. If a little terrifying. Oh, now talking of dramatic and, indeed, magnificent, I think we might have a leading lady. For *Letters*. She's called Eleanor Studely. She's beautiful, she's intelligent, she's a very fine actress and we can afford her. She's never quite made it in the top league. Best of all, she'd love to do it. So the whole project gets a bit nearer.'

'Rupert, I'm so pleased. Just let me know when you need something from me, won't you? Now look, I really must go to bed, I'm all in. Your room is all ready for you. It's up there on the top floor just opposite mine.'

'Darling, how exciting. To be sleeping so near you. I think perhaps we should keep quiet about this little assignation, don't you?'

'What assignation?' said Cassia, laughing. 'Rupert, you are ridiculous.'

'No, I'm not,' he said, and she could see that he was quite serious. 'I really don't think it would be a good idea if your husband – or, indeed, Edwina Moreton and her set – knew we had spent the night together under the same roof. You know how gossip flies about.'

'Yes, but—' She stopped, suddenly seeing it from other people's perspective: a young wife, a rich young wife, taking a house alone in London, away from her family responsibilities, and an old flame, one she had been famously devoted to for years, suddenly staying at her house. It was a strange and oddly disturbing thought; not just in its implications but its possibilities.

'Maybe you're right,' she said, standing up quickly, 'however absurd the idea.'

'Darling! Not too absurd, I hope. Am I really so decrepit?'

'No, of course not,' she said, looking at him (still so handsome, so very attractive, sitting smiling up at her, hers – in theory – for the taking). 'You're not in the least decrepit, and I adore you. Yes, all right, it shall be our secret. Goodnight, Rupert.'

'Goodnight, Cassia. Sleep well. And if I wander into your room in the night, send me very swiftly off to have a cold bath.'

'I certainly will,' she said, and went upstairs laughing.

But she couldn't sleep. The discovery of the pawn tickets, the oddly moving revelation that Harry had been with Leonora when she had actually died, Rupert's reference to what he called her performance at the Embassy, had all disturbed her. She opened her curtains and sat up in bed, staring out at the London skyline, thinking about all of it, remembering that night, remembering her performance, half ashamed even now at how she had behaved.

It had been Cecily's birthday, the year before Delia had been born. Benedict had telephoned and said he was going to take a party of friends to the Embassy to celebrate, and that Cecily had particularly requested that Cassia and Edward were there.

'We're going there because it happens to be a Thursday.'

'Oh, I see,' said Cassia, laughing. After four years of country-based domesticity she still remembered Thursdays at the Embassy, the night when everyone – 'but everyone', as Edwina would have said – was there. 'It sounds a lovely idea, Benedict, and thank you for asking us, but we can't possibly come.'

'Why not?'

Why not? Why not, indeed? So many reasons. She had nothing to wear. Edward's dinner jacket, the one he had had as a medical student, was so shiny now with wear it attracted jokes even amongst their friends in the village, and, besides, the Embassy was white tie. Edward would, in any case, refuse to go; or if he did, under enormous pressure, would spend the evening sulking silently until she wanted to hit him. They couldn't afford it, the inevitable expenditure, however much it was presented as a party and they as guests: taxis, at least one lot of drinks for everyone, babysitting, a present for Cecily, her hair would need cutting ... and Harry would be there.

'No, I'm sorry, Benedict, we really can't. We're—' A sudden anger struck her, as much at the impossibility of explaining as at not being able, never being able, to do anything like that, have any fun any more; anger at Edward too, for his absolute unwillingness to participate in her old life, in what she would enjoy; at having to avoid Harry Moreton at every turn, for fear of what he could do to her and her peace of mind. 'We just can't,' she said. 'Don't ask me why, we can't. I'm sorry,' and she put the phone down and burst into tears.

Five minutes later Cecily phoned. 'Cassia, please come. Don't say a word, just listen. Bring the children with you, of course. My hairdresser is coming here, he'll do your hair. Wear that black dress you wore last Christmas, it was divine. I'd give anything to be able to wear clothes like you do. If you want to bring me a present, nothing could make me happier than some cuttings of that perfect white rose for my terrace. Come without Edward, if he doesn't want to come. I want you here, it's my birthday, and you'll spoil it if you don't.'

Faced with such graceful, tactful, loving hospitality, how could she give the one remaining, overpoweringly important reason for her not going?

It had been fine at first, absolutely wonderful. There had been twelve of them. Rupert had come with his latest love, a very pretty girl called Yolande, who would have made Cassia jealous, and spoilt her evening, had she not told Cassia she was about to go to Hollywood with a three-year contract with Selznick.

They had found a partner for Cassia, a rather nice and funny man called Patrick Compton whom she had met before at the Christmas parties. He had sat next to her at dinner at the house and made her laugh so much she had twice choked and had to have her back banged rather over-heartily by an already drunk Benedict. Harry had been sitting at the other end of the table and had hardly spoken to her; he and Edwina had clearly had a row and he was not speaking to her either.

They had piled into cars at half past eleven and driven to Bond Street. The entrance to the Embassy at the Piccadilly end was down a long passage where a man stood all night selling gardenias to the guests. Patrick Compton bought Cassia one.

Luigi, the *maître d'*, greeted Cassia by name, which gave her a disproportionate amount of pleasure, and showed them to a pair of sofas, with ice buckets set beside them; she found herself settled between Patrick and Benedict, a glass of champagne in her hand topped up so regularly that she became swiftly confused and thought she couldn't be drinking any at all.

Patrick Compton was not a good dancer, but he continued to be funny, even on the dance floor; she danced with Benedict, who was superb, and then Rupert who was, of course, even better.

'You look marvellous,' Rupert said, kissing her hand tenderly as he led her back from the floor. 'Really very, very lovely. You light this dreary old place up, you know.'

'Oh, Rupert, honestly,' she said, looking around, laughing, 'dreary old place, indeed. It seems like heaven to me, absolutely packed with good-looking people, look at them all. You don't know what dreary is, Rupert. You should come to a social evening at the village hall, then you would.'

'If you were there it would be wonderful,' he said. 'Now let me give you some more champagne, and then I think the dashing Lord Wynford is waiting to claim you.'

Lord Wynford did indeed, and then another man and yet another. She felt dizzy, drunk with pleasure and the champagne and the freedom from her workaday life. And then finally, just as her pleasure peaked, she looked up and saw Harry Moreton standing in front of her. He half bowed.

'May I have this dance?'

'Yes, of course,' she said, taking the hand he held out, carefully not meeting his eyes.

He led her on to the floor; the band was playing 'Nice Work If You Can Get It'. That was good, that was safe. Nothing slow, nothing dangerous. She always forgot how well Harry danced, his heavy frame becoming somehow lighter, swifter, his sense of rhythm faultless. She told him so.

'I never forget how well you dance,' he said, and smiled at her. 'Or anything else about you, for that matter.'

The number ended. She pulled away from him, said thank you, made as if to leave the dance floor. The music began again, slower, more dangerous: not good, not safe. Harry pulled her back towards him, took her in his arms. She moved carefully, cautiously, holding herself just away from him.

'You can't do it, Cassia,' he said.

'Can't do what?'

'Avoid me. It doesn't work. Come on, why don't you just enjoy yourself? And me. Just for once.'

'Harry, I'm not avoiding you.'

'Of course you are.' He drew her closer, his arms very strong, their pressure impossible to resist. She gave in. He was very warm, as he always was; she felt alarmingly safe and happy suddenly. She smiled at him.

'That's better. Do you realise I haven't seen you since that rather exciting day at Brooklands?'

'Yes, Harry, I do.'

'I'm sorry about that.'

'There's nothing to forgive.'

'I mean I'm sorry we had to go home.'

'Harry, of course we had to go home.'

'We didn't have to. We didn't have to at all. But what I meant was, I'm sorry we had to go home too soon.'

'It wasn't too soon,' she said primly. 'It was hardly soon enough.'

'Don't be ridiculous, Cassia. You know what I mean.' He pulled her closer still, his mouth now in her hair. She began to give in to him, to the music, the sentiment, the nonsense – and the emotion, the longing, her own greed for him. She did know what he meant; and he realised it.

'We have to do something, you know,' he said suddenly, as the music changed again. 'Just the Way You Look Tonight': more dangerous still.

'What about?'

'About us.'

'Harry, I really don't know what you mean.'

'Of course you do. I really cannot contemplate spending the rest of my life entirely without you. It's a monstrous prospect.'

'Don't be absurd,' she said, half amused, half irritated. 'How can it be monstrous? We're both married now.'

'Well, that's your fault,' he said.

'Oh, Harry. You are ridiculous.'

'It's you who is ridiculous. Cassia, look at me.'

He had almost stopped dancing; his face as she looked up at it was as still as his body. Still, expressionless, except for his eyes searching hers. She felt them, those eyes, felt them as a physical force, deep within her, a powerful, probing energy. She was silent.

'Cassia, please! Stop running away from me. I can't stand it.'

Anger flooded her suddenly, anger mixed with frustration and a dreadful regret. 'Why do you do this to me?' she said, her voice very low. 'Why can't you accept it? Why won't you leave me alone?'

'You know why,' he said, 'and I can't and I won't.'

She wrenched herself free from him then, stood back from him filled with a blind rage that shut out everything but him; shut out the other dancers, the people watching from the small tables at the edge of the floor, the band ... 'You have to,' she said, 'you absolutely have to. It's awful what you're doing to me, Harry, horrible ...'

'It's your own fault,' he said then. 'You should have had more sense, more courage.'

And then she did lose her temper entirely, raised her hand and struck him very, very hard across the face. The sound was drowned by the music, but it could be seen, that blow, seen in the oasis of stillness, of violent emotion they had created on the crowded floor; everyone saw it, the whole place saw it. And mercifully misread it.

She had left him there, gone swiftly over to their party, holding the tears back somehow. 'Sorry,' she said briefly, smiling rather fiercely. 'Lost my temper. Sorry, Edwina, your husband said something that offended me. Very much. So silly of me. Sorry, Cecily, Benedict. Rupert, shall we dance?'

And Rupert, dear Rupert, already half standing up to greet her, his eyes anxious, careful, took her hand, led her back to the floor, where they danced for a long time, where slowly she calmed down, where carefully, tactfully, he asked her no questions of any kind. Harry Moreton had disappeared.

'Yes, all right, Cecily. I did it. I committed this terrible crime. I had lunch with Dominic.'

'Don't try and make it sound innocent, Benedict. I know it isn't.'

'For Christ's sake,' said Benedict. He lit another cigarette: it was the last in his case. It had been full when they had left home that evening, Cecily remembered him filling it. 'Foster is working on a housing development in which my firm, and indeed Harry's, has an interest. It was just a business lunch.'

'Really? In a small intimate restaurant in Chelsea? Why not Rules, the Savoy, somewhere nearer your office, or your club?'

'Because ... Jesus, Cecily, what is this, an inquisition?'

'Yes. Yes, it is,' she said, her voice rising. 'I want to know.'

'You don't want to know at all. You want the usual soothing platitudes. You've no interest in what I'm really doing, really feeling.'

'And what are you really feeling?'

He hesitated, almost caught in his own trap, then he said, 'I just told you, you don't actually want to know. What I feel is of no interest to you, providing I behave exactly as you want me to behave, toe whatever line your crazed imagination might have drawn. But I will tell you. I feel desperate, Cecily, stifled, hardly able to breathe. I can't react naturally to anyone, for fear of what you might think. I can't have the most lighthearted conversation with a man, make the most informal of arrangements, enjoy the most pleasant exchange. I do warn you, if you were seeking to drive me out of the house, you could not be going a more cast-iron way about it.'

'Oh, for God's sake,' she said. 'If you're going to—'

'No, Cecily, let me finish. I do everything you ask of me: I'm a devoted father, a perfect family man, a loving, loyal husband. I submitted to that appalling treatment for you, I have never asked you for a moment's sympathy or consideration for my own feelings—'

'Sympathy!'

'Yes, sympathy. Do you really think it has all been easy for me, that I have never felt any distress, any confusion?'

'Of course I don't. That's unfair. I forgave you, totally—'

'It's not forgiveness I want, Cecily. Forgiveness seems a very ugly word to me in this context. I want understanding. And I have never ever had that from you.'

He left the house after that; she heard the front door slam, his car drive away. She tried to turn her mind away from where he might have gone, and lay for the rest of the night, staring into the darkness, wondering where it would all, finally, end.

'As I told you,' said Mr Brewster, 'I visited your godmother twice in Paris: once to receive her instructions, that I might draw up the will with the power of appointment; once to obtain her signature and that of the witnesses, of course. Who, as you will recall, were her doctor and the priest from the neighbourhood church which she had been attending.'

'Yes, of course. I remember being a bit surprised by that. Leonora was never a churchgoer.'

'The most ardent atheists can become believers, confronted by their own mortality, Mrs Fallon.'

'Yes, I suppose so. And this was in ...?'

'Late March. I could check.'

'No, it doesn't matter. And how did she seem?'

'Well, clearly she was a very sick woman, but her spirits seemed good. As good as they could be under the circumstances, that is.'

'And she was being well looked after? There was no suggestion that she might have financial problems?'

He smiled at her almost reprovingly. 'She could hardly have bequeathed to you what she did, had she been hard up, could she, Mrs Fallon?'

'No, of course not. And this was in Passy?'

'Yes. As I told you, the most beautiful apartment, on the top floor of a building in a very pretty small square. I can give you the address, should you want it. And yes, in answer to your question, there was a nurse in attendance day and night, as well as a personal maid. I really don't think she could have been better cared for.'

'And she had been there for some time?'

'As far as I know. And she died there, of course. Mr Gresham, who set up the Maple Trust, wrote to inform me of the fact. He had spent quite a lot of time with her in those last few weeks, or so it seems. As had her cousin, Mr Moreton.'

'Yes, I had heard that. Poor Leonora.'

'Indeed. But may I say she was in many ways fortunate. So often these days the old are neglected by the young.'

'I would not have neglected her either,' said Cassia, a sudden lump in her throat, 'had I known how ill she was. But for some reason, it was kept from me.'

'Your godmother's own wishes, I believe.'

'So I'm told. Absurd. Anyone would think I was a child.'

Mr Brewster smiled at her. 'To our parents, and their generation, Mrs Fallon, we are always children.'

'And the trust, which actually held the money, what about that? Do you know who set up this Maple Trust?'

'You mean the trustees? I don't have their names immediately to mind, although again I could check. But they were appointed by Mr Gresham.'

'You know that for a fact, do you?'

'Yes, of course. I had to have sight of the terms of the trust and the document granting your godmother the power of appointment before I could draw up the document by which she could exercise it.' He smiled almost apologetically. 'I'm afraid it is very complicated.'

'So who did you deal with?'

'Mr Gresham's solicitors, who appointed the trustees.'

'So he had set up this trust, giving Leonora the power of appointment to leave me the money.'

'Yes,' said Mr Brewster carefully. 'I thought I had explained this before, Mrs Fallon.'

'You had. I'm just trying to get it straight in my mind. And then presumably there would have been interest from the trust fund?'

'Yes, indeed.'

'Which was payable to my godmother?'

'Yes. That was within the terms of the trust.'

She sighed. 'Well, it all seems perfectly straightforward.'

'It is, Mrs Fallon, within the perameters of a certain complexity. Is something troubling you?'

'No,' she said quickly, not really.'

Only it was, she thought, as she drove back to Walton Street; she didn't know what, but something was. She was aware of a tiny, but persistent fear that wouldn't go away. Something was not quite right, didn't exactly fit. Perhaps out of tune was the best way she could find to describe it. Only very slightly. But Cassia had a good ear, and discords troubled her.

'I'm so desperately sorry,' said Edwina. 'I just don't know what to say, Benedict. I did try to contact Leon all day, and you, but—'

'Don't apologise,' said Benedict. 'It was such a silly little thing anyway, absurd to make such a drama about it.' He pushed his hair back, clicked his fingers at the waiter. Edwina had phoned him in his office, asked if she could take him to lunch 'to make amends'. They had met at Rules.

Edwina studied him. He clearly hadn't slept, his face was puffy and very pale, and his hand as he picked up his martini shook. 'You look terrible,' she said sadly, 'really grim.'

'Thanks, Edwina. I feel it. I spent the night at the Turkish baths, at the Savoy.'

'Did you try to explain to Cecily?'

'There was nothing to explain. Quite rightly, she's suspicious of Foster, I mean suspicious that he's not – that he is – oh God.'

'All right, Benedict, I can imagine what he's not, or rather what he is,' said Edwina. 'She does sound rather unbalanced about it all, though. What's in a lunch, for God's sake?'

'She feels very strongly about these things, as I told you.' He ordered two more martinis: her second; his third.

'Well, you know what I think about it all.'

'Yes. The thing is, Edwina, I don't actually know what to do. I mean, I've reached the end of my tether. I can't go on like this, being watched all the time, like some bloody two-year-old. I do my best, I've done everything she asked, I'm in despair.'

'Poor Benedict.' It was rare for Edwina to feel concern for someone other than herself, but she felt it now. 'I wish I could help.'

'You can't, I'm afraid. Nobody can. I don't know what to do. I feel ...' He sighed, looked at her, smiled shakily. 'I feel so terribly alone. That's the worst thing.'

'You're not alone,' said Edwina firmly. 'You've got me. And Harry. For what that's worth.'

'I like Harry,' said Benedict, 'very much. He's a good chap. Don't underrate him, Edwina. It would be a big mistake. Let's have some food. It might help.'

The clinic was particularly busy that night: after three hours Mrs Barker, the receptionist, came in to report a waiting room 'still half full'.

Rupert had asked her if he could stay another night; he was seeing Eleanor Studely and Jasper Hamlyn for a drink that evening, to discuss the possibility of her doing *Letters*, and in the morning the three of them were seeing the management of the Second House theatre. 'I'm sorry to ask, darling, but it would be so much easier than going up and down to Brighton two more times. And I'll have a lovely supper waiting for you, like a good wife.'

'Don't talk about good wives,' Cassia had said with a shudder.

Now, the thought of him being there and the supper he would prepare – Rupert was an excellent cook – were the only things getting her through the endless evening.

On these occasions, particularly when she was tired – and she was very tired – Cassia began to feel she was hallucinating as the endless stream of women – mostly young, a few older, all with problems – came into her room. She only saw the more difficult cases: Nurse Hampton dealt with the straightforward ones. At about eight, there was a knock at her door.

'Dr Fallon?' said Joan Hampton.

However tired she was, being called Dr Fallon never failed to revive her. She smiled. 'Yes?'

'Bit of a difficult case here. Young woman in tears. She's got an infection, I think.'

'Send her in.'

The girl who came in: must have been about nineteen at the most. Cassia smiled at her. 'Sit down. What's your name?'

'Jane Ford, Doctor.'

'And what's the problem, Jane?'

'Well, it all hurts, Doctor. Really badly.'

She knew what 'all' meant. She smiled at Jane Ford encouragingly. 'How long has it hurt for?'

'Well, since I – I lost the baby, Doctor.'

'And when was that? And how far gone were you?'

'It was six weeks ago, Doctor. And I was almost three months.' She looked down, fiddled with her hands.

'Tell me about it. Did you just start to bleed? Did you have a fall?'

'I just started bleeding. Really badly.'

'Did you call a doctor?'

'No. My mum was with me, she said there was no need.'

'I see. And were you in a lot of pain?'

'Yes. Quite a lot.' She still didn't meet Cassia's eyes.

'And then what happened?'

'Well, after a while the baby just … just came.'

'Poor you. And did you go on bleeding a lot?'

'Yes, Doctor, quite a lot. It eased after a few days, but it's never really …' Her voice tailed away, she didn't look at Cassia.

'But you still didn't go to a doctor?'

'No.'

'And now you're in pain. Have you resumed intercourse with your husband?' She knew the answer to that one.

'Yes.'

'And it's very painful?'

'Yes.'

'Well, let's have a look at you. On to the couch here. I'll be as gentle as I can.'

The girl gripped the sides of the couch; Cassia began by palpating her abdomen, to relax her. She was hot; Cassia took her temperature. 'Jane, you've got a fever. A hundred and one. How do you feel generally?'

'Rotten, Doctor.'

She hardly needed to examine her any further; it was horribly clear. The cervix was inflamed and damaged; she was still bleeding slightly. She had obviously had an abortion.

'Jane, I'm sorry, but I really think you need to go to hospital. Don't look so frightened.' (As if she didn't know the reason for the fear.) 'Nobody will hurt you. I think you need some quite urgent medical treatment, possibly minor surgery – under anaesthetic naturally.'

'Oh, I can't do that,' said Jane Ford. 'Can't you just give me something for the pain and the bleeding? That's all I want. My husband's getting very – well, upset.' (Yes, he would be, thought Cassia.) 'He's been away a lot, you see, he's a commercial traveller and—'

'Jane, if you want to talk about this, you know it's all absolutely confidential. I mean, if there's something more I should know. It won't go any further and nor would it if you were to go to hospital.' Jane looked at her, and her lips folded very resolutely. 'No. There isn't any more, Doctor.'

Cassia gave up. 'Well, all right, but it's vital you don't even try to have any intercourse for at least two months. And you must rest, and pay very strict attention to your personal hygiene. Take these iron pills, and I'm going to give you what we call a douche, to use at least twice daily. I want you to come back in two weeks and see me again ...'

'That one'll never come back,' she said to Nurse Hampton, who had come in with the news there were still three more cases she'd like her to see. 'I'd bet everything I've got on her having had a little fling with someone else while her husband was away, got pregnant, went to a back-street abortionist. Now she's in ribbons, she's got a bad infection, and she'll probably end up sterile if she's lucky. If she's not, she might even die. If only there was something we could do for these infections as well; they're so terribly hard to treat. Oh, Nurse Hampton, sometimes I think we aren't making any progress at all.'

'Of course we are,' said Joan Hampton stoutly. 'At least we're here. And she might come back. Now, can you really cope with these last three? It's after nine ...'

'Yes, of course I can.'

She got home at a quarter past ten. Rupert was in the drawing room reading. He came down to greet her, settled her at the table and dished up a delicious fish pie.

'You look all in.'

'I am all in.'

'Oh God. My fault, isn't it? Keeping you up all night talking ...'

'Of course it's not your fault, Rupert,' she said, almost irritably. 'I'm all in because I've been sitting in front of an endless stream of wretched young women, most of them beyond my help.'

'I'm sorry. Here, drink this. It's a very nice wine, I bought it this afternoon from Berry Brothers.'

'Oh, Rupert, this is absolutely wonderful. Thank you.'

'Edward phoned,' he said.

'Edward!'

'Yes. Is that unusual?'

'Quite. Is there something wrong?'

'I don't think so. He sounded quite calm. Something about tomorrow?'

'I'd better ring him. Oh dear.'

Edward sounded coldly, horribly furious. 'Why is Rupert Cameron there?'

How could she begin to explain? 'Because he needed a bed for the night. And I offered him one.'

'How good of you. How convenient for him.'

'Oh, Edward, please! I'm exhausted. I've just done a six-hour clinic. Look, is there something wrong, otherwise—'

'Nothing really, no,' he said, clearly controlling his voice with a great effort. 'Maureen's father has been taken ill, she can't do her mother and baby clinic in the morning. I wondered if you could help, just with—'

Rage ripped through Cassia: fierce, dangerous. 'Just with what, Edward? Checking them in? Weighing the babies? Or something more difficult, like prescribing gripe water for them?'

'Cassia, please! God, I wish I'd never rung you.'

'So do I, Edward. But yes, I'll be there. Goodnight.'

'Bastard,' she said to Rupert.

He looked at her in silence, then said, 'Cassia, it's nothing to do with me, but—'

'No,' she said, 'it is nothing to do with you. Let's talk about something else, something more pleasant. How was Miss Studely?'

But it was hard to concentrate and she went to bed as soon as she had finished her supper: only to wake at two with indigestion and a terrible sense of unease.

'I'm going down to Devon for a few days,' said Benedict.

Cecily looked at him. 'Alone?' she said coldly.

'For heaven's sake, Cecily! Of course I'm going alone. I want to have some time to think.'

'About what?'

'About my life. Is that permitted?'

'Yes, of course.' She suddenly felt rather ashamed of herself; maybe he was right, maybe she was driving him away, putting him more at risk. 'I'm very sorry,' she said gently. 'I know I overreacted. It's just that—'

'I know what it is, Cecily, and I understand. But it's very hard to cope with. Very hard indeed. I wish you could trust me a bit more. That's all I ask.' Benedict looked at her. 'I think it's all been said. Over and over again. Anyway, I'm leaving tonight. I'll go straight from the office.'

'You haven't forgotten your son's christening, I hope? On Sunday week.'

'Of course I haven't bloody forgotten it,' he said. 'What do you take me for?'

'I wish I knew,' she said, and then would have given anything to be able to take the words back. Benedict looked at her in silence for a long moment, then walked out of the room, his face set, slamming the door behind him.

Fanny, who was running along the corridor to say goodbye to her mother before she went to school, bumped into him and was very surprised when he told her sharply to look where she was going.

She went into Cecily's room. 'What's the matter with Daddy? He looks very cross.'

'Oh, he's just worried about his work. Nothing serious. Come to give me a kiss goodbye?'

'Yes. Are you all right, Mama?'

'Absolutely all right, darling. See you later. Mind you don't forget your gloves.'

'I won't.' She gave her mother a hug, then picked her hand up and kissed it.

'I love you very much,' she said gravely.

'I love you too,' said Cecily.

If anything happened to Fanny, she thought, looking after her as she went, she would simply want to die. She loved all her children very, very dearly, but Stephanie was very often extremely silly, and Laurence too tiny to be – well, to be anything very much. Fanny, with her sweet seriousness, her gentle ways, her generosity of spirit, was, she knew (and admitted to herself, very occasionally), her favourite, a reflection of all that was best, and none that was worst, in herself. Just contemplating the intensity of her love for Fanny brought tears to Cecily's eyes.

She pulled herself together. She was overwrought because of Benedict and everything; it was just like the over-intense woman she had become, to start weeping over a happy, healthy little girl whose only problem in life was a very slight tendency towards plumpness. As had been her mother's: and still was, Cecily thought, slipping out of her nightdress, getting into the bath that was waiting for her. She must take herself in hand now that Laurence was being bottle-fed and there was no excuse for her to have second helpings of everything. She would begin eating less and doing some exercises that very day. No wonder Benedict hadn't been near her bedroom at night since Laurence had been born.

Perversely, Cassia was rather enjoying helping with the mother and baby clinic. It was all so cheerful: gurgling babies, happy mothers (even if they were tired), rosy toddlers. It seemed a very sharp contrast to the night before, and the pallid, hopeless women, all with seemingly insoluble problems. And the women seemed so pleased to see her, although a few, worryingly, seemed surprised.

'I haven't been away,' she said to one girl who actually told her it was nice to have her back.

'Haven't you? Everyone said you were living in London, gone to work there.'

'I'm only in London two nights a week. Who told you that, anyway?'

The girl looked awkward. 'Nobody actually told me, Mrs Fallon, everyone just seems to know.'

She knew she couldn't blame Edward, or even Maureen, for that; it was simply the rolling avalanche of village gossip.

'All right?' Edward came in, looked at her slightly warily at the end of the morning.

'Yes, fine. All gone now. No serious problems, except the couple I sent in to you.'

'Oh, yes. Davey Mortimer. He does seem to be quite seriously deaf. I can't think why his mother hadn't noticed.'

'Self-deception,' said Cassia briskly. 'No mother can bear the thought that her child is anything but perfect. And he was very good at lip-reading, didn't you notice?'

'No, I didn't.'

'Dear, oh dear.' She shook her head at him, pretending disapproval. 'Fine doctor you are. Just a joke,' she added hastily.

He even managed a smile. 'Thank you so much for doing that for me,' he said.

Cassia smiled back. 'It was a pleasure. Honestly.' It was nice to say that and mean it. It had been a long time, she feared, since she had given him anything but pain.

It was a beautiful midsummer day; after she had collected the boys from school, she gave Janet the rest of the weekend off, made a picnic, and took all the children and Buffy to the woods.

They sat by an almost-dry stream and the boys tried unsuccessfully to dam it; after the third breakthrough, she told them to give up. Delia insisted on standing in the water, giggling as it splashed over her small feet. 'Brond,' she said suddenly, tugging at her mother's hand, pointing downstream.

Cassia looked at William for translation. Delia had rejected the English language in favour of one her own; only William understood it.

'She wants to go down there, round that corner, there's a big branch that's made a bridge. She likes throwing things in the water. Nanny takes us there sometimes. We like it too.'

Cassia crushed the tiny germ of resentment at the thought of Janet doing things with her children that she had not even discovered, and said, 'Well, we must go, then. Come on.'

As they walked home, she said casually, 'So is it all right, then, me being in London those two nights?'

'Of course it is,' said Bertie. 'We don't mind a bit.'

'Course,' echoed William. 'Don't mind a bit.'

She was pleased they didn't; but a token protest might have been nice.

CHAPTER 15

'Dr Fallon?'

Cassia looked up, said 'Yes?' then realised both Edward and Maureen were looking at her oddly, half amused, half embarrassed. 'Sorry,' she said, flushing, angry with herself, shuffling her letters about on the breakfast table. 'It's just that I've got used to it at the clinic.'

'Oh, I see. Anyway, yes, Maureen?'

'There's a call from Mrs Rogers, Dr Fallon. Her husband. It sounds like pneumonia to me. Shall I go?'

'Yes, Maureen, you go. I've got a big surgery and I can see your patients for you, if necessary.' Edward continued to butter his toast, carefully not looking at Cassia.

Janet came in, smiling. She always looked so wonderfully well, Cassia thought, with her gleaming dark hair, her sparkling eyes, her perfect peaches-and-cream skin, with the healthy dusting of freckles on her nose and cheeks. She really was a very pretty girl, and almost absurdly good natured. She wondered how Edward could continue to dislike her so much.

'I thought I'd just see if there was anything special you'd like me to do today, or if I could take Delia out for a picnic. It's such a lovely day.'

'Yes, of course you can,' said Cassia, 'and, Janet, if you want to borrow my car, take her somewhere a bit different, you're very welcome.'

'Oh, thank you, Mrs Fallon. That would be nice. Yes, I might take her to the sea. She'd love that.'

'I'd really rather she didn't drive the children round in your car,' said Edward as the door closed on Janet.

'Why on earth not?'

'We have no idea what sort of a driver she is and—'

'Edward, she is a marvellous driver. I've sat with her several times. She's a lot safer than I am.'

'Well, I have had no personal evidence of that. They are my children as well and I would like to be sure of their welfare.'

'As you never go near Janet, or speak to her even, I think it might be hard for you to assess her driving skills.'

'Don't talk like that, Cassia, please.'

'Well, it's true. You're horribly rude to Janet, almost all the time, and she is incredibly patient and courteous in return.'

'I had understood that was how servants could be expected to behave. Of course, I wasn't brought up with them as you were.'

'Oh, Edward, please don't start that. Anyway, I'm perfectly happy for her to have my car, so—'

'So I suppose my wishes, as usual, are of no importance to you?'

Cassia struggled to keep her temper, changed the subject. 'It's the Trooping of the Colour on Saturday. I thought we might take the boys. As we'll be in London next day, we could stay in my – the house. You haven't even seen it yet.'

'Why on earth will we be in London on Sunday?'

'It's Laurence's christening. Edward, don't look like that, and don't say you've forgotten. And don't say you can't come either. I'm his godmother and it would look just appallingly rude.'

'Oh God,' he said, and sighed. 'Yes, all right.'

'And the Trooping the Colour?'

'I'll have to see about that. Now, if you'll excuse me, I have work to do.'

He went off, taking the *British Medical Journal* with him. Cassia wondered why, as he usually proclaimed it useless, and full of nothing but advertisements, preferring the *Lancet*. Maybe it was for Maureen Johnson. Bloody Maureen Johnson.

Edwina was sitting up in bed reading when Harry came in. He had been to a dinner, and he was clearly drunk. He pulled off his tie, looking down at her.

'Harry, please don't start dropping all your clothes on my floor.'

'You look very sweet. Very desirable. I've come to claim my – what's the expression? – oh yes, marital rights. If you'd be so good as to grant them to me.'

'Oh God,' said Edwina, and sighed lightly. But actually the idea appealed to her. They hadn't made love for quite a long time.

Harry was the only man she had ever been to bed with who seemed to understand a woman's body; after six years of marriage, she was still faintly surprised (having suffered at the hands – literally – of so many crass, inept young men, whose only ambition seemed to be coming themselves, and as quickly as possible) at the skill and patience with which he brought her to orgasm. And tonight he was particularly skilful, exceptionally patient; his penis moving in her, slowly, so slowly, his hands working on her with extraordinary, delicate skill, moving from her clitoris to her anus, moulding her buttocks, parting her thighs, his mouth on her breasts, her throat, her own mouth, and then, as she felt it, knew she was coming, felt the overlapping tumblings of pleasure, worked on, in her with great surging thrusts, until she thought she would break in half with their violence.

She fell asleep in his arms; woke to find him sitting up in bed, the bedside light on, looking down at her with an odd expression on his face.

She smiled up at him sleepily. 'What's the matter, Harry? You're not ill, are you?'

'No, of course not. I was just thinking about you.'

'Harry, you're ridiculous,' said Edwina, turning over, pulling the bedclothes more tightly round her. 'Goodnight.'

She woke again, two hours later; it was still dark, but Harry was gone. And now it was her turn to be wakeful, to lie, thinking of Harry; and especially of what he had said to her after her dinner party on the subject of their having children. And what on earth she was going to do about it.

Dominic Foster came out of the regular Wednesday meeting he had with his team of designers, extremely worried. The costings on the new development in Guildford were soaring; the capital sum he had originally agreed with the property company and by the various banks and financial institutions they were dealing with was simply inadequate. To proceed any further with the project would be at best misguided, at worst fraudulent; he would have to discuss it urgently with the principals of the property company.

He phoned Harry Moreton, its chairman, who was out of town for two days: 'In Edinburgh,' his secretary said; then Bernard Roach, the financial director, who was in Munich at a financial conference; and finally Benedict Harrington, the company's managing director, and on whose say-so a large number of City financial houses had been persuaded to invest in the development.

Mildred Waters, Mr Harrington's secretary, said that he was spending a few days at his estate in Devon. If it was very urgent, she could contact Mr Harrington and ask him to call Mr Foster. She was not permitted to give anyone the telephone number of the Devon house. Dominic Foster asked her to do that, put down the phone and swore loudly.

His secretary buzzed him immediately to say that Mr Stackforth, the officer presently in charge of the Guildford project, was pressing him for a final decision and, indeed, a signature. A rather uncomfortable conversation ensued with Mr Stackforth, the gist of which was that if no signature was forthcoming by nine o'clock sharp the following morning the contract would go to another company. Mr Stackforth added that he had been very patient, but that enough was enough, the delay had become unacceptable and that he could already sell every one of the prospective houses ten times over.

Dominic Foster, seeing not only his extremely large fee, but also the opportunity to become a household name as one of the seminal architects of the 1930s, vanishing fast, told his secretary to book him on to the next train to Exeter. He had already left for Paddington when Mildred Waters phoned to say that Mr Harrington was out riding, but that his housekeeper had promised to give him Mr Foster's message the moment he came back.

The main topic of conversation at Laurence Harrington's christening (to his mother's considerable irritation) was not how beautiful he had looked in the frilly christening robe that had been worn by Harringtons for five generations, nor how perfectly he had behaved, even at the moment the vicar tipped the water over his small head and intoned his four names – Laurence Henry St John Benedict. Nor was it of how exquisite the flowers had been in the church, how interesting a line-up the godparents were – an American merchant banker, a barrister, a countess, and a lady doctor – nor even how devastatingly pretty the baby's two sisters looked, dressed identically in lemon-coloured silk dresses. It was of what many had perceived as an assassination attempt on the King's life at the Trooping of the Colour the day before, and his great courage in carrying on with the ceremony after it, as if nothing had happened.

'We saw it,' said Bertie, jumping up and down with excitement, recounting the great adventure to Fanny. 'We were standing quite near the King as he rode past on his huge big horse, and we saw the man pointing his gun at the King and the police knocking it out of his hands.'

'And then what happened?'

'Well, then he just rode on,' said Bertie, clearly aware that the ending of the story was inevitably something of an anticlimax, 'but Daddy said it was really brave of him. Of course, if he had been shot,' he added, seeing a chance to create a finale, 'Daddy could have got the bullet out and saved his life. Couldn't you, Daddy?'

'Bertie, don't be silly,' said Edward shortly. Cassia was in another room with the parents and other godparents while the official photographs were being taken; Edward was standing with the boys, trying to restrain them, without a great deal of success, from eating too many of the sandwiches, sausages and other savouries that were being brought round by the staff. It was very plain that he was not enjoying himself.

On the other side of the room, standing near the christening cake, Sylvia Fox-Ashley looked at him and sighed. 'Such a dreary little man, Cassia's husband. Marcus, why don't you go and talk to him?'

'Why me?' said Sir Marcus, mildly indignant.

'Well, somebody has to. It might as well be you. Do go on, Marcus, it's so ill mannered leaving him there like that.'

'I will in a minute,' said Sir Marcus with a sigh. 'Just let me get my glass refilled. Edwina darling, how are all your projects going?'

'What? Oh, you mean my fashion show. Quite well. We've got the venue and most of the mannequins now. We need some music, I think.'

'Maybe I can help you there. I met an awfully nice chap the other night who plays the trumpet—'

'Marcus,' said Sylvia firmly, having organised the refilling of his glass, 'will you please go and talk to Edward Fallon. Where's Cassia? She ought to be looking after him.'

'Being photographed,' said Edwina, 'with all the other godmums and dads. She's certainly looking very good these days. The money suits her.'

The speech by the major godfather, the American banker, was long and tedious. Cassia glanced worriedly over at Edward. He was looking what she could only describe as difficult, standing next to Sir Marcus Fox-Ashley. She'd have to go and rescue him; maybe once the cake had been passed round they should go.

It had been a difficult weekend: he had made a great performance about getting Maureen Johnson to cover for him over the whole weekend, although that was exactly what assistants were for; had patently found her Walton Street house very hard to admire; had turned down her suggestion that they should all go and have lunch at Lyons Corner House at Piccadilly Circus, after the Trooping of the Colour had refused to go with the boys to the zoo, and had sat all evening reading up in the drawing room while she and the boys played Snap and Beat your Neighbour and Ludo on the kitchen table.

'The doctor doesn't seem to be enjoying himself over much.' It was Harry, smiling down at her.

She smiled back at him rather uncertainly. 'No, I'm afraid not.'

'Shall I send my wife over to talk to him?'

'Oh, no, I really don't think that would be a good idea,' said Cassia hurriedly.

'Oh really? Why not?'

'Harry, you know why not.'

'No, I don't,' he said, although of course he did. He knew that of all the people in the room, Edwina was the least likely to make Edward feel better, with the possible exception of her mother. 'She can be very charming when she wants to. And she flirts rather well, when she can be bothered. It's one of her few accomplishments. A great art, flirting, wouldn't you say, Cassia?'

'I really don't know, Harry, I'm afraid.'

'No, I wouldn't say it was quite your thing.'

'Thank you,' she said, slightly coldly.

'No need to get miffed. Women like you don't need to flirt. Another lovely hat. Really, Cassia, there'll be none of that money left soon.'

'Which would probably be no bad thing,' she said, and sighed suddenly, sharply, looking at Edward.

'Now why do you say that? It's not causing trouble between you and the doctor, I hope?'

'No, of course not. I—' She stopped, remembering suddenly her interrupted conversation with him at the dinner party, about Leonora. 'Harry, can I ask you something?'

'You can ask. I may not answer.'

'It's just that – well, Rupert said you were with Leonora when she died. That must have been terribly comforting for her.'

He looked down into his glass, clearly embarrassed at being caught out in a good deed. 'That's not a question,' he said finally.

'I know, but I hadn't realised. I just wanted to say thank you, I suppose. I wish I had been there too.'

'I felt I owed it to her.' There was a long silence, then he said, 'So what's the question?'

'All that time, when she was ill, before she died – was she being well looked after?'

'Yes,' he said, slightly impatiently. 'I've told you all this before. She had devoted staff, excellent medical care, and was as comfortable as could be expected.'

'So ... not in financial trouble?'

'Of course not. Why?'

'Well ... oh, it doesn't really matter.'

'Yes, it does. Tell me.' He sounded genuinely concerned.

She told him about the pawn tickets. 'It just doesn't add up with her leaving me all that money.'

'Which was how much exactly? Or should I not ask?'

'It was half a million pounds. Well, a bit more, if you're asking exactly.'

'A tidy little sum. Well, Rollo was – is – frightfully rich.'

'I know, but he'd left her.'

'He was very fond of her, wanted to see her well cared for. And he did see her well cared for. She had round-the-clock nursing, everything.'

She tried to feel comforted, to tell herself that she was worrying about nothing. 'Do you know where Rollo lives now?' she said.

'Haven't the foggiest. He keeps moving around. I think there was some rumour he'd gone to Venice.'

'But he went to Leonora's funeral?'

'In Paris? Oh, yes.'

'I see. Oh God, Edward is looking thunderous. We'll have to go.'

'What a shame. Well, goodbye, Cassia. I should stop worrying about Leonora and all of that, if I were you.' He bent suddenly, kissed her on the cheek. 'You look better every time I see you. It suits you, that money. We must go too – I'm flying to Le Touquet in the morning.'

'What for?'

'I'm in building a hotel there. It's a lovely place. You'd like it. Want to come?'

'Harry, of course I can't come.'

'Why not? It's not a clinic day, is it?'

'No, but I have things to do.'

'For the doctor, no doubt. Very worthy. Well, I'll have to take you another time. I've just bought a very nice little plane. Ah, Edward. I was just telling your wife how very lovely she was looking these days. What a fortunate man you are. You must excuse me, I have some champagne to drink.'

Edward looked after him, his face distasteful. 'Can we please go?' he said. 'I've got a terrible headache.'

'So have I,' said Bertie, 'and I feel sick. I've been drinking that fizzy stuff. It's very nice, though.'

'Oh, Bertie,' said Cassia, 'you are dreadful.'

They drove home in silence in Edward's car. His black mood was infectious: not even William could surmount it. When they got home, the boys went to find Janet to tell her about their weekend; Edward went into his study.

Cassia looked after him, anger rising suddenly in her. She followed him, knowing it was a mistake, knowing it would lead to trouble, feeling unable to help herself. 'Edward, do you think you could possibly tell me what the matter is?'

'The matter is, as you very well know, I had to go to that absurd affair today. I loathe all those people.'

'Well, if I didn't know it before, I certainly do now. I should think they do too.'

'Don't be ridiculous! As if they'd notice anything I said or did.'

'They wouldn't notice anything you said because you didn't say anything. I was embarrassed. It was just rude.'

'Rude! I think your friend Mr Moreton was pretty rude, walking away as soon as we had arrived, saying he had to go and find some champagne.'

'Yes, well, Harry was born rude,' said Cassia, 'but everyone else was making a huge effort – dear old Sir Marcus, and ...' Her voice trailed away.

'Yes. And who else? Next time, Cassia, please don't even try to make me come.'

'Next time I won't want you to come.' She walked out of the room and slammed the door.

'That went off awfully well, I thought,' said Cecily. She and Benedict were in the drawing room after dinner; she doing her tapestry, he working his way through a file of papers.

'Yes, I thought so too.'

'Laurence was as good as gold, and the girls looked so sweet.'

'They did.'

'I thought John Fisher's speech was a little dull.'

'A little.'

There was a silence. Cecily said, 'Benedict?'

'Yes?'

'Benedict, I am very sorry.'

'About what?'

'Well, that I was so angry about your lunch. With Dominic Foster. It was wrong of me. To make so much of it.'

'That's quite all right, Cecily.' He still sounded very distant; hardly smiled at her.

'Please forgive me.'

'There is nothing to forgive.' There was a smile then: a brief, courteous one. Cecily tried to see it as something more than courtesy and failed.

'Benedict—'

'Cecily, forgive me, but I have to get through these papers this evening. Perhaps I should go to my study.'

'No, please don't. It's nice to have you back. I've missed you.'

'I'm sorry, my dear, but I have to go away again. To Paris. Only for a week or ten days. One of the other partners in my firm, the stockbroking firm, that is,' he added carefully (he's making sure I don't think it's anything to do with property, anything to do with Dominic Foster, Cecily thought), 'is interested in forming a relationship with a French company. We're going to have a look at a few, talk to some of the people over there. He particularly wants me to go as I speak French.'

'Yes, I can see that would be an advantage,' she said lightly, smiling. 'What fun, of course you must go. I wish I could come with you.'

She waited for him to say (as he would have done once) that perhaps she should – could do some shopping, some sightseeing – but he was silent and then said, 'I wish you could too,' making it clear that closed the matter. 'Well, I will go to my study, I think, if you don't mind,' he said after a pause. 'See if I can make some headway with this.'

'When are you going?'

On Tuesday. We'll take the night train.'

'Yes, I see. Well, I'll see you later.'

'Oh, I'll be working quite late. I'll sleep in my dressing room. I won't disturb you.'

'I don't mind you disturbing me, Benedict,' she said, but he was already piling up the papers into a file, reaching for his cigarette case; either he had not heard her or he had chosen to pretend he had not. Cecily went back to her tapestry, but it was rather difficult: the small flowers she was working on had become very blurred.

Edward had left the dining room before Cassia and the children started their breakfast in the morning.

'The doctor said he had to get on, and to excuse him,' said Peggy, coming in with a dish of bacon and eggs. 'Now, do you boys want porridge? Because there's some in the kitchen if you're really hungry.'

'I'd love some porridge, Peggy, if it's not too much trouble,' said Janet Fraser. She was sitting with Delia, spooning Farex into her. 'It reminds me of being at home, and yours is so delicious, the best I've tasted outside Scotland.'

Peggy flushed with pleasure and went off to fetch the porridge.

Bertie picked up the paper Edward had flung down. 'Oh, look, Mummy, here's a picture of Uncle Benedict and that nice man with the cars and someone else. Look, here ...'

'Where? Oh, yes. Goodness, they look awful. Like a police line-up. What does it say?'

The article accompanying the picture informed her that the Moreton Construction Company, the chief officers of which were Mr Harry Moreton and Mr Benedict Harrington, both major investors in the Waterloo Bridge project, had just signed a very large contract to build a new 'Garden City' in the borough of Guildford. The architect for the project was Mr Dominic Foster, also pictured.

She remembered Dominic Foster now from Cecily's and Benedict's Christmas party, his dark good looks, his tall graceful body; remembered afresh Cecily's face as she had watched him then, her patent discomfort at Edwina's dinner party, when she had heard of the luncheon between him and Benedict. He was certainly alarmingly handsome: but homosexual? Who could possibly tell? Poor Cecily; her ongoing, near neurotic anxiety – totally understandable under the circumstances, but unfortunate none the less – must make life at best endlessly uncomfortable, at worst terrifying.

There was a scrunch on the gravel; Cassia looked out of the window. 'Bertie, there's the post, can you go and get it?'

There was the usual large pile: mostly circulars for Edward, a few now addressed to Dr M. Johnson, which afforded Cassia some pain, a couple of ordinary letters for Edward, and one for her, typewritten, postmarked London. She tore it open; the name and address of St Christopher's jumped at her from the top of the paper. It was from the Dean.

Dear Mrs Fallon,
I trust you are well. We are planning to make an announcement shortly about the inauguration of the Beatty Research Chair and there may even be a small ceremony; naturally, if that were so we would like you and your husband to be present.

I hear from Dr Richards that you are doing some very good work at the Brixton clinic. I wonder if you would like to come and see me? We have been discussing the possibility of expanding our postnatal surgeries, which we now hold weekly, to include some kind of contraceptive advice where it is felt medically necessary. It is only very tentative at the moment, but I felt you would be uniquely placed to be involved, given your experience with the Brixton clinic and your working knowledge of this hospital and the obstetric unit, and indeed some of the staff here. Naturally, I would stress, your role would inevitably be of a rather junior nature, but on the other hand, it would bring you back into contact with the hospital.

If you would care to write or telephone my secretary, an appointment could be arranged.

'Mummy, are you all right?' said Bertie. 'You've gone ever such a funny colour.'

CHAPTER 16

It must be a mistake, Edwina thought: a mistake or a practical joke. She moved the telephone to the other ear, sat down at her white desk. 'Perhaps you could repeat that,' she said. There was a sigh from the other end, an irritable sigh. 'I mean the very last bit,' she said quickly, 'about when you'd like to see me.'

'Oh, I see. Well, Miss Le Page is free on Thursday morning, or Friday. We'd like to see you as soon as possible. But would that give you time to do your critique?'

'Oh, yes,' said Edwina airily. She had no idea what a critique was, but she could do most things quickly. 'Thursday would be fine.'

'Splendid. Eleven, then. With the critique, of course.'

'Yes, of course. Goodbye.'

She put the phone down, phoned Venetia Hardwicke at her office at *Vogue* immediately. 'Venetia? It's Edwina. Look, is it true? Did you really tell those people to phone me? From *Style*?'

'I did, actually. I was at a show last week with one of their editors, and she said they were looking for someone well connected to do the shopping page. I told her about you and she sounded rather impressed and then rang me for your number. I didn't tell you before because I thought you'd be disappointed if it didn't work out. It's a piece of cake, Edwina, honestly. You just pick out a shop, or rather they'll pick it out for you, it'll be one of their advertisers, and you go and choose some things to write about and get them photographed. The thing about *Style* is, they have this very strong social bias, and they need editors who can get into people's houses and wardrobes and so on. I thought you'd be right up their street. And I've been awfully impressed by what you've done with the fashion show so far.'

'Oh,' said Edwina, 'I see. Well, it's hugely flattering, of course. I'd love to do it, but – well, I don't know whether I could. And what's a critique? And could I do it by Thursday? I said I could.'

'Edwina, you are priceless,' said Venetia. 'It's a criticism, a sort of review. I expect they told you to do one on the current issue? Yes, well, you go through it, bit by bit, saying which things you like and which you don't, and why, of course, and making suggestions for a couple of features.'

'What's a feature?'

'An article. Would you like me to come and help you?'

'Absolutely not,' said Edwina. 'I can perfectly well manage now I know what it is. What's she like, Miss Le Page?'

'Oh, terrifying. Works at being it, of course, as they all do. Absolute stickler for form, been known to sack a girl for not wearing a hat out to luncheon. But that's why she'll approve of you. Look, you get to it. Three days isn't long, and you know you've got the attention span of a gnat.'

'Thanks,' said Edwina, and put the phone down.

She went out and bought a copy of *Style*: it was like a cross between *Vogue* and *Tatler*, a fashion paper with a strong social bias, as Venetia had said, lots of pictures of people at parties. She had never bought it before, but she rather liked it, although the party section looked very stilted, no one looked as if they were having a good time. Why not photograph them dancing and drinking cocktails, instead of standing posed like dummies? And the shopping page was terrible, a selection of things all photographed separately, dumped down on two pages. Nobody would want to buy any of them. They'd look much better in a group, she thought; and the clothes should be worn by a model. Well, maybe that was the sort of thing she should put in her critique. She picked up her pen and the large pad of paper she had bought, and settled happily at her desk. This was going to be fun.

'What on earth are you doing?' said Harry. He had arrived home at six to find Edwina still scribbling furiously at her desk, great piles of paper all over it, the wastepaper basket spilling on to the floor.

'Writing a critique,' she said loftily. 'Of *Style* magazine. They want to see me about a job.'

'A job? What sort of job?'

'Shopping editor.'

'Shopping editor! You! How absurd.'

'Harry, you're such a beast. Why is it absurd?'

'One, you've never done a day's work in your life, you completely lack the discipline. Two, you have no idea how a magazine works. Three, and much more importantly, I don't like the idea.'

'Why don't you like the idea?'

'I don't. That's all. You're my wife. I don't want you doing some damnfool job. Certainly not at the moment.'

'Well, that's very unfortunate,' said Edwina coolly, 'because if I'm offered it, I shall certainly take it.'

'And what about this fashion show of yours that has dominated our lives for the past weeks? Is that to be forgotten in the light of this new game of yours?'

'Of course not. Everything is perfectly under control for now: the Dorchester booked; the clothes organised; Rupert is putting together some ideas for the presentation, and the tickets are being sold. Satisfied? Now could you leave me in peace, or at the very least bring me a drink, a gin fizz please, because I have a great deal of work to do still on this.'

Harry walked out and slammed the door. She looked after him and made a face, and then rang for Bishop. Clearly she wasn't going to get her drink brought by Harry. Bastard. Trying to tell her what to do, as if she were some kind of docile Victorian chattel. It was outrageous.

Cassia sat in the dentist's waiting room and tried to distract Bertie from the ordeal which undoubtedly lay ahead of him. He was only six and his teeth were terrible; he already had three fillings. He also seemed to have a very low pain threshold: last time, he had sat in the chair screaming, his legs thrashing about, as Mr Rankin drilled relentlessly into his baby teeth. That morning, knowing the day had arrived, that he couldn't put it off any longer, he had smiled at her rather tremulously over the breakfast table and said, 'I don't know if I'm brave enough to go to the dentist.'

Mr Rankin's door opened; the patient, a rather pale-looking woman, was ushered out. Bertie looked at her, envy burning in his eyes. Cassia sighed.

Mr Rankin beamed at them both. 'Ah, Bertie. Come for a ride in my chair?'

'Come on, Bertie,' said Cassia brightly, 'in we go.'

'Mrs Fallon, I think perhaps it would be better if you wait outside. Children are often better on their own, I find.'

She looked at Bertie. 'All right?'

He said nothing.

The nurse took his hand. 'In we go, young man. Show your mother how brave you can be.'

Bertie allowed himself to be led in, with a last desperate look at her. Cassia sat down with a pile of tattered magazines and tried not to listen to the sounds coming from behind the door.

There were the usual hotch-potch of publications from the usual hotch-potch of dates: *Good Housekeeping, Home Chat* and *Country Life*. Seeing herself in no way a good housekeeper or a home chatter, Cassia started leafing through *Country Life*, and became engrossed in an article about meadow flowers. It was quite a long article, and it took her right through the drilling part of poor Bertie's consultation; she realised she could relax for the next few minutes, and began to flick through the advertisements for houses.

There was a rather ugly castle for sale in Scotland and a sprawling bungalow in the Scilly Isles and then a house which seemed somehow rather familiar. It was very large and grand and extremely beautiful, a Queen Anne mansion in Wiltshire, set in what the writer of the advertisement described as three thousand acres of park land, with a dairy farm and agricultural outbuildings, a fine stable block and several staff cottages. It was advertised for sale by auction.

She sat staring at it, trying to work out why it was familiar, and then, as she heard Mr Rankin saying, 'Well, that wasn't so bad, was it?' and the door handle turned, she realised. It was Rollo Gresham's house. Leonora had shown her some photographs of it, taken long ago when Leonora, still married to Richard, had spent the weekend at a house party there.

Rollo Gresham selling his lovely house! Why? He had been so proud of it, Leonora had said – well, he would be, it would suit his self-importance, his pretensions at being an English gentleman. He had held the most lavish parties there, even while he and Leonora had been living in Paris. She had read reports of a couple in the papers, absurdly extravagant affairs going on for days, food and wine brought down from London, guests flying in from all over Europe in private planes, on to the airstrip he had had made for his own plane, well-known dance bands hired for days at a time, car races on the track he had also had built there, a string quartet playing at meals.

He had even been photographed in it for *Vogue* magazine. Leonora had sent her a copy, she remembered that too now: his heavily handsome face smirking against the background of its fine rooms and paintings. The paintings alone – like Harry's – had been worth a fortune. And he had kept his horses there, his cars. Surely, even if he did spend most of his time abroad now, he would want to keep so lovely a base in England? And it was very beautiful: not that he was likely to be able personally to appreciate such a thing, she felt sure, but he would know its value, its worth. Maybe it cost a lot to keep going for the occasional visit, even for someone as rich as Rollo.

Guiltily, quickly, and without really knowing why, she folded the magazine over and pushed it into her basket, and stood up smiling at

Bertie as he came through the door. He was white and drawn-looking, and clearly in no condition for ice-cream.

'Three fillings, I'm afraid,' Mr Rankin said. 'Never mind, very brave.'

Bertie was in a bad mood, resentful and tearful; she took him home and made him a hot drink and then sat reading to him and cuddling him, and forgot all about the copy of *Country Life* until the next day, when she found it in her shopping basket, couldn't quite think why she'd wanted to keep it in the first place, and tucked it into a drawer of her dressing table in case she remembered.

'This is very interesting, Mrs Moreton.'

'I'm so pleased you think so.' Edwina relaxed a little, allowed herself a sip of the lemon tea Miss Le Page had had brought to her. Miss Le Page herself was drinking only hot water, making Edwina feel that the infusion even of a little Lapsang Souchong into it was an act of the grossest self-indulgence.

She studied Miss Le Page as she flicked over the pages of her critique; she was tiny, birdlike in every way, with little fluttering movements of her hands punctuating her speech. She had very dark hair, framing a face of porcelain whiteness; her eyes were huge and dark, her mouth a scarlet gash. She was dressed entirely in black, apart from a red hat which exactly matched her lips; Edwina wondered if either the hatter or the cosmetic chemist had been briefed on that match. It seemed quite likely, given Miss Le Page's power.

As editor of *Style*, she presided over not only a circulation of over a hundred thousand, but a by-word in chic; only *Vogue* and *Harper's Bazaar* could challenge its authority. The battle waged between the three of them for advertising revenue and readers was savage; the three editors never spoke, never communciated apart from the briefest of nods as they took up their places at the couture shows. They each had their strengths; *Vogue* being the fashion bible, *Harper's* having a slightly greater breadth of vision, *Style* the additional input of the social pages. This had been the inspired notion of Aurora Le Page herself; although English, she had worked on American *Vogue* for five years before being brought in to rescue the ailing magazine, and had resuscitated it within a year.

The mixture it offered of gossip and fashion was irresistible; the editor of *Vogue* might pronounce it as common, the editor of *Harper's* denounce it as mindless, but its readers loved it and bought it in droves, in the hope of finding themselves contained within its stylish pages, photographed (and usually captioned 'enjoying a joke') at some cocktail party or hunt ball.

There were rumours that Drusilla Wyndham, the gorgon-like social editor, not only received invitations to parties and weddings with ten-pound notes fastened to them, she was frequently approached in restaurants, shops and even, famously, on her way back from the altar after taking communion at Chelsea Old Church, by mothers desperate to have their daughters' coming-out dances recorded in her column. Edwina had met Mrs Wyndham several times at functions, and rather liked her.

She looked up now as Aurora Le Page put her critique down and tapped it with talons that (inevitably) matched the hat and the lips.

'Quite interesting,' she said, 'considering you have no real idea what you're talking about.'

'No,' said Edwina cheerfully, 'how could I?'

'Absolutely. But I like some of these ideas. Especially your comment on the social pages. I believe you know Mrs Wyndham?'

'Yes,' said Edwina, 'we've met several times. At parties. She came to my dance, actually.'

'Yes, so she said. She said what a charming woman your mother was.' Which said a great deal about both of them, Edwina thought. 'Well, I certainly haven't seen anyone else who had any ideas at all. And you're clearly not unintelligent.'

'I hope not.'

'How soon could you start?'

Edwina hesitated, then, 'Tomorrow?' she said.

'Edwina, I forbid it,' said Harry, 'absolutely.'

'Well, that's fine by me,' said Edwina. 'You forbid away. I'm going to do it. If you don't like it, Harry, you can – well, what can you do? Divorce me? Hardly grounds, I'd have thought. Leave me? Perfectly fine. I mean, where are you living, in the Dark Ages? I'm not your chattel, I don't belong to you.'

'You know perfectly well why I don't like the idea.'

'Yes, I certainly do. You don't like the thought of me being just a tiny bit important. Having a life of my own, something to do other than run your household and trail around in your wake, listening to everyone saying how wonderful you are.'

'No, Edwina, that's not true. I have no quarrel with women working. As a matter of fact, I very much approve of it.'

'How very magnanimous of you.'

'But I don't want you to work at the present time because I want a family. Soon. As you very well know.'

'I didn't know that working prevented conception,' said Edwina coolly. She hoped he couldn't hear her heart pounding, prayed her colour wasn't mounting.

'Don't be absurd. You're being deliberately obtuse. Even more so than usual.'

'Really? Aurora Le Page said I was not unintelligent.'

'Who the hell is Aurora Le Page?'

'The editor of *Style* magazine. My boss.' She was sitting at her desk, in her white room, toying with a pen.

Harry had been standing by the door. He came over to her then, took hold of her wrist. His face was so taut with rage – and what? she thought, trying to analyse it. Frustration? – that he looked quite different. 'I have only one more thing to say to you, Edwina,' he said. 'If I find out that you are still, in any way – and I mean *any* way – avoiding pregnancy, I do assure you I will divorce you.'

'On what grounds?'

'Oh, never fear,' he said, 'I will find them. And they may not be very pleasant for you. Now I'm going out. I'll be late.'

When he had gone, Edwina reached for her cigarette case; her hands were shaking so much it was difficult to work the lighter. 'Oh God,' she said, leaning back in her chair, looking out at the golden summer evening that seemed to have grown suddenly darker. 'What am I going to do?'

'So sorry to have kept you,' said the Dean. 'Do sit down. Now then. Ah, yes. The Chair. We thought September was the time to inaugurate it, the beginning of the academic year and so on. What did you think about the idea of a ceremony? Something quite low-key, of course, a luncheon or something—'

'I'd rather not,' said Cassia, 'actually.'

He gave her one of his piercing looks; he knows, she thought, he knows why. 'Fine. But from time to time, it will be necessary to make announcements, as breakthroughs are, hopefully, made. It may be that you'll want to put your head above the parapet then. Anyway, as I said before, we're deeply grateful. And I'm sure much good will come of it.'

'I hope so.'

'Now, the other matter. An involvement with the postnatal clinic. How did that sound to you?'

'It sounded wonderful,' said Cassia simply.

'I thought it was a good notion. Mr Scarsdale and Sister Rigour tell me these clinics are proving extremely beneficial, and that there is scope, indeed need, for this area of yours.'

'Hardly mine,' said Cassia quickly, fearing that if the Dean gave the impression that birth-control clinics were somehow her idea, then she would become very unpopular very quickly.

'Anyway, birth control would seem to fit into the framework quite well.'

'Quite well, yes.'

'Of course it would have to be on a trial basis. It might not work.'

She was almost afraid to ask, but clearly had to. 'And where did you see me fitting into this scheme?'

There was a long silence; he just wants me to do the administrative work, she thought, or to give a bit of firsthand advice. He looked at her, smiled suddenly, the brilliant eyes under the jutting brows gleaming with pleasure

'Well,' he said, 'you're a doctor, aren't you? You passed your obstetrics rather well. You've had some experience now in the field. I thought it perfectly feasible you should be the doctor in charge. Of that side of things, that is. Naturally I'd have to clear it with the Board and Sister Rigour, it is a rather – what shall we say – revolutionary notion. Most of my colleagues at other hospitals are very sceptical, but I think that's largely due to the rather eccentric views and behaviour of Dr Stopes. No doubt you are familiar with all of that.'

'Yes,' said Cassia. 'We're actually much more influenced by Dr Helena Wright and her work in the Birth Control Association.'

'Ah, yes. She's a splendid woman. Although there again, you know, medical people are very sceptical. She gave a lecture at UCL, I think it was, and got a very hostile reception – might have been prophesying the second coming. But I personally don't see any problem in doing it here. And we are lucky to have a pioneering spirit on the board in the form of Lord Crowthorne, whose wife, as you may remember, was a midwife for several years, working at the Whitechapel Lying-in Hospital. It's given him a rather enlightened view of such things: Also, Mr Amstruther was interested in both the idea and your involvement when I mentioned it to him. In time, who knows, it might be possible for you to do some of the postnatal work yourself. But that would be up to Mr Scarsdale, obviously.'

'Yes, of course,' said Cassia, trying to sound and appear calm. She felt literally physically dizzy: partly at the undreamed-of prospect of working again at the hospital, in however lowly a capacity, and partly at renewed contact with Mr Scarsdale. He had been the obstetric surgical registrar when she had been a student; famous for his sarcasm even then. 'Were you thinking of getting that baby out today, Miss Berridge?' he had said to her once, as she had hesitated to turn a small pair of shoulders which had refused to follow the baby's head. 'Or shall we all go home and have a good night's rest and come back in the morning? Would that perhaps suit you better?' Now he was an Honorary, second in reputation only to Mr Amstruther; she could not imagine what he would have to say to the notion of her performing the most humble of tasks.

'Scarsdale was talking about you only the other day,' said the Dean suddenly, 'saying what a shame it was we'd lost you. Your name came up in connection with the Chair. He's pretty receptive to all this as well. You must see him one day, I know he'd like to thank you personally. And Amstruther, come to that. Well now, I suggest you make your way up to Rigour, see if you can find Sister, have a word with her about it. I have mentioned it to her.'

Cassia couldn't think of anything worse than being confronted by Sister Rigour. She, of all the sisters, had been particularly hostile to the infiltration of women into the hospital, seeing them as robbing men of their rightful position. Cassia had actually been on duty one day, and had overheard Sister Rigour on the internal telephone, an acute emergency on her hands, saying, 'I need a doctor, but don't send Berridge.'

It wasn't too bad; Rigour ward was quiet, three women lying in the peculiar rapture of the newly delivered, the remaining twenty-one reading, knitting or chatting cheerfully, and Sister had personally that afternoon managed the manipulation of a breech without recourse to any doctor. She was consequently in a mood of glowing self-satisfaction.

'Miss Berridge!' she said. 'How nice to see you.'

'I'm Mrs Fallon now,' said Cassia. 'I expect you remember my husband, he trained here as well.'

'I don't think so, no,' said Sister. 'Of course I only remember the outstanding ones. And the women, naturally.'

'Yes, naturally,' said Cassia, swallowing this double insult with good grace.

'I hear there's some question of a birth-control clinic here. I'm not very sure about the logistics. How it would work. But I certainly don't think it would do any harm, to put it mildly. I delivered a woman last week, sixth baby in five years. Her uterus is exhausted. And it's not as if she's a lone case. Anything that can improve that situation would be welcomed by me. I'm just not sure it has a place in the hospital. It would take up a lot of administrative time.'

'As I understand it, it would only be on a trial basis,' said Cassia, 'and it would contain its own administrative work, to a large extent.'

'That could be dangerous too,' said Sister Rigour. 'Autonomy has no place in a hospital. Still, we shall see. Now you must excuse me, I have a woman three weeks overdue to see to. No problems, apart from her blood pressure. OBE, I think, don't you?'

'Without seeing her, I wouldn't like to make a judgement,' said Cassia carefully, 'but, yes, it sounds like a good idea. If you think so, of course. And the baby's in a good position? Otherwise, if the induction makes labour faster, couldn't it be more difficult? Well, that's what we were always told,' she added hastily.

OBE stood for Oil (Caster), Bath and Enema. She had had one with Bertie and could still remember the misery. But she knew she would never hear the expression again now without a thud of sheer pleasure – at being caught up, for the first time for seven years, in hospital matters and at being asked, however cursorily, for her opinion.

'Edward, I have to talk to you,' she said, when she got home. She knew it had to be done, the matter confronted immediately. It was too important not to.

'Yes?' He looked at his watch. 'I may be called out. Old Tom Rickards is dying. I promised to go if he needed any morphine.'

'Oh, poor old Tom. I'm very sorry.' She was very fond of Tom: he had done some work in their garden; had played patiently with the boys; showed them how to whittle a piece of wood nail-sharp; how to blow birds' eggs; had dug vegetable patches for them, and then loyally cared for the seedlings when they had lost interest.

'Yes. Very sad. Anyway, what was it you wanted to talk about?'

He was extremely annoyed, annoyed and hurt. She had expected the annoyance: the hurt took her by surprise.

'So you saw the Dean, you say?'

'Yes. He asked me to go in.'

'I suppose it's this Chair nonsense,' he said. 'You've bought yourself back in.'

'Edward, I—'

The phone rang sharply; he went to answer it, came back into the room. He was very white, his face very drawn. 'I've got to go. I don't think there's much more to say, do you? Another day's absence from here each week won't make much difference, and no doubt you'll do what you want anyway. I'll see you in the morning. Goodnight.'

'I think you should tell him,' said Sylvia Fox-Ashley.

'Mummy, I can't. He'll kill me.'

'Why should he kill you? It's not your fault.'

'It's not my fault I'm sterile. Obviously. But I've known for quite a long time now. I should have told him. I've deceived him. Nothing makes Harry more angry than lies.'

'And how is he going to know that?'

'I can't ask Mr Fortescue to lie. Doctors don't.'

'Does he have to know you've seen Fortescue? Can't you just tell him you're worried, you think you ought to see someone?'

'I could for a bit. But then he'll want to know what investigations are being done, and he's quite capable of going into it all very thoroughly. Coming with me, asking questions, you know. Researching the whole thing.'

'Really? How extraordinary. Marcus would die rather than even think about my plumbing.'

'Yes, well, Harry's different. He gets totally involved in everything, you know he does. And our own doctor knows I saw Mr Fortescue.'

'I still think you could shut Fortescue up,' said Sylvia briskly.

'And Dr Prentice?'

'You're making a terrific meal of all this, Edwina. It's unlike you. I really don't know why you can't just tell him, say you're sorry, say you didn't want to upset him, say you'll see anyone he likes. Look, I'm sorry, darling, but I do have to change. We're dining at the Forty Three, have to leave in half an hour. I've given you my advice, I can't do more than that.'

'No,' said Edwina, and left. She was half relieved the conversation had been finished, even though she had intended to take it further: it was quite a difficult thing to tell your mother you'd had a pregnancy terminated three weeks before your wedding. Even a mother like Sylvia.

CHAPTER 17

'Odious woman,' said Mrs Wyndham. 'So vulgar.'

'But immensely chic,' said Aurora Le Page. 'Last time we ran a double page spread on her, we were spoilt for choice.'

'She's frightfully good at Canasta,' said Edwina. She had been discussing some ideas for her first shopping page with Miss Le Page when Drusilla Wyndham had stalked in with her social page photographs; talk had inevitably turned to Mrs Simpson and the King. They both turned and stared at Edwina.

'How do you know that?' said Aurora.

'My mother played with her. Last summer. In Biarritz. She was there in a party. The men were off all day playing golf and she was left with Mrs Simpson, so that's what they did.'

'How fascinating,' said Mrs Wyndham, 'but I'm not really surprised. It's a rather vulgar game.'

'Anyway, just look at these girls, being presented at the garden party. Don't they look frights?'

'They do a bit,' said Edwina. 'Those hats! How did it happen?'

'Well, because of the Court mourning, there was a backlog of six hundred of them, and it was decided to get rid of them, so to speak, at two garden parties.' Drusilla Wyndham helped herself to a cigarette from the box on Miss Le Page's desk. 'Absolute disaster, of course, apart from them all looking perfectly appalling: at the first one there was a thunderstorm and the King gave orders the presentations were to be taken as made, and most of them missed out, which was probably just as well; and then at the second one he just sat there looking like a sulky child. As you can see.'

'Yes, exactly. Pity there wasn't another thunderstorm. I'm sure the mothers were furious. Let's run that anyway, Drusilla, it's marvellously amusing. You don't happen to know what Mrs Simpson might be doing this summer, do you, Mrs Moreton?'

'My mother might. I'll ask her.'

'Please do. Now then, Drusilla, can we get through this as quickly as possible? I have a luncheon and then this afternoon a fashion sitting. Mrs Moreton, you'll have to come back in the morning, I'm afraid. I really haven't got time for you now.'

Edwina went back to the desk in the main fashion office which she shared with six other women. A gentler spirit than hers might have wilted in such an environment: Edwina's was thriving. The obsession with style, with originality, with the vital importance of the tiniest detail in a dress, a hat, a pair of shoes, a feather even, a deep conviction that not the deepest political crisis, the most momentous international event, could compare in significance with the latest collection from Monsieur Dior, the most recent pronouncement from Mr Hartnell: all these things seemed to her entirely reasonable and indeed sensible.

She felt herself, for the first time in her life, properly at home: she breathed in the heady air, savoured the extravagant taste, was careless of the often spiteful atmosphere. Acutely self-confident in any case, she accepted all criticism as constructive, saw most hostility as temporary; she was aware she had to prove herself and set about doing so with a refusal to recognise bitchiness, to hear the odd unpleasant remark, a capacity for hard work which surprised herself, and the rather thick-skinned good nature that made even those who disapproved of her actually like her.

All the other editors in any case came from a social ambience very similar to her own, while having admittedly more professional backgrounds; apart from anything else, no one could afford to work on *Style*, and certainly not dress to the required standard, had they not had another, primary source of income.

After an initial spat with the lingerie editor, one Frances Campbell-Moore, who accused her not only of muscling in on her patch but trying to buy Miss Le Page's approval by offering her house as a location for some ballgown shots – Edwina told her she had no particular wish to end her days lacing models into corsets and that if Miss Campbell-Moore could find a finer example of a classical staircase in London than her own, she would be extremely grateful, since her husband was about to divorce her for making the offer – she earned everyone's slightly waspish respect and was permitted to settle into her small corner of the fashion department and get on with her rather humble job in peace.

She did one day receive a brisk lecture from the fashion editor herself, a creature of an immense, hard-edged glamour that vied with Miss Le Page's own, when Edwina failed to wear gloves to an appointment with a fashion buyer. 'When you are on *Style* business, my dear,' she was told, 'you really must be properly dressed,' but recognising the failure was in herself, having left her gloves in her taxi that morning, Edwina apologised with unaccustomed humility and promised to keep a spare pair in her desk in future.

She loved the job, which was not nearly as difficult as she had feared. She was given a list of stores (usually that month's biggest advertisers), and told to go and choose whatever she liked from them and then get the resulting collection photographed. Having shopped for pleasure and with some fervour ever since she had been twelve years old, she found it hardly onerous.

The first fortnight was rather hectic, as the previous Counter Spy (the label over her name on the magazine's masthead) had left in a rage and there were two features to be prepared in the space of a week, but she found even that comparatively easy; by the end of her first month she felt herself quite on top of the whole thing. And happier than she could remember for a very long time: apart from the ongoing anxiety over Harry, her absolute inability to give him what he wanted, and what he might do when he found out.

'Cassia, I want to talk to you.'

Her heart wasn't just sinking, Cassia thought, as she followed Edward into his study, it was drowning. She had just returned from London, and an exhausting three days, to find Bertie and William in tears over the corpse of their beloved angora rabbit (choked, she was sure, on its own fur as a result of not being combed frequently enough) and Janet asking (quite reasonably) for two weeks off in August: 'I do realise it's difficult for you, Mrs Fallon, it being the school holidays, but my brother has asked me to go cycling with him in the Scottish Highlands and I really would like to go very much.' And now Edward: clearly, from the expression on his face, another difficult demand, probably unreasonable.

However, he sat down at his desk, indicated, with more courtesy than he had shown her for some time, the sagging leather chair by the fireplace, asked her if he should get Peggy to bring them extra coffee.

'No, I don't think so. Don't you have to go into morning surgery?'

'Maureen's taking it today. What I have to say to you is too important to be rushed.'

'Oh,' She felt nervous suddenly, almost panicky. Her mind ranged over the events of the past three weeks: she hadn't been away more than usual; the children had been apparently quite happy; she hadn't gone to any parties or christenings in London or, more importantly, asked him to attend any.

She had most carefully not mentioned her work – not even the day when Dr Rivers, the obstetric registrar, had succumbed to influenza, Dr Simmonds, the junior houseman, was assisting Sister Rigour with the delivery of premature twins, and the staff nurse in charge of the postnatal clinic had been called over to assist in the labour ward, where no less than three other mothers were delivering. Cassia had therefore singlehandedly taken the clinic, with the assistance only of a student nurse. It had been the hardest thing she had ever done, not talking about that; the day she knew she would look back on for the rest of her life as the one when she had actually returned to medicine. It had all been very mundane, of course: conducting pelvic and vaginal exmainations, palpating breasts, checking general health. But she had spotted one breast abcess, one inflamed pelvis and diagnosed what she was convinced was appendicitis, not what the patient told her were her monthlies returning – 'Ever so painful, Doctor, but what a blessing, I was worried I'd fallen again'. She had put in a call to one of the doctors on the medical ward and he eventually came over and confirmed it. Arriving back in Walton Street at seven o'clock, exhausted, she had thought she could not remember feeling so happy for a very long time.

And then her phone had rung and it had been Rupert. He had come up to London to see the director of *Letters*, and they were going out to supper. The director wanted to meet her, in view of her involvement, and would she like to come.

She had started to say no, she couldn't possibly, and then suddenly it seemed irresistibly attractive. They had come to collect her at eight, and taken her to a restaurant just off Sloane Street. It had a small courtyard at the back, and they had eaten out there, and she had sat listening to their extravagant gossipy chatter in the gathering dusk, while she ate deliciously baked trout and new potatoes and drank a little too much wine.

Later, lying in bed, the windows open to the warm summer night, she reflected on her day in all its colour and drama and wondered at all the drab and dull ones that she had endured over the past few years. Not, she thought, half shocked at herself, that they had been unhappy, for they had had their own richness, but she had often felt somehow adrift in them, as if she had strayed in by accident, had no real business there, and needed, in time, to find her way out of them again.

'I've been doing some thinking,' Edward said abruptly now, bringing her back swiftly to just such a day, a time, 'and I feel that neither of us is very happy with things.'

Cassia was shocked, alarmed, her first instinct to say that she was extremely happy. She bit that back, forced herself to be calm, to smile, to say, 'Go on.'

'I do realise,' he said, 'that I haven't always behaved very well. Recently.' His words came out somehow in staccato-style, telling of the difficulty he was having in voicing them, his determination to do so none the less.

'Well,' she said, anxious to be generous, to match his contrition with her own, 'neither have I. Not always.'

'It's been very difficult for me.' He smiled at her suddenly, a rueful, almost embarrassed smile; it took her back, that smile, back to their early days, when she had first known him, been happy with him.

'I know, Edward.' Don't be too apologetic, Cassia, don't say too much, you'll find yourself really in the wrong.

'The thing is,' he was warming up now, the words beginning to flow, 'I want to tell you something. Which I think will make me at any rate much happier. And I hope consequently you will be too.'

For God's sake; was he going to suggest divorce or something? She waited, willing herself not to speak. There was a long silence: then:

'I want to do something. Something very important to me.'

'Well then,' she said, carefully light hearted, 'you must do it. If it's very important to you.'

'Yes, but I would need your co-operation. Your support. You see ...' He looked at her awkwardly. 'You're not the only one with thwarted ambitions, Cassia. Mine have been too.'

'But Edward—'

'Let me finish. Then you can say whatever you like. Only I hope it will be what I want to hear.' Again, the hesitant smile. She waited; she felt rather sick. 'I always wanted, as you know, to be a surgeon. I buried that, under this practice. I told myself this was what I wanted.'

'But you did want it. This practice, I mean. You know you did. To be the community doctor, to be an important, a crucial part of it.'

'I know, I know. And it's been very good. I've enjoyed it. But now I want to do something more. I want to go back to medical school.'

'Medical school! But—'

'Yes, medical school. I want to study surgery again, get my MRCS. I had never dreamed such a thing might be possible, never let myself think about it, but of course, because of your legacy, things are different now.'

She was too astonished, too confused even to think. She had always assumed that Edward was perfectly content with his life, his medicine, with the position he held in the village, the respect and esteem it afforded him in the community, an esteem that reached something approaching awe amongst his humbler patients; the rich variety of the work, the constant challenge, albeit much of it on a rather mundane level, that he never failed to meet.

It seemed barely credible that he was prepared to sacrifice all these things for the harshly demanding and challenging prospect of a return to the life of a medical student, where he would have no authority, no respect, where his every utterance and, indeed, judgement would be challenged, questioned, often ridiculed. She had no doubt that given his extra maturity, and self-confidence, he would manage the work, would pass his exams well, would become a perfectly respectable surgeon. But the cost to himself, it seemed to her, would be inordinately high.

He was looking at her, an expression of impatience in his eyes. 'You look doubtful.'

'Oh, no. Well, not exactly. Go on.'

'In principle, though, do I have your support?'

'Yes,' she said, managing to sound positive, enthusiastic even. 'Yes, of course. You know your career was one of the things I first thought of, when I – we – got Leonora's money, that you could do something like that with it. Of course you have my support. And my co-operation.'

'Good. Because, you see, I've already applied for and got a place.'

'You've got a place? Where, how, why didn't you tell me before ...?' Her voice tailed away; she knew the inevitable answer to that one, didn't want to hear it.

'You're rather hard to talk to these days. To discuss things with. Away such a lot and so on.'

She let it go and waited; it was better not to answer, to argue.

'I've got a place,' he said, and the expression in his eyes was very strange now – wary, almost hostile, 'at University College Hospital, Glasgow. You may remember I went up there for a conference a few months ago. Or perhaps you don't. I got on very well with the Dean, it all went on from there. I did apply to a couple of London hospitals, but didn't get a place, and in any case, I liked Glasgow, the hospital, everything about the place so very much. I start – well, I hope to start – this autumn. For two years. And obviously I'd want you and the children to move up there with me.'

The words didn't mean anything, not at first. They were just words, sentences, put together: strange, odd. He couldn't really want her to go up there: there was the practice, Maureen, the new surgery. She said so.

'I've thought about that. Originally I did think I'd sell it, but I don't think that's wise. I'll get a locum in to run it. Make Maureen a junior partner, providing whoever comes in finds that acceptable. I'm sure there would be no problem, she's exceptionally competent. And I thought she could live in the house. It would be better than it being left empty. Of course she may want to leave.'

'Have you discussed it with her?' she said.

'No, of course not. I wanted to tell you first.'

'Yes, I see.' She tried to smile, to appear at least mildly enthusiastic, while thinking wildly, wretchedly, what it would mean to her: giving up her clinics – well, no doubt there would be one in Glasgow, that might not be too bad – but her postnatal work, her path back into St Christopher's, over almost before it had begun. And the house – no, the houses, she would have to leave Walton Street as well – and Rupert and ...

'How long have you been thinking about this?' she said, playing for time.

'Oh, a long time. Several months. I've actually been making applications to various places.'

'And there wasn't anywhere in London, or down here?'

'Nowhere in London, no. As I said, I did apply to a couple. And naturally I want to be somewhere with a reputation. UCH Glasgow has some very fine surgeons, they're doing a lot of very interesting work. If I'm going to do this, it's got to be properly, I don't want it going off at half cock. I mean, there's no point my going to Haywards Heath Hospital for instance.'

'No, of course not.' It was important she appeared positive, only put up reasonable objections. 'But what about the boys? Their school?'

'Well, Bertie will be off in a year to prep school. William can go to school up there. It's not a primitive community, you know.' He sounded bitter suddenly, bitter and cold.

She looked at him and saw that he knew, knew she didn't want to go, would find every excuse she could not to. And wondered suddenly why Glasgow, why now.

There was a long long silence. She sat, fiddling with a loose thread in her skirt, feeling him watch her, then he said, forcing his voice to sound cheerful, almost jovial, 'Well? What do you say?'

She waited: waited for help, for inspiration. It didn't come. Finally she said, quietly, carefully, 'It's a big decision, Edward. Very big. For me and the family.'

'I don't see why,' he said, dangerously quiet now.

'Oh, don't be absurd,' she said. 'Of course you must. Everything would change, everyone's lives—'

'Not drastically. The children would go to new schools. We would have a new house, make new friends. These are not unprecedented changes, Cassia. Many families make them, every year.'

'But the practice, suppose it didn't work out, suppose your locum didn't run it properly, then what would you do? You've put your life into that practice, Edward, you can't just throw it away.'

'Cassia, what is this? What are you trying to do, throw me on the scrap heap before I've even begun? If I do well, I won't come back to the practice. Perhaps you think that's unlikely.'

'Edward, of course I don't.'

'Just because I didn't do particularly well in my finals doesn't mean I'm incompetent. I used to suffer horribly from examination nerves, you've obviously forgotten.'

How could she, how could she possibly forget that, what it had done to her and her life? 'I don't think you're incompetent. I'm just trying to think of everything. And all your patients in the village, they love you, and trust you, you're letting them down if you leave them.'

'Cassia, my patients will be fine. They're not going to be abandoned in some way, left without medical aid.'

'Yes, I know that. But it seems so brutal somehow.'

'Oh, now you're being absurd. Sentimental and absurd.'

'Well, I'm sorry you should think that. I care about them all.'

'So much that you only live in the village half the time now.'

'Please don't start that.'

'Any other objections?' he said, after a pause.

She hesitated. 'Well, it's a risk. A big risk, for you.'

'For me!'

'Yes. Suppose you don't like it, suppose you find returning to student status more difficult than you think?'

'Cassia, I've thought of that, and I think I'm mature enough to cope with it. Given the importance of the end. And in any case, that's precisely why I'm holding on to the practice. It seems to me,' he said, 'you're not prepared to support me.'

'Edward, of course I am. That's not fair.'

'It doesn't sound like support. I'm disappointed in you, Cassia.'

She looked at him sharply, expecting pomposity, but he looked genuinely upset, hurt. Remorse hit her. 'Edward, please! Give me time. To adjust to the idea.'

'I didn't expect this,' he said, 'or perhaps I did. Let us say I hoped you'd be behind me, one hundred per cent. As I would be for you.'

'That's not true,' she said. 'Were you behind me when you took on

Maureen as your assistant? When I told you about the clinic at the hospital?'

'That's quite different.'

'Why?'

'Surely you can see why. This is my entire career we're talking about, not a few trifling clinics.'

'They are not trifling to me,' she said, and was shocked at the passion in her own voice, 'they are everything to me. My way back, my—'

'Ah,' he said, 'yes, I see. There we have it. This would interfere with your very important work, wouldn't it? Quite badly. All this touching concern for the practice and the village and the children. That's not what you're worried about at all. Not a bit of it. It's yourself, yourself and your own work and your bloody research Chair and your smart London friends—'

Suddenly she looked at him. There was grief on his face, grief and uncertainty. It was a long time since she had seen that; she felt, very surprisingly, tears behind her eyes. She got up, went over to him, tried to put her arms round him, but he pushed her away.

'Don't,' he said, 'please don't.'

'Edward, I didn't mean to upset you. Really. And I do admire what you want to do, and I admire you. Enormously.'

'Oh, for God's sake,' he said. 'How can you? I'm not successful, that's why this is so important to me, doing this. I'm not even particularly clever, I'm not certainly not witty and charming like—'

'Oh, stop it. Please. Stop being so sorry for yourself.'

'I feel sorry for myself,' he said quietly, 'desperately sorry.' And he walked out of the room and closed the door.

She heard the front door slam and watched him walk up the drive and out of the gate. He looked utterly dejected, his thin shoulders stooped, his head somehow sunk between them, his step slow and lifeless. She felt terribly ashamed of herself – and very, very unhappy.

Benedict turned away from Cecily; pulled the bedclothes up, almost to cover his head. He looked, in the bright moonlight, like a small boy, trying to hide. 'I'm sorry,' he said.

'It's all right. I understand.'

'Oh God,' he said, 'I wish you did.'

'Benedict, I do. Look, in future, perhaps it would be better if you always slept in your own room. This is wretched for us both.'

'Very well. If that's what you want.'

'It's not what I want. It's what seems best. To me.'

'Fine. Shall I go now?'

'No. I love you being here. Here, put your arms round me.'

'It's very hot,' he said. 'Let's just stay like this.'

Tears stung Cecily's eyes; she blinked them away. She couldn't ever remember feeling so humiliated, so wretched. And he must feel the same. What a wreck it was, this marriage of theirs, a hopeless, battered wreck. There seemed absolutely no hope for it, for them, no prospect of them saving it. And Benedict probably didn't want to. She wasn't even sure, these days, if *she* did. It would be horribly, dangerously easy to give up, give in. But they had three children, three young children; she couldn't do that. She couldn't. She lay there, her heart feeling literally heavy.

'What are you thinking about?' he said.

If she told him, hinted even that she might consider a divorce, then all really would be lost. He was probably waiting for that, for a cue, something that would release him. She searched frantically in her mind for something positive to say, found it, said in a desperate attempt to sound friendly, light hearted, 'I was wondering about the holidays, believe it or not. What about France this year? It's getting rather late to take the villa.'

'Much too late. Yes.'

'I wondered if we could go to Devon.' She wasn't usually very keen to go to Devon; that grieved him, she knew, he loved the place so much.

'Oh, I don't think so,' he said. 'The place is in a bit of a state. We must get it redecorated, possibly have central heating put in downstairs at least. And the gardens are running to rack and ruin, they look dreadful.'

'All the more reason to go there. I can set some work in motion.'

'Look,' he said, 'can we not discuss this now? I'm pretty tired. I think I will go to my own room. If you don't mind.'

'Of course not,' she said, and cried herself to sleep.

In the morning he was contrite, anxious to be placatory. 'I thought Scotland would be nice for a few weeks,' he said. 'We could go and stay with Jock Danvers at Ord. He's always asking us. The children would love it, and so would I. I could do a bit of fishing, maybe shoot …'

'I'm sorry Benedict,' she said. 'I hate Scotland and even more I hate listening to Letty Danvers talking all day while you and Jack go off killing things. I'd rather stay in London. You go if you want to.'

'No, no,' he said, 'I'm much too busy, I'll stay here too.'

But that night he said he had decided after all to 'go up for the Twelfth. It's so truly glorious up there, those first few days. If you don't mind'.

'I don't mind,' she said. 'We might go to my parents' house in Hampshire. Fanny loves it there, and she and Stephanie can have some riding lessons in the Forest.'

'Good idea.'

'Edward,' said Cassia. She had been screwing up her courage for days to have this conversation: had found it finally, from the heart of her desperation.

'Yes?' He was in the sitting room, staring out of the window at the dusk; he didn't even look at her.

'Edward, I've been thinking. About Glasgow.'

'You have?' His voice was lighter, hopeful even. She felt ashamed of herself, of not giving him, still, the answer he wanted.

'Edward, if I decided I couldn't come ...'

'Yes?'

'You could still go, couldn't you? You could take a house there, come home when you could. It might even be better, you could concentrate more on your work. Not many medical students have wives and families, after all.' She smiled, a bit too brightly.

'Oh, no,' he said, 'no. I wouldn't even think of that. I've told you, Cassia, I need your support. Your full support. Either you come with me, or I don't go.'

'But—'

'I can't do it without you,' he said. 'I need you with me, I really do. That's all there is to it. I hope very much you'll feel you can.'

It was almost dark in the room now; she couldn't see his face any more, but she could hear the genuine pain in his voice. 'Yes, I see. Well, I shall have to make a decision very soon, then.'

'Yes, you will,' he said.

That had been her last hope: and it had been very fully and dreadfully dashed.

CHAPTER 18

'It's blackmail,' said Harry briskly. 'He could perfectly well find a hospital much nearer London. Or he could perfectly well go without you.'

'I don't think he could. He lacks self-confidence, he's not a bit like — well, like you.'

'I devoutly hope he's not. Come on, let's go and dance.'

She hesitated.

'Come along. We can talk about it more later. I'm getting bored.'

What was she doing here, she thought wildly, following him on to the floor, here at the Four Hundred Club, alone with Harry Moreton? Had she gone absolutely mad?

He had phoned her at six thirty; she had just got in. 'Cassia? It's Harry.'

'Oh. Hallo.'

'Look, I remembered you were in town. How would you like to come to the theatre with me?'

'The theatre!'

'Yes, you know, place with a stage, curtains, people acting and so on. I've got two tickets for *The Barretts of Wimpole Street*. It's supposed to be rather good, I'm sure you'd enjoy it.'

'But can't Edwina—'

'Edwina can't, no. She's got some damn fool photo session this evening. Apparently the photographer got held up coming over from Paris and it has to be done by tomorrow. Bloody incompetent people.'

'I see. Goodness, she's taking this very seriously, isn't she?'

'Yes,' he said shortly. 'very. Anyway, I didn't want to waste the ticket, so I thought of you, thought you probably wouldn't be doing anything.'

'I'm sorry you should view me as a social disaster. I'm sorry, Harry, but I'm really very tired.'

'Oh, nonsense. It'll do you good. Get yourself ready, I'll be round at seven.'

She put down the phone and looked at it thoughtfully. She wasn't sure if the ease that was growing between her and Harry Moreton was safer or more dangerous than the highly charged antagonism that had been there before.

She thought the play was rather good, although Harry hated it. He kept yawning, and in the highly romantic third act, she suddenly felt something heavy fall on her shoulder: it was his head. She heaved it up.

'Do wake up,' she whispered fiercely, 'otherwise I'm going.'

'Let's both go.'

Two people in front of them turned round and said, 'Shush.'

Harry took her hand and pulled her up. 'Come on. Excuse me,' he said to the woman next to him, 'this lady isn't feeling well, could you let us past, please? Thank you so much.'

Outside in the foyer she glared at him. 'I was enjoying that.'

'Then you have worse taste even than I thought. Appalling rubbish. Real below-stairs stuff. Come on, let's go and have dinner.'

'Harry, I can't have dinner, I must get back.'

'What on earth for?' He sounded genuinely amazed. 'It's only ten fifteen. Come on, I've booked a table at the Ivy. We'll get there before the rush.'

The Ivy was full of the theatrical crowd; it was their unofficial club. Harry, amused at Cassia's frank fascination with them ('What a little bumpkin you are'), pointed out John Gielgud, who was dining with Peggy Ashcroft, Michael Redgrave, Alexander Korda. 'And over there, see, that's Lady Dudley. In the white silk. Do you know about her?'

Cassia shook her head.

'She was an actress once, called Gertie Miller. Wonderful character, still has her northern accent, I've actually heard her saying "ee ba goom". She runs the house absolutely beautifully, has wonderful servants, and has four of the most extraordinarily elaborate graves in the grounds for her dogs. She's rather fond of Edwina, we've been there once or twice.'

Cassia felt very dull suddenly, couldn't think of anything else to say.

'Come on, you're not eating,' said Harry after a moment, 'and have some more champagne. I know what you're thinking, and you're wrong.'

'Of course you don't,' she said irritably.

'You're feeling dull and provincial, aren't you? Don't look so astonished, I'm always telling you how extremely well I know you. And provincial you may be, but you're certainly not dull. Now look, over there, do you see that marvellously good-looking couple in the corner?'

'Where? Oh, yes. Goodness, is that Laurence Olivier?'

306

'It is. And the lady is the actress Vivien Leigh. Very beautiful and reputedly coming very fast between him and his rather nice wife, who is about to have a child. But I expect Rupert keeps you up to date on all this theatrical gossip.'

'I'm afraid he's not quite in this league,' said Cassia, laughing. 'I'm sure he could be, given the opportunity, and of course he'd love to be, but—'

'You're very fond of him, aren't you?' said Harry suddenly.

'Yes,' she said simply. 'Yes, I am.'

'He's much too old for you, you know.'

'Harry,' she said, laughing, 'I'm not having an affair with him.'

'Ah, but you'd like to, wouldn't you? And he'd certainly like to have one with you.'

'Of course he wouldn't,' she said, and held out her glass to be refilled. The conversation as much as the champagne was going to her head.

'Right,' said Harry, 'the Four Hundred.'

'Harry, no. This place is full of people who are obviously wondering what on earth we're doing here together, and ...'

'Well, they'll just assume we're having an affair. Nothing wrong with that. Give them all something to talk about. Come on. That dress is much too nice to waste. You wore it to Edwina's dinner party, didn't you?'

'Yes,' she said and gave in.

They arrived at the Four Hundred just before midnight; it was only beginning to fill. The *maître d'* bustled over to them. 'Mr Moreton, good evening. And madame.'

'Evening, Rossi. I trust you've got my table, we're in very good time.'

'Of course, Mr Moreton. Some champagne?'

'Please.'

The table was to the right of the door: Harry settled her at it, then sat down himself and smiled at her slightly complacently. 'People kill for this table,' he said, and just for a moment he was the pompous spoilt small boy again, demanding and acquiring everything he wanted. She told him so.

'Oh God. I was truly obnoxious, wasn't I?'

'Truly. I often wondered,' she said, sipping at her champagne, 'what it was that changed you, made you ... human. I mean, you went up to Oxford fairly awful still.'

'Thank you.'

'And then you changed, completely. Well, a lot, anyway.'

'Sex,' he said, leaning back in his chair, looking into his glass. 'I had the most amazing love affair with a woman quite a lot older than me in Paris; she showed me what a frightful little prick I was, taught me to laugh at myself.'

'Oh, I see,' she said, slightly uncertain of how to react to this.

'And she taught me a lot of other useful things as well,' he said, 'things best left to the imagination. For now, anyway.'

She was silent.

'Anyway, I'm glad you think I've changed, although I'm still extremely spoilt, of course. Good at getting what I want. And this is the best table in the room, famously so, and I do have to have it whenever I'm here. Good for seeing from. And being seen at.'

'Oh, Harry. What on earth will Edwina say?'

'Not a lot, I'm sure. She knows how cross with her I was.'

'Not as cross as Edward is with me,' she said, rendered indiscreet by the second – or was it the third? – bottle of champagne. Harry had drunk most of it, but still …

That was when she told him about Edward: Edward and her dilemma. And he made his pronouncement.

'I hadn't thought of it like that,' she said later, as they sat down again.

'Thought of what like that?'

'Edward's behaviour. As blackmail.'

'Well, it seems perfectly obvious to me. Rather clever, in fact. Machiavellian. I wouldn't have thought he had it in him.'

'Maybe there is an element of that, but he does genuinely want to go. He's always wanted it.'

'Why didn't he do it before, then? When he was a medical student?'

'He didn't do quite well enough in his finals.'

'Ah. So there we have it. And you did? Extremely well, I seem to recall.'

'That hasn't got anything to do with it.'

'No?'

'Harry, that's very unjust. Very unjust indeed.'

'Well, you know him better than I do. I'm happy to say. Anyway, I do hope you're not going to agree to go with him.'

'I don't know what I'm going to do.'

'If you do go,' he said, and his voice was very serious now, his eyes on hers, heavy, thoughtful, 'it will be the end of you. You know that, don't you?'

'That sounds very melodramatic. Not like you at all.'

'It's not melodrama,' he said, 'it's the truth. After all this time, you're beginning to get back, back to your career and your real self.'

'I'm also a wife,' she said, 'and a mother.'

'Yes, well, that can't be helped. But don't do it, Cassia. Don't give in to him. It's very wrong, what he's doing. Very. Anyway, don't let us talk about him any more. I want to dance with you again. A lot of people are watching us.'

'Oh God.'

'Don't be absurd. Now your provincial background is showing. Edwina won't give a toss. She never—'

'Never what?' she said curiously.

'Oh, it doesn't matter. And anyway, we're going away in a week's time, to Cannes. Staying with friends at the Carlton for a few days and then off with the Buchanans on their yacht. Going down to the Dalmatian coast. It should be fun. We shall be in good company: the King and his ladylove are cruising down there this year, on a yacht called the *Nahlin*. Only they are to be accompanied by two destroyers and we, I believe, are not.'

'What do you think will happen to them? The King and Mrs Simpson, I mean?'

'God knows. But apparently he is desperately in love with her – Sylvia's words, not mine – and he is not a strong character. And she is. But anyway, she is still married to poor cuckolded Mr Simpson.'

'You're sorry for Mr Simpson, then?' she said lightly.

'Yes, I am. It's a very public humiliation.'

'So people should be discreet about their infidelities, should they?'

'Indeed they should. Now let us go and dance again, in the most indiscreet manner that we can.'

They arrived back at Walton Street at four, in Harry's latest motor car, an extremely large black Buick.

Cassia laughed as they pulled up outside the house. 'This car practically fills the street. It looks like a hearse.'

'Thank you for that notion. I suppose if I lost all my money, I could hire it out for funerals. Or even drive it myself. I rather like that idea. Now I must go. I have to be at the Bank of England in just over three hours' time. Please excuse me. And thank you for a very nice evening.' He leant forward suddenly, kissed her very gently on the lips. 'Don't do it, Cassia. Don't give in to him.'

She sat staring at him, confused by the sudden change of mood, by his words, most of all by the kiss. Then he smiled, was himself again.

'I shall be away for three weeks,' he said. 'When I get back, I shall expect to hear that all is well with you. And if not, I may even go and see the good doctor myself.'

He got out, opened the door for her, kissed her again, this time on the cheek, and then he was gone: leaving her more confused, more afraid than ever.

Cecily sat in the great family Daimler on its way to Devon, hoping that Stephanie, who was always prone to car sickness, was not actually going to throw up, and trying to hear the more scurrilous details of Edwina's conversation with the photographer, which seemed to centre largely around whether Aurora Le Page actually kept cocaine in the cigarette box on her desk or not.

'And I tell you she's offered it to one of my closest friends,' said the photographer. He was a rather pale young man, dressed in black linen trousers and a cream linen shirt, with over-long pale brown hair that fell on to his open collar. Cecily decided she disliked him intensely.

'But not to you?'

'No. Not to me.'

'Well then, there you are,' said Edwina, sitting back with an expression of huge satisfaction on her face. 'It's always the same. Always a friend. Or a friend of a friend. I tell you, I looked in that box the other day and it was full of cigarettes. Turkish ones,' she added, as if that was relevant.

'Oh, darling, you're so naive,' said the photographer. 'Of course there are ciggies on the top of the box. There's a false bottom to it, everyone knows that.'

'Oh,' said Edwina uncertainly. 'Cecily, look out, I think Stephanie's going to be sick. Oh God, how disgusting, darling, not into my Hermès bag, there's a lamb ...'

Why on earth had she agreed to it? Cecily wondered, frantically mopping Stephanie and the mess up as best she could, calling to Preston to pull over; if she'd only said no, she'd be safely in Lymington by now, at her parents' country house; but somehow, the thought of having the house in Devon featured in *Style*, as the background to some wedding dress photographs, with her two little girls as bridesmaids, had been irresistible.

'They want somewhere with the sea as background,' Edwina had said. 'We were hoping to go to France, but Miss Le Page suddenly said there wasn't time – I think actually she didn't want to spend the money – and I thought of your house straight away. I mean, you can see the sea from the sloping lawn at the top, can't you, yes, I thought so, too perfect.' And anxious to have a diversion from her unhappiness, her loneliness, and with the added bait of Edwina's suggestion that the girls should be in the pictures too, Cecily had agreed.

Edwina had then proceeded to volunteer Benedict's Daimler in which to transport herself, the photographer and the clothes – 'Well, it is so wonderfully big, and much more comfortable for us all.'

Cecily had been surprised to find Edwina doing something so important as organising the photographs for what seemed to be a major article, but it turned out that the editor responsible for wedding dresses had been ill and Edwina had been co-opted on to the job, largely because of her ability to produce a large and beautiful house by the sea. 'But the fashion editor herself will arrive tomorrow and then we must all kiss the ground she walks on.'

'I hope not,' Cecily had said briskly, 'not when it's my own ground.'

There hadn't been time to contact Benedict, who was at a high-level conference in Munich, so she had just crossed her fingers and told herself that in any case he would be very proud to see his house all over the pages of *Style* magazine. She had telephoned the staff and they were preparing the house; and the girls were hugely excited at the prospect of being there, and bathing in the sea, never mind that of being photographed as bridesmaids.

They didn't arrive at the house until after six. Mrs Goss, the housekeeper, greeted them at the front door. She was like a caricature of a Devon farmer's wife, round and rosy, with an accent like golden butter; Cecily was very fond of her.

'Hocking's just finishing in the dining room now,' she said. 'He'll take your luggage, meanwhile I'll show you to your rooms. Hallo, my lambs,' she added, taking Fanny and Stephanie to her cushion-like bosom, 'lovely to see you.'

They both kissed her. 'I was sick,' said Stephanie, 'all over the car.'

'It smells disgusting,' said Fanny.

'Poor little blossom! No appley dumplings for your supper, then ...'

'Oh, yes, yes, I'm perfectly all right now. Come on, Fanny, let's go and see the cows.' They disappeared.

Cecily smiled at Mrs Goss. 'It's lovely to be here,' she said, 'and I'm sorry it was such short notice. You've met Mrs Moreton before, I believe.'

'Yes, I certainly have,' said Mrs Goss, bobbing briefly to Edwina, who managed the faintest of smiles before moving off round the house, peering up at it as if she were a highly critical prospective buyer. 'And this is Mr Everard,' said Cecily, glaring after her. 'He is taking the photographs tomorrow.'

Mrs Goss looked at Justin Everard slightly doubtfully, bobbed again. 'If you all follow me, I'll show you to your rooms. I'll feed the blessed lambs in the kitchen, if you don't mind, Mrs Harrington, and Hocking said to say dinner could be any time after seven thirty. Oh, and drinks are set out in the conservatory.'

Cecily led her guests into the hall and then let Mrs Goss take them upstairs. She went through into the drawing room and stood at the window looking out at the sea.

Merlins had been built two hundred years earlier, by the rather enlightened younger son of a Lord Jefferies, who had lived in the great and rather gloomy Elizabethan mansion five miles along the coast; he had employed a highly imaginative draughtsman, and told him he wanted the dramatic coastline, with its constantly changing mood, echoed in the house. The result had been a very fine but rather eccentric Georgian house, its interior fairly conventional apart from a panelled circular dining room, but with great windows almost the full height of the rear rooms, a vast conservatory forming what amounted to a semi-circular wing running cliffwards on the west side of the house, and a look-out tower on the east side, with a rotunda-style roof. Not only could the southern coast of Wales be seen from the tower on a clear day, but there was a breathtaking view at night of the heavens. Beyond the house, the lawns ran down directly into the heavily wooded cliffs; at the foot of the cliffs was a sweetly curving bay, from which the family bathed and sailed.

Cecily loved Merlins, would happily have spent much more time in it, but Benedict had a certain resistance to the family being there, seeing it as very much his own house. Which he then, Cecily had often observed, failed to occupy.

It was a beautiful evening, windy but brilliant; the girls were running down towards the woods, shouting loudly, excited by the sudden freedom. She smiled at their pleasure.

'This is a beautiful house, Mrs Harrington.' It was Justin Everard, down from his room, carrying a small camera in his hand. 'So unusual, such a very special atmosphere. May I take just a few snaps, get the feel of it all before dinner? And should we dress for dinner? I wasn't sure.'

'No, we don't very often dress down here,' said Cecily, smiling at him, at his appreciation of the house, 'only when we have very grand parties, which is about once every ten years. Please do, go ahead: or will you have a drink first? We always have drinks in the conservatory before dinner.'

'So enchanting!' said Justin. 'And look at those marvellous Lloyd Loom chairs. All of it, a fairytale palace. No, I'll wait for the drink, if I may. Those little girls are enchanting too, just look at them, lucky, lucky us.'

Any moment, thought Cecily, he's going to clap his hands. She supposed he must be queer, and wondered why the usual combination of distaste and panic didn't fill her. Probably because he was a photographer, which, being artistic, somehow made it seem all right.

Dinner was rather fun; Edwina complained briefly and tactlessly (considering she was enjoying its hospitality so fully) that the house looked rather shabby, and she didn't know what Camilla Marsden-Rose would say, but Justin assured her (equally tactlessly) that the shabbiness wouldn't show in the photographs, and then turned his attention to Cecily, demanding to know as much of the history of the house as possible. She said she knew very little, whereupon he said, 'Well, let's make some up, then,' and they took it in turns to add ever-increasingly extravagant and unlikely stories. Justin's were much the best: he added an errant princess (one of Queen Anne's daughters), a ghostly mermaid and a shooting star to establish the exact site of the foundation stone of the house. Edwina's were quite good too, and Cecily managed a bolt of lightning, thereby necessitating the rebuilding of the stables (a genuine puzzle, since they were very much Victorian in design).

Before they went to bed, Cecily led them up to the rotunda and studied the stars. 'Cassia should be here,' said Cecily, 'to show us her constellation.'

'Who is Cassia?' said Justin.

'Oh, a relative. Well, almost a relative – a friend.'

'How very confusing. And why should she be here?'

'Her name is Cassiopeia, and there is a group of stars called after her.'

'I should like to meet her,' said Justin. 'I've never known anyone with a constellation named in her honour.'

'Well, of course it's the other way round, really,' said Cecily, blushing, feeling suddenly silly.

'I prefer it your way. A better story, since this is the occasion for good stories. Well, I must go to bed. We have a long day tomorrow. Camilla threatened to be here at nine, which probably means eight. She's coming down in her own plane, so terifically smart, don't you think?'

'Don't talk about planes,' said Edwina with a shudder. 'Harry's just bought one. It's a nightmare, I know he's going to be killed.'

'Nonsense, darling, they're very safe. Cars are much more dangerous. Someone should establish a speed limit on the roads, it's too frightening these days. Goodnight, ladies, I'm off to the Land of Nod. Thank you again for your hospitality, Mrs Harrington.'

'Please call me Cecily. It makes me feel old, being Mrs Harrington.'

'You couldn't possibly ever be old, you look eternally young,' he said, and kissed her hand.

'Goodness,' murmured Edwina, as he disappeared down the spiral staircase, 'you have made a hit. He's frightfully hard to please usually.'

'I expect I remind him of his mother,' said Cecily tartly.

'Don't be so touchy,' said Edwina.

Camilla Marsden-Rose arrived at neither eight nor nine, but at seven thirty, landing her plane in a nearby field and striding across the lawns of Merlins in jodhpurs and a leather helmet, followed by Angela, the model, who looked green and very shaky.

'Too Amy Johnson,' said Justin, cramming the remainder of his toast in his mouth and rushing out to greet her. 'Camilla, darling, how wonderful you look!'

'Don't start that, Justin,' said Camilla Marsden-Rose. 'This house is an absolute gem, too marvellous of Mrs Moreton to have found it. Pity it's so shabby, but maybe it won't show in the pictures. Can you get this wretched girl a drink of water, she's been frightfully sick, and is there someone here who could clean out the plane?'

Cecily, who had followed Justin out to greet her new guest, thought that working on *Style* was hardly going to improve Edwina's manners.

It was a very long day; they had to photograph four different wedding dresses and sets of bridesmaids' dresses in four different locations. After the first one, Cecily retired to her sitting room to read and write letters; everything she suggested in the way of locations, and even the way the little girls had their hair done, was crushed most witheringly by Mrs Marsden-Rose. By lunchtime (delayed until three) Justin was flagging visibly, Edwina looked almost chastened and the children were bored and fractious.

'Fashion is a tough job,' said Camilla, bolting down an extraordinarily strong gin and tonic, and holding out her glass for a refill, 'not for the faint hearted. Is it, Angela?'

'No, Mrs Marsden-Rose,' said Angela, managing a smile, 'nor the faint stomached.'

'Oh God, don't remind me. Did your fellow manage to clean out my plane?' she said to Cecily.

'If you mean Hocking, the butler, yes, I think he was kind enough to do it,' said Cecily, 'although it really is not the sort of thing I would expect of him normally.'

'Is that so?' said Camilla, with a look that implied both Cecily and Hocking were seriously wanting in quality. She started eating from the buffet Mrs Goss had set out in the conservatory, adding that Angela was not to eat anything at all until the day's work was done. 'Your stomach is quite prominent already. Any more and you'll look as if you had to get married. And besides, I don't want you vomiting on the way back.'

Mercifully, Camilla left at six, bearing the unfortunate Angela (still forbidden so much as a cup of tea) with her. The rest of them collapsed in the conservatory and Cecily told Hocking to bring up some champagne from the cellar. 'I think we've earned it.'

The two little girls were highly relieved their day was over: 'She was so rude, that lady,' said Fanny. 'She said my face was too round, and she told Mrs Goss to get out of her way without even saying please.'

'Oh, she makes an art form of rudeness,' said Justin. 'I always expect to hear she's going to be exhibited at the Tate. The funny thing is to see her with Drusilla, though, isn't it, Edwina? She's such a monstrous snob, so keen to get in Drusilla's pages, she becomes frightfully deferential, seventeen thankyous a minute.'

'What does deferential mean?' said Stephanie.

'Extremely silly,' said Edwina briskly.

Cecily sat back in her chair laughing; she couldn't remember feeling so happy for months. 'I'm so glad you all came,' she said. 'You really have brightened my life considerably.'

'How sad it should need brightening,' said Justin. 'Now are you sure you want us to stay another night?'

'Oh, yes please.'

'Then consider your life further brightened. If you'll excuse me, I'm going to go up and have a deliciously long bath before dinner.'

'Of course. If you use the nursery bathroom, for some reason the water is hotter. It's up on the top floor, next to the playroom, where you were this afternoon.'

'The nursery bathroom it is,' he said, and stood up. 'I'll see you again down here at seven thirty.'

She was to remember that moment for the rest of her life.

'Letter for you, Mrs Fallon. Came by the afternoon post.'

'Thank you, Peggy. Could you possibly make me some tea? I'll be in the sitting room.'

'Yes, of course. You look all in, if you don't mind me saying so.'

'I feel quite a lot in,' said Cassia, smiling at her. 'Maybe not quite all.'

Peggy's face closed in as she tried to digest this rather complex thought; finally she smiled. 'Oh yes,' she said. 'Yes, I see. Well, the tea'll help, at any rate.'

'Yes, I'm sure it will. Where are the children?'

'Nanny's taken them for a picnic supper. Back about seven, she said.'

'How nice.' A stab of envy shot through her; of course it was wonderful to be working again, and it was lovely to have the house in London, and evenings like the one with Harry were – well, they were great fun. But picnic suppers in the woods, days by the sea, playing hide and seek in the house and the garden: she missed those. And found it hard to contemplate very closely the fact that her children were not missing them, were still enjoying them hugely, only with someone else. Well, if she went to Glasgow ...

She sighed, went into the sitting room, sat down on the window seat to open her letters. She was very tired: the strain of her split weeks, the complexity of her work, the early morning drives – although not quite so early now it was the school holidays – the agony of her dilemma over Edward, were all taking their toll. She was going to have to give him her answer soon: it wasn't fair to keep him hanging on. And the medical school would clearly be requiring an answer.

She looked at the letter. It carried a London postmark, SW1 – the hospital, she thought, tearing it open. The Dean had written: a handwritten note.

> Just to let you know that we shall be making an announcement about the Chair in the *Lancet* and the *BMJ* within the next couple of weeks. There is bound to be some interest, and various people in the profession will want to discuss it. Would you wish to have your name known at this stage, or to remain anonymous? I hear you are doing some very good work in the clinic: even Sister Rigour admits that your presence there is 'not unhelpful'. Well done!

Peggy came in with her tea. 'Nice and strong, Mrs Fallon, how you like it. And plenty of sugar, give you a bit of energy.'

Cassia actually hated strong tea, and particularly with sugar in it, but Peggy had somehow decided that was how she liked it; it would be horribly and impossibly hurtful to put her right.

'Thank you, Peggy, that's lovely,' she said. Peggy stood watching her carefully as she sipped at it, then went out, beaming with satisfaction.

A ceremony: announcing her bequest, presenting her as some kind of medical benefactor. How would Edward possibly cope with that? It was out of the question. Especially at the moment. He had scarcely spoken to her for days, even his rather distant politeness gone, looking at her when circumstance forced them to be together in the same room with a wall-eyed distaste. She kept hearing Harry's voice that night – 'It will be the finish of you' – and feeling a thud of fear and misery at the recognition that he was right, and then experiencing a sense of such self-loathing at being so terminally selfish that she felt sick.

'It's not fair,' she said, pushing her tea cup away fretfully, 'it's just not fair.'

'Sorry, Mrs Fallon?' It was Maureen; she looked rather flushed.

'Oh, nothing,' said Cassia, in the brisk tone she always adopted with Maureen. 'Just talking to myself. Would you like a cup of tea?'

'No, thank you. I have to get back to surgery. I'm taking it this evening. Dr Fallon has had to leave suddenly to accompany a patient over to the hospital, by ambulance, peritonitis by the look of her. But he asked me to tell you he would be back later, and he hoped you could have supper together.'

She knew what that meant: tight terror took hold of her somewhere between her heart and her stomach. She forgot all about an announcement ceremony.

Cecily was the first down in the conservatory. She had found a dress in very dark aquamarine silk that she particularly liked, and had forgotten about, very flattering, it made her look quite slim – she really wasn't doing terribly well with her figure, she must try a bit harder – and had pulled her hair back off her face with the aquamarine clips Benedict had given her the night they had become engaged, and which for some reason she kept in Devon. She smiled at her reflection in the mirror, sprayed herself lavishly with the Arpège that she loved, and wondered why she was going to so much trouble for Edwina and a homosexual photographer. Well, if the evening was half as much fun as last night, it would be worth dressing up for.

She was sipping her martini, mixed with surprising skill by Hocking, when Justin arrived, carrying his small camera. He smiled at her, kissed her hand.

'You look wonderful!' he said. 'I love that colour on you. May I take a picture of you, sitting there?'

'If you really want to,' she said, laughing. 'I don't think I can quite compare with Angela.'

'Of course you do. She's a model, and a rather stupid one, you're a real woman, a mother, a homemaker. And much more attractive, if I might say so. Now, just relax, that's right, and look at me …'

He took several pictures. Fanny appeared behind him and stood watching. 'Will you take one of me and Mummy?'

'Yes, of course. Go and stand behind her chair, put your arm round her, that's right. Now turn and rest your head on hers. Beautiful, enchanting.'

He took several more, then put the camera down on the low table. 'Right, I've earned my drink, I think. What a day. Oh, by the way, I found this up in the bathroom. It had rolled under the bath, came out when I tugged at the bath mat. I expect it's your husband's. So annoying to lose just one.'

Cecily held out her hand, and he dropped a cufflink into it. It was very heavy gold, rather large, flamboyant even. It wasn't the sort of thing Benedict would wear.

It wasn't Benedict's. And the initials embossed onto it were certainly not Benedict's either: not BH, however much she stared at them, and tried to make them so. They were something quite different, horribly, brutally different.

They were DF.

A dreadful sound came through the study door; muffled, but still audible. It was Edward, weeping. Cassia stood outside for a while, praying it would stop, knowing it wouldn't, dredging up the courage from somewhere to go in, to comfort him, afraid to do so lest, confronted by his pain, she gave in, told him what he wanted to hear. Finally, gently, she tried to open the door; it was locked.

'Edward!' she said. 'Edward, please let me in.' There was no answer; the sound stopped briefly, then started again. 'Edward! Please.'

Abruptly then it did open; he stood there, in the doorway, his face ashen, tear streaked, filled at the same time with both grief and rage. 'Just fuck off,' he said, in a low voice. 'Leave me alone, go to your own bloody bed.'

She knew then, from the language, how unbearably she had hurt him.

She had not actually known she was going to refuse to go until she was sitting down with him, across the table, trying to force food down a throat that seemed dry and swollen, trying to postpone the moment, asking him about the woman with peritonitis, about his other patients, the progress (as if she could not see it) of the beech hedge he had planted at the weekend – a screen between the vegetable garden and the back lawn, a long-planned project – whether the new greenhouse had arrived (as if she could not see that either), if he had ordered the new spectacles he had said he needed; and had he seen the news in the paper about the forthcoming march from Jarrow, and what did he think about it, this great and hopefully final protest against the crushing insensitivity of the government?

Finally he set down his knife and fork and said, 'Cassia, let us stop this absurd conversation. What have you decided? I really need to know.'

She had sat there for a long time, in absolute silence, and as if she were watching a film, every detail of it clear, saw her life, the life she would have to lead if she went with him. She saw the house – very nice probably, she would be able to see to that at least, and with as much domestic help as she had now, only without a nanny, for why should she need such a person? – in a strange new city, where she had no friends, no contacts, no life of her own whatsoever, merely a pleasant, bland day-to-day emptiness. Where any friendships and contacts would be forged entirely through Edward and his life at the hospital, and where her role would be once again entirely supportive, entirely subordinate.

And then she looked at her own life now, as it had become over the past year, in all its exhausting, challenging richness, and the scales tipped so devastatingly and with such speed that she closed her eyes, shocked at herself. For it was not just her work which mattered so much to her, and the subsequent soaring of her self-esteem, the fading of her misery and resentment – that was perfectly right and proper, that was by any standards absolutely acceptable – it was all the other things, bought at such cost, such emotional cost, her freedom, her house, the time on her own to be herself, the return of fun to her life, with Rupert and his probably vapid play, Edwina and her certainly foolish fashion show, things which she knew she should not value in the least and which she could see she was enjoying very much and valued very highly.

She had become herself again in the past year, with all that had been good and bad about her: strong, independent, clever – well, that was fine, that was good – but also opinionated, wilful, self-indulgent: and that was bad, it was appalling. And what she actually realised in those long moments was something infinitely frightening and fundamental: not so much that she had a great deal to give up, and it meant a great deal to her, but that she could not possibly love Edward, for if she did, then none of it would have meant so very much to her at all. She would have been deeply sad, horribly regretful: but she would, should, still have set it all aside.

And still she did not really know, was fighting the new Cassia – or was it the old? – trying to be noble, trying to be good, when Edward said, 'Look at me, Cassia,' and she had looked at him and he had said, 'You won't do it for me, will you, you won't come?' and that had shown her, given her the courage to say no, no she couldn't, she was sorry, she would do everything in her power to support him from here, but she could not relinquish her own life to him when – and at this point she heard Harry's voice in her head, telling her she was being blackmailed over it, lending her courage – she knew it wasn't actually necessary.

'I simply do not believe,' she said, 'that you need me, all of us, to be there, living with you, or even that it would necessarily be better if we were. I cannot see that, Edward, I really cannot.'

'Well,' he said, very calmly, pushing his chair back, standing up, 'at least I know where I am with you now. I think this time last year, Cassia, the answer would have been very different. You are not the same person, not the same person at all.'

'No,' she said, 'that is true, but I am the person you first knew, Edward, and that is greatly to the point, it seems to me. I have to be true to that person, not the one I had become. I'm sorry, but there is nothing more to be said. Except that I hope and pray you will still take this place at Glasgow.'

'How can I?' he said. 'How in God's name can I?'

'Very easily. We would all of us, the children and I, be behind you, all proud of you—'

'Don't start preaching family values to me,' he said, his voice quietly violent, 'you with your nanny, your job in London, spending half the week away from us all, going about with your wretched friends up there, involved with people like Cameron, the Moretons—'

'Edward,' she said, 'that has nothing to do with it.'

'Don't lie to me, Cassia,' he said, and his voice was so full of genuine pain that she felt sick. 'I am not quite as stupid as you so clearly think. Goodnight.'

CHAPTER 19

Cecily fought to keep her voice calm, level. 'Mrs Goss,' she said, 'last time Mr Harrington was down here ...'

'When would that have been, Mrs Harrington?'

'A few weeks ago.'

'Oh, well, now I wasn't here, Mrs Harrington, I was on my annual leave, went to stay over with my sister in Tiverton. But I do feel quite sure he was well looked after. May was here, of course, and Hocking, and—'

'Mrs Goss, I'm quite sure of that, of course. It was just that—' God, how did you say it, how did you say was anyone here with my husband, who was it, where did he ... 'The thing is, Mrs Goss, a friend of his came too. Or so I understand. And left something behind. Lost it, rather. A cufflink. He asked me to have a look for it. I just wondered if ...'

'Now where would that have been?' said Mrs Goss, her rosy face anxious. 'In the guest room, where he slept, I suppose. What would have been the name of this friend, Mrs Harrington? I could ask Hocking.'

'No, no, don't worry, I'll ask him. When my guests have finally gone. They're just packing now and I'm taking them to the station. Well, Preston is, and I'm going too.' God, she was rambling. Hardly surprising: she felt as if she was delirious, after a nightmare evening, pretending at first that nothing was wrong, then saying that she had a migraine and had to go to bed, a totally sleepless night, a growing sense of nightmare.

Mrs Goss smiled, picked up what was left of the breakfast things.

'I'll ask Mr Hocking,' she said, 'and then when you get back maybe the mystery will have been solved.'

'Yes,' said Cecily, 'maybe it will.'

She waved Justin and Edwina off at Exeter; Justin bowed and kissed her hand elaborately on the platform. 'It's been too wonderful,' he said, 'and thank you so much for your hospitality. Your house and your children are divine. I absolutely insist we meet in London.'

'That would be very nice,' said Cecily, looking nervously up and down the platform lest she saw anyone she knew, 'and thank you for being so appreciative. I'm sorry about last night.'

'Don't even mention it,' said Justin. 'Edwina and I were exhausted and quite pleased to have an early night. Weren't we, Edwina?'

'What?' said Edwina. 'Oh, yes. Cecily, I'll see you when we get back to London. Harry and I are off to Cannes in a couple of days. Thanks so much for everything.' She was looking strained, and pale; she had the curse, she had told Cecily, appearing after breakfast, terrible cramps, refusing everything but coffee, and swallowing what appeared to be a handful of aspirin; but she also seemed very distracted, Cecily thought, not herself at all. She wondered if she had told Harry yet about her inability to have children; she rather suspected not.

The drive back from the station seemed very long; she felt sick anyway, and the rolling motion of the Daimler made her feel worse. It was after eleven when they got back to Merlins; she went into the morning room and rang for Mrs Goss.

'Some coffee please, Mrs Goss, and could you ask Hocking to come in.' Better to get it over, she couldn't stand the suspense any longer.

Hocking came in looking anxious; he said he hadn't been able to find any cufflink.

'Look, you mustn't worry about it, Hocking, it's not particularly valuable, it's just that I told him I'd have a look while we were down here. It's probably in the room where he ...' She hesitated. 'That is, where Mr Foster slept.'

'Mr Foster, madam? There was no one here by that name.'

'Really? Are you sure?'

'Perfectly, madam, yes. Mr Harrington's guest was a Mr Fraser. An old school friend, Mr Harrington said. A very nice gentleman.'

Cecily sat staring at him, momentarily taken aback, hopeful even; then, hating herself, she said, 'Oh, how silly of me, yes of course, why on earth did I say Foster? Mr Fraser, yes. Tall and dark ...?'

'Yes, madam.'

If she had needed any proof, any proof at all that Benedict had been feeling guilty about Foster's visit, anxious even, it was that he had sought to disguise it, given him a false name. And then discouraged her from coming down here, possibly for a year while work on the house was carried out. It was so clever, so devious, so horrible.

She realised Hocking was staring at her now, his face puzzled. She smiled at him, a bright, cheerful smile, as if to imply that she was a silly, dizzy woman, frequently given to such confusion over the identity of friends.

'How silly of me,' she said lightly. 'I'm so sorry, Hocking. My mistake. Yes, goodness, I haven't seen him for years. Anyway, I'll have a look round the room, see if I can find it. Er, which one did he have?'

'The main guest bedroom, madam. Naturally.' He looked slightly disapproving now, as if she was questioning his professional skill.

'Yes, of course. Naturally. And he was here for how long?'

'Just the one night, madam.'

'Thank you, Hocking. Well, I'll go and have a look. As I said.'

She went up to the guest bedroom, shut the door behind her, stood leaning against it, breathing heavily; she realised she was crying now, quite loudly, like a child. It was a very nice room, with a wonderful view of the sea, one that she had had redecorated herself, in varying shades of blue and white to echo the brilliance of the world outside. She had always loved it, it had been her favourite room, even more than their own; now it seemed dark, threatening, horrible.

She went over to the bed, pulled the heavy cover off it, dragged furiously at the bedclothes, tearing them off, sheets, blankets, pillowcases, sobbing, gasping for breath, throwing them down on the floor. They were clean, of course, quite clean, she had known they would be, the bed would have been stripped immediately Dominic Foster had left, but she still needed to be rid of them, they were still contaminated by him, had replaced the sheets which had been next to his skin, had covered the mattress on which he had lain.

When finally she had finished, she sank down on to the floor, oddly exhausted, hugging her knees, her head thrown back, still crying, and tried to think whatever she should do.

'I'm sorry, Harry. I just don't think I can go tonight.' Edwina looked in her dressing-table mirror, saw her own face, glassy pale, saw Harry's beyond it, impatient, distasteful.

'What's the matter, why not?'

'I've got the curse and—'

'Oh God. Not again.'

'Harry, I can't help it.'

'I hope not.'

'What do you mean, you hope not?'

'Oh, nothing.' He looked at her, clearly trying to compose himself, to be more sympathetic. 'I'm sorry, you'd better go to bed. Shall I get Mildred to call the doctor?'

'I don't need a doctor. There's nothing seriously wrong with me. I just suffer from very bad menstrual cramps. I always have.'

'Yes but—'

'But what?'

'Oh, nothing. Forget it. But I think you'd better see a doctor anyway. It does seem to be rather bad. Most women manage to carry on, they don't have to take to their beds every month, like some sickly Victorian heroine.'

'Yes, well, other women are luckier. God, you're a bastard,' said Edwina. The pain was very severe; it was making her feel sick. And she knew what he was driving at: her failure, yet again, to conceive. That made her feel sick as well.

'I'm sorry,' he said again, 'sorry you feel so rotten. But I'd like you to try and sort it out. The whole thing. As soon as we get back from holiday. Now I'd better go, it's already after seven. I'll probably be late back. I'll see you in the morning.'

'So sweet of you to sympathise,' said Edwina under her breath as the door closed behind him. She climbed into bed and rang for Mildred; she felt too bad even to get undressed. 'Bring me a hot-water bottle, will you?' she said. 'And a hot drink, and some brandy, and some more aspirin.'

She lay down, turned on her side, pulled up her legs so that she was in the foetal position. The foetal position: that was an irony. God, it hurt. Harry was right about one thing: it was getting worse. Well, she knew what it was, Fortescue had told her, and there was nothing to be done about it, short of having a hysterectomy, and Harry certainly wouldn't agree to that. And it was all her own stupid, bloody fault. The pain suddenly worsened, shot through her, raw, piercing; she groaned aloud. And there would be hours of this before she felt better, most of the night, in fact. It wasn't fair: it just wasn't fair. Whatever she'd done. Other people got away with it, scot free: why not her?

For the first time, Cecily was thinking quite seriously about a divorce. She had always resisted it before, not least because in spite of everything, she genuinely loved Benedict. It was a rather odd marriage they had, obviously, pushed and pulled into some semblance of normality, and always with the overhanging shadow of her fear; but just the same, for much of it she had been fairly happy. She had her children, she had her house, her friends, a pretty good – albeit slightly anxious – social life.

She and Benedict got on very well, although they had little actually in common: he was so very clever, and she knew she was not; his idea of an enjoyable evening was the opera or a chamber concert, hers the cinema, or a musical comedy; he read Proust and Dickens and such modern writers as Spender and Cecil Day Lewis, she devoured Galsworthy, Daphne du Maurier and her new favourite, Angela Thirkell. But they both loved their children, enjoyed family life, were interested in their houses and in decor, looked forward to their holidays; in fact, she had often thought in the past, as she contemplated her marriage, it was no less, and possibly in many ways more, satisfactory than those of many of her friends.

And divorce was not a good prospect: it was still considered fairly scandalous, it would be appallingly bad for the children, and her own life, as a woman on her own, would be difficult and lonely. There was also the indisputable fact that were she to leave Benedict, he would be much more vulnerable to rumours, to scandal even. And what grounds would she give? Adultery, she supposed; and he would do the decent thing, no doubt, and provide the grounds, go to a hotel with some woman, having notified a private detective, get the necessary evidence, but it was all so horrible, so depressing, such an admission of failure.

But then, she thought, tossing endlessly, night after night, in the four-poster bed in their room in Devon, the marriage was a failure. Benedict preferred men to women, and at any one time, no doubt, one specific man to her: the treatment had been a failure, her own efforts to cure him with love and patience had been a failure, she was a failure. That last was the worst: the humiliation was intense, far more so, she was sure, than if she had discovered he was in love with another woman. It was a total rejection: he didn't prefer someone else to her, he found her very essence, her womanhood, distasteful, unattractive, undesirable.

Given that fact, it was very hard to hang on to any sense of self-esteem, self-respect even. Maybe she was only attractive to homosexuals, she thought, remembering Justin Everard and his very insistent, albeit charming attentions. That was a frightening thought in itself. But then what man would find her attractive? she wondered, studying her reflection in the mirror one morning after her bath, hating the plumpness, turning herself away from her own body, the full, heavy breasts, the rounded, loose stomach, the dimpled thighs. And no wonder Benedict of all people found her revolting. A man whose preference was for men, lean, taut men was hardly going to find any pleasure in her. Perhaps if she was more boyish, more like Edwina, Cassia even, it would be better. She kept meaning to eat less, to try really hard, but when you were unhappy, hunger was a most dreadful companion.

When she got back to London, she thought, she might go to one of

Syrie Maugham's diet luncheons. That would inspire her, perhaps, make it easier. She knew that Mrs Maugham had actually gone on a fast for six weeks and said she had never felt better; Cecily was sure that she would faint after six hours without food. Exercise might help, of course; she had heard that in Paris everyone was cycling: what had begun as a response to the taxi strike of the spring had become a craze, everyone was doing it. Or she could try tap dancing, that was supposed to be wonderful. There was a lady called Bunny Bradley who taught it, had been recommended by *Vogue*, apparently Mr Cochran sent his young ladies to her, yes, she'd try that ...

Oh God, Cecily, are you mad? she thought, pulling on her clothes, angry, almost tearful at herself and her own foolishness, as if the loss of a few pounds was going to make her attractive to Benedict, make him change, make him want her – and so she would start again, going round and round, wondering what to do, how she could bear it, whether she was better or worse off staying within this strange, difficult, hurtful marriage.

It was three days since Edwina and Justin had left; Benedict was due back from Munich in another two. He had no idea she was in Devon; she had decided to let him find out for himself. She almost enjoyed the thought of how terrified he would be to learn she was here. She would sit it out, his terror, wait and see what he did. She wasn't going to make it easy for him; she would force him to come to her. Only she had no idea what she would do after that: no idea at all.

For the first time in as long as he could remember, Rupert Cameron was feeling that most agreeable of emotions, self-respect. For much of his life he had done nothing he could be proud of: leads in light comedies in repertory in his youth, second leads as he had grown older, the occasional West End understudy, middleweight billing in provincial musicals, cabarets on ocean liners, so many Dandinis and Buttons in pantomimes, he had literally lost count. None of it added up to anything he could be pleased about, lived up to the early promise of the golden boy who had won the Shakespeare trophy at drama school and been summoned to Hollywood, only to find that the starring role promised by his London agent had been translated into a bit part by his American one, followed by still bittier ones, ninety per cent of the resulting film ending up on the extremely cluttered cutting-room floor.

Now, suddenly, there was *Letters* – a fine piece of writing, an original concept, a demanding part, and a production of very real quality – and it was making him very happy. He found it oddly moving that he had

Cassia to thank for much of it, Cassia, who was, as he often told her, the person he loved best in the world.

He phoned her one morning in late summer, choosing the time when he knew Edward would be entirely occupied with his surgery and was therefore most unlikely to answer the phone, to ask if he could, once more, stay at the house in London for a few days.

'I'm sorry to keep asking, but I'm a bit short of the tuppenny at the moment and—'

'Rupert, of course you can,' said Cassia. 'If I'm not there, Mrs Horrocks will let you in, she's there every morning from ten to twelve.'

'Bless you, darling. We're going to do the first full read-through of *Letters* on Wednesday, if you want to come along.'

'I'd love to, Rupert, but I don't think I can. I've got to go and see the Dean about the announcement of the research Chair, and then I'll just stay on and do my clinic in the afternoon.'

'All right. Probably better not, anyway, until we know a bit more what we're doing. Are you all right, sweetheart? You sound a bit subdued.'

'Oh, yes,' she said quickly, 'I'm fine. Just a bit tired.'

'I think you're overdoing it. I shall take you out to dinner on Wednesday evening – or perhaps cook you dinner – and talk to you like a Dutch uncle about it.'

'I'd like that,' she said, 'thank you. But it isn't work that's making me tired.'

Rupert had known that, of course: he knew exactly what was making her tired, wearing her down, hurting her; he had watched it, helplessly, for years. And the worst thing was that he felt, to some extent at least, to blame.

Cassia had hardly put the phone down that same Wednesday morning when it rang again; it was Edwina.

'Hallo,' she said. 'I hope this isn't too early for you.'

It was so unlike Edwina to say anything remotely considerate that Cassia was quite startled. 'No, it's fine. Honestly.'

'Good. I need a bit of advice.'

'Advice!'

'Yes. Sort of – well, gynae advice. I thought that was your sort of thing.'

'I'm not actually a gynaecologist,' said Cassia firmly.

'No, but I thought you might be able to tell me who I could talk to. I mean, you all know each other, you medical people, don't you?'

'Edwina, I'm not even on nodding terms with any of the sort of doctors you would want to see.'

'Oh, how boring,' said Edwina. She was clearly very put out: and she sounded something else, Cassia thought, slightly distraught.

'Edwina, is there anything wrong? What's the matter? Why do you want to see a gynaecologist?'

'Oh, you know. Just some rather bad curse pains recently. Harry's getting awfully fed up with it.'

'Harry's fed up with it! That is the limit,' said Cassia. 'Edwina, I don't wish to speak ill of that husband of yours, but I don't really think he deserves any sympathy over your pain.'

'No, but I keep having to not go out and—'

'So it's really that bad, is it? Doesn't sound quite right to me.'

'Well, obviously it's that bad or I wouldn't be ringing you,' said Edwina irritably. 'Anyway, you obviously can't help, so—'

'I'll do some research. I'm going to see the Dean this morning, and I'm working at the hospital this afternoon. I'll see what I can come up with, and ring you this evening, maybe?'

'Oh, that'll be much too late, we're going away tonight. I was hoping to get it organised before then. Look, you're obviously no use to me, I'll have to ask someone else.'

'If you're going away, you can't see anyone anyway,' said Cassia. 'I'll get a couple of names for you before you come back from holiday. Have a good time.'

'Yes, all right,' said Edwina, and put the phone down.

'Such pretty manners,' said Cassia lightly into the now dead receiver, and turned her attention to the day ahead.

The Dean was in rather high spirits; he said he had had dinner the night before with Sir William Beveridge and that they had had what he called a fine old fight. 'He's got all these ideas about what he called a National Health Service, whereby free medicine, or rather medicine paid for by the state, would be available to everyone. Well, he's a politican, so what would you expect?'

'I can't see what's wrong with that,' said Cassia. 'It sounds splendid to me.'

The principle's all right, but how is it going to be administered, eh? We'd all have to be employed by the government or the civil service or whatever, and what understanding would they have of medicine? No, it couldn't work, no doctor worth his salt would ever agree to it. We'd all be tied up in red tape before you could say consultant. Oh, now that reminds me. Mr Amstruther was asking me about you, saying if you ever wanted to go with him when he takes his students to one of the municipal hospitals he's consultant to, you're to ask him about it. It would be interesting for you, wouldn't it? Get another perspective on the field. Of course you must have gone as a student, but it's a few years since then.'

'It is indeed,' said Cassia. 'That would be wonderful. How very kind, thank you.'

'Not kind,' said the Dean. 'Nothing to do with me.' But she knew it was. 'Now about this announcement. How does this look to you …?'

She went to seek out Mr Amstruther when she left the Dean's office. He was operating that morning, she was told, but was due to finish at lunchtime; she should be able to catch him before he left for his consulting rooms. She waited patiently outside his room off the long corridor leading to theatre. Amstruther's list was long and he didn't emerge until almost two. He came striding towards her, scowled as he realised she wanted to speak to him.

'Can't stop now,' he said, 'I'm very late.'

'I'm sorry, Mr Amstruther, but the Dean said I could ask you—'

'The Dean doesn't understand about time pressures, pressures of any kind, come to that. Ask me what?'

'To take me some time with your students to one of the municipal hospitals.'

'Good Lord, did he? Yes, well, I can't see any problem with that. We're going over to Balford on Friday morning. Big obstetric ward there. That suit you?'

Cassia thought swiftly. Friday morning! When she went home. It was sacred, the children looked forward to it, she looked forward to it; lately in the school holidays they had developed a tradition whereby she took them all out to lunch, Janet as well. She really shouldn't. On the other hand, it was an incredible opportunity. If she said no, he probably wouldn't offer again. She'd have to make it up to them some other time. She took a deep breath.

'Yes,' she said, 'yes, that would be wonderful. Thank you.'

'That's all right. Starts at ten, the ward round. Don't be late.'

'I won't.'

'And don't expect any special treatment. You'll be one of my students, no more, all right?'

'Yes. Yes, thank you.'

★

Her afternoon clinic was long; she arrived back at Walton Street after seven to find Rupert waiting for her in the kitchen.

'Hallo, darling. You look tired. I've cooked us both a little chicken casserole.'

'How lovely. Goodness, what a treasure you are,' said Cassia.

'Well, it's the least I can do. To earn my keep here. Drink?'

'Yes, please. A sherry would be lovely. Incidentally, I think Mrs Horrocks thinks there's some serious hanky panky going on between us. Last time I told her you were coming, she said, "Perhaps it would be better if the gentleman had his own key, Mrs Fallon," and sort of pursed her lips. Too ridiculous.'

'Well,' said Rupert, 'not so ridiculous, perhaps. I did warn you right at the beginning.'

'It couldn't matter less really, could it? What she thinks?'

'My darling, how very naive you are. It's a well-known fact that domestic staff provide a great deal of evidence in divorce cases.'

'Rupert, now you're being ridiculous. I'm not getting divorced. Let's change the subject, I wish I'd never mentioned it. How was the read-through?'

'It was pretty good. Promising anyway. Eleanor is quite brilliant and Jasper Hamlyn has so many wonderful ideas. I really have very high hopes for this. Thanks to you.'

'Not just me, Rupert, I hope,' she said, laughing.

'No, of course not, but — well, I hope you know how grateful I am.'

'Of course I do. And anyway, I am looking for a return on my angelic money.'

The casserole was delicious; and after that he produced a large bowl of raspberries and a jug of cream.

She sat back, smiling at him across the table. 'I feel much better. Thank you, Rupert.'

He looked at her. 'Want to talk about it?'

'What?'

'Whatever it is. That's making you sad.'

'No. Yes. Oh, I don't know. I'd better ring Janet first anyway. I have some slightly awkward news for her.'

Janet, being Janet, took the awkward news extremely cheerfully. 'Friday will be fine, Mrs Fallon. Of course you must go, it sounds like a wonderful opportunity. We'll all go off on our bikes. I've had a little seat for Delia fitted on the back of mine. She loves it.'

'Janet, you are wonderful. Is everything all right down there?'

'Oh, perfectly all right, Mrs Fallon, yes. Dr Fallon is very busy, of course. He went straight from the surgery into his study, told Peggy to bring him his lunch in there, but he does that sometimes when you are away.'

'Does he? Oh, Janet, I am sorry.'

'Whatever for?' she said, her pretty voice with its soft Scottish burr sounding genuinely surprised. 'It's very understandable he doesn't want to eat with me and the children, it's a bit of a strain, not to mention a bear-garden. But apparently he's going to be out all day tomorrow. Leaving Dr Johnson in charge.'

'Poor Maureen,' said Cassia absently. 'How odd. I wonder where he's going. And what about the children?'

'Absolutely splendid. Bertie spent the afternoon with a little friend, riding. Says he wants to be a jockey. I said he'd have to ask you,' she added, laughing.

'Tell him he can't,' said Cassia, 'but he does love riding. I think he might like to have a pony. What do you think, Janet?'

'I think it would be a wonderful idea, Mrs Fallon. He has a natural seat.'

'Oh really? Well, I'll think about that one. Please give them all my love.'

'Do you want to speak to Dr Fallon?'

'No, I don't think so. He's obviously busy. Goodnight, Janet. And thank you.'

'She's wonderful,' she said to Rupert, putting down the phone, 'just once of the nicest people I've ever met. And Edward is so foul to her. It's embarrassing. He resents her being there, you see. Well, I can understand that, but it's not her fault and she never takes offence, just goes on and on being nice back. Anyway, I'm thinking of buying the boys ponies. Bertie would love it so much and, by some strange coincidence, the paddock next door to our garden is for sale. Good idea?'

'Yes, I'm sure. What does Edward say about it?'

'Edward doesn't say anything about anything to me, Rupert,' she said, and then burst into tears.

It was almost teatime when Cassia pulled into the lane leading to Monks Heath the next afternoon. It was very hot; she had put back the hood of the car, which might have made her feel cooler, but the roads had been thick with dust, most of which seemed to have settled on her face, she thought, catching sight of herself in the mirror. Well, it didn't really matter what she looked like: the children wouldn't care and Edward wouldn't even look at her.

It had been a very long week, and she was tired. The morning at Balford General Hospital had been fascinating but gruelling; she had tacked quietly on to the back of the crowd of students and followed Mr Amstruther's stalking figure into the vast, gloomy obstetric ward, and stood silent while he alternately bullied and coaxed them into their diagnoses of the conditions of silent, frightened women, who had already been through the trauma of describing the most intimate details about themselves to at least four different doctors.

The nursing staff were of an interestingly lower calibre than those at St Christopher's; harsher in their approach to the patients, less competent with their procedures. She watched one clumsily attempting to withdraw a catheter from a tearful young woman who had had a hysterectomy two days before, and had found it extremely difficult not to go up and show her how to do it properly, and listened in horror as Sister told a deeply wretched old lady she was going to give her an enema in front of all the students if she didn't stop complaining about her pain. Only the knowledge that it was strictly against medical practice and that Mr Amstruther would never ask her to join his round again kept her silent.

Mr Amstruther was, as always, rude to the nurses, and humiliated his students – 'Mr Ford, if you are of the opinion this lady has an ovarian cyst, why are you examining her in the area of her bladder?' – but surprisingly gentle and tactful with the patients, apologising if he hurt them and asking them if they minded the students examining them.

None of the patients objected, of course: apart from one feisty old lady who said she'd never had a man inside her yet who didn't know what he was doing and she wasn't going to start now, and cackled at him through her almost toothless gums. Cassia smiled at the memory, while thinking sadly at the same time that even that spirit was not going to withstand the onslaught of learning that she had a malignant tumour in her uterus, with secondaries in her spine; the most radical surgery could not help her, and the best that could be done was radiotherapy, to alleviate – in some small way – the pain.

She pulled into the drive at Monks Ridge, and Bertie came running towards her, shouting so excitedly that she could not distinguish one word of it. She got out, holding out her arms, picked him up, held him to her, burying her face in his soft hair, drinking in his warmth, and the sweet, fresh-air smell of childhood.

'Slow down, darling, start again, I couldn't hear you at all.'

'I'm going to school in September!' he said.

'Well, Bertie, of course you are, it's a new term. What's so exciting about that?'

'No, no, you don't understand. To my new school, to boarding school, next term. Isn't it exciting?'

'What? Bertie, don't be silly, of course you're not, not for another year, you're not nearly old enough.'

'But I am, you see, I really am. I can go, straight away, when I'm seven. Daddy's arranged it.'

She set him down then, icy cold in spite of the hot sun, and looked towards the house where Edward was standing in the doorway, an expression of chilling satisfaction in his eyes.

CHAPTER 20

Benedict had gone again, after a dreadful, hideous agony of a row that had raged for hours. Cecily could hardly remember a word of it now, certainly not a word that he had spoken, only the noise, the tears – his as well as hers – and the sense of absolute despair that had settled around them.

Once, little Fanny had appeared at the door of their room, her face troubled, frightened even; Cecily had gone to her, hugged her, told her to go and find Mrs Goss, that she and Daddy were talking.

'That's not talking,' Fanny had said, 'that's fighting,' and had pulled herself away from her mother and turned her small back on both of them and walked away, estranged from them for the first time in her short life. They looked after her, united, just for a moment, by remorse, sadness for their child, but the violence of the battle was too great to be contained. It gathered again, rose, engulfed them.

'I'm going,' he said, finally. 'I cannot and will not endure this any longer. I will be at the house if you want me.'

'Want you!' she had said, and in that moment, disgust for him, what he had done, was more powerful than anything she had ever known. 'You can be sure of one thing, Benedict, and that is that I shall never want anything to do with you, ever again.'

He had stood up and looked at her, and the expression in his eyes was so terrible, so filled with desolation and despair that even then she would have forgiven him, taken him back, had he not said, 'Well, in that case we are in accord at last. Goodbye, Cecily.' The door had slammed behind him and she heard him running down the stairs, heard him calling to Hocking, his voice raw with exhaustion and misery.

For a moment then, more than a moment, she felt remorse, pity for him even, and a pang of something close to panic. She rose in her chair, surprised at herself, wanting to call him, to tell him that at least, for her last statement, she was sorry, but she felt dizzy suddenly and had to sit down again, her head dropped on to her knees.

She heard the front door slam, and got up and looked out of the window, down at the courtyard, where he was putting things back into his car. He stopped when he had finished and looked up at the house briefly, and then suddenly in a gesture of total misery buried his head in his arms on the roof of the car. He looked somehow defenceless, childlike even; he looked up at the window and saw her, and she almost gestured to him to call him back, wanted to even, but something, pride, self-pity, stopped her and she turned away and sat down again in her chair. They might, perhaps, in time, be able to speak again, but for now the wounds were too deep, too terrible to staunch; any conversation would be so filled with the pain of them it would be meaningless, pointless. She heard his car starting, and the roar of its exhaust as he pulled out of the drive, and then, gradually, an absolute silence.

She had no idea how long she sat there; minutes or hours. Mrs Goss, clearly upset, came in to ask if she would like supper, but Cecily sent her away, and after a long time, pulled the heavy curtains across the windows, crawled into her bed, pulled up the covers and prayed for sleep. It did not come; not until the dawn had broken, the hideously early dawn, filled with birdsong, and dancing sunlight, when she dozed briefly, fitfully, for less than two hours, and even they were filled with ghastly, ghostly dreams from which she awoke, finally, to find her pillow drenched with tears.

Laurence Harrington, who had been left in London in the care of his nanny while his mother and sisters were in Devon, wasn't very well. Almost certainly teething, Nanny thought, and then of course he was undoubtedly missing his mother; but he had had a temperature now for over twenty-four hours. She'd called the doctor, and he was coming before midday, but she wondered if she ought to get in touch with Mrs Harrington. In the end she decided it would be better to see what the doctor said before worrying her.

Dominic Foster was having a problem with the design of the new development. Both Harry and Benedict had said he should base it on four major streets, forming a square, with all the secondary roads leading off them; but it wasn't working out satisfactorily with the formation of the gardens. The point was that the houses all needed quite large gardens, identical in size, it was one of the major concepts of these developments, and because of the overall shape of the site, that just wasn't possible. It was a matter of simple geometry. So either the houses had to vary in size slightly – which he had always argued for anyway, seeing a price differential as quite an interesting element in the overall package – or the gardens had to vary anyway.

He needed to discuss it urgently; Harry was away, and that meant Benedict. He knew Benedict was back from Germany: he had said he would be in London for a few days. He'd try the office; if he wasn't there it would have to be the house. And besides, he had another, more pressing reason to speak to Benedict. He would really like to see him, talk to him ...

He dialled the number of Simpson & Collins, asked to be put through to Benedict. Mildred Waters answered the phone. No, Mr Harrington wasn't there, although she was expecting him: she thought he would probably be in later. 'He only got back from Germany yesterday, Mr Foster,' she said, a touch of reproof in her voice. 'No doubt he is taking a few extra hours off to recover. I'll ask him to ring you as soon as he gets in.'

'Thank you. Can you tell him it is quite urgent?'

'I have several urgent calls for him, Mr Foster. I will add yours to the list.'

'Thank you,' said Foster again. God, he disliked this woman. Benedict always seemed to think the sun shone out of her arse, wouldn't hear a word against her. Funny relationship, men and their secretaries. Kind of second wives. Well, Benedict certainly didn't need a second one of those. One was quite enough.

The doctor finished examining Laurence and said that in his opinion he was almost certainly getting measles. 'See those little white spots in his mouth there? And that flush on his tummy? I'm afraid in another twenty-four hours he'll be very poorly indeed. Careful nursing will be needed, in a darkened room, because of the risk of damage to the eyes, regular sponging down, plenty of fluids. You should certainly tell his mother. I'll be back in the morning.'

Nanny thanked him and saw him out and then went to the telephone and asked the operator to get her the number in Devon.

Mrs Harrington sounded very strained, she thought, not at all how she should be after a week by the sea; and she was clearly upset by the news about Laurence.

'I'll come up at once, Nanny, naturally. I was intending to, anyway. I think the other children should remain here, don't you? To avoid any risk of infection. Such a horrible illness. Now if there's anything you need for him, do get it, of course, and naturally you must inform my husband. Or has he gone to the office?'

'Your husband isn't here, Mrs Harrington.'

'Oh. So he has gone to the office, then?' Her voice sounded rather sharp suddenly, sharp and uneasy.

'Possibly. I didn't realise he had returned to the house.'

'Well, maybe he hasn't got back yet. Stayed at a hotel, possibly, on the way. He did leave here quite late last night. Perhaps you'd let me know when he does get back, Nanny.'

'Certainly, madam.'

'And meanwhile I'll be on my way, as soon as I can. Poor little Laurence, is he very poorly?'

'Not too bad at the moment, madam, but Dr Rushton says he is bound to become worse.'

Cecily put the phone down, and went to find Mrs Goss. She was very sorry Laurence was ill, of course, but it was a relief to have an excuse to leave Devon and the children. The scene with Benedict had changed her perception of the house quite horribly, made it seem hostile and alien to her, instead of the lovely, peaceful, restorative place she had known; and the children, even Fanny, were grating on her raw nerves.

'Laurence is ill, developing measles, and naturally I must go back to London to be with him. I would greatly prefer it if the girls could stay here. I don't want them catching it, if I can help it. Now, is it too much to ask you to look after them, just for a few days?'

Mrs Goss said it would be a great pleasure. 'We had a wonderful week last year, when you and Mr Harrington went to the cows.'

Cecily wondered in her distraction what on earth she could mean, had a brief hysterical vision of herself and Benedict surrounded by a herd of Jerseys, and then realised – Cowes week – and smiled at her gratefully. 'Bless you. I'll send Preston back for them in a few days, when the worst of the infection is over.'

'Very well, Mrs Harrington. Er, is Miss Fanny all right now? She was a bit upset earlier.'

'Oh, I'm sure she's fine,' said Cecily quickly, 'but I'll go and find her, just make sure. I'm sorry about the – the argument last night, Mrs Goss. Married life, you know.' She smiled brightly at Mrs Goss, who patted her hand, her plump rosy face oddly relieved.

'I do know, madam. When Mr Goss was alive, we used to have regular

337

arguments, every Friday night usually, when he'd had a few. Cleared the air. And then of course, it's so nice making up afterwards, isn't it? Makes it all worthwhile.'

'Oh, yes,' said Cecily, trying to envisage a situation where she and Benedict ever made up. 'Yes, of course it does. Well, thank you again, Mrs Goss, I'll go and find the girls.'

They were sitting out in the stables; Stephanie was being a pony and Fanny a rather bad-tempered groom. 'Keep still,' she shouted. 'Keep bloody well still.'

'Fanny, darling,' said Cecily gently, 'that's not a very nice word.'

'You used it,' said Fanny, her small face hostile and flushed as she met her eyes. 'You used it last night. And Papa did. I'll say it if I like.'

'Fanny, I'm sorry about last night. If you were upset ...'

She tried to put her arms round Fanny, but she pushed her off. 'It's all right. Leave me alone.'

Cecily sighed and told them she had to go to London, that Laurence had the measles. 'But I don't want you getting it, so you're to stay here with Mrs Goss. That'll be fun, won't it?'

Stephanie, who had clear memories of a rapturous week of indulgence and overfeeding the previous summer with Mrs Goss, beamed at her and said, 'Goody, goody.' Fanny stared at her, morose, silently.

It was late afternoon, and they were driving through Wiltshire. Cecily told Preston to stop at the next large hotel they came to. 'I need to have something to eat. And I'd like to phone the house, see how Laurence is.' A sign said Marlborough five miles. That would do very well. There were several hotels there.

Preston pulled up at the Bear. She went in quickly, asked for afternoon tea, and if she could put a trunk call through to her house.

'Of course, madam. If you just take a seat in the lounge, we will call you as soon as we get through; there is a telephone you can pick up in the lobby.'

It seemed a very long time. Adams, the butler, was on the other end when she was finally called to the phone.

'Master Laurence doesn't seem too bad, madam. I will call Nanny for you.'

'Thank you, Adams. Is my husband there?'

'No, madam.' He sounded surprised. 'We haven't seen him since he left for Devon, yesterday morning.'

'Oh, I see. Well, no doubt he's taking the journey slowly. Or gone straight to the office perhaps.'

'Perhaps, madam. If he does arrive home naturally I will tell him you are on your way. I will have a supper tray set out for you. I imagine you will be home in two or three hours.'

'Yes, I should think so. Thank you, Adams. I'll speak to Nanny now.'

She sat there, wondering why her heart was thudding so hard, wondering what the reason was for the curling of unease in her stomach. Just about Laurence, of course. Of course.

Cassia sat in the study, staring at Edward. He was ignoring her, coldly and thoroughly, leafing through *The Times*; every so often he would look up at her, and give her a look of such intense and extraordinary hostility, she felt it as a physical blow. She had been sitting there for some time now, almost an hour, she realised, looking at her watch; she had gone in and said she would like to speak to him, she had to speak to him indeed, about Bertie, and he had said there was nothing to be said that was of any relevance or importance and he therefore saw no point in saying it.

'Edward,' she had said, 'I am not leaving this room until we have discussed it,' and he had shrugged and opened the paper and begun to read.

It was five o'clock; he had finished surgery early and walked through the hall, and she had been in the kitchen talking to the children, had seen him and excused herself and followed him. He had tried to close the door in her face, but she had pushed at it to prevent him; there had been a short, absurd physical struggle and then he had suddenly given in and she had followed him into the room.

They had scarcely spoken for days; she had gone into the house with Bertie, that Friday afternoon, holding his hand, listening to his excited chatter, had smiled at him brightly, said how exciting, had not hinted for one moment that she did not think it was exciting too, had sat right through supper doing the same thing, and it was only when they had gone to bed that she had said to Edward, fighting to keep her voice friendly, non-combative, 'Edward, why have you decided on this?'

He had said, not looking at her, picking up his book, 'I think it's time he went away, he's getting very mollycoddled here.'

'Mollycoddled, Edward, how absurd! He's only tiny and—'

'He is not tiny, that exactly proves my point. He's almost seven and he's treated like a baby.'

'Bertie is not treated like a baby, he has a very good life, lots of rough and tumble. St Joe's is splendid, he's playing games—'

'I don't like him being looked after by that nanny of yours,' he said, 'as you very well know. I think she babies him. With you away so much, I think he needs school.'

'Ah,' he said, 'so that's it. The nanny. And me being away.'

'Partly. But in any case, I have made the decision, it's settled. And I would advise you very strongly against undermining my authority in the matter in any way.'

'Of course I won't undermine it.'

'Oh, really? Of course you won't? I wonder why I find that just a little hard to believe. When you undermine most of my authority these days.'

'I do not. That's a lie.'

'Indeed? I rather think not. Well, please don't do it in this case. It would be very bad for Bertie, confusing for him. He's excited, he's looking forward to it, I don't want him upset.'

'You don't want him upset? Then don't send him away. Do you realise how lonely, how homesick, how frightened he's going to be? Of course he's looking forward to it, he has no idea what's going to happen to him. Cut off from all of us, from home, everything he knows and cares about, subjected to all kinds of things he's not ready for—'

'Don't be absurd. I was only just seven myself, when I went.'

'Yes, you were only just seven, and you've clearly forgotten what you've told me about it. The crying, under the blankets, the homesickness so bad you couldn't eat, the bullying by the bigger boys—'

'It didn't do me any harm,' said Edward shortly.

'I would disagree. I think it did you a great deal. Actually.'

He looked at her over his book, his face blank, and then shrugged, and returned to his reading.

'You are monstrous,' she said suddenly. 'Don't think I don't know precisely what you are doing, Edward, and why. I'm going to sleep in the spare room. I'll see you in the morning.'

She did see him in the morning, but he was gone, early, out on a call, and then came back and locked himself, literally, in the study, coming out only for meals.

They were invited out for supper that evening, with the Venables, where Edward talked comparatively animatedly about the practice, and Maureen's contribution to it, and his views on the much-mooted National Health Service. Mrs Venables studiously ignored Cassia, except to tell her that she imagined that with her high-powered work in London, parochial matters must seem rather tedious to her, while Mr Venables discussed his day's golf with her in enormous detail, hole by hole.

Sunday followed much the same pattern, except that the evening was spent first playing Ludo with the children and then by Edward listening to a concert on the wireless while she went to bed early, and then Monday had been absorbed for him by two long surgeries and a difficult birth that lasted most of the night. Now it was Tuesday afternoon and she was frantic, with suppressed rage, frustration and a determination to have the matter at least discussed.

Suddenly she lost her temper, walked over to him and snatched the paper from his hands. He looked up at her, his face thoughtful, and then he began, very slowly, to smile, and just for a moment he was the Edward she had once known and persuaded herself she loved: serious, tender anxious, with that slow, careful smile, and she was stopped in mid-emotion, shocked at the vividness of the memory and the sadness at how far they had both travelled from it. Then she looked again at him, and saw the smile was quite, quite different: not loving, not tender at all, but complacent, strangely triumphant. At that moment, and in this matter, he had won:

'It's no good, Cassia,' he said. 'I want him to go and he's going. The school will take no notice if you try to change anything, no notice at all. I am his father, you see. I am, in their eyes at least, the head of the family. I make the decisions.'

'It's so cruel,' she said, 'such an awful thing to do, just to hurt me.'

'Well,' he said, 'perhaps it's my turn,' and then just for an instant, remorse hit her, remorse and again sadness.

'Edward,' she said, 'what about Glasgow, what are you going to do?'

'I wouldn't have thought it was of any interest to you,' he said, 'but since you ask I have turned it down. The place. I have no intention of going on my own.'

'That's probably sensible, I think. It is a very long way away. I really can't believe you can't get a place nearer London, in London even—'

'Cassia, can we stop this, stop pretending you have any real interest in my future in any way? Now if you will excuse me, I would like to finish reading that article. It's most interesting.'

'I won't excuse you,' she said. 'I want to discuss Bertie, I want you to change your mind, I want him at home for at least another year, I don't see why you won't at least discuss it.'

'Really? Then you really have become very blind,' he said.

'You don't think it will be good for him at all, really, do you? You don't care about him in the least. You haven't even considered him. If I thought you had, I wouldn't mind so much but—'

'Cassia,' he said, 'just stop it, will you? You are not achieving anything.'

And then Cecily rang.

★

'Cassia? Look, I'm sure this must sound stupid to you, but you haven't heard from Benedict, have you?'

'No,' she said. 'Why should I have?'

'Oh, nothing. I mean – well, Laurence has measles, and I'm still not home, just travelling up from Devon now, we went down for a few days, I've stopped for tea. I thought he might have rung you, if he was worried, as you're a doctor and everything ...'

Her voice tailed away; Cassia heard the fear underneath it, misunderstood it. 'Cecily, you mustn't worry about Laurence. Measles is nasty, of course, but he's a tough little chap, he'll be fine. With careful nursing, he shouldn't develop any complications. Just make sure he's kept in a dim room because of the danger to his eyes, you know, and Nanny's so good ... Cecily, are you there?'

'Yes,' said Cecily. Her voice was very quiet.

'Look, I'll come and see him tomorrow if you like. Just to put your mind at rest. Not that I'm a paediatrician, but Bertie and William have both had it, Bertie terribly badly. I do know there are the most alarming symptoms, but they don't mean that much. Would you like me to come up tomorrow?'

'Oh, yes please. You're not working?'

'No, Janet is on holiday, I'm taking two weeks off. So a bit of a busman's holiday will suit me fine. I'm sure Peggy could look after Delia. I'll have to bring the boys, but as they've had it ...'

'Oh, Cassia, would you? I'd be so grateful.'

'Of course. Where are the girls?'

'They're in Devon, I left them there, didn't want them getting measles.' She hesitated. 'If you do hear from Benedict, you will let me know?'

'Yes, of course. Why? Has he—'

But Cecily had put the phone down.

Dominic Foster phoned the house at about the same time. Mildred Waters had told him in no uncertain terms not to bother her in the office again, that there was no point, she had the message, that if and when Mr Harrington came in, she would get him to telephone him at once. Benedict had told him not to ring the house, but since the wife was in Devon, there seemed little problem.

Adams, sounding slightly flustered, said that no, Mr Harrington was not there, that he had not yet returned from Devon, but that he was expecting both him and Mrs Harrington that evening.

'Are they coming up together, then?'

'No, sir, separately.'

'I see. Well, if Mr Harrington arrives first, please ask him to ring me, Mr Foster, on Sloane 687. It's about the development in Kingston. If Mrs Harrington is there, don't trouble him. I'll speak to him in the morning.' A nagging anxiety was beginning to uncurl in Dominic: similar to that experienced by Cecily.

Anxiety and a distinct sense of guilt.

Very similar.

Cecily arrived home at eight, exhausted and anxious. Adams let her in, took her things, told her that supper was waiting for her if she wanted it.

'No, not now, thank you, Adams, I'll go straight up to the nursery. How is Laurence?'

'Nanny doesn't seem too worried about him,' said Adams, 'but I'm sure it will cheer the little fellow up to see you.'

'Has my husband returned?'

'No, Mrs Harrington. Not yet.'

'Thank you, Adams. I'll be upstairs if he does.' She crushed the anxiety, and went up to the nursery.

It was ten before Laurence settled. He was fretful and very feverish, but his condition was clearly not actually serious. Nanny had had her bed moved into the night nursery and promised to call Cecily if he got worse in the night.

Cecily went downstairs slowly, into the dining room, picked listlessly at her supper, wandered into the drawing room. She wanted to ask if Benedict had phoned, but feared looking foolish; in any case, she knew Adams would have told her if he had.

She picked up a magazine, put it down again, switched on the wireless and switched it off. She felt restless, miserable, exhausted, yet totally unable to contemplate going to bed. She went out into the hall; it was silent.

On an impulse, she opened the door of Benedict's study and went in; it was in absolute order, the desktop clear. It was a very nice study, more like a small library, the walls and even the inside of the door lined with books. There was a fine, leather-topped pedestal desk, and a deep leather chair and a couple of tall wooden filing cabinets. They were not locked; she opened one. Every file was neatly labelled, every paper in place. One cabinet was entirely devoted to his stockbroking work, the other to his various companies, and a couple of the drawers to family matters. She pulled out the file labelled personal, simply to occupy herself rather than to pry or probe into his life, for she knew she would find nothing remotely incriminating there, and she did not.

There was his birth certificate – how long ago that sounded, 1888, part of history now – all his school reports, and what a good little boy he had been: captain of cricket and head boy of his prep school; and then he had been head of his house at Eton, passed his matriculation with distinction; gained an upper second in history at Cambridge; decorated in the war, having reached the rank of Lieutenant-Colonel. Where, in this catalogue of success, did she find the roots of his failure, when did the shadows gather, the darkness fall?

She went on: the deeds of both houses were there, and their marriage certificate, together with a few photographs. She looked at them, the pair of them, so happy, so hopeful, he so handsome, so beautifully dressed – she had forgotten how handsome he had been then: he had aged, sadly, over the past few years – she so innocent, ignorant even, she thought, gazing at that pretty virginal face, set beneath its crown of lace and flowers, dimpling at the camera, happy, triumphant even at the joy of her conquest, the splendour of her prize. And then, so soon after that, the disappointment, the sense of failure, the realisation that she had actually won no prize at all, and certainly made no conquest. Was that day really the last time she had been properly happy, pleased – in the best possible sense – with herself?

Cecily sighed, put the file away, went out of the room and closed the door.

In the morning, Laurence was worse: his little face scarlet with the high temperature he was running, his eyes hard and bright, even in the dark room. He was covered now with the rash, all over his small body, and he cried endlessly, waving his fists, a croaking wretched cry. Nanny had been bathing him hourly with bicarbonate of soda; she looked exhausted.

'Nanny, go to bed for a while, have a proper sleep,' said Cecily, who had hardly slept either. 'I will see to him, and the doctor will be here soon after nine – he just telephoned. And Mrs Fallon is coming up to see him today, just to reassure us – you know she is a doctor and both her boys have had measles – so I shall have plenty of support. Go on, off you go.'

There was still no word from Benedict. Carefully careless, she had phoned the house in Devon. The girls were being as good as gold, Mrs Goss said, and had been with her to visit her daughter and her year-old twins. 'I hope that's all right, Mrs Harrington. Hocking drove us there, I thought Miss Fanny particularly would like it, she loves babies, and she's wonderful with them. Oh, now there was a phone call, Mrs Harrington, from a Mr Foster. Looking for Mr Harrington.'

'Oh, was there?' said Cecily. A hot tide of rage and disgust rose in her throat; she could taste it physically sour, like bile. 'Thank you. What did you tell him, Mrs Goss?'

'Well, that Mr Harrington wasn't here,' said Mrs Goss. 'He seemed a bit put out. Very worried, as a matter of fact, I'd say. He said it was about business and if Mr Harrington did appear, could I tell him. I said I would. That wasn't wrong, was it, Mrs Harrington?'

'No, but if he rings again, perhaps you could tell him to ring my husband's secretary, not the house.'

'Yes, of course I will. And how is the dear little baby?'

Phoning the house! How dared he! How dared Benedict even allow him to think that he could? Tears of rage, of exhaustion, came into her eyes; she dashed them impatiently away.

'Anything wrong, madam? Master Laurence isn't worse, I trust?'

'No, Adams, thank you. He'll be fine. Adams, did a Mr Foster phone yesterday at all? For my husband?'

'He did, madam, yes. In the early evening, just after your own call. He left a number, would you like it?'

'No, it's perfectly all right.'

She stood there, trying to steady herself, to cope with this new assault upon herself and her dignity, when the phone rang sharply.

Adams answered it. 'Belgravia seven-two-nine. Oh, Mr Harrington. How nice to hear from you, sir. I trust all is well. Yes, she's here. Shall I—'

'No, Adams, please don't. I don't have time to speak to my husband now. Please tell him that.'

She had longed to hear from him, to speak to him; released from anxiety about him, raging at the new revelation that Dominic Foster was permitted to phone the house, she could not now bear even to hear his voice.

'Mr Harrington, I'm afraid Mrs Harrington is not available at the moment— Oh, yes, certainly, sir. I will tell her.'

He held the phone out to her. 'He says it's very urgent, madam.'

Cecily took the phone. 'Thank you, Adams. That will be all for now.' He went out, closing the door behind him. 'Yes?' she said, hearing her own voice very cold.

'Cecily?' His voice was raw, exhausted, strange. It seemed to echo her own feelings.

'Yes.'

'Cecily, I must talk to you. I must.'

'I don't want to talk to you at the moment. Benedict. I really don't have the strength. I'm sorry.'

'Would you consider coming to see me, meeting me?' She hesitated. 'Please,' he said, 'please, Cecily.'

He sounded dreadful. She remembered going through his things the night before, looking at their wedding photographs, remembered her sadness, her remorse. Then she thought of Dominic Foster, given their telephone numbers, given leave, still, to phone the house, and the fury rose in her again.

'I'm sorry, Benedict. I really find it impossible to contemplate. Besides—'

She had been going to tell him about Laurence, but he interrupted her. 'Very well, then. Goodbye, Cecily.'

She couldn't even bring herself to say goodbye; after a moment he put the phone down.

Cassia was with her when the police came, in the late afternoon, to say that Benedict's car had been found, parked in some woods near Camberley in Surrey. He had been in it, sitting in the driving seat, shot through the head; the pistol was still in his hand.

CHAPTER 21

There was an inquest of course; a verdict of suicide was brought in –
'while the balance of the mind was disturbed'.

Cecily gave evidence at the inquest, very calmly; she said that her husband had had a lot of worries of a business nature, but that in every other
way she would not have described him as depressed. The coroner asked
her if their marriage had been happy; she said it had been, very happy.

Harry Moreton, as Benedict's major business partner, broke his holiday
to attend the inquest. He stood, looking pale and rather angry, and said
that to the best of his knowledge, there had been no reason for Benedict
to take his own life, but that he was quite a volatile character.

'What precisely do you mean by volatile, Mr Moreton?'

Harry Moreton said that obviously he meant the dictionary definition
of the word, which was changeable. 'He was a very sensitive man. He
took things hard.'

'But he had no business worries? As far as you know?'

'Not so far as our own business affairs were concerned. Of course
nothing involving venture capital is free from anxiety; some of us
weather that sort of thing better than others.'

The coroner said that was indeed the case, and after a very short period
of deliberation, brought in his verdict.

Cassia had sat in the courtroom, holding Cecily's hand. Afterwards, they
all went back to the house, and Cecily went upstairs to lie down.

'That was mercifully brief,' Cassia said to Harry.

'Yes, I put a word in a few ears. Asked if it could be made quick. For
Cecily's sake.'

Cassia stared at him. 'Is there anyone you can't manipulate, Harry?'

He looked at her and half smiled for the first time that day.

'You,' he said.

There was a very small funeral at St Luke's in Chelsea. Just Cecily, the two girls, Cecily's parents the Forbeses, the Moretons, Rupert Cameron, and Cassia and Edward. Cassia had been surprised when Edward agreed to her request to come, but he had appeared badly shaken by Benedict's death, said he would like to come and pay his respects. Sir Richard and Margaret also came; this too was a surprise to Cassia, who had always observed Sir Richard's distaste for Benedict. But he said to her, as if sensing her question, 'He was a good man at heart, I think. And very good indeed to Leonora.'

She reached up to kiss him. 'I'm glad you're here, anyway. It helps. Both of them gone. It seems unbelievable.'

'Certainly to me,' he said.

'Those poor little girls,' said Margaret, looking over at them, their small faces white under their black hats, their eyes huge and tear stained. Stephanie was clinging to her mother's hand, but Fanny stood slightly apart, her expression somehow defiant.

'Yes,' said Cassia. 'They loved him so much, he was a wonderful father. Very sad. Oh dear, I'm afraid Mrs Forbes isn't helping Cecily much. I do think it might be better if she stopped crying.'

'Dreadful woman,' said Sir Richard, unexpectedly, for he was rarely outspoken about anything. 'I could have slapped her, sobbing loudly right through the prayers. If Cecily can control herself, then surely *she* should.'

'She likes drama,' said Cassia, smiling at him. 'I remember calling one day just before Cecily had Fanny, and she was discussing in the most grisly terms what poor Cecily was going to have to endure, as she put it, how she could remember every agonising moment herself. But I believe Stephanie is very fond of her, she might help her at least.'

'And how are those offspring of yours?' said Sir Richard. 'Doing well? The eldest must be ... what now?'

'Bertie is nearly seven,' said Edward, suddenly taking part in the conversation.

'Good Lord, going off to school soon, then?'

'Yes. This September actually. We thought it was about time, didn't we, Cassia?'

'Yes,' she said and turned away from them all, unable to continue with the conversation, unable to pretend she was part of this decision. She saw Harry standing on his own, staring across at the newly dug grave, his face dark and heavy. She went over to him. 'Are you all right?'

'Yes. I'm all right. I just can't believe they've both gone, though.'

'No,' she said, 'neither can I. I remember the day I first saw them

348

together at the Ritz. I thought they were the two most beautiful people I'd ever seen.'

'And the most doomed,' he said, and sighed. 'Damn shame. Damn shame.'

Cassia looked across at Cecily; she was talking to Edwina now, who was very pale and drawn, clearly shaken.

'Is Edwina all right?' she said. 'She looks dreadful.'

'Oh, yes, I think so. She was very upset, she was awfully fond of Benedict.'

'Yes,' said Cassia, 'I know she was. She seemed to ... well, understand. About him.'

There was a silence: small, heavy.

'I was a little afraid,' Cassia said then, 'that ... well, someone unsuitable might have turned up.'

'I told him not to, if you mean Forster.'

'That was – wise. Is he very upset?'

'Yes, of course he is,' he said shortly, 'and can't show it, poor devil.'

Cecily came over to them. 'I wonder if you'd like to come back for a drink and something to eat?' She seemed perfectly composed, almost cheerful, not the grief-stricken wraith Cassia would have expected. 'My parents are coming back and—'

'Perhaps very briefly,' said Harry, 'and then, Cecily, we have to go. We're making our way down to Wiltshire; we didn't fancy rejoining the party on the yacht, but the London house is locked up, none of the staff are there.'

'It was very good of you to break your holiday.'

'Don't be absurd. We had to come.'

'Of course we did,' said Edwina. She looked rather thin, Cassia thought, but very tanned. She remembered her request for the name of a gynaecologist suddenly, and also (with a pang) that she had forgotten all about it. She must put that right.

She turned to Edward. 'Would you like go go back to Cecily's for a short while?' She knew what the answer would be, but knew also that she mustn't assume it.

'No, I don't think so,' he said. 'I have to get back. Are you coming?'

'Yes, of course. What else would I do?'

'God knows,' he said and then bent and most surprisingly kissed Cecily on the cheek. 'Goodbye,' he said. 'Let us know if there is anything we can do.'

Cassia was astonished; she had expected the most token politeness from him. He seemed genuinely upset. She said as much on the train, but he looked at her blankly.

'I like Cecily,' he said. 'I feel very sorry for her.'

They were alone in the compartment. 'Did you … realise, then?' she said, very quietly.

'About Benedict?'

They had never discussed it: Edward was fiercely judgemental in such matters, and she had always been careful to keep any suggestion of it from him, fearing it would add to his distaste for Benedict in particular, and her friends in general.

He stared at her for a moment, as if he found it hard to believe she had asked the question. 'Yes, of course I did,' he said finally. 'Did you really think I wouldn't?'

'And was that why you disliked him so much?'

'It was one of the reasons,' he said, and then got out his paper and read it for the rest of the journey.

'You look upset,' said Eleanor Studely to Rupert after rehearsal that day.

'Yes. I went to a funeral this morning. Old family friend.'

'And was he? Old?'

'No, he was quite young, younger than I am anyway, three small children. It's very sad.'

'I'm sorry. What did he die of?'

'He killed himself, I'm afraid. A direct result of some of the barbaric laws in this country.'

'Oh, Rupert, I'm so sorry. How dreadful.'

'Yes. He was … do you mind hearing all this?'

'Of course not.' She smiled at him. She was by any standards a pretty woman, with dark hair and creamy skin, and very large hazel eyes, but two things turned that prettiness to beauty: one was her smile, which was extraordinary, very wide and sudden, transforming her rather serious face, and the other was her voice, which was low, husky, intensely musical. She could work magic with that voice, with apparently very little effort, make her audience cry, laugh, think, reflect, empathise with her; at this very moment it was soothing Rupert, easing his pain.

'Oh, darling, you're sweet. Well, you see, he was a homosexual, covered it up successfully for years, at Christ knows what cost to himself, and his wife for that matter.'

'Did she know?'

'Oh, yes. But not when she married him, she was a child bride. He had the usual blackmail threats, you know, survived them; but what did for

350

him, I truly believe, was the strain, the long years of pretending, and of fear.'

'It's appalling,' she said, after a silence, 'I do agree. All those lives wrecked, so needlessly. Why should he have had to marry, make her unhappy too? They have to change those laws, something has to be done.'

'Yes, but you see it's different for us. I mean, there are so many in our business, we understand it, see it for what it is. To his mother-in-law, for instance, his brother-in-law indeed, it would be something disgraceful, shameful, something he should be cured of, punished for.'

'And the wife? How did she see it?'

'I think she ... well, let's say she tried. Very hard. To understand.'

'Poor woman,' said Eleanor Studely, her lovely voice vibrant with sympathy. 'And was he related to your Cassia?'

'Only very indirectly,' said Rupert, 'only by God, as a matter of fact. He was her godmother's brother. And she's not my Cassia, as you put it.' For some reason the description irritated him: or did it make him anxious?

'Darling Rupert, I was only teasing. But you do seem terribly fond of one another. And spend a lot of time together. Jasper hinted that there was something going on between you.'

'Well, Jasper can mind his own bloody business,' said Rupert crossly. He stared into his glass, and did not see the expression of thoughtful amusement in Eleanor's eyes.

Nicola Foster stood outside her husband's door. She knew what grief, what agony lay behind it; knew also how helpless she was to comfort him. Just the same, she could not leave him there, the grief unacknowledged; she cared for him too much.

'Dominic,' she said, knocking gently, 'Dominic, please let me come in.'

There was a long pause; then she heard his footsteps, and the key turning in the lock. The door opened. He stood there before her, ashen, his eyes red and swollen. Nicola put her arms round him; silently, he responded to her.

'I've brought you some coffee. Here, come and sit down.'

'If only they'd let me go,' he said, 'to the funeral, if only I could have said goodbye.'

'Dominic, think sensibly. Think of the wife. How impossible it would have been for her.'

'She wouldn't have had to speak to me, acknowledge me. I would have stayed quietly in the background.'

'It wouldn't have worked. It would have made it worse. I do believe that. I'm sure Harry was right.'

'Well, maybe. Good bloke, Harry Moreton. He's such a mass of contradictions.'

'Most of the best people are. Here, drink your coffee.'

She poured it out and watched him: thinking how much she loved him, her husband, her best friend, thinking how well they suited one another, how lucky she was.

And how unlucky Cecily Harrington.

'Letter for you, Mummy.'

'Thank you, Bertie darling. Oh, it's from Sir Richard. You remember him, he lives in London in that great big house. My godfather. Sort of, anyway. He wants to come and see us, isn't that nice?'

'I thought you were looking a bit peaky at the funeral,' said Sir Richard, when she phoned him to say of course he must come to lunch. 'Hardly surprising of course. But you've lost a lot of weight. I hope you're not working too hard.'

'No, of course not. Anyway, I'm on holiday at the moment. We'd love to see you. Edward will be working, but he'll probably join us for lunch.'

'Good. I shall look forward to seeing the nippers, particularly that Bertie, he seemed a fine little chap.'

'He is a fine little chap,' said Cassia, feeling the horribly familiar lump rising in her throat at the very thought of Bertie, of their parting, of what he must endure, 'and he was very taken with you as well. Next Thursday, you said?'

'Yes. We're doing a tour of the South Coast, staying in Bournemouth a few days, then heading up to the Cotswolds. I wondered if Rupert might be at home if we went to Brighton that evening – we could take him out for dinner.'

'I think he might be,' said Cassia quickly, 'but he's spending a lot of time in London sorting things out for his new play. I haven't actually heard from him for a week or more. Have you seen Cecily?'

'No, she's keeping herself very much to herself. Margaret went to call, but she didn't feel she should stay long. She said Cecily seemed to be bearing up pretty well.'

'I thought she was wonderful at the funeral. It was almost as if ...'

'Yes, yes, I know what you're thinking. Well, who can tell? Poor woman, she's had a hard time. All right, my dear, we'll see you on Thursday.'

Just occasionally, Cassia let herself think about life before The Money. It was dangerous, because she had made so many decisions, taken so many irrevocable steps; there was no way now that she could step backward, become once again the woman who had had what seemed to be a good marriage, who had lived perfectly happily with her husband and her children, who had run the house adequately at least, who had been part of village life, who had turned her back on her own ambitions and desires and directed herself and her formidable energies towards the making of a happy family.

She had been perfectly all right, that woman; she had had her frustrations, her problems, her regrets, but in no way had she considered herself unhappy. And certainly none of her family had been unhappy. She had not been estranged from her husband, nor parted from her children almost half of every week, and nor was she about to be wrenched from her small son against her will and see him set down in a regime she passionately disapproved of. She had known more freedom, fewer responsibilities, less anxiety. And a great deal less guilt. Indeed, she had been a stranger to guilt, that woman, she knew nothing of it; she slept soundly, if exhaustedly, and woke every morning with only the day's duties and concerns in her head, not a mounting crescendo of conflict and self-reproach.

Today, because Sir Richard and Margaret were with them, because she was concerned only with domestic matters, and now, lunch over, was simply sitting in the garden in a deckchair, watching the children play, because everyone seemed happy, at ease, she did allow herself; and the view back across the dangerous divide looked golden, untroubled, sweet. She sighed suddenly.

Sir Richard looked at her, put his hand on her knee. 'Penny for them?'

'Oh, they're not worth that much. Honestly.'

'You happy these days?'

'Terribly happy,' she said, and of course that was true too: returned to her medicine, to old friends, granted freedom, power to do what she wished, and lovely, expensive toys, clothes, houses and cars to play with. 'Leonora would be very pleased with what she had done for me, I think.'

She smiled at him, meaning it, then remembered Benedict, a shadow across her pleasure. 'But oh, Godpa, how terribly terribly unhappy she would be. About Benedict.'

'Yes,' he said and then, echoing Harry's words, 'doomed, they seemed, the pair of them, God knows why. Sweet people, their parents, by all accounts.'

'My mother used to tell me stories about Mrs Harrington in particular. She had a great talent for dancing and would spend hours teaching the two little girls, Leonora and my mother, not just waltzes and so on, but ballet. And she loved flowers, did wonderful things with them, arranged bouquets into beautiful shapes and colours.'

'Yes, Leonora inherited that. The house always looked and smelt lovely when she was there.' He sighed, looked across at Margaret, who was rather surprisingly taking part in a game of cricket with Bertie and William. 'I don't suppose you can understand it, but I do still miss her. In spite of everything. And I feel very remorseful about how I managed the whole thing. But what else could I have done?'

'Nothing,' said Cassia, and in that moment at least meant it. 'It was an impossible situation. Except you might have spared her the awful Monk,' she added, laughing, 'That was mean.'

'I know. I do regret that. Terrible woman, in her way. But you know, quite extraordinary, she kept in touch with Leonora, went to see her in Paris even. Felt it was her duty. Who would have thought it?'

'Who indeed?' said Cassia, and felt her heart quicken suddenly. 'How very sweet of her. You know, I suddenly feel a certain sympathy with the Monk. Is she all right?'

'Oh, perfectly, yes. She lives in a little cottage in Surrey, bequeathed her by a maiden aunt – she would have had a maiden aunt, wouldn't she?'

'She would indeed. Do you know, I think I might write to her, or at least send her a Christmas card, she can't have many friends. Could you give me her address?'

'Yes of course. Before we go. Oh, well held, young fellow. I think I might join in this game myself, get into the slips. Will you excuse me, my dear?'

Well, thought Cassia, lying back, closing her eyes, maybe Miss Monkton was finally going to be of some use after all ...

Cecily took a deep breath and knocked, very gently, on the door. There was no answer. She tried again; still no answer. She turned the handle very gently, pushed at the door, but it was locked.

'Go away, *please*!' Fanny's pretty voice was hard, harsh with grief and hostility. 'I don't want to talk to you.'

'But darling, why not? I want to talk to you, especially as you're so unhappy.'

'Well, you can't help with that, can you? Not at all. Now go away and leave me alone. You can stay there all night if you like, I'm not coming out, not opening the door.'

Cecily turned away, walked back along the nursery corridor. On the way she saw Nanny, carrying a pile of nappies into Laurence's nursery. She smiled at her rather helplessly.

'I just came up to see Fanny,' she said, 'but she – well, she won't let me in.'

'She's very, very upset,' said Nanny. 'I've never seen a child in that sort of condition.'

'What sort of condition, Nanny?'

'I'd say she was shocked, madam, more than anything. And very angry about it all. I heard Stephanie saying her prayers the other night and then Fanny said, "I'm not praying to God any more. I don't believe in him." '

'Oh, Nanny. It's terrible. I want to comfort her so much and ...' She felt her own tears rising suddenly and bit ·them back: the tears she couldn't, wouldn't allow, for grief she had no business with.

Dominic Foster sat in his office, smoking endless Turkish cigarettes and drinking very strong coffee; he also would not allow himself to cry. Once he began, he would not, he knew, be able to stop. The guilt was the most terrible thing: knowing it was his fault. He hadn't even been able to tell Nicola about that.

And then there had been the sympathy. People who said they had been sorry to hear or read about it, that they knew he was a friend, that he must be upset, and then asked if he knew of any reason why Benedict might have done it. 'Pressure of work, I suppose,' he would say, smiling lightly, sadly. 'Gets to us all at some time or another.'

Worst were the ones who said did he think there'd been a problem with the marriage, had the wife been playing around? He'd said he didn't think so, while feeling the barbs gouging into the already hideous wound. The wife playing around: that was a joke. That was really a joke.

August was nearly over: Cassia watched the golden days, days where she could keep Bertie safe, unhurt, happy, slipping past, each one shorter than the last. He was alternately excited and growing frightened now; once or twice as they walked together, or she went to kiss him goodnight, he would say, 'I will miss you, Mummy,' or 'Do you think there'll be other new boys?' or 'It's a long time to be away, half a term.'

She would smile, brightly, reassuringly, and tell him that she would miss him too, but it would be lovely when he came home, and of course there would be other new boys, probably feeling a bit scared too, and half a term wasn't really all that long, only six weeks, and then he'd be home again with so much to tell them.

William was fiercely jealous, complaining about being left at home with Delia, already nagging to be allowed to go the following September.

'We'll see,' Edward had said.

'No, you'd still be much too young,' Cassia said.

She hardly spoke to Edward, such was the frighteningly cold distaste she felt for him; he did not seem troubled by it, hardly seemed to notice.

They had gone to Daniel Neal's, she and Bertie, and bought his uniform, his sports kit and a trunk large enough to hold him as well; plus, to his immense delight, a tuck box, which Mrs Briggs was already beginning to fill with biscuits, bars of chocolate – 'And I'll bake a couple of cakes for you later.'

Cassia had taken an extra week off, jealous of the time she had left with him. She surrendered herself to amusing him, keeping him happy, determined his last few days should be filled with pleasure. They went to the seaside, picnicking on the beach, savouring the delights of Brighton Pier, drove to London and stayed at the house, saw the Changing of the Guard, Madame Tussaud's, the Tower of London. He gazed into the room where the little princes had been, and said, 'Fancy keeping two little boys here, only a bit older than the little princesses, how could they be so cruel?' and she had hugged him to her, her own small captive-to-be, cold with her own betrayal, her own tacit cruelty, and said of course no one would do that now.

They actually saw the little princesses one day, scrambling out of their car followed by their nanny, and running into the house, 145 Piccadilly, where they lived. They were dressed alike in pale blue coats, white socks and button-up shoes, with straw flower-trimmed bonnets on their fair curls.

'They look very ordinary,' said William, 'not like princesses at all,' but Bertie said he thought they were pretty, especially Margaret with her great big blue eyes. The small crowd waved to them, blew them kisses, and the little girls smiled and waved shyly back.

The princesses' uncle David had returned from his cruise on the *Nahlin*; he was due to go up to Balmoral for the annual family holiday. Private gossip at the inclusion of Mrs Simpson and several of her friends on the guest list was intense, but the English papers were still held silent on the subject. In America, however, it was a different matter: the papers talked of little else but the King and his consort, and *Life* magazine showed a shot from a newsreel banned in Britain, of the pair bobbing about in the Mediterranean in twin rubber dinghies, and another of them sitting heads together in a nightclub.

Harry Moreton was reading *The Times* in the sunken garden of his country house one particularly beautiful morning when Edwina came flying out waving a magazine at him. The sunken garden, paved with very fine golden Cotswold stone and with a small fountain playing in its centre, was planted mostly with roses, but also an extraordinarily lush abundance of blue and white campanula and sprawling heathers and lavender. It was Harry's favourite place for reading, not because the air was so sweetly scented and so thick with birdsong and the deceptively lazy droning of hundreds of bees going about their work – for those were not the sort of things which would have permeated his consciousness – but because it formed something of a hiding place and was a warm and wonderful suntrap, even when spring was scarcely settled into itself or the days were growing cool in September or even October.

He found the interruption rather irritating: he had just settled to a rather satisfying analysis of the latest rise in share prices of companies connected with the building industry. However, he had been concerned about Edwina recently: Benedict's death had hit her very hard, and she did not look well, pale and even thinner than usual, her lovely face drawn, almost angular. And she had been listless, sleeping badly; he had been as close to worried about her as his impatient nature allowed. Harry did not love Edwina, he found her vapid and acutely irritating, but he was very fond of her. She was sexy and amusing and a clever hostess, and he certainly wished her no ill. He set down his paper and said, as indulgently as he could, 'Whatever have you got there, Edwina?'

'It's the latest issue of *Style*. It's got my first article in, look.'

Harry looked. It was only three quarters of a page, a survey of the accessory shops in Knightsbridge and Bond Street, but it had her name at the top of it. He studied it for a few moments before smiling at her and handing it back. 'Well done,' he said, smiling at her. 'I had no idea how clever you were.'

'There's no need to be so unpleasant.'

'Edwina, I'm not being unpleasant, you misunderstand me. I am genuinely impressed by this. It's just that I don't want to read it in detail. Not quite my subject. But I can see how satisfying it must be to you: especially to have your name at the top of the page.'

'So you've changed your mind about me working, then? You said you were very opposed to me doing a job. When I first got it.'

'The reason for my opposition was not to your working *per se*. I told you, I think it is excellent for women to work, to have something to occupy them other than their households. I like intelligent women and I am a great supporter of women's rights. As long, of course –' he paused and grinned at her – 'as long as it doesn't distract them from their duties to their husbands, in any way. Which was precisely my objection to this job of yours. It was because I felt your energies should be challenged into having a family. Have you seen anyone about that yet?'

'No. But I will. The minute we get back to London. I promise,' she said quickly: too quickly, he thought.

He frowned. 'Please do.' He went back to his paper.

'What are you reading?' she said. She had sat down in the seat opposite him, clearly making an effort to respond to his mood.

'Oh, nothing you need worry your pretty little head about. But since you ask, the shipping industry. I'm considering an investment in the dockland area.'

'I thought the shipping industry was bankrupt.'

'My dear! Such knowledge of current affairs. You must have been reading the newspapers. All this stuff about the Jarrow march. It has been bankrupt, but it's recovering. Slowly but steadily. And as such, a good prospect for investment.'

'Oh, I see,' said Edwina, and settled to read a rather more absorbing article in *Style* than her own, an analysis of all the latest theories about slimming and the importance thereunto of taking exercise.

'Cecily dear, are you listening to me?' said Ada Forbes.

'Oh, yes. Sorry, Mother.'

Cecily turned a cheerful face to her mother; they were sitting in the morning room, and Cecily was leafing through a magazine. Mrs Forbes had been up to stay for a few days: 'To try and take your mind off your grief,' she had said to Cecily when she had arrived, but so far she had observed little sign of grief in her daughter. Cecily had been brave and positive, chatting animatedly about all sorts of things – getting some new curtains made for the drawing room, putting Laurence's name down for Eton, starting Stephanie on riding lessons, a fancy-dress party the girls were going to, whether she should buy their winter clothes herself or send Nanny out with them ... Really, Mrs Forbes thought, it was as if she hardly cared that her husband had died, had never really loved him. In any event, there seemed little point her staying here with her; she had just said so, and said it again.

'No, Mother, I quite agree. I really am perfectly all right,' said Cecily.

'I can see that,' said Ada Forbes. 'Your father and I have a cabin booked on the *Queen Mary*, sailing to New York in a couple of weeks. Naturally I had told him I would not be going with him, that I felt my place was with you – he has to go, has business interests over there – but I really feel—'

'Mother, of course you must go,' said Cecily. 'Such a shame to miss the trip, you'd enjoy it so much.'

'So you feel you could manage without me being at least available to you?'

'Of course I could. Just bring me a nice new hat from Bonwit Tellers, I'm told they are the prettiest in the world, and I shall be perfectly happy.'

It seemed a very odd thing to say, as Mrs Forbes remarked to Mr Forbes when she telephoned him later that day while Cecily was out, seeing the lawyers about Benedict's will, but she had to agree that Cecily certainly seemed well able to manage without her. 'So I shall come home tomorrow, and we can start packing. Thank goodness you didn't cancel my passage.'

'Yes, indeed,' said Gerald Forbes, who had actually been rather hoping for a solitary trip to New York.

After Harry had gone to meet his business contact, Edwina telephoned Cassia; Peggy told her she wasn't there that day. Assuming she must be in London, she rang the Walton Street number.

Rupert Cameron answered the phone. 'No, Edwina, she's not here. Can I help?'

'Rupert, whatever is going on between you and Cassia? You seem to practically live with her these days. No, you can't help, I'm afraid. I need some advice from her. In her medical capacity. Nothing serious. Bye, Rupert. Don't get too carried away, will you?'

Later at dinner she said to Harry, 'Rupert seems to have taken up permanent residence at Cassia's new house. I'm beginning to think that's why she got it in the first place. They've always had a thing about each other, haven't they?'

'I really couldn't say, I'm afraid,' said Harry. He had been drinking from his claret glass; he set it down rather hard and the slender stem snapped. The glass fell over, spilling its contents all over the tablecloth.

'Oh, Harry, really!' said Edwina. 'That was my grandmother's.'

'I don't give a shit whose it was,' said Harry, dabbing at the stain rather ineffectually with his napkin. 'Just get me another glass, would you? That was a superb claret, appalling waste.'

359

He was in a very bad temper for the rest of the evening; Edwina presumed his business meeting must have gone badly. She knew better than to question him about it.

Bertie looked up at his mother, his small face fighting tears, his mouth shaping a trembly smile. 'Goodbye, Mummy,' he said politely.

'Goodbye, darling,' said Cassia, and smiled back at him. She thought of the other things that had been difficult and painful in her life: standing and staring at her mother as she lay, white and still and unbelievably dead at the hospital; sending Harry away from the house that night in Grosvenor Gardens; not screaming, somehow, as Delia, a breech baby, was delivered, because the midwife and all the nurses knew Edward and she felt that in some way she would be failing him, letting him down; nodding and agreeing politely on all the endless occasions when people observed that she must find it wonderfully fulfilling, being a doctor's wife; even – no, that was a forbidden memory, but it was surfacing most determinedly just the same – even telling Harry that she loved Edward that dreadful night when he came to see her. They all seemed nothing, those memories, mere trifles, slight discomforts or disturbances, compared to this one.

'You may kiss your mother goodbye,' said Mr Donaldson cheerfully.

Cassia bent down and took Bertie in her arms, felt his small, skinny body shaking with terror now at the ordeal that confronted him, kissed him tenderly on the cheek. She felt him clinging to her briefly, in panic, and pulled him closer, fighting back the tears. One fell suddenly, treacherously on his face, and she felt him recognise it, look up at her startled, saw him blink fiercely, and then they both smiled brightly, bravely, at one another, while she still held him, still wondered why she was doing this, why allowing it, why she had not fought it harder, and knew it was partly at least a result of her own guilt, her own sense that in this one way at least, Edward should be allowed some authority, some dignity.

'Come along now. Time to go and meet the other boys. Shake hands with your father,' said Mr Donaldson, in the voice of one who had absolute control – and of course he had now, over Bertie, over his life and everything to do with him, for most of the time and for many years.

Bertie pulled away from her, adjusted the grey cap that had become dislodged in the embrace, and held out his hand to his father. 'Goodbye, Daddy.'

'Goodbye, old chap. Have a good term. Work hard. You'll have the time of your life here, I certainly did.'

And Cassia smiled down at Bertie again, hearing Edward's voice telling her of that time, that time of his life, of all that he had endured at St John's, and how it had hurt him, damaged him, and wondered which of them was actually going mad.

'Right, well, shall we see your parents off?' said Mr Donaldson, and put his hand on Bertie's shoulder, as if to assert his ownership of him.

Cassia turned away from him swiftly, because she could not bear to look any longer, walked to the car in front of Edward, got in, put on her sunglasses so that no one could see the tears which were now streaming down her face.

'Bye, Mummy,' came the voice, the small, slightly shaky voice; he was smiling again now, very bravely, and waving. She managed to call, 'Bye, darling,' and smile, and to wave too, and then another car pulled in front of them, removing him from her vision for a moment, and when it had gone and she looked again he was being walked towards the school by Mr Donaldson, his head held staunchly high beneath the grey cap, set so neatly on his freshly cropped hair, his shoulders, in their stiff new grey jacket, bravely square, in the face of his misery and fear.

'Oh for God's sake,' said Edward, as she removed the glasses, wiped her streaming eyes, blew her nose. 'He'll be all right, he'll be fine, he'll have a wonderful time.'

'I hope to God you're right,' she said, her voice raw with hostility, and then, turning round to put her jacket on the back seat, saw Bertie's teddy, much loved, hugged half bald, lying there, and picked it up. The boys were allowed, officially, to bring their teddies; but Edward had said, very firmly, that he thought it was not a good idea.

The pain in her grew harder, coming in waves now, and she swallowed, hugged the teddy closer.

Edward turned to her and said, 'Cassia, do we have to go through this?'

'Yes,' she said, 'I'm afraid we do. Kindly remember whose fault that is,' and then said no more until they got home.

William (forbidden the journey to school by Bertie, who had clearly feared a failing of his courage in front of his younger brother) came flying out to meet them, and said, 'Was it all right, did he like it, is he playing games today?'

'He loved it,' said Cassia, holding her to him, 'really loved it, and he was perfectly all right, but I think we should all go and write a letter to him straight away so he gets it very soon ...'

Thirty miles away, as the boys of St John's sat at supper, it was discovered that one of the new boys, the very thin one, was having some difficulty eating his food; and when told firmly by the master on duty, the dreaded Mr Bosworth, that it all had to go, the boy gave him a desperate look and said something in a low voice.

'I'm afraid we don't allow that sort of fussiness here, Fallon,' he said. 'You're not a baby any more, you're at school, and at school we eat everything. It's good discipline. Unless your parents have written specially, you are not excused anything that is served.'

The new boy managed to eat a little of the particularly disgusting gristly mince, but then suddenly rushed outside retching. After a few minutes he was brought back in, scarlet faced, by Mr Bosworth and told to sit down again.

'You will stay there, Fallon, until you have finished. I will not allow this kind of nonsense.'

The boy sitting next to him whispered something and Fallon shot him a grateful look and managed to swallow the rest of his meal by way of washing down each mouthful of meat with water, rather as if it were a series of pills.

Later, as the bigger boys passed the lavatories, they heard vomiting sounds and Fallon came out, green faced, his lashes wet with tears. He smiled uncertainly at the boys, and said simply, 'I hate gristle, it always makes me sick.'

'Ah, diddums. Is Baby missing Mummy, then? Did she let him leave his nasty food? Poor diddums. Next time we'll get some extra for you, Fallon, get it put on your plate. Now get out, the bogs are ours until bedtime. Unless we call for you, and then you come jolly fast.'

Bertie's boarding-school career had begun.

CHAPTER 22

Somewhere someone was screaming. Loudly and persistently, a dreadful wailing scream. Everyone in the house heard it: it reached up to the nursery floor, where Nanny was bathing Laurence, along the corridor into the linen room where Susan was taking some clean towels for Mrs Harrington's bathroom, down to the ground floor, where Adams was setting out the newspapers and magazines in the drawing room, and on down to the kitchen where Cook was just beginning her preparations for luncheon.

The screaming came from the main bedroom. Nanny got there first, found her mistress lying on the bed, purple faced, not merely screaming but salivating horribly, punching the air, the bedclothes, anything within reach, which fortunately did not include Fanny, who cowered, terrified, against the window pulling the curtains about her, as if to hide.

'She just ... started,' she said, hiccuping breathlessly to Nanny,' I don't know why.'

Nanny walked over to the bed, pulled Cecily up to a sitting position and hit her hard, across the face.

The screaming stopped abruptly for a moment and there was absolute silence; then Cecily gasped, stared at her, and burying her head in her hands, began to sob less hysterically, but just as persistently.

'Fanny, run downstairs at once, tell Adams to call Dr Rushton. And get Susan to come in, please. Tell her to bring a jug of iced water, and some brandy. And then go on up to the nursery, I've left Laurence with Stephanie. I'll be up in a minute.' She looked down at Cecily's dark head, drew it to her large bosom, as if she were a child, rocking her, saying soothingly, 'Now, Mrs Harrington, hush, hush, that will do, you've been so brave, so very brave, you mustn't let yourself go now.'

However, Cecily continued to sob, loudly, frantically; it was only when Dr Rushton arrived, and after trying without success to calm her, to discuss things with her, gave her a sedative injection, and Susan and

Nanny tucked her tenderly up in her bed, and drew the curtains, that quiet fell on the house again.

'I fear she may be on the verge of a nervous breakdown,' said Dr Rushton quietly to Adams (he being the person of highest authority in the household), 'and if that is so, she will need very careful nursing. It may even be necessary for her to go to a nursing home for a while. Clearly I should discuss that with someone, as she is quite unable to take any such decision for herself. I wonder who you would suggest?'

'I would imagine, Dr Rushton, that her parents would be the best people to talk to. I can give you their address and telephone number.'

'Of course, what an excellent idea, Adams, thank you.'

Ada Forbes arrived next morning, bearing a rather formidable bunch of flowers and a large basket of fruit. She brushed past Adams and went straight up the stairs to her daughter's bedroom, dismissed Susan, who was sitting by the bed, and settled her own stout body there instead, holding Cecily's hand and weeping. After an hour of this, during which time Cecily neither moved nor spoke – 'not even to thank me for my gifts,' she said slightly plaintively to Mr Forbes later – she came downstairs again and told Adams that she would like to see Dr Rushton herself.

Dr Rushton came round within the hour, examined Cecily and said that in his opinion a good nursing home was the only answer. 'I would say she is very ill, Mrs Forbes, but I would be happier with your concurrence in the decision.'

Mrs Forbes wasn't sure what concurrence meant, but she did say that yes, she felt Cecily seemed to be in a very strange condition. 'But I would rather she wasn't moved just yet. There is nothing like a mother's presence, you know, by way of comfort; I feel after a few days she will respond.'

Dr Rushton said politely that he hoped she was right, but that she must be prepared for disappointment; meanwhile, he would make enquiries as to which nursing homes might be able to take her.

Mrs Forbes thanked him and telephoned her husband to say that she was extremely sorry but she was clearly not going to be able to accompany him to New York after all. 'My duty is here, with Cecily. I'm very sorry, Gerald.'

Gerald Forbes cleared his throat and said that of course Cecily was far more important than he was; and after waiting for what he felt was a decent interval, he sat down and wrote a letter to a certain Mrs Hardacre, a wealthy New York widow, to the effect that he would be alone in the city for a few weeks during November and would hope to be permitted to call on her.

Later that morning, after a rather longer session at Cecily's bedside, which yielded no more response than the earlier one, Ada Forbes came out of the room, dabbing at her eyes, to find Nanny waiting in the corridor.

'I wonder if I might have a word with you, madam. It's about Fanny.'

'Yes, Nanny. Is there a problem?'

'There is, madam, yes. She is very withdrawn, hardly speaks, and is refusing to eat. She was there, you see, when Mrs Harrington first – well, when she became so very upset, and she was already quite disturbed by her father's death.'

'Surely it's natural she should be upset?' said Mrs Forbes. 'I'm sure she will get over it soon, Nanny, and of course she must be made to eat. I will personally sit by her and feed her myself if necessary.'

'The doctor says we should not do that, madam, that we should leave her for a few days, see how she gets on.'

'Well, I suppose he knows what he's talking about, but I would tend to disagree; certainly we must try and tempt her. I will talk to her, we have always got on extremely well, I have a rapport with all children, and see if I can find out what is troubling her particularly.'

Nanny went on down to the kitchen, feeling more anxious than ever. Her observations of Fanny's behaviour did not encourage her to think that the kind of coaxing Mrs Forbes clearly had in mind was going to help. It was five days now since Cecily had collapsed, and all that had gone into Fanny's little body since then had been water. Of course she had been quite a sturdy little thing, but she was only a child, her resources were very slight. She asked Cook to make a milk jelly for the children's tea, 'In the shape of a rabbit. That just might tempt Miss Fanny.'

But later, as Fanny's rabbit jelly was returned to the kitchen, scarcely touched, despite Mrs Forbes's extremely energetic coaxing, Cook remarked to Molly, the kitchen maid, that she'd thought as much and that in her view forcefeeding was going to be the only answer. 'Stubborn she is, that one, gets it from her father. She'll die before she gives in, and I do mean die.'

Upstairs, Fanny lay in her small bed, wondering how long it would take before she could actually start to die, and also when the hunger pangs which assaulted her night and day would begin to ease. It hadn't been exactly difficult to reject the milk jelly, because she did want to die so much, and her grandmother sitting beside her telling her she must be brave and she must eat for her mother's sake, and that was what her father would have wanted, had certainly made her want to eat it a great deal less; but the memory of other milk jellies in the past, and how delicious they tasted, was still a little upsetting. She hadn't thought fasting would be quite this painful; but at least the terrible discomfort in her stomach was a distraction from the much worse one in her heart.

Being regarded, however inaccurately, as Cassia's possible lover, was worrying Rupert. He knew it was absurd, only lighthearted gossip; but lighthearted gossip had a way of becoming serious slander and, given the unhappy state of her marriage, he felt it was dangerous. It had also had another, absolutely unexpected effect; there was, he discovered, an erotic element in the rumour. It had aroused certain feelings and curiosities about her that he had thought long dead. Or at any rate told himself were dead.

They haunted him, those feelings, as he went through the days; he thought of her a great deal, more intently indeed than he had for years – her slender body, her deep blue gaze, her shining corn-coloured hair, and her rather fierce seriousness, her absolute integrity, her courage.

He had noticed and liked, he realised, the changes in her over the past year, changes that her money had brought: the chic clothes and the style with which she wore them, the ridiculously dashing car and her patent delight in it, her quiet, growing happiness in her work – and a certain detachment which she was so clearly fighting, not just from Edward but her domestic life in general. It was not a cool, careless detachment: it was a nervy one, troubling, unsettling, it lent her a certain tension, a self-awareness that was very sexy.

All these things had wrought a great difference in her, had delivered finally the beauty that had been promised, that had almost been hers in her youth and then slowly seemed to be lost in the early years of her marriage. She was, he thought, throwing stones into the sea one golden evening, trying (and failing) to make them skip across the surface, a dangerous woman these days, and she did not quite yet know it: lovely, fashionable, sensuous and – the greatest change of all – absolutely independent. She could do whatever she chose, go wherever she wanted, have whoever she desired.

She had not yet taken any real advantage of that independence, but she was undoubtedly aware of it, stood looking steadily at what she wanted and what she might have, waiting to make her decisions. And in the light of it, that freedom, and people's knowledge and perceptions of it, the fact that she could now find herself cast as his lover was truly dangerous.

Combined with their close, loving relationship, acknowledged by everyone who knew them, it was even more so. She must be warned of it, that danger, however slight, and it must be removed. He wanted to rescue her from it, and at the same time, he found it horribly beguiling, which was both dangerous and wrong. The monster must be confronted and slain.

'Darling, it's Rupert. Can I come and see you?'

'Yes, of course you can. I'll be in London on Tuesday, come then, or Wednesday. Stay if you want.'

What Rupert should have said then, what he knew he should have said, was that London was not where he should meet her, he would prefer to meet her at her home; but (beguiled yet further by the dangers, the sexy, sensual dangers) he heard himself saying that Tuesday would be excellent, he was up for two days' rehearsal, and perhaps he could come to the house in the early evening?

'I won't stay,' he said (showing, he thought, some common sense at least). 'I must get back that night, the house is in chaos, and I won't be late.' He put the phone down, feeling rather pleased with himself.

'Mrs Moreton, Miss Le Page would like to see you in her office. Immediately, please.'

God, what had she done? It occurred to Edwina, as she walked just a little too quickly along the corridor towards Aurora Le Page's office, resisting the urge to visit the lavatory on the way, lest she might be thought not to be obeying the command 'at once', that it was faintly ridiculous that here she was, the wife of one of the richest men in England, mistress of two large households, and with only the structure of her next dinner party, the redecoration of her drawing room, the restocking of her wardrobe to trouble her, until just over two months ago, suddenly returned to schoolgirl status, called into the study of her headmistress and called to account there.

She decided she must restore some balance to her relationship with Miss Le Page; indeed, it seemed absolutely reasonable that she should do so. She stood outside the office, checking her stocking seams, pulling her jacket straight, then realised what she was doing and walked straight in, smiling blithely at the secretary, a creature almost as awe-inspiring as Miss Le Page herself.

'Good afternoon, Miss Singleton. Here I am. Miss Le Page sent for me.'

'It was I who sent for you, Mrs Moreton,' said Joanne Singleton, sternly, 'if we are to be precise.'

She was middle-aged and a great deal less glamorous than her boss, but granted inevitably much of her authority. The name of Singleton at the foot of a letter or the head of a telephone message could imbue as much fear or excitement as Miss Le Page's own; her appearance in the office could inspire the same sort of tremulous silence. Her sternness now immediately crushed Edwina's resolution, turned the cheerful smile to a nervous smirk, made her recheck her seams, restraighten her jacket.

'Please wait. Miss Le Page is on the telephone to New York.'

Edwina sat down and waited.

Cassia had wanted to go straight to London after taking Bertie to school that Friday, so angry did she feel with Edward, so absolutely alienated by him that even courtesy seemed almost impossible, but she knew that would be hard on William, who was missing his big brother. Just the same, when Tuesday came, she left with relief.

The clinic was a long one, which pleased her, for she needed to be exhausted – sleep had eluded her since Bertie had left, haunted as she was by the thought of his own wakeful homesickness – and she wasn't back at her house until almost eight. She had forgotten all about Rupert's visit until she was driving down Knightsbridge; damn. He'd probably have left again in a huff. She rather hoped he would have done; she had been dreaming of solitude, to be allowed to fret over Bertie in peace. But as she pulled up in front of the house, she saw that the drawing-room windows were open, and the light over the door was on; and before she could even pull her key out of her bag, Rupert had opened it, was ushering her in, was kissing her on the cheek.

'You look tired.'

'I am tired. Rupert, can I smell supper? You are an angel, really, the people in this street must think we're married. Or that you're my lover at least. Oh, sorry, not funny.' She laughed, put down her bag, went into the kitchen. A pan stood on the stove, with eggs and tomatoes and herbs and olive oil by it, clearly destined to be one of Rupert's gourmet omelettes, and the smell of something wonderful reached her from the oven. 'Duchesse potatoes, my favourite,' she said, and turned to kiss him; he was looking at her slightly oddly. 'What's the matter, don't you love me any more?'

'Yes, of course I do,' he said, and smiled quickly, rather self-consciously, she thought. 'Come on, sit down, have a drink. Gin and tonic, martini, what?'

'Not gin. It makes me so melancholy, and I feel bad enough already. Let's have a glass of wine, and I'll sit and watch you make the omelette.'

'Why are you melancholy?' he said, taking a bottle of wine out of the fridge. 'What is it? Bertie?'

'Yes, he's gone and I miss him so much. Not that it matters what I feel, and I can only hope and pray he's all right, but I feel so angry with Edward, I can hardly bear to look at him, it was such an awful, horrible thing to do.'

'Revenge, I suppose,' said Rupert. 'Not pretty.'

'I suppose. Oh God, what a mess. Unhappiness everywhere: think of those poor little things of Cecily's, of Cecily herself ...'

'Yes, it seems she is very unwell,' said Rupert. 'Edwina was here briefly earlier—'

'Edwina! How extraordinary, why?'

'She said she wanted to ask you something. An earlier request. She said you'd know what it was about.'

'Oh God, yes, I do, and I keep forgetting. Oh dear. What was it about Cecily, then?'

'She's had some sort of nervous collapse, apparently. Her mother is staying—'

'Her mother! Well, that won't help, she is the most fearful woman.'

'She certainly seemed so. And Fanny is very upset still, scarcely eating, apparently.'

'I'll go and see them in the morning. Poor little Fanny, she loved her father so. And she was being very odd at the funeral, hardly speaking. It seemed natural at the time, but now I come to think about it, she wouldn't even touch her mother. Oh Rupert, what a mess.'

'I'm afraid so,' he said and sighed.

Cassia looked at him.

'What is it?'

'I'll explain later. But it's complicated. Now hold out your plate. Shall we eat in here?'

'Are you all right?' said Harry. His expression as he looked at Edwina was impatiently concerned; she had put down her fork, was sitting biting her lip, very pale.

'Yes. No. Well, you know. It's the usual. Christ, it hurts!'

'Oh God,' he said, and then, clearly sensing his reaction was harsh, uncalled for by any standards, 'Here, let me get you up to bed. Shall I ask for a hot-water bottle for you?'

'Yes, please. And some aspirin.'

'I thought you were going to see someone about this,' he said, trying not to sound irritable, as she lay back on her pillows, holding the hot-water bottle to her stomach.

'I am. I've asked Cassia to suggest someone. She was pretty useless actually, but she said she'd find out. I called at her house tonight, as a matter of fact, on my way home, to remind her, but she wasn't there. Rupert was there,' she added, swallowing a handful of the pills he handed her.

'Rupert? At Cassia's house?'

'Yes, I told you, he's always there these days. Anyway, he said he'd get her to ring me. Harry, do stop glaring at me, I've done my best. Oh, God, this is awful.'

'I'm not glaring at you,' he said, and turned and stalked out of the room.

Edwina clenched her fists, wondered how much more of this she could stand. They said childbirth was like period pains, only ten times as bad. If that was so, then perhaps it was just as well she wasn't ever going to have to go through it.

'Oh, Cassia, what have we done?' said Rupert.

She smiled at him, across the pillow; her hair was splayed across it, her face peaceful, her eyes very large, very dark blue. She put out a hand, pushed it through his silvery hair. 'What I've thought about for most of my life,' she said.

'Yes, but ...'

'But what? Rupert, don't look like that, it's not so very dreadful. Or was it?'

'No, of course it wasn't. It was lovely. You were lovely, but ... well, I'm just a bit worried about something ... as I said ...'

It had all been so totally unexpected – that had been the thing. They had had supper and finished one bottle of wine and she had felt suddenly better, braver about Bertie, more hopeful about Edward. 'I think,' she had said, 'perhaps we should have another of those. In fact, why not some champagne? So we can toast the future. Whatever that might hold.'

'All right,' he had said, 'and then I must go.'

'I wish you wouldn't. You're making me feel so much better. And it's getting awfully late.'

'Well, we'll see,' he had said.

There was a bottle of champagne, but not in the fridge. Rupert ran the cold tap on it for about ten minutes, then opened it. It wasn't cold enough and it wasn't even very nice, too sweet, not sufficiently sparkly. Cassia drank a glassful, failed to enjoy it, drank another and felt her own temporarily high spirits go as flat. She sighed. 'Oh, Rupert. I feel so ... so sad.'

'Poor darling.'

'No, I don't deserve any sympathy. Honestly. It's all my own fault. I pushed Edward out, don't you see, I got that money, that wretched money. I must talk to you about that, Rupert, as well, there's something ... Well, anyway, I got it and I started spending it.'

'So you should have done.'

'No, you don't understand. I started spending it, myself, in my own way, doing what I wanted. I didn't share it with him, not properly, not as I should have done. I took this house, that was a terrible thing to do. I didn't need it at all. I could perfectly easily get home, it was only an hour's drive. But I'd found out he'd taken on that awful Maureen, when he knew I wanted to work with him one day, and I did it as revenge, to get back at him.'

'Well, he should have considered you more.'

'Rupert, don't make excuses for me. I don't deserve it. And the car, I bought exactly the sort of car I knew would make him angry − flashy, obvious − and I started seeing all of you again, in London.'

'Cassia, we're your friends, of course you should see us, he had no right to stop you.'

'He didn't stop me, he just wasn't comfortable with you all, don't you see? He's shy, awkward with people, especially ... well, especially rich people, he can't help it. Oh God, have you got a hanky?'

She looked like a tearful little girl, he thought, and remembered the first night he had met her, sitting on the pavement in the street in Leeds, weeping into her school satchel, worn out with struggling to be good. The memory stirred him, led him on to others: the night she had gone to see him alone, in Manchester, made her clumsily graceful proposition to him, and then had been so appalled at his rejection, and then, her mouth under his in the train next morning, her hungry, strangely confident young mouth ...

Rupert wrenched his mind back to the present. 'Go on.'

'There isn't much more really. But I've estranged him absolutely, refused to go to Glasgow with him—'

'He should never have asked you to do that.'

'Why not? Don't answer, I know what you're going to say, and it's not true. I should have gone, it was the very least I should have done for him. And now this minute Bertie, poor little fragile Bertie, is lying in some cold, horrible bed, far away from me, and it's only happened because I've been so selfish, so thoughtless.' She was crying harder now, tears streaming down her face.

'Cassia, you're talking nonsense. Come over here, and have a cuddle.'

A cuddle: that was a safe word, a nice safe thought, cosy, unsexy. She joined him on the sofa, crawled into his arms, lay with her head on his chest, hiccuping gently. 'I'm sorry, Rupert.'

'Don't be sorry. It's sweet you're so remorseful. But quite unnecessary.'

'It isn't unnecessary. I'm so awkward and strong willed, I always have been, I want my own way so much, I know what's best for everyone ...'

'Cassia, for seven years, you had none of your own way. You lived with Edward, doing your wifely duty, gave up all your hopes for yourself, all your ambitions—'

'I had to marry him! You know I did. I was pregnant. And you said at the time, when I asked you—'

'Yes,' he said, very quietly, 'I know what I said. And hardly a day has passed since then that I haven't felt remorseful about it. It was pompous, self-righteous nonsense, what I said. I had no right to say it to you, and I feel a heavy burden of guilt about everything that's happened to you since.'

'Good heavens! Have you really?' She sat back staring at him; her face was tear stained, her hair ruffled.

'You look about fifteen years old,' he said simply.

'I was fifteen when I first met you.'

'And I was an old man of forty something,' he said with a sigh.

'I thought you were the most handsome, the most dashing thing I had ever seen.'

'Yes, I know you did. I knew it then, and I took the most appalling advantage of it.'

'Rupert, you didn't. I wanted you to, my God, I did, but would you? Even that night in Manchester, I ... well, never mind. I'll never forgive you for that.'

'Honeybunch, really! Do you honestly think I could ever have lived with myself, seducing a sixteen-year-old schoolgirl?'

'No,' she said with a sigh, 'I suppose not. But oh God, I felt silly.'

'I did try to save you from that.'

'I know, and you were lovely. And I do remember kissing you on the train: it set the standard for all the kissing I did for years. And no one ever came up to it.'

'No one?'

'No.' She flushed. 'And now I've just wrecked everything. Everyone's lives that I care about.' She had started crying again; looked at him, tried to smile. 'Oh, Rupert. Do you think I'm very wicked?'

'No,' he said, and meant it, 'I think you're rather good.'

'Good! That sounds so boring.' She took another swig of the flat champagne. 'This is horrible, not good at all. I do feel rather drunk suddenly, though. It's all the emotion, I suppose. So, darling Rupert, my lovely dashing love from the past, do you think I'm boring?'

'No,' he said, and suddenly common sense was gone, caution was gone, and all he knew was that he wanted her, fiercely and ferociously, as he had once, many times, had denied as many times. He looked at her, at those large, dark blue eyes, wet with tears, at her mouth, that full, sensuous mouth that he had once so long ago kissed and never forgotten, heard her voice just very sightly mocking, teasing anyway, calling him her love from the past, and he needed, more than he had ever needed anything, to make himself her love now, again, to feel young again, wanted again; and he put out his hand and pushed her hair back from her tear-streaked face, and pulled her head towards him and started to kiss her. He had intended just to kiss her, quite briefly, just to remember, just to make her remember; but her response was so lovely, startled for a moment, then so warm, so tender, so deeply sensuous, that he could not stop.

He went on, and the warmth became heat, their mouths harder, their tenderness sharply and dangerously desire. He moved one hand, felt for her breast; beneath her silk blouse, her thin chemise, the nipple was outlined, firm, erect; he felt her moving against him, closer now, determined almost, felt his own response, knew he must stop, must not, could not go on – and went on.

It was very lovely: she was at first tender, sweetly welcoming; became greedier, more passionate. He entered her quickly, the danger driving him; she began to move beneath, against him, he followed her, sensing a nervousness, an anxiousness almost. He felt her begin to rise, to climb to her climax quite swiftly; she was still suddenly then; he waited, and quite soon after that she did come, her body arched, he felt her spasms, heard her gasps, then her groans, and then as she eased, stilled, and his own climax began, her sigh. And then it was over: their sweetly gentle, deadly dangerous act, one they had both thought much of and never accomplished, and he thought as he lay there, holding her, feeling her, smelling her, that they had truly found themselves in a new country, new territory, and could not decide whether they had left or entered Eden.

★

'Fanny, if you don't eat you're going to die. Think how dreadful that would be for your poor mama. She has enough to bear with your darling papa gone to join the angels, that's why she's ill herself.' Fanny's small face closed; she turned it away from her grandmother. 'Come along, darling, here, just one spoonful, come along, for me, and poor Mama ...'

'I don't want it.'

'Fanny, I'm getting a little tired of this. You're wasting a lot of very good food, food which the poor starving children in Africa would be very grateful for.'

'Send it to them, then.'

'There's no need to be rude. Now come along, open your mouth, come on, that's it. And another. Now then, swallow it ... that's better. And again. There, you see ... Fanny! How disgusting, you horrible little girl. Nanny, can you come please! She's been sick, on purpose. I really cannot cope with this any longer, you'll have to deal with her yourself, I'm afraid. No wonder your mother is so ill, I would say you were partly responsible. Nanny, when is Dr Rushton coming?'

'At ten o'clock, madam. Come along, Fanny, let's go and change that dress.'

Mrs Forbes went up the stairs to Cecily's room. She was beginning to dread these encounters. Cecily would turn her head and look at her, then return to her habitual pose, staring out of the window, with dull, glazed eyes. She had not eaten or left her bed, except to have it changed and to allow Susan to help her wash, for over a week. Even when she did that, she clung to one of her pillows as if it were a child, refusing to surrender it; it was becoming grubby, but she would not have the slip changed. She no longer wailed, or even cried; she just lay there.

'Good morning, dear!' Ada Forbes still managed, with a great effort, to sound cheerful and positive; nobody seemed to understand what a great effort she was making both with Cecily and Fanny. It really was a little unfair. Still, she had to struggle on for both their sakes. 'Such a lovely one, here, let's open the curtains a bit wider, maybe even the window. How are you today? Have you got a smile for Mother? Come along, dear, just a little one. No? All right, then.' She sat down in her chair by the bed, and smiled even more brightly. 'Now Dr Rushton is coming this morning, and I do want you to make an effort for him. Otherwise, I'm afraid, dear, you may have to go to a nursing home. That won't be nice, will it?'

There was a long silence. Cecily stared at her briefly, then turned her attention back to the bed-hangings over her head. Ada felt a stab of violent irritation.

'Cecily, dear, I do think you might make a little effort. We all have to endure things, you know, I certainly have in my time, and it's no use just giving in. It's selfish and very immature. If you would only pull yourself together, then we would all be a lot happier. I know I would. I've given up this trip to New York so that I can be with you. Now I'm not complaining, naturally, I've done it gladly, and I don't look for any thanks for it, but I would like to see some kind of return for my trouble. Now come along, dear, do try to be a little bit more positive. Here, let me sit you up higher, and maybe I could brush your hair, it really does need washing, Cecily, I've always told you not to let your personal standards drop, it's the beginning of the end, standards, keeping up appearances is everything, in my personal opinion, it really is, and ...'

At this point, as she explained to Dr Rushton, Cecily suddenly opened her mouth and started screaming again, 'and hitting me, with her fists, it was actually quite painful. I really can't be expected to put up with this sort of thing, none of us can.'

Dr Rushton agreed, and (having given Cecily another sedative injection) telephoned the nursing home in Richmond which he had chosen for her (with Ada Forbes's tacit approval), saying that she would be arriving by lunchtime and that he was arranging for a private ambulance to bring her.

When Cecily had gone, when the ambulance had driven away, watched by Mrs Forbes and the staff standing on the steps, and by Fanny, frozen-faced from an upstairs window, Ada stood in Cecily's room, weeping quietly.

She rang for Susan. 'This bed should be changed again, Susan, and particularly this pillow. I noticed you had left it all week.'

'Yes, madam, I'm sorry, but Mrs Harrington refused to let me take it from her.'

'I do realise that, but standards have to be maintained somehow, perhaps when she was asleep ... anyway, here it is, take it.'

'Yes, madam. Oh, there's a letter here, tucked inside it, look, addressed to Mrs Harrington. I wonder if—'

'I will take that, Susan, thank you. And deal with it appropriately. Thank you, you may finish now.'

Later that afternoon, Dominic Foster received a phone call from a Mrs Ada Forbes, who told him she would like to come and see him. He was about to say that he was extremely busy and not seeing anyone at present, when she added that she was Mrs Benedict Harrington's mother, and that her daughter had been removed by ambulance only that morning to a nursing home.

'As you were such a close friend of my son-in-law's, or so I gathered from your letter, I expect you might like to send her some flowers, so I will give you the address.'

Dominic took it down meekly and arranged to see Mrs Forbes the following day.

Florence knocked at her mistress's door. 'Excuse me, madam, Mrs Fallon is downstairs. She'd like to see you. I explained you weren't well, madam, but—'

'Oh, I really can't— Well, maybe. All right, Florence, ask her to come up. Bring a tray of tea, would you, for two. And refill this hot-water bottle, it's half cold already.'

'Hallo,' she said listlessly to Cassia, as she entered the room. 'I'm not very good company, I'm afraid.'

'Edwina, I don't care. I'm not here for company.' She was looking very pretty, Edwina thought detachedly, it really had done a lot for her, getting that money. 'What's the matter, same old thing?'

Edwina nodded. 'It really is pretty bad.' She turned in the bed, winced. Cassia looked at her sharply. 'Edwina, have you told your own doctor about this?'

'Well, yes, of course I have.'

'And what does he say?'

'That it'll improve when I have a baby.' She laughed shortly. 'That's a joke.'

'Why is it a joke?'

'Oh, doesn't matter. Christ, I feel awful. Sit down, Cassia, Florence is bringing up some tea. I only came to see you because I thought you might have the name of someone I might see.'

'Yes, I have now. I'm sorry I've been so long about it. A wonderful woman called—'

'Oh, I can't go to a woman doctor,' said Edwina.

'Why on earth not?'

'Because Harry wouldn't think it counted. He doesn't believe in women doctors.'

'Well, that's very enlightened of him,' said Cassia coolly. 'I can't wait to ask him why not.'

'Yes, well, I can't help what he thinks. The point is, I've got to see someone to shut him up. Otherwise— Oh God ...' A knife-edge of pain shot through her. She turned her head away from Cassia. The combination of the pain and her misery at what she had to keep from Harry, what he was going to say when he finally found out, brought her very uncharacteristically to the edge of tears; she reached for a hanky, wiped her eyes. 'Sorry.'

'Edwina, this is not right. Honestly. Would you mind if I had a look? It's all right, I won't hurt you, I'm just going to feel your tummy.'

Edwina submitted herself to Cassia's attentions resignedly; she had to admit that her hands, warm and gentle, were a great deal more pleasant that Mr Fortescue's cold ones.

'That hurt there?' Cassia pressed gently. It did: horribly.

'Edwina, I think you've got an ovarian cyst. I can't imagine how your doctor could have missed it. Did you describe all these symptoms?'

'No, not really,' said Edwina. 'It didn't seem very important.'

'Well, it was very silly of you,' said Cassia briskly, 'but anyway, he should have examined you. It's quite obvious to me, the pain, the swelling—'

'Oh, don't start a medical lecture, for God's sake. I don't need it. 'Anyway, what is an ovarian cyst?'

'It's a growth on the ovary. Usually harmless, but horribly painful, and can cause all these problems you've been having. Anyway, it ought to be removed, and examined. Just in case.'

'Just in case of what?'

'Oh, that it might be something more serious. I mean it's very unlikely, but it has to go, then all these awful symptoms will stop. I really can't believe no one's spotted it. Have you ever seen a gynaecologist about – well, about anything? In the past year, I mean.'

'No,' said Edwina firmly. The last thing she wanted was a cross-examination by Cassia about why she had seen Fortescue.

'Well, you must. Go and see this woman, please, she's awfully good. Or if it must be a man, there's Mr Amstruther at St Christopher's. He has rooms in Harley Street. But he's a bit of a bully. I know who I'd choose.'

Edwina hesitated, then she said, 'Oh, to hell with Harry. Yes, all right, arrange it will you? Er, Cassia ...'

'Yes?'

'Could one of these cysts stop you getting pregnant?'

'It could certainly lessen the probability. Why? Were you worried about that?'

'No, of course not, not really,' said Edwina crossly. 'It's the last thing I actually want, it's just that I suppose I've got to think about it one day, that's all.'

'Well, you can talk to Miss Gerard about it.'

'Miss Gerard? I thought she was a doctor.'

'She is, she's a surgeon. If she were a man she'd be called Mr whatever; as it is she's called Miss.'

'It doesn't sound very impressive. I hope to God Harry will accept what she says.'

'I shouldn't worry about it,' said Cassia. 'I'm sure all he wants is for you to be better. And if I'm right, you will be. Now look, put that hot-water bottle back on your tummy and have some nice hot tea. I'll ring Miss Gerard straight away, shall I? When could you go, next week some time?'

Cassia stood at the telephone by Edwina's bed, waiting to be put through to Miss Gerard's secretary, and smiled down at Edwina. She really did look very good, Edwina thought slightly irritably, glancing at her own haggard reflection in her mirror; better than she'd looked for years, and it wasn't just the clothes (although the fine red wool suit she was wearing was very flattering, Lachasse almost certainly). She looked really young and sort of lit up. A bit as if she was in love, or at least having a really good affair: now there was a thought. She certainly deserved it, after all those years with that dreary husband of hers. Well, perhaps her half-joking remarks about Rupert were accurate …

The more she thought about that, the more likely and pleasing an idea it seemed to Edwina. Apart from anything else, Cassia's goodness irritated her; it would be nice to see it tarnished just a bit.

Fanny lay on her bed motionless, face down, willing some kind of unconsciousness to come over her. It did not. All she felt was a terrible gnawing remorse, even worse than the gnawing hunger pangs. The door opened and Nanny came in; she sat down on the bed, and tried to take her hand. Fanny snatched it back.

'Don't. Just go away.'

'Fanny, listen to me. Please. You really must try and eat something. You're making yourself ill, and Dr Rushton says—'

'I don't care what Dr Rushton says. I don't care what anyone says. Go away, Nanny, please.'

She heard Nanny sigh as she closed the door; she didn't want to be unkind to her, but really nobody could help. Her mother had killed her father − or certainly caused his death − and now she had killed her mother. She had to die herself; that was only fair.

'Right, Fallon. In you come.'

Bertie stood in the doorway of the lavatory. He was shaking with terror; the fact didn't escape his tormentors' notice.

'Ah, look, Mummy's poor little baby boy is frightened. Poor diddums. Is he missing Mummy, then? We did hear he was crying in bed last night.'

'I wasn't,' said Bertie staunchly.

'Course you were. Mellors told us. Pathetic little squirt. Anyway, we've got a cure for crying, haven't we? Every time you cry we're going to do this to you.'

'What?'

'This,' said Collins, the biggest boy; he was big for his age, not very clever, but a brilliant cricketer, and tipped to be captain of games the following year. 'Come here, squirt, bend over. Right, now put your head into the bog.'

'No,' said Bertie, 'I won't. It's disgusting.'

'Put your head down. Go on.' Collins pushed his head in, until his forehead and his nose were submerged in the water; he struggled, but it was no use, they simply pushed harder. 'Right,' said Collins, 'pull, Parkins.'

There was a rushing sound, a terrifying pressure up Bertie's nose, as Parkins, Collins's deputy, pulled the chain and the water flooded into the lavatory pan. For what seemed an eternity they held him there, then as the water slowly ebbed away, they released him. He came up gasping and fighting for breath, shrank against the wall of the lavatory.

'He's going to cry, I think,' said Collins, 'poor diddums. I hope he won't cry tonight, don't you, Parks?'

'Oh, I certainly do,' said Parkins.

'Otherwise we'll have to do it again. Only next time, Mummy's boy, we won't clean the bog first. We'll find one with some shit in it. Or maybe we'll make you shit first. Wouldn't be difficult, pathetic little squirt like you.'

'Collins! Parkins! Matron's coming.'

'Quick,' said Collins, disappearing into the lavatory, 'And you, Parks. And don't you say a word,' he said to Bertie, 'or you'll be really sorry. Not just a bit sorry, like you are now.'

Matron came into the lavatories, looked at Bertie. 'Fallon, how on earth did you get your hair so wet?'

'Sorry, Matron. I was washing my face and—'

'It looks as if you've been washing your whole head. Quite unnecessary, do be a bit more careful. And you should be up in the bathrooms by now anyway. Is there anyone else in here? I thought I heard—'

There was a loud flushing from one of the stalls and Collins emerged, looking angelic, went over to the basin and washed his hands vigorously. 'Good evening, Matron.'

'Collins, you're supposed to be at prep.'

'Sorry, Matron. I couldn't help it, Matron, got a bit of a tummy ache.'

Matron looked at him suspiciously. 'Right. Syrup of figs for you tonight. Come and see me at bedtime.'

'Oh, Matron ...' His tone was wheedling; he smiled at her, a wide, beguiling smile. He was at almost twelve already maturing; and very good-looking, with fair hair and brilliant blue eyes, one of Matron's favourites. 'That's the last thing I need, honestly.'

'All right, then, get along now. But don't let me find you in here again during prep. Otherwise it'll be two spoonfuls.'

'Yes, Matron.' He left, with another radiant smile.

Matron turned her attention back to Bertie. 'You're looking a bit peaky,' she said thoughtfully. 'Is everything all right?'

Sitting in his cubicle, Parkins held his breath for a moment as Bertie hesitated; then he heard him say, 'Yes, thank you, Matron, everything's perfectly all right.' Parkins smiled. Fallon was learning.

That Friday, Cassia went to have tea with Miss Monkton. She thought of taking William, but decided it would be boring for him, that he would be happier with Janet; Miss Monkton was hardly likely to have a rich store of toys to keep him amused, or funny stories to tell. However, she took Delia, who had become very clinging and whiny in the past two or three months; Edward had taken to commenting on it, and observing that in his opinion she was unhappy with Janet, and asking Janet very pointedly if she was sure she could cope with it. Cassia had observed even Janet's good nature becoming slightly strained under this new offensive.

She had written to Miss Monkton, telling her she would like to come, and suggesting a day; Miss Monkton had written back a short, stilted note saying that she would welcome a visit to her modest home and that one day was as good as another to her. 'It is not exactly a social whirl here. I suggest tea, as I have luncheon very early, due to my somewhat faulty digestion.'

Cassia could not imagine how eating earlier could aid a faulty digestion, but she preferred the idea of tea anyway. She felt sure that Miss Monkton's cooking would leave a great deal to be desired.

The village in which Miss Monkton lived was near Petworth, less than forty minutes away, but it was an Indian summer's day and the roads were hot and dusty. Delia whined for the first ten minutes, then fell into a deep sleep, lying on the back seat, her thumb in her mouth, her blonde curls stuck damply to her head. Cassia glanced at her and nearly hit a cyclist coming in the other direction: she would have to be more careful, concentrate a bit harder. She was finding it hard to concentrate on anything at the moment, ever since Tuesday night; the memories and implications of it, both good and bad, obsessed her.

For about twenty-four hours she had felt wonderful: blithely, confidently, sweetly happy, for the first time for years. And then reality had hit her, and with reality guilt and fear.

She wished she was clearer about her feelings on the subject; the only thing she was sure about was that she and Rupert had done something extremely dangerous and that life could never be the same again. The fact that it had been, at the time, very pleasurable, had seemed, had been indeed, absolutely irresistible, had nothing to do with the implications, which were terrifying.

She was even, she discovered, shocked at herself now: and that was an irony, too, she thought, looking back on the liberal creature who had argued with Edward that sex was never wrong, that it was only an expression of love, that all the taboos were nonsense. Of course she had not seen that argument extended to marital infidelity; although had she been asked, she thought, looking back at her confidently arrogant young self, she would probably have said as long as no hurt had been administered, there would be no great harm in that either.

The same confident, arrogant young person would no doubt have defended what had happened in her bed the other night – with all its undoubtedly attendant pleasures – and quite spiritedly too; but she would have been wrong, and besides, the arguments did not quite apply. In the first place, she was not in love with Rupert now, and she knew she was not. She had adored him once, he had been the focus of all her adolescent fantasies. He had known and to an extent encouraged that, and as a result there had continued to be a sexual frisson between them. Oh God, she thought closing her eyes briefly in anguish, a lot more now than a frisson. She loved being with him, still found him attractive, still adored him even; but she was not in love with him.

He was her confidant, her best friend, the person with whom she felt, probably, happiest in the world: but his place in her life was not as her lover. And she simply did not know what to do about it: neither of them did. The worst thing of all about it, she thought fretfully, watching the sun burning down on to the parched, early autumn countryside, was that because of what had happened, she had lost him, lost her best friend. Almost every crisis in her life until now she had discussed with Rupert, sought his advice, asked for his help. This time she could not do that; she had no one to turn to.

Of course, she told herself determinedly, the panic abating as it did from time to time, no one need ever hear about it, neither she nor Rupert was going to start talking about it, but her relationship with Edward was not good, to put it mildly. He was very angry with her, and if he even suspected what had happened, he was quite likely to insist on a divorce, on taking the children away.

No, thought Cassia, trying and failing to crush the panic which was rising remorselessly again, her whole life was threatened, darkened by this awful, reckless, stupid thing; she still found it hard to believe she had done it. Or that Rupert had done it, given what he had told her about all the snippets of gossip he was hearing about the two of them.

Edwina – who had already expressed her opinion on the subject, it seemed – had been to the house that very afternoon, found him there. Edwina of all people – what would Harry think? Not that she cared what Harry thought, of course, but he was so mischievous, so literally troublesome, he was quite likely to start talking about it, in public, in front of other people, Edward quite possibly, should the opportunity arise.

For the first time she felt she could agree with Rupert, when he had embarked on his routine of self-flagellation, started saying how he should have been shot, strung up, whipped. He should. But Rupert was helplessly, hopelessly fragile where sexual temptation was concerned; she knew that as well as anyone. It was actually part of his charm, his rueful, irresponsible, little-boy charm. How a man approaching sixty could possibly have little-boy charm, she wasn't sure, but Rupert did.

That apart, she should have known better, she was the sensible one; but she had been so low, so miserable about Bertie, so in despair about her marriage – and yes, all right, so sexually hungry. It had been weeks, months even, since she and Edward had made love; being suddenly confronted with the temptation of Rupert was like being offered some succulent meal after a long period on bread and water.

'So what happened to self-control, Cassia?' she said aloud, drumming her hands on the steering wheel; and then realised she had arrived at Miss Monkton's cottage and that for a while at least she would have to stop thinking about herself and the hideous tangled mess she had got herself into. Lucky old Miss Monkton: a frigid spinster, no dark secrets threatening her life. But who was to say Miss Monkton was frigid? she thought guiltily, switching off the engine; maybe that was another of her arrogant judgements, maybe she was a seething mass of frustration herself, had had lovers, married lovers, maybe her life had been one long sexual drama …

Cassia decided her own self-flagellation was getting slightly out of hand. She looked at Delia, still fast asleep, decided to leave her in the car and went and knocked on the door.

The cottage, as she would have expected, was not pretty: it was originally stone built, but had been pebbledashed and was painted a very ugly shade of grey, and the slate roof had been replaced by tiles. The path from the gate to the door was ramrod straight, and a few sickly-looking roses had been planted under both the front windows. Miss Monkton appeared at the slate-grey door.

'How nice to see you, Mrs Fallon. I get only a very few visitors, sometimes weeks go past without a word from anyone. Of course at my age, and without a family of my own, I must expect that, but loneliness is a very lowering thing.'

'Yes, of course it is,' said Cassia, turning her head away from her; the halitosis had certainly not been cured (so probably the series of lovers was unlikely, after all). In other ways she seemed much the same, too, the hair perhaps a little thinner, the hands just slightly more clawlike, and she was even wearing a dress that Cassia remembered, droopier and shabbier than ever, in black wool, with a lace collar and cuffs.

'Oh dear, don't say you haven't brought the children, I have made a cake for tea.'

'Oh, Miss Monkton, I'm sorry, I left William at home, he's so boisterous and noisy, he'd wear you out, and Bertie is at school. I've brought Delia, she's much quieter, but she's fast asleep in the car, I'll get her in shortly.'

They went into the front room; it smelt appallingly stuffy, and was rather sparsely furnished, with just two straight-backed chairs, a small table and a low bookcase. There were at least three fly papers, all covered with very dead flies, and several rather dismal pictures showing wildlife in various stages of death and decay, the most outstanding example being a large reproduction of *The Stag at Bay* over the fireplace.

'Now do sit down, Mrs Fallon. I won't offer you tea now, as we will wait for your little girl to wake up. Perhaps you'd like a barley sugar sweet, so refreshing, I always think.'

'Oh, thank you,' said Cassia, who was extremely thirsty and longing for a cup of tea, 'that would be very nice. Er, I expect you saw in the paper that Mr Harrington had died.'

'I did, poor soul. I could only think how thankful I was that Lady Beatty had not been alive to see that. It would have broken her heart. So sad, the pair of them gone. Mrs Harrington must be very upset.'

'Yes, indeed, and the children, of course.'

'I was so sorry not to have come to Lady Beatty's memorial service,' Miss Monkton said. 'Mr Harrington did invite me, but of course it was almost impossible for me to get there. I have very bad arthritis these days and there is no train station for many miles.'

There was a long silence, then Cassia said, 'We live not far from here, you know. Near Haywards Heath. My husband is a doctor.'

'Yes, I had heard that. It must be wonderful, I think, to be a doctor, to be able to heal the sick. You never completed your own studies, I presume?'

'Oh, yes,' said Cassia, 'but I didn't practise. I married Edward and the children came along.'

'A pity that,' said Miss Monkton, surprising her. 'I would like to see more women in the professions myself. I wanted to be a nurse, you know, but my poor father could not afford the training. I had to go straight into my work as a governess, after I had left school.'

'What a shame,' said Cassia, 'which reminds me, Miss Monkton; one of the reasons I wanted to come and see you was so that I could thank you personally for going to visit Leonora in Paris. When she was ill. I know she was well looked after, of course, but it must have been wonderful for her to see someone from home. Something of a daunting journey for you, I would imagine.'

'Not really,' said Miss Monkton, surprising her again. 'I had been several times before.'

'Really?'

She looked slightly reproving. 'You shouldn't assume that just because I am an impoverished and unmarried Englishwoman, I have never set foot outside these shores.'

'Miss Monkton, of course I didn't think that,' said Cassia, flushing, feeling foolish.

'I worked for a diplomatic family, when I was much younger, and we spent some time in Paris. And I had a cousin who lived there permanently. She is now deceased, very sadly. I used to visit her every two years or so. I know the place quite well.'

'Yes, I see,' said Cassia. It was hard to imagine anyone less like a practised visitor to Paris than Miss Monkton.

'So when I knew that Lady Beatty was there, I naturally went to visit her. I continued to feel some responsibility for her, you see. I was fond of her. And very relieved, of course, that I did go. Considering the circumstances in which she was living.'

'I'm sorry?' She had allowed her attention to drift, was watching the car. 'What sort of circumstances?'

'Well, Mrs Fallon – oh dear, she would have hated you to know, but I suppose now that she has passed away, it doesn't matter.'

'Was she in more trouble?'

'She was, yes. It was after Mr Gresham had left.'

'Yes, I knew they were no longer together. But surely she was – well, not in any difficulties?'

'Mrs Fallon, she was in serious difficulties. As you put it. And not well. Anyone could see she was not well, although she sought to hide it from me at first.'

'You mean she was hard up?'

'Extremely hard up, Mrs Fallon. Living quite alone, in a very modest place. Very modest indeed. I only discovered this from visiting her at the old address, near the Arc de Triomphe, when I was redirected.'

'And when was this?'

'It was January 1935. It was bitterly cold and wet, which made Lady Beatty's situation worse. The apartment was cold and—'

'Miss Monkton, how long had she been there?' The panic over Rupert was nothing compared to this.

'Oh, only a few weeks, she told me. "Purely temporary, this is, Miss Monkton," was what she said. "Just till I get back on my feet."'

'But didn't Mr Gresham – I mean ...'

'Mr Gresham had gone, Mrs Fallon. He was living abroad by then, I believe, possibly in Cairo.'

'Yes, actually, I have a poste restante address for him in Cairo, but I don't know if he's still there. I knew he'd gone, but I thought he left her well provided for.'

'No, I'm very much afraid,' said Miss Monkton, 'he lacked the wherewithal to do that. Mr Gresham had also become rather hard up.'

'But I don't understand. How could he have been? He was so extremely rich.'

'As I understand it, he had the same ... what shall we say ... affliction as Lady Beatty. He gambled, relentlessly. And in France, so much easier, of course, so many clubs and casinos. He had lost almost everything, I believe. And I am forced to say that Lady Beatty could not have been exactly a good influence. They had been reduced to considerably straitened circumstances, Mrs Fallon, considerably.'

'Oh God!' It was the heat in the room, of course, the stuffiness, the hideous fly papers, Miss Monkton's breath, that had made her feel so light headed, was making the floor heave slightly under her feet, not what Miss Monkton was saying, not what it meant.

'Mrs Fallon, are you all right, do you feel faint? Here, put your head between your knees.'

Cassia felt her cold, clawlike hands on her neck, forcing it downwards; it added to her sense of nightmare. She struggled against it, against the hand, the nightmare, then said, 'I'm sorry, Miss Monkton, I must have some fresh air.'

Cassia stood up, went out of the cottage door, sank down on the dried-up lawn. It was warm out there, she could feel the sun on her face again, hear the reassuring sounds of real life: a car driving down the lane, cows mooing, birds in the hedge, a lawnmower in the next-door garden. Gradually the nausea, the faintness, eased. She sat back, took a deep breath and managed to smile at Miss Monkton, who had followed her.

'So sorry, Miss Monkton, to have worried you.'

In the car, Delia began to cry. Relieved to have the distraction, Cassia went and got her out, sat her on the lawn beside her, smiling and chatting to her, and to Miss Monkton.

Later, while Delia picked the few daisies that had dared to grow on the lawn, she learned a little more: that Miss Monkton, distressed at what she had found, seeing Leonora clearly ill, had urged her to seek help.

'What sort of ill, Miss Monkton?'

Miss Monkton flushed. She was clearly hideously embarrassed. 'Her illness was of a … a female nature, Mrs Fallon.'

'Yes, I see. Did she tell you that?'

'Er, yes. And there was some evidence of it, in the bathroom, a pile of laundry … oh dear.'

'You mean she was bleeding a lot?'

'Yes,' whispered Miss Monkton. She looked down at her twisted hands. 'She said it was – well, her age, you know, nothing to worry about. I begged her to see a doctor and she said she couldn't, couldn't afford it, that it wasn't necessary.'

'Did you tell anyone?'

'She made me promise not to tell any of you about any of it. "Death rather than dishonour, Miss Monkton," she said, quite gaily. She was very brave. I said I wouldn't and I kept my word. I bought her a few things I thought might help her, some patent medicines, and so on, but I did tell my cousin in Paris, said it was quite desperate. She contacted her own doctor and he apparently went to see her. And quite shortly after that, I got a letter from Lady Beatty, from quite a different address, really a very nice district, the sixteenth arrondissement, near Passy, saying that she was fine, feeling much better, that an old friend had turned up and lent her some money and thanking me for my help. Now Delia, dear, if you can sit still and not fidget quite so much, I will give you a small piece of this cake that I baked for you ...'

The cake was very heavy; Cassia drove home, feeling it in her stomach like lead. She felt another weight, too, occupying the area somewhere between her head and her heart, that had nothing to do with the cake, with Bertie, with Edward, not even with Rupert; she could not analyse precisely what it was, but she did know that it contained a very large element of fear.

CHAPTER 23

'So how well exactly did you know my son-in-law, Mr Foster?' Ada
Forbes's expression was rather stern.

'Oh,' said Dominic Foster, tempted wildly, just for a moment, to tell
her exactly, 'pretty well. We worked together, of course, but we were
friends as well.'

'Quite. Well, it was tragic. Tragic. And my daughter is absolutely
devastated. She's had a complete nervous collapse, you know, is under
permanent sedation for the time being, in a nursing home. I really can see
no end to it. And the children ... well. What they would do without me
in that household at the moment I cannot imagine.'

'No, I'm sure they're very fortunate to have you,' he said.

'I fear they don't quite realise it. The children – one of them in
particular – quite distraught. Poor little thing, refusing to eat, there is
quite a lot of concern about her.'

'Oh, God.' He felt a stab of pure, stark remorse. 'Which one would
that be? The eldest, Fanny?'

'Yes. She adored her father, of course, and he her, she was definitely
his favourite.'

'Yes, I know. He told me.'

'How extraordinary.' She peered at him intently as if he were some
strange species of insect. 'You really must have been very good friends.'

'Yes, we were. Which is why ...' He hesitated, anxious lest he say too
much, make matters worse, then thought they were so bad he couldn't,
and said, '... why I wanted so very much to see your daughter. As I said
in my letter. You see, we had talked a great deal, Benedict and I, the last
few days before he died. I wanted to tell her about it. I thought it might
help. That's all.'

'That is quite out of the question, as you must realise. As she is so very ill. Are you – ' she leant forward – 'are you saying you think you might know why he did it?'

Dominic hesitated again, then said simply, 'Yes. Yes, I am saying that.'

'I see.' She was clearly desperate to ask him more; he sat, firmly silent. 'Well,' she said finally, 'I think all I can do is to tell my daughter, when she is better, what you have told me, ask her if you may go and see her.'

'Yes of course, what I have to tell her may help her a little. Even now.'

'Well, I think we are going to have to live with that, don't you? She is certainly far from reach to both of us at the moment. Poor soul.' She dabbed her eyes, then smiled rather weakly at him. 'It is very hard for a mother not to be able to help her child, Mr Foster. Are you married?'

'Yes, I am.'

'And have children?'

'No. No children.'

'Then you could not understand quite how I feel. Or your wife. Your own mother perhaps ...'

'My own mother is dead, Mrs Forbes.'

'How sad, I'm so sorry. And your father?'

'I never knew him.'

'Oh dear! Killed in the war?'

'No, Mrs Forbes. I was ... I am illegitimate.'

She blenched slightly, as he had known she would, not so much at the information as at the direct form in which he imparted it. 'I see. How very unfortunate for you.' Another silence, then, 'Well, I must be going now, Mr Foster. I will certainly pass your message on to my daughter. Good afternoon.'

He saw her out of the office and into the street and then went back and sat for a long time, staring into the space which she had occupied, thinking of Benedict, seeing him again, his tall, languid grace, his sudden brilliant smile, hearing his voice, easy, amused, amusing – and hearing his own, heavy, wretched, that dreadful night, telling him what he had decided, telling him the one thing that, clearly, Benedict had not been able to bear.

Cassia sat with her arms round Fanny, holding the pathetically thin little body, feeling the great sobs wrack through it, not saying anything, just waiting for the storm to pass. She was actually on her way to see Harry Moreton in his office, but was early, and having heard Cecily had been admitted to a nursing home, had decided to visit the house and see how the children were.

She had been quite surprised by the rapturous reception she got:

Adams had welcomed her in, almost effusively, his gloomy face creased into a smile; Susan practically fell into her arms, saying, 'Oh, madam, I'm so pleased to see you,' and Nanny came running down the stairs at the news that she was in the house, and ushered her into the morning room, telling her she had never been more relieved to see anyone in her life.

'I did think of telephoning you, madam, but Mrs Forbes was against it. She feels she is the best person to cope, and of course she must be, but—'

'Cope with what, Nanny? The children, I suppose?'

'No, not really, madam. Of course Stephanie and Laurence are miserable, but perfectly all right. Stephanie is back at school. No, it's Fanny, she is totally withdrawn, won't speak to any of us, and is refusing to eat.'

'Refusing to eat! Nanny, that's terrible, how long for?'

'Well, she's had precious little since Mr Harrington died, but since her mother had her breakdown, nothing. She's getting so weak, and her appetite has gone now, she just lies there all day. Even Dr Rushton is in despair, says we shall have to forcefeed her soon—'

'Surely not. That's barbaric. I would have thought some kind of … well, anyway. Where is she? Do you think she'd see me?'

'I really don't know, madam. She won't see her grandmother, that's for sure.'

'I think we should ask her. Go and tell her I'm here and I'd really like to see her. Tell her she doesn't have to talk to me or anything, but tell her Bertie's gone away to school and I'm really missing him and seeing her would cheer me up.'

Five minutes later, there was a gentle knock at the door and Fanny stood there. Cassia was shocked at the sight of her. She wasn't just thin, she was emaciated. Her little face, her round, glowing pretty little face, was waxy pale, her brown eyes huge and dark shadowed; her dress hung loosely about her, her legs, in their black stockings, stick thin. She really did look, thought Cassia, who was not given to exaggeration, who liked scientific exactitude, half dead.

'Hallo, Fanny,' she said, hoping her shock didn't show on her face, 'how are you?'

'All right,' said Fanny, and then moved, half ran across the room, and fell into Cassia's arms, crying.

'Promise,' she said through chattering teeth – she was very cold, Cassia noticed, and there was a slightly strange smell coming from her – 'promise you won't mention food.'

'I promise. Why should I anyway?'

Fanny looked at her, and her eyes were very sharp. 'Don't be silly, Cassia. You know why.'

'Sorry. Yes, I do. But I promise I won't. What's the matter?'

'I can't tell you. I really can't.'

'Well, it's not really so difficult for me to work out. You've lost your papa, who you loved so very much, and now your mama has gone away as well. It must be very terrible for you.'

'It's much more terrible than that,' said Fanny, very quietly. She burrowed her head into Cassia's chest. 'I think I could bear that.'

'Fanny, darling, nothing could be more terrible than that. What do you mean? Has something else happened? Has someone hurt you, or ...' Cassia's work at the clinic had opened her eyes to many dreadful things, things she would not have dreamed of a year earlier; she could not believe that Fanny could be the victim of any kind of abuse but ...

'No, no, it's not that. No one's hurt me.'

'Well, then – what?'

Silence. Cassia sat there, holding her, waiting. 'If a patient seems unable to describe a symptom, wait,' Mr Amstruther had told his students, years ago. 'Don't pre-empt his words. He'll find them in the end. Patience, that's the key.'

Fanny looked up at her; seemed about to speak, then turned her attention to a thread in her dress, sat picking at it. After a very long time she sighed. 'If I tell you some of it,' she said finally, 'you won't tell them, will you? I can't tell you all of it.'

'Them?'

'Nanny. Grandmama.'

'Of course not. I promise.'

'Well, you see, I – I made Mama ill. That day. It was my fault. And now she's going to die, and—'

'Fanny, who told you she was going to die?'

'She did.'

'Fanny, are you sure?'

'Yes. Quite sure. I heard her, I was there. And it was my fault.'

'You'll have to tell me a bit more, I'm afraid.'

'Well, you see, I gave her a letter. I saw it lying on the table and Stephanie said should she take it up to her, and Nanny said no, Mama was still asleep, she was very tired, and she needed lots of rest, because she was so upset. And I thought that was silly.'

'Why, Fanny?'

Fanny gave Cassia a look which shocked her; it was one of absolute contempt – not for her, but her mother. 'Because she wasn't upset. She was perfectly all right, she didn't care about Papa dying at all, she hadn't even cried.' She stopped.

Cassia took a deep breath. 'Fanny, sometimes people can't cry. They're too unhappy even to cry. I felt like that when my mother died. Did you know my mother died when I was only a little bit older than you?'

'No,' said Fanny, 'I didn't.' That was all, but she nestled closer to Cassia, sensing sympathy, understanding.

'She died, having a baby. The baby died too. And I couldn't cry, just couldn't. I stood there ...' She hesitated, wondering if she should expose Fanny to such a thing, then went on, 'I stood there, looking at her, lying there, white and lifeless and still, and I couldn't cry, it was too awful, too sad. And I know your mama was terribly unhappy about your father dying—'

'No she wasn't.' Again the hard contemptuous little voice. 'It wasn't like you – I can imagine that, I felt like that about Papa for a while – but Mama was happy about it, always on the phone, laughing with her friends. Don't tell me she was unhappy, she wasn't.'

'All right.'

'So I took the letter up, and she was sitting in her bed, reading a magazine. And she smiled and held out her hand and I knew she wanted to kiss me, and I wouldn't, and I – I threw the letter at her and said, "This came for you," and stood watching her. And she looked at it for a long time, and then she said, "I don't think I want to read this now," and I said, "Well, I'm going to read it to you, then". I picked it up and she snatched it from me and I tried to get it back and then I said go on, open it, and she did, very slowly, and read it a bit: and then she suddenly started screaming and screaming, it was so horrible, she went all stiff, and I went over to her bed and said, "What's the matter, what does it say?" and tried to get it again, and she said, "You can't have it, you can't, you should never have brought it," and then she said, "This is going to kill me,"and she started screaming again. Then they all came and – and then ...' The sobs were racking her again, the skinny little body convulsed.

'Shush, Fanny, it's all right.'

'It's not all right. If I hadn't brought the letter, and made her read it, she wouldn't have done that, she'd have gone on being happy. And now she's going to die.'

'Fanny, your mother is not going to die. You've got to believe that.'

'Well, what did she mean?'

'Darling, I don't know, but it wasn't what you thought, I promise you. People say all sorts of dreadful things when they're upset. I spoke to Dr

Rushton this morning and he said she was all right; she's had something called a nervous breakdown. Nobody ever died of that. It's not at all pleasant, and she will be in the nursing home for quite a long time, but she is very slowly getting better.'

'Oh.' There was a very long silence after that, then Fanny looked up at her. 'Is that really true?'

'It's really true.'

Fanny got off her knee, went over to the bookshelf.

'What are you doing, Fanny?'

'I'm getting the Bible. I want you to swear on it.'

Cassia sat there, her hand on the Bible, and swore that what she had told Fanny was true.

'Thank you,' said Fanny. She took a deep breath. 'Don't take your hand off yet.' This was a bit worrying; what was she going to ask next? 'Did you really want to see me because you were missing Bertie? Not because they told you about me not ... not eating?'

'No,' said Cassia, smiling at her, her heart lifting at the sight of a small upturn at the corners of Fanny's pretty little mouth, a faint sparkle of mischief in her eyes, 'no, I'm afraid that wasn't quite true. I was worried about you, but I am missing Bertie terribly and so is William. I tell you what, if your grandmama agrees, how would you like to come and stay with us for a few days?'

'Oh,' said Fanny, her voice resonant with longing, 'oh, Cassia, I'd *love* it.'

Ada Forbes was initially resistant to the idea. She owed it to her daughter, she explained to Cassia, to run the household and care for the children, indeed she had promised her that, even as Cecily was being lifted into the ambulance. Handing over Fanny, hugely agreeable as the prospect seemed, was not quite part of that agreement, and she felt she was failing in some way in her duty, admitting defeat. 'I'm not at all sure that would be best,' she said. 'This absurd refusal to eat, we have to overcome that. I certainly don't like the idea of her being away from Dr Rushton, and—'

'My husband is a doctor,' said Cassia carefully, 'so she could still receive medical attention if necessary, and maybe a fresh approach might deal with the eating problem.'

'I don't really see why that should be,' said Ada, stung at any suggestion that her own approach might in any way be deficient. 'I have worked extremely hard with Nanny over it and—'

'Mrs Forbes, you've been wonderful. No one would criticise that for a moment, but –' inspiration came to her: inspiration and the memory of

Mrs Forbes's frequently expressed view that London was no place for children to grow up – 'but the country air would surely do Fanny good. London is not healthy, and at the moment it can't be helping.'

She watched Mrs Forbes accepting this with patent relief. 'Well, that is certainly true,' she said. 'I do agree with you, the air in this city is appalling. Does your husband take that view, Mrs Fallon?'

'He certainly does. And I have an excellent nanny in Sussex, and my two younger children are there, so there would be lots of company for Fanny—'

This was a mistake. 'She doesn't lack for company here, Mrs Fallon, and she and I are great friends.'

'Yes, of course you are, but shall we try it, just for a week or so? Of course you'd want to check with Dr Rushton first.'

'I would indeed, but – well, yes, perhaps it would be a good idea. Just for a few days. I really do feel I need the break. I have slaved for this family over the past few weeks, literally slaved, and had no thanks for it. Yes, I think I might accept your offer. Providing Dr Rushton agrees, of course. Thank you, Mrs Fallon, it's very good of you.'

'Not at all. I'm terribly fond of Fanny. Er, Mrs Forbes, Fanny mentioned some letter that had upset her mother. Do you know of any such thing?'

'No,' said Ada firmly, 'I don't. I have checked through all my daughter's correspondence, each day, lest any of it needs attention. I have seen nothing that could remotely be described as distressing, I assure you.'

Later that day, as Ada supervised the packing of Fanny's things – she did feel Nanny was a little slapdash in her approach – she wondered if she had been right to lie about the letter, and finally decided she was entirely within her rights. It was one thing having Mrs Fallon become involved in Fanny's care; quite another in her daughter's affairs. Dominic Foster's involvement with Benedict had obviously been close, and she felt a certain possessiveness towards him, and also a sense of pride that he had confided in her. He clearly saw her as a person of discretion and common sense, and he certainly wouldn't want her discussing what he had told her with anyone else.

Because of her rather prolonged visit to the Harrington household, Cassia was late for her appointment with Harry. He was clearly in a very bad temper when his secretary showed her into his office. She had not visited him there before, and was intrigued and amused by it; it bore only the slightest resemblance to the conventional office, and was furnished more as a study, or even a small drawing room. It was in a building which he had bought in Curzon Street, a rather beautiful five-storeyed terrace house. The upper two floors were let as apartments; the three lower housed the Moreton Company and its subsidiaries, Moreton Construction, Moreton Investments and Moreton Overseas Ltd.

The entrance hall, tall and beautifully proportioned, painted and furnished entirely in black and white, and with black and white tiles on the floor, was occupied by an extremely pretty girl, dressed in a black and white check dress, sitting at the black desk, with a bank of white telephones on it. She smiled at Cassia, and after putting a call in to Harry's office, gestured towards the black leather sofa set against one of the walls. 'Miss Murray, Mr Moreton's secretary, will be down to collect you shortly, Mrs Fallon. Mr Moreton is engaged on a telephone call at the moment.'

Cassia sat down and picked up a copy of *The Times* which was on the low table in front of the sofa; Harry's telephone call lasted for the duration of two quite long articles, one on the futility of the forthcoming march from Jarrow, and the other on the proposed visit by the Prince of Wales to the depressed mining areas in the Welsh valleys.

When she finally was shown into his office by a rather cool Miss Murray, she was asked to wait again while he signed some letters. Harry sat at a leather-topped pedestal desk on which was set a stained glass Tiffany lamp.

'I will fetch some coffee,' said Miss Murray. She spoke as if this was extraordinarily kind of her, a gesture of immense goodwill.

She was really very good-looking, Cassia thought, watching her as she lifted one set of papers from Harry's desk, set down another, straightened an untidy heap of trade magazines that were dangerously near its edge; she was tall and slim, yet with a very full bosom, and was extremely well dressed, her ice-blonde hair drawn back into an ironed-neat chignon. She had rather fine features apart from her nose, which was too large, and she had extraordinary pale green eyes with very long dark lashes. She also had extremely good legs. Well, Harry was unlikely to employ anybody plain; even the kitchen maid in his house was pretty.

She sat down on another sofa, this one covered in heavy silk, one of a pair set on either side of a rather fine fireplace. Some extremely large and interesting modern pictures hung on the walls, two tall bookcases were set either side of the door, and there was a cabinet containing what she recognised as some very fine examples of art nouveau bronze figures.

Harry finally looked up at her rather coldly, pushed his pile of papers aside. 'You're very late,' he said.

395

'You've made that perfectly clear.'

'Yes, well, I can't be expected to hold everything up while I wait for you. You're looking rather tired, is anything the matter?'

'Oh, nothing I would want to trouble you with, Harry. Except, that is, for the reason which brought me here. And I'm sorry I'm late, I went to visit Cecily's children and Fanny isn't at all well.'

'Poor little thing,' he said, surprising her, 'appalling time she's having. What's wrong? Apart from what amounts to losing both her parents.'

'Like you,' she said, recognising the cause of his sympathy; the thought of his loveless, solitary childhood still had the power to distress her.

'Well, yes,' he said shortly. This was clearly not the time for emotional discussion. 'Anything else, anything physical?'

'She isn't eating,' said Cassia, 'or sleeping properly. Anyway, she's coming to stay with us for a few days.'

'How nice for her. How very good of you.' He looked at her again with something close to distaste.

Miss Murray came in with a tray of coffee and biscuits. Cassia accepted the coffee, waved away the biscuits, took a sip, and then said, 'Harry, is something the matter?'

'No, not really.' He made an obvious effort to be more friendly. 'I hear you've kindly arranged for Edwina to see some woman doctor.'

'Yes, Monica Gerard, she's a very fine surgeon and gynaecologist.'

'Well, as long as she can sort Edwina out, that's all I care about. I obviously wouldn't have chosen a woman myself, but—'

'Yes, Edwina said you had some strange prejudice against women doctors.'

'No, no, of course not,' he said, making a most uncharacteristic attempt at tact. 'It's just that—'

'You think men are likely to be better. Really, Harry, I'm surprised you don't employ a male secretary.'

'Oh, that's quite different,' he said, grinning. 'Secretaries play a supportive role. One women are better suited to. No, Cassia, I do assure you I have no quarrel with women having careers. I think it's splendid. In theory.'

She sighed. 'Well, anyway, I think Edwina does have a problem, but it's hopefully not very serious. I only wish she'd seen a gynaecologist before.'

'Yes, well, she didn't. Anyway, thanks for your help. Now what can I do for you? I really haven't got very long.'

'Yes. Yes, of course.' She took another sip of the coffee; it was very strong, but delicious. It would be: Harry was notoriously fussy about coffee, it had to be freshly ground, very strong, very hot. He was fussy about most things; Edwina's life couldn't be easy.

'Harry,' she said, fixing her eyes on his face very intently, 'I'm sure you told me Rollo left Leonora well provided for.'

His dark eyes did not change expression, did not even flicker. 'I did indeed tell you that, because it was patently true. When Leonora died, she was living in a luxurious apartment in Paris, cared for by highly qualified staff, and with an extremely expensive specialist overseeing her case.' He picked up his coffee, sat looking at her over it. 'Besides, I would have thought you had had the proof of her being well provided for yourself. That's another very nice suit.'

'I went to see Miss Monkton the other day,' she said, ignoring this. 'Oh, the Monk. Yes. Why on earth did you go and see her?'

'Because Richard told me that she'd been to see Leonora in Paris. I was very surprised, because I thought she disapproved of Leonora so much, but he said she had been very kind to her. And she lives quite near me, now, in Petworth. So I wanted to thank her.'

'Very admirable. What a saint you are, Cassia, doing good deeds all over the place.'

'Harry, please! Anyway, she said that ...' His eyes on her were thoughtful, probing: still with the odd, new coldness. She felt nervous suddenly, hurried on. 'Well, she said that Rollo was very hard up. That they had lost almost everything. He had left Leonora and she was living in very modest circumstances indeed.'

'Oh no,' he said lightly. 'Modest perhaps, compared to Miss Monkton's view of her London home, but—'

'Harry, she was living in poverty. That was Miss Monkton's word. All alone. And ill. Unable to pay for treatment.'

'This is absolute nonsense.'

'No, it's not nonsense. She was living in a nasty little apartment apparently in quite a poor neighbourhood, and with no medical help. No help of any kind.'

He did not move, did not seem in any way discomfited; he seemed completely relaxed, even mildly amused. 'Well,' he said finally, 'and then what happened? How was it, do you think, that by the next time I saw her, Leonora had come to be living in such pleasant and agreeable circumstances?'

'I don't know, Harry. I simply don't understand it. Leonora told Miss Monkton that an old friend had turned up and lent her some money.'

'Well, there you are, then.'

'No, it's not as simple as that. If the money was only lent, then surely that wouldn't explain the luxury, as you put it. She wouldn't have spent a great deal of it, would she?'

'No. Possibly not. But then, as you know, Gresham came back to her. Even he had some conscience. And I really cannot accept that he was penniless; the man was absolutely rolling in money, he had investments all over the world, it's absolutely inconceivable he had lost the lot.'

She was silent, then she said, 'Harry, you saw a great deal of Leonora, those last few months.'

'Not a great deal, as a matter of fact. I do feel a certain remorse about it. I was away a lot at that time. But I was with her when – well, at the end.'

'Yes, I know. So surely …' She stopped, unwilling to confront what was troubling her, unwilling to increase his already patent irritation.

'Look,' he said suddenly, 'why don't you come out with it, ask me what you really want to know. I loathe prevarication. Otherwise, as I've already told you, I'm very busy, I really don't have time for all this.'

Aware that she was still avoiding the real issue, her real fear, she said, 'It's just that I thought you would have talked a lot, she would have told you everything that had happened.'

'Cassia, I'm very surprised at you. You're a doctor, for Christ's sake, or so I have always understood. You must know that people are not entirely lucid when they are dying. Especially when they are heavily drugged with morphine, surrounded by large numbers of medical staff.'

'No, I realise that. But—' She stopped again.

'But what, Cassia?'

'Well, what about the money she left me?' she said, quickly, before she could prevent the words, leash in her fear. 'It was an awful lot, Harry. Surely if she'd been desperate, as she was when Miss Monkton saw her, she'd have spent some of it on herself.'

'Oh, Cassia, for heaven's sake. The money she left you was in trust. Have you no idea how hard it is to break a trust? That's the whole point of the things.'

'What about the interest? Mr Brewster, her solicitor, said she was getting that—'

'And no doubt seeing it off at high speed.'

She sat staring at him, cursing his ability to unsettle her, make her angry, lead her into a tortuous maze of inconsequential argument.

'Look, Cassia,' he said, 'I don't quite know what you're trying to prove, but whatever it is, I don't think I can be of any use to you. I'm sorry.'

'You could be of use to me,' she said, taking a deep breath, 'if you told me the truth.'

'And which particular bit of that rather dubious commodity would you like? Perhaps you'd tell me.'

'All right. Did you know Leonora was living there, did you rescue her from that place, that apartment? The one Miss Monkton found her in? And take her to the other one?' It was the most she dared to ask him, the rest was too dark, too dangerous even to reflect upon in that moment.

He looked at her, and his dark eyes were thoughtful; he paused for a long time as if wondering what to do. It was very quiet in the room, and utterly still; she could hear the clock ticking, even the creak of the radiators. Then he pushed back his chair and said, 'No, Cassia, I did not. Will that do for you? Now then, perhaps you'll be kind enough to leave this whole matter alone, and let me get on with some work.'

She stood up, afraid of him losing his temper finally, afraid of asking more, afraid of not asking more. Finally she said, 'Thank you very much for seeing me, Harry. For your time.'

'That's all right,' he said, 'but I do wish you'd stop all this nonsense, just let things rest. There really is absolutely no point in it, no point whatsoever. It seems to be wasting a great deal of your, and indeed my, time and energy.'

Miss Murray came in. 'Mr Moreton, there's a telephone call for you from New York – Mr Dysart. Can you take it or shall I tell him?'

'I can take it,' he said standing up. 'Mrs Fallon is just leaving. You really must excuse me, Cassia, I'm afraid. I have a business to run, as you see. I'm sorry I can't help you more. Good morning to you.'

'Good morning, Harry,' she said, holding out her hand, shaking his. His hand, his large, strong hand, was very warm, as usual; but his eyes meeting hers were still cold and hostile.

Walking down the street away from him, in the confused state of sexual tension and emotional outrage he always seemed able to arouse in her, she knew she had learnt absolutely nothing, gained precisely no ground, indeed had quite possibly lost some, for now he was on his guard against her, would be anticipating any future moves. 'Damn,' she said aloud, 'damn damn damn.'

Harry Moreton was too clever for her: he was too clever for most people – too clever for his own good, as her grandmother would have said. On the other hand, he had never actually lied to her, it was not in the nature of their relationship. Perhaps it was all true, perhaps Miss Monkton had exaggerated, perhaps it had been a temporary problem.

After all, if Rollo Gresham had abandoned her, left her unprovided for, he would hardly have come back. And Harry would hardly have lied about that.

If only there was someone else she could talk to, ask about it: Benedict had been close to Leonora at the end, of course, as he had throughout her life, but Benedict was dead, and she could hardly trouble Cecily, in her sad, haunted illness, with so distressing a subject. Perhaps she should just do what Harry said, try to let it rest. Perhaps he was right, and she was merely wasting time and energy …

At the thought of time, she looked at her watch, realised she was in danger of being late for her St Christopher's clinic. She could certainly let it rest for the next few hours.

'Have you seen anyone else about this?' said Miss Gerard.

'No,' said Edwina. 'Well, not recently.' Her voice tailed off. She wasn't sure what to say, how much she should confess to this strange, brisk, rather likeable woman.

'Not about the dysmenorrhoea?'

'I'm sorry?'

'The painful periods.'

'No. Well, my GP said that would clear up when I had a baby.'

'A very unrealistic attitude, in my view,' said Miss Gerard coolly. 'Besides, with a cyst such as this, your chances of conceiving would be considerably reduced.'

'Really?' A flood of relief overwhelmed Edwina: here was the explanation that she could offer Harry; not her fault, surely, this time, it couldn't be traced back to her … and perhaps she might become pregnant after all. 'And what causes the cysts?'

'We don't quite know. They just happen, some women are more prone to them than others. They are most commonly the result of the egg-producing follicle enlarging and filling with fluid.'

'But not – not an operation of some kind?'

'An operation? Good heavens, no. What sort of operation? You haven't had an appendicectomy, have you? No, of course you haven't, no scar.'

Miss Gerard looked at her, and Edwina could see that she had quite suddenly realised what she was actually talking about. She blushed and looked down at her nails, scrutinising the dark red enamel she had had painted on that morning by her manicurist.

'Mrs Moreton, if there's anything you want to tell me, you can. It would go no further, ever. A doctor's consulting room is like the confessional. We are bound by our professional code never to divulge anything that we hear.'

'Oh, no. No, there's nothing.'

'Good. Of course you can always talk to me again, if you have any anxieties. Now then, that cyst must be removed, and the sooner the better. I operate on Monday, Wednesday and Friday afternoons; I could fit you in next Friday, or the following Wednesday. Which would suit you better?'

'Oh, Friday, I think. Yes. How long would I be in for?'

'Three or four days. You'll be pretty sore for a day or two, and groggy of course from the anaesthetic, then you'll get better very quickly. And hopefully, provided nothing nasty shows up in the biopsy—'

'What's that?'

'We examine the cyst, make sure it's not in any way malignant. Highly unlikely. And then, as I say, all the pain and so on should be a thing of the past. Incidentally, this friend of yours, who spotted the cyst, is she a doctor? Or a nurse?'

'She's a doctor. Well, she trained as a doctor,' said Edwina, 'at St Christopher's.'

'Oh really. What's her name?'

'Fallon. Cassia Fallon.'

'Well, she obviously knows her stuff. It really isn't that easy to spot, not when comparatively small, as this one is. Tell her from me she's a clever woman. Well, good afternoon, Mrs Moreton. I'll see you next week. You'll have to come into the clinic on Thursday evening, so we can get you ready for surgery next day. My secretary will make all the arrangements.'

Bertie lay weeping in his bed, a sock stuffed in his mouth to muffle the sound, lest anyone should realise and exact retribution for it, and wondering how he was going to endure the five and a half weeks, or forty days, or 960 hours, until he went home for half term, and how even then he was going to manage not to tell his parents and his brother and sister that life at St John's was a painful, wretched, day-by-day torture and that death seemed preferable to spending the next seven years there.

CHAPTER 24

'He sounds quite happy,' said Cassia, passing Bertie's letter to Edward over the breakfast table.

'Of course he's happy, what did you expect? Plenty of other boys to play with, all the games he wants, how could he be unhappy?'

'Can I see?' said William.

'In a minute,' said Edward. 'Just let me read it.'

'But Daddy, I—'

'William, let Daddy read the letter. Bertie sounds fine: he's in the trials for the football team; he's singing in the choir, and the food is really nice. I'm so glad, I was worried about that. School food isn't good, and he simply can't swallow anything fatty, it makes him sick and—'

'Hysterical nonsense,' said Edward, 'isn't it, Janet?'

'Well, yes, in a way,' said Janet cautiously, 'but I do feel—'

'There you are. Even Janet agrees with me. Yes, Peggy?'

'It's Mrs Burton, Doctor. Mr Burton's scalded his hand really badly on the kettle, needs a dressing, she thinks.'

'Yes, all right, Peggy, I'm coming. Tell her I'll be down in ten minutes. Cassia, warn Maureen I may be late for surgery, would you?'

'Can I see Bertie's letter?' said Fanny, as Edward left the room.

'Yes, of course, darling.' Cassia smiled at Fanny. After only five days she looked a different child, still very thin, of course, but with some colour in her face and more importantly some life in her eyes. Being with William had proved the best medicine for her, and it had been nice for him too, he was missing Bertie badly. Fanny was a jolly little girl, took swiftly to playing football and was very good at card games. On Saturday afternoon, Cassia had taken them both to the cinema to see *Modern Times*, and Fanny had laughed so much she had developed terrible hiccups and had to be taken out before the end.

'Telephone for you Mrs Fallon,' said Peggy, coming in with her tray. 'It's Mr Cameron. Can I clear, please?'

'Yes of course.' She could feel her face burning, absurdly, her heart thudding; any mention of Rupert now filled her with a panic-stricken guilt, a blinding certainty that everyone must know what they had done. 'You children help Peggy, and then, William, we must go to school.'

Rupert wanted her to attend a rehearsal of *Letters*. 'I just haven't quite got it,' he said. 'Please come and watch a rehearsal, let me know honestly what you think.'

'Rupert, I don't know anything about the theatre – what help could I possibly be?'

'A lot. You're a fresh eye. And Jasper would love it, he wants to involve his major backer. Please, darling, do come.'

She hesitated; this was horribly difficult. She had told him several times she thought they should see nothing of one another for the time being, but he had been hurt, upset: 'I will, of course, get some digs for myself, but I can surely go on seeing you. I don't think one indiscretion should wipe out a lifetime's friendship. That would make me very unhappy. Don't you feel my friend any more?'

'Yes, of course I do,' she had said quickly, but it wasn't quite true. The uneasy agreement that nothing had really changed, that they should put that one night behind them, didn't, couldn't work; the old ease was gone, the happy flirtatious companionship, and with it trust. He had shifted totally in her life and the more he told her everything could be what it was, the more she knew he was wrong.

Maybe, she thought now, standing there in the hall, maybe through the play they could draw together again, it could provide a safe road to travel down, a most open and public association that nobody could misread; and so she agreed to come.

'Good,' he said, a touch of the old confident Rupert in his voice, 'and then you can see where your money has been sunk.'

She laughed. 'Not sunk, I hope. All right, Rupert. I'll be there. I'd like to. Thank you.'

Besides, she thought as she put the phone down, she wanted to see him for another reason: to tell him about Miss Monkton, her revelations about Leonora and her situation, Cassia's growing conviction that the money had come from another source – a dreadful, dangerous source. She needed advice, help, his easy confident way of talking her out of her fears; the habit of a lifetime, of confiding in him, was dying very hard.

'Good Lord,' said Harry Moreton. 'Look at this American magazine one of my colleagues has sent me. The bit about Mrs Simpson. See? According to them, at least, if Ernest Simpson decided to divorce her, the King could be sued for adultery in this country.'

'Of course he couldn't,' said Edwina. 'What a ridiculous idea. He's the King. That's just ignorant American nonsense. They don't understand the monarchy at all.'

'I rather like the idea of a royal co-respondent,' said Harry. 'It's pure Ruritania.'

'Well, I don't. And anyway, do you really think things are that serious?'

'I don't know, but if I were Ernest Simpson, I'd certainly want a divorce. Poor sod. Talk about public humiliation. And the King is absolutely besotted with the wretched woman. Apparently, he failed to open some hospital up in Scotland, sent his brother instead, the excuse being Court mourning — Court mourning, I ask you, when he's been frolicking round the Med for a month — and then went to meet Wallis off the train at Ballater in broad daylight that same day. Not tactful. Not the behaviour of a gentleman.'

'It's such a shame,' said Edwina. 'I just don't know why he can't be discreet about it, instead of upsetting everyone like this. What the old Queen must be going through, I can't imagine. And all this muck in the foreign papers, it's so bad for the Crown.'

'Most unusually, I agree with you. Well, he's lucky that Lord Beaverbrook is managing to keep the press quiet here. That can't last much longer, certainly not through a divorce.' He looked up at her thoughtfully. 'You look a bit pale. When are you going in to have your op?'

'Thursday evening,' said Edwina.

'Well, I hope that woman's competent.'

'Harry, of course she's competent. She's very highly qualified.'

'I think I'd like to have a word with her. What's her telephone number?'

'What sort of a word? Are you going to give her a grilling or something? Harry, I'd really rather you didn't. I don't want her feeling hostile towards me when she's wielding her scalpel or whatever.'

'Edwina, I shall be perfectly polite.'

'I rather doubt that. Anyway, if you really want to see her, the best time would be on Friday afternoon. She said she'd come and see me then, tell me what they'd found out. At least she won't be able to do anything dreadful by then. And I imagine you might be able to find the time to come and visit me, or will you be too busy?'

'Of course I'll come and visit you,' said Harry irritably.

Ever since she had first seen Miss Gerard, Edwina had felt she knew what the word lightheaded meant. The thought of being able to tell Harry that she was never going to be able to have children through absolutely no fault of her own was intoxicating; of course he would be disappointed, but he'd get over it and there was absolutely nothing she could do about any of it. She could get on with her life, untroubled by guilt; she had not realised how bad that guilt, how deep her fear of discovery, until it confronted her.

She did actually feel, to her considerable surprise, a certain sadness that she was not to know motherhood and its attendant pleasures, knowing that, realistically, the removal of the cyst would change nothing. Her emotions before had been largely coloured by her fear of Harry, of what she was to say to him, of him cross-examining her; now she had to confront her own feelings on the subject. And she did have some and they were not all relief. She had always viewed childbirth and, to an extent, pregnancy with horror, had felt none of the yearning to hold, to nurse, to succour a child that so many of her friends described. But she was a dynastic creature, she would have liked to see her line continue: that was immortality as she construed it.

She found it hard to believe that Harry felt a yearning for parenthood as such any more than she did; he appeared to regard most children with distaste. He had even said once or twice he would make an appalling parent (having had no family life of his own); but she did know that he felt he must have children, that he saw procreation as part of the inevitable process and progress of life.

Well, he had got all the other things he wanted, she thought, going up to her room to get ready for her day at *Style*: money, fine houses, valuable paintings, horses, cars, business success. This was just one thing he was going to have to do without. And it wasn't her fault. It absolutely wasn't her fault. Edwina ran up the last three steps singing 'Just the Way You Look Tonight' aloud in her rather tuneless voice.

There was an editorial conference that morning, in Miss Le Page's office. She held two each month: one for long-term planning, when each department head outlined the features she was preparing; one more detailed, when Miss Le Page handed out instructions in a voice more clipped than the languid one used for relating gossip or discussing trends. Today's was the latter variety, and the voice more clipped, the instructions more terse even than usual: the biannual circulation figures had come in the day before, and *Style*'s had gone down.

'Which means,' Francis Stevenson-Cook, the publishing director, had told her in his own deceptively languid tones, 'as of course you know,

Miss Le Page, that advertising revenue will drop. And after that who knows what will follow it: editors perhaps? Mmm?'

Francis Stevenson-Cook (born Frank Stephens) had risen from the ranks of office boy at *Style* to governing the empire which owned it and its sister magazines *Home Style, Wedding Style* and *Country Style*.

He was a bisexual, extremely handsome, and very stylish; it was said that the Prince of Wales himself had on occasions followed his lead (most notably into Fair Isle sweaters and two-tone shoes). All his suits, superbly tailored, were in shades of grey in varying patterns and tones, darker in the winter, lighter in the summer, all his shirts cream, in finest lawn, or silk; he wore his wavy brown hair a little long, flopping over his brilliant blue eyes, bow ties whenever he felt the occasion would permit it, and carried a silver-topped cane wherever he went.

He admired and appreciated women as much as he did men and had an extraordinarily finely honed instinct as to their taste; no one could spot a trend in a fashion collection, a colour in home furnishings, a concept in a garden, more swiftly and reliably than Francis Stevenson-Cook. He was brilliant, amusing, charming – and absolutely ruthless.

He had once famously lunched an editor, plied her with champagne and asked her which magazine she would next like to edit – and then, as he rose from the table, told her to apply for it, since she would no longer be editing her own.

He lived in a flat in Mount Street, refurbished and, to an extent, refurnished in a most lavish style every two years for nothing, by whichever interior designer was most eager to curry his favour. He owned an equally lavish apartment in Paris, threw the most outrageously extravagant parties, and was to be seen around London's smartest restaurants and nightclubs with a procession of beautiful young women, usually fashion models or minor actresses.

His sexual proclivities were a most bountiful source of gossip; his butler-cum-secretary, who lived with him and ran his life with steely efficiency, was widely rumoured to be also his boyfriend (a rumour which Stevenson-Cook encouraged in a mixture of mischievousness and pragmatism), but the fact was that that relationship was entirely platonic and he actually had lovers of both sexes. He was not, however, promiscuous (although he encouraged a rumour to that effect also); sex was actually a rather low priority in his life, and he preferred to conserve his considerable energies for his work.

All his editors were terrified of him with the exception of Drusilla, who pronounced him common (a fact which he had once told her he accepted wholeheartedly) and who he in turn recognised as the only member of his staff who was genuinely irreplaceable. Fashion editors came two, or at least one, a penny, as he was fond of saying; a woman who was on first-name terms with almost every titled personage in the land did not.

He was sitting in on the conference that morning, tapping one finely shod foot on the floor, resting both his hands on his cane, his brilliant eyes moving from face to face as its owner spoke, speaking only occasionally himself, and then to request that he might hear the utterance, whatever it was, again. The explanation given for this was so that he might consider it very carefully; in reality it was to impress upon the speaker that what he had heard was scarcely credible in its crassness.

Camilla Marsden-Rose had just finished describing her main fashion feature for February for the second time that morning, in tones rather less firm than usual, when Edwina realised that Francis Stevenson-Cook's eyes were on her; she met them rather coolly. Having been first the child, then the wife of a tyrant, she was unimpressed by the breed and knew precisely how best to deal with it.

'I think we have not been introduced,' said Stevenson-Cook, smiling just very slightly. 'Miss Le Page, could you ...'

'Yes, of course,' said Miss Le Page, interestingly flustered, Edwina thought. 'This is Edwina Moreton, a recent addition to our staff. Mrs Moreton is in charge of the shopping pages, and I did, of course, inform you of her joining us.'

'No doubt you did, but I prefer a personal introduction, as you know.' He bowed over his cane to Edwina; she smiled slightly, and inclined her head at him. 'Mrs Moreton,' he said, his eyes on her face rather intently, 'tell me, what in your view is the most important facet of the spring look?'

Edwina hesitated for a moment; she knew if she merely echoed Camilla Marsden-Rose she would sound foolish, especially as she did not quite agree with her; but if she did not, then retribution would be exacted for the rest of her stay at *Style*.

Then inspiration came to her. 'Charm,' she said firmly.

'Indeed? And how would you see this quality embodied in the clothes? As described by Mrs Marsden-Rose?'

'Well ... their essence. Of course in all the fabrics Mrs Marsden-Rose mentioned, the gauzes and organzas and so on, and the more feminine designs, but I think it's also a feeling in the air.'

'Do go on.'

God, what had she let herself in for? And why was he doing this to her, the newest, rawest recruit in the room? Precisely, of course, because she was the newest, rawest recruit in the room. She smiled at him very slightly.

'I think women are ready to appear more feminine again, Mr Stevenson-Cook, after the tailored suits and mannish hats. More what men might like. That's what the new clothes are really all about. It isn't change for change's sake. As Mrs Marsden-Rose said,' she added hastily.

'Well, she didn't quite, but let it pass. Very interesting, don't you think, Miss Le Page?'

'Oh, yes,' said Aurora Le Page. Her voice was very cold.

There was a long silence, then he said, 'I agree with you, Mrs Moreton. I would suggest your pictures get that feeling across, Mrs Marsden-Rose.'

'Well, naturally they will,' snapped Camilla. 'I had every intention of that.'

'Yes, no doubt, but I think I would take it further, with soft lighting and some artful accessorising, if I might be bold enough to make a suggestion. I would have men in at least some of the pictures as well. Being ... what was the word, Mrs Moreton? Oh, yes, being charmed.'

'But surely, Mr Stevenson-Cook, that could look rather cheap?'

He looked at her distantly, took out a silver cigarette case from his pocket, tapped the cigarette on it, then smiled. 'That must surely depend on how you handle the photographic session. Which is in turn surely your job. Anyway, naturally, this is only a suggestion. The final decision is yours. I would not dream of dictating to you. As you know. Now can we turn our attention to the advertisers? They are going to need considerable pampering in the next six months, that is, until we get our circulation figures back up. I would like to see more of the major wholesale people featured: Dorville, Harella, Jaeger, and the fabric manufacturers, Courtauld and Tootal. Very important not to make them feel second-class citizens, isn't it, Mrs Marsden-Rose?'

He leant towards Aurora Le Page, who was holding out her lighter to him, inhaled deeply, blew out a cloud of smoke towards the ceiling, his eyes never leaving Camilla's face.

'Of course not, Mr Stevenson-Cook,' she said, and managed to smile at him.

Edwina looked round the room filled with women, absurdly overdressed, or so most people would consider, for an office meeting, several of them in hats, all exquisitely made up, their hair beautifully done, looked again at Stevenson-Cook himself, with his silver-topped cane, his just slightly foppish bow tie, his elegantly autocratic bullying, and thought that for all its absurdity, it made for her a sort of sense. You could not dictate on style if you did not possess it. Francis Stevenson-Cook did not only run a magazine empire, she realised that morning, he was the head of what amounted to a school of style. And she liked that. She liked it very much indeed.

Cecily lay and looked out of the window of her room overlooking Richmond Park. It was a very nice room, and it had a very nice view; she could appreciate that fact at least. Unfortunately, that was where it stopped: she could take no pleasure from any of it, could find nothing to lift her spirits in the most modest way. Nothing could do that: not the beautiful flowers sent by friends that constantly filled her room, not the gentle kindness of the nurses, not the rather more robust care of her doctors, not the offers of visits from her friends, all of which she fretfully refused.

She wasn't desperate any more, not violently wretched; she was in a condition of heavy, black lethargy, which held her in thrall and from which she could never imagine any kind of release. If someone had come in and told her the building was on fire, she would not have had the energy, nor indeed the desire, to make the slightest effort to escape from it. Why should she, indeed? When all that lay ahead of her for the rest of her life was loneliness, guilt, self-reproach and the dislike of her children.

She knew that for as long as she lived, she would remember Fanny's little face, angrily hostile as she tried to hold her, comfort her after the funeral, telling her to leave her alone, and knowing why she had said it, knowing she blamed her for Benedict's death – and of course she deserved that blame, she had earned it very well – or Fanny's voice, harsh with rage as she thrust the letter at her, the awful letter, saying, 'Go on, read it, read it.' Fanny would not forgive her; Fanny should not forgive her, and in time Stephanie and even little Laurence would learn what she had done and would not forgive her either.

Her mother's visits were interminable torments, sitting there for as long as she was allowed – mercifully only thirty minutes, during which time Cecily's eyes never left the clock – brightly cheerful, telling her how well the children were, how expertly she was running the house, how there was no need to worry about anything, anything at all, how her father was having a very good and successful trip to New York, how gladly she had sacrificed going with him, and, as the half-hour drew mercifully to its close, how she did feel that Cecily really should try to pull herself together and show her gratitude for all that was being done for her.

The children were not allowed to come – it was felt they would exhaust her, and her condition would distress them, and she was thankful for it – but the little notes and drawings sent by Stephanie were a torture, accentuating as they did the absence of anything similar from Fanny. The stories which Nanny – another loyal visitor, more welcome than her mother – brought her were a torture too, stories of Laurence, of his daily progress towards crawling, chattering, waving, and, she thought wretchedly, staring blankly at Nanny, towards growing up to a comprehension of what his mother had done.

Edwina had written, asked if she might come, and Cassia; so, rather to her surprise, had Harry. The nurses read her their letters, in bright, encouraging voices, saying wouldn't it be nice to see them, and she always said no, she didn't think so, she didn't want to see them, there was no point, she was too tired. And she was tired: she could not sleep without pills, and even then the few hours granted to her were filled with demons, some foul and faceless, some recognisable. Those were the worst: her children, Benedict, horribly mutilated, hideous nightmares from which she awoke screaming, to find herself in the soothing, useless arms of the nurses.

Countless letters arrived from friends: she refused to read them, for she was in any case frightened of letters, frightened even of seeing that writing on the envelope, but the nurses insisted on reading them to her, saying they would surely cheer her up, and she listened to each one, holding the bedclothes tightly up to her chin so that in the awful, dreadful eventuality of hearing that name, she could take refuge beneath them.

She was having various treatments: pointless, exhausting treatments with drugs, with analysis – or what she supposed was analysis, a great deal of uncomfortable questioning from which ensued even more uncomfortable silences, as she refused to answer any of it – with sleep therapy – that had been quite nice, absolute oblivion from even the demons for what had seemed like hours, and had actually been days. It all seemed absurd, the doctors persisting in their view that there was something wrong with her, while she knew there was nothing, nothing wrong with her at all. It was merely that she had done something utterly terrible, and for the rest of her life she was going to have to live with the fact, and she didn't see how that would be possible.

She spent quite a lot of time wondering if she might kill herself, and indeed how; that seemed the only possible solution. She had refused to eat for a week, but they had forcefed her in the end, sticking tubes down her throat, and it had been so hideous, adding to her nightmares, a nightmare of its own indeed, that she had promised to eat again, had done so, although only very little, enough to make them leave her in peace. She studied her body detachedly sometimes when she had a bath. It was very different now: her stomach was almost flat, her breasts shrunken; her bony arms and legs eerily appeared longer. All her life she had longed to be thin, so that she could be chic and sleek, for Benedict; she had achieved it now, in a dreadful irony.

There was a new treatment being mooted, which frightened her: electric shock treatment. She was not supposed to know about it, but the doctors had discussed it with her mother, who had told Cecily, using the threat as a tool in her own amateur therapy, 'Very effective, but really rather unpleasant, dear, I believe. Now if you could only pull yourself together, get home, take up your responsibilities to your family, who do need you, then it would be far, far better for all of us, especially me. It's very hard for me to see you like this, you know.'

Her doctor had clearly been angry when he had discovered Cecily knew, when he had found her crying quietly and shaking with fear, and had promised he wouldn't use it without her consent, but she didn't quite trust him: it was so easy to drug her, render her unconscious and then do what they wanted.

Every day now she felt less in control, less connected with the person who lay in the bed, with her face and her name, and wearing her clothes. She hated her so much, that person, that person who had killed her husband, sent him to his death, hated her and was afraid of her, but she couldn't get away from her; she was chained to her for the rest of her life.

She ought to die, it would be much for the best; she deserved to die. Only actually she didn't even deserve that: dying was too good for her.

After a working lunch in Harry Moreton's office that day, during which both men most carefully avoided any subject other than the progress of the Guildford Garden Suburb, Dominic Foster finally asked how Mrs Harrington was progressing.

'Oh, pretty well, I think,' said Harry, who actually had no idea, beyond the bland assurances of Cecily's doctors, as passed to Edwina by Ada Forbes. 'The treatment they're giving her seems to be successful.'

'Good,' said Dominic, 'that's splendid.' At least if Mrs Harrington was recovering, he had a little less to reproach himself for, a little less to worry about: and there was also a less urgent need for him to talk to her, explain to her what had happened.

'My darling.' Rupert's voice filled the darkness. Cassia stiffened, tried to relax, wondered what she was doing here, why she had been persuaded to come. 'How wonderful it was to get your last letter. Life is so absolutely appalling here, so near to hell, we stand in mud all day, those of us who are still alive, and lie in it all night. The rats are our constant companions—'

'Rupert, you're overplaying it a bit.' The director's voice cut through the darkness. 'Too much drama. You're writing this letter in a state of exhaustion and terror; remember that. Very low key, a bit flatter, all right?'

Rupert began again. He was nervous, Cassia thought, panicky almost; it was under a month now to opening and he still was far from happy with his performance.

It was actually very intriguing seeing the play in the raw, watching it carved into shape. Not that there was a great deal of shape, with just two actors and almost no scenery; it was certainly very different from everything else in the West End at the time, full as it was of lavish productions, and the cinema, for that matter, a shrine to the musical. What had seemed exciting, different, when Rupert had first described it to her, now seemed rather more of a gamble. She hoped it was going to work; not for her own sake – she had no interest in seeing her investment pay off – but for Rupert. This was his big chance, albeit it rather late in life, his great play for success and fame, and he needed it, he needed it very badly. More now than ever, she thought, and sighed aloud.

Jasper heard her and turned his head and smiled. 'That sounded like a strong response, Mrs Fallon. I'm glad it's affecting you.'

'Oh, it is,' she said hastily, 'I really am loving it.'

'Good.'

'Dearest.' Eleanor's lovely resonant voice came through the darkness; she was a beautiful actress, she had great presence, could project intense emotion with the merest movement of her head, the slightest fall in her voice. 'I read your letter with such distress, such sympathy. If I could only share your sufferings in some tiny way, I would—'

'Mrs Fallon?' A voice came from the seat behind her.

'Yes?'

'I'm from the *Daily Sketch*. Could we have a quick word?'

'A word? What about?'

'Your involvement with this play. I understand you've invested some money in it. Mr Cameron said I could speak to you about it.'

She remembered now: Rupert had asked her, several weeks ago, had said the man was going to write an article about the play, that the publicity would be invaluable. 'I'd love it if you could say a few words, darling, just about how long we've known each other, why you decided to put the money into *Letters* ...' She had said then that of course she would, but that had been before ... well, before. Now she felt anxious, uncertain.

'I'll have to just check with him. Can we wait till this scene is over?'

Rupert said he would still be very grateful, that he knew the reporter, he was the *Sketch*'s show-business correspondent, very well respected, that anything that might make the article longer and more interesting would help.

'Not too interesting, I hope,' she said, laughing, and then turned to the young man and said, 'All right, go on, ask me whatever you like. Only could I read it first, before it's published?'

'Yes of course,' he said, getting out his notebook. 'Now then, what appealed to you about this play ...'

'Poor Mrs Harrington. She really is getting no better,' said Sister Lloyd to Dr Appleby, the psychiatrist in charge of Cecily's case. 'I worry about her, she is so terribly thin.'

'But she is eating now? Enough, I mean?'

'Oh, yes. Just enough. But she sleeps so badly, and has these appalling nightmares. She did ask me, and that is why I have come to see you, if she might have an extra sleeping pill each night, just for a while. She says the long sleepless hours, only relieved by the disturbed dreams, are simply making her worse.'

'I don't see why not. They're pretty harmless, and she does need rest. I think we may have to resort to the electro-convulsive treatment after all. It's so often the only answer in cases as severe as hers. But no word of it to her, or the dreadful mother, of course. Yes, very well, Sister. As from tonight, give her three pills.'

That night, Cecily carefully swallowed two of the pills, and then tucked the third into one of the lace hankies she kept in a small pile by her bed, and later transferred it to her washbag. The idea had come to her while she had heard two of the younger nurses discussing an overdose patient who had been brought in. 'She only took ten hypnotics,' said one, 'and that nearly killed her. Another two or three and she would have died.'

Cecily had thought about this a great deal over the next couple of days. Hypnotics were what she was given every night with her warm milk. It really wouldn't be so difficult to save a dozen or so up, and then swallow them all at once. And then it would be over: no more guilt, no more hatred, and she would be able to get away from the horrible, hideous person who inhabited her now scrawny body. If she could persuade them to give her a few extra, she could save them up without sacrificing what little benefit they did provide. She couldn't imagine how she could have failed to think of it before.

'So, darling, what did you think? What did you really think?'

Rupert's face was so anxious, so vulnerable in its fear, he looked like Bertie before the dentist. Cassia's heart wrenched in sympathy.

'I thought it was wonderful,' she said, raising her glass to him. 'Really wonderful.'

They were sitting in the pub at the end of the morning's rehearsal; Jasper Hamlyn and Eleanor Studely were still in the theatre, joining them a little later, after wrestling with a difficult passage in one of Eleanor's letters – although Cassia could not help thinking that it was Rupert's performance that needed the greater input.

'Really? Really and truly?'

'Yes, really and truly. I still think it's the most brilliantly clever idea, and—'

'Stuff the idea, Cassia. What do you think of the play?'

'I think that's wonderful too. Terribly moving and sweet and funny and – well, all the things you said. I loved it.'

'So you think it works?'

'Yes, I do. Of course I'm not really quite the person to pronounce on theatrical excellence, but—'

'You're prevaricating,' said Rupert gloomily.' 'You don't really like it. You thought I was bad. You think it's going to fail.'

'Rupert, you're being ridiculous,' said Cassia severely, 'ridiculous and negative. What is the point in my coming here and seeing it, and then telling you a pack of lies?'

'Because you're kind and sweet and generous and you don't want to hurt my feelings.'

'Oh, Rupert, really. I'm not like that, I'm a very truthful person. If I didn't like I'd say so.'

'And you didn't think I was bad, dragging down Eleanor's perform-ance?'

'No!' said Cassia, covering his hand with her own firmly, smiling at him (this was more and more like Bertie and the dentist). 'No, I didn't.'

'Because I'd much rather you said so, if you did.'

'Rupert, this is threatening to get ridiculous. Come on, let me buy you a drink now, and then—'

'Darling Cassia!' Jasper Hamlyn had come into the bar with Eleanor Studely and someone else whom Cassia recognised as the author, an intense young man called James Piggott. 'What did you think? No, no, let me buy the drinks. Go and sit down, and you, Eleanor. Now where is our boy? Rupert, don't look so despairing, it's all going to be fine, and James has come to just tweak a couple of your scenes.'

Cassia went and sat down next to Eleanor; she seemed smaller off the stage, and somehow younger looking.

Eleanor smiled at her.

'It's so nice,' she said quietly, 'to have another woman to talk to for once. These men are driving me completely mad.'

Cassia decided she liked her even more and settled into a soothing conversation about Eleanor's costumes, her young daughter − she was a widow, it transpired; Rupert had never told her that, clearly not nearly as important to him as the play and Eleanor's role in it − and the problems of working as a woman when you had children.

She was clearly not going to get a chance to talk to Rupert today about her anxieties about the money. The money ... and Harry.

'Come on, Bog Face.'

Bertie had thought he was safe, was hurrying past the lavatories on his way to prep; the sound of Parkins's voice made him literally retch. He stood there, heaving, praying someone would come along. They didn't.

'Bog Face, I said come in here. We haven't got long, you're late. Where have you been?'

'Football, Parkins.' He could hardly hear the voice himself.

'Where? Speak up, you little squirt.'

'Football.'

'Well, you'll need a good wash, then. Come along, in here. Put your head down.'

'Oh, Parkins, please!'

He knew that was a mistake, being seen to beg, to plead. One of the other boys who had been bullied had been talking about it in the dormitory the previous week. It was a sign of weakness, which the bullies were looking for, but he couldn't help it, it was all that was left to him; being brave, pretending not to care, had done no good at all.

'Aah! Did you hear that, Collins? Diddums said please. Very nicely. What a beautifully brought-up little chap he is. What do you think?'

'Well, I don't know.' Collins stood looking at Bertie consideringly; Bertie felt a stab of hope. Perhaps after all Collins was not so bad; perhaps he had made a mistake, trying to be brave. Maybe he just hadn't realised how badly frightened he was. Maybe ...

'You pathetic little turd. Think that'll do you any good? Come on, in here. Head down, quick. Right, Parks, pull the chain … now.'

When it was finally over, Bertie made his way towards the school building, his head bowed, his hands clasped firmly behind his back, lest he gave in to the temptation to wipe his eyes, was spotted doing it, either by the master who was walking towards him, or by Parkins or Collins. Whatever happened, he must not cry. Or tell. However great the temptation, he must not tell. Otherwise there would be no hope for him. No hope at all.

'Well now, Mrs Moreton.' Miss Gerard's face as she looked down at Edwina was expressionless. Edwina, lying back on her pillows, still feeling sick from the anaesthetic, tried to smile at her and failed. 'The cyst has been removed and sent for a biopsy, but I really don't think there is anything to worry about there.'

It was the 'there' that worried Edwina: clearly more was to come.

'However,' said Miss Gerard, 'if, as I believe I understood from you, you have had trouble conceiving, it is very plain why.'

'The cyst, I suppose?' said Edwina hopefully.

'No, not the cyst. They can and do cause infertility, although only in about ten per cent of cases, and generally temporarily. Not in yours, I would say. I'm afraid the surgery has revealed a far more serious problem.'

'What?' said Edwina. A cold tentacle of fear was creeping into her head.

'Mrs Moreton, I'm afraid your Fallopian tubes do show extensive damage.'

'What sort of damage?'

'They are grossly distorted. Quite clearly blocked. And there is considerable adhesion between the adjacent tissues.'

'Which would mean …?' said Edwina. She knew what the answer would be, but she wanted to postpone it, postpone the pronouncement she knew was coming – and the terrifying one subsequent to that.

'Which would mean conception will be virtually impossible for you, I'm afraid. Yes?' She turned, frowning; the door had opened.

Harry stood in the doorway, holding a very large bunch of roses. He scowled back at Miss Gerard. 'I'm Harry Moreton. This is my wife.' He went over to the bed, bent and kissed Edwina. 'How are you, Edwina?'

'I'm fine, Harry. Thank you.' She managed to smile at him.

He turned back to Miss Gerard. 'And you are …'

'I am Monica Gerard, your wife's surgeon, Mr Moreton. Sister really should have asked you not to come in just yet.'

'She did,' said Harry, and smiled at her. Edwina knew that smile; his most dangerous, his most challenging. Miss Gerard did not return it.

'I see. Well, perhaps you could be kind enough to step outside, just for a moment. I am in the process of a post-operative examination, and I would rather—'

'You appeared to be merely talking to my wife, Miss Gerard. If you wish to do anything more intimate, then I will of course withdraw. But I cannot imagine that you could be telling my wife anything that I am not entitled to hear.'

'Harry,' said Edwina, 'it might be better if you did go.'

'I don't think that would be better at all, Edwina. I wanted to talk to Miss Gerard, as you know. Now then, did you discover anything disagreeable, Miss Gerard? Any complications? Or can I assume my wife will make a full recovery?'

'A perfectly full recovery, Mr Moreton, yes. The cyst was, as far as I am able to tell, benign, and although it has caused your wife problems, they should now be a thing of the past.'

'Good. I'm delighted to hear it.' He turned and gave her one of his piercing stares. 'I heard you mention conception, did I not?'

Miss Gerard stared back at him. 'Yes, Mr Moreton, you did, but I really think this is not the best time to pursue this particular matter.'

'Why not? I would have thought it was the very best time, and you the very best person to pursue it with. Or does your expertise begin and end with the operation you have just performed, Miss Gerard?'

Miss Gerard looked at him very steadily. 'Mr Moreton, I'm sure you don't mean to be rude. Any more than I do. But I really would rather finish this consultation with your wife before any further discussion can take place as to her condition.'

'And I would rather you didn't,' said Harry.

Edwina struggled through the fog of her panic and the hangover from the anaesthetic. She had not lived with Harry for almost six years without knowing the boundaries within which he and his temper could be contained. This was not one; and she knew, too, there would be a hideous scene if she did not take charge.

'Miss Gerard,' she said, summoning all her considerable courage, knowing this was a definitive moment in her marriage, probably in her life, 'of course I would like my husband to hear whatever it is you have to tell me. Please do go on.'

Miss Gerard looked at her; her eyebrows raised just very slightly. It was more a warning than a question. 'Very well. I was just telling your wife, Mr Moreton, that her Fallopian tubes, those are the—'

'I am not entirely ignorant, Miss Gerard. I am aware of the existence of the Fallopian tubes, and their function. Thank you.' Animosity was so strong in the room it could be smelt, felt.

'Well, that makes this discussion easier. Your wife's Fallopian tubes are clearly dysfunctional. That means there can be virtually no chance of her conceiving a child. I'm sorry.'

'I see.'

There was a long, intense silence. Edwina was aware of her own breathing, slightly fast, within it, of the clock on the wall ticking, of a trolley moving down the corridor outside the room, of a car hooting interminably in the street below. Then Harry spoke again.

'And is there no treatment for this condition?'

'I'm afraid not, Mr Moreton, no. The damage is too extensive.'

'Damage? You mean this is not an inherent … defect?' The word was harsh, ugly; the look he gave Edwina the same.

'I would not quite describe Mrs Moreton's condition as a defect, Mr Moreton.'

'Indeed? What other label would you pin on to sterility?'

'Sterility – infertility, as I prefer to call it – is a most unfortunate thing, Mr Moreton. I would not call it a defect.'

'Well, I think I would. Anyway, what causes it? What has created these dysfunctional tubes?'

Now, thought Edwina, closing her eyes, waiting, waiting for the blow to fall on her, now what will she say? And heard, to her quite extraordinary, exquisite surprise, 'Mr Moreton, medicine is not an exact science, although we would all like it to be. There are any number of factors which could have caused this condition in your wife. I could not possibly be expected to answer that question without extremely extensive investigations into her history, general health :..'

'I would have thought you would, should indeed, have done that already, Miss Gerard.'

'Well, Mr Moreton, you would have thought wrong. Removal of an ovarian cyst is a straightforward procedure. Investigation of infertility is not. Now, if you would be kind enough to step outside the room for a few minutes, I would like to examine your wife.'

'Thank you,' said Edwina feebly as the door closed behind Harry, closing her eyes, willing away a wave of violent nausea, 'thank you very much.'

'As I said to you before, Mrs Moreton, the doctor's consultation room can be compared to the confessional. And I do not take very kindly to being pressured. But your husband is not a stupid man.'

'I'm afraid not.'

'Oh, come now. Very boring – stupid men.' She pulled the bedcovers back up, and smiled at Edwina. 'I would advise you to tell him the truth. In as palatable a form as you can find. That the damage could only have been caused by a pelvic infection, probably resulting from ... a surgical procedure. Of course you need not tell me anything at all, but if you would like to, if it would help, then I am happy to listen.'

'I would like to, actually,' said Edwina, 'but perhaps not just now. I'm frightfully sorry, Miss Gerard, but I think I'm going to be sick.'

Cassia was about to telephone the Harley Street clinic from her house, to see if she might visit Edwina before leaving London, when there was a thunderous knocking at the door. She opened it, half alarmed, half irritated.

Harry was standing there. He looked appalling, white-faced, dishevelled, and clearly extremely angry.

'Harry! What on earth is the matter? It's not Edwina, is it?'

'Yes, it's Edwina,' he said. 'Look, can I come in?'

'Yes, of course you can. She isn't – hasn't ...'

'She's fine,' he said, walking past her into the kitchen, sitting down at the table, his head in his hands.

'Well, then? What?'

'Can I have a drink? Have you got any brandy?'

'I think so, but it's not very good. Look, it's here, help yourself.'

'Good God,' he said, taking a cautious sip then examining the label, 'this is absolutely foul. Haven't you got anything better than this?'

'No, Harry, I'm afraid I haven't. I'm so very sorry.'

'She's had this bloody operation. As you know. I saw the bloody stupid woman who performed it. The one you recommended.' He glared at her.

'Whatever else she may be, Monica Gerard is not stupid.'

'No, I know. I'm sorry.'

Cassia tried and failed to remember Harry having used the word 'sorry' during the past ten years. She looked at him with some astonishment; he was clearly not himself.

'Anyway, she's removed the cyst or whatever it was. That was all absolutely fine. But as I arrived, she was talking to Edwina.'

He said nothing for a moment, looking down into the glass. He seemed defeated, utterly low. Then he took a deep breath, and said,

'Cassia, Edwina can never have children. Or not according to this woman anyway.'

'Oh,' said Cassia. 'Oh, I see.'

'Is that all you have to say?' he said, scowling at her again.

'No, of course not, I'm sorry. And I am so very sorry to hear that. It's – well, it's terrible. For her, for you.'

She looked at him, sitting there, holding the glass, somehow too big for her small kitchen, his head bent, his eyes fixed on his drink, his distress a tangible thing, and felt an almost overwhelming urge to go and put her arms round him. To counteract it, she sat on her hands.

'Did ... did Miss Gerard give a reason?'

'She said Edwina's Fallopian tubes were blocked. Very seriously dysfunctional, I think were her exact words. That there was nothing that could be done.' He looked at her. 'You know about these things, Cassia. Is that right? Is there really nothing that can be done?'

'Harry, I don't know. Without seeing the damage for myself, knowing more about it, I really can't answer you. And of course I'm not a surgeon. But—' She stopped.

'But it's unlikely?'

'Well, yes. I would think it probably is. From what you've said. I'm so sorry.'

'So what would cause that?' he said abruptly.

'Harry, I honestly don't know.'

'Well, have you any idea?'

She sensed danger, swerved to avoid it. 'I keep telling you, without knowing more about it—'

'You're all the fucking same,' he said suddenly, knocking the glass off the table with a violent fist. It fell, shattered on the floor; she stared at it, shocked.

'I'm sorry,' he said, pushing his wild hair back. 'Here, let me clear it up.'

'No, it's all right. I'll do it. Do you want some more?'

'Yes. No. Oh, I don't know. Oh Christ.' He put his head in his hands. Then he said suddenly, 'Could it have been an abortion?'

'What?'

'You heard me. I think she's had an abortion. I think she's probably had more than one.'

'Harry, that's absurd, why should she?'

'I'll tell you why she should,' he said. 'She doesn't want children, she's never been keen on the idea, she probably thought it would wreck her figure, more recently interfere with that damn job of hers.'

'Oh, don't be absurd. I know Edwina isn't exactly maternal, but she would never have ... You're over-reacting, it's absurd.'

'I don't think so,' he said. 'The years have gone by, and I told her a long time ago to stop taking precautions. Nothing's happened, and it seems to me more than possible that she's taken some active steps herself.'

'That's an outrageous thing to say. If her tubes are blocked, she can't conceive. It's as simple as that.'

'Yes, but why are they blocked? Answer me that.'

'Harry, I don't know. I have no idea. There could be any number of reasons. What I do know is you're talking absolute nonsense. Unfair, dangerous nonsense. I know you're upset, but ...'

He sat there, glaring at her; the hand holding the glass was shaking. 'Well,' he said, finally, 'we shall see. I intend to find out. Anyway, whatever the reason, it seems we are destined to be childless. And I – oh God, help me.'

She couldn't help it then: she put out her hands, both of them, took one of his. She was surprised at his intense distress, and said so.

'You don't understand me at all, you see,' he said, staring down at her hands wrapped round his. 'I wanted children very much indeed. I see them as the only reason for getting married. I wanted to see my line continue. I like children, although I can see that's a bit hard to believe. And I had that ghastly, filthy childhood, I wanted to have some children and give them a good one.' He looked up at her, and his dark eyes were so full of pain, she felt it too, winced.

'Oh, Harry,' she said, helpless in the face of it, of the pain, 'what can I say to you? Only all the stupid things which may be true: that there are other things, that often childless marriages are very happy—'

'Jesus Christ Almighty,' he said, staring at her, 'please don't let us go in for that kind of hypocrisy. Happy! Me and Edwina! Dear God in Heaven.' There was a very long silence.

'I'm sorry,' she said. 'I thought—'

'Of course you didn't,' he said, his voice harsh, brusque. 'How could you possibly think such a thing? How could you even suggest we were happy?'

She stared at him, genuinely shaken by the violence in his voice. 'I – well, I hoped you were.'

'You hoped!' he said, his voice loud, ugly with rage. 'You hoped that we were happy! That I was, that I could be happy with Edwina! Dear sweet Jesus, Cassia, spare me such drivel. You know why I married her, for God's sake, don't you? Don't you?'

She realised suddenly, with a sense of slight shock, that she was still holding his hand with both of hers. The physical contact, so gentle, so tender, was oddly at variance with the violence of his mood. She looked down at them, at their hands; felt afraid, tried to move one of hers away.

'Don't,' he said sharply. She put it back and was still. 'I married her,' he said, very slowly and distinctly, as if anxious that there might be no misunderstanding in the matter, 'simply because I could not marry you. No other reason whatsoever. As of course you very well know.'

This was danger: terrible danger. She was afraid to speak, afraid to move, just sat there, looking at their hands, feeling in some strange confused way that if nothing was disturbed, if the silence could continue, they might move away into safety.

After a long silence, he said, his voice steadier, less raw, 'You did know that, didn't you, Cassia? Yes, of course you did. You knew it then, and you know it now. So please don't start mouthing obscene platitudes about us being happy, because I don't think I can bear it. Not today, today of all days.' Still she was silent.

Suddenly he stood up, wrenched his hand away from hers, brought it down violently on the table. 'Damn you,' he said loudly, 'damn you, Cassia.'

'Don't,' she said.

'Why not? Can't you see that I have an absolute right to be angry with you?'

'No,' she said, 'I don't think I do. And I think perhaps you'd better go.'

'Oh no,' he said, 'I'm not going. You're always telling me to go, Cassia: you told me to go that night when I came to Leonora's house and first kissed you; you told me to go the night when I came to tell you not to marry Edward. And I did what you said, I went, and both times you were wrong and I should have stayed. You're very fond of saying I'm arrogant, but in fact you are immensely arrogant yourself, probably far more so than I.'

'I'm not arrogant.'

'Oh, but you are. You know so well what's best, don't you? You always have done. Best for you, best for me, best for everyone. You're arrogant, and you're stubborn, and you're ruthless and—'

'Stop it,' she said, standing up, 'stop this. I will not listen to it, and if you won't leave, then I will.'

'Don't be absurd,' he said, pushing her back into her chair, 'and sit down again. And that's something else: you won't listen, you only hear the things you want to. I would like you to hear this, Cassia, and I would like you to reflect upon it. Here we are, the two of us, locked into miserable marriages—'

'Mine is not—' she started, and then stopped.

'Of course it is,' he said. 'Don't lie about that, of all things. It's miserable, desperately so. You should never have married him, it was an appalling mistake, and you should at least have the grace to admit it to me.'

'I won't admit it.'

'Very well. As I said, you are appallingly, dangerously stubborn. And had it not been for that stubbornness, we could have been perfectly happy together. One happy marriage instead of two wretched ones.'

'Oh, now, Harry, that is really absurd.'

'Is it? Why?' He sat down again, his eyes probing hers.

'Well,' she said, aware that she sounded slightly foolish now, that as always he was getting the better of her, 'you can't blame me for you marrying Edwina. You didn't have to marry anyone.'

'Oh, but I did,' he said. 'I did have to marry someone, because I wanted to hurt you. I wanted to hurt you more than anything in the world; indeed, it was the only thing I wanted.'

'That is an appalling thing to say. To have done,' she said, genuinely shocked at the savagery in his voice.

'Really? Why? When you were wilfully hurting me.'

'This is ridiculous. I wasn't marrying Edward to hurt you, I was marrying him because I was pregnant with his child. I told you that. How could I do anything else?'

'Easily,' he said, 'very easily. That was no reason to marry him, when you loved me. We could have solved that problem, very minor in comparison with—'

'Minor! A child!'

'Cassia,' he said, and his voice was very low, but still violent, 'Cassia, I would have taken Edward's child. Of course I would. Not easily perhaps, but I would have done it. I would have seen it as a small price to pay for you.'

'Oh,' she said, 'oh, I see.' She felt devoid of emotion; an empty, shocked shell.

'I hope you do,' he said. 'I hope you believe me.'

'But if—'

'Yes? If what, Cassia?'

'It doesn't matter. It really doesn't.'

If you knew I loved you, she had been going to say, why did you let me do it, let me go? But she knew the answer, and she did not want to hear it again: it was her own arrogance, her own stubbornness, her certainty that she knew best, knew what had to be done; she would not have listened to him. And who would? How many women, pregnant with one man's child, would have listened to another when he said he loved her, that he would take her, even with that child, would have admitted that she loved him?

She felt grief fill the void, the empty shell of her, a dreadful, hungry grief, felt tears rush to the back of her eyes. She dashed them impatiently away, looked away, at the blank wall, fighting down the sobs.

'Now, you must not cry,' he said, his voice gentle suddenly, reaching out, as he had done once before, so long ago, arresting a tear in its journey down her face, looking at it on his finger, 'not unless you want me to stay with you. You know what happens when you cry, don't you?' And again, remembering, showing her that he remembered, he raised the finger to his lips and licked it, very tenderly, his eyes fixed on hers. 'I find your tears absolutely overwhelming, Cassia. And I wouldn't leave you this time, you know. I wouldn't and I couldn't.'

And she sat there, staring at him through her tears, and felt the emptiness, the void, filling swiftly, with something quite different, something very strong, very dangerous, a desire so violent, so intense it was pain, so urgent that she moved, curved her body towards him, and then she reached out both her hands, across the table and took his face between them and leant forward and kissed him, on the mouth, very hard, very deliberately, her tongue seeking his; and then pulled away as swiftly and said, 'No, Harry, don't go, please don't, please stay.'

He stood up then and held out his hand, his face strangely expressionless, his eyes fixed on hers, and led her out of the room.

What happened between them then, passed everything she had ever known, every expectation she had ever had. She had no idea how long they were there, in her bed, for darkness fell and the streetlamps came on. She heard once through the tumult the phone ringing, and once a knock at the door, and it meant nothing to her, nothing at all: her entire being, not just her body, but her mind and her heart and what she supposed she would call her soul, was focused on Harry, on how much she loved him, on what was happening between them at last.

So frantic was she, so desperate for him, that at first she could not, would not wait, lay there like a whore, arms held open for him, legs splayed, ordering him into her. She could not have begun to imagine that moment; as he entered her, she felt not only herself, but her life, all the years behind her, filled. Her climax began almost at once, rising, clenching, pulling at her and 'Wait,' he said, easing himself up from her, 'wait a little.'

'I can't wait,' she said, 'I can't,' and felt it immediately break, shatter deep, deep within her, heard herself cry out, in a long harsh cry, fell half sobbing, half laughing back on to the bed.

'Oh God,' she said, 'Harry, I'm sorry, so sorry.'

'That's what the man is supposed to say,' he said, smiling down at her. 'I told you you were arrogant. Are you always like that?'

'No,' she said, smiling back, 'no, I am not always like that, I am never like that.'

'Well now,' he said thoughtfully, looking at her, tracing the shape of her breasts, of her pubic hair, with his finger, 'well now, let us see.'

He began again, then; lay away from her, kissing her, kissing her mouth, her ears, her throat, her hair, moving down to her breasts, her stomach, her thighs, settled into her with his tongue; she held his head, pushing it into her, feeling the bright, brilliant darts of pleasure, moaning at times, crying out at others, climaxed slightly, sweetly again.

'You are having this all your way,' he said then, and moved into her, heavily, slowly, and with infinite care; she lay there, feeling him, deep, so deeply into her that his body became a part of hers, every movement, every tremor; she felt herself lost then, in a strange, wild new country, her progress measured only in the great swooping arcs of pleasure that she rode, now moving forward, now circuiting back on herself, and her body did not only feel, it could see and hear, it knew darkness and brilliance, noise and silence. She came not once, but several times, always higher, deeper, fiercer, the echoes each time fading only as the next began; she felt him come, heard him call out, cry her name, a great primeval cry, and when at the end she finally lay still, exhausted, and at peace, new knowledge, new instincts within her body, her prime emotion was awe at the pleasure they had known, and their power to unleash it.

She fell asleep then, briefly; and awoke to find him watching her, his eyes thoughtful.

'Now what are we to do?' he said.

CHAPTER 25

Cassia thought at first she must be mishearing; stood for a full minute outside the dining room, listening, but yes, it was as she had thought; Janet was telling Edward something, something about William wanting to play cricket on the football pitch, and Edward was laughing. She wasn't sure which was the more welcome fact; that Edward should listen sufficiently courteously to Janet, or that he was capable of laughing these days. She could hardly remember the last time she had seen him smile.

She took a deep breath and pushed open the door, smiling determinedly herself. Edward's expression froze and he promptly disappeared behind the *Telegraph*. Janet smiled back at her.

'Mrs Fallon, good morning. I was just suggesting to Fanny here that we should maybe read some poetry together this morning. It's dull for her when William is at school. She was telling me how much she enjoyed the Edward Lear verses; the Jumblies in particular. I love them too. So later on, when Delia is asleep, and if it's all right with you, Mrs Fallon ...'

'Janet, of course it is. It's sweet of you.'

'I'm not too keen on Lear myself,' said Edward suddenly from behind the paper. 'Lot of bloody nonsense.'

'But, Dr Fallon, that's the whole idea,' said Janet, her pretty mouth twitching.

He looked at her and for a moment Cassia thought he was going to scowl. Then he smiled his slow reluctant smile – God, thought Cassia, what that used to do to me, that smile – and said, 'Yes, I suppose so. Touché. Well, I must get into the surgery, I can't sit here talking all day.' The implication that they all could was very strong.

'Now,' said Janet, advancing upon Delia and the hideous mess she had made on the tray of her highchair – rusk mingled with blackcurrant juice and lightly boiled egg – 'let's get this mess cleared up – I hope some of it at least has gone into you, Delia – and then I think I might take you out for a bit. Do you want to come, Fanny?'

'Oh, yes please. That'd be lovely. I do like the country.'

Cassia looked at her fondly; she was almost herself again now, although still quieter, less talkative than she had been. 'You don't feel … ready to go home yet, darling?'

Fanny shook her head violently, and her large dark eyes took on their haunted look. 'No, I don't. I love it here so much, Cassia, please let me stay.'

'All right, Fanny. You can stay.' But not indefinitely, she thought, walking out into the hall to greet the postman. She would have to go back to London one day, when her mother came home perhaps. Poor Cecily; the news of her was not very good. Really, she ought to go and see her – she *would* go and see her. But not just yet. She couldn't think about it yet.

She couldn't think about anything at the moment: except Harry. He consumed her, occupied all her senses, every waking moment of the day and most of her dreams as well. It was as well, she thought, that she and Edward now slept in separate bedrooms, given a certain propensity of hers to talk in her sleep. Even her work, her distraction and comfort from all her troubles over the past year, seemed unimportant, not quite real. She had stopped fretting over Bertie, her marriage, Rupert: none of it mattered. Only Harry. Harry and being with him.

'Mrs Moreton, good afternoon. I trust you are quite well again.'

Edwina looked up startled from her desk: Francis Stevenson-Cook stood in front of her. He was looking particularly resplendent, in a suit in very dark grey wool under an even darker grey overcoat, with a velvet collar. He carried his cane and a top hat.

'Good afternoon,' she said, 'and yes, thank you, I am quite well now.'

'Excellent. I came to ask you to have luncheon with me tomorrow. Are you free?'

Edwina had actually agreed to have lunch with Justin Everard, to discuss a photographic session, but she knew that if Stevenson-Cook asked you if you were free, you were free. 'That would be delightful,' she said. 'Thank you.'

'Good. If you come downstairs at twelve forty-five, my driver will take us to the restaurant. Good afternoon to you.' He turned and left the office with a wave of his hat.

Edwina sat staring after him.

'Don't get excited,' said Betty Farquarson, the accessories editor, coolly, 'he takes everyone to lunch at least once.'

Edwina knew this was not true, but she smiled sweetly at Betty and said, 'I do realise that,' and picked up the phone to cancel her lunch with Justin.

'And how is your delightful friend?' he said after agreeing (albeit reluctantly) to come to the office for the meeting instead.

'My friend? Oh, you mean Cecily. She's not at all well, I'm afraid.'

'I'm sorry. What's wrong? I read about her husband of course: such a tragedy.'

'She's had a nervous breakdown,' said Edwina.

'Oh, how frightful. Poor her. I shall send her some flowers.'

'Justin, how terribly sweet of you.'

'Well, I liked her very much. And I thought she was very attractive.'

'Really?'

'Yes, really. And you can take that surprised note out of your voice. She was beautiful, I thought, and really rather ... sexy.'

'Justin! Surely not.'

'Surely, indeed. Well, perhaps sexy isn't quite the word. Sensual. Yes, that's better. And very very warm. You stick-insects of ladies shouldn't dismiss her type. We poor men rather like it.'

'Justin, you really do talk absolute nonsense,' said Edwina, 'but anyway, I'm sure poor Cecily would adore to get some flowers from you. I'll give you the address.'

She left for home a little early; she felt tired. It was a fortnight since her operation and although she felt quite recovered, she did seem to need rather more rest than usual.

She had had a long conversation with Monica Gerard the next day, and told her everything. Miss Gerard had been totally pleasant and nonjudgemental, but said that she was afraid Edwina's history did confirm her original opinion. 'Miracles do happen, I am told, but I have personally never experienced one. Your tubes really are damaged beyond repair, and you cannot lay the blame for that on the cyst or the operation to remove it. The infection you describe, following the termination of pregnancy, would have accounted for it, without doubt.'

'Yes, I see,' Edwina had said with a sigh.

'How do you feel about the prospect of childlessness yourself, Mrs Moreton?'

'Oh, you know,' Edwina had shrugged. 'I suppose I'd have quite liked a sprog or two, but I'm certainly not going to break my heart over it. I've got loads of other things to fill my life with. My husband's rather more keen, I'm afraid.'

'I gathered that. Well, I would advise a frank conversation. He is obviously an intelligent man. Presumably this operation took place before your marriage.'

'Oh, yes. Yes, of course,' said Edwina hastily.

Miss Gerard had looked at her sharply. 'I feel sure that it did. Quite a few years before. That will naturally make it rather more acceptable to him. Now then, if I could just examine those stitches ...'

And so she had returned home, braced for a conversation, an inquisition, indeed, from Harry: and found none. He greeted her kindly, but abstractedly, told her she must be sure to rest and take things easily, and after seeing her into her bed, disappeared to his club.

Since then she had hardly seen him; on the occasions when she had, at breakfast each day, and over a long weekend in Wiltshire, almost all of which he had spent either at race meetings or playing golf, he had been polite, solicitous – and with no apparent desire to pursue the question of her childlessness. Even at bedtime, when she sat, dreading the sound of his footsteps approaching her room, the sound seldom came, for he was out a good deal, as always, and when it did, he knocked at her door, came over to the bed and kissed her goodnight – after asking her how she felt – and left again. It was a huge relief; but it was none the less still rather odd.

Francis Stevenson-Cook took her to lunch at the Caprice; he had inevitably his own table, tucked into a corner. There was a bottle of Veuve Cliquot in an ice bucket beside it.

Edwina, who had a strong head, exclaimed with pleasure over this – 'It's absolutely my favourite champagne' – and drank three glasses before the first course arrived, a fact which appeared to give Stevenson-Cook great pleasure.

'I admire women who can drink,' he said, 'but now that the food has arrived, we will leave the rest. Nothing worse than ruining champagne by disturbing its taste. They do a very fine white burgundy here, I think we will have that. So vulgar, this restaurant, isn't it? All the pink? But I do rather like it.'

'I quite enjoy vulgarity,' said Edwina, nibbling thoughtfully at a stick of asparagus, 'providing it's terribly, terribly expensive.'

'What a very interesting view. I think I agree with you. Well, it is certainly terribly terribly expensive here. And certainly the food is not vulgar in the least.'

He was a charming and attentive host; regaled her with gossip – including the news that Mrs Simpson had introduced the three-decker toasted sandwich to the King's guests at Balmoral and that Prince Aly

Khan now kept three mistresses at the Ritz on three separate floors – laughed at her jokes, and admired her dress and particularly her hat.

'Do you like it? One of Miss Swirling's creations,' said Edwina.

'I thought it might be. How is she? Such fun, isn't she? The last time I walked down Bond Street – a very rare occurrence – I did think of going to see her, but I feared I might be interrupting a session with a client.'

'I'm sure she wouldn't have minded,' said Edwina. 'Hard to imagine an interruption she'd like more, in fact.'

'Maybe, but I do have a great respect for people in their working environment, Mrs Moreton. I feel it's rather vulgar to intrude, to trade on one's position. Don't you agree?'

'Oh, absolutely,' said Edwina. It seemed to her that of all the people she had ever met, Francis Stevenson-Cook traded on his position most thoroughly and ruthlessly.

On the way back to the magazine offices, he said, 'I understand you are mounting a charity fashion show.'

'Yes. In just over a month's time. Of course it won't interfere with my work at *Style* in any way.'

'Of course not. Are your plans for it complete? Is it all under control?'

'Well, more or less,' said Edwina carefully, anxious he should not think the fashion show was occupying too much of her time and attention; in fact, she was horribly behind with the arrangements, and had even wondered, since her surgery and consequent tiredness, if she should cancel, or at least postpone it.

'And which charity is it in aid of?'

'St Christopher's Hospital. A very close friend of mine works there, and she—'

'She? Is she a nurse?'

'No, she's a doctor,' said Edwina, who had always been a trifle hazy about Cassia's role at St Christopher's, largely because she never listened properly to anything she said about it.

'A woman doctor! How very unusual. She must be extremely clever.'

'Yes, she is. Anyway, that's how it happened. Well, indirectly. It's being held at Grosvenor House. In the Great Room. The one that was the ice-rink, you know.'

'I do know. I went to the Hallowe'en fancy-dress party there in 1930. I went as a mermaid. Of course that made skating impossible, but I was on a sleigh.'

'How glorious,' said Edwina, genuinely entranced by this picture. 'I do wish I'd seen you.'

'I have some photographs. I'll show you some time. Now, back to your fashion show.'

'Well, we have the clothes all organised, and the mannequins – a few professional, and some friends—'

'Oh dear,' said Stevenson-Cook with a very slight sigh. 'Amateur mannequins are always a disaster in my view.'

'Oh, no, they're all quite good. I have a lot of very stylish friends,' she added with a touch of complacency.

'I don't doubt it. And is your friend the doctor taking part in any way?'

'Yes, she's modelling.'

'Modelling! So she is elegant as well as clever. What a paragon. I should like to meet her. I shall meet her. Now I should like to propose that *Style* becomes involved in this show of yours.'

'Oh!' said Edwina. She was astonished: astonished and wary. 'Well, of course that would be very nice, but Miss Le Page feels—'

'I know what Miss Le Page feels,' said Stevenson-Cook, 'and I happen to feel differently. This will clearly be a very superior affair. Association with it can do us nothing but good. I would propose that the magazine takes a table at the event, and advertising space in the programme. We could give copies of the magazine to each lady present. And I imagine there will be a tombola of some kind?'

'Yes. Very important, always raises lots of money.'

'Then a year's subscription to each of the magazines as prizes. How would that be?'

'That would be splendid,' said Edwina. 'Thank you, Mr Stevenson-Cook. Thank you so much.'

'Don't thank me, Mrs Moreton. I see this as something of mutual benefit. In more ways than one.'

'You must leave him,' said Harry.

'I will leave him. But not yet.'

'Why not yet? You've wasted quite enough of our lives, Cassia, I can't allow it to go on.'

'Harry, I haven't wasted our lives!'

'Of course you've wasted our lives. Entirely your fault.' He grinned at her. 'I seem to be able to forgive you, God knows how. Tell me why not yet.'

They were lying in bed together in the house in Walton Street; they had an arrangement to meet there for lunch each of the days she was in London.

'Lunch?' Cassia had said when he first proposed it, smiling at him.

'That seems rather a waste of time. Especially as I seem unable to eat at all at the moment.'

'Lunchtime, then. We shall take a little nourishment to replenish our energies. I shall see to that. You are to be ready for me when I arrive.'

And she was, each time: lying naked in bed, feverishly impatient. He would appear in the doorway, his arms full of flowers, presents, champagne, would hurl them down, tear off his clothes, and join her there. Join his mouth to hers, her body to his; join thoughts, hopes, fears, laughter; join their lives.

They would stay there for an hour, two if they each had time; they would eat something that she or he had bought, something suited to the dining place: a sliver of cheese, strawberries, some ice-cream; she stocked her kitchen with fresh coffee beans, the variety that Harry preferred, and bought a grinder. Harry would drink champagne, which she would not, because she was almost invariably going to work, and she would drink the coffee while she opened her gifts.

He bought her wonderful things, some rare and thoughtfully chosen books: an antique history of medicine; a first edition of *Gray's Anatomy*; some modern, lavishly illustrated books about India, Egypt, China, all the places he said he would take her; poetry books from which he made her read to him; the complete works of Pliny, Socrates, Virgil, from which he read her fragments.

'They are important to us, these works, it was the night I came to tell you about my First that you realised I loved you, don't deny it, you did.'

And he bought her jewellery, a triple length of pearls – 'which you are to wear always, you were wearing pearls when I first realised you were so beautiful, at your dance, remember? When I behaved so appallingly? Yes, of course you do' – a diamond watch and clips, an emerald necklace, a set of three gold bangles.

He bought her other things – silk négligés, scarves, robes. 'These are mistress's things, Harry,' she said, laughing, taking the latest offering out of its tissue-lined box.

'Quite right,' he said, 'for that is what you are, just for the moment, and what better than to be my mistress? You know what the proper definition of mistress is? I looked it up today.'

'No,' she said, 'what?'

'A woman with power to control. That is what you have, Cassia, the power to control. To control me. It's a rare talent, don't waste it.'

'Of course I can't control you,' she said, half irritable, 'nobody can.'

'Oh, but you are wrong,' he said, taking the things from her hands, setting them down, pushing her gently down on to the pillows, kissing her breasts, 'you do control me, you always have. There have been times when I have tried to take control of you, but failed. From the first moment I saw you, standing there considering me, in that tartan dress and black stockings, your hair hanging down your back, you have controlled me. I have not done a single thing, since that day, without considering you and how it might or might not please you. If that is not control, tell me what is.'

She didn't argue, she could not, he was too clever for her; merely pulled him down on to her and kissed him. But his words – the brilliant, beautiful words with which he courted her, made love to her – moved her, moved her physically as much as his body, his mouth and his hands, and they filled her head, so that when they were apart she remembered them, all of them, examining them, delighting in them.

'Why can you not leave the doctor yet?' he said again, picking up a strawberry and examining it.

She hesitated. 'It's all so ... difficult now. We have to think of how best to manage it all. Edward is so hurt, so unhappy already—'

'So he should be,' said Harry briskly.

'Harry, that is very harsh. It isn't his fault I don't love him. I've done him so much wrong.'

'Indeed? How? He's had seven years of you, more in fact, you've given him three children—'

'Which I plan to take away from him.'

'Of course. He can marry again, have more. He can marry that other appalling-sounding doctor person.'

'If we are not very careful, I will lose the children. He's already sent Bertie away from me.'

'Cassia, I will hire the best divorce lawyers in the land. You will not lose your children. I promise you that.'

'You can't promise that,' she said, 'you really can't. And then I have failed him, refused to go to Glasgow with him. I'm his wife, I should have gone.'

'Well, we shall have to disagree on that. It was a disgraceful piece of behaviour, in my opinion. Next? You haven't convinced me yet. I may have to pick up the phone and instruct my lawyers now, before I leave.'

'Oh, Harry, really!' She smiled at him, picked up his hand, kissed it. 'Please, please be sensible. We must take our time. And besides, there's Edwina.'

'Oh, she won't mind,' he said easily, 'as long as she gets enough money.'

'Of course she'll mind. She's very fond of you.'

'Only quite, I would say.'

'Why did she marry you then?'

'She was dying to marry me,' he said. 'She knew I didn't love her and she didn't hesitate. And why should she have, indeed? She was getting my money, my houses, my position, my cock—'

'Don't!' she said. That had hurt her.

'Oh now, don't come over all virginal, Cassia. The good doctor got you, in all your loveliness – ' he stroked her thighs tenderly, bent and kissed them – 'and Edwina got me. There is no sense in pretending none of it happened, that we remained in some strange way chaste for one another. Is there now?'

'No,' she said quietly. 'No, of course not.' She pushed herself up suddenly, lay away from him, considering him, then she said, 'Anyway, we have to be careful, cautious. Please, Harry, be patient. There are so many dangers.'

'Very well, I promise. Just for a little while. But not for long. There you go, you see, controlling me, as always. I told you you did that.'

She looked at him sharply, the fear surfacing suddenly, the half-formed fear she kept so well buried, that she had thought was buried. 'And have you never tried to control me? In any way?'

'Good Lord no,' he said, turning away from her, pouring himself a glass of champagne. 'I know my limitations.'

Nanny was finding life extremely difficult: difficult and worrying. It would have been bad enough without Mr Harrington, but losing Mrs Harrington as well was dreadful. Mrs Forbes was a nightmare, never stopped criticising her, her and all the staff, and when she wasn't criticising them, she was talking to them, outlining her own misfortunes, her absent husband – Nanny would have put quite a lot of money on Mr Forbes positively relishing his solitude – the difficult time she was having with the children, her daughter's own ingratitude. And Stephanie was missing her sister and her mother and was behaving extremely badly. Only the baby was cheerful.

She also found herself in a position of strange authority; not only Susan, but the rest of the housemaids looked to her for direction, They were under-employed, and miserable at what had happened to the household; it was difficult to keep their morale high.

Even Adams was low; he was having as much trouble with the kitchen staff, particularly Cook, who had developed a fierce dislike for Mrs Forbes, and he confided to Nanny occasionally over their late-night tipple of whisky in hot milk that he was not sure how much longer he could consider remaining in the house. 'Naturally I would not wish to let Mrs Harrington down, and I would not dream of leaving until she is quite better. But it is an odd household, without a gentleman to head it. And Mr Harrington was such a very considerate employer. God rest his soul.'

And then things began to get worse.

'My daughter is not to know this, naturally,' Mrs Forbes said to her, one evening, meeting her on the first-floor landing as she hurried upstairs with a pile of clean nappies for Laurence, 'but they were talking about electro-convulsive therapy for her again at the nursing home today. I was not supposed to hear them, although naturally they take me into their confidence about most of Mrs Harrington's treatment, but I was rather alarmed. Most extreme, and very unpleasant, of course. It is a measure of how seriously they are taking her illness.'

She then went on to describe electro-convulsive therapy to Nanny in some detail; she listened in horror.

'If only there was some key. That is what the doctors are looking for,' Ada said with a sigh, 'some slight thing, that might lift this terrible depression. Guilt, you see, over poor Mr Harrington's death. She blames herself, which is absurd, but it's natural, all widows feel it apparently, the doctor was telling me about it. Of course my daughter is very sensitive, she gets it from me ...'

'Cassia?'

She had been sitting in the dining room, writing to Bertie – only a week now till half term – safely, virtuously contained in her other life. Her real life. His voice was a physical shock: she felt dizzy.

'Harry!' She crushed the instinct – the incriminating instinct should she be overheard – to tell him he must not do this, must not phone her at home, and said, her voice pleasantly level, 'How nice. How are you?'

'Lonely. Miserable. Concupiscent.'

'And how is Edwina?'

'Do you know what concupiscent means?'

'No.'

'So ignorant, you are. It means lustful, filled with desire. What are you doing?'

'I'm writing to Bertie.'

'How very virtuous. As always. I'm flying to Le Touquet tomorrow. I want you to come.'

'That would be very nice, and please thank Edwina for inviting us,' she said, acutely aware of the many people who might be listening to this conversation, 'but I'm afraid we can't—'

'Of course you can. If you don't I shall come down and tell the doctor some of the appalling things you've been doing over the past few weeks. It's the last time we'll be able to do it this year, a beautiful Indian summer's day is forecast, and you are to come. I want to fuck you on French soil. Find some excuse. I'll collect you from your house in London in the morning at six.'

'I'm afraid it will be quite imposs—'

The line had gone dead.

'Edward, I'm so sorry, I have an urgent extra session tomorrow. In the morning. One of the other doctors is ill. It means my going up to London tonight, I'm afraid.'

'Fine. Don't worry about us.'

She wondered why she had even bothered to tell him, and went to warn Janet.

Janet said that would be perfectly all right. William had extra choir practice and Delia was going to a party. 'Don't worry about it, Mrs Fallon. It's only an extra half day.'

She went down to the post office to make the next call: to tell Mrs Jennings, the secretary at the clinic, that she had a domestic crisis and simply couldn't make the next day's session.

'That's all right, Dr Fallon. It looks like a quiet day, anyway. I hope things get sorted out for you soon.'

'Thank you. I'll see you on Thursday, then.'

She could hardly believe her own irresponsibility. Irresponsibility and wickedness. She told Janet she would collect William from school and spent the entire evening, up to suppertime, doing all the things she most hated, as a sop to her conscience: standing in goal while William fired his football at her in the garden, reading Delia's favourite picture book, *Babies on the Farm*, to her over and over again for the best part of half an hour, and then tidying all the kitchen drawers while they ate their tea, patiently untangling pieces of string from skewers, old birthday cake candles from shoe-polishing cloths. She watched herself in wonderment, thinking that she was a rich, a very rich woman, there was no need for her to be doing this, and then that she was also a very wicked one and that what she was doing was a highly inadequate penance for it.

Ada had gone out, to meet Stephanie from school and take her to a party.

Nanny was enjoying the peace and quiet when the phone rang in the hall. It was Edwina Moreton.

'Oh, Nanny. I need your help. Have you got a moment? Look, before Mrs Harrington was – well, ill, she was selling some tickets for me. For my fashion show, you know. I'm sure Mrs Harrington will have told you about it.'

Mrs Harrington hadn't, of course, and Nanny said so.

'How extraordinary. Anyway, I need some information, and it's very important. I need to know how many tickets she's sold. She'll have a record of it somewhere, in her desk, I expect. Could you go and have a jolly good look for me, please, and then ring me back? What? No, I'm at *Style* magazine, surely you realised I worked there? Well, look, take the number down, it's Regent 444. Got that? And then ask for me. Thank you; Nanny.'

Nanny went into the morning room, and started rummaging through Mrs Harrington's desk. It was all in very neat order, as she would have expected, with files labelled things like 'schools', 'ballet classes', 'tennis lessons', 'dinner parties'. But there was nothing, nothing at all connected with a fashion show. She sighed. Mrs Moreton would be furious. Maybe it was somewhere else.

She went up to Mrs Harrington's room. There was a small escritoire in the corner; that might produce something. However, it had been used for sewing, each drawer neatly filled with cottons, fabrics, needles and pins, elastic and hemming tape. Not a scrap of paper in it.

She left the room, and wandered out on to the landing, where she found Susan with some flowers.

'Oh, hallo, Nanny. Everything all right?'

'Yes. Well, Mrs Moreton just telephoned me, about some fashion show she's running. Apparently a list has been mislaid, of the number of tickets Mrs Harrington has sold. I have searched her desk, and it's not there: is there anywhere else she might have kept papers?'

'She sometimes used the little rolltop in the guest room,' said Susan, 'the one where Mrs Forbes is sleeping. You could try there. And I do know Mrs Forbes is out at the moment.'

'Good idea,' said Nanny. 'Thank you, Susan. I'll have a look there.'

She knocked at Ada's door, just to make sure she wasn't in the room, and went in. The little rolltop desk was open; Ada was obviously using it too. She certainly didn't seem as orderly as her daughter: there were piles of assorted papers all over it, envelopes with their contents spilling out, bills from the nursing home, from the girls' school, a pile of unanswered letters. Nanny pushed those aside and looked in the pigeonholes at the back.

This was better: lots of correspondence in Mrs Harrington's writing, with correspondence from friends, all neatly slotted in, in alphabetical order. Nothing that looked as if it was connected with the fashion show, but she could try the drawers: the top one yielded. A small accounts book, some bank statement and – yes! A file labelled 'Fashion Show'. She pulled out the contents: it was all there. A list of people approached, neat ticks by the ones who had bought tickets, a second list headed 'Table guests?', again with ticks. Mrs Moreton would be very pleased. She pushed the drawer shut again carefully, and in the process dislodged one of Ada's piles of papers. They fell on the floor in a flurry.

'Damn,' said Nanny, and bent down to retrieve them. She tried not to look at them, of course, but she couldn't really help it. There were a couple of letters from Mr Forbes which began 'My dearest Ada', and which contained details of his trip to New York; very dull accounts, too, he seemed to be on his own most of the time. More letters, mostly from Mrs Forbes's friends, telling her how wonderful she was to be doing so much to keep the household together – well, I like that, thought Nanny, tearing it apart more likely. That was about all. Oh no, there was another. Nanny pulled it out from where it lay under the foot of the desk.

She recognised the name on the top of the letter heading: it was the architect Mr Harrington had been working with, he'd telephoned the house a couple of times, Dominic Foster. What on earth was he doing, writing to Mrs Forbes? Then she saw he wasn't writing to Mrs Forbes: the letter was to Cecily.

Dear Mrs Harrington,
I was so desperately sorry to hear of Benedict's death. It goes without saying that my thoughts are with you at this sad time.

I would very much like to come and see you. I realise you might not find this a welcome prospect, but there is something I would like to talk to you about, in connection with Benedict, and the time leading up to his death. I do realise this might be painful, but I think in the long run you might find it helpful. If you can find it in your heart to allow me to visit you, I would be so very grateful.
Yours sincerely,
Dominic Foster.

'Poor man,' said Nanny aloud, 'what a sweet letter.' She put it back carefully, wondering if Mrs Harrington had indeed seen him, and then went downstairs to tell Mrs Moreton that she had the information she was looking for.

She almost had enough tablets now, Cecily thought: ten. To be on the safe side, she would get twelve, then there would be no chance of her being brought round. She wanted to make quite sure they didn't even try: the girl who had taken the overdose had had to have her stomach pumped, and Cecily had heard the nurse describing it. It sounded appalling, even worse than the forcefeeding. But if she took the twelve pills, plus her own three, at bedtime, and no one checked her until morning, it would be much too late. There would be no point pumping her stomach, because she would be quite, quite dead. Dead and safe.

Cassia ate supper with the family, forcing down mouthfuls of stew and trifle, pressing a monosyllabic Edward for details of his day, listening to Fanny as she recited the Edward Lear poem she and Janet had read together that day, and finally, after tucking William up in bed and taking Edward his coffee, kissed everyone goodbye and said she was so sorry to have to go tonight, but she had a very early start and it would be impossible to get there in time through the ever heavier rush hour traffic. That at least, she thought, was true.

'I have to go to France tomorrow,' said Harry, 'see how my project in Le Touquet is coming along.'

'The hotel? I might come with you. I'm looking for a location for a sportswear sitting, and—'

'Oh, you can't. Sorry. I'm taking a designer with me, no room in the plane.'

'Very well. Not Dominic Foster?'

'No, why?'

'I just wondered. Cecily is still terribly ill, apparently, about to have electric shock treatment.'

'Poor woman,' said Harry.

Only four more days, Bertie thought, burying his head underneath his pillow (not that it was necessary any more, he was past crying, past anything except an exhausted, resigned misery), and then he would be home for half term. Home to his mother, to William, to love; home to his father; to safety, to warmth; home to food he did not have to finish, to a bed where he could sleep in peace; home to Buffy, to Peggy, to freedom. Home. He fell asleep smiling.

439

He awoke, in the thick darkness, to find himself itching violently on the stomach. He scratched it for a bit, threw off his covers to get cool and went back to sleep. And awoke again, as the bell went, hot, itching all over, everywhere, stumbled into the bathroom scratching, feeling dizzy, looked in the mirror.

'Chicken pox, you've got chicken pox, Fallon, I'm afraid,' said Matron firmly. 'Come along with you, up to the san. Bad luck, you won't be able to go home for half term with that. Still, never mind, there's a few others up there, you won't be on your own. Now come along, don't cry, great big boy like you.'

Cassia was waiting for Harry on the doorstep when he arrived, wearing a beige gaberdine jacket and jodhpurs with high brown boots, a cream silk shirt and his pearls around her neck.

'You look beautiful,' said Harry, slamming the door of the car, getting in beside her, revving the engine loudly, hooting at a wandering cat. Thank God it was still dark, she thought, telling him to be quieter, and then lay back in her seat and gave herself up to pleasure.

He kept his plane at a small airfield in Heston, just off the Bath Road in West London; walking towards it, observing how small it was, feeling his arm heavy on her shoulders, she felt, irresistibly, like someone in a film, half expected the scene suddenly to change, to find herself on a beach or in a nightclub.

'It's very ... nice,' she said doubtfully, as Harry demanded her admiration for the plane, studying its pretty lines, its worryingly lightweight-looking wings, the curved hood over the cabin, the jauntily upturned tail. 'What make is it? And what are those things fixed on the wheels?'

'It's a Vega Gull Gipsy Six. To be absolutely accurate. And those things are called spats. The longer ones, like those over there, are called trousers. They're for streamlining.'

'Oh, I see. Is this the same as Rollo Gresham's plane? That he flew in that day, at Brooklands. I don't suppose you remember.'

'Of course I remember,' he said. 'How could I ever forget that day? But anyway, no, it's not the same, his was a Leopard Moth.'

'And has he still got it?' she said casually, seeing an opportunity to learn something of Gresham, of his movements; but Harry's face was blank. Too blank? She was beginning to know that look rather well.

'I'm afraid I have no idea,' he said smoothly. 'I expect so.'

'Because—'

'Cassia, if we are to spend the day discussing Rollo Gresham, I think it would be better for us not to go. Now get in, and keep quiet for a bit.'

She climbed into the cabin, settled herself into the passenger seat, buckled herself in. Harry got in beside her, started fiddling with the instruments, checking them, shouting at the mechanic down on the ground. He switched on the engine; the plane filled with noise, and then moved slowly forward across the grass. She felt briefly scared, thinking how irresponsible she was being, thinking of the considerable risk she was running, the risk not only to herself, but her family; and then that lifted with the plane, became excitement, freedom, a sense of heady, wonderful adventure ...

It was extraordinary going up, just rising through the air so easily, so smoothly, moving towards the blue sky, watching the ground shrinking beneath her, watching trees, houses, roads, become tiny toy things. She gazed down at them enraptured, feeling dizzily safe.

'It's wonderful,' she said, smiling at Harry. 'I can't believe it.'

'Glorious, isn't it? You feel so free up here.'

They seemed to be moving quite slowly; she said so, and he laughed. 'Not terribly. She does a hundred and sixty easily.'

They reached the coast, and she looked down at model cliffs, tiny ships, a sea even bluer than the sky. 'I love it,' she said.

Harry reached across, took her hand and kissed it. 'I'm glad you do. I might have gone off you if you hadn't.'

'Harry, do concentrate,' she said, trained as she was to road travel and its dangers, 'we might hit something.'

'I can't think what,' he said, laughing, 'unless some stray seagull. It's hardly crowded up here. We have it all to ourselves. That's a major part of its charm.'

The French coast appeared with astonishing speed, the long straight beaches of Normandy, the lush flat green of northern France, studded with toy cows. They flew on, into the shining day, following the line of the sea, and then Harry suddenly said, 'There it is, there's Le Touquet now. Pretty, isn't it?'

It was very pretty: a vast and beautiful beach, the great stretches of impossibly perfect green golf courses, glorious maritime pines.

'It's known as Le Touquet Paris Plage,' said Harry, 'because it's so chic that half Paris is here on the beach. And half London as well.'

They turned into a wide estuary; the plane banked, then settled again. The grass of the airfield seemed to reach up to them suddenly, and then they were down.

'Welcome to France,' he said. 'I hope you enjoy your stay.'

'I'm sure I shall,' she said, smiling.

There was a car waiting for them, with an English driver. 'Morning, Mr Moreton. Good flight?'

'Excellent,' said Harry.

'Where to, sir?'

'The Links Hotel.'

In the suite at the Links, apparently reserved for his exclusive use, he ordered coffee, orange juice, champagne, ran a bath. 'It feels like evening already. Or the start of another day. Take that lovely suit off and come and join me.'

'I'm glad you like it. It seemed appropriate.'

'It's wonderful. Very Amy Johnson. But, now, I would prefer it hanging over a chair.'

She sat in the bath with her back to him, his arms round her, holding her breasts. He began to kiss her shoulders, her neck; she dipped her head, kissed his arms, his hands.

'I love you,' she said.

'I love you too.'

He lifted her very slightly, in the water, settled her on to him; she felt him sinking in her, felt strangely taut around him in the hot water.

'You're beautiful,' he said, 'so beautiful,' and began to move, lazily, easily. She felt her own rhythms begin, gently, almost reluctantly at first, then growing in strength, in violence. She leant back against him, her arms flung wide, her head turned to the ceiling, and felt him pushing into her, harder now, urgently. Rippling circles of her own, deep within her, echoing the ones in the water, began to spread, reaching through her, outwards, upwards: she tensed, was still, and then quite suddenly came, in huge, hot breaking waves of pleasure, and cried out again and again as she did, as he came too, that she loved him.

'Well,' he said, passing her a glass of orange juice with one hand, of champagne with the other, 'that is the first objective of the day accomplished.'

'Having a bath?' she said, smiling.

'No,' he said, 'not having a bath. I told you I wanted to fuck you on French soil.'

'But it wasn't soil,' she said, 'it was water.'

'You are appalling,' he said, draining his champagne glass, refilling it, 'a

442

literal-minded pedant. I don't know that I can spend the rest of my life with such a person.'

She shrugged. 'You must please yourself, of course.'

'That is exactly what I am doing,' he said, coming over to kiss her. 'Pleasing myself. Pleasuring myself.'

'And pleasuring me.'

'Naturally. That is part of the pleasure. You have not had enough of it, of pleasure. In its broadest sense, that is, not simply the sexual one. I intend to see you get a great deal more.'

'Well, that will be very nice,' she said.

'I trust it will be more than nice. You really must try to extend your vocabulary, Cassia. I see you are about to tell me I am arrogant,' he added, laughing at her, 'and I suggest you find a new word for that as well. I am going to buy you a *Roget's Thesaurus* as soon as we get back to London, and make you learn ten new words a day. Don't look so cross, you know I don't mean it. You are quite, quite perfect. Well, almost, anyway ...'

Nanny was haunted by the letter from Dominic Foster. She knew it was nothing to do with her, but she felt a sense of responsibility, having seen it, and if Mrs Harrington was really as bad as Mrs Forbes said, then it would be wrong not to make sure at least that Foster had been allowed to speak to her. Bravely, aware that she might quite justifiably incur Mrs Forbes's wrath, she broached the subject early next day.

'Mrs Forbes, I wonder if I might have a word.'

'Yes, Nanny?'

'I do hope you won't think this ... interfering, and I do apologise for what might seem a breach of etiquette, but I was looking for something of Mrs Harrington's yesterday, something to do with Mrs Moreton's fashion show ...'

'Oh, yes?' said Mrs Forbes. She looked slightly less benign. She didn't like Edwina Moreton, Nanny knew. 'And did you find it?'

'Yes, I did. I had to look through the desk in the spare room, though. I do hope you don't mind, it was Susan's suggestion—'

'Well, that was very wrong of you. Many of the letters in there are private. I am more than a little surprised at you, Nanny.'

'I'm sorry, Mrs Forbes, but Mrs Moreton was in a considerable hurry and—'

'Mrs Moreton is always in a hurry. It's a very unattractive quality. Anyway, do go on.'

'Well, I did find the file. About the fashion show. But I just couldn't help seeing a letter to Mrs Harrington from – from Mr Foster.' Oh dear, this was beginning to go really badly: Mrs Forbes had an ugly flush on her face, and her eyes as she looked at her were very hard and glittering. 'It sounded as if – well, as if he might be able to help Mrs Harrington. Make her feel better. And I thought – as she was so very ill – that anything ...' Her voice faltered.

'Nanny, I have to tell you I am very shocked by this. By your behaviour. It far exceeds anything that might be expected of someone in your position. It was very wrong of you to go through my desk, and even more wrong to read my personal correspondence.'

'I'm sorry, Mrs Forbes. Very sorry. But ...' Indignation gave her courage: it wasn't Mrs Forbes's desk; it hadn't been her personal correspondence, far from it. 'But it just seemed, under the circumstances, too important to ignore. I mean, did Mr Foster go and see Mrs Harrington? Because I really think—'

'I told you, Nanny, I am not in the least interested in what you think. I am rather surprised and very disappointed in you. When my daughter is better, I shall certainly see it as my duty to inform her of it. But since you ask, and as it happens, I told Mr Foster there was no question of him seeing my daughter at the moment, she is far too ill. And he was quite happy to accept my decision, naturally. Now perhaps you should go to the nurseries and confine your energies to your duties. On all future occasions.'

'Yes. Mrs Forbes. I'm sorry.'

Nanny left the room flushed and near to tears; in the ten years she had worked for the Harringtons, in the twenty years she had worked for the family before that, she had never been spoken to so harshly. Of course she had overstepped the boundaries of her position – she was aware of that, had apologised profusely for it – but the situation was serious enough and her affection for Mrs Harrington deep enough to warrant it; moreover, she had no intention of stopping now.

The more she thought of poor Mrs Harrington lying in the nursing home, about to endure the rigours of electric shock treatment, the angrier she felt, and the more she thought she ought to do something about it. But what? Who could she go to? She could ring up Dominic Foster herself, of course, but he was hardly going to override any decision of Ada Forbes. Or was he? It could make matters worse.

Then she thought of Edwina Moreton. She was very sensible really, related to Mrs Moreton by marriage after all, she would care, she would be able to help. Yes, that was a good idea. She'd telephone Mrs Moreton at her magazine, once Mrs Forbes had finished her breakfast, and retired

444

to the lavatory for the half-hour session there that followed her breakfast every morning, and talk to her about it.

But Mrs Moreton wasn't there: neither at home, nor her office. She was out for the day, the secretary in the fashion department said, in a very bored voice, on a photographic session. 'But if she does get back, which is extremely unlikely, I'll ask her to give you a call.'

'Thank you.'

Nanny sighed; it would just have to wait. At least until the evening. She wondered wildly if she should ring Mr Moreton, but she was much too frightened of him to contemplate it seriously. One more day wouldn't matter, surely.

Harry and Cassia walked along the wide promenade of Le Touquet, holding hands, not talking very much. It was a glorious day, white and blue and becoming windy; the air was headily clear.

'This is lovely, so lovely,' she said. 'I feel ...'

'What do you feel?'

'Perfectly, absolutely perfectly happy.'

'Good,' he said briskly. 'That's exactly what I want you to feel.'

Later they had lunch in one of the small streets of the town; she had become slightly cold, and the restaurant, small, dim, seductively rich smelling, was wonderfully welcoming.

'I've turned into such a wicked person,' she said suddenly with a sigh, reaching for his hand, stroking it across the table.

'Really? In what way?'

'Oh, selfish, deceitful, irresponsible, all the things I most disapprove of.'

'And what has brought about this change in you? I hope you are not laying the blame at my door.'

'No, of course not,' she said. 'This – us – is merely the manifestation of it. Of the wickedness. No, it was the money, I'm afraid. It has done terrible things to me.'

'Nonsense,' he said briskly, 'that money has only done one thing to you: given you some courage. Courage to be yourself. I'm delighted with it, your money.'

'I dare say you are,' she said, looking at him thoughtfully, grateful for the slightly confusing effects of all the wine she had drunk, that she could allow her brain to pursue this. 'So are you implying I was always wicked, always deceitful and selfish?'

'I think,' he said, raising her hand to his mouth and kissing it, 'I think you are neither entirely wicked nor entirely good, merely interesting.

Extremely interesting. And the interesting person was being stifled, crushed. Now she is emerging, in a most satisfactory way. How does that sound?'

'Totally unreassuring,' she said, laughing, 'but I'm too drunk to argue with you.'

'It's never a good idea to argue with me, drunk or sober. I always win,' he said, waving at the waiter, asking for the bill. 'And now you must excuse me, I have my business meeting. Will you be all right? Go and look at the shops, they're quite wonderful, the very best are on the rue de Paris. I'll meet you back in the hotel at four. Take a taxi. Then we can have tea, before going back.'

'I don't want to go back,' she said. 'I really don't want to.'

'That's because you are not being sensible, and coming to live with me. I have no sympathy, no sympathy at all.' He reached to kiss her across the table. 'Goodbye. I'll see you later.'

Cassia wandered out of the restaurant, found the rue de Paris, which was indeed wonderful, bought herself a silk sweater and a white silk scarf for Harry, then walked back in the direction of the promenade, wanting to breathe in more of the sea, fill herself with it, make it part of her, part of this lovely day.

She stopped at a café for a hot chocolate, then reached for a guide book she had picked up in the hotel. And read of the casino, a very fine casino (it said), and found the thought absolutely irresistible. The Casino du Palais, one of Leonora's old haunts.

She went out of the café, found a taxi.

She hadn't meant to go in, of course, merely to look at it, but admiring its splendour, trying to imagine Leonora, her friends, Rollo Gresham, in there, she did walk in through the door, stood slightly uncertainly in the foyer, looking round her.

A man came over to her, clearly some kind of hall porter, shook his head.

'*Madame, je regrette, c'est fermé.*'

'Oh, no matter. Do you speak English?'

'A little.'

'I thought you might remember my godmother, Leonora Beatty. She came here quite often, I believe.'

'Ah, Lady Beatty. A most beautiful and very lovely lady. So sad, I was so sorry to hear that she had died. She died in Paris, I believe?'

'Yes, that's right.'

'Yes, she would come here, in a big party in the old days, with

Monsieur Gresham and their friends. She was always very kind to me, always asked how I was.'

'She was always very kind to everyone,' said Cassia soberly. Coming on the high emotion of the day, talking about Leonora in such vivid terms, upset her; she was surprised to find tears at the back of her eyes. She smiled at the man. 'And do any of them come here now, her friends, Mr Gresham perhaps?'

'Some of the friends, yes, but not Mr Gresham. We have not seen him for some time now.'

'Oh really? I wonder why not.'

'I really could not say, madame.' He seemed awkward, even slightly embarrassed, suddenly. She was intrigued, pressed on.

'Well, is there some problem, is he in trouble?'

'Madame, you must ask the friends of Lady Beatty. They will know perhaps, they will have news for you.'

'I'm afraid I don't know any of those friends,' said Cassia firmly, 'so I would like you to tell me what you know. Is Mr Gresham ill perhaps? Because if he is, then—'

Another man, in morning dress, clearly more important, appeared through a door in the foyer. The doorman looked at him gratefully. '*Est-ce qu'il y a un problème, Henri?*'

The doorman spoke rapidly to him in French, looking sideways at Cassia from time to time. She heard the names Beatty and Gresham, and suddenly felt rather sick. Too much wine at lunch, no doubt: or maybe the oysters Harry had insisted on feeding her ('although God knows why: you of all people have no need of aphrodisiacs').

The second man came over to her, looked at her slightly coldly. 'Madame, good afternoon. I understand you were enquiring about Monsieur Gresham?'

'Yes. He was a great friend of my godmother, Lady Beatty. She has died, as I believe you know.'

'Indeed. Please accept my condolences.'

'Thank you. And I have heard nothing from Mr Gresham for quite a while. I just wondered if he might still come here.'

'No, madame, he does not. We also have not seen Monsieur Gresham for some time.' There was a note in his voice she didn't like, or even understand: heavy, almost hostile.

'Oh. Oh, I see.' She waited. There seemed to be no more to come.

He gave her the same distant smile. 'Is there anything else I can do for you, madame?'

'I was hoping to make contact with Mr Gresham. I have written to him, at the only address I have, but received no reply. I thought perhaps you might—'

'I know nothing of Monsieur Gresham's whereabouts, madame. Unfortunately.' Again the hostility. 'I would suggest you ask his friends, perhaps.'

'I can't really do that,' she said, aware that she sounded foolish, not caring very much. 'I don't know any of his friends.'

'Well, then I'm afraid I really cannot help you. And now if you will excuse me ...' He clearly wanted to be rid of her, saw her as a tedious and potentially embarrassing force.

'Yes, of course. I wonder if I could leave my card here. You could give it to one of these ... friends. Ask them to contact me.' She handed it to him.

He took it, looked at it disdainfully, turning it over in his hand. Clearly the addresses on it were not of the calibre he would have looked for.

'Of course, madame. If I do see any of them.'

'Thank you.' The card would, no doubt, go straight into the waste paper bin. He bowed to her. 'Good afternoon, madame,' he said, and disappeared back into his office.

Cassia thanked the man on the door and turned away. She felt odd: physically and mentally. A second wave of nausea hit her, nausea and dizziness; she looked round for a chair, saw one by the door and half walked, half staggered over to it. She sank down, and put her head between her knees.

The porter hurried over to her, looking concerned. 'Madame, are you all right? Can I get you anything? A glass of water, perhaps? Call a taxi?'

'No, no, it's quite all right.' She'd probably caused the poor man enough trouble – she'd get him the sack if he had to go to any more trouble for her. 'Just a dizzy spell. I'm fine now.'

'May I suggest, madame, the café, just down the street. You could get a coffee there perhaps, a brandy.'

'Yes. Yes, I'll go there, thank you.'

'And madame – ' he hesitated – 'the patron there, he knew Monsieur Gresham well. He might have some news of him for you.'

'Oh, thank you.' She smiled at him. 'Thank you very much.'

Sitting in the café, sipping iced water – why couldn't you ever get iced water in England? – and strong coffee alternately, she felt better. When the waiter came for the money, she said, 'Is the owner of the restaurant here? I would like to speak to him, if he has time.'

'One moment, madame. I will ask.'

They all spoke English so well, she thought irrelevantly. Presumably it was in their interest to do so: there were a great deal of English visitors, spending a great deal of money. There was a small group of women in the corner now, drinking cognac, well dressed, talking loudly, a pile of shopping bags set at their feet.

'Madame? You wished to see me. No problem, I hope?' A short, stout man, the patron had dark hair and black eyes, and had clearly been rather good-looking in his youth. He smiled at her.

She returned the smile, said no, no problem at all. But the man at the casino, he said you might have some news of a friend of mine. Well, not exactly a friend. A lost acquaintance ...'

'Indeed, madame? Perhaps. And what is the name of this acquaintance?'

'Gresham. Mr Rollo Gresham.'

'Ah, Monsieur Gresham. We miss him, he was a very ... cheerful gentleman.'

'He was indeed,' said Cassia politely, trying to equate the loud vulgarity of Rollo Gresham with cheerfulness. 'So he never comes here now?'

'No, madame. He never does.'

'You don't know why that is?'

The same awkwardness again, then he said, 'Well, madame, he – well, he had some problems. But you will know of them, I expect.'

'No,' said Cassia, her heart beginning to race uncomfortably. 'No, I didn't. What sort of troubles? Were they – ' God, she shouldn't be doing this, it was dangerous, deadly – 'were they financial?'

He hesitated. 'It is really not for me to say, madame. I'm sorry.'

'Please!' she said. 'It's important to me. My godmother, Lady Beatty, you know, she was ... with him, for the last few years of her life.'

'Ah, Lady Beatty. So beautiful a lady, so kind. I was so sorry to hear she had died.'

'Yes,' she said, 'yes, thank you. But you see, she died in Paris, and I didn't know until it was too late, and I am trying to find out what happened to Mr Gresham since then. If he's really in trouble I need to know.'

He looked at her as if trying to assess her, the reasons behind her need to know, then said suddenly, 'He was in some financial trouble, madame, yes. He had – what is the word, *il manque de l'argent* – ah yes, debts. Everywhere here. Many people knew that, there is no harm my telling you.'

'Yes, I see,' she said. 'And were they large debts, do you know?'

449

He smiled. 'What is large, madame? To me it is a hundred francs, to you, perhaps a thousand, to Monsieur Gresham maybe a million.'

'A million! He had debts of a million francs?'

'*Non non*, madame, I do not say that. Merely that if you are very rich, it is possible for your debts to be very large. I do not know the size. I can only tell you there was a problem, that we do not see him any more.'

'Yes, I see,' said Cassia again. She was finding it hard to say anything remotely coherent. 'And how long has it been since you have seen him? Can you remember?'

'Oh, not so very long, madame. A year ...' He paused. A year would be all right, she thought, a year would be perfectly all right. 'No, more than that, of course, it must be two years, *ah, le temps est disparu*. It was the summer the Prince, your King now, of course, was in Biarritz. Monsieur Gresham and Lady Beatty had met him there, I remember Monsieur Gresham telling us.'

Yes, thought Cassia, he certainly would have told you about it, he wouldn't have let that go unremarked. But two years ... the time ground into her brain. 'And you haven't seen him since?'

'Oh, perhaps a little, madame. But not ... not as we did.'

There could still be explanations, Cassia, of course there could; temporary difficulties, they did happen, and then people recovered again. She heard a voice from the past year, at Benedict's and Cecily's villa in France, a man's voice saying, 'Isn't that Gresham's house down there?' and another answering, 'He's sold it now.' And the house in England, the one in *Country Life*, that too on the market ...

'And you don't know where he is now?' she said, her voice sounding rather loud, loud with fright.

'I believe he is living in North Africa, madame. That was the last story I had heard.'

'North Africa! Goodness, why?'

'It is not such a strange idea for a man who loves France,' he said quickly, smiling at her. 'The food is French, or some of it, French is spoken in all the cities, many many French people go there. And it is very beautiful ...' He smiled.

'Yes, I can see that. But you don't have an address for him there?'

'No, madame. I do not. I'm so sorry.'

'Well, if you see any of his old friends, perhaps you could ask them to be in touch with me? Here's my card, look, there are two addresses.'

He bowed. 'Thank you, madame. I will do my best,' but she got the same impression: that the card would not be passed on, that she would not find Rollo Gresham this way.

What was it all about, what had happened to him? She sighed.

The patron smiled at her. 'And now, madame, another coffee, a brandy perhaps? You look a little pale.'

'A coffee perhaps, thank you. And thank you for your help. I'm so grateful.'

She sat there for a long time, staring on to the street, trying to make a little sense of it at least, to persuade herself that sense could be made of it: trying and failing.

Dominic Foster was working on a new building for the City of London when Harry Moreton phoned him late that afternoon.

'Dominic, *bonjour.*'

'You sound very cheerful, Harry. Awful line, though – I can hardly hear you.'

'Sorry, I'll shout. Look, would you be interested in doing some work over here? It could be a very nice job. I want to put up a second hotel, further along the coast.'

'Which coast? Where are you?'

'Le Touquet.'

'For Christ's sake, Harry, no wonder I can't hear you. Look, phone me when you get back. The short answer's yes, of course.'

'All right. I'll be back tonight. *Au revoir.*'

Dominic put the phone down and sighed. It seemed a very long time since he had felt cheerful.

'You're very quiet,' said Harry. 'What's the matter?'

'Oh, nothing. Honestly.' She smiled at him. They were in the car, driving back to the airfield, through wide streets set with huge villas. It was cloudy now, stormy-looking, and her mood had changed, changed with the day, with what she had learnt.

'Cassia, if there's one thing I cannot stand, it's being told there's nothing the matter when there clearly is. Especially by a woman. Now what is it?'

'I just don't want to go back,' she said. She could face neither a further fight with him over her anxieties, nor confronting them herself.

'Oh Christ.' He had been sitting with his arm round her; he withdrew it, pulled away from her.

'What? What have I done?'

'Told me a lie.'

'I haven't told you a lie,' she said. 'I don't want to go back.'

'You have told me a lie. That's not the problem. Not this one, anyway.

451

Now please can we get it out of the way, or shall I just get on with some work? I have no intention of sitting here trying to coax something out of you.'

'I'm sure you don't,' she said shortly, 'and there's no need. Could we perhaps discuss the weather or something straightforward like that?'

'It's not straightforward, as a matter of fact,' he said, looking out of the window, up at the sky. 'It looks quite stormy. It might be a difficult ride back.'

'I don't care,' she said, and meant it. A difficult ride would suit her mood.

It was almost five o'clock. The sky was extraordinary, rolling black clouds, drenched with great shafts of light here, poured over with red and orange there, and occasionally stretches still of pure aquamarine blue.

'Bit stormy up there, Mr Moreton,' said the mechanic, pulling up some steps for Cassia to climb into the cockpit. 'Could be an exciting trip.'

'Excellent,' said Harry. He climbed into the pilot's seat, buckled his straps, looked across at her.

'You all right?'

'Yes, of course.'

They skimmed across the airfield, took off in an easy, smooth lift from the ground, seemed to slide through the lower clouds into the drama beyond. It was like another country up there, another landscape, such as Cassia had never seen. She clapped her hands with pleasure like a small child at the sight of it: great cliffs and seas of clouds, grey and orange waterfalls tumbling into black, sudden sheets of white, an apparent infinity. It was as if they were on a great highway, driving rather than flying, their way ahead easily charted, as if the great banks and cliffs of cloud were landmarks; she looked at Harry, as he sat at the controls, absolutely absorbed and intent, and thought that she had only seen that look before when they were in bed.

A mass of something hard struck the windscreen: she jumped.

'Hail,' he said briefly, and then there was a huge engulfing flash of light and a monumental sound that seemed to enfold them, swallow them up in itself, and they dropped suddenly, in a perpendicular descent that left her shocked, physically and mentally. He put out his hand, briefly, clasped hers. 'It's OK,' he said, 'only a storm, don't be frightened.'

'I'm not,' she said, as the sound came again and they dropped once more, and she wasn't, she was excited, exhilarated, intensely alive.

On they rode, through the churning clouds, the noise, the dazzling light, and it was like sex, she thought, exactly like sex: an endless series of

452

peaks and swoops, on into infinity, brilliant light, then shadow, then greater brilliance still, and more than once she heard herself, as she did in bed, cry out with the strange, fierce pleasure of it.

It was over, in the end, and, also as with sex, they moved into quietness, a clearer, simpler sky. She could see now the field below them, its colour somehow strange and unfamiliar after the country they had left behind, and the plane landed lightly and with extraordinary ease. And as it came to rest, she looked at Harry, and he at her, slightly shaken, both of them, at what they had shared. They smiled at one another and Harry reached out again and took her hand as he had earlier and lifted it to his lips and kissed it.

'Dear God, I love you,' he said.

CHAPTER 26

'Where the hell have you been?'

'You know perfectly well where I've been. I told you. I've been to Le Touquet.'

'I mean this evening. You said you'd be back for dinner. I waited over an hour and a half, I wanted to talk to you about something.'

'I've been in the office. Discussing things with Matthew Hardacre. Is that all right, or do you want to phone him and check?'

'Don't be absurd.'

'Well, you're acting like a jealous wife.'

'Now you are being absurd. I just find it rather irritating to delay dinner for you and then have you not turn up.'

'I do have a company to run. It can't always revolve round your domestic arrangements, I'm afraid. Anyway, what did you want to talk about? Your fashion show? Your job? Your next dinner party?'

'No,' said Edwina, 'Cecily.'

'Oh, really?'

'Yes, Cecily's nanny telephoned this evening. She'd been trying to get hold of Cassia, but apparently she wasn't either at her house or the clinic.'

'Edwina, am I supposed to be answerable for Cassia's whereabouts as well as my own?'

'No, of course not. The point is, Nanny was worried. Apparently, she found some letter that Dominic Foster had written to Cecily, asking her if he could come and see her, to talk about Benedict's death. He seemed to think it was important, that it would help. Anyway, Nanny asked the dreadful Ada if he had been to see Cecily and she said no.'

'This is all extremely interesting, Edwina, but I do have other things to attend to.'

'Harry, don't be so bloody callous.'

Just for a moment he looked contrite, then he said, 'Well, what would you like me to do?'

'I do think, given that Cecily is so very ill, about to have this horrible treatment, we should at least find out what it is that Dominic has to tell her, don't you? I mean, it might help.'

'Oh, I don't know.' He pushed his hair back wearily. He was looking very tired, Edwina thought, tired and distracted. 'Do we have to get involved?'

'Nanny thinks it's important. She must do, poor soul, she's got into frightful trouble with Ada, doing all this. It's a measure of her devotion to Cecily she's carried on with it. And I can see why.'

He looked at her sharply. 'You really are worried, aren't you?'

'Yes, I am, and if you don't talk to Dominic, I will.'

'All right. I have to phone him anyway, about a new project of mine in Le Touquet. Can you ask Bishop to bring me a brandy? I'll be in my study.'

Edward's voice on the telephone was coldly polite. 'I tried to get you at the clinic, but I was told you weren't there this afternoon.'

'No,' she said quickly, 'I was at another one. I told you, it was an emergency.'

'Ah, yes. So complex, all your arrangements. Now, I'm afraid I have some slightly unfortunate news. Bertie has chicken pox.'

'Oh no! Poor little boy. He ought to be at home if he's ill.'

'He's being perfectly well cared for, I'm sure, but he won't be able to come home for half term apparently.'

'Not come home? But Edward, why not? It's not a dangerous illness. I can collect him in the car and—'

'Cassia, the school rule is that anybody with an infectious illness must remain in the sanatorium until quarantine is over. I can understand that. However, they have said that we may visit him.'

'Well, that's extremely kind of them.'

'So I told Matron that you would phone and make the necessary arrangements.'

'Don't you want to be involved?'

'I will join you if I can. I think that is best.'

'Yes, all right, Edward. I expect I'll go tomorrow.'

'Surely you have a clinic tomorrow?'

'I can cancel it. Easily. Bertie is much more important.'

'How very curious your work seems to be, Cassia. One clinic is so pressing you have to leave the house the night before to be there on time, another of so little importance you can simply cancel it at a moment's notice.'

She was silent; she dared not start an argument over this of all things. 'I'll phone you, then.'

'Very well. How was your day, by the way?'

'My day? Oh, all right. Bit difficult. How about yours?'

'Much the same as usual. Pretty tedious, actually.'

'Edward, I still don't know why— Oh, look, I'd like to talk to you. Maybe on the way to the school?'

'Maybe. I can't imagine what we might have to talk about, but yes, if you want to.'

She phoned the school. Matron said Bertie was very uncomfortable and miserable, but, as of course Mrs Fallon would know, her husband being a doctor, chicken pox was the least serious of all the childhood illnesses.

'I am also a doctor, as a matter of fact, Matron,' she said, unable to help herself, shocked at her own pettiness.

'Indeed? I had not realised that.' She sounded disapproving rather than impressed. 'Well, be that as it may, I do know your son would like to see you. He's very upset about not coming home for half term.'

'Yes, well, I'd like to talk to you about that. Could I come tomorrow?'

'That would be perfectly all right, Mrs Fallon. In the afternoon, perhaps?'

'Yes, fine. Goodnight, Matron. Please – ' 'Give Bertie a kiss from me,' she had been going to say, but then didn't, afraid he might be thought foolish, should anyone else hear the message, a mummy's boy. 'Please give him my love. Tell him I'll see him tomorrow.'

Rupert read the article first. He was sleeping badly, fretting over the opening of *Letters*, now only a week ahead, had woken early, his stomach churning, and gone for a walk, down towards the Embankment. He stood there on Albert Bridge, oddly calmed by the loveliness of early morning on the Thames, the mist rising off it, the eerily beautiful light, the heavy industrial craft working their way slowly through the water, the great stretch of buildings on the banks, the Houses of Parliament gleaming in the sun.

It was a cold morning, as well as a beautiful one, and after a while he bought himself a cup of tea from a stall, and then saw a newspaper stand just beyond it, asked for *The Times*, and saw on the front page of the *Sketch* a strapline advising him that they had done a round-up of all the West End shows, both new and longstanding, in an easy-to-view guide. He bought that too: maybe, maybe they would have mentioned *Letters*. His friend had promised he would get the piece in if he could. He had.

'CHILDHOOD SWEETHEARTS UNITED IN WEST END VENTURE,' Rupert read (the headline set above smudgy photographs of the childhood sweethearts in question), and then in growing, crawling horror, an account of Cassia's involvement with *Letters* that implied a relationship between them at least as passionate and illicit as that between Laurence Olivier and Vivien Leigh:

Rupert Cameron, star of the highly original new production *Letters*, has been the most important figure in Cassia Fallon's life since she was an impressionable young girl of fifteen. He was her father's best friend, and she used to long for his visits on tour to Leeds, the city where she grew up, so that she could see him on the stage, and even more excitingly, in his dressing room afterwards. He stayed in the family home when he was playing in Leeds, rather than in theatrical digs, and was a thrilling addition to family life for the young girl, who would wait up for him to come home, while the rest of the household was asleep, to ply him with hot chocolate and to hear his stories of the night's performance. He was her confidant and mentor, encouraging her to train as a doctor, and although she is now married and has a young family, it is Mr Cameron she regards as her 'very best and dearest friend'.

Recently, Mrs Fallon came into a large sum of money which enabled her to invest in *Letters*, the play in which he is finally launching his West End career, something which before her intervention was denied to him. As the major backer, she is an important part of the production, which is an unusual show, tracing the close relationship between two people who have loved and remained faithful to one another over a span of many years, despite marriages to other people. There could be echoes here of real life for Mrs Fallon and Mr Cameron!

When I arrived at the theatre, I found Mrs Fallon sitting in the empty stalls transfixed by her 'dearest friend's' performance; indeed, she refused to speak to me until the scene was over. She told me it was her greatest ambition that the play might be successful and Mr Cameron become a star. 'It is so very exciting to think that I have been able to help make this possible.'

Mrs Fallon, who is a very attractive young woman, and was a leading debutante in her day, now lives in the country with her family, and also has a house in London where she spends much of the week: 'This makes it possible for me to see more of Rupert –

and the rehearsals, of course,' she added with a gay laugh. 'But of course we are only good friends, nothing more than that.'

Letters opens in a week's time at the Second House theatre on the Embankment. Mrs Fallon will, of course, be at the first night, although her husband, who works hard in his country practice, is not expected to be there.

'Oh my God,' Cassia half whispered, looking at Rupert across the kitchen table. 'This is appalling. How on earth did it happen? I said so little.'

'Did you?' he said. He was white, shaking, smoking, most unusually, cigarette after cigarette. 'Did you really?'

'Rupert, I hope you're not implying this was in any way my fault.'

'So how did he know all this rubbish, about you and me being alone in the house, when everyone else was asleep, and you living in London, away from your husband? And where on earth did they find that photograph?'

'I don't know: some old copy of the *Tatler*, I suppose, I was only about eighteen. And I suppose I told him those things. But they were so unimportant, meant to be funny, some of them. He's twisted them, made them into something quite different. We can sue them, can't we? I'll ring a solicitor, there's surely something we can do.'

'There's nothing we can do, Cassia. There's nothing here that's not true, and nothing you didn't tell him.'

'It's so unfair,' said Cassia, getting up, pacing up and down the kitchen, 'so terribly unfair. I was only trying to be helpful, and he promised to let me read whatever he'd written. I'm going to complain to his editor.'

'Cassia, they always promise to let you read it. Oh God, I should never have let you talk to him—'

'Let me! Rupert, you made me talk to him, you asked me to because you said it would help.'

'I know, I know. I'm sorry.' He pushed his hands through his hair. 'Whatever will Edward think?'

'God knows. Or what he'll do, and as for—'

'As for who?'

'Harry,' she had been going to say, bit the name back. 'Oh, you know, Janet, the village, the children, all our friends. Maybe they won't see it, Rupert, maybe—'

'They'll see it,' he said. 'They'll see it all right.'

'Cassia?' It was Harry. 'What is this wonderful story in the *Sketch*? I love

458

the vision of you as a theatrical angel, buying some illicit passion. With a rather elderly lover, it must be said. Your father's best friend, indeed.' He was laughing; she supposed that at least was something to be thankful for.

'Harry, it isn't funny.'

'Isn't it? I find it extremely funny. Can I have lunch with you, somewhere very public, gain notoriety from my association with you?'

'No, you can't,' she said irritably. 'I'm keeping very well out of sight, and besides, I'm going down to see Bertie at school this afternoon, he's got chicken pox.'

'Poor little brute. Can I come too?'

'No, Harry. Don't be ridiculous. I've got enough problems ...' She heard her voice shake; heard his own change to one of concern.

'You're really upset, aren't you? It isn't so very important. Particularly under the circumstances.'

'What circumstances?'

'Well, you hardly want to preserve your marriage, do you? This could be quite helpful if it was read out in your divorce suit, I'd have thought.' He was laughing again.

'Oh, Harry, don't! Please don't.'

'All right, I'm sorry. Incidentally, talking of divorce, did you see another item in the newspaper? Of rather less national interest, of course, but still quite intriguing. Mrs Simpson was granted her decree nisi yesterday. At Ipswich Crown Court. Now we shall see feathers fly. Read it, it might distract you. Look, let's have a drink before you go. I'll meet you in the bar at the Dorchester at twelve. No, don't argue. You need some Dutch courage, before having to face the doctor. I presume he's going to Bertie's school with you. I'll see you then.'

One of the younger nurses at the nursing home saw the article, recognised Cassia Fallon's name as that of the lady who had brought over several things for Mrs Harrington when she had first been brought in and had telephoned several times since, and read it excitedly to her colleague over breakfast.

'She seemed such a nice lady. Who would have thought it? She didn't seem that sort of person at all. And her husband a doctor. Poor man.'

'What difference does that make?'

'Well, I don't know, it just seems more ... wrong somehow. A leading debutante, she was, you know what that means, very spoilt—'

They were interrupted by Sister, who had come in in a very bad temper, having received a dressing-down from Matron in her turn, to complain about the state of the linen room. 'You can put that newspaper away, Nurse, and go up and see to Mrs Harrington. I want her bed changed. She's got two visitors coming this afternoon, two gentlemen – Mr Moreton and Mr Foster – but you're not to mention that to her, Mr Moreton said when he telephoned.'

'Yes, Sister. No, Sister. Certainly, Sister.'

As if it did any good saying anything to poor Mrs Harrington: she never took anything in.

Cecily had not, of course, seen the article; but she was taking little in that day. She felt strangely elated, almost happy. She had saved enough pills now, and tonight she would take them. This was her last day; it was almost over.

Nanny saw the paper lying in the kitchen when she went down to fetch Mrs Forbes a cup of herb tea after breakfast. Poor Mrs Forbes was not feeling at all well, said she could feel one of her bilious attacks coming on; so great was her misery that she had clearly decided to let bygones be bygones with Nanny. Or rather, Nanny thought grimly, so that she could use Nanny to run around after her, nursing her. She really couldn't imagine how so unpleasant a woman should be the mother of so sweet and kind a daughter.

Cook took the *Sketch*, and had been reading the article about Cassia and Rupert aloud to a goggle-eyed Susan when they heard Nanny's footsteps on the stairs. Cook threw it hastily down on the table and attacked a ball of pastry with her rolling pin. Nanny, waiting for the kettle to boil, saw the headline and, not wishing to show an unseemly interest in what she called the guttersnipe press, managed to read the entire article upside down. She was very shocked.

In the village of Monks Heath, there was talk of little else, every inhabitant, from Milly Hascombe, who took in washing, to Mrs Venables, reading her cook-general's copy while pretending not to, much as Nanny was doing in London, was consumed with excitement by it. 'Poor doctor,' was the phrase on everyone's lips, followed by some variation on the observation that everything had been perfectly all right until Mrs Fallon had come into that money.

Dr Fallon conducted himself with great dignity; only Maureen had witnessed him cracking a cup as he set it down with quite extraordinary violence on his desk in the study, and hurling a copy of the *Sketch* into the waste paper basket – and more poignantly, dashing a brusque hand across his eyes as she asked him if he would prefer to take surgery, or go down to Mr Harrison in the Drift Cottages, who was complaining of violent chest pains and difficulty in breathing. Wisely, she thought, he opted for Mr Harrison. There were at least five copies of the *Sketch* being read in the waiting room.

Francis Stevenson-Cook also saw the article. He made it his business to skim through all the papers before leaving for the office, very often sitting in his extremely large bed and consuming what served him as breakfast – a raw egg beaten up in milk – along with the news and gossip of the day.

It was Rupert Cameron's name that actually attracted his attention, for he remembered Edwina telling him that Rupert had choreographed some of the fashion show. He read the piece with interest and growing amusement, and picked up the magnifying glass he kept by his bed, the better to study Cassia's picture. It had clearly been taken many years earlier, at some debutante party, but it was still possible to discern a beautifully shaped head, a fine neck, a tall slender body. He could see how Edwina Moreton could have cast her as a mannequin in her fashion show. She sounded a rather interesting person, if a naive one; he looked forward to meeting her, and picked up the telephone that stood by his bed.

His unfortunate secretary, whose working day began at any time from seven onwards, said that yes, she would certainly arrange for Mrs Moreton to be available for lunch that day.

'The only thing I mind,' said Harry, raising his glass to Cassia, 'is having Rupert established as your childhood sweetheart. When really of course it was me. Perhaps you could ask the *Sketch* to publish a correction to that effect tomorrow.'

'Oh, Harry, please! It isn't funny.'

'I think it's extremely funny. So does Edwina. She phoned me from the offices of *Style* to make sure I'd seen it.'

'Oh God!'

'What do you think the doctor will have to say?'

'I don't know. Not a lot, I expect. He doesn't say anything much to me at all these days.'

'Well, I think he might break his rule about this. Pretty distressing stuff, I'd say, for a husband to read over his breakfast egg.'

'Do you really think so?'

'Well, of course I do. It does more or less describe an adulterous

461

passion. The irony being, of course, that your adulterous passion is for someone quite different.'

'Yes,' she said listlessly, 'I suppose so.'

'The other irony is,' he said, leaning back in his chair, his eyes amused, 'that a few weeks ago I was extremely irritated by a suggestion of Edwina's that you and Rupert were having an affair.'

'Oh, really?' said Cassia. The dizziness and nausea of yesterday seemed to have returned. She finished what was left of her martini rather too quickly and tried to smile at Harry.

'Yes. I tried to be grown up about it, of course. To tell myself you were after all childhood sweethearts, as the *Sketch* expresses it so elegantly. And then a couple of days after that she mentioned she'd called at your house one evening and that Rupert had been there. She saw that as proof positive, and I must admit even I found it a little unsettling. Then things took a rather different turn, as you know, and I forgot all about him. Until today. Poor old Cameron. One of life's losers, I'm afraid. Is this play any good, incidentally? We ought to attend the opening night, I think. Show some solidarity. I'll tell Edwina to get some tickets.'

'Yes, it seems very good. What I saw of it.'

'Ah yes, at the rehearsal. Where you were ... what was the word? Transfixed. You see how I have committed the article to memory. Well, it must be good to transfix you.'

'It is,' said Cassia again, 'very good.'

'You really are worried about it, aren't you?' he said suddenly. 'You shouldn't, you know, nobody really takes any notice of the tabloid press.'

'It seems to me, Harry, that everyone takes a great deal of notice of it,' she said.

'Oh, not really. A little cheap amusement, and then tomorrow, someone else.' He leant forward, took both her hands in his. 'It's nonsense, that's all, a bit of fun. Try and see it like that. Amusement for the masses. And as there's absolutely nothing in it, what. can—' He stopped quite suddenly, just sat there, absolutely still, his eyes fixed on hers.

She looked at him, and she could see his expression change. And in spite of the warmth of the Dorchester Hotel bar, of her new sable coat, bought in a fit of sexually induced extravagance the day after she and Harry had first made love, she shivered.

'There isn't anything in it, is there?' he said after a long silence. 'You're not in love with him?'

'No, of course I'm not.' She smiled, hoping, praying he would leave it, leave the subject. He did not.

'And you haven't … had an affair with him?'

She was silent.

'Recently?'

Still, silence. She sat there, her eyes meeting his steadily, not moving, not speaking.

'Dear sweet Jesus,' he said, 'you have, haven't you? You've been to bed with him. Edwina was right. Well, haven't you? Answer me, Cassia, please.'

'Yes,' she said, her voice very low, 'yes, I have. But it wasn't like you think.'

'Oh, really? Is that really so?' His expression, his voice, were calm; just for a moment she was hopeful, hopeful that he would believe her, would listen to her. Then he leant forward, grabbed her wrist, twisted it upwards, and sat there holding her by it.

'Do tell me how it was not how I think. I would very much like to know. Does his cock grow backwards? Does he make love standing on his head? Or is—'

'Harry, please! Please!'

'You are disgraceful,' he said, standing up, releasing her wrist with a violent gesture. 'Disgraceful. I would not have believed it of you. Can this be the woman who expressed great distress the other day at the notion of me sleeping with my own wife?'

His face was white, his expression somehow fixed, rigid. His eyes, brilliantly dark in that whiteness, were full of a dislike and distaste so strong she could feel it like a physical force.

'Well', he said, finally, 'I have clearly been deluding myself. Aided and abetted by you. It seems that even my wife's morals are of a higher calibre than your own. Goodbye, Cassia. I do hope very much we never meet again. In fact, I feel a very strong compunction to be out of this building immediately, if you are going to remain in it. Perhaps you would be kind enough to settle the account. Whores are very highly paid these days, I do believe. But, of course, you would know that …'

CHAPTER 27

Dominic Foster was trying to concentrate on a drawing, and to distract himself from his natural nervousness at the prospect of visiting Cecily in the nursing home that afternoon, when Harry Moreton phoned him. He sounded extremely strained.

'Dominic? Look, I'm sorry, I can't make this afternoon after all. Something's come up. I've asked Edwina if she'll go with you, but she's got a luncheon or some bloody nonsense. Can we postpone it?'

'I'd rather not. Actually. I think it's very important. Could we go later?'

'No, I don't think so. I really can't, not today. You could go on your own, of course.'

'You know I can't do that, Harry.'

'Well, it'll have to wait, then. Sorry.' And he put the phone down.

Dominic sighed, and returned to his drawing. He was torn between relief and a sense of anticlimax. He had been wanting to get this over for a very long time. Perhaps he should, after all, go on his own. However, it seemed quite possible to him that if he did arrive unannounced, his presence unalleviated, in Cecily's sickroom, he might do a great deal more harm than good. And Nicola was giving a dinner party that evening. No, he'd wait for Harry. It really would be much better. There wasn't so much of a hurry, surely …

Cassia drove much too fast towards St John's school and Bertie. She felt in some strange way she was putting a distance between herself and her unhappiness, and going there, visiting him, was the one thing she could do that was useful, helpful, that would not hurt anyone.

Even her work hurt people, she realised, negotiating a roundabout with rather reckless skill. It forced her to neglect her children, upset her husband. God, she was a wicked woman. What was Harry's word for her? Disgraceful. A strangely paternalistic adjective, thrown at her in that voice, harsh with distaste, but it was a good word, the right one. She did indeed lack grace, in the purest sense of the word, the religious sense. She had fallen from it.

Thinking of words and their pure meaning made her think of Harry, of him instructing her in them, as they lay in bed, through all those lunchtimes, smiling at her, teasing her about her illiteracy, her pedantry.

'Oh God,' she said aloud, and pulled over to the side of the road suddenly and burst into tears. There was a screech of brakes and a squeal of tyres as a car which had been following her rather too closely had to swerve violently; she looked up dully through her tears and saw him shake a fist at her. She didn't care. She almost welcomed it: she deserved to have fists shaken at her, stones thrown even.

After a while, she started the car again and drove on. It wasn't going to help Bertie if she was late.

She was, of course, going alone. An icily courteous Edward had said he was far too busy to come.

'Yes, I see. But Edward, we do need to talk, when I get home.'

'Oh, you're coming home, are you? How very good of you. In the middle of your working week. And do I take that to mean that you have no rehearsals to attend either?'

'Edward, that is just so much nonsense, that article, so ridiculous.'

'Indeed? I had thought it was I who was ridiculous. Or rather had been made to look so. Yes, I agree, we do have something to talk about. Several things.'

Rupert had phoned her just before she had left the house to visit Bertie. She was crying, quite hard, her voice thick with sobs as she answered the phone.

'Oh, my darling, don't. I feel so very dreadful, so responsible for all this.'

'It's all right. It's my fault, really.'

'Was Edward so very upset?'

'Yes,' she said, for that explanation seemed simpler, easier, less ... disgraceful.

'Shall I phone him, try to explain?'

'No,' she said sharply, 'no, don't. That would make things much worse. Look, Rupert, I've got to go. I'm going to see Bertie at school, he's ill and—'

'Oh, darling, as if you haven't got enough to cope with.'

'Rupert, it doesn't matter. Honestly. Bye.'

Misery engulfed her then, so thick, so stifling, she found it physically hard to breathe.

'Company for you, Fallon,' said Matron, smiling. 'One of the big boys has got chicken pox now. Come along, Collins, into bed here, beside Fallon. You can cheer each other up.'

Bertie looked through crusty eyes at Collins, who was smiling bravely up at Matron. 'Thanks, Matron. I feel a bit sick, could I have a bowl, please?'

She bustled off, and Collins looked at Bertie.

'You little turd,' he said, 'this is your fault I'm here, it's your filthy germs I've got. You see that pot over there? I'm going to fill it up and make you drink it, you little piece of shit. Oh, thank you, Matron, thank you very much. Don't worry about me, I'll be fine now, I feel a bit better now I'm lying down. Me and Fallon'll be fine, won't we, Fallon?'

Bertie didn't speak; he just lay looking at Collins, in a state of terror so abject he actually felt as if he was going to mess the bed.

Matron hesitated. Then she said, 'No, I think I'd better stay for a bit. In case you are sick. I've got some sewing to do. Are you all right, Fallon? Your mother will be here soon.'

'Yes, thank you,' said Bertie. His voice sounded faint and shaky, even to himself.

Matron put her hand on his forehead. 'You're still very hot,' she said thoughtfully. 'You've got a really bad dose of this. I might get the doctor to look at you again when he comes to see Collins. You're not drinking enough,' she added severely, looking at the jug by Bertie's bed. 'It's important. I'll just get my sewing and I'll be back.'

'I'll see you a drink a bit more,' said Collins, smiling his angelic smile across at Bertie. 'Gosh, I'm looking forward to meeting your mother. There was an article about her in the paper, did you know? The housemaid showed it to me.'

'What?' said Bertie. His misery just for a moment was forgotten.

'It said she was shagging some bloke. Who isn't your father. Basically.'

'I don't know what you mean,' said Bertie, who didn't.

'You really are an ignorant little squirt aren't you? Screwing, Fallon, having sexual intercourse with. That's what it means. You know what that is, don't you?'

'No,' said Bertie. 'I don't.'

'I'll tell you later. When you've had your drink. Oh, hallo, Matron. What a lot of socks. Are you going to darn them all?'

'Are you happily married?' said Stevenson-Cook suddenly to Edwina. They were coming back in his car from luncheon, prior to meeting Rupert at Style House.

'Well, you know. I'm still married after six years, so I suppose it must be all right. We suit each other pretty well.'

'You don't have any children?'

'No, I can't have any,' said Edwina abruptly. She was surprised she could tell him such a thing, when she had known him for so short a time. He really was dangerously easy to talk to.

'How sad.'

'Yes, I suppose so. It would have been nice, of course. I'm not exactly the maternal type, though.'

'No, you don't seem it,' he said, smiling at her. It was clearly intended as a compliment. She smiled back. 'Tell me about your friend Mrs Fallon, the doctor. I saw something about her in the paper today.'

'Oh, yes. Pretty ghastly, that. Poor Cassia.'

'Is it true, do you think?'

'Oh, I really don't think so,' said Edwina thoughtfully. 'She's a frightfully virtuous sort of person. Always doing good works and so on. I can't imagine her having an affair with anyone. She has always had a huge crush on Rupert, though. They're terribly close. And they do spend a lot of time together. He stays at her house quite often and so on. I have to say I wouldn't really blame her. Her husband is just too dreary for words.'

'Well, I shall look forward to meeting her. And Mr Cameron, of course.'

'Yes, he's very charming. You'll like him. Best not mention the article, though.'

'Mrs Moreton! Or perhaps I might call you Edwina? Away from the office environment, of course.'

'Please do, yes.' She was surprised, but rather pleased.

'And you are to call me Francis. Anyway, of course I won't mention the article. I do have some delicacy, you know.'

He smiled at her. He had extraordinarily nice teeth, she noticed, very white and even. He was extraordinarily good-looking altogether. Those wonderful blue eyes. And extremely amusing and civilised. She liked him more and more.

'Hallo, Bertie.'

She looked so lovely, so much more beautiful even than he remembered. Her lips as she bent to kiss his hot, itching face were so cool, her hair as it fell on to his forehead so soft, she smelt so lovely. It was more than Bertie could bear. He burst into tears, careless of Collins's eyes on him, and sat up, winding his arms round her neck.

'Mummy,' was all he said, over and over again, repeating it like a mantra. He felt not happiness, but as if his heart was going to break.

Cassia sat holding him, her face buried in his soft brown hair, noticing his extreme thinness – surely he had had more flesh on him than this? – his burning temperature, the rather frantic clasp of his arms. Something wasn't right; she knew it wasn't.

'I'll get you a cup of tea, Mrs Fallon,' said Matron, who had been watching this scene with a touch of disapproval. 'Come along now, Fallon, be a big boy, let your poor mother sit down.'

As Cassia sat down, a very good-looking boy in the next bed, much older than Bertie, smiled at her.

She smiled back. 'Hallo.'

'How do you do, Mrs Fallon. Aren't you going to introduce me to your mother, Fallon?'

'Oh, yes,' said Bertie, brushing away his tears. 'Mummy, this is Collins. He's probably going to be head boy next year.'

'How very important,' said Cassia.

'I've been keeping an eye on Fallon,' said Collins, 'as he's so new. Tried to help him a bit. Haven't, I Fallon?'

'Yes,' said Bertie.

'How very kind of you.'

'Oh, not really. The least I could do. And it's really lucky there's two of us in here, to keep each other company. Isn't it, Fallon?'

'Yes, it is.' His voice was low, slightly shaky.

Cassia looked at him thoughtfully. He didn't seem himself. Well, he wouldn't be, he clearly wasn't at all well. He had chicken pox very badly. A couple of the spots on his face were slightly infected; she remarked on this to Matron.

Matron clearly saw this as a reflection on her professional skills. 'Naturally I am aware of that, Mrs Fallon. I have been attending to them.'

'I'm sure you have, Matron. It's just that there's a danger of scarring with chicken pox. That would be a shame.' She smiled encouragingly at Bertie; he stared back at her, trying to smile and failing. She put out her hand, took his, pushed back his hair. Even his scalp was covered in spots.

'Poor old chap. Look, I've brought you some fruit and a few books. Would you like some grapes now? Collins, what about you?'

'Oh, that would be awfully kind of you, Mrs Fallon.'

She sat there for an hour or more, chatting to Bertie, reading him a story. He remained tense, watchful, his eyes huge in his blemished face. She felt increasingly uneasy.

'Darling, I'll be back in a minute. I'm just going to have a word with Matron.'

She found Matron sorting what looked like an impossibly complex pile of socks. 'What a job! A bit like Pelmanism.'

'Indeed,' said Matron. She was clearly still feeling stung by Cassia's criticism.

'Matron, I really would like to take Bertie home. He does seem absolutely wretched.'

'Mrs Fallon, I'm afraid that will be quite impossible.'

'I know it's against the rules, But I can't quite see why, to be honest. It is half term, and extra work for you, of course. I just wonder what the point is of him staying here. I'd love to have him home with us, and I'm sure it would do him good. Of course you're looking after him beautifully, but there's nothing like your own family when you're ill. And he does seem very ... tense.'

'Well, he is, of course, a very highly strung child, Mrs Fallon.'

'I know that. All the more reason to have him home, nurse him back to health there. We're both doctors, you know, my husband and I—'

'Yes, Mrs Fallon, so you told me.'

'Look, could I have a word with the headmaster? I can see it's not your decision.'

'If you wish, of course. But I'm quite sure he will agree with me.'

The headmaster did. Politely, firmly, very slightly patronisingly, he told her it was out of the question, that other boys' parents were less willing, less capable to care for sick children, that it was far better to have one rule for all, that justice might be seen to be done. 'I'm sorry, Mrs Fallon, but in the long run, it could make life more difficult for your son if he is allowed to break the rules.'

Cassia sighed. She could see the logic of that if nothing else.

'Mrs Fallon, I wonder if you will excuse me now. I have a great deal to do, other parents to see ...'

She went very slowly back to the sanatorium. Bertie was alone; Collins had disappeared.

'Hallo, darling. I'm back.'

'Mummy?' He put out a hot little hand, held hers. 'Couldn't I possibly come home?'

'Darling—'

'Please! Please!'

'Fallon,' said Matron, coming in again. 'Don't upset your mother. You know the rules.'

469

'Look,' said Cassia, hating herself for what she knew, deep down, was weakness, what she was telling herself was conforming, best for Bertie, 'look, darling, maybe when you're better. But school rules have to be kept. They really do. They can't make exceptions for one small boy. However miserable. Can they, Collins?' she said to Collins who had come back into the room.

'No, of course not,' said Collins.

'I've got to go now, darling, but I will come back in a day or two. Maybe even tomorrow.'

'Mummy, please!' There was a desperation in his voice, in his eyes.

She struggled, managed to hold firm. 'No, darling. Not today. Now I must go. I've got to go home and see the others and Daddy, of course. I'm sorry.'

She bent to kiss him again, felt him turn from her, heard him stifle a sighing sob. It hurt; it hurt horribly. She stood up, quickly, before she weakened, said goodbye again, waved quite gaily to Collins and half ran from the room.

Bertie looked helplessly at Collins. He could feel the hot tears running down his face; he couldn't help it, he didn't care. He didn't care about anything any more.

'Diddums,' said Collins very quietly, 'poor baby diddums. Come on, over here, have a nice drink, that'll make you feel better. I've been piddling all afternoon, just for you. Matron's gone to take supper. Come on, in with your head ...'

Cassia was halfway down the stairs, when she realised she had forgotten her gloves. She thought at first she would leave them, didn't want to upset Bertie by returning, raising his hopes however briefly. But it was a frosty evening, and her car was very cold; she found it hard to drive with cold hands. Reluctantly, she turned and went back upstairs.

She could hear strange sounds as she started to open the door: a stifled groan, a splashing, a retching noise, a wail of misery. She pushed it wide open, saw two empty beds, saw two figures in the corner of the room, saw Collins standing over Bertie, pushing his head into a chamber pot ...

'What on earth is he doing here?' said Edward, as she carried Bertie into the house, wrapped in blankets. 'I thought the rules at his school were—'

'No longer his school, Edward,' she said. 'He's left it. As of this afternoon. And don't even try to argue with me, please. I've told the headmaster that he and the matron and Bertie's housemaster, and quite possibly a few of the parents, will be extremely fortunate not to find themselves the subject of a further interview with me in the *Sketch* newspaper. A copy of which I found, somewhat to my distress, on his desk. That is, if we don't receive a very full written apology, a confirmation that a boy called Collins and his cohorts have been expelled, and a full refund of the term's fees. Janet, would you help me get Bertie up to bed, please?'

'I rather liked your friend,' said Rupert. He and Edwina were sharing a taxi from Style House; he *en route* to the theatre, she for her house. 'He has great style. Rather appropriately.'

'Doesn't he? I like him too. Hardly my friend, though. Much too grand for that.'

'Oh, Edwina, come along. He clearly admires you greatly. What are his sexual proclivities, do you suppose?'

'Heaven knows. I haven't really thought about it. I suppose he's a fairy. But quite a sexy one. Anyway, it's thrilling he's helping so much with the fashion show. It will make a huge difference. I just hope he thinks it's good enough, that's all. Otherwise I'm in serious trouble. I keep forgetting to do the most crucial things. It was all right until I had my job, but now I'm so busy I just haven't got the time. I'm so grateful for your help, Rupert. That idea of the all-red scene was wonderful. And I thought we could have some children in the finale, it would bring the house down. Isn't that a brilliant idea? We'll have Fanny and Stephanie but I must find some more chums with tinies, mobilise them. You'll choreograph that, won't you?'

'Yes, of course I will,' said Rupert, and sighed. 'God, Edwina, what a mess all this is. This stuff in the *Sketch*, I mean.'

Edwina put her hand out, patted his. 'Poor you. Beastly, they are, the press. Still, take a positive view, it's all good publicity, isn't it? God knows what Edward must be saying to Cassia. He'd take it all so seriously. He'll probably challenge you to a duel at dawn.' She giggled.

'Thanks,' said Rupert, 'thanks a lot. What are you going to do now?'

She looked slightly embarrassed. 'I'm having dinner with Francis, actually. We're going to discuss the fashion show.'

'Oh, yes? Whatever will your husband say?'

'Nothing at all, I should think. He's gone off to Munich for a couple of days, got one of his endless projects there. He's in the most frightful bait. I really don't know what's the matter with him.'

'I'm very tired,' Cecily said to the nurse who came to wash her, and to

471

ask her what she would like for supper. 'I really don't want any supper. Could I just have my hot drink and settle for the night early?'

The nurse went to ask Sister, who said that it was just as well Mrs Harrington's visitors hadn't come, she really wouldn't have been up to seeing them, and that, yes, it probably would be a good idea to get her settled early for the night.

'Take her her hot drink at eight 'o clock, Nurse, please, and her pills. But try and persuade her to have a little supper in the meantime. It will do her good and it helps the pills to work.'

Nicola Foster had been feeling unwell all day; she was prone to migraine, and by five o'clock the flashing lights that heralded a fullblown and hideous attack had arrived. She decided she would have to cancel her dinner party. Her friends were sympathetic and understanding: her appalling headaches were well known. She phoned her husband last; he had been about to leave his office.

'I'll stay on awhile, I think, and work,' he said, 'if that's all right.' He found her sufferings rather distasteful, even while he sympathised with her, and there was nothing he could do for her – all she wanted was to be left alone in her darkened bedroom.

He stayed in his office, working, and then at six o'clock went over to the cupboard where he kept a bottle of whisky and poured himself a large one. He and Benedict had often sat at the end of the day, at this window, overlooking the Thames, drinking whisky; Irish whiskey it was that they both liked, whiskey spelt with an e, Benedict called it. They both took it the same way: with just a little very slightly warm water, and they drank it slowly, savouring it, and nibbling at salted almonds. The other drink they both liked was white port: Benedict had some friends in Oporto, and they had introduced him to it.

Benedict had had friends everywhere; everyone loved him. It wasn't just that he had been charming and amusing, he was genuinely kind and almost insanely generous. Of course everyone said it was easy to be generous when you were very rich; but Dominic knew plenty of very rich people who were decidedly mean. God, he missed him.

He thought about Cecily and what she had endured; it was truly terrible for her. She had had her faults as a wife, of course, but she had been brave and loyal, and Benedict had loved her very much. He wondered if she knew how much; he hoped so. Somehow he doubted it. It was one of the things he had been intending to tell her.

He thought of her lying in her nursing home, sick and alone, and felt very remorseful suddenly. He should have gone today; he really should.

It had been cowardly of him not to. The worst that could have happened would have been that Cecily would have abused him, ordered him out. He could have survived that. He really could. And he might have been able to help her.

He looked at his watch. It was still only half past six. Perhaps he should go. Visiting hours at these places were usually from seven to eight; he could be in Richmond in half an hour. He picked up the phone and dialled the nursing home's number.

Edward was waiting at the bottom of the stairs when Cassia came down from settling Bertie.

'He's asleep,' she said, 'poor little boy, poor, poor little boy.'

'Please come in here,' he said, leading the way into the sitting room; she followed him in and shut the door.

'Have you gone quite mad?' he said quite quietly.

'No, Edward. I have come to my senses.'

'You kidnap a child from his school—'

'Edward, really.'

'You listen to some no doubt exaggerated story about his bad experiences there, make a complete fool of yourself in front of the headmaster—'

'Edward—'

'Now what do you think is to become of him? Where is he to go now? Who will take a child who has been taken out of a perfectly good prep school halfway through the term just because he's homesick and can't cope? Perhaps you'd like to answer me that.'

'Edward, that is not a perfectly good prep school. It's an appalling place. How do you think it's possible that a small boy is subjected almost nightly to a brutal torture—'

'Brutal! Cassia, really.'

'Shall I tell you what they were doing to him, those boys? Holding his head down in the lavatory and pulling the chain. Every night. Threatening him with worse if he told. Told anyone. Today, one of them was forcing him to drink urine, out of a chamber pot. Actually in the sanatorium. And no one keeping an eye on a small boy, a new, very small boy, the youngest in the school, to make sure he was all right. Now don't tell me nothing like that had ever happened before, Edward, that they should not have been alert to it, and don't tell me that is a good school.'

He was silent. Silent for a long time. Then he got up, went over to the fireplace and stood there, staring in at the blazing spitting logs. 'Scene of another incident of boyish torture, a fire,' he said. '*Tom Brown's Schooldays*, you know. Oh, God.' He looked across at her, his face drawn. 'What have we done to him?'

'Well,' she said, choosing to ignore, with agonising generosity, the 'we', 'of course you thought it was for the best, but he can't go back, Edward, he really can't. He's too small. No one should have to cope on their own, in an alien environment, at the age of six.'

'He's almost seven.'

'He's six.'

'I suppose you're right. But I'm afraid it may be very bad for him psychologically to think he can run away from trouble.'

'I don't see it like that. I see it as being good for him to know that we're prepared to admit we made a mistake.'

'I wonder if the other place will take him back.'

'Of course they will. And if they won't, there are others.'

'Yes. Yes, I suppose so.'

He looked utterly exhausted; his thin shoulders drooped as he stood there, his face etched with new, deep lines, his eyes sunk beneath his bony forehead. She felt stricken suddenly: she had done that, or much of it, and he had not deserved it. The word 'disgraceful' worked its way back into her head.

'If we were divorced,' he said suddenly, 'I could probably get custody of the children. Have you thought about that?'

Cassia's guts literally lurched; she swallowed hard, took a deep breath, said, 'Edward, why are you talking about divorce, for heaven's sake?'

'Because I've been thinking about it.'

'Because of this nonsense in the paper?'

'Is it nonsense?' he said, his voice heavy. 'Is it really nonsense?'

Another deep breath. Never admit anything, Harry had said a lifetime ago: you can't unadmit it. 'You know it's nonsense. Surely. The only real truth in that report was that I've known Rupert all my life. Everything else was innuendo, they distorted what I said. You must see that.'

'Oh, I suppose I do, yes,' he said, surprising her. 'It isn't exactly pleasant for me, but ...'

'I know,' she said, her voice low. 'It was stupid of me to talk to the reporter. I'm sorry, Edward, so very sorry.'

'Well, what's done is done. But in any case, I have been thinking about at least separation for some time. It has nothing to do with Rupert Cameron, or indeed anybody else. It's that I don't really see any future in our marriage. You have no time for me, no interest in me—'

'That's not true!' she said.

'Of course it's true.' His voice was less exhausted now, there was anger coming back into it. 'You're so wrapped up in your own life you won't even consider making a temporary move in order that I can get a qualification that would transform my career. Is that really so very much to ask?'

'No,' she said quietly, 'not if you put it like that. And I would love you still to do that, you know I would.'

'Do I?' he said. 'Do I really know that?'

'You should. But you could have got that qualification anywhere, Edward. In London, quite possibly. It really wasn't necessary to uproot us all, was it? Be fair, we could have all stayed here, you could have lived at home—'

'And you could have continued not to live at home. To have taken off each day for your smart little house in London, pursuing your own interests. Very convenient for you.'

'Edward, I—'

'This is a fruitless conversation,' he said suddenly. 'I need to be on my own. I think I might go out for a walk.'

'Edward, please! Please listen to me. It's so important.'

He sat down again, looked at her, his face, everything about him, hostile. He said nothing. She presumed this meant she should speak.

'Edward, I know I've not always behaved very well. Since – well, since I got the money.'

'I think that's an understatement,' he said. Thank God, she thought; he didn't know how much.

'Yes, I suppose it is, and I'm very, very sorry. But I just want you to try and see it from my point of view. It may be that our marriage is over, but if it is, then we should approach that constructively. It won't do us or the children any good not to.'

'Perhaps you should tell me,' he said, his voice heavy, dark, 'about your point of view.'

'I'd like to. It might help. Might make you feel less hostile to me. I wasn't really properly happy. Before.'

'Oh, I see. And do you think I was?'

'I have no idea, although of course I should have done, but – oh, Edward, I wanted to work so much. So so much. I could have been such a good doctor. I know I could. It's probably too late now. But I gave up any chance I had, came here with you, lived with you, as your wife—'

'Very good of you,' he said.

'Please listen. I gave up my dreams of surgery, of obstetrics, for you and our future. Not easily, of course, but I was very happy to do it. And anyway, there was Bertie. But I could have worked locally, on a part-time basis, I could have helped you, here, in this practice, only you wouldn't let me, God knows why. That hurt me so much. There I was, running, or trying to run the house, doing something I hated badly, when I could have been doing something I loved well. Only you wouldn't let me, you stopped me, blocked me at every turn. Why, Edward, why?'

He was silent.

'And then I did miss my friends, they were so important to me, Leonora, and Cecily and Benedict and—'

'Harry Moreton?'

She felt herself flush, looked down, then met his eyes. 'Yes. Harry, of course, and Edwina. They were my family, really, as Rupert was. And you kept me from them, too, you must admit that. You always refused to come and see them with me, made it awkward for me to see them, you were hostile if they came here. I was lonely and frustrated and bored, Edward, even if I did have the children and you. And so when I could take things for myself, I'm afraid I was tactless and impatient and greedy. And when you took Maureen on, I could hardly bear it. I could have killed you both, first her, and then you. It was so unjust, so cruel. Or it seemed so. I'm sure it seemed different to you.'

Still he was silent.

'That was why I took the house, you know, to hurt you back. And so it went on from there, Edward, didn't it? I hurt you and then you hurt me. That was why you sent Bertie away, really, wasn't it? To hurt me – you didn't really want him to go, I know you didn't – because I had hurt you when I wouldn't come to Glasgow. But I still want you to get that qualification, Edward, I really do. I hate it that you're not doing what you want either. I'd love you to do it in London, or at least somewhere nearer, so you could come home often. I'd support you in every way I could, but don't ask me to give up what shreds of my own career are left. Please.'

Eventually he stood up. 'I'm going for that walk now,' he said. 'I need to be on my own. I'm very sorry to have been such an unsatisfactory husband. Sorry you've been so unhappy.'

'Edward, that's not what I said. You're distorting it. Please, please, try to understand it.'

'Oh, I do,' he said, 'I do. All too well. It reinforces my own view of myself, which is not a pretty one. God in heaven, Cassia, do you think I'm so stupid that I couldn't see all those things for myself? Do you think I am proud of myself for sending Bertie away, for my jealousy of you?

476

My inability to relate to your friends? Of course I'm not, but—' He stopped; she realised there were tears in his eyes.

Remorse moved in her, a great raw wound. 'Oh, Edward,' she said, moving towards him, wanting to hold him, to comfort him, as if he were one of the children.

'No,' he said, moving away from her, moving his arms as if to ward her off, 'no, don't. It's too late, Cassia. Too late for both of us. We can't negate everything that's happened. It's been too much, gone too deep, too much has changed. It's hopeless, there's no future for us together any more.'

She stood there, staring at him, feeling guilt and misery settling into her, heavy, inescapable, staring at the ending of her marriage, listening to its death knell.

He walked past her and out of the room; she heard the front door slam.

CHAPTER 28

Sister stood in the hall, looking at Dominic rather severely. 'It's rather late,' she said, 'for visiting. You were coming, I had understood, this afternoon.'

'Yes, I'm extremely sorry. Mr Moreton, Mrs Harrington's cousin, you know, we were coming together. He was called away suddenly, and I was held up in the office, but I would still like to see Mrs Harrington. If at all possible.'

'Well, I'm not sure that it is, Mr Foster. Mrs Harrington is very tired, she is being settled for the night now.'

'How is she?'

'Not at all well, I'm afraid.'

'I think,' he said, 'I really think I can help her. I knew her husband very well, I have some knowledge of what was in his mind when he – well, when he died. Please let me see her.'

Sister hesitated. She looked at her watch. It was after seven thirty; Mrs Harrington had been bathed, her bed changed, she was virtually ready for sleep. She had picked at her supper, Nurse Jenkins had said, but she was calm. Her medication and a hot drink were already being prepared for her. A visitor now might upset her; and in spite of what he might think, whatever it was he had to say could upset Mrs Harrington rather than cheer her up. It seemed very unwise.

'I'm sorry,' she said, 'I really don't think it's a very good idea. Mrs Harrington is very fragile. Another day, perhaps, and if you could try to come earlier ...'

'Yes,' said Dominic humbly. 'Yes, of course.' He wasn't sure which was the stronger emotion: relief or anxiety. He decided it was relief. No one could say now that he hadn't tried, hadn't done his best. 'Well, perhaps you could give her these.' He handed Sister the bunch of white roses he had brought and he went out of the front door.

The nursing home was on Richmond Hill, near the gates of the park. It was quite dark now, and a full moon was rising; against its brilliance in the frosty sky was etched the shape of the great Cedar of Lebanon that stood just inside the gates. It was hauntingly beautiful. Benedict would have loved that tree, Dominic thought; he adored trees, had spent a lot of money planting them down in Devon. 'These are my immortality,' he had said to Dominic, once, patting one of them affectionately, 'here to look at for centuries ahead.'

Dominic had parked his car under the tree; he walked over to it, wondering if he would ever be able to forget what he had done, forgive himself; if Benedict, wherever he was, would forgive him.

He looked up at the nursing home, wondering which room was Cecily's, and saw the curtains being slowly pulled half aside at one of the first-floor windows, and then Cecily's face at the window, looking out. He could see her quite clearly: the light over the front door illuminated her, and so did the moon. She was wearing a white nightdress, and her dark hair was loose, hanging over her shoulders. He could not see the expression on her face, of course, but her stance, the despairing droop of her shoulders, the way she leant her head on the windowpane, spoke of an intense and dreadful misery. Then he saw a figure come up behind her, a nurse, saw her put an arm round Cecily, draw her away from the window, close the curtains.

Afterwards, things seemed rather hazy to Dominic; he remembered running back to the house, ringing urgently at the bell, remembered a nurse telling him he was too late, that visiting time was over, remembered even moving her gently but firmly aside. He could just remember racing up the stairs, hesitating on the landing, working out which was Cecily's room, remember drawing breath, dredging up courage just briefly outside it before knocking and then going in without hearing her respond; could just remember her face, white, horrified, frightened, remember her shrinking back on to her pillows. After that, no details, no details at all.

'It was really awful,' Nurse Jenkins related to a breathless common room. 'I was in the corridor, and I followed him in, of course, and he went over to the bed, poor Mrs Harrington was so frightened, I thought she was going to scream, and then she did start to scream, and he put his hand over her mouth, and I almost screamed myself then, I thought he was going to rape her, but I didn't, I stayed calm somehow. I was surprised at myself, just pressed her bell, you know, and then went over and tried to pull him off her, and then I heard him shouting something at her, saying it had been all his fault that her husband had died, and she just went all quiet, and lay there staring at him, and then she started to cry, but not that awful screaming she does sometimes, just ordinary crying, and he sat down on her bed, holding her hand, and saying, "There, there." Then Sister and Matron arrived, and the porter, and told him the police were on their way, and she said in a really strange voice, "There's no need for that, no need at all," and then he got off the bed and knocked over her tray and I went for a towel from her bedside cupboard and, of course, that was when I found all the pills ...'

'I thought we might go to the Forty Three later,' said Francis Stevenson-Cook. They were dining at the Savoy; had been dancing in between courses. He danced extremely well, if in a slightly showy way, and it amused her, the showiness, she enjoyed it even, found it easy to adapt her own style to it. He looked very good in his white tie; even his tailcoat was, she realised, not black but very, very dark grey. She shuddered at the thought of what Harry would have to say about such sacrilege.

'I'd adore to go to the Forty Three,' she said.

'It really is the best music in London, don't you think? And the best cocaine as well, of course, if you want it.'

'I don't,' she said firmly. She had tried cocaine a few times, unbeknown to Harry who fiercely disapproved of drugtaking, and had enjoyed it, but it was not something she was going to reveal to a virtual stranger, and particularly one who was her boss.

'Nor me,' he said lightly, 'I don't really enjoy it. I don't enjoy anything of that sort. I like to stay in control. At all times.'

'I had noticed,' she said, 'that you don't drink very much. Is that for the same reason?'

'It is. I do enjoy what I have, of course. I adore wine. But one, possibly two glassfuls from a bottle is enough. How about you?'

'Well,' she said laughing, 'as you know, I drink rather a lot. I adore it.'

'Of course. But I meant, do you prefer to control or to be controlled?'

'I'm not sure. Actually. I have a very controlling husband.'

'Indeed?'

'Yes. I suppose being controlled absolves one of responsibility.'

'It does indeed, but that also implies a certain – what shall we say – frailty of will. I would not imagine your will to be frail, Edwina.'

'No,' she said, 'no, I don't think that it is.'

'That is a wonderful dress,' he said suddenly.

'Thank you. Hardy Amies.'

'Do you not patronise the Parisian couturiers?'

'Not really,' she said. 'To be honest, I don't know any of the houses there. My mother does, she buys from Balmain, occasionally, and my coming-out dress was from Mainbocher, but I find plenty to my liking here.'

'I think you should buy in Paris,' he said suddenly, 'it would suit your style. Are you going to the collections in January?'

'What, for the magazine? Goodness, no, I'm not nearly important enough, you should know that.'

'You are quite important enough,' he said, 'in my opinion.' He picked up her hand suddenly and kissed it, his brilliant blue eyes fixed on hers. 'I should like you to go. I shall tell Aurora Le Page.'

'Oh, Francis, please don't, it will cause the most awful trouble.'

He looked at her thoughtfully. 'Well, perhaps. But I would like you to go. I would like to go with you, I think it would be fun. We shall see. Now, shall we summon the dessert trolley?'

'I'm frightfully sorry, I couldn't eat another thing.'

'Don't be sorry. I neither. I have to watch my weight very carefully. More control, you see. I did try the Poincarré diet, but I found it very tedious. What about you?'

'Never tried it,' said Edwina, 'although I did do the thing of his, you know, of saying every day in every way ...'

'Getting better and better! I too. Like a mantra. I chant it, lying in bed, before I turn the light out. Sadly, I don't think it has taken. Now, shall we have coffee, or go on to the Forty Three? That won't cause problems with your husband, will it?'

'Oh, no,' said Edwina vaguely. 'Anyway, he's abroad.'

'Good. I don't like upsetting husbands. I do pride myself on my sixth sense on a marriage, though. I have rarely found myself entertaining a truly happily married lady.'

'Oh, really? So I'm not truly happy? Is that what you are saying?' She laughed, took out her cigarette case, offered him one.

'No, thank you. I smoke only in bed. And yes, I would say you are not truly happy. In your marriage, that is.'

'Ah,' said Edwina.

The Forty Three was packed. Everyone was there: the Mountbattens with Charles Chaplin, Max Aitken, Penelope Dudley-Ward, the Sweenys ... 'Did you know,' Francis hissed in her ear, as he smiled and bowed across at the ravishing Margaret Sweeny, 'that she'd had twenty-one affairs by the time she was twenty-one?'

'Is that all?' said Edwina.

There was a sudden stir through the place; not a sound, not even a movement, just an almost imperceptible concentration on the entrance.

'It's the King,' said Francis. 'Look, he's just joined the Mountbattens.'

'Good heavens. But not her.'

'No, apparently he's been told not to be seen in public with her. Not in the week of her divorce, at any rate. I'm told, though, that things are reaching something of a climax. Scenes with the old Queen, talks with Baldwin, with the Archbishop ...'

'He can't actually think he can marry her, surely?'

'I imagine,' said Francis soberly, watching the King move on to the dance floor with Mrs Dudley-Ward, 'he thinks he can't do anything else. And there's going to be frightful trouble. The Duchess of York is incandescent with rage about the whole thing, apparently. And the press can't be held down much longer. The American papers are full of nothing else. "King buys gems for Wally" was one of the more genteel headlines there last week.'

'Well, she has great style,' said Edwina, 'that's for sure.' The band struck up with 'Let's Call the Whole Thing Off'. 'Come along, Francis,' she said, standing up, 'this is absolutely my favourite number at the moment.'

They left the Forty Three at two, and he escorted her home, kissed her hand on the doorstep and then got immediately back into the car. She waved at him, watched until the car reached the end of the road, and then went thoughtfully inside. This was extremely interesting. He could surely have no sexual interest in her – although there were rumours of affairs with women, rather than just social events – but he clearly liked to be with her, to be seen with her. Well, fairies always did. She appealed to them, she was never sure why. And she liked them: so undemanding, so much fun. And Harry was hardly going to make a fuss about it: it was all rather ideal really.

Cecily woke up feeling deeply, terribly sad. It was so different, that sadness, from the other wretched emotions that she had lived through during the past weeks: the rage, the horror, the remorse, and the dreadful, horrible guilt, that it seemed almost sweet. She lay there, on her pillows, thinking about Benedict, able for the first time since he had died to do so; remembering him, the way he had been, so kind and gentle always, so good a father, so loyal a friend, so amusing and attentive a host – and so good in so many ways a husband, and it was the purest pleasure to be able to do that.

She found herself calling up memories, happy memories: the evening they had met; the night he had proposed; the day of their wedding; the afternoon Fanny had been born and he had come to her room, his face drawn with the anxiety of the day, his eyes brilliant with pleasure at its joyful resolution, the resolution that lay, yelling loudly and indignantly in her frilled cot. They made her smile, those memories, and then they made her cry, but it did not matter, they were good, healing tears; there was no need for Nurse Jenkins, who was sitting with her, to rush over to the bed, to ask if she was all right, to offer to call Sister, the doctor.

She knew there was no point trying to explain, explain that she was only crying because of the happy memories, that the only ones she had known before had been dreadful, hideous ones, because they would not have understood. She simply smiled through her tears, and patted Nurse Jenkins's hand as if it had been she who was upset, and said she was quite all right, there was no need to worry.

She was forbidden visitors that day, for which she was grateful; it was explained to her that she had had a shock from which she needed to recover and she said that she understood, that she did not, in fact, feel quite up to seeing anyone, even (least of all, but she did not say so) her mother; but she also said that she might like to start seeing people quite soon now, as soon as they felt it might be possible, she would like to see her children very much, all of them, and Mrs Fallon, and she would like to see Harry Moreton.

She didn't think she would like to see Dominic Foster again, or not for some time; his courage in coming to see her, in confessing, with all its attendant risks, had impressed and moved her greatly, but her prime emotion towards him was still hostility, less harsh, but still strong; it could not have been otherwise. Jealousy suffused her still, that it had been Dominic's faithlessness that in the end Benedict had been unable to live with, rather than any failing of her own.

His confession had not absolved her from all her feelings of guilt, of course: how could it? She had still been, she knew, intolerant, uncompassionate even, and at the last, unforgiving. She would carry that and her memory of it with her for ever, she knew. Had she been otherwise, then even the pain of Dominic's rejection might have been bearable for him, the appalling conflicts of his life eased. But as she had sat there, hearing Dominic telling her, in a quick, urgent voice, that Benedict had always, in his way, loved her, loved her very much, had wanted to continue with their marriage with all its failings, had even at their last meeting talked lovingly and gratefully of her, the worst of her remorse, her self-hatred, had fallen away.

Something else came into her consciousness too, for the first time, something healthy and strong: anger at Benedict that in taking his own life he could have subjected her and their children to such horror and such pain. He had been, of course, a little, possibly even very, mad. The doctors themselves had explained that to her endlessly from the beginning, saying she must understand that no sane person would have done such a thing, but she had not believed them then, feeling, preferring even, to take all the blame on to herself, convinced that even if he had been mad, then she had made him so; now she felt able to accept it, and even in accepting it, felt angry. The combination was strangely healing.

She also realised, as the medical staff told her she should see no one that day, that they had a problem themselves: in enabling her to hoard and hide her pills, they had been guilty of a lack of proper supervision, a kind of neglect. If that were revealed, there could be serious trouble, and she did not wish that for them; they had been so kind to her, kind and interminably patient, and her skill in concealing her pills (moving them about, from her drawer to beneath her pillow when they were cleaning the room, to her sponge bag as they made her bed, from her sponge bag to the commode cupboard as they took her for her bath) had been pathologically cunning. She did not want them to be in any way blamed, and she wanted them to know that.

After lunch that day (having eaten almost half a plateful) she asked to see Matron, and the doctor if possible. Matron came in, looking sternly uneasy like a guilty child; Cecily smiled at her and told her how much better she felt, and that there was no need for the story of the pills that she had forgotten about to go any further, as far as she was concerned, she didn't want people to know she was so stupid, and she would be grateful if Matron would convey that to the doctor and also to any of the other staff who had come to know of it.

'It was certainly through no fault of anyone here that I became so absent-minded; and since I never wish to see another sleeping pill as long as I live, I see no risk of it ever happening again.'

Matron said she was extremely glad she was feeling so much better, and that she was grateful for the kind words expressed by Mrs Harrington, which she would pass on to the doctor.

Later the doctor himself came to see her and said that although medical etiquette required him to say in his report on her that she had not always taken her pills and that they had been found in her room, he was satisfied himself that no more than absent-mindedness, due to her general unsatisfactory mental state, was to blame, and that she herself, he presumed, would not wish her family to suffer any more than they already had from a mistaken idea that she might have planned on taking an overdose.

'And I will explain this to the rest of the staff, and, of course, should you wish to do the same, particularly to Nurse Jenkins, who found the pills, then there would be no objection to that, indeed it might even be welcome.'

'Thank you. I will. Now I am very tired and ...' She felt her eyes fill suddenly, with exhaustion and the strain of the two interviews, as well as sadness. She swallowed hard, reached for a handkerchief. 'I would like to sleep for a while. But there is no need for Nurse Jenkins to continue to sit with me, Dr Meredith; I really can be quite safely left, and I do value my privacy at the moment.'

Dr Meredith patted her hand and said that as from that moment, she should have it, 'on condition that you notify me immediately if you feel any return of the old symptoms. The mind does not recover quite as steadily as the body, and you may have setbacks.'

'I don't think I will,' said Cecily politely, wiping her eyes, 'because a major reason for my symptoms has gone. Of course I am still very unhappy, but I can see now that I shall in time recover. But, yes, I do promise to let you know if I feel a setback coming on.' She closed her eyes. 'How I could ever have needed to have pills to send me off to sleep I find it hard to imagine.'

She woke up three hours later, in the early evening dusk, to find a very large bouquet of roses in a vase by her bed; the card read simply, 'Thank you for listening to me. Dominic.'

In a few days, when she really felt stronger, she would write to thank him.

Rupert had forgotten an enormous number of his lines. The prompter was patient, Eleanor soothing, even Jasper Hamlyn tactful – 'I know it's only stage fright, happens all the time. You'll be fine next week.' Nevertheless, at the last runthrough, with the dress rehearsal the following Monday, prior to the first night on Wednesday, it was not the sort of thing that inspired self-confidence. Having left the theatre alone (convinced that Jasper was even now confiding in Eleanor that he was seriously considering closing the show before it had even opened), he went into the nearest pub and had three double brandies before going back to his digs and telephoning Cassia. He didn't care if it was unwise; he only knew he needed support and succour and she was the only person who would provide it.

She didn't answer; not then, which was (he ascertained after a rather prolonged study of his watch) seven thirty, nor was she half an hour later, or half an hour after that. Rupert found this unbearable; in his loneliness and panic, he decided to go to the house in Walton Street and wait for her there. She couldn't be very much longer, surely.

He went out into the street and hailed a taxi and directed it to Mrs Horrocks's house. Mrs Horrocks held a spare key to Walton Sreet and had lent it to him before, at Cassia's instigation; she did so now, and was quite overcome to receive, in return, two complimentary tickets for the first night of *Letters* for herself and Mr Horrocks, along with the information (conveyed just a little unsteadily) that Rupert would very much like them to come round to the dressing room afterwards and take a glass of champagne with him and any other visitors who might be there.

'Pissed,' said Mr Horrocks briefly as the door closed behind him. Mrs Horrocks told him not to be so rude, and that it was a great honour to be asked to a first night, and whatever was she going to wear.

'You reckon he's humping her?' said Mr Horrocks, pouring himself a glass of beer.

Mrs Horrocks told him to wash his mouth out and that Mrs Fallon was a beautiful lady, and married with a lovely family.

'I didn't say she wasn't. He's humping her, you mark my words,' said Mr Horrocks, embarking on the rather lengthy task of lighting his pipe. 'What do you think he's doing when he stays in the house with her, practising his lines?'

Mrs Horrocks, who had had the same thoughts from time to time and kept them to herself, told him that he ought to be ashamed of himself and then started fretting over her wardrobe and its inability to provide anything for her to wear to the theatre.

Rupert let himself into the house – Cassia surely couldn't be long – and tried to concentrate on the script he had brought with him, to revise his lines. It proved absolutely pointless: as fast as he had fixed one forgotten letter in his head, the next one slithered out of it again.

By nine thirty he was in despair; by way of alleviating it at least a little, he found a bottle of Cassia's very nice Burgundy and drank three large glasses of that. He then began to feel very odd indeed, and in need of lying down; he settled himself on the sofa, his eyes fixed on the wireless, which he had tuned to a very nice symphony concert. He would have liked to close them, but every time he tried it, the room started spinning in a very vicious way; it reminded him of being on the waltzer at the Brighton funfair to which he had taken a delirious Bertie and William the year before. They had been so happy then; all of them.

The memory of that happiness, spinning ever further away from him (rather like Cassia's drawing room), made Rupert suddenly want to cry; the fact that the last letter he had tried to learn, the one which was presently fixed in his head, was the one his character had written to Eleanor's on hearing of her marriage while he was at the Front (under the illusion that he had been killed eighteen months earlier), did not help.

'I cannot imagine living for even one other hour, let alone a day, or, God help me, the duration of this war, without the thought of you and your love to sustain me. I lay in that hospital bed, in what was at times agony, and the only thing that got me through it was thinking of you, and the happy memories, worn threadbare with overuse, that were the stuff from which our rather modest love affair was woven. Modest! Was it so modest, my darling? So fragile that you could tear it apart, return it to the separate threads that were there before we met, before it began. Surely not; surely there was strength, steel in those threads? Surely ...'

At this point Rupert fell asleep: to dream not of the play, not of the first night, not even of Cassia, but of Eleanor Studely, and her lovely voice.

Cassia had not gone to work that day, had phoned the clinic, citing the same domestic crisis that she had on Monday, able to elaborate on it quite truthfully that day, saying she would come in on Friday instead; and serve me right for lying about such a thing, she thought gloomily, putting down the phone, they'd sack me if there was any justice.

She could hear nice Nurse Hampton frowning sympathetically down the phone, shocked to hear of Bertie's misfortunes, reassuring her that she must only come back when he was quite well enough to be left. Which was probably in about ten minutes, Cassia thought, listening to the shrieks of laughter that were coming from Bertie's bedroom, the endless loud thuds that were William demonstrating his new prowess at gymnastics to Bertie, and Delia's high-pitched squeals of 'Me now. Me now. *Me now!*' – such normal, happy sounds.

The clear sense of happiness reached out to her, clearing just for a while, at least, the sense of panic that had taken over her life. It was stronger than anything else, that panic: stronger than sadness, remorse, self-distaste, stronger even than the raw, wracking misery that had filled her ever since she had watched Harry walking away from her in the Dorchester, heard his voice over and over again, calling her a whore.

As long as she lived she would never forget that moment, never even begin to forget it. It had provided a scourge with which she chastised herself, night and day, over all her behaviour: not merely the foolish fatal incident with Rupert, the all-consuming selfishness of her adultery with Harry, but − perhaps most − the savage wilfulness with which she could see, and with horrible clarity, she had destroyed her marriage. She loathed herself for that: her cruelty, her selfishness, her rejection of the kind, gentle, loving man she had married, married so wrongly, and the brutality of her behaviour to him. That was what created the panic: not that her marriage was ruined, Edward damaged beyond repair, Harry and her chance of happiness lost to her for ever, but that she could actually be the creature who had wilfully, knowingly, brought about all those things. A creature she had to live with for the rest of her life.

She went upstairs and into Bertie's room. Fanny was sitting at the end of his bed, and Bertie was lying back on the pillows. Tears streamed down both their faces, not of misery, but laughter, and William had collapsed upside down on to the floor, his legs and arms helplessly entangled with Delia's and those of Buffy, who had followed Bertie up to his room when Cassia had carried him there last night, and had been there, with occasional forced absences while William marched him round the garden, ever since. Buffy had not liked Bertie being away; he didn't like any sort of change. And quite right too, Cassia thought, patting his old, slightly balding head absent-mindedly; dangerous stuff, change.

'Hallo, Mummy.' Bertie managed to stop laughing for a moment. 'Can I have some more toast?'

'Of course you can. You're obviously feeling better.'

'I'm feeling much better. Hardly any itching and not hot at all. Just starving, starving.'

'Starving,' said William, beating a rhythm on the floor with his feet. 'Toast for me too, please.'

'Starvy,' said Delia, 'toasty, toasty.'

'All right. I'll be back in two ticks.'

'Two tickles, you mean,' said William, giggling at his own wit. 'Two chicken poxy tickles.'

'Chicken tickle,' said Delia, 'chicken tickles, chicken tickles.'

Cassia went downstairs smiling; Fanny followed her, saying she thought she might go and read in the sitting room for a bit.

'Good idea, darling. They are very noisy, aren't they?'

'Well, they're very young,' said Fanny sagely, from all the height of her eleven and a half years.

It was extraordinary, Cassie thought, how quickly children recovered. Dying one day, in the rudest health the next. Or even the next hour.

She took the toast back upstairs; Bertie was quieter now, told her to sit on the bed. She did and he took her hand. 'Don't I really have to go back to that school? Never?'

'Never,' said Cassia, 'never, never.' She held out her arms.

He cuddled up against her. 'It was horrible,' he said simply.

'I know. I'm so sorry.'

'Wasn't your fault. Or Daddy's,' he added firmly. 'He thought I'd like it. I thought so too.'

How generous children were, she thought, turning her head, resting it on his, how quick to forgive. It became lost, much of that generosity, somewhere along the way to adulthood, round about puberty. 'I know, darling. We made a mistake.'

'Yes, well, it doesn't matter. It's worth it to be home again.' There was a silence, while they watched Delia feeding Buffy her toast, and Cassia thought rather half-heartedly that she ought to stop him licking her small fingers, that it was rather unhygienic.

'Mummy?'

'Yes, Bertie?'

'What does shagging mean?'

'What?' She was half shocked, half amused.

'Shagging. What does it mean? Because Collins said there was an article in the paper, that said you were shagging some bloke who wasn't Daddy.'

Cassia looked at him, at William who was looking at her enquiringly, and prayed for inspiration. It did not come. 'Well,' she said finally, 'if it was the article I'm thinking about, it was a very silly one. It was about how I've lent some money for Rupert's new play. And then it was about what good friends we are, which is true, of course, but the reporter got a bit carried away and seemed to think I was his girlfriend.'

'What, you and Rupert?'

'Yes.'

'So is shagging being someone's girlfriend?'

'Sort of, yes.'

'Well, that's really silly,' said William. 'I mean you can't be anyone's girlfriend, because you're married to Daddy.'

'Yes, of course. I told you it was silly.'

There was a silence, then Bertie said, 'Two of the boys at school, their parents were divorced. I suppose then you could shag someone else, if you were divorced?'

'Well, yes, I suppose you could. Incidentally, Bertie, shagging isn't a very nice word. Not one I'd use.'

'OK,' he said cheerfully. 'Anyway, you're not divorced, are you?'

'No, of course not.'

'I'd hate that so much,' he said, burying his head against her again. 'This boy, Davidson, he was in my dorm, he used to cry about his mother leaving his father, getting divorced. I'd rather go back to that school than you get divorced, you and Daddy, I really would.'

'Don't be daft,' said William, thumping him with a pillow, 'of course they're not going to get divorced. Hey, Mummy, want to see Delia do a cartwheel?' He picked up Delia by her plump legs; she squealed with pleasure.

'Yes,' said Cassia, her voice rather quiet, 'yes, I'd like that very much.'

She decided not to go up to London to work next day; she told herself, and indeed everybody else, that it was because Bertie still wasn't very well, and she wanted to stay with him, but the real reason was an increasing sense that she was fast losing any semblance of control over her life, and staying within her own four walls gave her a sense, probably illusory, that she was halting that process just a little.

CHAPTER 29

Harry glared at Edwina across the dining table. 'I am not going to the bloody thing, and that's the end of it. Please don't mention it again. Take your new boyfriend. He'll probably enjoy it. Now I'm going to the office. I don't know when I'll be back.'

Edwina looked after him thoughtfully. He had been in a filthy temper for days. Not that that was anything unusual; but she did wonder if his remark about Francis was a clue. Maybe he did mind. She'd told him about dinner and going to the Forty Three when he'd got back from Munich, simply because he always got so angry if he discovered such things for himself. He hadn't semed remotely interested, simply shrugged and continued to read the paper; he hadn't seemed remotely interested in anything she'd said or done for weeks. In a way the bad temper was a return to normality.

Well, if he wasn't going to come to Rupert's first night, she certainly was. She was actually rather dreading it, but she'd promised Rupert and, apart from anything else, she needed to keep him on her side because of the fashion show. But it certainly didn't look as if it was going to be the theatrical event of the Season; the bookings were very modest, even for the first week.

She wondered if she might actually take Francis, or at least ask him if he wanted to go. It was quite a good idea of Harry's. She supposed Cassia would be there; Edward obviously wouldn't. Rupert's mother was going, full of excitement at her son's West End debut. She was a game old bird; she must be at least eighty.

She'd spoken to Rupert at the weekend and he'd sounded utterly distraught, said the whole thing was going to be a disaster; but then that was probably the artistic temperament. She'd seen a great deal of the artistic temperament since she'd been working at *Style*, and rather to her surprise felt she absolutely understood and sympathised with it. If you were struggling to do something superbly well, it created huge tension and strain, which inevitably surfaced. Just the same, Rupert might be right, the play could be dreadful: maybe it wasn't such a good idea to ask Francis.

In the event Francis raised the subject himself. He'd phoned her about the fashion show and then asked when Rupert's first night was. 'Tomorrow,' she said. 'He's frightfully nervous.'

'Well, he's chosen an auspicious day. London will be packed. The Jarrow marchers are arriving, poor desperate things, there's a Communist rally, and it's the Opening of Parliament. The new King's first performance. Oh, and the forecast is heavy rain. Is Rupert getting a full house?'

'Only if all the Jarrow marchers decide to shelter from the rain, I should think. Very poor bookings, apparently. I honestly don't know that it's going to be very good.'

'Poor fellow. We ought to support him, don't you think? Show solidarity. Specially as he's doing such sterling work for us. Look, can you get me a ticket or two? I could bring some chums along.'

'Funny you should say that,' said Edwina.

Cassia was taking Fanny and Stephanie to *Letters*; Edward had, of course, refused to come. Afterwards, Rupert had suggested they all went out to supper together, 'And I can either drink champagne or a phial of poison.'

'I might join you in the latter,' said Cassia.

A letter came for her that Monday morning, a letter with a French postmark. It was from M. Jean Berrez, the patron of the café in Le Touquet. He had seen one of Rollo Gresham's old friends, and had managed to get an address for her: he was living in Marrakesh, in the French quarter of the city, known as the Ville Nouvelle, near the Jardin Majorelle. 'It seems M. Gresham has not been well, so he would, I am sure, like to hear from you.'

Cassia sat down and wrote to Rollo Gresham immediately – none of her other miseries and anxieties had removed what still seemed to her a most crucial and pressing one – and then went out to post the letter. On the way she saw Mrs Venables; she smiled at her, and said good morning, and received a very icy nod of the head in return. The article, she thought with a sigh: she'd received a lot of icy nods over the past few days.

The November morning dawned, as Francis had said it would, to torrential rain. It did a great deal to depress everyone's spirits, that rain:

Rupert's as he lay, awake from dawn in an agony of terror, listening to it lashing against his windowpane; Cassia's as she drove up to London with Fanny, forced to take a circuitous route to her house, on account of large areas of London being cordoned off for the state procession to Parliament; Harry Moreton's as he stood scowling at his office window, staring out at it whilst shouting instructions at the unfortunate Margot Murray; those of the loyal subjects of His Majesty who had been waiting patiently for several hours to see the state procession and to wish him well on his way to his first parliament; and of all the weary men who had been marching for over a month now from Jarrow and had chosen that day to present their petition to Parliament, that it should 'recognise the urgent need that works should be provided for the town'.

It did not help anybody either that the King cancelled the state procession and travelled to the Houses of Parliament by car (thereby making the detours virtually unneccessary, and the loyal waiting totally pointless), although the men of Jarrow, having held their public meeting, were able to watch the arrival of the King at Westminster from a good vantage point (where, with the good nature that had characterised the entire march, they cheered him most enthusiastically).

Cassia, who had stopped off at Eaton Place to leave Fanny with Nanny, and stayed to witness her touchingly joyful reunion there with her brother and sister and, indeed, the staff, arrived rather late at her clinic, to find Nurse Hampton's patience with her and her unreliability finally bending, if not actually snapping.

'I'm so sorry,' she said humbly, 'so very sorry. It's just that—'

'Never mind what it is, Dr Fallon. It's a relief that you're here. Although luckily, with the rain it looks like a quiet day. Now shall we get started? We've a lass in there with five children under six, all with her, all creating, so the sooner she's seen the better.'

Sometimes, Cassia thought, putting her head round the waiting-room door and asking the mother of five – who was clearly a great deal younger than she – to come into her consulting room, just sometimes, she wondered if her job was worth it. Then she looked at the girl's greyish-white face, at her thin hands, clasping her youngest child in his distinctly threadbare shawl, listened to her voice, tired, anxious, explaining how one more and she thought she'd go mad, and knew it was.

The Second House theatre at seven fifteen was not exactly packed. Cassia and Rupert's mother, a most daunting old lady who had defied her doctor and her Brighton nursing home to attend, together with Stephanie and Fanny and Eleanor Studely's daughter, a rather serious little girl with her mother's dark beauty called Portia, sat alone in the front row. Mrs Cameron kept looking behind her with an expression closer to anger than anxiety and said to Portia, who was doing much the same thing, 'Don't worry, people always come late to first nights.'

'It's such a pity Uncle Edward couldn't have come,' whispered Fanny to Cassia. 'It would have helped. And Janet, she would have liked it.'

'Yes, it is,' said Cassia, who wished she'd thought of inviting Janet herself, 'yes, it's a terrible shame.'

In a hideous way she was almost relishing the evening and its potential horror; it pierced through her own troubles, made them seem at least a little distant. Then she thought here was more proof still of her absolute self-absorption, and felt freshly ashamed of herself.

The Horrockses, who had arrived at half past six, lest they might be late, sat in the row behind them, with six people who seemed to be friends of Eleanor's, and there was a group of Rupert's theatrical chums up in the front row of the circle. Two couples, one of whom Cassia recognised as the other backer, joined them in the front row; a few more distinctly damp, and what Mrs Cameron described in a loud whisper to Cassia as arty-looking, people took their places halfway down the stalls.

Jasper Hamlyn, a greenish-pale James Piggott, and a group of friends came down the side aisle, talking and laughing loudly and bravely. Jasper came over to Cassia, kissed her hand and told her theatrical history was about to be made, before leading his friends to their seats. Two men, who were obviously journalists, one with a camera, arrived and complained about the seats they had been given. Jasper Hamlyn moved them into the second row, next to the Horrockses.

And that was all.

Cassia looked at her watch; it was already seven forty. Curtain up couldn't wait much longer. It wasn't going to get better.

She felt sick; a small trembling hand slid into hers. It was Portia's; her own, responding to it, squeezing it comfortingly, was clammy with sweat. It just wasn't fair. Poor Rupert, he'd be going through the tortures of the damned backstage. And where on earth was Edwina? It was too bad, when he was doing so much for her, her and her wretched fashion show.

And then, just as the lights were going down, there was a great noise outside, the doors opened and at least two dozen people came in, headed by Edwina and an exotic-looking man wearing a scarlet-lined cape, and carrying a silver-topped cane. They all looked as if they were going to a party, the men in dinner jackets, the women in long dresses; in some strange and hugely welcome way, they seemed to illuminate the drab little theatre, fill it with excitement and pleasure.

'Can't possibly find our seats in the dark,' the exotic man said in a whisper that could be heard throughout the theatre. 'Let's just sit where we can.'

They seemed to fill the stalls, those few people, separating into small groups; Cassia's saw Mrs Cameron's stern face relax, felt a lump in her own throat, then turned her attention and determined to concentrate very hard on the play. In the event it was not in the least difficult.

From the moment the curtain rose on the two of them, Rupert and Eleanor, sitting on chairs on either side of the stage, the set a simple Victorian-style drawing room, cleverly designed with a few items of furniture – a jardinière, a chair, a low table, to make a division of sorts in it – to the moment when it fell an hour and a half later (there was no interval), the entire theatre was utterly silent. Nobody shuffled their feet, nobody coughed, nobody rustled sweet papers; the story, so simply, so movingly, at times so wittily told, took hold of the fifty or so imaginations laid before it and did not release them. It smiled, that audience, it sighed, it wept, it held its breath; and when the last letter was signed off in Rupert's beautiful voice – 'All my love, for what I truly believe to be eternity' – and the curtain came down, there was an absolute silence for what seemed a long time, before applause rose, its noise out of all proportion to the size of the audience.

In the balcony Rupert's friends stamped their feet: Portia looked back up at them, her small face flushed with joy, and then joined in, the other children following her lead. One of the journalists shouted 'bravo', and clearly wishing to set his own mark on the occasion, Francis Stevenson-Cook rose to his feet and clapped more loudly still. Other people followed him, until the entire audience was standing; Cassia watched Rupert holding Eleanor's hand and taking bow after bow, his face raised into the spotlight, his eyes brilliant with tears. There were cries for the author, the producer, some flowers arrived from somewhere for Eleanor; in all they took nine curtain calls. And at the last Rupert looked out into the front row, where they sat, and blew Cassia and his mother and the children a kiss.

'Oh dear,' said Mrs Cameron, wiping her streaming eyes, 'that was lovely. If only, if only my husband had been here.'

As Mr Cameron had died when Rupert had been a small boy, this seemed a little excessive even by theatrical standards; but Cassia smiled at her and said carefully that it was indeed very sad, but how wonderful that Mrs Cameron had been able to see it.

'As if I would have missed it,' she said with a sound that approached a snort. 'Well, it's taken him long enough, but he's managed it at last. Thanks to you, my dear. Now come along, come on, everyone, we must go backstage.'

'Marvellous, wasn't it?' said Edwina, linking her arm through Cassia's as they walked round to the stage door. 'What a triumph. Cassia, this is Francis Stevenson-Cook. Francis, my frightfully clever friend, Cassia Fallon. You could say she made this evening possible,' she added carelessly, and then disappeared into the mêlée of people kissing Rupert.

'Ah, the famous doctor!' said Stevenson-Cook. 'I am delighted to meet you at last. I've studied your picture in the paper, heard of your huge success in your career—'

'Oh heavens,' said Cassia, half irritated, half amused, 'no success at all, and it was a very old picture.'

'Well, you look every bit as beautiful now. If I might be allowed to say so.'

He was very good-looking, this friend of Edwina's, although possibly, she thought, a homosexual; it had been he, she realised, who had led the crowd of people in late, the crowd who were now fluttering and swooping about the corridor kissing everyone within reach, the immensely stylish crowd, overdressed for the occasion, but bestowing upon it a chic, a sense of social importance, that had undoubtedly contributed to its success.

'It was very nice that you all came,' she said suddenly. 'Thank you so much. Rupert will be terribly grateful.'

'No need for gratitude, our pleasure entirely. It was marvellous. And one must look after one's own, after all. Now tell me, how was it exactly that you made this evening possible?'

'I didn't do anything of the sort. I just put a bit of money into it.'

'Oh, yes, of course. I remember the article.' She could see him studying her, examining her for signs of an adulterous passion. 'And is your husband here?' he said carelessly after a moment.

'Oh, no. No, he's working. As usual.'

'I see. How sad he should miss such a success.'

'Terribly,' said Cassia, and then in an effort to escape what was clearly to develop into an inquisition, 'You must excuse me, I have three little girls here, all in need of supervision.'

'I adore children. I'd love to meet them,' he said, surprising her.

'Of course. I'll round them up and bring them over.'

★

They never reached a restaurant. After a while, the Stevenson-Cook crowd departed 'for another party, too boring', although he and Edwina, of course, remained. They all moved to the stage; more champagne was brought in, and a hamper of food materialised apparently from nowhere: canapés, tiny sausages, smoked salmon sandwiches – 'Francis's idea,' said Edwina to Cassia. 'He had it in the car, said we might need it.'

'He's very nice,' said Cassia, 'and this is all terribly generous.'

'Don't you adore him? He's such fun, and really been so kind to me.' She hesitated. 'No Harry, then?'

'No, he's been in the most frightful bait as usual, for days. Refused flatly to come, even though he had told me to get tickets. I'd have been quite sunk without Francis this evening, been here on my own un-escorted. Like you,' she added, 'but, of course, it doesn't matter for you.'

'No, I suppose not,' said Cassia (wondering why not: too dull? too unattractive?).

'Who are those extraordinary people standing over there, next to old Mrs Cameron? Isn't she marvellous?'

'Oh, they're the Horrockses,' said Cassia, laughing. 'She does for me, in London. I don't quite know why they're here, I suppose Rupert invited them.'

'Too heavenly of him, but they do look a bit out of it. I'll go and talk to them for a bit, put them at their ease.'

'Do you really think that's a good idea?' said Cassia.

'Of course. I'm marvellous with working-class people, it's a knack I've picked up from Mummy.'

Mr Horrocks, who had had several glasses of stout before he had even left the house, and several of champagne since, found himself having a rather bewildering conversation with Edwina.

'I thought you looked a bit out of your depth,' she said, smiling at him sweetly, 'but really no need. It's too thrilling you're here, and it's marvellous to think people like you can enjoy the theatre. Do you get up this way often?'

'Not very often, no, but Mrs Horrocks does, of course, looks after Mrs Fallon's house for her.'

'Yes, so I understand. She must enjoy that. And Mrs Fallon is a charming person. I've known her since we were debutantes, you know.'

'Is that so? Well, she seems very nice. And Mr Cameron, he's a charming gentleman.'

'Oh, you've met him, have you?' said Edwina. 'Here, have some more champagne. It's a tiny bit warm, but I don't suppose you'll mind too terribly much.'

'Not too much, no,' said Mr Horrocks. He drained the champagne glass, held it out slightly uncertainly to Edwina for refilling. He gave her a wink, drained the glass again. 'Mrs Horrocks has met Mr Cameron a lot more often. He's at her house all the time. Stays the night quite often.'

'Really?' said Edwina. She clearly found this very interesting. 'Are you sure about that?'

'Course I'm sure,' said Mr Horrocks, slightly indignantly 'Came round only the other night, last Friday I think it was, for the key. Brought it back in the morning, looking terrible.' He paused, grinned at her, winked again. 'Well, they're all the same these theatricals, aren't they? No better than they should be. It's the artistic licence, Mrs Horrocks says, don't you, Bets?'

At this point Mrs Horrocks dug him hard in the ribs. 'Time we went home, Alan,' she said, 'you've had far too much of that stuff. Come on, let's go and find Mr Cameron, say thank you.'

Edwina watched the Horrockses weave their way across the room, and then stood looking at Cassia thoughtfully. How very interesting. Goody goody Cassia. So the article hadn't been so far wrong. You never could tell with people. She couldn't wait to tell Francis.

The party finally ended after one. Cassia, looking round at the almost surreal scene that had formed on the stage, felt as if she was part of some theatrical performance herself: Fanny and Stephanie, apparently tireless, were playing blind man's buff with Jasper Hamlyn and his friends; Rupert was standing with his arm round Eleanor's shoulder, a bottle of champagne in each hand; Mrs Cameron was sound asleep in one of the Victorian chairs; Francis was engaged in intense conversation with James Piggott, and Edwina was doing a charleston with Portia, to the accompaniment of a mouth organ played most expertly by the stage doorman.

'Come on!' said Cassia, clapping her hands, beckoning to the children. 'It's terribly late.'

There were violent protests; Edwina told her not to be such a prude, and said why didn't she and Rupert come to the Embassy, with her and Francis.

'No, I don't think so,' said Cassia. 'I am responsible for these two, and what are we going to do with your mother, Rupert? I thought she was supposed to go to a friend in Victoria at the end of the play?'

'Oh, she can come back to my digs,' said Rupert. 'I can settle her there, and then I'd love to come to the Embassy. Eleanor, why don't you come with us?'

Eleanor, who was clearly longing to go, said she couldn't, what about Portia, and Cassia said that was fine, she could stay with them. 'One more little girl won't make any difference.'

'Yes, but then where can I stay? I can't go all the way home to Croydon tonight.'

'You can stay at our house,' said Edwina. 'Absolutely no problem, and we'd love to have you with us. All right? Come on, everyone. Francis, you ready?'

Cassia took the children back to Walton Street alone; in spite of her pleasure at the night, at Rupert's success, she felt suddenly rather depressed.

She was woken by a small hand tugging at her sleeve. It was Fanny. 'Cassia, wake up. Portia's terribly worried, she says she has to go to school, she's got to play in a lacrosse match, she's lacrosse captain in her year, isn't that wonderful? She's awfully nice, I think. Anyway, her mother's at Aunt Edwina's, isn't she? Could you ring her, Cassia, please, or do you know where Portia's school is?'

Cassia didn't; through a considerable haze of pain from a throbbing head, she dialled Edwina's number. The butler answered the phone.

'Oh Bishop. Sorry to bother you, but could you possibly ask Mrs Studely, who is staying there, to come to the phone? It's rather important. Only tell her,' she added hastily, mindful of the ongoing anxiety felt by all mothers, 'tell her Portia's perfectly all right.'

'One moment, madam, please.'

A long pause, then a sleepy voice came on to the phone. She felt briefly guilty, then thought that Eleanor really should have remembered her daughter's lacrosse match.

'Oh, God,' she said, 'oh dear, how awful of me. I did forget; I can only plead temporary insanity. Brought about by my considerable anxiety. Oh dear, Cassia, is she terribly upset?'

'Well, a bit,' said Cassia, looking at Portia's anxious little face, her small hands wringing at her hanky. 'I think she really should go if she can. Where does she go? Shall I take her?'

'Oh, no. She's at St Margaret's, in Clapham. I'll get dressed quickly, come and fetch her, in a taxi. Oh, dear, how dreadful of me.'

'Look,' said Cassia, her heart going out to Eleanor in her guilt-ridden anguish, 'if she has to get to Clapham, it's terribly out of your way to come here. I'll drop her over to you, that'll save you at least quarter of an hour. And then you can have the taxi waiting. And don't start putting on

499

your sackcloth and ashes yet,' she added, 'I've done much worse than this to my children.'

'Have you really?' said Eleanor. 'Thank you so much for saying that.'

It wasn't until she and Portia were in the car that Cassia realised where she was going: to the Moreton house. The thought of seeing Harry was literally terrifying. Well, maybe Eleanor would be waiting outside. Or Harry would still be asleep – it was very early.

The Moreton house looked blessedly dark and slumbering; Eleanor was not, however, outside. Cassia waited a few minutes, then knocked gently on the door and ran down the steps again, like a naughty child. Eleanor was probably in the hall. At worst, Bishop would open the door.

Harry Moreton opened it. He was fully dressed, his overcoat slung round his shoulders, carrying his briefcase. He looked down at her, his face initially startled, shocked even, then coldly, horribly distasteful. 'Why are you here?' he said.

Cassia felt as if someone had picked her up and shaken her physically; she stood there for a moment, knowing she was blushing, feeling hot, horribly sick, even for a dreadful moment as if she was going to be sick. Then she swallowed hard, and said, 'I've come to collect Eleanor Studely.'

'Who the hell is Eleanor Studely?'

'She's a a friend of Rupert's. An actress.'

'And what is she doing in my house?' It was an expression of such hostility, such disgust that anyone connected with Rupert, or indeed her, should be within any property of his, that she winced.

'She stayed here. She was out with Edwina and her friends last night. It was after the play. You know.'

'Oh, that. Yes.' Again the absolute distaste. 'Well, you'd better go in and find her. I'm leaving.'

He stood aside so that she could walk into the house; as she passed him, the sense of him, this man whom she had known so intimately, whose body had become so utterly familiar to her, pulled at her, and she felt it, that remembered intimacy, that pleasure, felt it as a violent physical force.

She looked up at him then, she couldn't help it, looked at his face, at his eyes; they met hers, and she could see, just for a moment, that he felt it too, the pull; there was emotion there, strong emotion, not love, not even liking, but a response to her, and then it was gone and the dark eyes lost everything, even hostility, became utterly, deadly blank.

Eleanor suddenly appeared. 'Sorry, Cassia, I'm so sorry. Oh, good morning, you must be Mr Moreton, do forgive me …'

Harry said nothing, said nothing more to either of them, ran down the steps, and got into his car, drove away, the tyres screaming through the morning silence.

'Oh dear, he seems very upset,' said Eleanor.

Cassia didn't even try to answer.

Later that morning she went to see Cecily. The news that Cecily was better, wanted to see her, had touched her deeply. She decided not to take Fanny and Stephanie, and drove them over to Eaton Place to Nanny. They were still high with pleasure at having been at such a dazzling affair as the party on stage the night before. Rupert had telephoned to say that three other journalists from three other papers had asked for tickets for that night, and that Saturday night was already a sell-out. 'So you'll get your investment back at least, my darling, and probably ten times over.'

Cassia told him rather wearily that that was the last thing on her mind, but she was very, very happy for him. The thought of having any more money, she realised, made her feel sick.

Cecily was sitting up in a chair at the window when Cassia arrived at the nursing home. She turned and smiled at Cassia, held out her hand. 'It's so lovely to see you,' she said simply.

'It's lovely to see you too,' said Cassia, shocked at her appearance: she must have lost two stones at least, the creamy skin was parchment dry and pale and the dark eyes sunk deep into her face. But they were serene, the dark eyes, they had lost the frenetic brightness that had been there at the funeral, and the dreadful staring vacancy of the morning of her breakdown.

Cecily smiled, clearly reading her thoughts. 'I look awful, don't I? I do know. But you should have seen me a week ago. This is fat by comparison. Fat and rosy.' She laughed. 'I never ever thought I'd be trying to put on weight.'

'Cecily, I'm so pleased you're better.'

'I do feel better,' said Cecily, her voice slightly surprised. 'It's lovely. I – well, I really did want to die, you know. Until the other day. Now I'm just sad, sad and lonely and full of regrets; but not frantic any more, not in despair.'

'What happened? To make you feel differently?' said Cassia. 'Was it the drugs, do you think, or the treatment, or just time?'

'No, none of those things helped at all. No. Dominic Foster came to see me.'

'Dominic Foster!' said Cassia, trying not to sound too astonished. 'But, Cecily, I thought – that is, you—'

Cecily smiled. 'I know what you thought. But he – well, he told me something that made all the difference. He was very brave, actually. He came here, and insisted I saw him. He told me lots of things, actually, but one in particular and I – well, I realised it wasn't all my fault. It wasn't all his either, of course, which is what he thought – we both contributed – but most of all I realised it was the awful conflict Benedict just couldn't cope with. The conflict with himself, with me, with all of us, with his – his instincts, but most of all, what society does to him, him and people like him. I never thought I'd come to think this, Cassia, but you know I do now agree with you about the laws about—' She hesitated, obviously finding it hard to say the word; Cassia waited. 'About homosexuality,' Cecily said finally. 'I have come to see it's dreadful that they drive people underground, make them subject to blackmail, all that sort of thing. Think of that awful Norman Duvant, what he was able to do to Benedict.'

'Yes,' said Cassia quietly. 'Just think.'

'I mean I still feel odd about it all. I still see it as an illness, a sickness, which I know you don't. But maybe you're right, and maybe I'm getting there. I'm trying to, anyway.'

Cassia leant forward and kissed her. 'You don't have to feel anything, get anywhere,' she said.

'No, but can't you see? That's part of feeling better. It's hard to explain. Anyway,' she smiled again, 'thank you so much, so very, very much for everything, but most of all for looking after Fanny all this time. I know it must have been difficult.'

'It wasn't,' said Cassia truthfully, 'not in the least. She's a darling child. We've loved having her, she's been no trouble at all. I do think, though – ' she hesitated – 'she's ready to come and see you now, to talk. I think it's a bit like you and Dominic and everything: she can see she might have got it wrong, but she needs to be helped to work out how and why. And she does miss you. Terribly.'

'Yes, well, I want to see her too. I've already seen Stephanie and darling Laurence, that was easy. Fanny did seem more of a problem. She wouldn't even speak to me, you know.'

'I do know, but I think that's over now. She'll just be pleased to see you, be with you,' said Cassia, 'and she's got such a lot to tell you, which will help – Bertie's come home, you know, wait till I tell you about that, poor little boy – and then she's very full of Edwina's fashion show, I think that's helped her a lot, given her something to focus on, specially as she hasn't been going to school. They're going to be in it, you see, her and Stephanie and little Portia – she's Eleanor Studeley's daughter—'

'Cassia, you're going too fast. Who's Eleanor Studely?'

'Oh, Rupert's leading lady. So nice, and so beautiful. She's a widow.'

'Do you think he might fall in love with her?' said Cecily hopefully.

'No, no chance at all. You know he likes little starlets.'

'He likes you, darling.'

'No, he doesn't,' said Cassia firmly – too firmly. Cecily looked at her thoughtfully. 'Not like that. Of course he doesn't. But anyway, back to Fanny. I do think she could go back to school as well now. She's much much better.'

'When is it? The fashion show.'

'Pretty soon. Three weeks, Saturday the twenty-eighth. Edwina's got the most extraordinary man helping her with it, well, he's her boss, actually. I can't make out if he's—' She stopped suddenly, aware that Cecily was far from ready for a discussion about whether Edwina's new escort was a homosexual. 'If he's in love with her or not.'

'In love with her? Cassia, what are you talking about? What about Harry? She hasn't left him, has she?'

Cassia looked out of the window, felt herself flush, aware that she had been foolish, and more than foolish, expressing a dangerously strong bit of wish-fulfilment. 'Of course not,' she said hastily. 'You know Edwina, the way she exaggerates, rambles on about things.'

'Yes, I suppose so. Goodness, I can see I have a great deal of gossip to catch up on. Incidentally, it was so sweet of Edward to send me those flowers. Please tell him I'll write to him when I feel better.'

'Edward! Sent you flowers!'

'Yes, didn't you know? Oh dear, I hope you don't feel put out. Yes, he sent me two lots, actually, one just after the funeral, and one while I was ill. And a sweet note, too.'

'Oh, yes, of course, he did mention it,' said Cassia hastily. She could hardly have been more surprised if Cecily had told her Edward had come in to see her wearing an evening dress and high heels. And then thought that would really have been very inappropriate indeed and giggled.

Edwina looked at Harry slightly nervously across the dining table. His temper had clearly not improved; he was eating silently, rather fast, studying some papers as he did so. She would not normally have cared, would have simply fetched a magazine to read, but she had to ask him something that he might just not agree to. Finally, she cleared her throat and said, trying to keep her voice light, 'Harry, I'm so sorry to interrupt your reading, but I would like to speak to you just for a moment. If you can spare the time?'

'Yes?' he said. He looked up at her, his face still closed and heavy.

'We want to do some photographs next week, of some thick stockings, country shoes, that sort of thing.'

'We?'

'The magazine. And the idea I had was that we should use cars. As background.'

He frowned. 'You're planning to hang stockings over cars? It sounds a little bizarre.'

'No, of course not. No, naturally models will be wearing them. But standing on running boards, getting into the cars, that sort of thing.'

'Oh, I see. Yes. Well, it could look quite interesting, I suppose. Is that all?'

'Not quite, no. Harry, do stop being so irritating. Anyway, the point is, I wondered if we could use a couple of your cars? The prettier ones. The Hispano, for instance, it's so lovely. And the deLage. Possibly the Bugatti ...'

'Oh no,' he said, 'not the Bugatti. But yes, the others, if you like. On condition Manning is there. He'll have to get the deLage up from Brooklands, anyway. And I don't want anyone else driving any of them. Not even you. Certainly not you.'

'Yes, of course,' she said. She was amazed at the ease with which he had agreed. 'That's very good of you.'

He shrugged. 'It's no great hardship.'

'Well, thank you,' she said again, and then, feeling she should show a little interest in him, out of gratitude said, 'What are those papers you're reading?'

'Oh, company reports. Very dull. Coffee?'

'Please. The play went off very well last night.'

'Oh, really? And then where did you go? You weren't at the theatre, I imagine, until after three. Unless it was an extremely long play.'

'Oh, at the Embassy. With some friends. Rupert Cameron and his leading lady—'

'Yes, I saw her, unfortunately. This morning.'

'Oh, did you? She's rather beautiful, didn't you think?'

'I really hadn't noticed, I'm afraid. More cream?'

'No, thank you. Incidentally, I heard the most delicious bit of gossip last night.'

'Really? Do I have to listen to it?'

'Yes, you do,' she said, 'it's about Cassia.'

He said nothing, merely sipped at his coffee.

'You know what that article in the paper was saying? About her and Rupert?'

'I seem to remember something, yes.'

'Well, it does seem as if it's true. Her char was there last night, don't ask me why, I suppose because she's so drearily socialist, Cassia, I mean. Anyway, her husband said—'

'Cassia's husband?' His eyes were watchful suddenly.

'No, he wasn't there. Of course. No, the char's. He said that Rupert stays at Cassia's house all the time. That he stayed there only last Friday, the old chap gave him the key. Isn't that extraordinary? Well, you know what they say, no smoke without fire.'

'Indeed not,' said Harry.

Cassia was trying to concentrate on some reports she had to write for the Birth Control Association next morning when Edwina arrived at the door. She felt a wave of terror at the sight of her, as she had ever since the first night with Harry, terror and guilt, but Edwina looked perfectly cheerful and friendly.

'Can I come in? I want to ask you something.'

'Yes, of course. Why aren't you at work?'

'I am, sort of. I wondered if I could borrow your car next week?'

'My car! Why?'

'For a photograph. It's so pretty, that wonderful yellow, and we're already using two of Harry's, both blue. I thought it would complete the set. Would that be all right? I'll take great care of it, of course. In fact, I'll get Manning to pick it up, and drive it and so on, he's seeing to Harry's, naturally.'

'Well, yes, of course you can. If you want.'

'Thanks. Wednesday, it'll be, you're in town, aren't you? I can lend you my car for the day in its place if you like.'

'Oh, I don't think that'll be necessary. There's a rehearsal for the fashion show that evening, isn't there?'

'Yes. At Style House, in the studio. Such a godsend, that. Francis is being such an angel about it all.'

'He's very nice,' said Cassia carefully.

'Isn't he? I just adore him, such fun, always in a good mood – or nearly always. Unlike my own dear husband. Who is being – well, vile is the only word for it, at the moment. Filthy tempered, doesn't even speak at meals. I don't know, Cassia, I really don't, I sometimes can't see the point of our marriage at all. Specially now—'

'Now what?' said Cassia, quickly. Too quickly, she feared; but Edwina hadn't noticed anything.

'Well, now he knows about the children. You know?'

'What children?'

'That I can't have any.'

'Oh, I see,' said Cassia. She struggled to sound merely polite, lightly interested. 'When did you find that out?'

'Ages ago, actually. But I hadn't told Harry until I had that op, you know? Your Miss Gerard pinpointed the reason, actually. She's awfully nice, Cassia, I must say. Blocked tubes, apparently.'

'Blocked tubes. Oh, Edwina, that's very unlucky … Why on earth should you have blocked tubes?'

'Oh, you know.' Something in her face was intriguing; Cassia felt she had to go on.

'No, I don't know.'

'Oh, I suppose I might as well tell you. We're such old friends, after all. And you're not going to tell anyone, are you? Medical etiquette and all that.'

'No, of course not,' said Cassia. She didn't think it necessary to explain to Edwina all the ramifications of medical etiquette.

'I had an abortion,' said Edwina casually. 'Well, I had two actually, but the first was when I was only sixteen. Anyway, that was all right, but the second was just before I got married.'

'*Just* before?' said Cassia. 'You mean it was Harry's baby?' She knew pressing Edwina like this was dangerous, but she simply couldn't help it: it was one of the most fascinating conversations she had had in her life.

'No, that would have been all right. Obviously. No, Harry had been away, in New York. I had dinner one night with Roddy Buchanan, you remember him, such fun, I always had such a thing about him, cried buckets when he married Yolande. Well anyway, he was terribly miserable, said he'd made an appalling mistake, that he should never have married her, she was fooling around with some Indian prince, she'd gone to Paris, and we both got fearfully drunk and – well, one thing led to another, and a couple of weeks later I realised I was in the club. I felt absolutely dreadful, anyone would, it had only been the smallest, silliest mistake, I was so excited about marrying Harry, but there was nothing else for it, I had to get rid of it. Harry would have known, and anyway I couldn't possibly have – well, anyway. So I had an abortion. And it wasn't awfully well done. I mean the chap was perfectly competent, and it was in a pukka nursing home, not a backstreet thing or anything, but I got an infection of some sort. I felt lousy for weeks. It was hell on the honeymoon, I can tell you: I had to pretend to Harry I'd got flu and a really bad curse. Anyway, that was what did it, apparently. Simple as that.'

'Terribly simple,' said Cassia.

'Does that make sense to you? As a reason for the blocked tubes, I mean?'

'Oh, yes,' said Cassia, 'yes, I'm afraid so. I see it all the time. It must have been quite a bad infection, though.' She felt rather dazed, as if everything in the world had shifted.

'Yes, it was. Terribly painful, luckily that got better more or less before the wedding, but then I just felt awful, generally.'

'So,' she tried to sound detached, concerned, 'so Harry just thinks you're – well, that you can't have children. Doesn't know why.'

'Yes. I thought he was going to quiz me about it, after the op, you know, but he never did. He seems to have accepted it. It's a terrible shame, of course, but it's him that really minds. I mean, I do feel a bit of a failure, but I'd have made a lousy mother, don't you think? Anyway, it does seem to have taken a lot of point out of the marriage, really. Specially for Harry, it seems. We never were madly in love, just rather fond of each other, I suppose. And we suited each other. And got on pretty well. Now we don't seem even to do that. On the other hand ... oh, I don't know. I don't really fancy divorce, do you?'

'I haven't really thought about it,' said Cassia faintly.

'Oh, you must have done surely. Specially now, with all this about Rupert and so on.'

'Edwina, that has been hugely exaggerated. Honestly.'

'Oh, really? Not entirely, though, as far as I can make out. Come on now, has it?'

'Well,' said Cassia helplessly, 'not entirely, no, but—'

'Oh, darling.' Edwina looked at her and smiled. 'No need to cover up to me. Specially not after what I've just told you. Anyway, I won't say a word, obviously. It's entirely your affair. Literally.' She leant forward, patted Cassia on the arm. 'Look, I must go. Thanks so much about the car. Terribly sweet of you. See you soon.'

Cassia stood staring out of the window for quite a long time after the sound of Edwina's high heels clacking down the street had faded, and the sight of her brilliant red coat and hat had disappeared. She felt absolutely shattered, rather, she imagined, as one might after struggling to stay on a very wild horse for a long time, before falling off on to very hard ground. Her life generally seemed to resemble a very wild horse at the moment. She really wasn't sure how much longer she could continue to ride it.

But one thing at least had changed, importantly: any guilt she had felt about Edwina in connection with her affair with Harry had completely disappeared.

It was decided at a meeting in the boardroom of Boodles that morning, that several memberships which had come up for review could not be allowed to continue. One of the letters which went out later that day, informing him with great regret that this was the case, was to Mr Rollo Gresham. It was sent to the only address they had for him these days, a small service flat in Bath; the housekeeper there, who had just sent on one set of mail, put it aside to forward, when she had a few more letters, to his house in Marrakesh.

CHAPTER 30

Such tiny threads, our lives hang on, Cassia reflected, as she edged her way across London towards Balham in the grey November mist: a mist that was already thickening into a dark, woolly fog. Sixty years ago, her grandmother had met Leonora's mother at a tea party; without that tea party, Leonora would not have become her godmother, she would not have met Harry, quite possibly would not have been able to go to St Christopher's, and would therefore not have met Edward, would certainly not have inherited the money: the whole train of thought was frightening. As she pursued it, in all its complexities – where might she be living, who might she have married, who Bertie would be – cutting across an intersection just a little too fast, she almost ran into the back of a horse-drawn milk float, barely visible in the mist. She jammed on her brakes, and sat breathing rather fast, her heart thumping uncomfortably; she would clearly have to concentrate harder, if she were to reach the clinic alive.

A tiny thread was at that moment linking another life to hers, starting on another complex weave of events: Barbara Perkins, a twenty-two-year-old mother of three who had been putting off her visit to the birth control clinic for some time, largely on account of it being against her husband's wishes, discovered her youngest with the kitchen scissors, happily shredding up the new jumper that her mother-in-law had knitted for him. This was the last straw, added to several earlier ones, which included the eldest having fed her precious breakfast egg to the cat, and the middle one developing what looked suspiciously like mumps to Barbara's unpractised eye – not to mention the fact that she had thought she'd fallen again and had lived through three weeks of terror until her period had finally, blessedly arrived. And then her mother arrived somewhat fortuitously so that she could leave the children with her, and Barbara decided that a visit to the clinic was more important than her own nervousness or her husband's objections.

She had heard there was a new and very nice lady doctor at the clinic, really easy to talk to, her friend Joanne had said, didn't make you feel embarrassed at all; so maybe it wouldn't be too awful.

She'd been feeling rotten all day, which had probably added to her general desperation; the pain which had accompanied her period had been quite bad and was still with her, she couldn't think why, and she felt oddly shaky and weak.

She got to the clinic feeling so nervous she forgot about the pain; a young, rather smartly dressed woman followed her in, rummaging frantically through her bag as she did so. Barbara was very surprised to hear the large, cosy-looking nurse who sat in the waiting room saying that no, Dr Fallon, she hadn't seen the keys to the store cupboard anywhere. Well, she couldn't be much of a doctor, Barbara thought, hardly older than she was, and might have made that the excuse to leave again, had not a fresh wave of intense pain suddenly struck her and left her leaning on the cosy nurse's desk, trying to breathe deeply as they had told her she should when she was in labour.

'Are you all right?' It was the doctor, her face concerned.

'Yes,' Barbara said, 'I'm fine, just a bit of indigestion.'

'Here,' said the doctor, producing a tablet from her bag, 'chew this, they're really good. I'll try not to keep you waiting long, shouldn't be too busy this afternoon, with the fog and everything.'

She did seem very nice, Barbara thought, although her indigestion tablet didn't do much good – about as much good as the deep breathing had in labour – but she sat and read an advertisement in a magazine about the Aga cooker and how it would keep both husband and wife happy, the husband because it used so little fuel and would provide much better meals, the wife because it would mean Cook was in a good temper all the time.

'Bloody rubbish,' said Barbara aloud; her neighbour looked at her and raised her eyebrows. 'Sorry,' she said meekly, and turned the page to an article which told her that women were not necessarily the weaker sex, even if they couldn't change electric plugs or read train timetables. This both pleased and distracted her for a while, but then the pain began to increase in intensity again, and so did the weakness, and by the time she was finally called in to the doctor's office, she was feeling so bad she thought she might actually faint or be sick.

'Right,' said Cassia, 'do sit down, Mrs Perkins. Now just let me get a few details – address, age, and I presume you're married.'

'Too bloody right,' said Barbara.

Cassia looked up at her in amusement and saw that the face in front of her was very white, and that she was biting her lip. 'Are you all right?'

'Think so,' said Barbara Perkins, 'just got this pain still.'

'Where is it? show me.' Barbara indicated her lower abdomen. 'Is it very bad?'

'Quite bad, yes. It'll go, it was bad this morning as well.'

'Come and lie down on the bed. That's right. Now can you just pull your panties down a bit, so I can feel your tummy ...' She palpated Barbara's tummy gently; it was clearly very tender. There was a slight swelling on the right-hand side, almost imperceptible, in the area of the ovary; as she pressed that, Barbara winced. 'Sorry. Does that hurt a lot?'

'Yeah. A lot. And I feel a bit bit sick.'

She had an appendix scar: it wasn't that, then. A cyst perhaps? 'When did the pain start?'

'Oh, about a fortnight ago. On and off, not like this.'

'Have you had a period recently?'

'Yes, doctor. About two weeks ago.' Not a miscarriage threatening, then.

'Was it heavy?'

'No, not very bad at all. It was a relief, though. I did think—' She hesitated.

'Yes?'

'I did think I might have fallen again. We'd been – well, you know, we'd ...'

'Had intercourse?' said Cassia helpfully.

'Yes. At the wrong time. And he doesn't like – you know, the ... things.'

'No, they don't,' said Cassia. She sighed. 'Well, you're in the right place to get everything sorted. I think you could have something called an ovarian cyst. It isn't serious, but it can cause bad pain. I'd like to refer you to the hospital, you might have to have a very minor operation. Don't look so worried, a great friend of mine had it done recently, and she was back at work in a week or so. Anyway, let's get the other business sorted out and I'll give you a letter for the hospital.'

She measured the girl for a diaphragm, trying not to hurt her, worrying about the intense pain she seemed to be in. 'Right, then, get dressed and then come and sit at the desk again. I really think—'

There was a loud crash: Barbara Perkins, having stood up, had fainted. Cassia yelled for Nurse Hampton, lifted Barbara on to a chair, bent her forward, put her head between her knees.

Barbara Perkins yelled out.

'I'm sorry,' she said through chattering teeth, sitting up slowly, throwing her head back, 'it's bloody agony. It really is.'

Cassia looked at her; she was sweating, and a ghastly colour. 'Barbara, are you sure you had a period recently?'

'Yes, course I'm sure. I never was so glad to see anything in my life.'

'And when did you have this unprotected intercourse?'

'I don't know, about seven, eight weeks ago, I suppose. God almighty, this is horrible.'

Cassia thought fast, then she said, 'Excuse me a moment. Nurse will look after you.'

She went to the outer office, dialled St Christopher's, asked to be put through to Mr Scarsdale. God, if he was delivering a baby she'd scream. She was lucky: he wasn't, merely taking a clinic, a fact of which he informed her in an extremely impatient voice.

'Mr Scarsdale, I'm terribly sorry to bother you, but I need your help. It's Dr Fallon.'

'Yes, I had been informed of that.'

'Sorry. The thing is, I'm in my clinic in Brixton. I've a young woman here, and I'm pretty sure she's got an ectopic pregnancy ... What? Severe abdominal pain, tenderness, she's sweating badly, her pulse is a bit fast. Temperature slightly up, just under a hundred. BP's OK at the moment. Oh God, hold on a minute ... Yes, Nurse Hampton? Sorry, Mr Scarsdale, apparently she's just started bleeding. No, not a lot. No, it's not an appendix, she's had that out. Of course. Would you? I'd be so grateful. Thank you. Yes, I'll call for an ambulance from here. If you could be in Casualty when we get there, that would be wonderful. It would save time. Thank you so much. About twenty minutes, I suppose. Although with this fog ...'

She rang for an ambulance, then went back into her room. Nurse Hampton had laid Barbara Perkins on the bed, was holding her hand, wiping her sweating face.

'I think you just might have something called an ectopic pregnancy, Barbara,' said Cassia. 'That means the baby is growing not in your womb, but in one of your Fallopian tubes. Unfortunately, it can't possibly survive there.'

'Thank Christ for that,' said Barbara, her eyes meeting Cassia's with a flash of humour.

'Well, yes,' said Cassia, smiling back at her, 'maybe. But it could be dangerous unless we get you to hospital very soon. I've called an ambulance, and I'm going to come with you to St Christopher's Hospital. It's not the nearest, but it's very, very good and I happen to know the gynae staff there, I trained there. Just hang on, and in an hour or so, hopefully less, the worst will be be over.'

'I'll try. God, this is like labour, only worse. I was just reading an article about how we weren't the weaker sex. Too bloody right we aren't.'

The phone rang; Nurse Hampton went to answer it. 'I'm afraid we have a problem,' she said. 'That was St Christopher's. Because of the fog, ambulances are having a lot of trouble getting anywhere at all. It doesn't seem like a very good idea, taking Mrs Perkins over there.'

'Where's the nearest, then? Thomas's, I suppose. That's not a lot nearer. Oh wait, there's Queen Alexandra's, of course, why didn't I think of it? We can take her there ourselves, probably quicker than waiting for an ambulance. Barbara, if you lean on us, do you think you can walk out to my car?'

'I think so. Just.'

Cassia looked at her again; her colour had worsened. 'I'm just going to have another look at your tummy, if you don't mind. And take your blood pressure.'

The blood pressure was lower; she felt Barbara's abdomen carefully. It had changed; become hard, rigid even. Which pointed to a haemorrhage into the abdominal cavity. It must be an ectopic, couldn't be anything else. And if it had ruptured it was life threatening. Simple as that. She smiled at Barbara, patted her hand.

'You'll be fine. Come on, let's get you into my car. The hospital's very near.'

The fog was settling fast, but it was still not yet of the confusing, direction-losing variety. It had merely slowed the traffic to a crawl. They settled Barbara on the back seat, and Nurse Hampton crouched on the floor beside her. She was still only bleeding a little, but her teeth were chattering.

'Pulse?' said Cassia briefly.

'Quite steady,' said Nurse Hampton in a bright tone. 'BP dropped a bit. Nothing to worry about.'

It wasn't actually a very long journey from the clinic to the Queen Alexandra Hospital; up the Brixton Road for about a mile and then left and left again, doubling back into the Clapham Road. It was perfectly straightforward. In normal circumstances it would have taken ten minutes, fifteen at the most. But these were not normal circumstances. Cassia looked at the traffic ahead of her, and decided to take a back route: she knew the area fairly well, it had to be quicker. She turned left, started on a progression of left and right turns, leading her in the direction of the Kennington Road. God, she hoped she wasn't going to get lost now. It was extraordinary how swiftly you became disorientated in the fog: she could have sworn she should have passed that school, King George's Infants, about quarter of a mile before, and there it was now, looming up at her. And surely there was another left turn she could take almost immediately: it seemed to have totally disappeared. No, there it was. Thank God. At least they were making progress: the streets were virtually clear, and strangely silent, movements slowed, sounds muffled by the fog.

'Shan't be long now,' she said cheerfully, into the driving mirror. 'Two or three minutes at the most. How's the patient?'

The patient was silent. 'Pulse just a tiny bit unsteady,' said Nurse Hampton, her voice quiet with suppressed panic.

Cassia glanced over her shoulder. 'Blood pressure?'

'Ninety over sixty.'

'Bleeding?'

'About the same.'

No doubt about it now: internal haemorrhage. It was the only explanation for so fast a drop.

Someone shouted. She turned her attention back to the road just too late: great yellow lights seemed to rear up at her through the fog, and a large van, driving in the middle of the road, exactly as she was, rode relentlessly into her. There was the awful noise of screeching brakes, breaking glass, crunching metal: and then silence.

'Oh, Christ,' she said, getting out.

'Stupid bloody woman,' shouted the driver, 'sitting in the middle of the bloody road.'

'You were in the middle of it too,' said Cassia, surprised by her calm, 'and I'm very sorry, but I've got a woman in the back of my car, who'll die if we don't—'

'I don't care if you've got the bloody Queen of Sheba in your car, what are you going to do about my van?' The van looked astonishingly rather worse than the Jaguar: it was collapsed on to the road, its bonnet completely stove in, its front wheels buckled, and half resting on its mudguards, as if on its knees.

'Oh, God, I'm so sorry.'

'Sorry doesn't do me any good, does it?' He was shaking with rage and shock.

'Dr Fallon!' It was Nurse Hampton. 'I'm a little concerned.' That was code for desperate.

Cassia went over to the car; Barbara Perkins appeared unconscious.

'She's just vomited. She's in severe shock. Blood pressure's down again. And her abdomen is becoming extremely rigid.'

It was years since Cassia had been involved in a medical emergency; the last time had been a breech birth, resulting in a blue – although not dead – baby. The absolute concentration on the moment, the consideration of nothing else, the total lack of emotion, the clear insight into what had to be done, returned to her now with a thud of recognition.

'Nurse Hampton, you run to the hospital. It's not more than five minutes away by foot. Tell them she'll need immediate surgery, give her blood pressure and pulse rate, say there's internal haemorrhaging. Get them to bring a stretcher: we can't move her or carry her, it will do more harm than good. I'll stay here with her. You go down there, first left, then it's straight ahead of you. Good luck. And you – ' she said to the man – 'if you can't be useful and go and ask anyone in any of these houses for some towels and pillows, just sit down in your van and be quiet. I'll buy you a new van, I'll buy you two new vans if you like, but just stop shouting at me and making a bad situation worse.'

Whether it was hearing the magic word 'Doctor' or her tone, or the sight of Barbara Perkins lying on the back seat, apparently very close to death, the man set off obediently towards the nearest front door; at least it occupied him, Cassia thought, kept him from shouting at her. She felt for Barbara's pulse, and for a long time couldn't even find it. When she did it was weak and fluttery and very fast. She took her blood pressure again: seventy over fifty. Barbara's eyes flickered open suddenly, looked into hers. Cassia managed to smile.

'You're going to be fine,' she said, and, there being nothing else left to her to do, decided to try prayer.

Prayer worked. Less than ten minutes after Nurse Hampton had left the car, she first heard, then saw the miracle: a stretcher on wheels being pushed at a run by two orderlies, then a doctor and a nurse, followed by Nurse Hampton breathing very hard, but moving surprisingly quickly on her stout frame.

'Quick,' said Cassia, the words coming out in an oddly staccato manner, 'here, in my car, she's very, very bad, needs plasma immediately, emergency surgery, ectopic pregnancy, ruptured, I'm sure, pulse now failing, blood pressure seventy over fifty, severe rigidity of the abdomen—'

'Fine,' said the doctor, 'absolutely fine. We've alerted Theatre. Now if we can just lift her out … We've got plasma with us, if we can get a vein up. Excuse me, please,' he said with surprising courtesy to the van driver, who was standing, his arms holding what must be, Cassia thought, at least a dozen towels, and as many pillows, his face a mixture of fascination and horror as they lifted Barbara Perkins out of the car and settled her on to the stretcher.

'You'd better come with us,' she said, 'and I'll write you a cheque for the van once my patient is safely in hospital. And you might as well bring those towels. We could still need them.'

No one, thought Barry Andrews, following the strange procession through the streets, one nurse holding up the bag of fluid, the doctor firing questions at the posh woman with the flashy car, no one would believe this when he told them about it that night in the pub.

There was another thread being drawn towards the others in this particular weave that afternoon: Harry Moreton's chauffeur, Arthur Manning, who had had a very long, tedious morning waiting for his employer to emerge from a meeting which had overrun by an hour and a half, and then an extremely frustrating afternoon endeavouring and failing to get from the Reform Club to Curzon Street in a West End thrown into chaos by the fog, and being shouted at from the back seat for his pains, decided that what he needed to restore his spirits, before what threatened to be an even more difficult evening, was a piece of Cook's pork pie and a cup of tea. He went down to the kitchen in Mount Street where Cook was having her afternoon nap, and found the kettle simmering on the stove and a large piece of pie on the table. He was halfway through it when Nancy the kitchen maid came in and said she wouldn't really advise eating the pie, Cook had said it was off and was going to give it to next door for their dog. Manning said cheerfully that it tasted fine to him, much too good for a dog, and continued to eat it enthusiastically.

Cassia was drinking a cup of coffee in the waiting room when a tiny, rather stern-faced woman doctor dressed in a heavy tweed suit under her white coat came over to her.

'Dr Fallon? I'm Monica Gerard, consultant obstetric surgeon here.' Of course: it was Miss Gerard's hospital. She'd forgotten.

'Is she going to be all right?'

'Yes, she is. Very dicey at one point, and she needed a lot of blood, but everything's steadying now. Ectopic, as you said, ruptured, and we've had to sever the tube, but yes, fine. That was clever of you. Not easy to spot. As for getting here in this fog ...'

'Yes, it wasn't too good. You should see my car.'

'Oh dear. Well, you did better than a lot of ambulances. And I hear your lass arrived on foot.'

Hearing the redoubtable Nurse Hampton described as a lass made Cassia smile. 'Yes. She was marvellous.'

'I know your name, and can't think how.'

'I suggested a friend of mine came to you. Edwina Moreton.'

'Ah yes.' The small stern face softened. 'Mrs Moreton. Is she quite well now?'

'Quite well,' said Cassia quickly.

'Good. So where do you work?'

'Oh, nowhere much,' said Cassia, 'just a couple of birth control clinics and the new postnatal at St Christopher's. I trained there.'

'Oh, did you? Why aren't you doing a decent job somewhere?'

'Well, I got married and ...'

'Foolish woman.' Monica Gerard almost smiled. 'Ever regret it? Terrible thing to do, you know, wasting all that training.'

'I know,' said Cassia humbly. 'So I was told in no uncertain terms. By Mr Amstruther, you know?'

'I do indeed. Old friend. So you trained under him, did you?'

'Yes, I did. I wanted to do obstetrics but ...'

'Hmm. So you're fitting lasses up with diaphragms all day. Dear, oh dear.' Miss Gerard looked at her watch. 'I must go. I've got a section to do – twins, one a breech. Look, we should talk some more. Ring my rooms and make an appointment.'

It clearly didn't occur to her that Cassia might not wish to talk to her. But then, thought Cassia, it wouldn't. And it shouldn't.

'I don't feel too good,' said Manning to Mrs Manning, falling on to his bed with a groan at one that morning, having delivered Harry Moreton safely and finally to his door.

'Well, you shouldn't have eaten all that cheese,' said Mrs Manning, 'it always gives you indigestion.'

'Wasn't the cheese,' said Manning, and then suddenly shot out of bed and into the small bathroom next door. He emerged five minutes later looking green, and then had to rush back again before he even reached the bed.

Mrs Manning sighed. It was obviously going to be a long night.

Edwina was just reflecting how wonderfully lucky it was that the fog had cleared in time for her photographic session in Hyde Park with the cars, when Bishop came into the dining room. Harry, whose temper could always be measured at breakfast by the amount he ate (worse meant more), was just buttering his third piece of toast.

Bishop cleared his throat. 'I'm very sorry, Mr Moreton, but Mr Manning will not be able to drive you today. He is indisposed.'

'Oh Jesus,' said Harry, 'what a bloody awful nuisance. Well, I'll have to use taxis, I suppose. Get me one, would you, Bishop? In about fifteen minutes?'

'Certainly, sir.'

'Harry,' said Edwina, 'you might at least think of me. I've got my photographic session with the cars today. How am I going to manage without Manning?'

'I have no idea,' said Harry. 'Do it another day perhaps?'

'I can't. You just don't understand. The models have been booked, and the photographer and—'

'Edwina, I really can't be held answerable to your magazine and its arrangements, I'm afraid. And although its administration is fascinating, I unfortunately don't have the time to listen to the details now. You must excuse me.'

'Oh, Harry, really. Well, I'll just have to drive them myself, one at a time, and get taxis back. Or maybe—'

'Edwina, are you out of your mind? Do you really think I'm going to allow you to drive those cars through the streets of London?'

'What else can I do? I've got to have them. Simply got to. I shall be fired if I don't.'

'Dear me,' said Harry. He stood up. 'You must excuse me, I'm afraid.'

'Harry, please! It's so important. Look, it's not so far from your office, is it? Couldn't you drive one at least, the Hispano, and then get a taxi? And maybe you could trust me with the deLage?'

'Oh God,' he said and sighed, then looked at his watch. 'Yes, all right, Edwina, I'll drive the Hispano. But you're not driving anything. Bishop, you drive pretty well, will you follow me with Mrs Moreton in the deLage? To Hyde Park. And then hopefully Manning will have recovered later and will be able to collect the cars.'

'Certainly, sir. It will be a pleasure, sir.'

It did not seem to have occurred to either of them, Bishop thought, to enquire after Manning, or the nature of his indisposition. There were occasions, and this was one of them, when Bishop's unquestioning loyalty to his employers was shaken. Nevertheless, he was delighted at the prospect of driving the deLage. He had done it once before, when one of the other cars had had a breakdown on the Great West Road, and Harry had needed to be transported to Oxford urgently. He had never forgotten the sheer heady pleasure, not simply of feeling such an enormous amount of motor car under his control, but the expressions of awe and sheer naked envy on the faces of the other drivers as he waited beside them at traffic lights and crossroads.

Cassia woke up late, and phoned the Queen Alexandra to enquire after Barbara Perkins. She was recovering, they said, but would not be able to go home for at least two weeks. Cassia, remembering the flushed, fleshy features of Mr Perkins scowling at her on the doorstep when she called to explain, clearly seeing Barbara's near death as something designed to inconvenience him, and her mother's whining voice saying she couldn't be expected to drop everything and look after their children just like that, felt a pang of pity for the Perkins children; and then, remembering her own, and the fact that Delia had been fractious the day before and that Janet had remarked, with a dazzling smile, that it looked as if she might be getting Bertie's chicken pox, telephoned Monks Ridge.

'Yes,' said Janet, as if she were imparting the news that Father Christmas had just arrived early, 'yes, she is poxy. And a tiny bit irritable. But nothing to worry about, Mrs Fallon, we're all absolutely fine here. No need to rush back.'

'Oh, well, if you really think so. And how was school for Bertie?' Bertie had returned to his old school on that Monday; the first day had been fine, but she had still been worrying about him, worrying that the other boys might tease him, think he was a cissy.

'Splendid still. It's as if he'd never been away. Already back in the football team, and I've asked a couple of his friends here for tea, after team practice. I thought that would be a nice positive thing for him.'

'Oh, Janet, how clever you are.' Now why couldn't she have thought of that? 'Thank you. Well, see you tomorrow.'

'Yes, Mrs Fallon. And don't worry about Delia, she'll be fine. We're going to do lots of painting, take her mind off it.'

'Thank you. And Dr Fallon? Is he all right?'

'He's fine, Mrs Fallon, yes. You remember he has a meeting in London tomorrow, at the College of Physicians, something to do with the proposals for this new Health Service?'

'Oh, yes.' She hadn't remembered, of course. 'Well, tell him I'll see him tomorrow evening, would you?'

Cassia put the phone down feeling inadequate and depressed, her sense of panic rising within her again. Sometimes she wondered if it would matter if she never went back to the house at all, if indeed it might be better for everyone if she did not. She forgot everything these days, everything except her own problems and – oh God. She'd forgotten something else now. Edwina's photographic session. Well, there was no way she'd want her car now. But she should have told her.

She dialled the number. Florence, Edwina's maid, answered the phone. No, Mrs Moreton had left, and so had Mr Moreton, and Bishop with them, taking two of the cars somewhere, Hyde Park, she thought. Yes, definitely Hyde Park, near the Serpentine, Mrs Moreton had said.

'Oh God,' said Cassia. There was nothing else for it, she'd just have to go up there herself.

The car still went, surprisingly well. It looked dreadful, rather like a child with a bloodied nose, with its lovely headlamps crushed and its radiator bent in, and its bumper broken in half, but it would be easier to drive it to Hyde Park – at least Edwina would be able to see for herself that it was unusable. Otherwise she'd argue for hours. She pulled on her sable coat – it was terribly cold – and her gloves and went out to her car.

'Look, Edwina, I'm going now,' said Harry. 'Don't on any account move that car or let anyone else move it, apart from Bishop. All right?'

'Yes, all right,' said Edwina crossly. The morning so far was not going well. Justin was in a bad temper, the models were late, and one of the two borzoi dogs she had hired for the day had just slipped its leash and plunged joyfully into the Serpentine. 'But— Oh my God. Just look at Cassia's car. What on earth does she think she's doing? Oh, it's too bad.'

'Looks as if it's been used as a war amublance,' said Justin. 'Really, darling, this is all we need.'

'I'm so sorry, Edwina,' said Cassia, hurrying over to them. 'Oh, hallo, Harry. I didn't think you'd be here.'

'Neither did I,' he said shortly, 'nor do I want to be. I'm just leaving, in fact and – oh Christ, get off me, you filthy, fucking animal.' The borzoi had tired of the Serpentine and its delights and decided to return in search of its trainer and the small biscuits she carried with her as rewards for good behaviour. On its way, it saw Harry; all dogs liked Harry, as did cats and the fact that he loathed both species deterred them not at all. The borzoi was now leaping up at him, attempting to lick his face, its once luxuriously white, perfectly coiffed coat slimy and matted, leaving a trail on Harry's camel-wool overcoat.

Cassia tried not to laugh and failed; then she met Harry's furious eyes and said, 'Sorry. I'm really sorry. It's not funny.' He said nothing.

'What on earth happened to your car?' said Edwina. 'I can't imagine how you could be so stupid.'

'Well, you see, I collided with a van yesterday, I had a woman in it, she'd collapsed in the clinic – she was desperately ill, we had to get her to hospital, and because of the fog the ambulances weren't getting through so—'

'So it was being used as a war amublance!' cried Justin, clapping his hands. The story seemed to have completely cheered him up. 'How divine. I think we should use the car, Edwina. As a kind of witty aside. You know?'

'No, I don't,' said Edwina irritably. 'It's appalling, and look at the inside, God, it's disgusting, Cassia, really.'

'Well, I'm sorry,' said Cassia, finally indignant. 'I didn't do it on purpose, Edwina, and I forgot till this morning—'

'You forgot! My photographic session! Cassia, how could you?'

'Edwina, you really are monstrous,' said Cassia. 'You might spare a moment's thought for me – and my patient, come to that. Since you're so very concerned, I have to tell you she survived emergency surgery. Performed by Miss Gerard, as a matter of fact. Although she nearly died, and would have done without my war ambulance. Well, I'll take it away. I'm so very sorry to have inconvenienced you.'

'Oh, don't be so ridiculous,' said Edwina. 'Of course I'm glad the wretched woman didn't die, but it's just so – well, so difficult for me.'

'It was quite difficult for me as well,' said Cassia. 'And I did love this car, and just look at it.' She sighed, and patted the bonnet of the Jaguar tenderly.

'It hardly matters, though, does it?' said Harry Moreton suddenly. His voice was extraordinarily hostile: even Justin turned to look at him. 'I mean you can buy another one, after all, can't you? You can buy a dozen more if you want to. Edwina, I'll see you later, no doubt.' And he turned on his heel and walked away from them.

It wasn't the hostility that had made Cassia realise – she was growing used to that – it was the bitterness, the awful, naked bitterness on his face as he'd said she 'could buy a dozen cars if she wanted. It had been curiously personal, that bitterness, it had come not from his head, not from a straightforward observation, but from his heart, an emotional plaint; it had shaken her, shocked her even. And finally decided her, after all, that she could not let matters rest.

CHAPTER 31

'Cecily, you look wonderful. Doesn't she, Justin?'

'Beautiful!' said Justin, taking Cecily's hand and kissing it.

'Of course I don't,' said Cecily. 'I look frightful. But at least I'm thin. For now, anyway. I'm eating like a pig.'

'Cecily,' said Justin severely, 'you could never look frightful. Not with those eyes. Could she, Edwina?'

'Absolutely not. So Cecily, when are you leaving here?'

'I've promised Fanny to come to your show,' said Cecily, 'so I suppose that means in a week. I'm – well, I'm a bit frightened. To tell you the truth.'

'Frightened!' said Edwina. 'What on earth about?'

'I know exactly what,' said Justin. He smiled at her. 'You've been in here, safe and sound, for a long time.'

'Yes.' She stared at him, surprised at his understanding. 'Yes, that's right, but—'

'You'll be fine,' he said. 'We'll all look after you, won't we, Edwina?'

'Oh, yes,' said Edwina. She sounded rather less enthusiastic than he did.

'It would be marvellous to have you there on Saturday,' said Justin, 'seeing your lovely little daughters in their moment of glory.'

'Yes, I know,' said Cecily. She had been regaled by Fanny for a very long time about the most recent rehearsal of the fashion show, almost to the point of losing concentration, indeed had been accused of not listening.

It formed a wonderful bridge, the show, spanning the gulf between her and Fanny, easing them back into closeness; she was almost herself again now, this small, beloved daughter of hers, although a little thin, and still, it had to be admitted, a little wary of her; and Cecily knew she had to find the courage to go, to see her, that that would close the gulf completely.

She realised Edwina was talking again; also about the fashion show. It did seem to be absorbing an awful lot of people's time and energy; she hoped it would be worth it for them all.

'Anyway,' Edwina was saying now, 'we have another full rehearsal on Sunday, with all the clothes this time, if Leon de Rosay has managed to finish the bridesmaids' dresses, all the girls are coming, the professionals are doing the rehearsal for nothing, which is sweet of them, don't you think, and – Cecily, are you all right?'

'Yes, I'm fine,' said Cecily, wiping her eyes on a rather inadequate handkerchief. 'Sorry, it was just hearing Leon de Rosay's name reminded me of – well, it was a bit of a bad evening, that one. That's all.'

'Poor you,' said Justin. He rummaged in the pocket of his jacket and produced a very large handkerchief. 'Here you are, this is clean, I promise. The worst thing about what you've been through is that every single occasion, or place, or piece of music, or anything, is a memory. Everything hurts, life's a minefield.'

'Well,' said Edwina, looking at them, half amused, 'I think I might leave you two together. I've got an awful lot to do. Cecily, if you need any help, you know, getting home or anything, I can always send Manning.'

'Thank you so much,' said Cecily, and giggled. Her emotions were so raw still, so mixed up, that laughter followed on tears with hideous ease.

'I can't see why that's funny,' said Edwina, bending to kiss her. 'Anyway, lovely to see you out of bed. You need a few new clothes, don't you, though? That's really not very flattering, so baggy, although I suppose you'll grow into it again. Bye, then. Justin, are you really sure you want to stay here on your own?'

'Yes,' said Justin, 'yes, I'm quite sure. I'll see you tomorrow, darling.'

As Edwina left, they looked at one another and laughed.

'She really is a monster,' he said. 'She thinks not only the world, but the universe, centres around her. But one has to like her, goodness knows why. Now, shall I ring for some more tea, and biscuits? We have to feed you up a bit.'

'Oh, yes please!' said Cecily. 'But I'll have to stop eating like this soon – I'll be the size of a cushion again in no time.'

'Nonsense. You looked lovely before, I thought. I get very tired of these stick insects of ladies. I'm sure your husband didn't want you to look like them.'

'Oh, I don't know,' said Cecily. 'I don't know what he wanted – from me at any rate,' and burst into tears again.

Justin wiped her eyes tenderly on the handkerchief again. 'Another minefield exploded,' he said. 'It's important to talk about him, you know, remember him properly. When my wife left me—'

'Your wife!' said Cecily. She was so surprised she could feel her mouth dropping open; she shut it hastily.

'Yes. She left me for some rather unpleasant Italian, and I was very unhappy for a very long time. But in the end I learnt that I had to remember the happy times, otherwise all those years were wasted, thrown away. You must do the same. It's—' The door opened and a smiling student nurse came in with a heavily laden tray. 'Oh, my goodness, now what do we have here? Warm scones, how wonderful. And cream! Cecily, come on, let's eat mountains of it all.'

After he had gone, she sat looking out at the cedar tree and wondering about his marriage. Presumably his wife had left him for all the reasons she had nearly left Benedict. It was very odd that she found him such good company, so extraordinarily soothing and comforting. Odd and really very nice.

Cassia sat in the waiting area of Miss Gerard's rooms in Harley Street reading an article in *The Times* about the visit of the King to the horribly depressed areas of South Wales. He had visited the labour exchange at Merthyr when it had been full of men waiting hopelessly for work, and spoken to a great many of them personally, and then insisted on visiting the steel works at Dowlais, where hundreds of unemployed men who had been waiting for him had stood up and sung an old Welsh hymn. The King had, the reporter said, been patently moved, and had turned to an official saying, 'Something must be done to find these people work.' *The Times*, remarking on his capacity for sympathy, said he had spoken words that had ensured him a place in history.

Cassia remembered the evening in the South of France, so long ago now it seemed, when she had sat in the soft, scented darkness, listening to Harry defending the King and his capacity for sympathy and indeed his great talent for communication with the ordinary man. It was an extraordinarily vivid and painful memory; when the secretary told her to go in to Miss Gerard she found herself disorientated and upset.

Miss Gerard's brisk voice brought her back to the present. 'Dr Fallon. Yes. Nice to see you again. Your young woman is recovering very well. And when I told her she would be almost certainly unable to have any more children, she appeared about to leap out of her bed and embrace me. I'm recommending a ligature of the remaining tube, just in case.'

'Good,' said Cassia. 'I'll go in and see her if I have time.'

'Do. She was very complimentary about you. As was Horace Amstruther when I spoke to him. Two pretty good recommendations, I'd say.'

'Well, both a bit prejudiced, I'm afraid.'

'My dear girl,' said Monica Gerard, 'if you think it is easy to prejudice Horace Armstruther in your favour, you have him very wrong, I assure you. Never was a man more monstrously prejudiced against women. Or men, for that matter, should they happen in some minute way to fall out of his rather exacting standards. So well done. Now then. Proposition for you.'

Cassia's heart lurched. A proposition! From Monica Gerard, FRCS DObstRCOG, one of the most highly regarded women obstetricians in the country, possibly the world. This was not what she had envisaged when she had phoned her rather nervously. The most, the very most, she had hoped for had been a few words of advice and just possibly encouragement.

'I'm enlarging the department at Alex's. Got the backing of the board, although God knows how all this National Health Service business might affect it. Mind you, I'm not against all that; in fact, I'm rather in favour. Anyway, that's by the way. I'm recruiting a new team. I'm looking for young, talented people, surgeons, women preferably. I get a strong gut instinct about the sort of people I want to work with, and you're one. I'd like you to come on board.' Cassia sat staring at Monica Gerard, felt her face flush, felt tears rising behind her eyes. She blinked them hastily away; she was sure those fierce dark eyes had not harboured tears, except possibly of exhaustion, for several decades. She felt as if someone had come into the room and tossed the moon into her lap, told her she could keep it, yet felt at the same time quite calmly confident, as if she had been coming to this moment all her life, as if it had been waiting for her patiently, almost as if it was her due. She forgot about Harry, about Edward, even about her children. She knew only the same sense of fierce concentration and singleminded purpose so long forgotten and brought back to her the week before as she had steered Barbara Perkins through her crisis. Her response did not mirror this sensation.

'But I never even did a house job,' she said.

'I'm perfectly aware of that,' said Monica Gerard. 'More fool you, of course, but what's done is done. Or rather not done. You can do it here. Providing you can square your domestic arrangements, I see no reason why not. Then you can move straight on to registrar status. All right?'

'I – well ...'

'Oh, now come along,' said Miss Gerard, a touch of impatience in her voice. 'Surely you can sort out a few children? Horace Amstruther said you weren't short of money. You'll have to live in, of course, but you should be able to get home fairly regularly. A good nanny, surely, a London house ...'

Her mind was racing, veering about now, contemplating the children, Edward, resiting Janet, resiting all of them, hauling their lives around, contemplating possibilities, assessing probabilities. 'Well, I suppose—'

'Good,' said Miss Gerard briskly, holding out her hand. 'Splendid. We can get you in after Christmas, that should give you plenty of time. I must ask you to leave now, I'm afraid. I've a frightfully demanding woman coming in, seven months pregnant, prima gravida, big baby as far as I can establish, tiny pelvis, refusing a section, so far at any rate, terrified of anaesthesia, insisting on natural birth, all that silly nonsense, although of course the first twinge and she'll be screaming. I know her sort. I dread her confinement more than I can tell you. Perhaps you should come along. Well, you might even be at Alex's by then. We'll see. Anyway,' she stood up, held out her hand, 'delighted. Keep in touch, let me know when you've sorted yourself out.'

Cassia walked out into Harley Street not sure if she was in heaven or in hell.

'Anyway, our marriage is over,' said Edward. 'That's one thing I am sure about.' He looked at Cecily rather helplessly. He was not usually given to personal revelations, but she was so gentle, so encouraging, so nonjudgemental, had been through so much herself, it suddenly seemed rather easy.

He had been to see her on an impulse; he had volunteered as a member of the Sussex branch of a committee being organised to study the proposals for the National Health Service and the reaction of GPs to it, and there had been a committee meeting that morning. Cassia was at her fashion show rehearsal with her friends and Janet had taken all the children to visit an aunt in Hastings; he had no wish to sit alone at Monks Ridge reflecting upon the wreckage of his marriage.

Cecily smiled at him, and reached forward, patted his hand. 'I don't think you should feel that,' she said. 'It's much too early to say. And if it's all this nonsense about her and Rupert ...'

'Oh that!' he said, frowning at her. 'No, it's not that. I don't give a toss about that. I don't like the man very much, but ...' Edward realised with a sense of slight shock that he had no reason whatsoever to dislike Rupert: he was a charming and courteous man who had never shown him anything other than friendship. 'I suppose it's just because Cassia is so fond of him. Always has been. I don't actually believe all this stuff about them having an affair, but I do mind that she is so close to him, tells him everything.'

'That's not his fault,' said Cecily mildly.

'No, I know. And I also know that compared to him I must seem very dull.'

'To me you don't seem anything of the sort,' said Cecily. 'I actually find Rupert rather irritating, between you and me. I'm very fond of him, of course, but that endless charm of his, and that rather fake self-flagellation he goes in for – well, I would rather tell everything to you. If I were Cassia,' she added hastily.

Edward sat with his head bent, fearfully embarrassed now. He should never have embarked on this discussion, he thought, and wondered wildly if he should not pretend a sudden pressing engagement, a train to catch. It would appear callous, though, callous and rude; especially when Cecily was trying so hard to help him.

'Cassia is a very special person, you know,' she said, 'very special. She is headstrong and self-centred at times, of course she is. But she is brave and clever and an extraordinarily loyal friend. As of course you are: I owe you a great deal for taking Fanny in when I was so ill.'

'It was nothing, really,' said Edward, thinking remorsefully of the complaints he had made about Fanny, about having her to stay.

'It was a lot. And you have to remember,' she added, leaning forward and in her earnestness taking his hand, 'it can't have been easy for Cassia, coming into all that money. It sounds like a dream come true, but actually it's also a nightmare. Very hard to handle. For you, of course, but also for her.'

Edward stared at Cecily; her hand in his was very gentle and warm and her eyes sweetly sympathetic. He felt as if he had been tossing about on a bed of barbed wire and someone had come along and said, look, if you just shift over here a bit, it's softer and quite warm and you'll be a lot more comfortable.

'I've been a terrible husband to her,' he said suddenly, 'really terrible, but it was so hard, when she – oh God.' He felt tears rising behind his eyes, swallowed hard, horrified at himself.

'Of course you haven't. Well, sometimes no doubt you have. As I was sometimes a terrible wife. But I've learnt – well, I'm learning,' she corrected herself hastily, 'to admit it and to admit the good things too. You must do the same, otherwise it's not fair on anyone.'

Edward left her shortly after that, and drove back to Sussex feeling much happier. He was still quite sure that his marriage was over, but he no longer felt quite so bitter about it. Or so self-reproachful.

'Well, thank God for the myth about dress rehearsals,' said Rupert finally, collapsing into a chair in Francis Stevenson-Cook's rather grand office on the corridor below the photographic studio. He had made it available to the cast for the evening, and it had become an unofficial green room, set with bottles of wine and glasses and Thermos jugs of coffee and tea. It was after ten; and the last model had departed, and Francis and Edwina had gone off with several of the non-professional models to calm their nerves, as they put it, at the KitKat Club.

'Do you think it is a myth?' said Cassia. 'About dress rehearsals, I mean?'

'Oh, darling, I'm afraid so. I've been to some magnificent dress rehearsals which have become magnificent shows, and some terrible rehearsals which have become terrible shows. It's actually quite rare for the opposite case, but it keeps people calm.'

'It was rather awful,' said Cassia, 'when Venetia Hardwicke kept tripping over that trailing hem. And that other girl, that friend of Edwina's with the long hair, you know, went on and on coming in at the wrong time. I was listening to some of the professionals up here later, they were *so* disapproving. Mind you, the bride wasn't exactly wonderful – I wouldn't have thought a couple of twirls while those adorable children danced round her was so very difficult.'

'Oh, don't. I'm surprised Evelyn Brunel didn't actually hit her at one point. I'm actually quite relieved now that the ballet is down to her. Now, Cassia, let's get drunk.'

'Don't let's,' said Cassia. 'It caused rather a lot of trouble last time.'

'Oh, darling, I'm so desperately sorry about that.'

'Well, Rupert, it was hardly rape,' said Cassia with a sigh. 'Anyway, let's not talk about it, Rupert, please. I can't bear it and I have other problems, much worse ones.'

'Tell me about them,' said Rupert, leaning forward, wiping away a tear that was trickling down her face. Things had eased between them recently, mostly, he knew, because of an increase in his own self-confidence: he no longer felt obsessed with his failure in every possible direction – even with women.

'No, honestly, it won't help.'

'Very well. Let's talk about me, then. Such a very agreeable subject. Bookings are now solid up to March. Isn't that wonderful?'

'It is wonderful, Rupert. And I've really enjoyed being involved. It's been very exciting.'

'Well, you obviously have an eye for a good play. You should back some more. This one is clearly going to make you very rich.'

'Oh, don't talk about being rich,' said Cassia. Her voice was irritable, fretful even. 'I don't think I'm very good at it, not very good at all.'

He looked at her curiously. 'You've stopped spending it, haven't you?' he said. 'No new cars or frocks or houses even for ages. Why? Nothing more you want?'

'Oh, no. Lots of things, actually. I was thinking quite seriously about buying a plane. I went flying with – well, with someone, and it was wonderful. And I plan to buy the boys ponies, it's just that ...' She smiled at him; her old shaky, reluctant smile. He knew that smile very well: it preceded confidences of some magnitude. This was no exception. 'I've stopped spending it because I think – well, I think I might have to give the money back.'

The room seemed to sway a little. Rupert stared at her and it was if she were suddenly speaking Swahili, for all the sense it made. He took a large swig of wine to steady himself.

'Give it back!' he said finally. 'Cassia, darling, who on earth to?'

'I'm not sure,' she said, 'but if it's come from where I think it has, I'm not keeping it. Not any of it.'

'And where do you think that might be?' he said, determinedly keeping the conversation light. 'The Bank of England?'

'No,' she said simply. 'Harry Moreton.'

The room did not sway this time: it froze into a silent stillness. He said nothing himself for a long time and then, finally, forcing himself to smile, 'Well, I can't believe he needs it.'

'Of course he doesn't,' she snapped, ignoring his attempt to treat her remarks as in any way humorous, 'but he's going to have it. If it is his. I certainly don't want it.'

'Cassia,' he said gently, 'I'm a simple fellow. Very simple. I need to have things explained to me very clearly. Could you please tell me why Harry Moreton should suddenly have handed over half a million pounds to you, and pretended it came from Leonora?'

'He likes to be in control of people,' she said, her voice very low, 'and he wanted my marriage to fail. I think he thought this way he might manage that.'

'But, darling, how, for God's sake?' Rupert was beginning to feel he was on some kind of emotional quicksand; moreover, that he was sinking into it very fast.

'Well, he has managed it. If it was him. The money has wrecked my marriage. It's over, Rupert, absolutely. Isn't it?'

'Here,' he said, handing her his handkerchief, putting his arms round her. 'Cry, if you want to, but then listen to me. You've got to stop blaming yourself for all this. I've said it before: your marriage has failed because you and Edward are basically unsuited, not because you suddenly came into a lot of money.'

'Rupert, if I hadn't had that money, I'd still be with Edward. Perfectly happy – all right, not perfectly,' she said, seeing his face, 'but pretty happy, and I think Harry knew that would happen.'

'I still don't see why Harry should have done such a thing. I know there was always a lot of animosity between you, but that seems a little extreme.'

Cassia was clearly finding the conversation increasingly difficult. 'It's not really animosity,' she said finally, 'it's something quite different. The one thing I've never told you.'

He had never even suspected it: that was what hurt most. That he had thought he knew her so well, and this thing, so central to her, had remained a secret, too important to entrust even to him. 'Well,' he said finally, his voice carefully light, 'I must say I was never quite deceived by your affirmations that you hated Harry. Methought you did protest a bit too much. But I had no idea … Lucky old sod, that's all I can say.' It was probably the most difficult speech he had ever had to deliver, and there had been no rehearsal for it. But he got through it, and clearly successfully: he saw her relax suddenly, smile.

'Well, not really lucky. Not any more. We've quarrelled.'

'Darling, you've been quarrelling all your lives. I can't remember a time when you weren't.'

'No. This is different. Final. Let's not talk about it.'

She was keeping something from him still; he decided to leave it for now, managed to smile at her again, say still in the same, light voice, 'I'm sorry, darling, but I don't think much of your plot. Purest melodrama, if you ask me. Don't take up script writing, whatever you do. Not even I would take a part in such a drama. If Harry had wanted to manipulate you, he could have done it far more easily – and cheaply, I would have thought. And do you really think even he is rich enough to cast such an enormously expensive piece of bread upon the waters? And that Leonora would agree to such a piece of connivance? Of course she wouldn't. Honestly, darling, your imagination has been not just running, but galloping away with you.'

'I can see it sounds insane, although you're wrong about Leonora: she was very unhappy about my marriage too, and she was a great mischief-maker, dearly as I loved her. And I still don't see how the money can have come from her. Every bit of evidence I've got seems to show that she and Rollo were in financial difficulties.'

'But darling, Leonora was always in financial difficulties. She'd have been in them if she'd been married to Midas. And what evidence, anyway?'

'Oh, various things. I told you about the pawn tickets, then Miss Monkton, you remember her, she found Leonora living in extremely difficult circumstances in Paris. All alone and ill. I'm quite sure it was Harry who rescued her from that, not Rollo at all.'

'Have you asked him?'

'Yes, and he denied it. Obviously. But he's so clever, so devious.'

'Yes, well, you should stick to simple chaps. Like me,' he said. The pain was beginning to worsen; combined with all the wine he had drunk, it was making him feel rather sick. She looked at him, he saw concern in her eyes.

'Rupert, the way I feel about Harry has nothing whatever to do with how I feel about you. Nothing. I still love you terribly, you are my dearest—'

'Friend,' he said, no longer trying to disguise the bitterness, the sense of rejection he felt. 'I suppose that's all we ever were. I thought perhaps – the other night ...'

'Oh, Rupert, darling! How many times have we said the other night was a sort of madness? A lovely, happy madness, that shouldn't have happened, that nearly spoilt everything between us.'

And because he did love her so much, because he could see that this was the moment, the turning point, when he could either lose her for ever or have her back as a loving friend, he managed to smile again, to say, drawing warmth, tenderness into his voice, 'Yes, of course we have. And it was. I regret it as much as you do, lovely as it was. I've hated that it spoilt things between us.'

'Not just between us,' she said suddenly.

'You and Edward?'

'No. Funnily enough, it didn't seem to bother him very much.'

'Was this the reason for the quarrel, then?' he said suddenly. 'This final quarrel between you and Harry? Was that what you wouldn't tell me before?'

'Yes,' she said quietly. 'Yes, it was, I'm afraid. He accused me of being a whore.'

'You mean you told him?'

'Not exactly, but he's very good at getting the truth out of people.'

'Oh dear, Cassia,' he said, half amused, half shocked, 'your honesty will get you into trouble one of these days.'

'It already has,' she said, trying to smile at him. There was something wrong in this account, he felt, something illogical; had it been a scene in a play he would have said it didn't make absolute sense, needed rewriting. But he couldn't quite think what it was.

'Well, I'm terribly sorry,' he said eventually, still struggling to keep his voice light. 'I certainly would not have wished to come between you and the love of your life.' Suddenly he couldn't bear it any longer, any of it. 'Look, I'm awfully tired, and so are you. Shall we call it a night?'

'Yes, I'm sorry. Thank you for listening to me, Rupert. As always, I feel better. Much better.'

They went out into the street, found taxis, kissed one another goodnight. Rupert went home to his small, lonely room and lay awake for a long time, thinking that for the first time in his life he could empathise with Edward Fallon. He was deeply, horribly jealous of Harry Moreton too. Only Edward had had the sense to recognise the fact, and the reason for it, if subconsciously, where he, Rupert, had been extremely and foolishly blind.

'I really should go home,' said Edwina, 'it's almost midnight.'

'Don't go home,' said the man sitting next to her, whose name was St John Vincent. 'Our little gathering will be greatly diminished if you do, and I was going to ask you to join us at a small party.'

'Well, sweet of you to say so. But I have to go to work in the morning, don't I, Francis?'

'Indeed you do. As do I.' He smiled at her rather indulgently, almost as a father would. 'And we've both been working today, not pursuing pleasure idly as I'm sure you have.'

'You don't look as if you've been working. Not tired at all,' said St John Vincent slightly irritably.

'Then our looks belie us,' said Francis. 'I do assure you that I for one am quite exhausted.'

'You need a small fillip,' said Vincent. 'Come along, just for an hour or so. Janine has one of her gatherings going on. Myrtle, darling, do tell Francis and this perfectly divine creature that they absolutely must come to Janine's with us.'

Edwina had taken rather a dislike to Myrtle. She was dressed with enormous splendour in a heavily sequinned and emboidered robe and a beaded turban. Her face was dramatically made up, her eyes ringed with kohl, her lipstick almost black, and she smoked constantly through a very long cigarette holder. She seemed to have a somewhat proprietary relationship with Francis and kept stroking his face; they had been appropriating the dance floor for much of the evening, dancing a series of rather showy tangos. She looked at Edwina now and said, 'St John, if she wants to go home, then she should. Never try to corrupt virtue. Isn't that right, Francis?'

'I thought you knew nothing about virtue, Myrtle,' said Francis.

'I don't, actually. Only that it's boring,' said Myrtle.

Edwina met her black-rimmed eyes and smiled recklessly. 'Well, I'd hate you to think me that. All right, I'd love to come. Francis, what about you?'

He hesitated, looked at her for several moments, clearly trying to establish something in his mind, then apparently resolved it. 'Yes, very well,' he said, 'just for an hour or so.'

It was Monday night, and they had been sitting in a nightclub that was new to Edwina, called Jack's, for a while. Francis had phoned her in the office, told her he wanted to discuss various aspects of the fashion show, and suggested dinner. Harry was at the White City with friends, and she saw no reason to refuse. They had had an extremely nice evening at Daphne's in Sloane Avenue and Francis had suggested they moved on 'just for a short while. There are some people there who might amuse you.'

They did, and the people had amused her hugely. Two men, both undoubtedly homosexuals, and three women – two of them rather vulgar, but great fun, and the exotic Myrtle. Edwina had drunk a great deal of champagne, danced with all three men, and told a couple of extremely filthy jokes, which had been received with great enthusiasm. She would never, she realised, with a slight sense of shock, have done such a thing in public before: with her intimates perhaps, both Harry and her mother had a penchant for dirty jokes, but never with people she did not know.

She wondered if she was changing in other ways, and decided she was. She certainly felt different, quite different, quite a lot of the time: freer, not just in what she did, but in what she thought. She had always been liberal, nonjudgemental, but in a rather reactive way; now she found herself consciously in search of new ideas, new attitudes, felt almost an impatience to do so, lest time, opportunity, might be lost. She felt on the brink of some vast discovery about herself, and she looked back at the person she had been only a few months before, concerned only with the running of her household, the conduct of her social life, with something close to contempt.

And now, she found, she wanted to go with them all very much, with these interesting new people, rather than returning home to the predictability of her house and her bed, and she smiled at St John Vincent and said, 'Come on, then, let's go.'

Janine lived in Chelsea, in a very pretty house just off Cheyne Walk. They went down in Francis's car, all six of them; there was not enough room, and she sat on St John Vincent's knee and became aware suddenly of his hand moving smoothly and very confidently along her thighs, and wondered if she had perhaps been wrong about his sexual orientation.

A tiny, sliver-thin woman opened the door to them herself, dressed in a pair of wide silk trousers and a very long silver sweater. 'Darlings, how lovely! Lovely, lovely to see you.' She kissed them all, then stood studying Edwina. 'And St John, who is this nice new friend?'

'This is Edwina,' said St John Vincent, 'a friend of Francis's.'

'Francis, you do find the most wonderful-looking people. Do you work on one of his magazines? You must do, you have that look about you.'

'What sort of look?' said Edwina, laughing.

'Oh, hard to explain. As if you had something to say, perhaps? Which I'm sure you do. Anyway, welcome.' She reached out and took Edwina's hand. 'The main thing is, Francis never brings anyone boring. Come and meet some people.'

The house was quite wonderful, Edwina thought, very, very modern; the drawing room particularly was exquisite, all white: white walls, white curtains, white carpets, white sofas, chrome-framed mirrors, chrome wall lights. There were some very fine modern pictures on the walls. She recognised a couple of the artists, fashionable and immensely expensive: Otto Dix, Paul Klee – Harry had some of their work – and a huge Alberto Sarinio, the Surrealist, with his extraordinary animal heads on human bodies.

The room had only perhaps two dozen people in it, all extremely well dressed, the men in dinner jackets or smoking jackets, the women in evening dress or the new palazzo pyjamas; someone was playing the piano rather well, a few people were dancing. Edwina realised, with a stab of something half shock half pleasure, that two of the couples were women.

Janine took her hand, 'Let's get you a drink. Cocktail? Champagne? If you want anything stronger, ask St John, he'll show you. Now, let me see, who can you meet ...? Ah, yes, now this is Marcia, Marcia Bryanston, and this is her brother, Ivor. Well, more than her brother, of course, as you can see, her twin. Ivor, darling, do go and get some more cigarettes, would you? Turkish, if you can find them.'

Edwina could indeed see they were twins, the likeness was extraordinary: two tall, blond, rather androgynous creatures, their hair identically cut in slightly long Eton crops, straight noses and very brilliant blue-green eyes. Ivor, like Marcia, seemed to be wearing mascara. And how sensible, thought Edwina suddenly, when his eyes are so amazing and it suits him so well. He looked, if anything, the more beautiful of the two. He was wearing a black velvet jacket and a very large loosely knotted tie, which exactly matched his eyes; Marcia's dress, long and very narrow, was the same colour. It was very clear, from the nipples etched clearly against the crêpe fabric, that she had nothing on underneath it.

Janine put her arm round Marcia's shoulders. 'Marcia, this is Edwina, Francis brought her, Edwina ... sorry, I didn't catch your surname.'

'Moreton,' said Edwina, but she found it odd saying Harry's name, she felt it suddenly no longer hers at all, felt, for some reason that she could not have explained, that she had shed it, shed her old life, indeed, as she walked into this room.

'Marcia paints,' said Janine, 'dreadfully naughty nudes mostly. Do be careful, she'll try and persuade you to model for her.'

'I've never been painted,' said Edwina, and then said, finding it was true, 'I'd rather like it, I think.'

'Well, now is your chance. But I do warn you, not for your drawing room.'

Marcia stood studying Edwina for a moment, and then smiled at her. It was a brilliant, strangely seductive smile. 'Come and sit down,' she said. 'I want to know all about you.'

'You're beautiful. So beautiful.'

Edwina shivered, shuddered with pleasure; the tongue in her mouth was very gentle, exploring it, the fingers encircling her nipples intensely skilful. Delight shot, spread through her body; she shut her eyes, forcing herself to concentrate absolutely on the moment and its pleasures. They were in another room now, upstairs, a dark room full of people and throbbing music; she could not quite remember getting there, only a long conversation with Marcia, intriguing, enthralling, then dancing with Ivor, slowly, languorously, aware that Marcia was watching her, watching every move she made, and liking that fact, excited by it, and then Marcia joining them, dancing with them, and finally Marcia's hand taking hers, leading her away from her brother, out of the white room.

The music seemed to have taken possesion of her, its rhythms become her own. This was more than dancing: not yet sex, but a strange amalgam of the two, smooth, fluid, absolutely compelling. She moved her own hands slowly down the body pressed against hers, lingering on the stomach, feeling for the mound below it, moved her hands round the narrow hips, felt for the slender buttocks. They were quite high, high and firm; she stood there, feeling them, kneading them, excitement hot, liquid, flooding her, her breathing very fast and hard, and then the voice came again: 'Oh my God, you're so beautiful.'

It was strange, so strange, to feel this intense sexual pleasure and desire, and then in the midst of it, the tumult, to hear a female voice.

Later, she looked for Francis. He was sitting in the drawing room, a little apart from the rest, talking to Janine. Edwina was momentarily anxious, that this might seem an aberration to him, that he had in some way not known, might even be shocked, in spite of bringing her here; but he smiled at her, almost imperceptibly blew her a kiss, and continued his conversation. Whatever she was doing clearly did not matter to him.

Marcia had left, saying she had to work early on a painting, that she would see her again, and Ivor was dancing with her now. She found his likeness to Marcia confusing and erotic; the same full, sensual mouth kissing her, the same brilliant, amused eyes looking at her, his hands moving on her in the same skilful way.

Later St John joined them, danced with them, kissed them both, caressed them both; a confusion of pleasures, of sound, of touch, of taste, possessed her. She wanted them both, she could have them both; she felt love, warmth, an intense happiness. Sexual pleasure, sexual excitement had taken hold of her brain; she felt drunk, drugged, and knew she was neither.

Next to her two women danced, kissing, caressing, and somewhere dimly beyond her consciousness she saw another couple still; a man and a woman – how strange, she thought, how very strange – were moving into yet another room, the room where she and Marcia had lain and discovered one another's soft, sweet, pliant bodies, had moved and moaned and cried out with pleasure, seeking out, knowing precisely what the other had wanted, where the delights lay.

She had no real idea where she was, or where she should have been, she could hardly have told anyone her own name, but an energy possessed her, a new warm, vivid energy; she felt strong, safe, inviolate.

★

At some point later, she was dancing with Janine, talking with her, laughing with her, and noticed the clock: it was almost five. The night had vanished, consumed itself in a confusion of pleasure. She looked for Francis again; he had gone. Anxiety stabbed at her.

Janine read the anxiety and smiled. 'Don't worry about Francis. He said to say goodbye, that he'd see you tomorrow. He seldom stays for long, just arrives and leaves again. He just likes to see us all, to feel part of us. We're a very happy little group.'

'So I see,' said Edwina.

She arrived home at six thirty, removed her shoes on the doorstep, fled up the stairs, praying she would meet no one, and fell into bed, fully dressed. She lay there, wide awake, in a state of wonderment, exploring her feelings and the memories of her night and marvelling that she could have lived without such pleasures for so long.

CHAPTER 32

Cassia's hand, holding the telephone receiver, was wet, slippery with sweat, her heart beating so fast she felt the person the other end must be able to hear it. The room seemed to be rather dark, and there was a pain somewhere tight in her chest. She wondered idly if she might be having a heart attack, even hoped that she was. It would solve a lot of dilemmas, save so much anguish.

'Yes? Miss Gerard's secretary speaking.'

'Oh, is she there, please? It's Cassia Fallon.'

'No, Mrs Fallon, I'm afraid she isn't. She's operating this morning.' The secretary clearly felt Cassia was in some way incompetent not to know this.

'Oh, I see.' Relief flooded her, sweet, soothing, the room lightened. Execution had been stayed.

'She will be back this afternoon, though. Can I give her a message?'

'No, I'll ring back.'

A very brief reprieve, then: only a few hours. Only a few hours left before she was branded as incompetent, unreliable, probably in Miss Gerard's eyes contemptible, before she had to set aside, and be seen to be setting aside, what she wanted so much that it was a bodily hunger, a physical pain, before she had to face finally that success in her career was not to be hers, that she was condemned to a professional lifetime of compromise, of dissatisfaction.

Of all the elements in the scenario, she dreaded Miss Gerard's reaction most. She felt she was failing not only her and her expectations of her, the risk she was prepared to take in offering her the job, but all the women before her who had struggled for a voice, a place in the professional world, fought to be something more than wives, more than mothers, more than a support system to men. She felt feeble, nerveless, dreaded being branded so.

She wondered briefly what her own mother, so staunch a supporter of the female cause in her own gentle way, would have advised her to do, whether she would have been disappointed in or proud of a daughter who put her family before a quite possibly brilliant career, and a career, moreover, that would bring benefit to hundreds, thousands, of other, less fortunate women. And lent courage to the next generation: what might the small Delia, considering her own career in the years ahead, think of a mother who had turned her back on professional success? Would she despise her, sneer at her even, for wasting her talents, her education, rejecting her opportunities – or would she be grateful that, in doing so, she had given her the security, and thus the self-confidence, to make her own decisions and cut out her own path?

There was no real decision to be made: Cassia knew that. She had three small children, one of whom had already suffered a considerable trauma, and all of whom were about to have to endure the pain of seeing their parents' marriage come to an end. For that really was indubitable; there was no alternative to it. She and Edward had nothing left to say to one another, no emotion remained but a wary affection. The shared enthusiasms and ambitions of their youth had been destroyed by the extraordinarily powerful amalgam of professional jealousy, and personal dissatisfaction. She, and Leonora's money, had hastened the process, but it had only been a hastening, she could see that now; in the years ahead, as the children grew up, her bitterness and frustration would have increased, as would Edward's sense of inferiority and need to overbear. They needed to part: he, as well as she, would be happier and stronger for it.

The children, however, would be bewildered, wretched, torn in their loyalties; they would need absolute security and endless attention if they were to begin to recover, not a mother who came home once a week, exhausted and self-obsessed. No, there was no help for it, she had no choice; but Monica Gerard would not see it that way, and her scorn, both personal and professional, would be hard to bear.

It was Wednesday; she had hours to kill before she started her clinic. She went out and bought a newsaper, sat reading it. There was much discussion of the position of the King, not in his relationship with Mrs Simpson, on which the press with extraordinary restraint was still remaining silent, but with Parliament and the country; what some saw as a simple desire to help the less advantaged of his subjects, others read as a conscious rift with his ministers – the same men who might stand between him and his personal happiness. And how, thought Cassia, would the King finally decide? Would he choose personal happiness or professional duty? The thought of the two of them, herself and her King, struggling with moral dilemmas, amused her, quite cheered her up.

Later she went to see Cecily. As Cassia drove through the gate of the nursing home, she found her walking in the grounds, looking very much better, still thin, still a little frail, but quite cheerful, her face rosy in the frosty morning. She walked over to Cassia as she parked her car.

'Heavens, Cassia, what have you been doing to this poor, beautiful thing?'

Cassia told her. 'But I can't get it fixed, I need it too much, and at least it still goes.'

'That's ridiculous,' said Cecily. 'You can borrow my car, just go over this morning and get it, I'll telephone Preston. Or better still, I'll tell him to take it over to your house. Now come along, let's go in and have some coffee. I need some support, I'm packing to go home, and half excited, half terrified.'

'The children are so excited about you going home,' said Cassia, helping to fold the few dresses Cecily had brought in with her. They all looked too large for her new, slender shape.

'I know. I feel so guilty about what they've suffered, poor little things, what they'll go on suffering, but I'm determined to be a good mother to them now, somehow.'

'You always were a good mother,' said Cassia, smiling at her.

'Maybe, but they've been alone a lot lately. And I do realise the combination of Nanny and my mother is not ideal. Stephanie has got very spoilt, and as for Laurence ... well, quite impossible. It's funny, isn't it,' she said after a pause, 'how whatever happens to you, whatever you want or don't want, once you've got children, they remain the most important thing?'

'Yes,' said Cassia. She had no desire to get into a discussion on the maternal instinct that morning – her own had been wearing her out. 'Cecily, can I ask you something?' She took herself by surprise with that question, had not thought it was currently in the forefront of her mind.

'Yes, of course.'

She wondered why Cecily looked startled, awkward at that, at her relief, when she said, 'It's about Leonora.'

Cecily said that, yes, she had heard from Benedict that Leonora had been in financial difficulties at one point, that she had kept it from him, from all of them, that Harry had told him about it. 'He went immediately over to Paris to see her.'

'Harry?' said Cassia. 'Are you sure it was Harry who told him?'

'Yes, of course. I remember him telling me about it, Benedict, I mean.'

'So how did Harry know?'

'I'm not sure. I think he just went to see her.'

'And when was that, can you remember?'

'Well, it was after Christmas, I do know that. It was terrible weather when Benedict came back, fearfully rough crossing, and you know what a bad sailor he was, and the heating had gone wrong on the Golden Arrow and he said it had been absolutely freezing. So I suppose very early spring. Yes, that's right, the spring before she died.'

'And where was she living then?' said Cassia. 'When Benedict went over? Was she in the awful place that Miss Monkton found her in?'

'Miss Monkton? Oh, I don't know anything about her. No, she was in a very nice apartment by then, apparently, one of those ones with a *porte cocherie*, you know, built round a lovely courtyard garden.'

'And Gresham was back?'

'I don't know if he was actually back, but he'd certainly arranged for her to have some more money, and for medical care and so on. She was abslutely all right by then. Honestly, darling, I do think it was only for a very short while she was in trouble. You mustn't feel bad about it.'

'Well, I do,' said Cassia fretfully, 'I feel bad about all of it: about not knowing how ill she was, not going to see her more. If only I'd known, I'd have visited her before she died. I do wish you'd all told me.'

'In the end she died very quickly, though. It happens with cancer sometimes, you must know that. It was a shock for all of us. And you were down there, in the country, with all those tiny children. I think we all kept putting it off, telling you, not wanting to distress you.'

'Well, I feel distressed now,' said Cassia, 'I feel terrible. And about her being in difficulties. I could have helped somehow. And I'm not so sure it was such a short time ...'

'Oh, I'm sure it was. Cassia, you know what Leonora was like, so irresponsible, so hopeless with money, so incapable of looking after herself. And it can't have been anything very serious, could it, or how could she have done what she did for you?'

'So everyone keeps saying,' said Cassia shortly. Her misery was making her irritable.

'Benedict was clearly exasperated with her, as well as upset and worried. He felt guilty that he hadn't kept more of an eye on her, but he did write to her very often.'

'Where did he write to her? At the avenue Foch?'

'I think so. Well, obviously, because he had no idea she'd moved.'

'So you didn't ever visit her, those last few months?' said Cassia.

Cecily flushed. 'No, I didn't, and I do feel ashamed about it, but –

well, you know, I always had a rather difficult relationship with Leonora. I was jealous of her, she was always so close to Benedict. And she knew about his – his problems, of course, knew why he'd married me. I found that very difficult to cope with. I knew I should have gone, but I kept putting it off, there was always some excuse, the children, and so on. And then, as I say, her death in the end was rather sudden. Even Benedict was here, in London, he was terribly upset.'

'Yes, of course. And Benedict didn't tell you more about any of it?'

'No. I don't think there was more to tell, I really don't. She got herself in a mess and Benedict found out about it and tried to help, as he always did. His patience with her was incredible.' Her voice was almost hard.

Cassia looked at her sharply, but she wasn't really surprised: the antagonism between Cecily and Leonora had always been quite deep.

She drove back to her own house – where Cecily's small Daimler was already waiting for her – feeling thoughtful. Her conversation with Rupert had eased her worries, shifted them – her carefully constructed theory about Harry did now seem a little foolish – but she was still very far from happy.

She decided to go to Paris: to do some research for herself.

Harry's rages were very noisy affairs, Edwina thought. She had been listening to him from her room where she was reading: his brakes screeching as he pulled up outside the house; the car door slamming; hearing him shouting for Bishop as he came in; heard his study door banging shut, echoing through the house. She took no notice; they had been the background to her life for as long as they had been married, those rages. She almost enjoyed them in a way – or she had in the old days. They provided some drama, some light and shade in her life. Which now, looking back on it, seemed very monochrome.

She went back to her reading: American *Vogue*. It was more hard-edged in its glamour than the English version, she liked it. And there were some extraordinary, almost surreal photographs inside by Man Ray; she thought she might talk to Francis about using him. Of course he'd be expensive, but if it gave them the edge over *Vogue* ...

She was so engrossed she didn't consciously hear the study door slam, the pounding footsteps on the stairs, the same footsteps moving along the corridor, only her own door wrenched violently open, and Harry's voice telling her he wanted to talk to her.

She put her magazine aside with exaggerated patience. 'Yes, Harry?'

'Edwina, you are to give that damnfool job up. Immediately.'

'Don't be ridiculous. Why should I?'

'Because I wish it, that's why you should.'

'Well, I'm sorry, Harry, but I don't wish it. I enjoy my job, in fact I love it.'

'Yes, so I see. And your relationship with that – creature Stevenson-Cook, and some other fairly unpleasant characters as well, it seems.'

'I don't have a relationship, as you put it, with Francis Stevenson-Cook.'

'Of course you do. You dine with him night after night, you've been seen at nightclubs with him, you could at least have the grace to employ a little discretion. And don't start telling me he's a homosexual, because I know at least two women personally who have had affairs with him. Whether or not you've actually been to bed with him is of no interest to me, but I will not be publicly cuckolded, I will not have my wife linked in London gossip with such a person.'

'Such a person!' she said. 'Harry, you sound like Edward Fallon. I'm surprised at you.'

'At least Edward Fallon has a moral code of sorts,' he said, 'which is more than can be said of you.'

Edwina felt her cheeks begin to burn, felt fear, an icy trickle somewhere deep within her.

'I know where you were the other night,' he said. 'I heard about it, and your behaviour. With Marcia Bryanston and that twin brother of hers. Edwina, how could you?'

'Very easily,' she said, her courage up as always when she was cornered. 'I liked them both, they were interesting and amusing.'

'No doubt. And degenerate and decadent. Her paintings are pure pornography, and he sleeps with every homosexual and bisexual in London. They are both cocaine addicts. And those are the sort of people Stevenson-Cook numbers among his frends. I will not have it, Edwina, I really will not.'

'And how,' she said, leaning back in her chair looking at him, 'will you stop it?'

He came over to her then, leant on the arms of her chair, put his face quite close to hers. She could feel the rage in him, smell it. 'I have endured a great deal from you,' he said. 'Your lack of affection, and then there is your lack of interest in everything I do, your rendering yourself sterile—'

'Who told you that?' she said, too shocked to be careful.

'Nobody told me. I worked it out for myself. But of course it's true. I thought it must be.'

She felt a new, violent rage herself. 'That was a filthy trick. Trying to trap me.'

'With every justification, it seems. So here I am, denied my right to children, denied my marital rights much of the time, although God knows I have little interest in them, and now the foolish centre of a storm of very unpleasant gossip. I don't like it, Edwina, and I will not endure it. Either it stops or you will find yourself the guilty party in a very ugly divorce suit. You can make your own mind up, it is entirely up to you. But I have no intention of letting things go on in this way.'

Edwina sat in her room after he had left, and tried to decide what to do. She wondered who had told him about the other night, at Janine Sobel's house. Someone in the art world, obviously: gossip flew there, even faster than in her own circle; it was a tiny, convoluted world, and Harry knew everyone in it. And she could not imagine Marcia troubling herelf to be discreet, still less Ivor. It had been foolish of her to behave as she had, foolish of Francis to take her; she wondered idly why he had, whether he had had some kind of ulterior motive. She didn't trust him; she didn't trust any of them. She just liked them, wanted to be ... well, if not quite one of them, to be accepted by them.

The world for Edwina had shifted totally on its axis that night at Janine Sobel's. A process that had begun when she had started work at *Style*, fallen in love with its philosophies, its standards, its extraordinary passions, a process that had given her an entirely new viewpoint on life and what she wanted of it, had been completed in those hours; she had been brought to an entirely new viewpoint on herself. The person she had thought she was no longer existed; in her place was a stranger, an intriguing stranger, stronger, cleverer, bolder. She felt she had been freed, that night, from the constraints of her old life, and that moreover those constraints were foolish, unnecessary; she had walked through a series of doors and found herself in a dazzling new landscape and she could not and would not go back.

Discretion in her social circle was the ultimate virtue: with its help any extramarital relationship could be conducted, any passion pursued. Husbands would look away as their wives took lovers, wives smile sweetly upon their husbands' mistresses. It was a pragmatic philosophy and there was much to be said for it: households – and fortunes – were preserved, children protected, and very often a kind of functional affection, if not love, was able to survive. Marriage was seen as a business which must be run efficiently and conscientiously, and a degree of hypocrisy was a perfectly acceptable element of that business.

Perhaps because Edwina had never loved Harry, nor he her, because they had married for reasons that were at best dubious, perhaps because they had never treated one another with anything more than an affectionate tolerance, or perhaps because Edwina had been born with a genuinely more questing and straightforward nature than the social mores of her generation allowed, she suddenly found herself exasperated by these conventions.

Harry did not love her, he had no real interest in her, he spent a great deal of his time away from her, and she saw every reason to behave in a way that would redress those facts, and no reason at all to protect him and their increasingly unsatisfactory relationship. If she wanted to spend her solitary evenings with her own friends, doing what interested and amused her, then she felt she had a right to do so.

She said all this to Francis Stevenson-Cook next day over lunch in his office – for she dared not be seen in public with him, she really was too frightened of Harry for that – and he listened to her carefully, then smiled and refilled her glass.

'I was right,' he said with great satisfaction. 'I read you exactly right.'

Manipulative so-and-so, she thought with a mixture of amusement and irritation. She was under no illusions about Francis. He picked people up and played with them for a while and then tired of them and set them down again. She had realised that finally the other night at Janine's, watching him surveying the scene with that strange indulgent detachment. The danger was in not realising it: but she did, and he knew she did, and therefore she was safe.

That same afternoon in London another woman had found herself confronted with a new angle on her marital dilemma: Mrs Wallis Simpson, lunching at Claridges with Esmond Harmsworth, son of Lord Rothermere, owner of the *Daily Mail*, was asked if she had ever considered the possibility of a morganatic marriage. Within this framework, Mr Harmsworth explained, she could marry the King but would not take his rank, and nor would any children have the right of succession. It could provide a solution of sorts: might she suggest it to the King?

'Good God,' said Edward.

Cassia looked at him across the kitchen; he was reading a letter, was rather pale. The hand holding the letter was shaking. 'What? Is something wrong?'

'No,' he said slowly, 'no, not wrong. Not wrong at all. Just – well, a bit of a shock. That's all.'

'Can I see?'

'Yes, of course.' He handed it over. They had, in the calm of their tacit decision to separate, become more friendly, more able to communicate; rage, resentment, jealousy even, seemed to have left them, leaving only a great sadness and regret that was easier to bear.

'Oh, Edward,' said Cassia, and she felt her eyes filling with tears, saw the words '… able after all to offer you a place as registrar as from next April, and we understand you will be doing your MRCS.' She took in the name of the hospital: St Mark's, Clapham, a good teaching hospital. 'Edward, I'm so pleased. You will accept this one, won't you?'

'Yes, of course I will.'

She moved forward, put her arms round him. For the first time for months he didn't shy away, but returned the embrace, and then walked into the study, smiling foolishly at his letter, and shut the door.

Not even her own anguish about Miss Gerard's offer could dent the happiness she felt for him.

Later he came to find her. 'I think we should talk, don't you?'

They talked for a long time: agreed that they should part, that they were no longer remotely able to make one another happy; that he at least could not bear the imbalance of their relationship, knowing she did not love him; that they should, could hopefully, remain friends.

'I'm so truly happy for you,' she said, kissing him gently on the cheek. 'Nothing could please me more.'

'I know,' he said, 'I can see that. Thank you.'

He would be living in at the hospital; there was no question of him doing anything else. It would make the transition for the children far easier, would help to explain his absence. They agreed the practice should probably be sold, that the family also should move to London, that Cassia should buy a large house there.

'But we still have to tell them,' he said, 'we can't pretend. Oh dear,' he said, and sighed heavily, 'it's all so sad, isn't it?' He dashed his hand across his eyes suddenly. 'Sorry. Bit emotional.'

'Me too,' she said, and looked at him; saw suddenly not the Edward who was sitting there now, drawn and pale, deep lines etched in his face, his eyes heavy with the hurt of it all, but the Edward she had seen that first day in Casualty, young and hopeful and happy, his brown hair flopping over his face as he bent over her ankle, bandaging it with slow and infinite care, and then sitting back on his heels, smiling his slow, sweet smile at her for the first time. She burst into tears and cried, cried for a long time.

When Peggy came out to find them and tell them it was lunchtime, Edward was sitting with his arm round her.

'They seem much happier,' she said to Mrs Briggs later. 'I think maybe they've come to their senses after all.'

Cecily was waiting for the car to take her home that Thursday afternoon, feeling sick. The thought of being away from the doctors and nurses who had cared for her for so long was terrifying. She almost wished she could be sick, to delay her departure. She saw a taxi coming in the gate; someone visiting some fortunate patient, one who could stay a little longer. And then watched in amazement as Justin Everard got out of it.

'I thought you would need company,' he said, walking over to her, giving her a kiss, 'company to lend you courage. Come along, give me that attaché case. Oh, look, here is your wonderful car now. I shall never forget our journey down to Devon in that car, with your little girl being sick all over Edwina's bag. So enchanting.'

'It didn't seem very enchanting to me,' said Cecily, laughing.

Justin held her hand all the way home, telling her funny stories about sessions he had been on, the fashion show, the dreadfulness of Edwina, the even greater dreadfulness of Madame Brunel; she forgot all about her nervousness.

The children and Nanny were waiting outside on the steps of the house, holding a big white banner that read 'Welcome Home'. Mrs Forbes stood behind them weeping openly. As they walked into the hall, her arms round the two girls, the first thing Cecily noticed was the smell of flowers, and then she looked about her and laughed with pure pleasure: vases of roses, of lilies, of freesias, stood on every conceivable surface; glorious white and scarlet azaleas filled the jardinières; trailing greenery was draped over the doors.

'It's wonderful,' she said, 'simply wonderful.'

'Justin did most of it,' said Fanny.

'Did you really?'

'Well, I and a few underlings,' he said modestly. 'Edwina helped as well.'

'You are so kind to me,' said Cecily, 'so very very kind, I can't think why.'

'I'm very fond of you,' he said simply. 'I think you're wonderful.'

★

547

Later she phoned Edwina to thank her.

'Oh, honestly, it was all Justin really,' she said. 'He absolutely adores you.'

'It's rather ironic, isn't it? Since he's – well, he's ...'

'Cecily,' said Edwina, amused, 'you really are ridiculous.'

'I am not ridiculous,' said Cecily. Weariness and emotion had brought her near to tears. 'I think he's wonderful too. I'm terribly fond of him. But I don't think I could cope with—'

'Cecily, if you mean he's a fairy, of course he's not. I really thought you understood that. He puts it on because people expect it of him, in his profession, but he's one of the biggest wolves in London.'

'Oh,' said Cecily. 'Oh, yes, I see.'

'I'm thinking of getting a divorce,' said Edwina. 'I thought I'd better tell you.'

'Oh, don't be so ridiculous. What on earth for?'

'Mummy, it's not ridiculous. We just make each other miserable.'

Sylvia Fox-Ashley stared at her, pulled a cigarette out of its case and lit it. 'I have never heard such nonsense,' she said. 'You mean neither of you is having an affair even?'

'Not exactly. I mean he might be, but I don't think so. And I'm certainly not.'

'Edwina, I think you must have taken leave of your senses. You're giving all that up, all that money, just because you're miserable. You'll be a great deal more miserable without it, I do assure you.'

'I don't think I will, actually. And anyway, I won't be without money. Harry has terrible faults, but he's extremely generous. And he won't want to look mean. To him it's the ultimate sin.'

'Believe me, darling, no man is generous when it comes to divorce. And Harry is so charming, so interesting. I don't know what your father will have to say, he's so fond of him. What are you going to do all day without a house to run?'

'Mummy, you don't understand. I'm leaving Harry because I want to lead my own life, do my job. He won't let me go on with that and—'

'Quite right too. Nobody in your position should be working, I told you that at the beginning. And I know you think it'll all be rather exciting, living on your own, but it won't, it'll be extremely lonely. Nobody asks single women to dinner parties, they see them quite rightly as a threat. And what happens when you get tired of that job, as of course you will? I cannot tell you how horrified I am, Edwina, and don't think I can't imagine what this is really all about. Now if you have any sense at all you'll go home and tell Harry you're extremely sorry, that of course you don't want a divorce and that you'll do it upside down tied to the bedpost if that's what he wants.'

Edwina laughed aloud. 'Mummy, this has nothing to do with sex.'

'When a marriage goes wrong it's always to do with sex,' said her mother. 'Now, please, Edwina, do rethink this crazy idea. You'll regret it for the rest of your life.'

'Perhaps you're right,' said Edwina thoughtfully.

'What's the matter, Rupert?' said Eleanor Studely. They were sitting having a glass of wine after the performance as they often did; he had hardly spoken.

'Oh, nothing. Just a bit low.' A bit low, he thought; what a stupid, inadequate phrase. When he had been feeling, ever since the conversation with Cassia, so deeply and heavily depressed he found it a physical effort to do anything at all. The play had gone badly that night, he knew it had. The power his work usually had to remove him from himself had failed him; he had had to drive out his performance, rather than making a journey through it, as he usually did.

'Come on,' he said, 'tell me. A trouble shared and all that.'

'Oh, I'm being ridiculous. A foolish old man. As usual. I shall get over it, no doubt, but this one was rather special.'

'Oh, I see.' She sounded amused. 'Real love, was it, this time?'

'Eleanor,' said Rupert, 'I don't want to be rude, but if my misery is so amusing, then perhaps we should end this discussion.'

'Rupert, don't be silly. Of course I don't find it amusing. It's just that I've known you quite a long time, although not intimately, of course, and I've seen you tumble in and out of love so many times.'

'I'm afraid this is rather different,' said Rupert coldly. He knew he was being unpleasant, but he couldn't help it, that most unattractive of qualities, self-pity, distorting his judgement and his behaviour. 'Perhaps you have forgotten how it feels to be rejected, Eleanor. By someone you really care about.'

The minute he'd said it, he was horrified at himself; he looked at Eleanor, saw high colour flash into her face, saw her eyes dangerously brilliant, saw the shake of her hand as she put down her glass.

She stood up. 'I think I will go home now,' she said. 'I'm very tired. Goodnight.'

'Eleanor,' he said, 'I'm so desperately sorry. Do forgive me. Christ, I don't know what came over me.'

'Whatever it was, I would rather not hear any more of it,' she said, opening the dressing-room door. 'Goodnight, Rupert.'

This was the woman, he thought, who had watched her much-loved husband die from tuberculosis while being forced to carry on working in order to support all three of them for six desperate months; who had, in the three years since, managed to care for her daughter, all on her own, without the benefit of any family whatsoever. And who, most remarkably, had managed to remain positive, generous and tranquil. Who had had the courage to risk coming into their funny, dangerous little project. Whose gaiety and perseverance had seen them through many dark hours. And he had shown her in return bad temper and meanness. All because his pride had been hurt. He had seen that in the instant he had spoken. He ought to be put up against a wall and shot for it: or maybe that was too good for him. Hanging, drawing and quartering would be more in line.

'Mummy,' said Bertie, 'can we come and watch you all on Saturday? Please?'

'Bertie, you'd hate it,' said Cassia firmly. 'Lots and lots of ladies just walking up and down in silly frocks.'

'No, but you'll be walking up and down too, won't you?'

'Only about twice.'

'Well, we'd still like to see you, wouldn't we, William?'

'Course we would.'

'It's out of the question,' said Edward sharply. 'You'd be bored to tears after five minutes and someone would have to look after you.'

'You could look after us,' said Bertie. 'You're coming, aren't you?'

'No,' said Edward. 'No, I'm afraid I can't.'

They both stared at him. 'But don't you want to see Mummy on the stage thing?' said Bertie finally. 'With Aunt Edwina and everyone? And Fanny and Stephanie dancing?'

'Yes, and Rupert's doing something for it, too,' said William, 'and you wouldn't let us see his play, you've got to let us come to this.'

'Perhaps Janet could take them?' said Edward. He looked at Cassia with an expression that was close to desperation.

'Well,' she said thoughtfully, 'I think that's a very good idea. I'm sure Janet would love to see the fashion show, and as long as Peggy and Mrs Briggs could look after Delia, then that's the answer. Janet, would you like that?'

'Oh, I'd love it,' said Janet, her face flushed with pleasure. 'Thank you very much, Mrs Fallon.'

'Good,' said Edward, 'that's settled, then. You must excuse me now, I've got things to do.'

He walked out of the room, and Cassia went after him. 'Edward, it's time we told them. I think it's a good moment.'

'There's never a good moment.'

'All right, but it's as good as any.'

Afterwards she had no idea whence had come that conviction, that panic-stricken conviction, or the courage to see it through, but he gave in, agreed with her, and they did it, somehow, they got through it. They sat on the sofa by the fire, holding hands, Cassia's arm round Bertie, Edward's round William, and told them first that Edward had a very exciting new job which meant living in a hospital all the time for two or three years, and then that after that she and Edward would not live together all the time.

'You see, we don't seem to make each other happy any more,' said Cassia, wiping the tears that were rolling silently down Bertie's face.

'Don't you like each other?'

'Yes, of course we do. Very much. But we disagree about so many things, we keep quarrelling, you know we do, you've heard us, and if we don't live together all the time, then we think we can stop quarrelling and just be friends.'

'When we quarrel you tell us not to be so silly,' said William. 'Why can't you stop being silly?'

'It's very hard to explain,' said Cassia with a sigh. 'It's different when you're grown up: you need to live with someone you don't quarrel with.'

'So are you going to live with different people?' said William warily.

'No,' said Edward, 'of course not. Well, I am, but only other doctors. In the hospital. And I shall come and see you lots, every weekend that I'm not working.'

'We'll get a new big house in London,' said Cassia, 'and—'

'In London? Why not here?'

'Well, we'll be nearer Daddy in London, and – and my work. I won't be away three days a week any more.'

'No,' said William, 'I like it here, and what about Buffy?'

'Buffy can come too. We'll have a garden, a big garden.'

'No. I like it here.' His small face was working, his eyes filled with panic. 'This is our house, I don't want to leave it.'

'Nor do I,' said Bertie, 'I won't leave it, not ever, whatever you say, and you said we could have ponies, we can't have ponies in London.'

'All right,' she said soothingly, aware that she was making life still more difficult for herself, desperate to soothe the panic, ease the pain, 'we don't have to go to London, we can stay here. If that's what you want, if that will make you feel happier about it. And have ponies.'

They were both silent; Bertie was sucking his thumb, watching them warily. 'And will you stop going to London to work?'

She hesitated, then said quietly, 'If you like, yes.'

'So it'll be like now really, only the other way round? You'll be here all the time and Daddy won't.'

'Well, sort of like now, yes. But, Bertie, you must understand that—'

'And you won't be shagging anyone else? Not either of you?'

'Bertie!' said Edward. His face was rather pink.

'It's all right, Edward. He picked that particular expression up at school. I explained it meant being someone's girlfriend. Or boyfriend.'

'Oh. Oh, I see. No, Bertie, certainly not.'

Bertie looked up at them both, an expression on his face that Cassia had never seen before. Analysing it, she realised with something of a shock that it was cunning. 'So you really are still friends?'

They looked at each other.

'Yes,' said Cassia firmly, 'we're still friends. Very good friends.'

'Want to prove it?'

'Yes,' said Edward.

'You come to the show thing as well on Saturday, then. Come and see Mummy. Otherwise I won't believe you.'

Finally Edward said, 'Yes. Yes, all right.'

'We can't tell Janet she can't come now,' said Cassia firmly.

'No, that's all right. We'll all go.'

'Good,' said Bertie. He smiled at his father rather uncertainly.

He was very shaken, Cassia thought, but he'd taken it better than she had hoped. They both had. She wasn't so foolish as to think it was over; she knew there would be many tears, much grief yet, and that the small piece of cunning Bertie had exhibited was only the beginning. They had lost security, her children, in that hour in the sitting room, by the great roaring fire, lost a degree of innocence; but if she did what she had said, if they both did, if they kept their promises to them, they would recover, they would survive. And as she sat there, trembling, still holding Edward's hand, she suddenly realised what she could just possibly do now, and found in it some consolation for herself at least.

CHAPTER 33

Cecily did not sleep very much on the night of 27 November; she spent much of it reading, and when she did go to sleep it was to restless dreams in which Fanny fell off the catwalk and ruined her precious dress and, indeed, the entire show. She lay in the slightly shaky peace that follows waking from a nightmare, telling herself it was ridiculous that she should be so worried about any of it, and realising at the same time that she must be very frightened of the ordeal ahead of her.

She was just wondering if she could actually face it, if there was any way at all she could make an excuse and not go, when Susan came in with her breakfast tray.

'There's a telephone message, Mrs Harrington, from Mr Everard. He says he's going to come and collect you, take you to the fashion show tonight himself. He says not to ring him back because he'll be out all day, but he'll be here at six thirty sharp. Only can you be ready because he'll be in a bit of a hurry. Mrs Harrington, are you all right? You look a bit flushed.'

'I'm fine, Susan, thank you. I think I might go out shopping this morning, find myself something to wear. Could you tell Preston, please?'

Rupert had also slept badly; in fact, he had scarcely slept at all, so deeply ashamed of himself did he feel. Every time he closed his eyes he saw Eleanor's face first flushed with anger, then white and drawn with pain; he could not imagine how he could put things right between them. Clearly a simple apology, some flowers, would help; but something more was needed. Dinner perhaps? A full-scale abasement? Throwing himself upon her mercy, asking her for forgiveness? But in the end, he realised that only one thing was going to begin to explain his behaviour, and that was making Eleanor understand the depths of his misery and humiliation – the misery that had driven him to make his remark. And it must be done quickly: he must not put it off. Eleanor's hurt had been too severe to be left untreated for a minute more than necessary.

Sitting in his taxi on the way to her small house in Balham, a large bunch of flowers in his hand, he reflected not for the first time how unfortunate it was that Eleanor was in no way the type of woman to whom he was attracted; nothing could have been more convenient, more suitable, than for him to be in love with his leading lady, moreover a leading lady who was beautiful, intelligent, interested in what interested him, caring about all the things that he cared about. But life was not convenient, or suitable; if it was, he would have spent less time in the company of dizzy young blonde things who had no interest in him whatsoever beyond his ability to provide them with a good dinner, a few bunches of flowers, possibly the odd bit of jewellery – and very occasionally a sexual experience which they probably found at best moderately satisfying. He might even now be married and have the one thing he increasingly yearned for as the years went by: a proper home and a family of his own.

He spoke of this yearning to Eleanor, as they sat drinking some very good coffee that she had made in the kitchen of her enchanting little house, after he had made his stammering explanation and she had accepted it with a grace and generosity that he knew he did not deserve.

'I do know,' she said, 'that in spite of everything, I am very blessed. Portia gives my life a stability and a meaning that it would not otherwise have. And I did love Walter very much, so I have very happy memories to see me through as well. We were very happy, in a strange way during those last few months; we said all the things we wanted to one another, all the misunderstandings were cleared up ... Rupert, are you all right? What is it?'

It was the word misunderstanding that did it: it made Rupert suddenly see what had been wrong with the explanation Cassia had given him about Harry's anger with her, about their brief liaison. Harry had misunderstood: not about *what* had happened, but *when*. He stood up suddenly, pushing his chair back.

'Eleanor, I'm so very sorry, but you must excuse me. I've just realised I've been rather stupid. Well, not just I, Cassia also. Do please forgive me, I have to go and see someone urgently. Thank you for your generosity. I'll see you later, at the fashion show. Goodbye. So sorry, so very sorry ...'

After he had gone, Eleanor cleared away the coffee cups and took them into the kitchen, staring out at the grey November day. She did feel better: much better. She had appreciated Rupert's self-abasement – while being more than a little aware that he was giving what amounted to a very good performance of a self-abasing man – but nothing was going to ease the much deeper pain she was experiencing: that of unrequited love. She had fought it for a long time, knowing it was hopeless, recognising Rupert's golden charm for the dangerous thing it was. However, she had now stopped fighting it, had given in to it, admitted it. And it hurt. It hurt a lot.

Harry Moreton was standing staring down into the street from his study, wondering morosely whether he should take his plane and fly across to France, or drive down to Wiltshire and stay there until the lunacy that was the fashion show was over, when he saw a taxi pull up outside and Rupert Cameron get out of it. As Rupert was the last person in the world he wished to speak to, be near even, as the simple sight of him produced in him certain very distinct emotions – rage, jealousy and distaste being only three – he called out to Bishop that he was not to be disturbed under any circumstances and slammed the study door very firmly shut. Rupert, who had looked up at the house (rather nervously, for he did not relish the task before him in the very least) and seen him, was neither deterred nor deceived by Bishop's announcement that Mr Moreton was unavailable, and, indeed, Rupert stood in the hall saying so quite loudly – so loudly that the sound reached Edwina who was in her sitting room.

Edwina's nerves were stretched very taut; an argument in the house between her butler and a guest pulled them tauter still, and after trying to ignore it for a little more than thirty seconds, she ran downstairs and told Bishop that of course Mr Moreton was available and that he was to show Mr Cameron into the study immediately.

'It really is too bad when I'm trying to work and have so much on my mind. Rupert, he's in there, although why you or anyone else should wish to speak to him, I cannot imagine. Now can I please have some peace and quiet?'

Harry looked up from his desk, where he was pretending to be heavily engrossed in some work, and scowled as the door opened and Rupert Cameron came in, an apologetic and nervous Bishop behind him.

'I'm sorry, Cameron,' he said, 'but I'm awfully busy, and I really have nothing to say to you whatsoever.'

'You don't have to say anything,' said Rupert, 'but I'd be really awfully grateful if you'd listen.'

Edwina was at her desk only a little later, going over the checklist for what seemed like the thousandth time, when Harry walked in.

He looked rather odd, she thought, as if he didn't really know quite where he was; but he smiled at her, albeit distantly, and said, 'Look, do you still want me to come to this thing tonight?'

As his last words on the subject had been 'Don't think for one moment I am coming to that fucking show of yours, because I do assure you I would rather spend several hundred years rotting in hell,' she was slightly taken aback.

'You must please yourself of course,' she said coolly, 'but it would be rather nice for all those of our friends who have bought tickets to find you there.'

'Yes, all right,' he said, 'I'll be there. I've got to go out now. I'll see you later on.' He left the room and shut the door very quietly behind him. Edwina sat staring at the closed door and tried to imagine what could have happened. She failed totally.

Cassia had an appointment at Leon de Rosay's salon at eleven for a final fitting of her dresses; she had lost weight over the past month and they had had to be taken in. She had intended to get up early, but she had fallen into an exhausted sleep at four, having lain awake until then, fretting over the children. Having told them, she was suddenly unsure that it was the right thing to do; she wondered if she and Edward should not have allowed the realisation to creep up on them. It would have been so easy, with him being away in London, but she herself had hated being deceived as a child and had never trusted the deceiver again.

Bertie was almost seven, no longer a baby, no longer gullible; he had become aware of divorce at school, he knew it happened, he would wonder and fret at his father's absence, his rare appearances. She heard his voice over and over again, saying, 'I'd rather go back to that school than you got divorced,' and felt extremely sick. What kind of parents were they to have allowed something like that to happen to him, something he viewed with more horror than being homesick, being bullied, being afraid? But in the end it had been Edward who had insisted on the separation, who had said he could not contemplate spending the rest of his life in a marriage where he did not feel valued. She could not argue with that.

But then, she thought, tossing miserably on her pillows, checking the time yet again – still only half past two – if she had behaved better, treated Edward better, he would still feel valued, would want to stay with her, with the marriage.

She wondered if she would have been having this debate with herself if she had not quarrelled with Harry, if their affair had still been going on.

556

She rather feared she would not. Harry, how she had felt about him, how she had loved him, how she knew he had loved her, had blinded her, stupefied her, wiped out sense, sensibility, virtue. They had been cataclysmic, those few weeks; she knew she would never recover, never be restored to herself again.

For as long as she lived now, everything that happened to her, every emotion she experienced, would be set against it, judged by it; there was to be no denying it, no escape. It still hurt, the loss of him, the pain was frightful; it was in everything she did, everywhere she went. She kept expecting it to ease, to dull even, but it did not; each day's pain was as fierce, as awful as the one before. The best that could be said was that she was growing used to it.

At least she had phoned Miss Gerard; the children's anxieties had made that comparatively easy. It had still hurt, just saying the words had hurt: 'I'm sorry, I can't accept your offer,' and then proffering the reason, the incomprehensible excuse – incomprehensible to a childless woman – hearing the long, exasperated silence, the sigh, the terse 'I see,' and then after a pause, 'Well, there seems nothing more to be said. I hope you won't regret it too much. Goodbye, Mrs Fallon.'

She had put the phone down then and cried: cried for a long time, as much over Monica Gerard's disapproval as the lost opportunity. It had been one of the hardest things she had ever done; but having done it, she had felt better, easier, had bought off a little of her guilt at least. And now she had her new idea, her new scheme, consolation of a sort. If only she could persuade Edward, make it work. Thinking of her new scheme, how she might make it work, Cassia fell finally asleep.

She woke in a panic, to brilliant daylight. Ten o'clock. She shook her clock, hurled it across the room. She must have either slept through it or failed to set it properly. Probably the latter; she had been very distracted when she had gone to bed. And before she left, she had to phone home, make sure everything was under control, that Janet and Edward were communicating properly, that Peggy really was able to look after Delia.

She still felt confused, heavy with sleep; it was hard to hurry. She looked at herself in the mirror, at her pale drawn face, her eyes dark ringed, somehow deeper in her face than they used to be. Hardly the face of a mannequin; she wasn't going to do much for Edwina looking like this. God, she was dreading this thing: if only she could get out of it. But she couldn't; short of a heart attack there was no excuse.

She thought of Amstruther's rather beady joke that the first symptom of heart disease was often sudden death and then it was usually too late ...

God, what would he say if he knew she'd turned down yet another opportunity? Well, no doubt he would know – he and Miss Gerard were friends – would be putting her on a very black list indeed.

She pulled on the dress she had worn the day before; it had spent the night on a chair and was very creased. There was no time to do anything about her face; maybe she could do her make-up at Leon de Rosay's. She even had smudges of mascara under her eyes from not cleaning it off properly the night before; she licked her finger, tried to rub it off and made it worse. She dragged a comb through her hair, pushed her feet into her shoes, realised she had laddered one of her stockings. Well, what did it matter? Who, as her grandmother would have said, was going to look at her?

She grabbed her handbag and her keys and ran out of the front door, down the steps and into her car; it had come back from the garage, pristine and gleaming, quite restored to its original beauty. If only she could do the same for herself, she thought, catching sight of herself again in the driving mirror. God, she looked terrible.

She started the car, set off down Walton Street with a screech of tyres. She was dimly aware that another car, an extremely large car, was coming up behind her; as it drew nearer, as she braked at the bottom of Walton Street, waiting to turn into Draycott Avenue, it hooted at her, hard. Some bloody man, no doubt, irritated by the sight of her car, by the fact it was being driven by a woman, it happened quite often. Deliberately not so much as looking into the mirror, let alone taking any notice of it, she pulled out and roared down Draycott Avenue. The car followed, still hooting. She tried to ignore it, to think where she was going, how best to get there. Leon de Rosay's salon was in Tite Street; down the King's Road, turn left down Flood Street then—

'Oh shut up,' she shouted irritably into her driving mirror. The car was a black Bentley; whoever owned it clearly felt he should have the road to himself. She turned right into the King's Road, drove down much too fast. The car was still behind her, continued to hoot. What was the matter with him? Ah, thank God, there were some traffic lights ahead, just changing. She could shoot through them, leave him stuck behind, with a bit of luck. Then she was practically at Leon's. She put her foot down, shot the lights; they were just changing. Good.

'Oh God,' she said, as the Bentley followed her through; she had been so engrossed in his behaviour she had not been concentrating on what was in front of her, had to swerve to avoid another parked car. Another hoot: was he a maniac or something? It was a huge car, black, trimmed with chrome; it was rather like Harry's Bentley. Another ostentatious vehicle, another autocratic driver. Another hoot: the Bentley suddenly accelerated, shot past her, pulled in sharply in front of her and stopped; she almost ran into it.

She sat for a moment, breathing rather hard, shaking violently, then got out of the car on legs that were weak, could scarcely hold her, walked towards the Bentley. The King's Road rang with hooting horns, people shouting; a car coming the other way had practically run into it, the one behind her had slewed across the road in its effort to avoid her, and hit a lamp-post. The driver was clearly mad: completely mad.

'Are you completely mad?' she shouted, as the door opened and a large frame began to emerge from it.

'Yes,' said Harry, 'probably. My God, you look dreadful, Cassia, what on earth have you been doing? And why aren't you wearing my pearls?'

It was that day that the regular batch of letters from England arrived at Rollo Gresham's house in Marrakesh, coinciding with a bout of the periodic joint pain and fever which characterised his illness. One of the letters caused him particular distress; the coincidence of that with another, less threatening in nature, but as distressing to him for the memories it evoked, resulted in one of his violent rages.

When finally he fell asleep, Mehdi, his servant, found the two letters as he moved silently round the room clearing up the worst of the chaos, the broken jugs and ornaments, the spilt wine, the spattered food, and instructed the rest of the household to make sure that in future any communication from either of the sources must be intercepted and kept from the master at all costs.

At Fort Belvedere that same day, Mrs Simpson was with the King, enjoying briefly the eye of the storm that they had created, the King having only a few days previously informed his mother and his brothers that he was prepared to 'go out quietly' if a way could not be found to enable him have the wife he so desperately wanted.

Meanwhile in London in the homes of the King's ministers and the Lords of the press, the arguments raged as to the advisability or indeed feasibility of the morganatic marriage proposal, which Mrs Simpson and consequently the King favoured and which was now the subject of formal discussion. The ministers were, on the whole, against it, as was Baldwin, but he was anxious that it should at least be fairly considered. The Dominions, he informed the Cabinet, were being urgently consulted on the matter, and there was much talk of a 'set', which possibly included the press Lords, backing the marriage. And still the press was held silent.

★

Cecily had already changed into three different dresses and was trying to decide whether she should consider a fourth, when Justin arrived at the house.

'Oh dear,' she said, hearing the door-bell peal, 'that's Mr Everard, I had no idea it was so late.'

'It isn't late at all,' said Susan, who already had done her hair, and stood proffering dresses, expressing the opinion that each was even prettier and more suitable than the last. 'It's only a quarter past six, no need to worry about the time. I should go for the blue,' she added, 'it always did suit you.'

'That's just the point,' said Cecily fretfully. 'I've worn it a lot, everyone will remember. I want to feel confident, look really nice.'

'Well, if they remember,' said Susan with simple logic, 'they'll remember how it suited you. So it's obviously a good idea. Come on, let's try it on again.'

'No,' said Cecily, suddenly decisive, 'no, not the blue. I'll wear the cream. It's more eveningy, and then I can wear the fox jacket over it. And that means the pearls, Susan, the double string, I think, that Mr Harrington gave me for our tenth wedding anniversary.'

She was very surprised she had managed to say that: surprised and proud. It was the sort of thing an ordinary woman might have said, a confident woman, albeit a widow, who had nothing to be ashamed of, nothing to fear from what lay ahead of her, a woman who was looking forward to an evening with old friends who would almost certainly be pleased to see her, would not turn their backs on her, not shun her, not treat her like some sort of a pariah.

She was still managing to retain this mood of optimism and courage – albeit with some slight difficulty – when she went into the drawing troom to greet Justin. Expecting one of the ecstatic greetings that she had come to expect from him, she was taken aback by him being clearly impatient.

'I did say you should be ready,' he said, a touch of reproof in his voice. 'I've left the rehearsal to come and fetch you.'

'Well, you didn't have to,' said Cecily, too annoyed to be upset. 'I'm perfectly capable of getting across roughly a mile of London on my own.'

'I wanted to,' he said, his voice not quite its warm, charming self, 'but I didn't want to be long, that's all. I'm taking pictures at this thing, and—'

'I'm sure they can wait ten minutes for you to get back,' said Cecily. 'Now I've got some champagne on ice for us, and we can—'

'Cecily, darling,' said Justin, the 'darling' coming out with a clear effort, 'I do not have time for champagne. I've left my assistant in charge of a very tricky sequence and I must get back to it.'

'Well, it's a pity you didn't send your assistant for me,' said Cecily sharply, 'and I want some champagne, so you'd better just go back without me. Go on, Justin, I'll follow. And you needn't worry that I won't come, I have far more pressing reasons for being at this thing than arriving with you.'

She wasn't looking at him as she delivered the last bit of this speech, so she didn't see the hurt in his eyes; but she heard the drawing-room door slam behind him as he walked out and felt a stab of pain herself. She sat down in a chair and rang for Adams, thinking that Justin had not even told her how nice she looked, and irritation disposed of the pain again. After all the trouble she had gone to. However busy Benedict had been, he had always had time to compliment her, was never in too much of a rush to take a glass of champagne with her if she wanted one before they went out.

'Oh, Adams,' she said, hearing her own voice rather cool, very confident. 'Bring in the champagne, would you? Mr Everard didn't have time to wait for me, but I would like a glass in any case. And tell Preston I shall need driving to the Dorchester after all. Thank you.' And she glanced at her reflection in the mirror, thinking how nice she did indeed look, before sitting down again by the fire with a glass of exquisitely chilled Veuve Cliquot.

Justin sat in his taxi, shaking quite literally with rage. To think he had left one of the most important sessions of his life, risked it going wrong, just to find himself on the receiving end of a lot of upper-class nonsense from a spoilt, over-indulged woman. How could she possibly not realise how crucial it was? How could she not appreciate him tearing himself away from it, just to collect her? He had thought she would be grateful, that she would be able to see that he was supporting her in her hour of need, that he understood the need uniquely. It appeared she felt neither gratitude nor understanding.

Of course it was hardly surprising she was spoilt; he had heard her husband had been one of the richest men in England. You only had to look round that great house of hers, at the servants, the paintings, the absurdly lavish furnishings. Well, he wasn't going to spoil her; he had no intention whatever of pandering to that sort of thing. Either she accepted him for what he was, appreciated the limitations of his job and lifestyle, or their relationship was over. Then he realised that their relationship existed only in his hopeful imagination and that, in actual fact, it had no future whatsoever.

★

'Oh, Cassia, there you are. I do think you could have got here earlier. I could have done with someone to help me sort out the seating arrangements.'

Cassia looked at Edwina across the ballroom of the Dorchester, the chaos of the room: men up ladders fixing lights, more men fixing trailing cables, more men still putting a red baize cover on the vast catwalk that extended two thirds of the room's width; various models drifting about in dressing robes; several children sitting surprisingly quietly in a corner; a young man with long brown hair who was clearly upset bending over his camera, shouting at one of the models; a large woman putting the final touches to an incredibly elaborate urn of flowers; a pianist playing what was clearly supposed to be soothing music and which was having no effect whatsoever — and the wife of her lover glaring at her across the chaos. All these things seemed to go some way towards restoring her to reality.

Until then, she had not felt herself rooted in reality at all. She had experienced in the course of the day a flow of such extraordinary and violent emotion that she was by then utterly spent: exhausted, bleached of feeling, able only to proceed at a most basic and undemanding level. She had managed to collect the dresses from Leon de Rosay half an hour earlier, to thank him for them, to say, yes, they fitted beautifully now. Was he able to tell, she wondered, as he studied those dresses on her, one by one, with fierce attention, could he see by looking at her, what had been happening to her in the hours between the morning appointment and the evening, the hours that his seamstresses had spent feverishly unpicking and restitching, the hours that she had lain in her bed in her house in Walton Street with Harry?

Could he tell that the body on which he now studied his creations had arched, thrust, throbbed, soared into pleasure, not just once, but again and again, as morning became afternoon and afternoon evening. Could he tell that the voice that assured him with courteous calm that the dresses were perfect now, quite perfect really, had cried out repeatedly, loudly, with wild primitive pleasure, that the ears in which he pinned first this style of earring, now that, had heard words so extraordinarily, so powerfully carnal that merely remembering them made her body clench with delight?

And perhaps the most extraordinary words of all, given that they were on Harry's lips, were, 'I'm sorry,' not once, but again and again.

'I'm sorry,' he had said, as she stood there staring at him, scowling at him, still shaken from the chase, the near crash, 'I was only trying to catch you, attract your attention.'

'And quite possibly kill me, yourself and several other people besides into the bargain,' she said. 'Really, Harry, you are cretinously stupid. You'd better talk to that man, the one in the Riley, I think he's going to hit you.'

'I'm sorry,' he said to the man in the Riley, the bonnet of which was virtually enfolding a lamp-post, 'frightfully stupid of me, of course you must allow me to pay for any damage, here is my card.'

And 'I'm sorry,' he said to her, as she sat in the Bentley, still scowling, 'sorry I said you looked dreadful, but you — well, you do. I've never seen you like that. Did you sleep in that dress or something?'

'No,' she said.

'Well, it looks like it,' he said, and then reaching out for her face, stroking under her eyes, first one then the other with his forefinger, 'and what is this?'

'It's smudged mascara, that's all. I was too tired to clean it off properly last night.'

'And laddered stockings,' he said, tracing the snaking shape of it with his thumb, from her knee down to her ankle. Really, Cassia!'

'Well, I'm sorry you find it all so shocking,' she said irritably (while noticing and trying not to notice that even the simple fact of his thumb moving idly up and down her leg caused reverberations in other places in her body, invisible, horribly responsive places).

'Not shocking, just surprising,' he said, and then, 'I'm sorry, Cassia. I'm sorry I misjudged you. Leapt to conclusions. About — well, about Cameron.'

And while she sat there, staring at him, amazed at this most extraordinary and unexpected of all his apologies, he said, clearly with excessive difficulty, 'I do tend to be slightly hasty. At times.'

'Well,' she said, in response to this generosity, eager to meet it with her own, trying not to smile at this most considerable understatement, 'there had been some grounds for it. For the misunderstanding. I can't let you think there wasn't.'

'I realise that,' he said, 'of course I do. And I'm not going to pretend I don't care about it. I do. But I can live with it, I think. Let's say I don't care about it enough to stop loving you.'

Until that moment she had not been sure where this exchange was leading, whether he was simply having a discussion, clearing the air between them, removing unnecessary animosity. Now happiness flooded her, drenched her; she stayed very still, afraid to speak further, afraid even to move, lest she shattered it, this seemingly fragile truce.

'Good chap, Cameron,' he said, sitting back in the driving seat, looking rather distantly out of the window. 'Very good. Good friend to have. He came to see me, you know. No, of course you don't. This morning. To explain.'

'Oh, I see,' she said.

'It can't have been easy for him. Christ, I couldn't have done it. Apart from anything else, I'd have felt such a fool.'

'So what – what did he tell you?' she said nervously.

He looked at her consideringly for a moment, then half smiled. 'Oh, now,' he said, 'here is a pretty situation. I have the opportunity to be judge and jury. To hear your evidence and set it against his. Shall I do that, Cassia, would you like to give me your version of what he told me? Might it be different in any way, do you think?'

'You are monstrous,' she said, anger rising in her, 'absolutely monstrous. I will tell you what happened, not to gain your bloody approval, Harry Moreton, but because I want you to know, and if it does differ in any way from his, then that is not my fault, and if you care to bring in a verdict of guilty, or guiltier, then that is entirely up to you. Rupert and I got drunk one night in my house in London, months ago. I was very upset about all sorts of things – my marriage, my own bad behaviour towards Edward, Bertie being sent away to school – and he was lonely and miserable about his life and his lack of success. We have known and been very fond of each other ever since I can remember and – well, you know the rest. And it was an absolutely isolated incident long before you and I ...' She turned and started to open the car door. 'I don't think I quite like the turn of this conversation, Harry, you must excuse me. I have a great deal to do.'

'Don't be ridiculous,' he said, reaching over, pulling the door shut again, 'I wasn't entirely serious. I seem to be far more anxious to gain your bloody approval, as you so elegantly put it, than you are to gain mine, for some reason. I can't help being jealous of the bastard, Cassia, but I can live with it. I've said I'm sorry, for fuck's sake, what more do you want?'

She looked at him and smiled. Everything seemed very simple suddenly, and she felt utterly happy; she felt it must be visible, that happiness, that she must somehow shine with it, that people passing that car would look in and see it, feel warmed by it themselves.

'You,' she said, 'I want you and as soon as possible.'

For Edwina the entire evening had blurred. Somehow the chaotic room cleared into order, rather like a speeded-up film; the catwalk standing pristine at its centre, the gilt chairs ranged round it, the great urns of flowers standing either side of the models' entrance. The hubbub cleared, the music began, the pianist running through his repertoire of Gershwin, Cole Porter, Irving Berlin. The models arrived one by one, the amateurs excited and chattery, the professionals rather more languid, moved into the huge dressing room, each with her own clothes on a rail, her own running order, her own dresser, the hairdresser moving swiftly and easily between them all. The children, summoned earlier for a final rehearsal and allotted another dressing room, appeared for her approval, transformed from rather ordinary little girls into a myriad of befrilled and beribboned bridesmaids; the chief model, who was to be the bride, looked at them darkly and said she could see who was going to get the best press.

The gilt chairs began to fill; peering through a gap in the curtains Edwina saw countless friends, saw Cecily enter alone, looking terribly nervous, then saw first one, then another, then a crowd of people go over to her and greet her (but where was Justin, for heaven's sake? He had promised to look after her). She saw Francis arriving, with Aurora Le Page and Drusilla Wyndham; saw Edward Fallon with the two little boys and an extremely pretty, dark girl who Cassia said was their nanny; saw the Whittakers settle themselves, Lady Whittaker looking interestingly nervous; her own parents, her mother looking quite wonderful in beaded black; saw Leon de Rosay slip into the back row, having driven everyone in the dressing room completely crazy; saw Justin appear from behind the scenes and set up his camera on a tripod next to Leon; and then time really took a rush forward, and she had made her announcement, welcomed everyone, and then it was starting and the first girls were gliding in the most professional manner along the catwalk, even Venetia Hardwicke, who swore she had two left feet, and then ...

'Silence!' said Francis Stevenson-Cook. 'Pray silence for Mr Rupert Cameron, who will read aloud from tomorrow's newspaper, which through my unrivalled contacts with Fleet Street I have managed to acquire. It says it all.'

Rupert stood up, smiling, waving a copy of the *Daily Sketch*, and began to read from it in excessively dramatic tones.

'Huge Success at Charity Fashion Show. The cream of London society and the fashion and theatrical world met last night in the new ballroom in the Grosvenor House Hotel where a fashion show in aid of St

Christopher's Hospital was staged by Mrs Edwina Moreton, a fashion editor on *Style* magazine—' very loud cheers.

Edwina felt thankful that neither Aurora Le Page nor Drusilla Wyndham were at this party, organised by Francis in a large private dining room at the Dorchester.

'Seats for the show were totally sold out, and guests staying in the hotel who did not have tickets were prepared to stand and watch for its hour and a half duration. Many of Mrs Moreton's friends, including Mrs Cassia Fallon, a doctor at St Christopher's Hospital—' loud cheers and wolf whistles – 'modelled the clothes, which were by London's top couturiers, along with a large number of professional mannequins.

'The finale of the show was a wedding sequence, including a children's ballet choreographed jointly by Madame Evelyn Brunel of the well-known Brunel Academy and Mr Rupert Cameron, the actor, star of the new hit play *Letters*—' this to deafening applause. 'One of the very pretty bridesmaids was ten-year-old Portia Studely, the daughter of Mr Cameron's co-star, Eleanor Studely.

'The evening raised over £1,000 for the hospital, and Mr Stevenson-Cook, the publishing director of Style Publications, who presented the cheque to Mrs Mary Whittaker from the hospital committee, paid tribute to all Mrs Moreton's hard work – ' cries of 'well done, Edwina' – 'and said he was proud to have *Style* magazine associated with the show.'

A few people were not at the party: Edward Fallon, grateful for an excuse to avoid it, had returned to the house in Walton Street with Janet Fraser, saying (with perfect truth) that the boys must be got home, they were exhausted and needed to go to bed. He and Janet then spent the rest of the evening drinking cocoa and playing canasta.

Edward was surprised, as he drifted off to sleep, by how much he had enjoyed the whole occasion, even the fashion show; for some reason the foolishness of Cassia's friends, the strain of contact with them, had been eased by Janet's smiling, sensible presence, her occasional sharp comment. And she was wonderful with the children (who had been swiftly bored, asking at regular intervals and in loud whispers when it would be over), reminding them firmly how much they had wanted to come, how important it was to their mother that they were good, feeding them boiled sweets at regular intervals from a seemingly bottomless paper bag in her pocket; he really had been very impressed by that. And by her insistence that Cassia went to the party afterwards, and her tactful recognition that he, Edward, would love to escape it, 'but maybe if Daddy could come with us, that would help me a lot'.

It had all been very impressive.

Cecily had not been at the party, and nor had Justin; they had returned to the house in Eaton Place together (having apologised to one another almost in unison in the interval of the fashion show) and had drunk another bottle of the champagne she had had put on ice for their earlier consumption. She had then gone up to bed, pleading a genuine tiredness, but very happy none the less, and resolved to try to understand the demands of a life hitherto unimaginable to her, and he had walked all the way home to his flat in Clapham, scarcely noticing the distance and equally resolved to try to understand the effect of a life equally unimaginable to him, and its power to spoil even the sweetest and most unselfish of people.

Eleanor Studely was also not at the party; she had insisted that she and Portia, who had a nasty headache and was very over-excited, should go home to the peace and quiet of Peckham. It was very peaceful and very quiet there: Eleanor sat drinking a strong cup of tea and tried to tell herself that being at the party, watching Rupert Cameron flirting with the enormous number of pretty young women who would be there, would be more painful than sitting here all alone, thinking about it. She was not terribly successful.

Edwina, looking round the table in the private room Francis had taken for the party, experienced a sense of surprisingly quiet and almost private satisfaction at what she had accomplished.

She looked across at Harry, who was watching her thoughtfully, his eyes full of a rather unfamiliar emotion. It was admiration. He raised his glass to her and smiled.

CHAPTER 34

'Cecily.' Cassia's voice was urgent, oddly excited on the telephone. 'Do you speak French?'

Cecily shook her head, to try and rid it of the rather woolly sensation that filled it, and struggled into a sitting position. 'Yes,' she said, 'yes, I do.'

'Good. I want to ask you something. You know you once said you didn't know how to thank me when I went to see Norman Duvant with you? Well, I'm about to tell you.'

Three days later, as Cassia lay in their twin cabin in the Golden Arrow, as it made its way through the dark stretches of northern France, Cecily snoring in a rather unexpected way in the berth opposite her, she felt a strange mixture of elation and terror. Making Cecily her accomplice had been a stroke of genius, she thought; desperate to go, completely incapable of thinking of any excuse to present to her family and, indeed, Harry for doing so, the inspiration had come to her as she lay uncomfortably on the sofa at Walton Street after the party, not wishing to wake Edward and inevitably acquaint him of the fact that it was almost three o'clock. And it had worked beautifully; Cecily had been excited, intrigued, had promised absolute discretion, had completely understood her reasons for wanting to go (presented more as a mild curiosity as to Leonora's situation in the last few months of her life than a burning, desperate need to understand it), had suggested they present the trip as a treat for Cecily and a chance to buy the new clothes she so desperately needed. None the less, she came close to being tempted to cancel the trip many times in the days following the fashion show. Her children had been querulous about it, her husband disapproving, her lover outraged, but she had faced them all and told them it was only for two days, that she had promised now that they should go, that Cecily had specially asked her, that she had been having a horrid time lately, that it was all booked and arranged, that they would be home for the weekend.

Her anxieties about the money would not go away. They extended their tortuous, ill-shaped shadow into every area of her life, and she could not rest until they were at best removed and at worst realised. She wanted more than anything in the world to discover that she was foolish, neurotic even, that everything everyone had told her was true, that Leonora had indeed died a rich woman, her spell of hardship short lived and easily explained; but until she had proved that to her own absolute satisfaction, she could not rest, she felt she was cheating, living in a mirage, enjoying a spurious happiness to which she not only had no right, but which she did not even want. Certainly did not want.

They were staying at the Ritz. 'My treat,' said Cassia firmly, 'it's the least I can do. We're going to have some fun as well.' And as she unpacked her things, looking out of the window of their suite on to the place Vendôme in all its splendour, as they sat in the bar and ordered Bellinis, as they sipped their drinks looking on to the lovely area, half conservatory half garden, beyond it, studied the absurdly elaborate menu for luncheon, she wondered why she had not indulged herself more in the time since she had become rich. In the eighteen months or so of its duration, she had indulged herself in very little luxury: some clothes, her car, what was really a very modest house – that had been the extent of her extravagance. It was rather absurd, she thought, that a fortune which could have bought her mansions, yachts, strings of racehorses, a vault full of jewels, should only have extended to such things.

There had, of course, been the requirement for tact with Edward, a requirement she had scarcely fulfilled, she reflected with a stab of misery, the fact that she had been overwhelmed by the extent of the money, both unable and unwilling to convert it into objects, possessions; but there was, of course, something else, something which initially had not been a factor but increasingly now was: a sense of unease about it, a sense that it was not properly hers, that she had no right to it.

Perhaps the trip would give her the right to it, but she was very much afraid it wouldn't.

After a lunch of lamb noisettes so tender they seemed quite literally and in the approved manner to melt in the mouth, and a champagne sorbet that did indeed taste exactly like finest Veuve Cliquot *brut*, they walked out into the brilliant streets of pre-Christmas Paris.

Cecily knew Paris well, she had spent six months there just before she had done her London season, and she acted as guide. It was like a celebration of fashion, that walk: careless of the exquisite buildings, the infinitely graceful shapes, the charming boulevards of Paris, they walked into the Faubourg St Honoré, and then back to rue Cambon, down the rue Royale and across the place de la Concorde into the Champs Elysées and thence into Avenue George Cinq; they passed the salons of Lanvin, Chanel, Givenchy, Laroche, vast shimmering department stores, tiny jewel-like boutiques. They bought clothes, perfume, hats for themselves, presents for everyone else; stopped every hour or so for lemon tea, hot chocolate piled high with *crème chantilly*, and when they were hungry, and to restore their flagging energies, wonderful pastries, fruit tartlets, chocolate éclairs.

They took a taxi back finally to the hotel at seven and collapsed exhausted into hot baths; having changed and re-energised themselves with cocktails, they went out to dine in the art nouveau splendour of Maxims, and sat happily weary, eating lobster thermidor and observing chic Paris at play: groups of impossibly thin women in narrow black dresses, with tiny hats or extravagant decorations in their hair, and absurdly handsome men oozing sex, all of them talking more loudly than might have been considered acceptable in a London restaurant, and greeting friends constantly at other tables with much kissing and cries of pleasure.

'The thing about Paris,' said Cecily thoughtfully, 'is that everybody is much more self-confident than they are in London. So they're not worrying about what everybody else thinks all the time. Oh, I am enjoying myself, this was such a lovely idea.'

'You're not tired?' said Cassia anxiously, but Cecily said, no, she was not in the least tired, she felt less tired than she could remember for a very long time.

'Now, enough fun: let's talk about tomorow. What are we going to do?'

'Well, first of all, I want to go down to this place, the Auteuil district. Do you know that?'

'A bit. It's near Passy. Not exactly a slum, but not at all chic. That's where Leonora was living? How awful.'

'Yes, and then she moved up to Passy itself,' said Cassia, 'and it's her apartment there that I want to visit after that. I just thought we might find someone who could tell us a bit more about it all, who visited her and so on. Now, shall we have crêpe Suzette?'

'Maybe just this once, but I so want to stay thin, Cassia, it's so lovely. Although Justin says ...' Her voice tailed off; she looked at Cassia awkwardly, blushed. 'He seems to understand me. It's so strange, because our lives are so different.'

'It sounds as if he's in love with you to me,' said Cassia, smiling in genuine pleasure, 'how lovely.'

'Oh, I don't think so. Now, come on, let's have a crêpe. They look so wonderful.'

Cecily could have taken the opportunity, Cassia thought, to have questioned her about her own shaky marriage; but she didn't. It was not Cecily's style; years of acute discomfort in her personal life had taught her delicacy about such matters. Delicacy: and absolute discretion.

In England that day, 1 December, something had happened which many people read afterwards as an omen of the end of the King's brief reign: the Crystal Palace, that monument to Victorian tradition and values, was burnt down. On the same day, as if in response to that particular sentiment, the Bishop of Bradford spoke at his diocesan conference about the forthcoming coronation and expressed his pious hope that the King was approaching the event in a spirit of piety and self-dedication. It was the first time anyone in official life had seen fit to comment on the royal affair to any degree whatsoever; and it was the first tiny snowflake in the avalanche of comment that was so shortly to follow.

They took the Metro next morning to Porte d'Auteuil. Cassia emerged from the Metro station feeling slightly nervous; she had half expected to find herself in the middle of a slum, a sort of Parisian Whitechapel, and was relieved to find a district that, although not beautiful, and extremely noisy and busy, was still quite respectable. The chief difference was in its colour: where the Paris she knew was all shades of white and golden stone, the Auteuil was drab, uncompromising grey with new apartment blocks rising on every corner.

She stood in the street, staring at them, at the greyness, imagining herself Leonora, arriving here completely alone, ill and anxious, from the glorious tree-lined sweep of the avenue Foch, with its tall, eighteenth-century houses set behind ornate railings and lush greenery, and felt sick.

'Down here,' said Cecily, who had been studying her map, 'the rue Molitor we want, look, it's that main road at the bottom, and those must be the apartments there. Goodness! Poor Leonora. Rather her than me.'

The apartment block in which Leonora had lived for those months was a vast rectangular concrete structure, built in the new functional style, with a plaque reading '1934' set at each end, extending a full block about a dozen storeys tall, set with small, square windows; there was a door leading straight off the street every thirty yards or so, each one firmly locked. 'She was number one hundred and ten,' said Cassia, 'it must be about halfway along. How on earth are we going to get in? There's no central door, no porter.'

'We'll just stand there,' said Cecily. 'Someone's bound to come out sooner or later. Then we can simply walk in.'

Not for the first time since they had arrived in Paris, Cassia looked at her with a certain admiration.

They had to wait almost half an hour; it was very cold and the street was narrow and made dark by the tall buildings. Eventually an old man emerged, a parody of a Frenchman in his beret and blue overalls, a cigarette adhering to his bottom lip; he glared at them and tried to pull the door closed. Cecily gave him a dazzling smile, put out her arm quickly and stopped him.

'*Bonjour, Monsieur. Comment allez-vous? Nous visitons notre grandmère au cinquième étage.*'

The old man glared at them, removed his cigarette and spat on to the pavement; but he let them through.

Inside, the building was even less savoury: long cold concrete corridors, with iron-railed stairs leading up a central well. It was clean, but incredibly ugly. The apartment was on the fourth floor; it seemed quite a long climb.

'Think of hauling your shopping up here,' said Cecily. 'And she was ill when she had to do this, and no lift. I can't bear it.'

They knocked on the door of 110; no answer, nor to those on either side of it, nor the two doors opposite. The silence was somehow theatening; the only sound the echoes of their knocking.

An old woman came slowly up the stairs towards them, breathing heavily, carrying a very full shopping basket. Cecily went down to meet her, held out her hand for the basket and said, '*Puis-je vous aider, madame?*' The old woman looked at her suspiciously for a moment, then grunted and handed the bag over. '*Dans quel apartement est-ce que vous habitez?*'

'*Numéro cent sept.*' She set off along the corridor. '*Là bas.*' She spoke very fast, and rather gutturally: Cassia thanked God once again for Cecily and followed meekly.

Numéro 107 was quite a long way down the corridor from 110; when they got there, Cecily set down the basket while she fumbled for her key, and then said, '*Madame, est-ce que vous connaissez la femme qui habitait dans cet apartement-là? Numéro cent dix? Une femme anglaise?*'

'*Non,*' said the old woman very firmly indeed. '*Non, je ne l'ai jamais connu.*' She turned away from them, walked into her apartment; Cecily put a small, elegant foot against the peeling door.

'*Vous êtes sûr? Lady Beatty? Ou peut-être vous la connaissez comme Madame Gresham?*'

'*Non, mademoiselle. Pas du tout. Non.*' She slammed her door on them with a final glare.

'Oh dear,' said Cecily, rubbing her ankle which had been struck by the door. 'Sorry, Cassia.'

'She must have known her,' said Cassia, 'or known of her. Cecily, tell her who we are. Tell her Leonora has died, that we're trying to find out who looked after her when she was here, so that we can thank them. Or even – ' inspiration struck her – 'reward them. Here, write that old woman a note, push it under her door. Saying what I told you to. I bet it'll work.'

It did work; five minutes later they were sitting in the old woman's apartment, being poured large cups of very bitter black coffee from a tin jug.

The apartment was very basic: one fairly large room and a kitchen and bathroom leading off it. It was dark, the only small windows looking out from the living room on to another huge block directly behind it: and it was cold. Again and again Cassia tried to imagine Leonora living there, Leonora with her extravagant tastes, her love of luxury, her beautiful clothes, tried to imagine what she must have endured, what desperation must have brought her there – and failed.

It was a strangely frustrating experience, sitting there, asking Cecily to ask questions, important questions, not sure if she had asked exactly the right one, not sure if she had interpreted its answer correctly. But a story did emerge; Leonora had moved into the apartment just after Christmas, and had stayed only a few weeks. So that part of the story at least was true. She had been unwell, a doctor came two or three times, then no more.

A young man who had lived next door had befriended her, done some shopping for her, the old woman herself had taken soup in from time to time. She had been visited by an English lady, Miss Monkton, Cassia supposed, then shortly after that a friend had come and taken her away and they had not seen her since, although she had written to thank them both, herself and the young man.

'Ask her –' Cassia felt sick suddenly, sick and shaky – 'ask her if it was a man or a woman. The friend.'

What seemed like an endless exchange followed; she sat biting her lip, willing herself not to interrupt, struggling and failing to understand the rapid, guttural accent, straining her ears for familiar words, words she did not want to hear, a name she dreaded recognising.

'It was a woman. A young woman. A French woman, she thought, anyway, she spoke perfect French.'

Relief, absurdly, flooded Cassia, blessed warm relief. The bitter coffee tasted sweet suddenly.

The young woman had been tall, blonde, very slim, it seemed. Nice legs. Well dressed. Obviously well off. The old woman cackled with laughter, made a cupping gesture with both hands. Cecily smiled.

'She had a rather large bosom, apparently.' At least, not a tall, heavily built Englishman with dark hair.

'But she doesn't know her name?'

'No.'

'Cecily, ask her why she didn't want to talk to us, didn't want to tell us anything.'

The old woman's face became guarded, then she spoke at some length, in staccato sentences.

'Apparently, Leonora was frightened of people finding her. Finding she was here. She owed money, madame thinks. In the end, she couldn't even pay the doctor, that's why she stopped calling him.'

'What was the matter with her? Does she know?'

Another long exchange. There were gestures, a hand on the abdomen, the breast. 'She says she thought women's troubles. Quite bad. And something else as well, perhaps, but she wasn't sure.'

'Oh, God. Poor Leonora. Does she know the doctor's name?'

The doctor's name was Bertillon, his surgery in the rue Chanez. 'It's just up the street apparently.'

'And this young woman, she came for Leonora when?' Before Easter: that was the most accurate date they could get.

She stood up. 'We must go, Cecily, not trouble her any longer. She's going to run out of patience with us. Ask her what she would most like from us in the way of thanks for what she did for Leonora – food, wine, money, whatever …'

The old woman shook her head, looked disdainful. 'She doesn't want anything. She said Leonora was her friend, that it was a pleasure.' The old woman was talking again, her dark eyes gleaming; Cecily listened, then laughed. 'She says perhaps a bottle of Benedictine would be very welcome.'

Dr Bertillon was a charming, rather handsome young man with dark eyes and dark curly hair; he even spoke rather halting English. He was not, however, able to be of very much help to them, since the Dr Bertillon who had treated Leonora was his father, at that time away on a visit to relatives in Tours.

'Thank you, Dr Bertillon,' Cassia said. 'Perhaps I could telephone your father when he gets back next week?'

'But of course, madame. I am sure he will be pleased to speak to you.'

The apartment in Passy was, as everyone had told her, beautiful. In fact, everything was exactly as everyone had told her, she thought, and wondered why that irritated her. It was on the top floor of a most lovely eighteenth-century house, set high above the Trocadero Gardens, its entrance through a *porte cocherie*, and with an exquisite central courtyard that even in the cold December light had a golden summery quality. The porter's wife, who had greeted them like old friends, took them up to the apartment adjacent to the one Leonora had lived in – hers, it seemed, was occupied – so that they could admire the view, both over the courtyard at the back and out on to the Luxembourg Gardens at the front. The Eiffel Tower dominated the view, the whole area indeed, set down as if by some giant Gulliver in Lilliput, an absurdly oversized addition to a toyland of tiny cars, boats, buildings and parkland.

The porter's wife said something to Cecily in French. 'Apparently, Leonora used to like to walk in the Trocadero Gardens when she first came here. Then later, she couldn't get down, was confined to the balcony, she spent all that spring and summer until she died lying out there.'

'Who visited her? Does madame know?'

More rapid French: then, 'Several gentlemen and a very nice, kind elderly English lady.'

'And who brought her here? Ask her that.'

Cecily asked the woman. 'A French woman, quite young. You see, it all seems to be true. Cassia, let's go and have lunch, I'm starving.'

'Yes, of course,' said Cassia, 'but I want to know if there's anyone still living here who knew Leonora? Who I might talk to?'

There was: a lady who had lived on the floor below, a Madame Christophe. They had become quite good friends. She was out for the day, would be back that evening. 'And she speaks English. Cassia, please can we get some food? I'll faint soon.'

They lunched at a restaurant Leonora had taken Cassia to on one of her visits and loved, La Closerie des Lilas, in Montparnasse. Cecily had been delighted: 'Lovely idea. It's where all the most interesting people

575

eat. Terribly chic. The whole area is one long party, how clever of you to think of it.'

The Closerie was packed; they had to wait for a table, and sat in the rather dark bar, all mahogany and brass, watching Paris's smart literati coming and going, greeting one another, holding long intense conversations, some of them reading or even writing at the tables; they moved to the restaurant and its more conventional atmosphere almost reluctantly.

After lunch, Cassia told Cecily to go back to the hotel to rest, and when she had seen her into a taxi, turned back up the boulevard Montparnasse. She had another reason for coming to the area.

The Montparnasse Cemetery was where Leonora was buried; walking through its neat, grid-like layout, along gravelled paths, half amused, half impressed by the elaborate tombs and effigies, she wondered why it had been chosen for Leonora. There was a cemetery in Passy: why bring her here? It seemed to extend for miles, a forest of crosses, of marble angels, of vast, raised tombs. She recognised several famous names, Baudelaire, Maupassant, Saint-Saëns, smiled at a sculpture of a couple in bed on one, a copy of Rodin's *Kiss* on another.

She found Leonora's grave finally, marked with a simple white marble cross, carved only with her name, and the dates of her birth and death: June 1886–May 1935. So she had been almost fifty: it was somehow a surprise, that; she had known it of course, when she stopped to think about it, but she always thought of her as much younger.

There were some dead flowers lying beneath the cross; she wondered who could have put them there, wished she could thank them, placed the bunch of small white roses she had purchased on her way next to them, unwilling to remove the others for fear, absurdly, of appearing ungrateful.

It was very cold; she pulled her coat up round her neck, and stood there, thinking of Leonora lying there beneath the hard frosty earth, in the cold she had hated so much, trying to recall her as she had known her first, before the shadows had gathered properly about her, lovely, charming, amusing, adored by her husband, loved by her friends – and yet doomed to become a lonely, sad exile. Finally she moved away, walked slowly back to the Metro, thinking how apt a phrase 'heavy at heart' was. Her own that day seemed literally to weigh her down.

Madame Christophe offered Cassia pastries and coffee, more than happy to talk about Leonora. She was pretty, plump, well dressed, wearing a lot of jewellery; she had been widowed very soon after she had moved to the apartment, which was one of the things that had drawn her to Leonora; they had both been lonely, both living in their pasts.

'She was so brave, so very brave. She was in much pain and yet she never complained. Except at how she had lost her looks; she hated to see people, people from her past, she said they would find her ugly. That seemed to distress her very much.'

'I wish I had seen her, wish I'd know how ill she was. She must have thought so badly of me.'

'Oh no, madame.' Her face was shocked. 'She thought nothing but good of you, she loved you so. She would talk about you for hours, you and your *maman*, the fun she had with you, when you were a debutante, and she was so proud of you, of your success as a doctor.'

'Oh, was she?' said Cassia, hearing the bitterness in her own voice. 'I'm afraid there was very little to be proud of there.'

'She did not think so. She thought you were wonderful.' She smiled. She and her cousin, Monsieur Moreton. He admired you greatly too. I think Lady Beatty would have wished that you and he had married. He was here a great deal during those last few weeks.'

'Really?'

'*Mais oui*! He was so good to her, so gentle, so *tendre*. And when she was dying, he sat by her bed for thirty-six hours, never left her for more than a few moments until she was *sauve*. She was very afraid of dying, of being put in the cold. She hated the Passy cemetery being so near, it's just down there, you know, behind the gardens. She used to say, "Soon I shall be down there unable to escape", and in the end she made Monsieur Moreton promise that she would be taken somewhere else, that this would be a place where she was only alive, not lying still and cold.'

So that was why she was at Montparnasse, thought Cassia. Madame Christophe wiped her eyes, smiled at Cassia rather weakly. 'He was so very good to her. When she was still well enough to go out, she liked to go down the steps into the gardens, he would take her, walking with her so patiently, and towards the end he would carry her back up the stairs in his arms. I'm sorry, this upsets you.'

'No,' said Cassia, 'don't be sorry, I like to hear these things.' She thought of Harry, so arrogant, so impatient, walking slowly through the gardens, carrying the sick Leonora up the stairs, sitting with her through the long hours as the death she feared so much became inescapable, giving her courage, and realised how much he must have loved her, what a capacity he had indeed for love, thought how strange that was when he had known so little, what an extraordinary and complex person he was.

'Madame Christophe, who else was here? Did you meet a young

woman, a Frenchwoman? Tall, blonde? It was she who brought her here in the first place.'

'No, I never met such a person, but in the early days there were quite a few visitors. I did not know Lady Beatty so well then.'

'What about her her brother, Mr Harrington, did you meet him?'

'Yes, I did. A charming man, I thought. He was not here as much as Monsieur Moreton, but still he made many visits.'

'And did you meet Mr Gresham?'

A long, agonising silence, then: 'Ah, yes,' she said at last. 'A big man, yes? Very big, very – what do you say, jolly?'

'Yes, I suppose so. So you did meet him?'

'I did, but only once. And then only in the *vestibule*, with another gentleman, an Englishman, a business compatriot, as I understood it.'

'Oh, I see,' said Cassia. She wondered who that might have been: a lawyer probably, possibly even Mr Brewster – no, he hadn't met Gresham. Well, it wasn't important. 'I'm surprised you didn't see more of him, I thought he was here quite a lot.'

'Perhaps he was here more than I thought, madame. Time is *compliqué*, is it not, our memory plays tricks with it. As I say, he was not so friendly toward me as the other two gentlemen. Perfectly pleasant, *bien sûr*, but ...' She shrugged.

'Yes, I see. But not towards the end; he wasn't with Leonora when she died?'

'No, madame, no one was with her then, except her doctors and Monsieur Moreton, of course. I went in, to bid her farewell, and so I know that.'

'And did she speak well of Mr Gresham?'

'Oh, yes, madame. She had nothing but good to say of him. That he had always cared for her, left her well provided for. I think she was very sad that they had decided to part, *mais c'est la vie, n'est-ce pas?*'

'Yes,' said Cassia absently. '*C'est la vie.*'

She took a taxi back to the Ritz; she felt tired and curiously discouraged. She had learnt nothing that day, nothing at all to indicate that things were not as she had been told: perhaps it was time to bury her anxieties, let them rest. Leonora had plainly had a great deal of money lavished on her during the last few weeks of her life: before that there had been a period of temporary discomfort, lasting at the most a couple of months, during which time she had presumably overspent hopelessly on the income from the trust fund, and was too proud to admit to it. It did make sense, that Benedict had found her fecklessness increasingly exasperating; and if

Rollo was living abroad, having settled some large sum of money on her, the interest from which was more than sufficient to keep her in some luxury, he would not be inclined to look indulgently on her asking for more. Perhaps she had told Miss Monkton that Rollo was in financial difficulties so that she wouldn't start pestering him – she would have been quite likely to do so – and then the young Frenchwoman, whoever she was, her friend – she must have taken it upon herself to sort things out, move her to the new apartment, summon Harry. It was all perfectly reasonable.

Not for the first time, she wondered if Rollo Gresham would ever contact her: it had been a very pleasant letter she had written to him, merely asking how he was, expressing regret that she had not been able to visit Leonora during the last few weeks of her life, telling him she would always be pleased to hear from him, or indeed see him if he came to London; she had been surprised to receive nothing in reply. Perhaps he had moved on again from Marrakesh, was living some-where quite different. Whatever the reason, it was very frustrating; he really would be able to give her some information. She looked down at the piece of paper, which the porter's wife had given her, with the name of Leonora's last doctor on it. She would just ring him, make sure – what on earth was she going to make sure of, what could she even ask him?

'You're getting obsessed,' she said aloud, and turned her mind to the evening ahead and what she and Cecily might do.

'I'd like to get the divorce proceedings set in motion as soon as possible,' said Harry. 'I presume that will be acceptable to you.' He spoke quite calmly and casually, as if he were discussing taking her out to tea, and smiled at her almost benignly.

Edwina smiled back, slightly uncertainly. His mood had changed again so swiftly in the past week, so totally that it was unnerving. All his rage, his animosity towards her, seemed to have gone; he was relaxed, cheerful, albeit distant. Maybe he did have someone else: maybe the whole thing, all the fuss about having children, his rage at her going around with Francis Stevenson-Cook, and even her indiscretion at Janine Sobel's, had been an elaborate cover-up. The thought gave her a stab of alarm; she had not seriously considered it before. It was one thing to walk away from a marriage because it no longer held any interest for her, quite another to appear foolish: the deceived, unwitting wife.

'I'm perfectly happy to provide grounds,' he said, 'of course, so I'll speak to Geoffrey Partington, shall I? Get things moving?'

'Well ...'

'Naturally, I wouldn't argue about money. I have no desire to see any wife of mine in straitened circumstances, nor to go through any kind of vulgar scene in court. I'd want you to have a nice little house and an allowance which I don't think you could find ungenerous.'

'Harry,' she said, hearing her mother's voice, 'you do realise, don't you, that we should – would have to discuss terms, very carefully.'

He looked at her, clearly considering what she had said. Alarm flashed briefly at the back of his eyes.

'The thing is,' she said, 'I haven't actually quite made my mind up yet. I mean about your ultimatum. About giving up my job and so on.'

She had, but she wasn't going to hand it to him on a plate. Making grandiose gestures and statements was one thing; putting them into practice, walking out of a marriage that had, however she looked at it, considerable advantages, in terms of wealth and status, suddenly seemed very much another. At worst, she intended to walk out with a great deal more than she had walked in. And if there was someone else in his life, which suddenly seemed rather likely, it might be easier to ensure a really generous settlement – misbehaving at a party hardly constituted grounds for divorce. The case would go in her favour and the other woman, that dark, avaricious creature, seldom brought a large dowry to a marriage. Of course Harry was extremely rich – she had never been quite sure about the extent of his fortune, although his assets alone had to run into millions – but she wanted a lot of that fortune. If he was anxious to become free as soon as possible, she could make a great deal of capital from that. Capital being the operative word, she thought.

'Well,' he said, and his eyes were blank again, 'do make your mind up soon, Edwina. I don't enjoy the present situation very much at all. As I explained to you.'

'Well, that's unfortunate for you, Harry,' said Edwina, 'but I must ask you to endure it a little longer, I'm afraid. I'm sure you wouldn't want me to end our marriage lightly.'

She walked out of the room, shutting the door rather firmly, stood leaning against it, feeling slightly sick, and then went into her sitting room and sat down at her desk. She wondered if indeed there was another woman, and who she could possibly be. And if she realised what a formidable opponent she had.

'And how was Paris?' said Justin Everard. 'I've missed you a lot.' He had suddenly turned up on her doorstep the day after her return, said he had been working at a studio in Chelsea and could she give a poor artisan a cup of tea?

'It was wonderful, we had the best fun and I've brought you something I think you'll like.' It was an antique camera she had found in one of small streets off the rue de Rivoli, wooden with brass fittings, absurdly expensive, very beautiful.

Justin was overcome by it, kept turning it over and over, stroking it as if it were some kind of beloved animal. 'I adore it. How lovely, how generous you are.'

'I just wanted to say thank you,' she said simply, 'for everything.'

'You do that by simply being. Now, you have missed a lot of wonderful gossip. Have you seen the *News Chronicle?*'

'No,' said Cecily, 'only *The Times*, which I could hardly follow, and the *Telegraph*, which was very firm on the matter. Said the King must put duty first and give Mrs Simpson up.'

'Quite right. Terrible woman. Well, the *Chronicle* has this extraordinary story that he should be allowed to marry her but she shouldn't be queen. Did you ever hear such nonsense?'

'Oh, I don't know,' said Cecily, 'I do feel sorry for him. He obviously loves her.'

'Darling Cecily, you're such a romantic. Which is why I adore you so much. I agree he loves her, but he can't have it all ways. Apart from the fact that you can't have a divorced woman married to the head of the Church, the people won't accept her. You mark my words.'

'I suppose not. But he's so popular, everyone adores him.'

'Only because he's so dashing and handsome and seems to sympathise with the miners and so on. If he did something which our very moral nation disapproved of, it would all change in a flash. The English like things to be proper. Now look, I came to see you for two reasons: one, because I missed you, and two, to ask you to have dinner with me.'

'What, tonight?' said Cecily.

'Don't sound so frightened. Tonight or tomorrow night or the next night. Whenever it suits you. I am at your disposal. I just want you to come.'

'Well, I don't know,' said Cecily. She felt genuinely alarmed by his invitation. Being visited by him at the nursing home, chatting and laughing with him at the fashion show – that was all right, she could cope with that. But dinner: dinner was quite different, dinner was a statement, it had a sexual content, it was ...

'All right,' he said, laughing, oddly able to read her thoughts, 'suppose it was lunch. Would that frighten you less?'

A rush of affection, of gratitude to him, flooded Cecily. His ability to understand her fears, to read her thoughts, and, moreover, to sympathise with them, still amazed her. Benedict had not been nearly so perceptive – probably, she thought, because he was so concerned with his own fears and thoughts. Justin was, despite his rather absurd manner – which now Edwina had explained it to her, she quite enjoyed – formidably straightforward. After twelve years of tension and secrets, his company was, to Cecily, like walking out into the sunshine. And then he was such fun, so full of gossip and jokes, and he seemed to find everything she said amusing or interesting or both. That in itself was a novelty.

And on top of all that, she had to admit, he was rather good-looking, in a slightly effete way, with his heavy brown hair and soulful dark eyes. Edwina had told her he was terribly popular with women, that all the models adored him, loved being seen with him; she could not imagine what he could possibly find attractive about her. Maybe she was just a novelty. Maybe she was just charity work. Maybe once he was satisfied she really was better, he would disappear from her life. Anyway, in the meantime, she should just enjoy it; it was all very heart-warming and morale-boosting.

'No,' she said, 'no, not lunch, I'd like to have dinner with you very much. Thank you.'

'Splendid. Tomorrow, then? Friday is always a nice night. Somewhere quiet, I thought, I'll find somewhere. Bye, darling.'

She couldn't simply be charity work, Cecily thought, he didn't have to buy her dinner, tell her he adored her, call her darling. He could just have gone on coming to call. She smiled rather foolishly in the mirror at herself and started fretting over what she should wear.

'I suppose,' said Harry, running his finger idly down the length of Cassia's abdomen, lingering tenderly in her pubic hair, recommencing its journey upwards again, 'I suppose we should think about telling people soon. Otherwise the rumours will begin.'

He had sent her a telegram to the Ritz: 'IMPERATIVE YOU RETURN TO WALTON STREET EARLIEST STOP,' it said. 'URGENT BUSINESS NEEDS YOUR ATTENTION STOP. CONFIRM TIME OF ARRIVAL FRIDAY. MORETON.' She had cabled back, saying, 'MEETING IMPOSSIBLE', and another had come within the hour saying, 'REPEAT, WALTON STREET MEETING IMPERATIVE STOP. ALTERNATIVE VENUE MONKS RIDGE STOP. PERHAPS WITH DR FALLON STOP. MORETON.'

She had given in then, as of course he had known she would, had cabled back again saying, 'WALTON STREET MIDDAY STOP. VERY ANGRY ABOUT TERMS STOP.'

She and Cecily had parted with some regret; they had grown very close in those two days and she had been impressed again by Cecily's clear loyalty, her generosity, her refusal to press her for an answer to questions she must have. One day, when she had all the answers herself, she would pass them on; meanwhile she knew she had no need to worry that any confidences would be betrayed.

They arrived to a London alive with excitement about the King and Mrs Simpson; now that the silence of the press had finally broken, nobody talked of anything else. If you sat listening on a bus, by the counter in a shop, on the Underground train, it was the only subject under discussion: would he marry her, should he be allowed to marry her, who was she, why had an affair with a divorced woman been allowed to get out of hand, what must the old queen be thinking about, how much could the government control what he did? It had become, in the two and a half days they had been away, a national obsession. The vast majority of ordinary people had known nothing about it and the news had dropped into the nation's consciousness with a suddenness that had taken most people by surprise. She remarked on this to Harry who threw up his hands in mock horor.

'None of that, please. I have severe *ennui* on the subject. I presume you know what *ennui* means, having just come from France.' He was waiting for her, sitting naked in bed, a bottle of champagne on ice beside him and a basket of roses in the fireplace so huge it dwarfed the room.

'Hurry up,' he had said, as she stood there, half laughing half angry with him still at the danger of his peremptory telegrams, his assumption that she would be so instantly available to him. 'I want you in here beside me, with absolutely no clothes on, in less than thirty seconds. We've wasted quite enough of our lives already.' This was a constant cry of his.

'Harry, of course we can't tell people,' she said now, sitting up in her alarm. 'Tell them what, anyway?'

'That I love you. That you love me. That we're going to – what are we going to do, Cassia? Get married? Live in splendid sin?'

'Neither,' she said, 'not for a long time, anyway.'

'Why in the name of heaven not? We've wasted so much time already on our disastrous marriages. At this rate we'll be in our dotage before we even get to holding hands in public.' He spoke lightly, but there was a thoughtfulness behind his eyes.

She took his hand in hers, kissed it, said, 'Harry, I do love you. I love you more than I ever thought possible, but we can't do anything about it yet. I have the children to worry about.'

'The children! I thought you and Edward had agreed to part. I intend to institute divorce proceedings immediately, why can't you?'

'Have you really?' she said, appalled at the speed with which he was acting.

'Yes, of course. I can't see the slightest point in waiting. Although Edwina is behaving with sudden and rather suspicious loyalty. No doubt with her lovely eyes on my bank account. But I've agreed to provide grounds, as a gentleman should.'

'Naming me?'

'Of course not you. That wouldn't be gentlemanly, would it? No, with some floozy in a Brighton hotel. Like poor Mr Simpson. I see she has fled the country, by the way.'

'I thought you were bored with the subject. Well, yes, Edward and I have agreed to part. But we haven't actually even agreed to divorce. We have to let the children get used to the idea, they'll hate any notion of him being replaced, they adore him.'

'They'll adore me,' he said carelessly. 'Children always do.'

'Harry, you are unbelievably arrogant. These are another man's children. They'll be jealous, wary, resentful. It'll be very hard for them. Do you know what Bertie said to me the day I rescued him from that terrible school? He said he'd rather go back there even than Edward and I got divorced, that there was a boy in his dorm whose parents were divorced and he cried every night.'

'Poor little sod.'

'Yes, well, there you are. You've got to understand that.'

'Oh yes, I do,' he said, suddenly agreeable, surprising her as he so often did. 'I'm prepared for all sorts of difficulties, of course. Just the same, they do like me already. That has to be a help.'

'They like you now. They won't when they know. Honestly.'

'Well, all right. We'll begin our marriage with three difficult, hostile children. A small price to pay, to my mind. Under the circumstances. Any more objections?'

'Well, yes,' she said slowly, 'there might be. I can't tell you yet. It's a bit complex. It might not come to anything.'

'But if it does, it would affect you and me?'

'No. It would affect me.'

'Well, then, it would affect me too. Everything to do with you affects me Cassia, it always has. Surely you realise that. You don't seem to understand the nature of love very well.' He smiled at her rather warily.

'Now I have to go. When am I going to be allowed to see you again? Before Christmas? Or some time next summer?'

'Harry, please don't be difficult.'

'I'm afraid,' he said, 'that if wanting to be with you because I love you is difficult, then I shall most certainly continue to be so.' He looked at her and smiled, then said, 'What was it exactly you were doing in Paris?'

'I told you, shopping, Christmas shopping mostly. Cecily asked me to go with her and I thought it was the least I could do. I have something for you by the way, it's a—'

'Cassia,' he said, 'I hope that's all you were doing.'

'Of course it was.'

'Good,' he said lightly, 'then you may give me my present.'

Edward Fallon had an appointment that Friday afternoon to meet some of the board at St Mark's Hospital. He was already viewing his new life with some anxiety; he was not an adventurous creature, and he knew that the personal traumas he would be undergoing at the same time, the separation from his family, would add to his difficulties. Neither did he have any illusions about the kind of struggle that lay ahead of him: his was not a brilliant mind and, although he had a certain facility for the mechanics of surgery, he was aware of a shortfall in the diagnostic element.

Nevertheless, his desire to do it was stronger than his fear; he would not have dreamed of drawing back now. He would become a surgeon: perhaps not a brilliant one, but one none the less; and it would be infinitely more challenging than running a country practice. He would miss the country practice, though, he had been thinking about it that morning, as he worked his way through his surgery. It was sad to be leaving it, sad to think of all these patients being attended to by another doctor, another doctor not familiar with their histories, both medical and personal, sad to think that the pregnant women he was now looking after would be delivered by somebody else, the mortally sick eased out of life by other, less familiar hands.

Maureen, he knew, would be glad to leave; she was restless now, wanted something more challenging, an urban community, preferably working class, ideally in one of the really rough districts, she had said, her eyes shining with zeal. So there would be no continuity there. His patients would be his no more, they would have to learn about the new doctor as the new doctor would have to learn about them: and they might prefer the new doctor, find him more satisfactory, their own health dramatically improved. No doubt some would, others would not; in either case, he would lose them, lose control over their health and ultimately part of their lives.

And the thought of the surgery moving physically was distressing too: it had always been at Monks Ridge, and now it would have to be down in the village, away from the house – for he could not expect Cassia to endure the presence of a stranger at the house, a daily stream of patients through her front door – away from the sense of home, of family that so many found reassuring.

But then he would be doing more important, more ultimately healing things, removing cancers, diseased organs, repairing broken limbs; his life would be enthralling, challenging, as it could never be in Monks Heath. In time, he hoped, it would help to heal his shaken self-confidence, his loss of self-esteem – and a heart that in spite of everything, every bit of common sense, and the certain knowledge that living with Cassia was no longer in any way right for either of them, ached for a great deal of the time.

The board meeting went well: he was welcomed, introduced to the theatre staff, had a long talk with the three consultants who had interviewed him briefly six months ago – and had, at the time, rejected him.

'Glad this has worked out,' said one of them, shaking him vigorously by the hand. 'Personally I wanted you at the time, but we took that young woman on. And of course she's leaving, got married. God, it's a waste of money training women. What are you views on that? Purely personally, of course.'

Edward said that purely personally he thought women made very good doctors, but were inevitably inclined to find their personal lives getting in the way of their careers, that it was as a pity, but—'

'Yes, of course it's a pity, so is heart disease and cancer, but it's a fact of life. No, I hope if this new National Health scheme comes in, women will get themselves into nurses' uniform if they want to look after the sick. I really think to spend public money on training them as doctors would be little short of a crime. What about your wife, Fallon, will she be moving up to London with you?'

Edward was mercifully spared from answering this question by the arrival of the Matron, who had expressed the desire to meet him; after that, he could hardly wait to escape again to the peace and quiet of Monks Heath.

He telephoned home to see if Cassia could meet him, since Maureen had his car that afternoon to make some rather distant calls. Janet said

Cassia was out walking the dog and was then going to visit someone in the village, but her car was in the drive and she would come and collect him if he liked. Edward said that would be very kind and she said not at all, there was plenty of time before she had to get the children's supper, and she had them all busy making Christmas decorations.

There was no doubt that Janet had a gift for home making, Edward thought, for creating warmth and dispersing chaos at the same time; it was a very pleasant quality. And it was a gift, like any other; he had loved Cassia desperately, but he could see she had certainly not had that gift: Monks Ridge had certainly lacked neatness and order under her, and she had been hopeless with the staff, over-indulgent and reluctant to find fault. It had to be said that under Janet, in Cassia's absence, things were run a great deal better.

CHAPTER 35

I can't actually be doing this, thought Cassia; I can't really be lying here on the floor, the floor of an office, without any clothes on, it just isn't possible – and then she lost sight entirely of what might or might not be possible as Harry launched an assault on her senses that wiped out any kind of thought, any kind of reason, any notion of where she was, where she should have been, indeed.

It was his office they were in, and it was after midnight; she had allowed herself to be persuaded by him to go out to dinner despite her reservations, her fear that they would be seen – the talk would start, the rumours begin to spread – and she had allowed it because she wanted it so much.

'But not here, Harry, because I've offered Eleanor Studely a bed for the night, she's having dinner with someone late after the show, and somewhere very quiet, very discreet, not the West End, for heaven's sake.'

'I'm not very good at discretion,' he had said, 'but I'll do my best.'

He had phoned her back in half an hour. 'You are to come here, to the office,' he said, 'at eight o'clock. I have a very nice restaurant in mind. It's all right, it's totally discreet, you're not to worry about it.'

When she arrived, nervous, he opened the door to her himself; there was no porter on duty.

'I have given him the night off,' Harry said, taking her hand. 'Poor fellow, he was looking very tired. It is almost Christmas, after all. Come along upstairs.'

'Harry!' she said, beginning to suspect. 'Harry, whatever have you—'

'Be quiet,' he said, 'wait and see.'

She followed him up to the first floor, along the corridor, into his office; and then laughed aloud, for there, laid out on the floor, complete with cloth and wicker hamper and some bottles of wine, was a picnic.

'I did it all myself,' he said proudly. 'I phoned Fortnum's, and ordered all this. And here – ' he went to a cupboard, opened it, brought out an ice bucket and some champagne – 'can't have a picnic without champagne, and then to follow we have some very delicious-looking pastries. Really, Cassia, do stop shaking your head, you should be congratulating me on my originality and domestic skills. Not to mention my sense of occasion. Now take your coat off, and your shoes, and sit down on the rug. That's right. In a little while, you are to take your dress off as well, and then your stockings and so on. I have it all planned, you see. I see a sort of intramural *Déjeuner sur l'herbe*. Champagne?'

She sat down laughing on the rug, took the glass he handed her.

'You look very beautiful,' he said, his face suddenly serious. 'I do like it that you are so beautiful.'

'Harry, I'm not beautiful. I'm quite ordinary really.'

'Oh no,' he said, sitting down beside her, leaning across to kiss her, 'there is nothing ordinary about you, Cassia. Nothing at all. Least of all what you look like. I remember, even that first time, when we were children, thinking how annoying it was that you were taller than me. I so wanted to look down on you.'

'Well, you do now,' she said, 'you look down on everyone.'

'True. In more ways than one. Do you find me very arrogant, Cassia?'

'Very.'

'Well, clearly you like arrogant men. The doctor is arrogant, in his own way. Are you ready to disclose this breathtaking secret of yours yet?'

'No,' she said quickly, 'no, I'm not.'

'I want it all settled,' he said, leaning forward to kiss her again. 'I want it settled very quickly.'

'Harry, I've told you, that isn't possible. We have to wait.'

'Well,' he said, beginning to unbutton her dress, 'I suppose I have waited seven years for you. I can wait a little longer.'

He bent his head, began to kiss her throat, his mouth thoughtful, careful, very determined; the stabbing, the glorious, stabbing probes of pleasure began to stir in Cassia. Her thoughts, her senses flew ahead, to the delight; she clung on to sanity, the present, with a huge effort. 'Harry, not here, not now, someone might—'

'Don't be prudish, Cassia. Your provincial background is showing. No one might anything. And of course here, of course now. We will make this little room an everywhere. John Donne, as I hope you know. "The Good Morrow." And so very appropriate. Listen: "I wonder by my troth what thou and I did till we loved." What did we do, Cassia? How did we spend the days, pass the time?'

The dress was half off now. His hands were caressing her shoulders, moving towards her breasts, his thumbs seeking out the cleft between them.

'I don't know,' she said, smiling down at the thumbs, at the pleasure they were able to give her. 'I really don't.'

'I waited,' he said, his face very serious suddenly, 'that's what I did. Of course I always loved you. Always. But it was a little hard to do anything about it. Much of the time. We have a lot of making up to do.'

'Yes,' she said, 'yes, I know.'

It was two o'clock when they left the building; she was exhausted, sated with pleasure. She had looked down at her body, as she finally dressed again, looked at its neat lines, its slender self-containedness, and marvelled that it could break into such tumultuous disorder, so many splintered fragments of piercing near-pain, could take leave of itself and its normal duties to behave with such absolute unpredictability, that all its parts could merge, fuse, become one, an absolute concentration of delight: and then reassemble, become itself again, something that could stand and walk and have clothes hung upon it, something over which she had control.

She looked up at him as he closed the door on to the street and smiled; he looked back at her, in a moment of absolute intent, and then bent and kissed her, gently, lightly, put his arm round her shoulder, and she turned her head, kissed his hand as it lay there: and thus they walked along the street to where she had parked her car.

Justin Everard, coming back from a long and exhausting session in his darkroom, where he had been trying to perfect a process of very high-contrast printing, saw them and realised he was not actually very surprised.

'Edward, may I talk to you? After surgery this evening, perhaps?'

He looked up at Cassia, clearly surprised. 'Yes, all right,' he said, 'but I may be quite late, and I may have to go out if there are any calls – Maureen has gone for an interview.'

He looked tired, she thought, and very strained; it was hardly surprising, of course, but he had seemed rather more cheerful lately. Guilt rose in her, reaching almost panic proportions: God, what harm she had done him, what havoc she had wrought in all their lives.

'You ought to have a break,' she said, concentrating on the present, on what she could do about that, 'before you start your new life. A short holiday. It will be very hard to cope with if you're worn out before you start.'

'Yes,' he said with a sigh, 'yes, that's what Janet said.'

'Janet!' She would not have been more surprised if he had said he had discussed his situation with Sylvia Fox-Ashley.

'Yes,' he said shortly, avoiding her eyes. 'She obviously knew about it, and with people coming to see me about the practice – well, she was very understanding about it. And interested.'

'Edward, I thought you couldn't stand Janet.'

'You misunderstood me,' he said, 'as always. I didn't like the idea of having a nanny for the children. I thought you should have looked after them yourself. I always found Janet perfectly pleasant and, indeed, extremely good with them. And I have to say that in your frequent absences she does run things here extremely well.'

'Oh,' said Cassia. She felt rather put out suddenly. 'Well, I'm delighted, Edward. Anyway, do think about taking a break. If you can.'

'Yes, well,' he said, 'it all depends on when I can get someone. I haven't seen anyone I liked sufficiently yet.'

She went and asked Peggy to make shepherd's pie for supper: Edward's favourite. She wanted him to be in the best possible mood for their discussion.

Later that afternoon Harry phoned her. 'I found your gold neck-chain on the floor of my office. I can't imagine how it came to be there.'

'No,' she said, and the room was suddenly brilliant with memory, the memory of pleasure, 'no, I can't either.'

'I expect you'd like it back. I have to go to Paris for a few days. I'll leave it with Miss Murray, you can pick it up if you're passing.'

'Thank you. Thank you very much. Have a good trip. I mean, *bon voyage*.'

Saying that reminded her of Dr Bertillon. He would be back the next day, she would phone him. Or perhaps she wouldn't. There really didn't seem very much point.

Fleet Street was in turmoil that afternoon; it had received a statement issued by Mrs Simpson from Cannes, in which she stated that she would be willing, 'if such action would solve the problem, to withdraw from a situation that has been rendered both unhappy and untenable'. The ambiguity of this statement, implying as it did that this was a decision removed from the personal sphere and into the constitutional, fuelled rumours of the 'King's camp' led by Winston Churchill, and the

Beaverbrook–Rothermere press, of a government hostile to the King for reasons more sinister than that of his *amour*, of something approaching a coup from within the royal circle.

Mrs Simpson, banking on the King's popularity, had suggested the King take the country into his confidence, with a broadcast that was the equivalent of one of President Roosevelt's 'fireside chats', and that the people should then decide what might be done; that Baldwin had crushed this merely fuelled the talk of coups and camps.

The whole story was fast acquiring qualities that were quite literally epic: reporters were dispatched to wait at the gate of Fort Belvedere, contacts dredged, stories taken to the edge of what might be found acceptable to a shocked country. Crowds began to gather outside Buckingham Palace, Downing Street and St James's Palace: but at Fort Belvedere, the King had summoned his brother, the Duke of York, to tell him of his decision.

After supper, at which Edward expressed pleasure both to Peggy and to Janet, who had contributed an excellent apple pie, they went into the sitting room. Cassia felt absurdly nervous. 'Coffee, Edward?'

'No, thank you,' he said, 'you know I don't drink coffee after supper these days. I have trouble enough sleeping as it is.'

'Do you, Edward?' she said. 'I'm sorry.' More guilt: that she had not realised he had given up coffee, that she was not able – because of their estrangement – to realise that he couldn't sleep.

'Well,' he said, 'there's a great deal to worry about. It isn't going to be easy, what I'm going to do.' The words 'without you' hung in the air. She tried to ignore them.

'No,' she said, 'but I know you're going to love it, Edward. And do terribly well.' It sounded patronising; she hated herself.

'And obviously I've been worrying about the children,' he said, 'as I expect you have. And then there's the practice.'

Cassia took a deep breath. 'Edward, that's what I wanted to talk to you about.'

'These are lovely, Justin,' said Cecily, smiling at him. 'Thank you. The one of Fanny is specially nice.'

'She's very photogenic. Like you.'

'I'm not photogenic, Justin, don't be silly.'

'Darling Cecily, you are immensely photogenic. The camera likes you, as they say. Look at you here, at the fashion show. Lovely.'

She looked; she had to admit she did look much nicer than she would have expected. She was talking to Edward, laughing; she looked carefree, young again, her eyes alive. Edward, by contrast, looked strained, awkward.

'Poor Edward. He does hate social gatherings.'

'I'm not surprised,' said Justin, 'he's very dull.'

'Justin, that's horrid. He's not dull, he's just quiet. Quiet and shy.'

'Well, we're all shy,' said Justin. 'I'm shy.'

'You!' said Cecily. 'Justin, that is the most ridiculous thing I ever heard.'

'Why?' he said, He looked quite hurt.

'Well, you're – you're the opposite of shy. You're so self-confident, you love being the centre of attention ...'

'Well, that's where you're wrong,' he said. 'I do get dreadfully nervous, quite often. Especially when I have to do an important shoot. But I've learnt to hide it. That's why I'm so noisy, it's camouflage. Don't look like that, it's true. If I let people see, I'd be done for. That's why I love you, my darling,' he added seriously, 'you make me feel safe, I can forget about myself. I don't have to put on my act with you.'

'Oh,' she said. She felt rather confused by all this, deeply touched and not quite sure if she believed it at the same time.

'No, shy is one thing,' said Justin firmly, 'not making an effort quite another. Edward Fallon doesn't make any effort at all. He had that pretty girl with him, the nanny, and he had those two dear little boys with him who obviously adored him. It wasn't as if he was there all alone. I'm sorry, Cecily, I really don't think very much of him. Maybe I'm just jealous. I can see you're very fond of him.'

'Don't be silly. I mean I am fond of him, but – well, not in that way.'

'What way? In the way you're fond of me, you mean? And how would you define that exactly? Oh, this is lovely fun.'

'Oh, Justin, don't tease me.'

'I'm not teasing you, I really want to know. I'm very very fond of you. As you must very well know. Is it absolutely one sided? Because if it is, I might go out and throw myself in the river. Oh, sorry, my darling, not tactful.'

'It's all right,' said Cecily, laughing. Nothing could have made her realise more clearly how much she had recovered from Benedict's death than that moment. She leant forward and gave Justin a kiss on the cheek. 'I'm very fond of you, of course I am, but you are wrong about Edward. I think it is especially hard for him. Cassia is so lovely and so self-confident these days, and—'

'And a little bit naughty, from what I've observed,' said Justin, 'and who could blame her?'

'What? Justin, what are you talking about, what sort of naughty?'

He looked at her and smiled, a wicked, conspiratorial grin. He looked rather like one of the children, she thought.

'Justin! Tell me.'

'Well, let's just say that if you'd been coming down South Audley Street the other night, or rather at about two o'clock in the morning, you'd have seen her and Harry Moreton. Coming out of a building. Kissing, cuddling, obviously having just had a *very* nice time.'

'Cassia! And Harry!' Cecily was so astonished she literally found it hard to breathe. 'Good heavens! Are you quite quite sure?'

'Quite quite *quite* sure. It was hardly crowded in the street. And then she got into that lovely car of hers, which is all beautifully mended now, and drove away. After another rather long kiss.'

'Good heavens,' said Cecily again. She had been standing up; her legs felt feeble suddenly, and she sat down on the sofa rather heavily.

'Are you all right?' Justin's face was concerned. 'I'm sorry, I shouldn't have told you, it was obviously a shock. I always forget how utterly virtuous you are ...'

Cecily ignored this. Her mind was whirling. Did Edwina know? She was sure she didn't. And Edward, poor, poor Edward, surely he couldn't. Of course Edwina had always behaved rather wildly – this new job of hers, and everything – but she had never heard any rumours whatsoever about her. Or Harry, come to that. And Cassia – she was the most unlikely candidate for his affections, she would have thought. So independent, so different from all the women in his social circle. Anyway, she'd always implied that she hated Harry, there had certainly always been a lot of animosity between them in the old days.

'I'm sorry, Justin,' she said, 'this really has been rather a shock.'

'Darling, you'd better go and lie down,' he said, his face concerned. 'I'm beastly and thoughtless. I just assumed you wouldn't mind very much, I thought it would amuse you. Here, come along, I'll take you to your room. Where is it?'

Cecily gave him her hand, allowed him to take her upstairs, to settle her on her bed. He bent over, kissed her forehead tenderly. 'Shall I ask your maid to come up?'

'Yes, please.' She felt very foolish, very unsophisticated, reacting in this way; she supposed perhaps she was not as emotionally stable as she had thought. It was just that – well, it being Cassia! Cassia, whom they had all admired so much, looked up to for her independent views, admired for her cleverness – and considered so extremely virtuous. She felt angry suddenly, angry and stupid at the thought of all she had done for Cassia, going to Paris, promising to keep her secrets – and all the time she had had this huge dangerous one and had not told her. It wasn't fair. And now, she thought, what should she do: should she tell Edward and Edwina or not? Surely not, that would be terrible.

Who could she talk to about it? she wondered. Maybe it was a mistake, maybe they had just been fooling about. Justin didn't know either of them very well. Who would know, whom could she ask? And then she thought: Rupert. Rupert would know, he knew everything about Cassia, he was her best friend, she told him everything. And if she hadn't – well, it was probably just not true.

She waved rather feebly at Justin, who was standing at the door blowing her kisses, and reached for the telephone.

Maureen Johnson stood waiting slightly impatiently for Dr Fallon to finish his surgery; she needed to get away, she had a second interview for a junior partnership in a practice in Euston that afternoon, and was running late already. In the early days she had admired his patience, the long time he spent with everyone; now it had begun to irritate her. He had begun to irritate her altogether with his tendency to self-justification, to over-explanation; it was as well events were moving them apart.

'Ah, Maureen!' He came out and smiled at her. 'Time for a coffee? I can ask Peggy—'

'No, really, Dr Fallon, as I explained to you, I have to get a train to London in half an hour, the taxi will be coming very shortly—'

'Of course. Do forgive me. Well, I'll be brief. I just wanted to discuss something with you.'

'Yes, Dr Fallon?'

'My wife has suggested – proposed to me rather, that she should take over this practice. When I take up my new post at St Mark's, Clapham. I wondered what your reaction to that would be.'

'Well ...' Maureen hesitated. She was very surprised on two counts: one, that he should be even considering such a thing, and two, that he should be asking her opinion on it. She disliked Cassia intensely; she had found her arrogant, condescending, self-interested from the first day she had met her, and nothing that had happened since had changed her mind. She had watched Dr Fallon become increasingly depressed and lonely and had felt extremely sorry for him; she was delighted at the news that he was to move to London and achieve something more satisfying for himself.

'You're not sure?' he said, watching her carefully. 'That's interesting, neither am I. Could you perhaps give me your reasons?'

'Well ...'

'Let me give you mine. It's all about confidence, is it not, medicine? I feel the patients here trust me – and you, they know us as doctors, as respected, successful doctors. If they bring us a problem, they think we can solve it. They only know Mrs Fallon as my wife. The fact that she is herself a qualified doctor—'

'Yes, but that's all,' said Maureen quietly.

'I'm sorry?'

'She is qualified. She has passed her finals. Very well, I know. But she has no experience, apart from her London clinics. Of course they must have been very challenging, but—'

'Very limited in their range. Indeed. So you're saying she would need a period as an assistant, a junior partner at the very least, are you?'

'Well, yes, ideally. I would have thought it would be very difficult for her simply to begin to practise here, without any practical experience. But that would obviously be very hard to arrange – impossible, really – while she was here.'

'Yes, it would. Although she would be working alongside me for a couple of months. And then she is very familiar with the village, with the patients, with their histories. She has known most of the children here all their lives. And of course they know her, very well.'

'They do,' said Maureen, 'but, as you said, not as a doctor. And surely that is how they would need to see her. If they were to have any confidence in her at all. I don't see how they could have that confidence. Oh, dear, I do feel rather disloyal, talking like this.'

He looked at her and smiled rather wearily. 'I'm sorry. I shouldn't have asked you, it's very difficult for you. But I think simply talking to you has helped me to make up my own mind. You're a very good sounding-board, Maureen. I've found it in many different situations, you have a gift for listening. Very valuable, in life as in medicine. Thank you. You must go and get your train. In fact, is that your taxi now?'

'I think so,' said Maureen, 'yes.'

'Good luck this afternoon, then.'

'Thank you.'

If she hadn't been in such a hurry, she would have seen Bertie, home from school with a cold, who had been in the hall for some time, ostensibly doing up his shoelaces, but actually listening very attentively to the conversation through the just open study door.

'Ah, Mrs Fallon, good afternoon.' Margot Murray smiled at her graciously. 'Mr Moreton did say you were coming in.'

'Yes, I somehow managed to lose my necklace here, so stupid of me ...' Her voice tailed away.

She felt confused, embarrassed, sure somehow that Miss Murray must be able to know perfectly well what had been going on between her and Harry, stared at the carpet where they had lain, thinking that such intense carnal pleasure must somehow linger in a room, the sense of it, that an area normally given over to shorthand dictation and typing letters and the taking of telephone messages could not possibly contain sights and sounds such as had taken place there there other night without conveying something of it to whoever was in it afterwards.

'Indeed, yes, it is here, in my desk, in an envelope. Here we are, I think you will find it in order, do check it, won't you?'

She spoke as if Cassia might suspect her of stealing some of the links, or substituting it with another of inferior quality, as poor Leonora had done.

'I'm sure that's not necessary,' she said hastily. 'Thank you so much, Miss Murray.'

'Please think nothing of it. Now I have something else for you, a note from Mr Moreton, if you could just bear with me while I get it from the file – oh, excuse me. Mrs Fallon, I'm so sorry.'

The phone had rung; Cassia smiled at her, picked up a copy of *The Times* which was lying on the low table, to show she was not troubled by the delay, started to read the personal column, as if she found it deeply fascinating, while still thinking about Leonora and the fate of her jewellery.

She became aware that Miss Murray was speaking French, was actually speaking perfect French, absolutely perfect, better even than Cecily's, she would have thought ... perfect, perfect French ... Cecily, Leonora, their trip to Paris ... the old woman in the Auteuil describing the woman who had come for Leonora, taken her away ... realising that Miss Murray was slim, tall, blonde, had good legs, did have a rather large bosom, actually ... remembering the old woman gesturing with her hands, to describe such a thing ...

'Mrs Fallon, are you all right? You look a little pale.'

Cassia smiled carefully. 'Oh, yes, yes, thank you. Just a bit – well, faint.'

'Do sit down,' said Miss Murray graciously. 'I will fetch you a glass of water. It is rather hot in here.'

She came back with the water, made Cassia drink it slowly, watching her rather severely. She would have made a wonderful matron, Cassia thought.

'Thank you, Miss Murray. I must go now. I'm working at St Christopher's Hospital at two, I run a clinic there, you know.' God, why was she telling Miss Murray all this? She must think she was completely demented.

'Of course. Well, if you are sure you are well enough. I admire your attitude: punctuality, timing, is so important, I feel.'

Another memory, another French voice, time is *compliqué*, our memory plays tricks with it ... time, timing, this whole thing was about time, what happened when ...

Margot Murray was speaking again, handing her something. 'Here is the letter from Mr Moreton, Mrs Fallon.'

'Thank you.'

Standing in the lift, she tore open the letter; it was a large sheet of paper, and simply said, 'I love you,' in Harry's sprawling writing. She found it surprisingly difficult to read, for some reason, and then realised as she got outside that she was crying.

Rupert was eating his lunch, prior to going to the theatre for the matinée, when Cecily phoned. She sounded very upset.

'Rupert, can I talk to you?'

'My darling, of course you can. Now? On the telephone? Tell you what, I have to be at the theatre in half an hour; do you want to come and talk to me there, in my dressing room, while I get ready? It's a very automatic process, you mustn't think I won't be concentrating on you.'

'If that would really be all right. Yes, thank you. I'll get a taxi and meet you there.'

Now, what could that be about? thought Rupert. He couldn't imagine, couldn't think of a single area in Cecily's life in which she would not have far better advisers than he. Perhaps Fanny wanted to go on the stage: sweet little thing, she was. Definitely not an idea to be encouraged. He finished his omelette – a light meal was essential to a good performance – and went out to find a taxi.

Fortunately, he was looking into the mirror applying his base make-up when Cecily finally managed, rather haltingly, to ask him about Cassia and Harry. Even so, he knew, his eyes flicked to meet hers, knew she had seen that; then he smiled at her quickly and easily.

'Darling, what a wonderful rumour. If rumour it is. I wish I could help, tell you it's nonsense, but I can't. I would have to do some detective work of my own.'

'I'd have thought,' said Cecily just a little coldly – she knows I know, he thought, she can tell – 'I'd have thought you could just have asked her. I thought you and she told each other everything. And you suffered enough from rumours yourself, didn't you, a few weeks ago? I'd have thought you'd be rather sympathetic about getting such things scotched. If it's not true. It is true, isn't it?' she said suddenly. 'I can see it is, and I can see you knew. I'm surprised at you, Rupert, I really am.'

'Cecily, what was I supposed to do about it?' he said, realising there was no point in pretending. 'Tell Edwina, tell Edward? Of course not. That is for them to do, not me, it's their affair – literally. I can only be here if Cassia needs me.'

'Needs you to lie for her, you mean.'

'No, I don't mean that. Cassia would never ask that, anyway. She's very direct.'

'Oh, very,' she said.

Rupert looked at her; she was flushed, clearly upset. 'Cecily,' he said gently, 'don't be too hard on her. She – well, she's been very unhappy. For a very long time.'

'Oh, really?' said Cecily. 'Well, so was I. For a very, very long time. Most of the time I was married, actually. I didn't start having affairs with other people's husbands, though, to make myself feel better.'

Rupert sighed. 'Of course you didn't,' he said, 'but we all manage differently.'

'Yes, well, making other people unhappy doesn't seem a very good way of managing to me. You would stick up for her, Rupert, you adore her, she can do no wrong in your eyes. I think it's awful, dreadful of her, poor gentle Edward, never hurt a fly ...'

'Cecily, it's very dangerous to pronounce upon other people's marriages. You don't know, none of us knows, what went wrong in Cassia's marriage. People are never what they seem. I'm not trying to make excuses for her.'

'Yes, you are,' said Cecily, 'and I don't want to hear any more. I think it's awful of you to defend her, actually, I don't think she deserves defending. I'm going home. Oh, don't worry, Rupert, I won't tell anyone. But I'm going to find it very hard to be nice to Cassia in future. And Harry, for that matter.' She walked out of the dressing room, slamming the door after her.

Rupert sat staring at it. 'Oh dear,' he said aloud, 'oh very very dear.'

Cassia sat in the small drawing room at Walton Street, trying not to scream while the operator asked her to hold the line while she connected her to her Paris number. She wasn't quite sure why she was so upset:

Harry might not have been telling her the whole truth when he had said he hadn't rescued Leonora from her apartment in the Auteuil, but it hardly meant that the whole story was lies, that Leonora had really been in serious financial trouble, that it had been Harry and Harry alone who had bought her out of it and then ...

She shut her mind off from the rest of that scenario and tried to concentrate. A series of bleeps and clicks and a sort of grinding noise was going on at the other end of the phone; the international operator said, 'Putting you through now.'

A voice in French informed her she was speaking to Dr Bertillon's surgery; she asked if she might speak to him.

'Le Dr George Bertillon? Ou le Dr Pierre?'

'Le − le père?' said Cassia hopefully.

'Dr Pierre. Un moment, madame.'

Another wait: more clicks, then, 'Ici Pierre Bertillon. Bonjour.'

'Bonjour,' said Cassia, and then, hopefully, 'Do you speak English?'

'A little, madame.'

'My friend and I came to see your son last week. Two English ladies.'

'Ah! Two beautiful English ladies. My son has told me how very charmantes you were, madame.'

'Well, thank you. So did he tell you what it was about?'

'Only a little. Lady Beatty, n'est-ce pas?'

'Yes. The thing is, I didn't realise how ill she was, what difficulties she was in until she died. If I had, I would have come over, helped her, I feel so terrible about it. Anyway—'

'Madame, forgive me, but you must speak plus lentement. I have only a little English.'

'I'm sorry. Well, there were two things, really. One, I do hope there are no medical bills of any kind outstanding, because if so—'

'No, madame, of course not.'

'I know − she told you to stop coming after a bit. Because she couldn't pay you.'

'Yes, madame, although I did call from time to time in any case. I was concerned for her, fond of her by then.'

'That was very kind of you,' she said. 'Thank you.' Something jarred here: what was it?

'But the gentleman, of course, he pay me. Immédiatement.'

'Oh, I'm glad. And you didn't look after her once she was in Passy, did you?'

'No, madame. The gentleman found another doctor. A more

fashionable one.' He laughed. 'Madame, I do not mind. And in any case, it is better to have a doctor who lives near you, *bien sûr*.'

'Yes. Well, you were certainly very near her before.'

'The last few weeks, indeed, very, very near.' Something else. What was it? Probably just the French translating oddly. 'And of course the new doctor, he was a specialist. In her condition.'

'In the cancer?'

A long pause, then, sounding slightly awkward, 'Yes, madame. Yes, of course.'

'So you don't think she suffered too much?'

'I hope not, madame. I did my best.'

'Well, thank you. Thank you very much. For all you did. It must have been so hard for her, managing on her own, in an awful place like that.'

'Oh, it is not really so bad, madame. Not the rue Molitor. The other place ... well! That was not good.' His voice seemed to be coming from rather far away.

'The other place?'

'Yes, madame. In the rue Cauchon.'

'I'm sorry. She was living in another apartment? Down there, in the Auteuil?'

'Yes, madame. You did not know?'

'No, of course not. I mean, no, I didn't. When was that?'

'For the whole year preceding. That was very, very bad. I was shocked to find her there. It was I who was able to secure the other apartment for her, in the rue Molitor. A patient of mine had died and—'

'Oh dear,' said Cassia. 'Oh dear.' It was all she could find to say, that inadequate little phrase, so deep was her shock.

'Pardon, madame?'

He must think her completely barmy; she struggled to come back to him, to explain. 'I'm sorry. You see, I thought she was only in difficulties for a couple of months. We all did.' (Didn't we, Harry, didn't we?)

'Oh, no, madame. Sadly, that was not the case. She first came to see me – let me see, in late 1933.'

'Oh God. But that means ...' It all made sense now, the strange phrases about growing fond of her, the references to 'the last few weeks'. Only the rest of it didn't make sense at all.

'Dr Bertillon, was it a Mr Gresham who paid you? Paid your bills?'

A pause: a very long pause. Then, 'No, madame. I do not recognise that name at all. It was a Monsieur Moreton who paid them all. I have the receipts here.'

★

Edwina had left three messages for Cecily that morning and was told she was out; when she rang a fourth time, and was told she was back but busy, she became exasperated.

'Please put me on to her, Adams. It's a very quick matter. I just want to ask her if I can take a photograph in the drawing room, for my magazine, and I have to speak to her soon because she might put her Christmas tree up. Or is it up already?'

'No, madam. It is only the sixth of December, after all.' His tone was mildly reproachful.

Edwina sighed. 'I'm aware of that, Adams, thank you, but my photograph is for the March edition of my magazine and it is therefore imperative that the tree doesn't go up until I have done it. I just wanted to make that quite clear. She might have been going to do it this afternoon.'

'I do not imagine so, madam, but I will enquire now. And endeavour to find Mrs Harrington, in order that she may speak to you.'

'Thank you,' said Edwina, 'and please tell her it is urgent. Oh, and that it won't take more than a few minutes. If she's really busy.' Which she wouldn't be, she thought. Cecily didn't know the meaning of the word, it was probably half her problem. It didn't occur to Edwina that until six months earlier she had not known the meaning of the word herself.

Cecily came on to the line. 'Edwina?'

'Yes. What on earth have you been doing, Cecily? I've been trying to get hold of you all morning.'

'Sorry. I've been out.' She sounded odd, Edwina thought, strained.

'Oh, I see. Well, look, I need to use your drawing room for a photograph. Or rather your fireplace. I want to display some things on it. Under that divine mirror. I thought you wouldn't mind.'

'Oh, Edwina, I'd rather not.'

'Why, for heaven's sake? Justin will do the picture, I thought you'd be pleased. Only for God's sake don't put your Christmas tree up yet, this is supposed to be March.'

'Well, I wouldn't be pleased,' said Cecily, 'and I'm sick of having my houses used as photographic backcloths. What's wrong with yours? And if I want to put up my own Christmas tree in my own house, I will.'

It was so totally unlike her to be rude that Edwina was shocked.

'Cecily,' she said, 'Cecily, are you all right?'

'Yes. No. Oh, I don't know.'

God, maybe she was going to have another breakdown, Edwina thought. How awful if it was her fault. Small things could trigger them off, she did know that. 'Look,' she said, 'don't worry about the photograph. It doesn't matter, honestly. I can ask someone else. Um – are you sure you're all right?'

'Oh, Edwina, I'm sorry,' said Cecily. She sounded very contrite suddenly. 'I didn't mean to be rude to you. Of all people. Upset you. I'm just a bit upset.' And she burst into noisy tears.

'Don't worry about being rude to me, upsetting me,' said Edwina, anxious to divert her, to cheer her up, 'I'm quite used to it, I live with the rudest man in London, don't forget. And the most upsetting, I should think. Specially at the moment, do you know what he's—'

She had been about to regale Cecily with Harry's ultimatum, his insistence she should give up her job, purely to distract her from her own troubles, but, 'Oh, Edwina,' said Cecily, 'so you know, do you? I thought perhaps you must. I'm sorry. So sorry.'

'Know? Know what? Cecily, what on earth are you talking about?'

Mr Brewster was enjoying the quiet cup of tea and the two digestive biscuits he always had at four o'clock, when his secretary informed him that Mrs Fallon was on the telephone. 'She sounds rather distressed, Mr Brewster.'

Mr Brewster set aside the biscuits, which he knew would give him indigestion if he ate them too fast, and took the call at once. Mrs Fallon did indeed sound very distressed and it took him some few minutes to ascertain exactly what she wanted, and even having ascertained it, was not able to respond immediately, but had to ask her if he might ring her back. This being apparently impossible, since she was working, she said she would ring him back within the hour.

'Will that give you long enough, Mr Brewster?' Mr Brewster said he hoped so, and set himself to the task.

When Mrs Fallon phoned back, sounding more agitated still, an hour and a half later, he was able to give her the information that the document by which Rollo Gresham had set up the Maple Trust and thus empowered Leonora to make her deed of settlement upon Cassia, had been dated 3 May, 1935. 'And the will, drawn up by me, in which she exercised her appointment, was signed a fortnight later.'

He told Mrs Fallon that he had not appreciated that there was any significance in the date of the first document, that it certainly held no legal importance of any kind, and tried to reassure her that there was no need for her to be anxious about it, but he could tell that he had failed.

As he finally put the phone down at almost six o'clock, he realised he had still not eaten his digestive biscuits.

★

Janet Fraser was trying to persuade William to eat the scrambled egg she had cooked for his tea when the telephone rang in the kitchen. She took the call herself; Peggy was not well, Maureen was out delivering a baby and Dr Fallon had gone to see old Joe Carter who had slipped on some ice and broken an ankle, which was not serious, but he had now according to his daughter come over very queer. She assumed the next call must be from yet another victim of the influenza epidemic that was cutting a very unpleasant swathe through the village, and thought what a shame it was that Dr Fallon would not be able to settle to his supper in peace since he was so very tired; it was therefore a pleasant surprise to find it was Mrs Fallon. She sounded rather agitated.

'Janet, I'm so sorry to bother you, and I know you'll think I'm quite mad, but up in my room, in the bottom drawer of the chest of drawers, is an old copy of *Country Life*. Could you go and fetch it and tell me the date of it, please? Thank you.'

Janet checked that Delia was still safely imprisoned in her playpen and that William was making at least some inroads into his egg, and ran up to the room which Dr and Mrs Fallon ostensibly still shared, although to her certain knowledge they had not slept together in it for several weeks. She found the magazine at once, and took it downstairs again.

'I have it here, Mrs Fallon, yes. Now the date is, let me see, yes, April thirtieth, 1935. Is that all you want to know? Good. No, everything is fine here, everyone perfectly happy. William has been practising his solo verse for the carol concert next week and it is simply beautiful, and Bertie's cold is much better. No, that's perfectly all right, don't worry at all about anything, and we shall see you tomorrow, shall we? Oh, good. Very well, Mrs Fallon, goodnight.'

As she put the phone down she heard the door open and Dr Fallon came in; he was very pale. He saw her looking at him and tried to smile.

'Hallo, Janet.'

'Hallo, Dr Fallon. Is everything all right?'

'What? Oh, yes. Well, no. Not really. Poor old Joe died; went into heart failure, died in my arms.'

He looked desperately upset, Janet thought; she felt a pang of concern for him. 'I'm so sorry,' she said, 'so very sorry. Do come in and sit down, I'll bring you a cup of tea.'

'That would be very nice,' he said, 'thank you. Silly to get upset, but I've seen him through so much – pneumonia, pleurisy, the arthritis – and then it's a broken ankle that gets him. I can never help being distressed by a death of a patient. I'm sorry.'

'Dr Fallon, please don't apologise. I can quite appreciate how very sad it must be. But at least you were there, you didn't arrive too late. I'm sure you eased his passing and, of course, his family must have found it comforting and helpful. I'll go and get that tea now.'

When she got back with the tea he was sitting at his desk, his head in his hands; he didn't hear her come in. She felt so sorry for him that, without stopping to consider whether or not it was acceptable for her to do such a thing, she put her arms round his shoulders. 'Don't be too distressed, Dr Fallon,' she said, 'it was surely time for him to go. As we say in my village.'

He looked up at her, half startled, half grateful, and she saw there were tears in his eyes. He managed a smile and patted one of her hands awkwardly.

'What a comforting thought, yes. Yes, indeed it was. And we doctors really should be able to take such things in our stride. It was just, as I said, having seen him through so much and ... oh dear, you must think me rather a fool.'

'Of course I don't, Dr Fallon,' she said, 'I don't think anything of the sort. I think it's extremely nice that you should care so much about people. Extremely nice. Now drink your tea, and just let me know when you want supper. I've made a casserole, in Peggy's absence, so it's very flexible.'

'How nice,' he said, taking the tea, smiling again, and then, 'Whatever did we do without you, Janet? I really can't imagine. I mean that very sincerely.'

She knew exactly what he meant; and she was touched. From such a proud man, it was a very big concession.

Cecily was alternately pacing her sitting room and trying to settle to her book – *Northanger Abbey*, by Jane Austen, an author she had shunned while in the charge of her governess and had now rediscovered with considerable delight – while Nanny bathed Laurence and the girls ate their supper. She was feeling very odd; her initial distress at discovering the affair between Cassia and Harry easing just slightly and making way for a rather more uncomfortable emotion, which, try as she might to deny it, she recognised as envy. Of course she was still shocked, especially at Cassia's behaviour; Harry, she thought, could be assumed to have found his way into many beds other than his own, with other women than Edwina. It had to be expected, and besides, no one could regard Edwina as a model and submissive wife, her behaviour was often outrageous, her attitudes always unconventional, and her attitude towards Harry hardly tender and loving.

But Cassia: so kind, so fiercely honest, so brave, so clever, and married to an unarguably hapless man, whose every attitude and utterance told of a moral conformity, a most dutiful attachment to his family – that she should be indulging in an illicit sexual relationship with a man like Harry Moreton Cecily found very shocking.

She also – and this was where the discomfort came in – found it strangely exciting; it had ruffled her own sleek moral feathers, made her aware of her own long-dormant desires. She felt herself suddenly dull, sensually dreary, sexually deprived; she looked back on her sex life with Benedict, so unsatisfactory for the most part, remembered all the nights she had lain throbbing with frustration either after some brief encounter with him, or more usually after none at all, and a surge of self-pity and discomfort rose in her. She had hardly known sexual pleasure; she knew of it, she had read of it, but had never experienced herself more than a flicker, an echo of it. And she wanted to, she wanted it very much; she had felt the longings, the physical yearnings in her body, never more than now, recovering from her unhappiness and remorse over Benedict, discovering pleasure, sexual awareness with Justin – she wanted it desperately.

She found Justin extremely attractive; she was surprised and even slightly shocked to discover how much she thought about him, not merely his company, his charm, his extraordinary gentleness and consideration towards her, but his tall, slender body, his beautiful hands, his rather oddly good-looking face, his brilliant eyes, his expressive mouth. Sometimes, as he had kissed her briefly, tenderly, on the lips – the full extent so far of their sexual encounters – she had longed for him to go further, to feel his mouth working on hers, his tongue exploring her, had even thought of taking the initiative – but shyness, delicacy, and a fairly strong conviction that she was very little more to him than a loving and loved friend, held her back.

Tonight, with sexual infidelity filling her head, sexual excitement strong in the air, she longed for Justin, longed for him not only to kiss her, but to go further, longed for his hands on her, his mouth moving over her, not only on her lips; longed for ...

At this, this realisation, she threw down her book, and ran up the stairs to the nursery floor and endeavoured to occupy her thoughts and, indeed, her entire self with her children and the care of them. They were her future, her interest, her excitement now; she was a matron, a widow, and a failed wife, and she had not only no business but no right to to be looking for anything more from life than their happiness.

'You look awfully pretty, Mummy,' said Stephanie, coming into the nursery bathroom, smiling at her, 'prettier every day. Justin said that, didn't he, yesterday? I wish I had a boyfriend like Justin.'

'He's not my boyfriend,' said Cecily, and, to her horror, burst into tears.

Rupert Cameron was eating his second light meal of the day, prior to leaving his flat for the evening performance, when Cassia telephoned him. She sounded almost hysterical.

'Rupert, I've got to see you, I've got to talk to you.'

'Oh, darling,' he said, 'has Cecily been on to you?'

'Cecily? Why ever should Cecily be on to me?'

'Oh, no matter,' he said quickly. 'What is it? What's the matter? Is it this business of taking over the practice? What did Edward say? I hope he didn't turn you down.'

'No, no, not at all, he seemed to quite like the idea.' She had forgotten about that, it seemed of absolutely no importance whatsoever. 'It's ... oh, Rupert, I can't tell you on the phone. Can I come over now? I've just finished my clinic.'

'Come to the theatre. I'm going over there straight away.' If he didn't forget his lines tonight, he thought, it would be something of a miracle.

She was looking terrible: pale, tense, literally hollow eyed. She also looked as if she had been crying.

'Darling, sit down there, have a drink, I've got some perfectly foul sherry.'

'I don't want a drink, Rupert. I want you just to listen to me.'

'I'm listening' he said.

'You know what I told you before? That I thought Harry had something to do with my money?'

'Ye-es.'

'I know he did now. I know it. Leonora was poor for a year and a half before she died, not just a few months. Don't tell me that was extravagance. The awful place she was living in, I went to see it when I went to Paris. Well, apparently, that was nothing compared to the one where she was before. And it wasn't a friend who rescued her finally, it was Margot Murray. Harry's secretary, you know?'

'I don't, but—'

'And then, Harry had paid all her medical bills. Not Rollo at all.'

'Darling, none of this is exactly proof of anything. Simply that they couldn't find Rollo straight away. Don't you think?'

'No, no, I don't. Rupert, think, think, please.'

Tears of what seemed like fright were rolling down her face; he held out a handkerchief to her. 'Try to keep calm, darling. This is quite hard to follow, you know.'

'Sorry.' She blew her nose, took a deep breath. 'The thing is, if she was short of money all that time, if Harry rescued her, then it must mean Rollo had no money. It must. There was no trust fund then, no interest.'

'Cassia—'

'No, I know there wasn't. I found that out today as well: the trust fund was set up just two months before she died, two weeks before she willed it all to me, or settled it on me or whatever. It's so complicated, I don't understand it myself.'

'But if he had no money, then how could he do that anyway? I still think you're making no sense.'

'It doesn't make sense, I know that. But that same month, Rollo's house and estate here went on the market. He did still have that. And also he sold his house in Cannes that summer. I know that too. It's desperate stuff, not the action of a man who had so much money he could settle half a million pounds on his mistress, a month or so before she died. I don't think the money was his at all, Rupert, I still think it was Harry's.'

'Cassia, that is ridiculous. I told you so before. It's crazy, absolutely crazy, the stuff of melodrama, darling, honestly, you've been reading too many novels.'

'I don't read novels. And Richard, even he knew she couldn't have had all that money: he looked utterly shocked when I told him, he would have known—'

'Cassia, you must calm down, try to think logically. You're in a state of panic.'

There was a knock on the door. 'Twenty minutes, Mr Cameron.'

'Oh God. I must start getting ready. Don't go away, Cassia, it's perfectly all right.'

She looked at him. 'Do you still really think so? That the money couldn't be from Harry?'

'Yes, I do. I think it's absolutely out of the question.'

'Well, how do you explain it all, then? Where did this money come from suddenly? Why should Rollo Gresham suddenly hand it over, start selling all his assets?'

'I don't know. I can't imagine. But there must be a reasonable explanation for it. There always is. Maybe he just wanted to get out of England, settle in — where is it, Marrakesh?'

'Yes, but why, if he was so hard up, and everyone knew that, I told you about him owing money in Le Touquet, I bet that wasn't an isolated case, why give Leonora money then? When she was dying? It's all mad.'

'Maybe he didn't know how ill she was. Maybe they thought she'd live much longer. I always had the impression it was something of a shock to everyone, not just you. Can't you ask Harry?'

'No. Well, I already have, about some of it at least, and he's lied to me, that's one of the things that makes me so suspicious still, and he'd just go on lying, of course he would.'

'Perhaps you should go and see Gresham,' said Rupert cheerfully, 'he'll put you straight. Don't look like that, my darling, it was only a joke. Anyway, what made you suddenly think of the dates on all these deeds and trust funds? Why didn't that come to light before?'

'It just didn't, it didn't occur to me that it mattered, I suppose it wouldn't have. Even Mr Brewster, the solicitor, you know, he hadn't thought to go into it. I mean, he'd seen the document, but hadn't taken any particular notice of the date, and we'd all assumed that Leonora had had the money ever since Rollo left her. It was something a French woman said, someone who lived in an apartment in the same house as Leonora: she said time was complicated, that our memories played tricks with it. I was thinking this whole thing is about time, not *what* happened so much as *when* it did: when Leonora moved away from the avenue Foch, when she was rescued, when Gresham sold his houses, it all weaves together – and there are some great big holes in the cloth. Oh, Rupert, I hate this so much. If I'm right, if Harry has done this—' Tears stood in her eyes; she looked frightened, like a small child.

Another knock on the door: 'Ten minutes, Mr Cameron,'

'Darling, I'm sorry, but I'll have to start concentrating. Can you wait here? It's only an hour and a half, we can have dinner later. There's something else I want to talk to you about as well.'

'Yes, all right,' said Cassia, 'good idea. I'll go home for a bit, and then come back. Thank you, Rupert.'

But he could see, as she went out of the door, that she was distracted, not really concentrating on what he was saying at all. Perhaps not a night to warn her that Cecily had found out about her and Harry after all. It could wait; Cecily had promised not to say anything. Anyway, for the next hour and a half they would all have to fade into the background; what he had to do on the stage must be reality now.

Half a mile away, in Mount Street, Edwina, having tried and failed to get hold of Harry in Paris, and filled with a sense of outrage and anger that

609

surprised her, decided that she would speak to Cassia instead. There was no reply to the house in Walton Street; she decided to try Monks Ridge.

Edward answered the phone; he sounded tired.

'Oh, Edward. This is Edwina Moreton here. I'd like to speak to Cassia.'

'Good evening, Edwina. I'm afraid she's not here. She's in London.'

'No, she isn't. I've tried. So I thought she must be down there.'

'I'm sorry, Edwina. She isn't. She's away. As is so often the case.'

Edwina suddenly wondered if he knew. And saw life through his eyes, just for a moment, and with a flash of very rare imagination, saw how unsatisfactory for him it must be, married to Cassia, Cassia with all that money, Cassia living in London, free as a bird, the cover being her work. Her work! Well, he must be very naive, Edwina thought, and then realised she too must be naive to swallow it all, all that nonsense. Who needed a house in London, a conveniently small house, too small for her family, ideal for just one person, one independent person? Just so that she could work for a few hours each week at a hospital or a clinic or whatever it was Cassia was supposed to do. Maybe she wasn't doing anything, maybe the whole thing was a front, an elaborate cover-up for the affair with Harry. What a marvellous idea, and how they must have enjoyed it, the two of them, having duped their spouses.

It was suddenly borne very strongly in upon Edwina that she and Edward, whom she had always so despised, found so dull and so unworldly, had been deceived in exactly the same way by exactly the same people: and she felt not only angry but extremely foolish. And she didn't like feeling foolish. It suddenly became rather important to her to get hold of Cassia, to deliver a few extremely well-chosen words.

'So do you know where Cassia is?' she said. 'I mean, is she coming back tonight?'

'No,' said Edward, and he sounded exasperated now as well as tired, 'she won't. She's just phoned to say she won't be back until the weekend. Some panic or other at the hospital.'

'Oh, really?'

Harry also wasn't coming back until the weekend. It seemed not unreasonable to think that the two of them were together somewhere. In fact, it seemed very unlikely they were not. Edwina suddenly felt more foolish still: foolish and very, very angry.

'Edward,' she said, 'Edward, I wonder if you realised something ...'

CHAPTER 36

Cassia was not to be found. Not by her husband, who had phoned the house in Walton Street immediately (having put down the telephone on Edwina) and repeated the process every hour until midnight, when he had fallen exhaustedly asleep, and then recommenced his task at six a.m.; not by Rupert, who, worried by her failure to return after the performance, had also phoned the house several times and then tried Monks Ridge as well, to have the phone picked up by a hugely agitated Edward; not by Harry Moreton, who had telephoned her from Paris almost as frequently through the night as her husband; not by Nurse Hampton, who had wanted her to start the clinic earlier than usual on the Thursday, owing to an exceptionally heavy attendance on the Tuesday; not by the Dean, who wanted her approval on the press release he had prepared for the medical journals on the subject of her research Chair, and had found himself talking to an irate Edward; and not by Edwina Moreton, who had decided the only thing that was going to make her feel better was a confrontation with Cassia, and the sooner the better.

All these people, or most of them, began eventually to telephone one another: and as the morning of Thursday 10 December wore on, it became apparent that the last person to have seen Cassia was Rupert. Rupert said he had no idea where she was either, and told all of them the simple truth: that she had come to see him the night before at the theatre and had then promised to return so that they could have dinner together, but that she had not done so, and had not been at her house, as far as he had been able to ascertain; but as time went by, he became anxious enough to start examining and re-examining his conversation with her for some clue as to what might have happened to her.

By the fifth call of the day, which was from Harry Moreton, the examination had led him to a remark he had made shortly before she had left, partly in jest: 'No, I would say almost entirely in jest,' he said to Harry, 'that she should go and see Rollo Gresham in Marrakesh. Of course I don't think she intended to do any such thing, and anyway, how could she? But it seemed worth mentioning, that's all.'

'Sweet Jesus,' said Harry, 'surely, surely she wouldn't try to do that. She couldn't be so foolish, so unutterably stupid.'

'She was very upset,' said Rupert carefully, 'and more than ready to be foolish. Or unutterably stupid.'

'What was she upset about? Come on, Cameron, you'd better tell me.'

Rupert told him.

Cassia was at that very moment walking across an expanse of very wet grass at Croydon Aerodrome towards an Air France plane. It seemed very strange, she thought, that a journey that was to end in a place as exotic as Marrakesh should begin in one as mundane as Croydon, but in a way rather reassuring, it seemed to make her adventure in some way more sensible.

She had only ever been in a plane once, and that had been Harry's; she had no idea what a commercial aircraft might be like, and imagined it inside at least to be simply a larger version of his Vega Gull. In the event, it proved to be extraordinarily reminiscent of a train, with pairs of armchair-style seats on either side of the central gangway, complete with linen-covered headrests, a hammock-style luggage rack, and a white-jacketed steward taking orders for lunch.

Cassia herself could not imagine eating lunch, eating anything indeed ever again; she was in a strange, uncomfortable state, agitated, excited and distressed all at the same time. It seemed somehow familiar to her, that state, and partly to distract herself from her nerves, she raked through her memories to try and define why. She remembered as the propellors whirred and the plane taxied briefly down the airfield, then rose rather majestically into the sky: it was the most excruciating stage in her first experience of childbirth, before the midwife uttered her exhortation to start bearing down, and after reaching the absolute certainty that what she was being asked to endure was unendurable. She smiled at that memory; she could only hope that her current adventure would have as happy an ending.

She could still hardly believe that she could have come to be living the adventure – or in her own foolhardiness or courage in undertaking it – but events, relentless and irresistible, had led her to it, and in the end it had seemed the only reasonable course. Having left Rupert, she had gone back to Walton Street and sat drinking extremely strong tea and trying to think what she might do; his exhortation to go and find Rollo had seemed absurdly, almost dangerously, impossible, but on the other hand also strangely sound. No one else was going to tell her what had happened, no one else could explain events; and as she sat there, the telephone rang and it was the Ritz in Paris phoning to say they had found a pair of gloves which she had left behind and that they would send them on unless she was planning another trip to Paris in the very near future.

Cassia asked them to send her gloves, and then, reflecting upon the fact that it was absurdly easy to telephone a place so far away, realised that she could, conceivably, phone Rollo Gresham in Marrakesh.

A feverish hour later, with the help of a very nice operator, she was listening to the phone ringing in what she presumed was his house.

A man answered the phone: a servant, she presumed. 'House of Monsieur Rollo,' he said. The line was appalling, crackly and frequently interrupted by a high-pitched buzz; she could hear, too, she thought, a child crying somewhere.

She had asked to speak to Monsieur Rollo, and the man had said, 'One minute. Who is calling, please?'

'I'm calling from England,' she said, speaking very slowly and clearly, 'and I am a relation of of Lady Beatty, a good friend of Monsieur Rollo. Could I speak to him, please? Is he there?'

'One minute, please. Will see.'

Another long wait; and this time a child shouting, loudly, sounding aggressive, then an angry adult voice, a woman's. Perhaps Gresham had married, or had a woman out there, had children; God, she knew so little about him, it was absurd to think she could have a conversation with him across all these miles, a complex, emotional conversation.

'Name please, madame,' said the man's voice.

'Fallon,' she said, 'Mrs Cassia Fallon.'

'Wait again.'

Another long wait, while she dreaded being cut off again; finally he returned. 'Monsieur Rollo is not here,' he said quickly, too quickly, then, 'Is ill.'

'Not there? Or ill? Which?'

'I'm sorry. Not here. Ill. Goodbye.' The line went dead.

She sat there, staring at the phone, taut with frustration, knowing he was there, that Gresham was there, had refused to speak to her, could imagine him telling the servant, 'Say I'm ill, say I'm not here, just get rid of her,' knowing he could tell her what she wanted to know. That was when she decided after all to take Rupert's advice.

In London that morning, the brief reign of Edward VIII ended, as the Instrument of Abdication was signed and witnessed by the King's three brothers, as was the King's message to the House of Commons, and arrangements made for their distribution throughout the Empire.

Queen Mary, speaking probably for millions, remarked, 'To give up all this for that.'

The newly designated ex-King, no longer constrained by government, announced that he would broadcast to his people, as he had wished to do much earlier in the affair, the following night.

The plane was very noisy; much noisier, or so it seemed, than Harry's small one, and seemed to be making rather lumbering progress, but proved actually astonishingly fast. They were in Paris by midday, at Le Bourget airport, where she and a handful of other passengers changed into a very different plane, a Dewoitine, the steward told her proudly, as if he might have built it himself, with only eight reclining seats and each with its own small table. They were to go on to Toulouse, where they would spend the night, reaching Casablanca at midday the following day.

'From there, you can take a train, or a car, of course, it's only about a hundred miles,' the nice young man at Thomas Cook had said, having entered rather thoroughly into the spirit of her adventure, and thinking how he was looking forward to telling his girlfriend about the beautiful young woman in the sable coat who had been waiting outside the door of their Knightsbridge office as they opened, and demanded to know how she could get to Marrakesh 'as soon as it's humanly possible, and, yes, I have my passport with me.'

'And if you want to stay in a hotel, then you must go to the Mamounia,' he had added. 'It's extremely beautiful and luxurious, often described as the most beautiful hotel in the world. Winston Churchill often stays there. The gardens once belonged to royalty. I could send a cable if you like.' Cassia said she would like.

By the time they reached Toulouse she was completely exhausted. The noise of the aircraft, the constant juddering, the realisation finally of what she had done, in all its inescapable folly, overwhelmed her; she almost fell down the steps of the plane and into a bus, along with her fellow passengers, most whom seemed to be travelling in irritatingly jolly groups. She was borne through the darkness to a hotel, the standard and location of which was of no interest to her, so long as it provided her with a bed on a steady and silent floor. In the event it was modestly luxurious, the dinner served more than adequate, and the bed comfortable; she sent a telegram to Edward to tell him where she was going, and that she was quite safe – and then went to bed and slept dreamlessly.

She woke at five to the darkness, feeling very alone and very afraid, and half tempted to fly home again, and was only prevented by the thought of how much she would hate and despise herself if she did, and that she would forfeit for ever any chance of finding out the truth. And of course that she would have made several people extremely worried and angry to no purpose whatsoever.

In London that morning, the ex-King awoke early to complete his speech and arranged to lunch with Winston Churchill in order to show him the draft and bid him farewell; and, while discussions continued as to his future rank and titles, made arrangements to join Mrs Simpson at the house of the Baron Eugene de Rothschild in Vienna.

Justin Everard also lay awake in the long dark winter dawn, reflecting upon his future and where Cecily Harrington might be placed in it. He had been immensely surprised the previous day by her reaction to the news of Cassia's and Harry's liaison: surprised and distressed. He was distressed on two counts: one, that he should have inflicted any unhappiness upon her, and two, that it served to pinpoint yet again the great cultural gulf that yawned between them.

He genuinely loved Cecily; he found her deeply attractive both physically and emotionally; he loved being with her, he enjoyed the atmosphere of warmth and caring in which she seemed permanently to move, and he found her far removed intellectually from her often vapid peers. She was intelligent, thoughtful and well read, her interests frequently coincided with his, particularly in the arts, and indeed he had noticed a pleasing and growing self-confidence in her own intellectual views, despite her still shaky emotional state.

Increasingly, over the past few weeks, he had found the thought of consummating a physical relationship with her immensely intriguing; her body, regaining now its lush plumpness – why did modern women all feel they had to look like adolescent boys? – her full, lovely breasts, her surprisingly slender legs and neck, her large dark eyes and full mouth, her gleaming cloud of dark hair, were beginning to obsess him. The women with whom he spent his working days, with their flat figures, their cropped hair, their neat, bored little faces, bored him sensually, he found them dull. And, aware though he was of Cecily's emotional vulnerability, the dreadful wrong he would be doing her should he disturb her, arouse her without proper consideration of the consequences, he had begun to plan, in the nicest, kindest possible way, her seduction; the thought even of kissing her, really kissing her, of feeling that mouth under his, that throat, of his hands in her hair, inspired in him extremely distinct physical symptoms.

Nevertheless, the events of the previous day had worried him. Was there really any future in a relationship between the two of them? Between two people, one of whom regarded the sexual frissons between people married to other people amusing and diverting (even while probably not approving of it for themselves), the other finding it shocking and distressing; between two people, one of whom moved in a world not only of sexual freedom, but sexual anarchy, and to whom homosexuality was a simple fact of life, a blithe accident of biology, potentially even a happy one, and the other to whom it was something abhorrent and who, having discovered it in her husband, had regarded it as a shameful sickness.

Two people, one of whom had come from a level of society that was modest, to put it mildly, and for whom the earning of a living was not only satisfying and pleasant but essential, and the other from its upper echelons and rich beyond the dreams of most of the population.

Could emotional concern, sexual fulfilment, even the most ardent love, possibly counteract all those difficulties, render them at worst unimportant, and at best nonexistent? Or would there be, after a short time, the first rapture having passed, resentment, unhappiness, discontent, disillusion?

Lying there, staring into the darkness, Justin found no comfort in the answers that came to him.

'Could we have lunch together today?' said Edwina.

She could tell from the silence that followed, she had overstepped the mark, crossed some important boundary of protocol, that not only should she not have taken the initiative in this instance, that while Francis Stevenson-Cook might enjoy her company, find her attractive, in whatever sense might be relevant, might invite her to lunch, to dinner, to nightclubs, to parties, invade her life, ride over her marriage, introduce her to his friends, friends with whom she might then indulge in every kind of sexual deviation, he remained, in spite of all those things, her employer, and she ignored that fact at her peril. It did not strike her as particularly unfair even: that was her place, however privileged, in his hierarchy, and she would do well to remember it, if she wished to retain the status quo.

'I'm sorry,' she said quickly, 'forgive me, I expect you're busy. I just wanted to talk to you. I'm sorry, Francis, very sorry.'

He recovered at once, on her apology – the most abject she had ever made to anyone, Edwina thought, if only he knew – recognising it as his due. 'That's perfectly all right. It's just that I have a very heavy day, preparing for the American contingent who are arriving in a week. I was taken aback. You sound upset, perhaps cocktails later, in my office? Then we would have plenty of time.'

'Yes. Yes, that would be very nice, thank you. I'll wait for your call.'

She was in a strange new country these days, she thought; she was still learning her way about it.

Later, as she sat at her dressing table, applying her make-up, Harry phoned.

'You,' she said briefly, 'are contemptible.'

'Really?' he said. He sounded rather cheerful, she thought.

'Yes. You and Cassia.'

'I see. And you and the Sobel crowd, the Bryanston twins – I suppose that's something quite different.'

'Of course it's different. Cassia is my friend. Or so I had thought.'

'Well, at least we are equal now, Edwina. Anyway, I phoned to tell you I'm not coming home for a few days.'

'Good,' she said, 'and when you do, my solicitor will be waiting for you. Do give my regards to Cassia. Tell her she's very welcome to you.'

'She's not with—' he began, but she had slammed the phone down.

'Where's Mummy gone now?' said Bertie.

Janet looked at him thoughtfully; for the very first time he sounded plaintive, upset about the situation, about what must seem his mother's endless absences, what indeed *were* her endless absences, she thought rather sadly. She would have hoped, given the children's sadness at their parents' marriage ending, that Cassia would have tried to be at home more for a while, would have put her job on hold until after Christmas at least. It seemed terrible for children to be unhappy at Christmas.

'She's got some very important work to do,' she said, 'terribly important. She can't just turn her back on sick people, any more than your father can. They're doctors, their patients' lives often depend on them.'

'She doesn't have to be a doctor,' said Bertie, 'she could just be a mother again, like she used to be. Then she wouldn't have to worry about her stupid patients.'

He got up from the kitchen table, where he had been doing some drawing, and walked out of the room rather slowly, his thin shoulders drooped. Janet looked after him and sighed.

It was the smell that Cassia noticed first about Morocco, the strange, fierce, potent smell that somehow fused with the heat; years later, discussing those few extraordinary days with someone who had visited Morocco frequently, he said, 'Ah, yes! Woodsmoke, camel dung and incense, wonderful.' She wasn't sure about the wonderful, even then, but she could, in memory, pick out all those elements.

And after the smell, the literally pressing proximity of bodies, of brown grinning faces, of people proffering, offering her things – lengths of fabric, jewellery, ornaments – a sense of panic, almost of claustrophobia, and then after that the relief and promise of order as her driver, the driver she had hired in Casablanca, shooed them contemptuously away as if they were little better than the mangy, scrawny dogs who ran everywhere, ushered her into the car and shut her away, briefly safe from it all.

He had driven her then along a hundred miles of painfully rough, red, sandy roads, through plains which seemed to her to be desert, ever less fertile, through occasional squalid villages where they were stared at by children playing in the dust and watched morosely by wretched-looking donkeys, tethered in the blazing sun.

The car had been large and comfortable, but the heat was stifling, she had been feeling very sick, and the driver had talked to her virtually incomprehensibly all the way: he had started talking when they left Casablanca and was still talking when they arrived in Marrakesh and she became aware of the tall city walls, built with the red mud of the plains, the extraordinarily intricate roofline of domes and turrets and minarets, and carved out behind them in the blue sky, the unbelievable sight of the snow-capped Atlas mountains. They looked impossibly, tantalisingly near, those mountains, cool and reassuring, a note of clean sanity in what seemed to her the hot near-hell of these streets, filled with apparently starving animals, donkeys piled high with loads three times their own height, their bones jutting so sharply through their skin that it was painful to look at them, dogs and cats slinking in the gutters, close to death.

Cassia had sat shrinking into the corner of her car, absurdly fearful of what was outside, her mission almost forgotten, her only concern reaching some kind of civilisation that she could recognise as such, despising herself for her feebleness and her chauvinism.

And then her car pulled into the entrance gates of La Mamounia, and she smiled with pure pleasure, feeling almost at once herself again, so lush it was, and filled with palm trees and brilliantly flowering shrubs and grass, an oasis of calm, of peace, of green, wonderfully green, after the red of the mud and the dust.

The hotel itself was pale pink with a large curving courtyard in front of it, parked with a few extremely large and expensive-looking cars. Her driver picked up her one piece of totally inadequate baggage – a servant was removing what looked like a dozen matching pieces, including hatboxes, from the boot of a white Rolls Royce – and led her into the hotel, where it was so cool, so quiet, she could scarcely believe she was in the same country, never mind the same city, as the one outside.

They took her up to her room, with its vast bed, its balcony overlooking the gardens, its basket of fruit and huge vases of flowers, and left her there. She felt suddenly, in her exhaustion and anxiety, rather as if she was in a hospital or convalescent home, recovering from some dreadful illness, and that they were not hotel staff but medical, there to nurse her back to health and strength.

She could not possibly go down to dinner, she could see that – she had only the crumpled clothes she had been wearing since leaving London, and a simple black jersey dress which would certainly not serve for use in the extremely grand dining room, with its black marble pillars, its vast windows, its exquisite mosaic floor – so she had a bath and then ordered a meal of smoked salmon and salad and fruit from room service, and ate it sitting in her bed, feeling slightly decadent and miraculously more cheerful.

She tried to make a phone call to England, but the lines were all busy, so she sat gazing at the great range of mountains, forming their incongruous snow-capped background to the palm trees.

She must have slept then, for she woke in the dark, extremely cold (having left all the windows and the french doors on to her balcony open), and remembered the young man in Thomas Cook's warning her that Morocco was often called a cold country with hot sun. She rang room service for some tea and went round shutting windows and doors, piling extra blankets on her bed, pulling on the sweater she had been wearing when she left England, and a pair of socks, and then lay slowly growing warmer, wondering a little fearfully, but with a degree of intense excitement, what the next day might bring.

Other English guests in the hotel tried without a great deal of success to tune their radios to the BBC in order to listen to what was arguably one of the most historic broadcasts ever made: that of the ex-King of England, introduced now as His Royal Highness Prince Edward, speaking from

Windsor Castle and telling his people that he had discharged his last duties as King and Emperor, and declaring his allegiance to the new King, his brother, the Duke of York.

The whole of England heard that broadcast. The country was almost entirely silent for its duration; families everywhere gathered round the wireless, some distressed, others surprised, all of them, whatever their views on the matter, deeply moved.

In Monks Ridge Edward Fallon sat with his arms round his two little boys, Janet Fraser opposite him in Cassia's chair, strangely subdued, and Peggy standing in the doorway, weeping openly, as they were told that the King found it impossible to carry the heavy burden of responsibility without the help and support of the woman he loved.

In London, Cecily Harrington sat in her drawing room, also with her children, thinking how desperately the King must have loved this woman, hoping that he had indeed been comforted by his mother and his family, as he was claiming he had been, feeling a pang of intense sympathy with him as he described the 'matchless blessing enjoyed by my brother and so many of you, and not bestowed upon me – a happy home with his wife and children'.

Rupert Cameron, who had also not had that blessing bestowed upon him, listened to the broadcast in his dressing room, his heart heavy, for he had always felt a certain empathy with his sovereign, had defended his right to follow his heart.

As he sat there, the door opened quietly and Eleanor came in. Her eyes were full of tears; she was clearly deeply upset. She looked at Rupert and he at her, wondering in this moment of very raw emotion why he had never been more moved by her beauty, her gentleness, and, telling himself he was acting purely in friendship, stood up and took her into his arms, in order to comfort her.

Justin Everard, listening to the radio while he worked in his darkroom, had not thought he would care very much at all about the King and what he did, but he found himself actually rather affected by the intense emotion of the moment and especially touched by this reference to the 'greatest kindess he had been treated with by all classes, wherever he had lived or journeyed through the Empire' and his gratitude for it.

And even Edwina Moreton, listening to it with Francis Stevenson-Cook in his flat in Mount Street, felt a lump in her throat as the voice, clear and very strong now, wished the new King 'and his people, happiness and prosperity with all my heart. God bless you all. God save the King.'

At which point Francis poured them both a glass of champagne and raised his, echoing the last words himself.

But Harry Moreton, flying across southern Europe through the darkness, heard nothing of it at all.

CHAPTER 37

Absurdly, Cassia found herself worrying as to what she should wear to visit Rollo Gresham. She had nothing remotely suitable for the situation and, more relevantly, for the climate either. It wasn't unbearably hot, the temperature was that of a pleasant English summer day, but it was humid, and neither a tweed suit nor a black jersey dress was going to be in the least comfortable. She put the dress on as the slightly better option, as she at least knew it suited her, and rang for breakfast; and then, because she could not possibly postpone it any longer, went down to the lobby and asked them to call her a taxi.

Justin did not often work on Saturday, but there was a general air of panic at Style House at the moment, and everyone who worked there, whether fulltime or freelance, was in a state of acute tension; the Americans, who ran the sister company in New York and who were both financially and stylistically the overlords, were arriving for their annual visit at the beginning of January and there was an absolute need to get Style House in order by then. The magazines always ran late, all of them, the panic-induced adrenalin producing better, more interesting work, but the Americans would expect to see dummy issues, work in progress, photographs, layouts clearly ready in plenty of time; this meant virtually doing two issues in the time they usually spent on one, which meant, in turn, a six- or even seven-day week.

Consequently Style House that Saturday morning was operating as if it were a weekday, and Justin was just leaving to go and take some photographs in Edwina Moreton's drawing room when the telephone rang, and his assistant told him that it was for him.

Suzanne, the secretary, who spent most of her days booking models and arranging sittings and who was consequently privy to some of the richest, most scurrilous gossip in London, looked up at him with a knowing smile. 'It's your rich lady friend,' she said, putting her hand over the mouthpiece. 'Keep in with her, Justin, and you'll be able to give up work altogether in a month or two.'

Justin scowled at her and took the phone.

'Hallo?' he said cautiously.

'Justin, hallo, it's Cecily. How are you?'

'I'm very well,' he said.

'It can't be much fun working on Saturday. I'm sorry.'

'Oh, it's all right,' he said, 'but we're all in a panic here, everything's running terribly late. I'm about to rush off and do some pictures for Edwina, so I can't be long.' He sounded more impatient than he actually felt: partly because he was irritated by Suzanne's remark and and partly because his mind was actually fixed on the difficulties of the morning ahead, and taking pictures of a drawing room that he knew to be the wrong location for the job. He had wanted something ornate, almost baroque, rather like Cecily's own drawing room, but Edwina's was contemporary in style and filled with her husband's aggressively modern pictures.

'Oh, I see. Yes. She wanted to use my house for those, but I refused, I'm afraid.'

'She did?' Damn. Extremely tantalising. It was yet another pointer to the differences between them, the differences he had been thinking of so much lately. Cecily would not wish her drawing room to be photographed; it would not be the sort of thing she would feel comfortable with, seeing it as somehow rather vulgar, commercial, an invasion of her privacy, not something that was to him absolutely everyday, part of his normal working life.

'Justin, if you'd rather use my house, I—'

'No, no,' he said shortly, 'it's all arranged now, it really doesn't matter at all.'

'Oh.' She sounded taken aback, then rallied. 'Well, I actually phoned to say would you like to come and have supper here tonight? At the house? Nothing formal, just me and the girls. A little – well, a little thank you. For everything.'

'Oh.' Justin hesitated. Nothing could have appealed to him more: supper at Cecily's, delicious food, no doubt a bottle of superb wine, a warm, easy, family atmosphere, the little girls to tease and flirt with, sitting in the drawing room after dinner by that great fire, playing some silly game with them all – it would be exactly what he would most like after a difficult day with an extremely prickly Edwina. The uncomfortable conversation he had had with himself two nights ago, the conclusions he had been forced to reach, suddenly resurfaced; and he saw this as a rather clear turning point. If, as he had almost decided, he and Cecily were not right for one another then the sooner he started to ease out of the relationship the better, however much it hurt him to do.

He took a mentally deep breath and said, 'I'm sorry, Cecily. I'm busy tonight. Working in the darkroom, you know.'

'Oh, I see. Tomorrow perhaps?'

God, this was going to be difficult. 'No, not tomorrow either, I'm afraid. It's Sunday, I have to go and see my mama. Sorry. Maybe some time next week, that would be very nice.'

'Yes,' she said, and he could hear the hurt in her voice, 'yes, all right. Maybe next week. Goodbye, Justin.'

'Goodbye, Cecily,' he said, and hoped she couldn't hear the hurt in his.

Rollo Gresham lived in the part of Marrakesh known as the Ville Nouvelle, the area built under French colonial rule; off the avenue d'el-Jadida, and very near the Marjorelle Gardens. Cassia had been told about those gardens by a helpful porter in the hotel as she waited for her taxi, told she must go and see them, that they were 'very very very beautiful' and designed by the French painter Jacques Marjorelle in the 1920s, who had also done some work on the Mamounia.

Removed from the peace and tranquillity of the hotel grounds, and confronted again by the twin terrors of Rollo Gresham and Marrakesh in the raw, she began to feel very sick; the lurching taxi, the powerful smells of the city made her realise she was about to vomit: she told him to stop, leant out of the door and threw up repeatedly. Mercifully, they were no longer in the crowds; they had already reached the Ville Nouvelle, and the street was wide, tree lined and almost deserted. The driver was surprisingly kind: he got out, held her head, passed her a handkerchief that was only slightly grubby, and offered to fetch her some water.

'No,' she said, 'no, really, it's all right. I'm so sorry. I'll be all right in a minute. Where are we?'

'Marjorelle Gardens through there,' said the drive, indicating a small side road. 'Avenue d'el-Jadida along street. Very very near.'

'Yes, I see. Thank you. I think I'll walk the rest of the way. I need some air. You go.' She gave him his fare and a tip worth twice as much.

He gazed at her, his wizened face with its deeply etched lines still concerned. 'Will wait for you.'

'No, no, don't. It's perfectly all right. I might be hours. Please, I'll be fine. But thank you for everything. You were very kind.'

It was horribly hot in her jersey dress; the sun was beating on her unprotected head. She crossed the street slightly unsteadily, hoping she wouldn't be sick again, and walked down the street towards the avenue d'el-Jadida.

Harry Moreton taxied down the airfield in Casablanca in that combination of exhaustion and exaltation which seems almost hallucinogenic; he could have flown no further, even had he known of an airfield in Marrakesh, which he did not.

He climbed out of his plane on legs which threatened to fail in their function, and walked across to the control tower with his papers. And an hour later was asleep in a surprisingly comfortable train.

'What on earth is the matter with you, Justin?' said Edwina irritably. 'This whole thing should only have taken an hour or two at the most, and here we are, nearly lunchtime and we're still setting it up.'

'Oh, shut up,' said Justin. 'I get so bloody tired of editors telling me things should only take an hour or two. If the lighting was wrong, if the beastly pots didn't look right, you'd be the first to complain. It's very difficult in this room, you knew perfectly well I wanted somewhere that was basically darker, less modern looking.'

'Yes, well, at forty-eight hours' notice, that was a little difficult to arrange,' said Edwina, 'and I'm afraid I didn't have time to restyle my drawing room for you. I'm so sorry. If your girlfriend had been a bit more co-operative—'

'If you mean Cecily, she is not my girlfriend. Far from it. I never heard anything so absurd.'

'Really? Well, in that case, all I can say is you'd better stop leading her up the garden path, encouraging her. She's going to get frightfully keen on you, and it's not fair. And besides, it will come back to reflect on me if she starts getting serious about you and then you ditch her. I introduced you to her, after all.'

'That would be really serious, wouldn't it?' said Justin. 'I'd hate to mess things up in your perfectly organised life, Edwina. Anyway – Edwina, are you all right?'

'Yes, I'm fine,' said Edwina, dashing a hand impatiently across her eyes, pulling her cigarette case out of her bag, flicking at her lighter with a hand that shook. Do you want one?'

'No, thanks. I hate those things. Are you sure you're all right, Edwina?'

'Yes, I think so,' said Edwina with a sigh. 'It's just that my life is very far from perfectly organised, as you put it; it's in total chaos, and I don't quite know what to do about any of it.'

'Well, you're not alone,' said Justin. 'Tell you what, let's have supper together tonight, shall we? We can give each other lots and lots of perfectly terrible advice and—'

'Marvellous idea. But would you mind eating here? I really don't want to go out. I'll tell Cook to do something wonderful. Now, in the meantime, can we please get this thing going? Otherwise I'm going to start screaming. Very loudly indeed.'

Cassia had no way of knowing whether Rollo Gresham's house was that of a rich man; she was so disorientated by her travelling, and by being in a place so alien to her, that it was impossible to put a value on anything: but it looked to her fairly modest, the size of a detached suburban villa in England. It was certainly a very pretty house, set back from the street, not a Moroccan-style street, but quite wide and lined with jacarandas. The house was deco in style, white stucco with curved lines and a flat roof, and the lovely front garden was overflowing with flowers. A man was watering the shrubs with a long hosepipe; he grinned at her as she walked in, showing the largely toothless mouth she was growing swiftly familiar with. She smiled uncertainly back.

'You want Monsieur Rollo?'

'Er, yes. Yes, I do.'

'I call Mehdi. You wait.'

She moved to the shelter of the arched porch and waited. She felt sick again.

Mehdi appeared, clearly a more important servant, better dressed, in white tunic and trousers, with more teeth. 'You want to see Monsieur Rollo?'

'Yes please.'

'Your name?'

'Mrs Fallon. Mrs Cassia Fallon.'

'Wait, please.'

Three children came out, two boys and a girl. They looked at her uncertainly, and the younger boy smiled, a glorious, beautiful smile. He was altogether beautiful: fairly light skinned, with dark shining hair, only a little taller than Bertie, but clearly older. The little girl looked younger, probably only about seven, clinging to his hand. She looked as if she had been crying.

Mehdi appeared, waved them away as if they were dogs, said

626

something incomprehensible. The older boy said something back, nodded, then they all ran. Mehdi looked at her. 'You alone?'

'Yes,' she said, surprised at the question. 'Yes, of course I'm alone. As you see.'

'Wait again.' He went back into the house, reappeared. 'Monsieur Rollo says ...'

He's going to tell me I can't come in, Cassia thought, can't see Gresham. I'll have come all this way, and still I can't see him, won't know. She was so sure that was what he was going to say that when she actually heard the words 'come back in two hours' it meant nothing to her, nothing at all. She just went on standing there, wondering wildly if she could creep round the back, work her way through the gardens, get into the house some other way.

'Two hours all right?'

'What?'

'Come back in two hours, all right? Three o'clock.'

'Oh, yes. Perfectly all right. Thank you.'

He bowed, the garden boy bowed, grinned at her, and she went out into the street.

Yes, they told Harry at the Mamounia, Mrs Fallon had indeed checked in, but had gone out shortly after breakfast; she had said she might and might not be back for luncheon. Would Mr Moreton require luncheon, would he perhaps wait in case Mrs Fallon returned?

Harry went to the bar, ordered a large whisky, issued a short prayer that Mrs Fallon would indeed return and tried to decide what he should do in case she did not.

Cassia had thought she would return to the hotel for the intervening two hours, and then realised that she had no idea how to get there. There were certainly no black cabs, or their equivalent, she couldn't walk, certainly not in this heat, and if she didn't faint or throw up again, she was bound to get lost and probably be attacked or at best pestered on the way. She couldn't stand around here for two hours. It was hideous. Maybe the taxi would still be waiting; he had insisted on staying for what he called a very few minutes. It hadn't been that long.

The taxi driver had indeed waited: he had been concerned for her. She was so young, clearly not well, and he didn't like to see women travelling about Morocco on their own. It was very unwise.

He knew the house, as he knew so many of the houses in the town, knew it was lived in by an Englishman, knew the Englishman was ill, knew what he was suffering from, knew even who his doctor was.

He watched from the corner as she went through the gates, pulled forward cautiously as she disappeared; he saw her speaking to the gardener, then waiting in the doorway for the houseboy. And he watched the children coming out: Arab children. Pretty children, no doubt brought in for the Englishman.

He looked at his watch – it was already almost a quarter to one – and then remembered he had to be back at the hotel by one, for an important booking, some American ladies who wished to go to Asni to see the market. He could not afford to upset the head porter at the Mamounia; his livelihood and that of his very large family depended upon it. And besides it would be a big fare. He put down the clutch, swung the car round with a scream of tyres on the hot road and headed back to the other side of the town.

Cassia came out of the gate to see him disappearing round the corner. For a moment she panicked again, and then she remembered, with a thud of pleasure, the Marjorelle Gardens; she could go and sit there for a while.

She retraced her steps, paid her entrance money and went into the gardens. And immediately felt quite quite different, no longer in the least sick, but almost dizzy, dizzy with visual delight. The gardens were quite extraordinary in themselves, incredibly lavish, thick with palms and bamboo, planted with nasturtiums, geraniums, bougainvillaea, set with pergolas, lily-covered pools and brilliantly coloured paths painted in pinks, lemons and greens. The air was also lush, rich with sound, the sound of water and birdsong, but the most extraordinary thing of all about it was the colour of the walls, the walls of the garden and of the main building within it, an amazingly brilliant, stinging mauvish blue, a blue she could never remember seeing ever anywhere before and which she thought she might never see again.

She sat down on a bench by one of the pools, feeling better now, soothed and excited at once by this place, which must, she thought foolishly, resemble the Garden of Eden, thought also it had been worth coming here simply to see it; and composing and recomposing her thoughts for the interview ahead. This was a much better idea than returning to the hotel.

Lunchtime by any stretch of the hopeful imagination having come and gone, Harry tried to decide what to do. Presumably Cassia was at Gresham's place; how she had got the address, heaven only knew. Not for the first time since this whole insane adventure had begun, he was filled with intense admiration for her. He could only think of one other woman in his acquaintance who would have embarked on such a trip on her own, and that was Edwina. He seemed to find himself attracted to extremely strong women, Harry thought, and found the thought amusing, ironic even; then returned to his dilemma.

There was no point in trying to get into Gresham's house: he would be thrown out if he so much as put a foot into the garden, probably shot. He could wait around outside, in the hope that Cassia had either not got there yet, or that when she came out she would not try to shoot him herself. After a few more minutes he decided that was the only course.

He called for a taxi, looked at his watch: two twenty-five. He could be there in less than half an hour. He wished to God now that he had gone straight there, not wasted time in the bar. If he'd missed her, if she got to Gresham first, things could get very nasty indeed.

Cassia decided she should leave the sanctuary of the gardens and make her way back to avenue d'el-Jadida. It was ten to three; she didn't want to be late. Rollo Gresham might keep to a very strict timetable, might even be going out, might use her lateness as an excuse not to see her. She felt much better now, in command of herself and events. She stood up, straightened the increasingly unchic and unsuitable dress and set off towards the house. She would be five minutes early, but that wouldn't matter. She could wait in the street, just by his gates. Nobody would accost her there.

'*Yallah!*' said Harry, throwing himself into the taxi.

The driver was neither moved nor impressed by this Moroccan exhortation. 'Yes, boss,' he said, and proceeded towards the Ville Nouvelle at his normal rather sober pace. He had a new car; he wasn't going to risk it for anyone.

The roads were surprisingly clear; they would be there, Harry reckoned, in less than fifteen minutes, if only this fool would put his foot down a bit. He fumbled in his pocket for some notes to wave at the driver, pushed them over the man's shoulder, and said, '*Vite, plus vite.*'

The driver shrugged, increased his pace imperceptibly, just enough to indicate he might increase it further.

'For God's sake,' said Harry, fumbling for some more notes. The man half turned again to him, assessing their value: and then it happened.

A donkey, carrying what appeared to be the contents of an entire house on its back, and the tiny cart it was pulling, slithered suddenly on the road. Its small legs gave way beneath it, and it lay spreadeagled in the road, its owner flogging it and shouting at it uselessly. A car coming towards it in the opposite direction slammed on its brakes and collided with a horse-drawn cart, whose load of several dozen chickens escaped and ran clucking joyfully all over the road. In rather less than sixty seconds the entire street was impassable, resembling a disorderly farmyard.

Harry's taxi, pulling out, swerved to avoid the largest contingent of chickens, and struck a large rackety van coming in the other direction. Harry, who had been leaning forward, shouting at the driver, was thrown right forward, hitting his head very hard on the dashboard; the last thing he remembered before losing consciousness was a large chicken clambering in through the driver's open window.

'Janet,' said Bertie, 'Janet, do you think Mummy will be back on Monday evening? For my carol concert? And to hear William's solo? She will, won't she? A patient couldn't matter more than that.'

Janet smiled at him brightly. 'Yes, of course she will. I'm *absolutely* certain. She wouldn't miss that. Not for all the patients in the world.'

'I hope not,' said Bertie.

Later, when he was outside playing, she went in to see Edward. He was in the study, scowling over some papers at his desk.

'Dr Fallon, I'm so sorry to trouble you, but Bertie is very anxious that Mrs Fallon might not be back by Monday evening. For the carol concert. It's very important to them both. I wondered when she would be back. What I could tell them.'

'God alone knows,' said Edward wearily. 'She's abroad, in some godforsaken city in North Africa, can you believe it. She says she's leaving again tomorrow, but God knows if she will.'

Janet received this information in characteristic style, rather as if Edward had told her Cassia was in Cheltenham or Leamington Spa. 'I'm sure if she says she will, she will,' she said cheerfully, adding, 'North Africa, how very interesting. My father lived in Algiers for a few years in the twenties and made a few forays down there. Delightful people. Well, Delia and I are off now for a walk. We'll see you later, Dr Fallon.'

Edward, watching her through the window as they set off down the lane, Buffy on the lead, Delia chattering up at her happily, thought that she would have created calm and order out of a hell as visualised by Hieronymous Bosch.

Rollo Gresham was obviously quite ill, Cassia thought, looking at him carefully; he was a bad colour, and clearly short of breath. He was also extremely thin, a shadow of the rather grossly handsome man she remembered. He had had her brought through to a terrace at the back of the house and ordered tea. He had greeted her with courtesy, expressed pleasure, kissed her hand; she wondered why he had ignored her letters.

He sat in a large, high-backed wicker chair, with his feet on a stool, and she noticed that his ankles were puffy and swollen. Heart disease, clearly. He was wearing loose, light trousers and sandals, and at one point he pulled his leg up to swat a fly on his ankle; the trouser leg slipped up and she saw a dressing on his leg.

'So what do you think of Marrakesh?' he said.

'Oh, it's very ... interesting.'

'It's an acquired taste. It becomes rather fascinating when you know it. Have you been to the square yet, to the Djemâa el-Fna?' He gave it the Arab pronunciation.

She had no idea what he meant, but she shook her head. 'I've only seen the gardens. The ones near here.'

'Well, you must go to the square. It's incredible. You step back in time, hundreds, possibly thousands of years. Snake charmers, fire-eaters, preachers, whirling dervishes – it's truly marvellous. Go tomorrow.'

'I'm going back to England tomorrow,' said Cassia.

'A very fleeting trip.'

'Yes.'

A silence, then, 'So how long have you lived here?' she said.

'Oh, on and off for several years,' he said carefully. 'I like it. This does me well enough.'

'Yes,' she said politely, 'it seems very nice to me.' She thought of the house in England, the one advertised in *Country Life*, with its cottages and stables and parkland and woods, and tried to imagine how he must feel about it.

'Of course,' he said, 'it's hardly what I was used to. All those years. My estate, in England. But one has to adjust. As, no doubt, have you. Learnt to adjust. I was thinking of going into politics in England, you know,' he said suddenly.

This was so absurd she found it hard not to smile. 'No, I didn't know that,' she said. 'How ... interesting.'

'Yes. I felt it was something my talents were suited to. I always liked public speaking, that sort of thing. But of course I shall never get the opportunity now.'

'No, I suppose not.' She hesitated, then said, 'I'm sorry you are not well.'

'Oh, I'm perfectly well. Just a temporary indisposition, here – ' he indicated the leg – 'and of course in our old age we grow less ... vital. I don't have the energy I used to. And this climate is not ideal, to put it mildly.'

'No, I can see that. Are you well cared for?'

'What do you mean?' he said, his face wary suddenly. 'What do you mean by that? If you mean the servants, they aren't much good, you know. They're two a penny here, everyone has them, it doesn't mean anything. It's not like having servants in England. When I think of my household there ... well. They're not the same out here, not the same at all.'

She was puzzled by his change of mood, of direction. 'Actually, I meant medically, are the doctors good?'

'Not bad,' he said, 'not as good as English doctors, but they're cheap, of course.'

'Ah.'

'So why the hell are you here?' he said suddenly. 'Eh? Tell me that, why are you here?'

'Well, I – that is, I wanted—'

'Wanted what? More? I hope you don't think you can get any more out of me,' he said, sitting back, looking at her with an expression of odd bitterness on his face, 'because there isn't any. It's all gone. As you see.'

'I don't know what you mean,' she said, 'of course I don't want any more. Of anything.'

'Then what the hell are you doing here?' He put his cup down, leant forward, his expression harsh. 'Have you come to check up on me, to make sure I'm well and truly done for, eh? Is that what this is about?'

'No. No of course not.' Was this normal anger, justifiable hostility? Or was this some kind of paranoia, a dementia? She watched him, half intrigued, half nervous.

'Did Moreton send you? Did he tell you to come and try again? Is that it? I bet he did, I bet this is what it's about.'

'No, Rollo, of course he didn't. He has no idea I'm here. And I've no idea what you're talking about. Please calm down. Please.'

He did then, he seemed to relax; he lay back in his chair, reached for a cigarette and lit it. His hand shook slightly. He reached up to swat another fly, one that was buzzing round his head. His hair had become very thin, she noticed; it had been thick in the old days, thick and very wavy. Lounge lizard's hair, Edwina had once described it.

She smiled at him awkwardly. 'Those children looked very sweet,' she said, by way of finding some safe, neutral ground.

'What children?' His eyes were angry again: not so safe, then.

'The children I saw here this morning. Three of them. Are they the servants' children?'

'Yes. Yes, that's right.' He seemed to have seized on the explanation gratefully. 'Yes, servants' children. They cost me nothing. Nothing at all.'

'No, of course not.' The same fierce obsession with money, with a need to impress her with his penury; it seemed bizarre.

'Well,' he said finally, 'what does bring you here, then?'

His voice was heavy, exhausted suddenly. He clapped his hands, the manservant, Mehdi came in; he spoke to him in rapid French. Mehdi left the room, came back with a tray of drink: brandy, whisky, soda, glasses.

'May I offer you a drink?'

'No, thank you.'

'Oh, come along,' he said impatiently, 'I have to drink alone most of the time. You could do that for me at least. Come along, Cassia, have a drink.'

She had once interviewed a seriously ill mental patient; she had found the mood swings, the sudden lurches into reason and then away from it again, and her need to accommodate them, to go along with them even, highly disorientating. She remembered and recognised that disorientation beginning in her now. She must be careful. 'Yes, all right, then. Thank you. I'll have a brandy.'

'A good choice, I will have the same. Soda? No, it wrecks a good brandy, much better on its own.'

He poured the brandies, very large ones, raised his glass to her. His hands shook, she noticed, wondered if he had Parkinson's disease as well as his other problems. He was clearly a very sick man. 'To you. You were always pretty,' he said suddenly, 'now you are beautiful. She would have been proud of you.'

'Thank you,' she said carefully. 'You mean Leonora?'

'I do mean Leonora. Yes. Perhaps we should drink to her. A little late but ... to Leonora.'

'Leonora.' She drank, obediently.

'You still haven't told me why you're here.'

'I wanted to see you,' she said.

'I am flattered. It's a very long journey, however did you come?'

'I flew. With Air France. To Casablanca.'

'Very enterprising. And Moreton isn't with you? Didn't send you?'

'No. No, really he didn't.'

'I hope not. Well, then. Tell me what you want.'

She decided to be at least partly honest. It could surely make things no worse. 'I have come here to clear up a mystery,' she said. 'I can't get the truth from anyone else.'

'A mystery?'

'Yes. About – well, about Leonora's circumstances, when she died.'

'When Leonora died she had a great deal of money,' said Rollo Gresham, 'as you know. A great deal of money.'

'Yes, I do know. Which she then left to me.'

'Of course. Very neat. First she had it, and then you had it.'

'Yes,' she said, 'yes, that's right.'

'Not really,' he said, and his face was ugly again suddenly, 'not really right at all.'

'I'm sorry, I—'

'Oh, it doesn't matter. Look, I'm getting rather tired of this. Tell me what you want to know and then I must ask you to leave.'

He seemed to be growing hostile again.

She took a deep breath. 'What I want to know is – where the money came from. That Leonora left me.'

'Why do you want to know that?' he said.

'I want to know because I – I'm afraid it can't have come from her.'

'Oh, come along!' He was smiling suddenly, seemed almost amused. 'Of course it did. It was her money, wasn't it? You must have seen the papers.'

'Yes, but—'

'But what? I am finding this rather interesting, getting your view of events.'

'You see, I found out she was living in rather bad circumstances a year, eighteen months before she died. She was very hard up, and ill, of course, so how could she suddenly be so rich?'

'Yes, that is a mystery, isn't it?' he said, and smiled at her suddenly, a cunning, rather ugly smile. 'I can see you would find that intriguing. Well, who do you think it might have come from?'

'I don't know, you see. I didn't think it could have come from you ...'

'Oh, indeed? And why not?'

'I thought that you were – well, not in possession of that sort of money. By then.'

'I see. And how do you know that?'

'I just heard some rumours.'

'Oh, you did? Dear me, what a lot of detective work you have been doing, Cassia, to be sure. I wish you would drink that brandy, isn't it good enough for you? That's better. Now tell me, where did you hear these rumours? In London, was it? Have they been talking about me

634

there? Who did you talk to, who did you track down? And did anyone help you, I wonder, in this quest?'

'No,' she said firmly, 'nobody helped me. It was a chance meeting with Miss Monkton, she seemed to know—'

'Miss Monkton!' he said, sitting back and smiling again. 'Poor old withered, frustrated Monk. With her wispy hair and her bad breath. What a dance Leonora led her. Leonora and I.' He stopped smiling, his face darkened again. 'How the hell did she know what money I had and hadn't got, eh? Was she spying on me too?'

'Rollo, neither of us has been spying on you. It was just that she had found Leonora living somewhere rather wretched, and Leonora told her.'

'Told her what?' he said, his voice suddenly loud, very loud. 'What did she tell her? Eh?' He reached forward, grabbed Cassia's wrist; his face was very close to hers. His breath was foul, hideous.

She tried to smile at him, not to turn her head away. 'Just that you'd lost a lot of your money,' she said steadily.

'And nothing else?'

'No. Nothing else. Really.'

He sat back, seemed to relax. 'Oh, I see. Just that. Well, she was quite right. I had. A great deal. Leonora helped me lose it, what's more. She had a great talent for that: losing money. I hadn't realised quite how much.'

'And so I just didn't understand how Leonora could have had so much money to leave to me. I couldn't see where it might have come from.'

'But you have an idea, don't you?' he said, his eyes narrow, glittering. 'I can see you have an idea. Do you want to tell me what it is?'

'No,' she said, oddly frightened now, without being sure why. 'No, really, I don't have an idea. That's why I'm here. I thought you might know.'

'Didn't you see the document?' he said, releasing her suddenly. 'The deed of settlement?'

'Yes, I did, but—'

'Well, then. You do know. It came from me.'

'But did it? Did it really?'

'Well, if not from me, then whom?' he said impatiently. 'Who else could it have come from?'

She was silent.

'Come along, Cassia. Who, in your clearly crazed imagination, could have, would have handed over half a million pounds to Leonora, if it wasn't me? Who, who, who?' His face was thrust into hers now, he was breathing heavily. She felt trapped, terrified. 'Cassia, who do you think that money came from?' He raised his hand, and she thought he was going to hit her.

She decided to tell him: things could hardly get worse. 'I thought perhaps – from Harry Moreton.'

'Harry Moreton! Sweet Jesus! Dear sweet Jesus. That's very rich. Very rich indeed.'

He released her, sat back in his chair and started to laugh. He laughed for so long she was alarmed. It was hysterical laughter, totally uncontrollable, crazy, his face growing red, and then, finally, it turned to coughing, ugly coughing, then choking, a horrible fighting for breath. She watched him in alarm, then stood up, bent his body forward, banged him hard on the back. The coughing slowly eased; she poured him some water, held it to his lips.

'Thank you,' he said finally, sitting back, wiping the tears from his eyes. 'What a fine doctor you are. There was much talk of you and your medicine, I seem to remember.'

'Really?' she said.

'Yes. Leonora was very proud of you. And sad that you had not pursued your career.'

'Was she? I'm surprised, I always thought she found it a little puzzling. That I should want to do it.'

'Oh, no. It saddened her. Anyway, let us return to your idea. Your strange idea. No, my dear Cassia, the money did not come from Harry Moreton. Most unfortunately. It came from me. That's why I'm living here in this stinking, flyblown hellhole of a place, far from home, from my friends; that's why I can't come home, why I have no home any more; that's why I'm going to die out here – because the money came from me. Not Harry Moreton, Cassia, although—'

He stopped, looked at her with such absolute hatred that she shivered. He noticed and smiled. 'You're not frightened, are you? Yes, I think you are. Good. I quite like the thought that you are frightened. I've been very frightened, quite often, out here.'

'I'm sorry,' she said, 'but I still don't understand—'

'Oh, for God's sake,' he said, 'just get out, will you? Leave me alone. You'd better ask your friend Harry Moreton if you want to know any more. He can tell you all about it. Although he promised not to, promised not to tell anyone. They both did.'

'Both?'

'Yes, the two of them. Thick as thieves, they were, those two. A very appropriate expression that, under the circumstances. Don't you think?'

'I don't know.'

'I often wondered about them, didn't you?'

'Wondered what?'

'Oh, come along. You can't be that naive. If they were lovers. What do you think, eh? It makes a sort of sense, doesn't it? What do you think, Cassia? I never could decide.'

She stood up then, lost in a new panic, literally shocked at the idea, felt herself, despite the shock, examining it. Was it possible, was it? It had never, in her wildest imaginings, even occurred to her: the implications were hideous.

'I really have no idea,' she said finally.

'Oh, I have an idea,' he said. 'It seems to me not impossible. Quite neat, as a matter of fact. Think about it. His devotion was very intense. Too intense to be filial, I would have thought.'

She thought of Harry, caring for Leonora in her last days, paying for her medical care, carrying her up to her apartment, out into the Trocadero Gardens, sitting with her as she died, and felt very sick. Then she steadied. She would have known; surely she would have known.

'I'm sure you're wrong,' she said, 'and now I must go. I'm sorry to have taken up so much of your time.'

'No,' he said, 'sit down again, Cassia, you haven't finished your drink.'

'I don't want it,' she said, 'thank you. I haven't been very well today.'

'Really? I'm so sorry to hear that. The heat, I expect, and the strange food. It's so important to be careful. Would you like to lie down for a while? Should I call my doctor perhaps, ask him to see you? Here, let me call Mehdi ...' He was suddenly his old charming self, almost the Rollo she remembered; again, as he swung into sanity, she felt herself descending into madness.

'No,' she said, 'no, really, I'd rather go back to the hotel.'

'Do you have a taxi waiting? You won't get one here, you know, they don't come passing by.'

'Well, no. Perhaps you could call me one.'

'Yes, of course. Or I could send you in mine. It's not much of a car, I'm afraid, not what you would have expected me to have once. Has Moreton kept all those cars of his? The Bugatti? Does he race that still?'

'Yes. Yes, I believe so.'

'Well,' he said, 'I suppose he would. He would have everything still. His houses, his paintings, his cars. Very nice for him. I raced my cars, you know. I had a very fine Alfa Romeo. I was very successful.'

'Yes, I remember. I remember that day at Brooklands—'

'When I beat Moreton. Yes, that was a good day. I enjoyed that. Well, he's beaten me now. Well and truly.'

She longed to ask him what he meant, was too afraid. 'I'm sorry. Anyway, if you could ask your servant to get a taxi for me perhaps ...'

'Yes, yes, I will.' Relief flooded her for a moment. Then he said, 'But I'd like you to stay for a while. Until you feel better. Have a meal with me, please.'

'No, Rollo, really, I—'

'Now come along,' he said, 'I think you owe me a little pleasure. When I have given you so much. Don't you? I have little enough these days.'

He went over to the door, called through it; Mehdi appeared, and Rollo spoke to him in Arabic. Mehdi bowed, backed away, and Rollo closed the door, stood against it, barring her way.

'I'm glad I had this idea,' he said. 'I think we can have a very nice evening together. I apologise for my earlier inhospitality. Now let us begin with another drink. More brandy? Cassia, do sit down, try to relax. I want you to enjoy yourself. I really do.'

CHAPTER 38

Cecily had slightly reluctantly accepted a last-minute invitation to supper with Venetia Hardwicke. She had been reluctant on two counts: first, that she was still upset about Justin's refusal of her own invitation, and second, she really didn't feel she could cope with a dinner party, but Venetia had persisted, and in the end it seemed churlish to continue to refuse.

In the event, it was a very pleasant evening: a simple supper, as Venetia had promised, in the Hardwickes' very pretty dining room in their very pretty house in Keat's Grove, Hampstead. Everyone was so nice to her, so kind, so clearly and genuinely pleased to have her with them; and she did have to admit that it was nice to be with people again, other than her own family, which had begun to feel a little claustrophobic. To her great surprise and pleasure, she found herself chatting quite easily to them all, Paul Hardwicke in particular, whom she had always liked, almost sparkling indeed, and enjoying his mild, but unmistakable flirting with her. So high were her spirits that by the end of the evening she felt quite optimistic about Justin again, able to tell herself that he really was extremely busy, and he had after all proposed a meeting the following week. She really couldn't believe he had been just pretending to like her all this time.

By the time she took her leave of the Hardwickes, just after ten thirty, she was extremely happy, and also rather drunk. She had had quite a lot of Paul's extremely good champagne when she had arrived, drinking it out of nervousness, and then had moved rather effortlessly on to the very nice white Burgundy he was serving with the food.

Preston was waiting for her with the car, and having enquired if she had had a nice evening, proceeded to become rather pompous, and held forth at great length about the abdication, and how he would never have believed it of the King, that he should have put pleasure before duty to such a disgraceful extent. She became a little sleepy as the car drove

639

southwards, and woke with a start to hear Preston hooting loudly at something.

'Sorry, madam,' he said, 'two young gentlemen who seemed to feel the middle of the road was the best place to walk. Nearly home, madam.'

'That's all right, Preston, where are we?'

'Just coming into Lowndes Square, madam,' said Preston, and looking out of the window, as they drew level with the Moretons' house, she saw the door open and Justin coming out of it: he turned and kissed Edwina who had followed him on to the doorstep.

Had she not had such a good evening, had she not had, indeed, quite so much to drink, Cecily might have acted quite differently; in the event, outrage and a lack of self-consciousness filled her in equal measure and she told Preston to stop and got out of the car.

Justin and Edwina watched her in a frozen fascination as she stalked across the pavement and stared up at them.

'I do hope you've both had a nice evening,' she said. 'I wasn't aware you had a darkroom in your house, Edwina. Next time you prefer someone else's company to mine, Justin, I'd be grateful if you could be honest with me. I'm neither half-witted nor so emotionally broken that I can't cope with the truth. And in any case I can't imagine why you thought I'd mind so much. I suppose you thought I'd have another nervous breakdown. You flatter yourself, you really do. Goodnight.' With that, she turned and went back to the car.

Preston, who had been standing by it rather nervously, opened the door for her and then, clearly wishing to enter into the spirit of things and put up a good show for his mistress, closed it again with something of a flourish and drove away with a rather firm piece of acceleration.

'My God,' said Justin, gazing after them, 'I had no idea she had so much style.'

Harry Moreton woke up in his room at the Mamounia to find one of the hotel staff and a uniformed nurse both looking at him rather anxiously. He looked at his watch, which said nine thirty, and sat up suddenly, swinging his legs over the edge of the bed. Pain hit him ferociously, followed by nausea.

The nurse pushed him firmly back on to his pillows. 'Lie still, please,' she said, 'and I must call the doctor.'

'The doctor! For God's sake, I'm not ill.'

'You are concussed,' she said, 'and I have instructions to call the doctor when you wake. He has been up already several times.' She moved over to the house phone, spoke to the operator rapidly in French.

'Concussed!' said Harry, glaring up at her. 'Of course I'm not concussed. I just dropped off to sleep for a moment. I've flown from England, I'm extremely tired. Now I have to go—'

'Monsieur Moreton you are concussed. I'm sorry. You had a very bad blow on the head, and although you were not unconscious for very long, you have been sleeping on and off for several hours.'

'Of course I haven't. I drifted off briefly, that's all. I do seem to remember some damnfool doctor at the hospital insisting on an X-ray, which was perfectly all right, apparently. I'm sorry, but I really do have to go.'

'Monsieur Moreton, please! Please keep still. The doctor will be here shortly.'

'I can't wait for any doctor. What I have to do is very urgent. Please let me go.'

The nurse stood back rather helplessly. Harry stood up cautiously, pushed his feet into his shoes, reached for his jacket – and then rushed for the bathroom. He emerged feeling very shaky and slightly foolish.

The doctor had just entered his room. 'Filthy head,' said Harry to him conversationally, 'but I feel much better now.'

'Good,' said the doctor, 'that is good. Please lie down again.'

'I can't,' said Harry, hearing the desperation in his own voice, 'I really can't, I have to be somewhere. Now, at once.'

'Monsieur Moreton, you are not well enough to be anywhere. If you tell me what is the problem, I will try to help, but you really cannot leave this room. If you do, I cannot be held responsible for the circumstances. You have had quite a serious concussion, and you must remain quite still and quiet for twenty-four hours.'

'Oh, don't be absurd,' said Harry. 'While I'm remaining still and quiet, my—' he hesitated, then said firmly, 'a woman is in serious danger. Now will somebody please help me out of this place.'

Cassia started to cry. She knew there was no point in it, that it would probably make things worse, but she felt she had been brave quite long enough and she really couldn't help it.

She couldn't ever remember feeling so alone: even in the moments of greatest crisis in her life, such as when her mother had died or when she had finally sent Harry away, or she had made the decision to give up her medical career, there had always been someone there, even if they had been the wrong person, even if they didn't properly understand. Now there was no one: no one at all.

It was ridiculous, too, she told herself, to be quite so distraught: she was only lost. Only lost: in a strange and seemingly dangerous country, where she did not speak the language, where nobody knew her, and she knew nobody, where she could not ask directions or even find out where she was. The nearest she had to a friend was the taxi driver of this morning, and she was very unlikely to see him again. And worst of all, she had, of necessity, left her handbag behind at Rollo Gresham's house and had no money.

She took a deep breath, fighting down the tears and the panic, and tried to think what to do. She had been walking for at least two hours, and in absolutely the wrong direction, it now appeared; she seemed far from anywhere, wandering along a road which clearly was heading out of the city, rather than into it, cold now and utterly exhausted. And the worst thing was that if a car, or indeed a pedestrian, came in sight, she simply felt terrified, and tried to hide, either in a gate or doorway, or even behind a tree or a shrub.

She had, at one point, been hopeful that she had found the direction at least of the train station, having heard a train starting up not so very far away, but had clearly taken a wrong turn after that, for the sound had never come near again.

The suburbs of the Ville Nouvelle were long lost to her; she seemed to be in some no-man's land, with fewer and fewer houses, fewer people, even – and this was merciful at least – fewer stray dogs and cats. She should walk in absolutely the opposite direction, simply turn round and retrace her steps, but she had done that several times already, and got nowhere: no road seemed to run straight, they all curved confusingly about, leading back on themselves. Or so it seemed in the dark and the cold.

Escape had been simple by comparison: she had sat there, patiently, admirably calm, she thought, drinking with Rollo Gresham, watching him top up his own glass, sipping at her own with minuscule sips; quite quickly he became confused. He was reminiscing much of the time, talking about the old days, in the grandiose terms that alternated with the paranoia, talking of grand social connections, his association with the highest in the land – absolute nonsense, she knew, he had always been a rather dubious figure – telling her how a knighthood had been on the cards. She had sat listening, responding politely, determinedly keeping panic at bay, panic and the inevitable questions, and had finally asked if she might go to the lavatory. He had been surprisingly agreeable, had told Mehdi to show her the way, and she had followed him, carefully noting the location of the front door – it was, in any case, a fairly small house.

She had used the lavatory, flushed it, and then started running taps, so that they would assume she was washing her hands, and then, leaving them running, had come cautiously out. There was nobody immediately outside; she had walked, rather than run, to the hallway, smiling politely to someone she presumed was the cook, carrying dishes across from one room to another, and then simply carried on walking out of the front door.

The gardener was still at work although dusk was falling – that was a dangerous moment – but she smiled at him, cheerily, waved even, and walked quite steadily to the gate and then out into the street. And then she had run, run and run until she was absolutely exhausted, and still run on, waiting, dreading every moment to hear shouts, feet running after her – but they did not come.

A crowd of people were leaving the Marjorelle Gardens. She plunged into their midst, where she was camouflaged, but they then all climbed into a fleet of taxis and she was left alone and exposed once more.

By now it was becoming clear that no one was coming after her, and after all, she thought, feeling almost foolish suddenly, why should they? Rollo had had no evil designs on her, had not planned a kidnapping or even a seduction; she had been behaving like a classically hysterical woman. She imagined him discovering her departure, first angry, then resigned, but hardly likely to pursue her. He would probably return to his brandy sad, but no more than that, sad and lonely, deprived of someone to talk to. She felt, in that moment, almost ashamed of herself.

Osman Jamal was very tired. It had been a very long day, and the American ladies he had taken to Asni that afternoon had been both ungracious and ungrateful. Now he was taking a couple back to the Mamounia after a very long wait for them and their guide outside the Medina where they had dined at the Yacout restaurant, the present favourite amongst tourists. All he wanted to do was go to bed; and indeed that was what he planned to do, but as he got back into his car, having said goodnight to the couple and expressed enormous gratitude for a very modest tip, one of the porters told him that the English lady he had driven up to the Ville Nouvelle that morning had failed to return and that an English gentleman who had arrived was very concerned about her.

Jamal enquired why it was not possible for the Englishman to be out looking for her, and was told that he was confined to his room on medical orders, having been involved in a car accident that afternoon. Someone from the hotel had been sent to an address the Englishman had given, but she had not been there. A small party had been sent out looking for her; there was even talk of involving the police.

Jamal was concerned; he had liked the English lady very much, she had been charming and generous and unusually polite to him. He felt it his duty to go and look for her himself; he would not be able to sleep if he did not. He knew what she looked like at least, which most of the rescue party would not.

He swung his car out of the Mamounia courtyard and in the direction of the avenue d'El-Jedida.

Harry Moreton had phoned Rollo Gresham's house; had spoken to a servant, had been told that his visitor had left a couple of hours earlier. Monsieur Rollo was indisposed, the doctor had been sent for and he was under sedation: there was no question of him being disturbed. But the lady had been perfectly safe and well when she left, although had left her handbag behind; if Monsieur Harry cared to come and collect it, he was very welcome, or it would be brought to the hotel in the morning. For some reason, that above anything else convinced Harry that he was speaking the truth. But it didn't find Cassia for him.

He had tried several times to get up, planning to get a car and simply drive round the streets looking for her, but each time the terrible nausea and pain overwhelmed him; he was literally helpless. And so he lay, fretting and wretched, trying to keep his mind turned away from the vision of her being raped or beaten in some dark alley somewhere and trying also to believe that the search party that had been sent out from the hotel was doing as much as was humanly possible, and had as good a chance as any of being able to find her.

Cassia was walking rather automatically now in the direction she could only pray was the right one, away from the outer darkness of the town as far as she could tell, stumbling slightly in her weariness, shivering violently with the cold, when she heard footsteps behind her. She told herself first that they were nothing, then that they were simply those of another night walker, and hastened her own just a little: and heard them hasten also. She slowed down: so did they. Otherwise the street – wide, empty, menacing, with nowhere to hide – was deserted: it was almost midnight. She felt fright rise in her throat, a physical presence, like bile, felt her guts flushed with hot terror.

She took deep breaths, closed her eyes briefly, then continued to walk, firmly, steadily, towards what appeared to be some streetlights. The footsteps behind her, equally firmly and steadily, were getting nearer.

After a few minutes calm deserted her; she looked over her shoulder, saw a man in white djellaba and turban only about thirty yards behind her, and began to run. At first he continued to walk; then as she began to feel safe, to tell herself he was actually only walking home himself, he increased his own pace. She ran faster: so did he. She could hear him now, hear his breathing, then his voice, speaking incomprehensibly to her.

She turned to face him, said, stupidly in English, please leave me alone, and he grinned, the awful half-toothless grin of Morocco, and moved nearer still. She could even smell him, the now familiar smell of spice and strong cigarettes; she winced, turned her head away, began to run again.

He followed her, lightly, easily, in his soft shoes; she, in her high-heeled English ones, was helpless. She bent down to take them off, and as she bent, she felt a hand on her back, below her waist. She screamed, turned, lashed out at him with her shoes, caught him in the face with them, and began to run again.

He caught her in moments, grabbed her, grabbed her wrists, swearing at her, grinning at the same time; there were no streetlights, but the moon was full and the white walls of the street reflected it. His eyes were glittering, under the turban, his face etched with deep lines, he could have been any age. He certainly wasn't old and he certainly was strong.

Cassia did the only thing left to her, followed the age-old instinct of women in physical danger: she raised her knee swiftly and kneed him in the crotch; because she was so tall, she was able to inflict a considerable blow. He cried out with pain and bent over, releasing her, and she was able to run then, run faster than she had ever thought possible: and then, dear God, she saw another man coming along fast, faster than her assailant even, overtaking him, there were two of them now, how could she survive this, how, why had she ever come to this hideous, awful place, she would be raped, tortured, mutilated, murdered.

She turned to face this new attacker, raised her hands to ward him off, sank on to her heels, crying, whimpering with fear. And heard his voice, familiar, gentle, wonderfully kind saying, 'Madame should have let me wait. Come with me now. Come with me, Madame is safe.'

In the car Jamal had blankets, a bottle of water, a flask of tea; he wrapped her up tenderly, drove quickly in the direction of the Mamounia. Amazingly, she had been only a mile or so from Gresham's house; she had obviously been wandering through the streets, some larger, some small, in ever-more rambling circles. Her method of constantly retracing her steps had worked to an extent, then. She asked him where the station was; he pointed behind them. It was possible, she supposed, that at one point she could well have been near it. She had been walking for hours, she could have been anywhere.

'However did you find me?' she asked.

Jamal shrugged. 'I want to find you,' he said simply, as if that explained everything. 'I will drive until I find you. Many many people worried.'

In that moment, her entire perception of Morocco changed.

They pulled in to the courtyard of the hotel to find a reception committee; she had been sitting, half asleep, shivering still, a combination, she supposed, of shock and the cold, and looked up to see not only the familiar pair of porters flanking the door, but behind them, pushing past them now, the manager, and following him, confusingly a nurse in a rather dated uniform, and behind her again, a large, looming, slightly unsteady figure.

'How could you have been so abysmally, so criminally stupid?' said Harry Moreton's voice, and she looked at him and did not really find it in the least peculiar that he was there, it seemed no more or less surprising than anything else that had happened to her in the last few days, and everything seemed to polarise in that moment, and the entire reason she had come was focused in him, in what he might and might not have done, and because one of those things had become the most important, the most crucially important of all, and heedless of all the other people standing there, the staff and the uniformed nurse and a couple of curious guests: 'Harry, were you and Leonora lovers?' she said.

She did not hear his answer: he had collapsed with a groan on to the steps, his head in his arms.

'Did Gresham tell you that?' he said a lot later, when, distracted from her own shock, she had settled him into bed, had assured the nurse, who at the doctor's suggestion had taken the precaution of giving Harry a sedative, that she would personally see he stayed there, had drunk several cups of strong tea herself and wolfed down a large club sandwich and a bowl of exquisitely crisp, salty *frites*. She found herself suddenly feeling rather cheerful and pleased with herself.

'He – suggested it.'

'And what did you think of the suggestion?' he said, glaring at her from his pillows.

'I didn't know. It seemed ... possible. Suddenly. I'd never thought of it before.'

'Well, thank God for that at least. No, of course I wasn't her lover. It's just the sort of filth he would dream up. I'm horrified you should even consider it a possibility. What the hell do you think I am, that I'd behave like that?'

'I don't know what you are,' she said wearily, 'that's the whole point. I don't understand you, you won't tell me things.'

'What things? What won't I tell you?'

'You know perfectly well,' she said. 'You won't tell me about the money. All along, you've ducked my questions, laid false trails, told me half-truths—'

'Oh, indeed? So that renders me capable of any kind of hideous behaviour, does it? Incest or close to it ...'

'Harry, don't. Please!'

'I cannot bear this,' he said. 'I thought you loved me.'

'I do love you. That's the whole point, why I cared so much. Harry, please, please, try to see things my way.'

'It seems to me,' he said, 'that trust is a large part of love.'

'Of course it is. That's what I wish I could make you understand.'

'Well, let me try,' he said. 'Would you like to give me an example of these false trails, these ducked questions, that you speak of so graphically?'

'All right. I will. You told me you didn't rescue Leonora. From that awful place.'

He stared at her. 'I didn't.'

'No, but your secretary did, Margot Murray did. Didn't she, Harry? Come along, tell me the truth. Just for once, tell me what really happened.'

'Yes, all right. She did. You didn't ask me who rescued her, you simply asked me if I did. I didn't.'

'But you told her to. You sent her.'

'This is ridiculous,' he said, turning fretfully away from her on his pillows, closing his eyes briefly, 'a ridiculous conversation.'

The sedative was clearly beginning to take effect.

'I quite agree.' She looked at him and longed suddenly to hit him; the frustration was so awful, so strong. She wondered, as she had wondered so often, if this compulsion to manipulate, to play games with people, was a legacy of his strange, undirected childhood, the lack of example, of any kind of moral guidance: she supposed it was. If so, it wasn't going to change; and she would either have to learn to cope with it, or walk away from it and him altogether. She sighed. This was not the moment for a decision of that magnitude.

'What do you really want?' he said suddenly.

'I keep telling you. I want the truth. Someone has to tell me the truth. About the money.'

'Ah,' he said, 'that.' His eyes closed again, then opened, fixed on her very steadily. 'And did you get that? The truth? From Gresham?'

'No, well, not all of it. He talked so much nonsense. He's a little mad, I think.'

'Cassia, he's absolutely mad.'

'No, not absolutely,' she said slowly, 'and I still want to know ... Harry, you look terrible, are you all right?'

'No, I'm bloody well not all right,' he said. 'My head hurts like hell and I think I'm going to be sick again. And this inquisition of yours isn't helping, I can tell you.'

'Harry, it's hardly an inquisition.'

'It seems like it to me.' There was a pause, then he said, 'Oh, let's get on with it, tell me what you want to – Christ. Help me to the bathroom would you, Cassia?'

Five minutes later, back in his bed, he was asleep. She looked at him and sighed. She clearly wasn't going to learn very much from him for several hours yet.

Cecily woke up early on Sunday morning, feeling dreadful. Her head ached, she felt sick and, worst of all, she was experiencing considerable humiliation and remorse. How could she have done that, made a scene in the street, shouting at Edwina and Justin? It was appalling. Whatever must they have thought of her, what must Justin particularly have thought of her? She didn't care so much about Edwina. And to think that she had been sorry for Edwina, concerned about her huband's infidelity. That was a joke. Well, she had done it now, as far as Justin was concerned, he would never admire her or respect her again. Not that it mattered; he was clearly having an affair with Edwina. And all this time, all this time she had thought he liked her, found her attractive, possibly even might love her. Of course he and Edwina were far more suited to one another, working in that ridiculous world of theirs; a world she didn't really understand, didn't want to understand even. No doubt they had been saying exactly that to each other that evening: that she didn't understand it, was too dull, too bourgeois, laughing about her, saying how dreary she was ...

'Oh God,' said Cecily aloud, and flung back the bedclothes. She would have a bath and then take the girls to church. And then they were to go down to Dorking to have lunch with her parents; her mother had been very reproachful when she had telephoned, complaining that after all she had done for Cecily, all she had sacrificed for her during her illness, she was clearly now forgotten, cast aside. Yes, she would have a really dreary, dutiful day. The sooner she got back into her virtuous, matronly lifestyle, the better.

Justin woke up feeling also very wretched. The thought of the pain he had inflicted upon Cecily, the humiliation, hurt him terribly; he cared so much for her, had tried so hard to care for her while she had been ill, worked upon increasing her fragile self-confidence patiently and lovingly. And now it had all been undone in one single, savage moment. How could he have been so stupid? Not that she could have been expected to come through Lowndes Square late at night, but he had handled his refusal of her invitation clumsily, had clearly upset her by that. She would probably never speak to him again now, certainly not wish to be with him. He had as little chance of re-establishing their relationship as – well, as of being asked to take the cover photograph of *Style*, an ambition so long held he sometimes felt he had been born with it. The very least he could do was say sorry.

Justin was nothing if not brave. He would try, he would go round, take her some flowers, and if she wouldn't see him, then he could leave them for her. And if she did agree to see him, and then proceeded to berate him, he would deserve it. And he might even get a chance to explain. The only thing was, where could he get flowers on a Sunday? All the shops would be shut, it was hopeless. And there were none that he could pick, not in December, and all he had in his house was a half-dead bunch of roses that he had taken home from some photographic session.

What else could he take her, then? What present was even remotely suitable? Champagne perhaps? He had a bottle of very nice champagne, Veuve Cliquot, that Francis Stevenson-Cook had sent him recently to say thank you for some photographs he had taken at incredibly short notice, of a set of evening dresses on the stage at the Royal Opera House against the set of *La Bohème*. He could take that to Cecily. Of course it wouldn't mean that much to her – her cellar, or rather Benedict's, was stacked with the stuff – but it would be a great deal better than nothing. And certainly better than a bunch of half-dead roses.

He spent over an hour writing a two-line note to accompany it, and then decided he would take it immediately before his courage failed him.

Just as he was leaving his telephone rang: it was Aurora Le Page.

'Justin, darling, sorry to bother you on a Sunday, but I thought you might like to know, I've just left Francis, and he and I both agree that one of those pictures at the Opera House would make a perfect cover ... Hallo? Justin, are you still there?'

'Oh, yes,' said Justin, 'I'm still here, darling Miss Le Page, and I do like to know. I like it very much, in fact I can't believe it. Thank you very very much. And I'd like to tell you, I do see it as a most wonderful omen. Wonderful.'

'Most wonderful what?' said Aurora Le Page, but he had gone. She put the phone down and sat shaking her head at it. Photographers became more absurd every day.

Cecily stood in her bedroom, struggling to do up a skirt, with hooks which proved themselves just slightly unequal to the task. The skirt, bought only a few weeks earlier, was a little tight for her. All the new things she had bought were quite tight, and soon she would be back in her old clothes; she would be fat again, fat and matronly. She looked at herself in the full-length mirror, standing there in her chemise: there was no doubt about it, the old Cecily was coming back, the Cecily with the full breasts and the rounded hips and the dimpled thighs; her brief spell as a sleek, chic creature was over, over for ever.

It wasn't fair, she didn't eat that much, she never touched chocolates, and seldom ate cakes; Edwina wolfed down whatever she wanted and remained sliver-thin. No wonder Justin preferred her, she thought wretchedly, Justin who spent his days with all those beautiful models with their narrow hips and their flat chests, they must be his ideal women, not someone like her.

She tugged again at the hooks, and one of them bent, and the fabric next to it ripped slightly. She pulled it off and threw it across the room, near to tears. She felt absurdly, disproportionately miserable at the sight of it lying there, useless, hardly worn, bought only a month ago.

Dimly, she heard a taxi pull up in the street below, heard the bell ring, who on earth was that, Adams must get rid of them, and then she heard Fanny's voice suddenly, ringing out, laughing, heard her saying, 'Just a minute,' heard her footsteps pounding on the stairs and along to her room, then the door opened and Fanny said, 'Mama, whatever are you doing? You look ever so funny.'

Cecily burst into tears; loud, noisy tears, and then was aware of Fanny looking at her in terror, backing away, her eyes huge, realised just a fraction of a second too late why, that she thought she was having another breakdown, rushed after Fanny as she ran hysterically downstairs, calling, 'Come, quickly, come to Mama's room, quickly,' and she stood there, shocked at what she had done to Fanny, not just then but in the past, over the months before and she cried harder, and went back into her room: and so Justin found her, standing flushed, huge eyed, tear streaked, her hair dishevelled, her skirt still hurled into the corner.

He stopped absolutely still in the doorway, gazing at her, his eyes moving over her, first concerned, then tender, and then something else, something changed, there was something else in his eyes, something she was largely unfamiliar with, but recognised none the less as wonderfully, unbelievably welcome, recognised desire.

He turned to to Fanny who was standing behind him breathing heavily, her small face ashen, and said, 'Fanny, she's fine, don't worry, she's absolutely fine, aren't you, Cecily?'

'Yes,' she said, 'yes, of course I am. I just pricked my finger badly on a pin, the pin of my skirt, it hurt me a lot,' and watched Fanny's face change, grow relieved, relax and then smile.

Justin said, 'I expect she'd like a cup of tea, though, and some biscuits, perhaps. Do you think you could go and ask Cook for that?'

And when Fanny had safely gone, running down the steps, lightly now, shouting happily to her sister that everything was all right, Justin moved forward into Cecily's room and pushed the door shut behind him, still staring at her, his eyes brilliant, and stood in front of her, staring at her as if he had never seen her before, and then he put out his hands and took her face in them, and began to kiss her, really kiss her, kiss her mouth, so that she felt invaded, in every inch of her body, with a flooding warmth and a sweet, curiously uncomfortable pleasure, kissed her on and on, over and over again, and then moved his hands down, very slowly, down her throat, over her breasts, feeling them, stroking them, caressing them, and bent his head and kissed them too.

'You are beautiful,' he said finally, standing up again, standing away from her, smiling into her eyes, 'very, very beautiful. And I love you.'

'I really don't know that we're in the best place for this interview,' said Harry Moreton. 'It's much too pleasant.'

They were sitting on the terrace at the back of the hotel, under one of the striped umbrellas, drinking coffee which he professed strong enough even for his taste. The sun was climbing, the air warm, the bougainvillaea round the swimming pool dazzling, the palm trees' neatly graphic shapes etched against the white-capped mountains.

'It seems a very good place to me,' said Cassia, 'and why shouldn't it be pleasant? And anyway, I know what you're thinking: that you can postpone it yet again, and then again. I won't have it, Harry, I really won't.'

He sighed, leant his head back. Cassia looked at him sharply; he was rather pale, and the lump on his forehead was very large. Perhaps he was right, perhaps he wasn't well enough.

'I don't think you ought to drink that coffee,' she said. 'It's not good for you when you've been concussed.'

'Oh, for God's sake,' he said, 'stop nannying me. It's superb coffee and I shall drink what I like.'

'No doubt you will,' she said, and decided he was perfectly well enough. 'Now please, Harry, please tell me everything. Otherwise I shall go back to London and you will never see me again.'

'Very well, but I would like some more of that excellent orange juice first. Thank you. And perhaps some fruit—'

'Harry, *please*! I have a plane to catch in a very few hours.'

'Very well,' he said, with a sigh, clearly resigning himself finally to the occasion, 'I will tell you. Where shall I begin?'

'At the beginning. It seems a sensible place.'

'All right. Well, Leonora finally contacted me, that spring, shortly after Miss Monkton found her. I think she was too sick, too wretched to struggle on any longer.'

'So you hadn't been to see her that whole year, after she left the Avenue Foch?'

'Once or twice. I was very busy at the time, away a lot, I had no idea she was ill, and when I did go to Paris, she insisted on meeting me in restaurants. You know what she was like, a superb actress, she was always very gay, always full of stories about her life, what a wonderful time she was having. I could see she was thin, pale, but when I asked her if she was all right, she told me that of course she was, that I must remember she wasn't as young as she once was, that when women reached a certain age they became less ... robust, I think was her word. Fussing always made her cross, you know it did. And I saw her in London, once, briefly, in the late autumn, she was staying at the Basil Street Hotel, she seemed pretty well.'

'That must have been when she came over to pawn what was left of her jewellery.'

'Yes, I suppose so. Anyway, when she did finally ask for help, I was away, I was in America. Margot cabled me, I sent her over to Paris, told her to sort things out, find an apartment for Leonora, and went to see her on the way back. It was pretty awful. What she'd been through. I felt very ashamed of myself.'

'As did I. Still do. But, Harry, what – what was it, what had happened?'

'Well ...' He looked at her. 'This isn't a pretty story, Cassia.'

'Oh, for God's sake. I'm a doctor, Harry.'

He hesitated, sighed, then said, 'She had syphilis.'

'Syphilis! Oh my God.'

'Yes. She'd had it for three, four years, apparently. It's a funny disease, I expect you know, it proceeds in stages. She'd come through the first and the second, and it had been latent for a long time, but by then it was getting pretty nasty. She had recurrent fevers, terrible joint pains, and the tissue destruction had begun.'

'Oh, Harry. So it wasn't cancer at all?'

'Oh yes, she had that too. Poor Leonora. Uterine cancer, spreading very rapidly.'

'Oh dear,' said Cassia. She looked down, fighting tears, filled with horror at what Leonora had so stoically endured.

Harry reached over, covered her hand with his. 'You all right?'

'Yes, I'm all right.' She felt angry suddenly, angry and ashamed. 'Why shouldn't I be? I've always been all right, we all have, and all the time poor Leonora was there going through this ...'

'Yes, I know. Anyway, she had contracted it from Gresham, of course. Who knew, knew he had it, had had it for years, didn't tell her.'

'Oh God.'

'Yes, he's a charming fellow.'

She thought of him, as he had been the day before; it all made sense suddenly: the dementia a very specific form with syphilis, the delusions of grandeur, the tremors that she had thought might be Parkinson's, the skin ulcers, the signs of heart failure.

'Anyway, she found out when she first developed the symptoms herself. Then she challenged him and he told her. He'd got it out here, it's pretty rife, as you might imagine.'

'But why did he come out here in the first place? I don't understand.'

Harry hestitated, then he said, 'He's a paedophile, Cassia. He likes little children. They cater for this sort of thing out here, life is cheap.'

'Oh, Harry. I can't bear this.' She thought of those children, the ones she had seen yesterday, so tiny, so pretty, being brought to the house for—

She tried to focus on the mountains, the palm trees, while her brain adjusted to this horror; they were blurred, shifting in her view. A fly settled on her plate, got to work on the crumbs of her croissant; she looked at it, as it went about its disease-spreading task, and thought it seemed to symbolise everything she was hearing, this ugly, evil story. 'Go on,' she said.

'He told her then. She challenged him, about the syphilis, and he told her – not about the children – he presented it as a bad-luck story, he was very good at that. She was horrified, of course, but she felt she had no choice but to stay: she had no money, nowhere to go, and she was still fond of him, in her own way, I'm afraid.'

'Yes. Yes, I think she was.'

'It didn't emerge about the children for some time, until she opened a letter of his one day, by mistake, from a friend out here, and discovered what had been going on. She told him she was leaving, and he told her, of course, that she would get nothing from him if she did. He was losing money hand over fist anyway; and she was helping. She was an appalling liability, financially; I don't think he realised it for quite a while.'

'Yes, I see.'

'Anyway, she left, moved out, sold what jewellery and so on she had. She was all right for a bit, lived somewhere quite nice: then she got through that money, the illness began to resurface, and the cancer was making itself felt and – well, you know the rest.'

'No, Harry. I don't. And why, why on earth did she keep quiet about it? Why didn't she tell us?'

'Cassia, think. Think if it had been you. She'd run away from home, from her husband, to live with a man nobody liked, nobody approved of, and who turned out to be a sexual criminal. One minute she was ensconced in millionaires' row, the next in a hovel, suffering from a sexually transmitted disease. She had committed an unutterable, an unspeakable folly: would you admit to that?'

She was silent.

'Anyway, I went to see her, as soon as I got back, and finally she told me. I think I would have killed Gresham, if he'd walked in that first week. As it turned out, I think he's suffered more. I hope so.'

'So what did you do?' Fear, cold and clammy, was heaving into her stomach.

'I tracked him down. Got him to Paris. I told him I knew about his filthy predilections, and what he'd done to Leonora, that I'd make sure everyone in England, in the world, knew about them. And he was terrified. It would have meant disgrace, imprisonment, if I acted quickly enough. And Leonora didn't want it. She didn't want the disgrace, and I'm afraid she still cared about him.'

'She couldn't have.'

'I think she did. She felt he'd rescued her from a miserable fate in England, given her some good years, unbelievably she felt some kind of gratitude. Pretty stupid creatures, women, I have to say.'

'Oh, Harry, don't. Don't joke.'

'I'm not joking. I'm perfectly serious. Unfortunately.'

'So what happened then?'

'I didn't actually have to do anything. He came slobbering in, said he'd do anything, anything at all to make it up to Leonora, give her money, set her up in style again, he said he hadn't got a lot left, but he'd sell his house in England, give her the money from that, his house in France, anything at all. He'd been disinherited by his father – dreadful old man he was, chip off a most unpleasant block, was young Rollo – but there was still a lot of money about. He said he could get at that as well if he really had to. I just sat there, listening to him, watching him sweating and shaking, and I realised it would hurt him more than anything, to do that.'

'Not as much as the disgrace, if people had known.'

'Perhaps not, but that would have hurt Leonora.'

'While she was alive. Not afterwards.'

'Cassia! Of course it would. It would, it *did* terrify her, to think of people laughing at her, shocked at her, of her name dragged through every sort of dirt, even after she'd died. She made me promise never to tell, and I did promise. I never told anyone at all – except Benedict, of course. He had to know. Not Edwina, not Richard, not anyone. It seemed important to me. Perhaps it was wrong of me, perhaps I should have had him arrested.'

'I think you should. It would have saved some children, at least,' she said soberly.

'I know, I know, and it tortures me, that. Of course he promised it would never happen again, and I swore that if it did I would see him in jail, but how could I be sure? I knew in my heart that I couldn't be sure, but ... I don't break my promises, Cassia. I really don't.'

'Harry, I saw some children at the house yesterday.'

'Christ, did you?'

'Yes, I did. Something has to be done, Harry, it really does. I can't bear to think of that going on and on, with him—'

'It would be very difficult,' he said. 'They see things differently here, you know. The Pasha himself delivers native children to his guests, as gifts, should they so desire. Along with hashish, opium, diamonds ...'

'That's no reason not to try, is it? Anyway, you'd better go on.'

'So I just said, fine, but I wanted that money, all of it, for Leonora, and that I wasn't going to forget about it. I made him put the houses on the market, I made him keep me informed of progress – I made him sweat,' he said, sitting back, looking at her with an expression of great self-satisfaction on his face.

'Yes, I see,' she said again, 'but Leonora was dying, you must have known she was dying.'

'She was dying. But nobody realised how quickly she would go. In the end it was very quick. It was partly the syphilis, it weakened her heart, you know. But that wasn't the point. I wanted to get the money away from him: he deserved it, deserved to lose it, deserved to be brought down as low as she had been, as he had brought her.'

'And then?' she said after a long pause. 'Then what happened? I mean, about the money. And me.' The last word came out very quietly, almost shakily.

'You.' He smiled at her. 'Well, that was the happy bit. For her. She sat there one night, and started crying, became very distressed – she was very frightened of dying, you know – and I was trying to comfort her. She said what should she do with all the money, having got it, how useless it was, in fact, that she hadn't really wanted it, didn't see the point. And I said there must be something, something useful she could do with it. We didn't have to think very long.'

'You thought of me.'

'Yes.' He smiled at her again, the same complacent, self-satisfied smile. 'We thought of you. We thought what it would do for you, how it would rescue you – shall we get some more coffee, it's really awfully good here —'

'Harry, for God's sake! I think this is rather more important than coffee. What do you mean, rescue me?'

'Sorry. I mean rescue you. From your lousy, dreary marriage, your wasted life, your frustrated ambitions.'

'Oh, I see. Do, please, go on.'

He looked at her just slightly uncertainly, then said, 'She loved you so much. And she knew I loved you. I'd always told her everything, she knew why I'd married Edwina, all of it.'

'So the money was from her, after all? From Leonora? Or so you would like me to think?'

'Cassia, what is the matter with you? Yes, of course it was. She loved the idea of giving it to you. She saw it as a way of making things right.'

'For her.'

'Well, yes. And for you, surely?'

'I don't know,' said Cassia slowly. 'I mean, I don't know that it has.'

'What on earth do you mean? It's done all the things we thought it might do for you. It's given you your life back. It's made it possible for you to have a career again. I've got you back.'

'Exactly. You've got me back, and all the other things you wanted, you thought were right for me, you and Leonora.'

'What do you mean?'

'Harry, I don't know how you see this, but I see it as a piece of appalling manipulation. Manipulation of my life. The thought of the two of you sitting there in Paris, saying this will do it, this will be good for her, this will break up her marriage, her family—'

'You're being ridiculous,' he said, slamming his glass down.

'Am I? Am I really?'

'Yes, you are. It was – is a legacy, that's all. Lots of people come into money, are left it by relatives, they don't start rambling on about manipulation ...'

'This money isn't quite like an ordinary legacy, though, is it, Harry? In the first place, it's horrible money, I hate the thought of it, where it came from, and in the second, it seems to me it was acquired by slightly dubious means.'

'Dubious! What on earth do you mean by that?'

'I'm afraid I mean it smacks of blackmail to me. What you did.'

'Cassia, you really are crazy. Blackmail! That man helped to kill Leonora, abandoned her, continues to conduct his disgusting life, about which he begged me, literally with tears in his eyes, to remain silent.'

'Exactly. He bought your silence.'

'Of course he didn't. I kept silent for her sake, because I promised Leonora.'

'That's a matter of interpretation, I would have thought. Actually.'

'Well, this is rich!' he said, leaning back in his chair, staring at her. 'You'll be telling me next that he doesn't deserve such treatment, that you're going to go round there and mop his filthy brow and give him his money back.'

'I'm not going to mop his brow, but I shall probably give the money away. No, not to him, he shouldn't have anything, he should be locked up, I want him locked up, but—'

'But what? Now I've heard everything. Everything.'

'Harry, I don't want that money. The very thought of it now makes me feel sick.'

He sat looking at her, an expression on his face of such total bafflement that she almost laughed.

'You just don't understand, do you?'

'No. No, I don't.'

'Let me try and explain again. There you sat, you and Leonora, with this vast, this obscene amount of money to play with. Saying what shall we do with it. And then saying let's give it to Cassia, because she's unhappy, she's got her life all wrong, and we know how to make it all right again. We know what's best for her, we know what will happen, she'll leave her husband and go back to her career, and maybe come back to London and then might even embark on an affair with me, Harry Moreton—'

'Jesus, Cassia, what is this? You really are mad, you know.'

'I'm not mad. Didn't it occur to you, enter that great arrogant ego of yours, that I might be perfectly capable of taking charge of my own life? Didn't it? No, it wouldn't, because you don't really know me at all. You never really listen to me and you never really think about my life, you just think of what you want me to do, want me to be. Harry, if I'd really really wanted to change things or go back to medicine, I'd have done so anyway, without your interference.'

'No, you wouldn't,' he said, and he was starting to shout now. The occupants of the other deckchairs and umbrellas turned to look at them. 'You were too bloody stupid and too much under the thumb of that pathetic, half-brained man you're married to.'

'Don't talk about Edward like that, Harry, please.'

'Oh, so you're becoming loyal all of a sudden, are you? I don't recall much loyalty when you lay in my bed and told me you loved me, I'm afraid. When you moved back to London for days at a time. When you—'

'Shut up,' she said, 'just shut up.'

'I will not shut up. What did you want us to do, Leonora and I? Say look, Cassia, if you like we'll give you some money to play with?'

'There you are,' she said, 'you've just admitted it, that you were both giving me the money, the pair of you, plotting it together. That's what makes it so ugly. You cold-bloodedly discussed what the money might do to me and my life, and decided it was a good idea.'

'But what,' he said, and he was patently trying to be calmer, to understand her, 'what would you have liked us to do?'

'I'm not sure, but the very fact that it was all surrounded in secrecy, in strange half-truths, proves that you felt guilty about it, that I wouldn't be happy with it—'

'That's a filthy lie. It wasn't surrounded in secrecy, it was a perfectly sound, legal arrangement. I felt it better, safer for the money to be in trust for Leonora, I had no idea how long she was going to live, how soon she was going to die, it was only because you developed this obsession—'

'Yes, and I was right. I'm sorry, but I can't accept any of what you say, even if you believe it yourself, which I very much doubt. You and Leonora have made me a pawn in your rather perverted chess game and I don't like it. God, when I think of the appalling fuss you made about my one small indiscretion with Rupert – that really is pathetic. Well, I'm not going to play your game any longer. I'm going home, and I'm going to try and put things right there, and I shall be extremely grateful if from now on you excise me from your life, as I shall you from mine.' She stood up. 'Goodbye, Harry.'

He looked up at her and gave her a rather odd smile. 'I shouldn't bank on the doctor taking you back,' he said, 'letting you back into his house even.'

She stared at him. 'What do you mean? The marriage may be over, but I have my children to think about, and besides, I'm going to—' She was stopped by a gentle tap on her shoulder.

'Madame Fallon, your car is here. To take you to Casablanca. And we have your handbag in reception, Jamal went to collect it this morning for you. If you are ready, madame ...'

'Yes,' said Cassia, 'I'm quite ready. Thank you. I've nothing left to do here.'

And she turned her back on Harry and stalked into the hotel.

CHAPTER 39

Cecily lay in the large, soggy, slightly lumpy bed in Justin's house in Clapham and wondered how something so extremely physically uncomfortable should provide such extreme physical pleasure. She had spent several hours in it now, had gone to the house as soon as she had seen the girls off to school – and it was now, she realised, looking at her watch with a certain sense of shock, almost time for them to come home for tea.

'I shall have to go soon,' she said, reaching out her hand, pushing Justin's floppy hair out of his eyes; he caught the hand and kissed it.

'But you will come back?'

'Well, not today, but would you like to come to supper this evening?'

'No, my darling. Correction, I would like to, but I really do have to do some work. And not at Edwina's house, either, don't look like that. Tomorrow night perhaps?'

'Tomorrow night. The girls will be thrilled. It's nice you and they have such a mutual admiration society.'

'Not as great as the one you and I have, I hope.'

'Maybe not.'

'I love you,' he said simply, 'very much. And you are – well, magnificent.'

'Don't say that,' she said with a shudder, 'it sounds fat.'

'Cecily,' he said, leaning over her, kissing first one breast then the other, 'you must rid yourself of this obsession about being fat. You are perfectly, beautifully, sensuously divine. I adore your body, it's luscious and glorious and I drown in pleasure in it.'

'You do talk nonsense,' she said, laughing.

He looked hurt. 'I do not. It's all true, every word.'

He lay back, gazing into her eyes, his own probing hers, and memory, physical memory, stirred Cecily literally; she turned to him, imperceptibly thrust her body towards him, the trickles of desire, so recently spent, beginning to flow, unbelievably, again.

He reached out his hand, placed it on her stomach, began to massage it with immense tenderness, his thumb reaching down into her pubic hair; Cecily moaned gently, put out her own hand and he took it, kissed it, guided it down, down to his penis, erect again now. She smiled, half embarrassed, for until today lovemaking had been swift, furtive, scarcely acknowledged, she had had no experience of the looking, the smiling, the talking, the delight of it all.

Justin, reading this, laughed aloud, and said, 'My darling, don't look like that, don't you like what you see?'

'Yes,' she said, shyly, 'very much, of course I do but—'

And he said, 'I'm sorry, sorry to tease you, come here, quickly, now,' and then he was in her again, smoothing, pushing her slowly, gloriously into the dazzling new country she had discovered that day, a country of light and shade, noise and silence, surging waves to be scaled, up, up into the great white churning brightness and then a rolling surf of pleasure to be ridden down again, tumbling down, down into the sweet peaceful quiet below.

'That was wonderful,' she said afterwards, 'so wonderful.'

'No, you were wonderful,' he said. 'I can't believe how wonderful you are, in every way. I can't believe I've found you.'

'Nor I you,' she said, and was silent, smiling at the unlikeliness of it all, of the unhappy, unfulfilled woman she had been, transformed into this joyful, easy creature who lay beneath her lover and cried aloud with pleasure: and perhaps more importantly still, who felt valued, desirable, and the absolute centre of someone else's life. It might not last, it could not last, she felt, but for now at least she could make the most of it, learn from it, learn to be happy.

'I shall never let you go again,' he said, as if reading her thoughts.

'Don't be foolish,' she said soberly, 'our lives are so different, we are so different, how could we—'

'Shush,' he said, putting his fingers over her lips, 'don't say it. Of course we are different, that's what makes it so wonderful, we are indeed so different, but each exactly what the other needs.'

'In some ways,' she said doubtfully, 'but—'

'But what? There are no buts. Cecily, I need you. I need you to make me feel safe. That's the most important thing, more important than anything, more important even than love. And how do I make you feel, tell me that?'

'Safe,' she said.

'Well, there you are, then,' said Justin.

She didn't argue any more. She still felt he might be wrong; but for the foreseeable future she didn't care. And the unforeseeable future could take care of itself.

Cassia reached Croydon at lunchtime the following day; she was faintly surprised and immensely relieved to see her car still in the parking area. She was short of time: Bertie's concert was at four. If anything happened, if she got a puncture or broke down, she would be late, and he would never forgive her.

She was so exhausted, she couldn't even think, certainly couldn't feel. Her only conscious emotion was an appreciation of the weather, which seemed to her to be wonderful: cold, grey, windy. That in itself was a great relief.

The events of the past four days were somehow tangled in her head, she was unable to make any sense of them, incapable of even reflecting upon them. She felt neither happy nor unhappy, peaceful nor angry; she had no capacity within her for any emotion whatsoever. It would return, no doubt, she would surface to pain, awful pain, as from an anaesthetic, but for the time being she was safe from it − it could not touch her.

'Look, look,' shouted William, who had been at the window since lunchtime, 'it's Mummy, she's here, she's here,' and Bertie, who had been up in his room reading, refusing to show any interest and concern any more, so certain had he been she would not come, threw his book down, slid down the banisters and into her arms, occupied already by William, with whoops of joy.

Edward, who had been in the study, doing accounts, had heard the car, and the whoops, but refused to get up to go and greet her.

Janet put her head round the door. 'Mrs Fallon's back,' she said, smiling, 'so she'll be able to go to the concert with you. Isn't that good news?'

'I suppose so,' he said, 'yes, yes, of course it is. But you will come too, won't you?'

'Dr Fallon, I can't. Who will look after Delia?'

'Peggy can look after Delia,' he said firmly. 'You've kept this household going these last few days, and I want you to come.' He went back to his accounts.

After a few minutes, the door opened and Cassia stood there, an arm round each of the boys.

'Hallo, Edward.'

'Hallo,' he said shortly.

'Mummy's been to Africa!' said Bertie, his eyes shining with pride, rather as if Cassia had discovered the entire continent herself. 'On an aeroplane, isn't she clever?'

'Oh, extremely clever,' said Edward, standing up, stalking past them, not even looking at Cassia.

Bertie looked up at them, startled, his small face anxious; then he recovered, took Cassia's hand, dragged her into the sitting room saying, 'Tell me all about it. How big was the aeroplane? Were the people all black? What language did they speak? Could you understand them ...?'

Janet appeared. 'Welcome back, Mrs Fallon, we're so pleased to see you, and just in time too. Dr Fallon has asked me to come to the concert as well, and leave Delia with Peggy. Will that be all right with you?'

'Yes, of course,' said Cassia. She was too exhausted to wonder at the strangeness of Edward requesting Janet's presence anywhere.

William sang beautifully, the descant verse of 'Oh, Come All Ye Faithful', his sweetly rich voice reaching out and up into the darkness, the tallest reaches of the church. Cassia sat between Edward and Janet, watching him intently through rather blurred eyes, watching his face, fiercely serious, his eyes fixed on the organist, and thought how extraordinarily literal was the phrase 'lump in the throat'. Opposite him in the choir stalls, with the bigger boys, stood Bertie; equally serious, equally intent, but occasionally daring a glance at her, as if he could not be quite sure that she was really there, had not vanished again. She smiled at him, each time, reassuringly, examining him foolishly for signs of all the trauma she had inflicted upon him; finding, equally foolishly, none.

She sat absorbing this moment, this utterly English occasion, in the dark, cold, candlelit church, the great Christmas tree standing to the right of the choir stalls, the crib to the left of it, the organ playing carols, tunes as familiar as her own name, surrounded by smiling mothers and stiff-faced fathers and smaller siblings, unnaturally neat and well dressed, contrasting it with what she had left behind only yesterday – the heat, the smells, the dust, the dark faces, the flowing robes, and her own fear – and unable to believe very fully in any of it.

The solo, the whole concert ended; and the church emptied gradually, people shuffling out of pews, looking for their children, greeting one another, smiling, saying how hard it was to think it was Christmas again. Edward stalked ahead, looking neither to right nor left, but Cassia moved more slowly, chatting, receiving compliments on behalf of William, saying to this person, yes, they would love to come for a drink over Christmas, to another that, no, she hadn't done all her Christmas shopping yet, and moving finally out into the cold and the darkness, where Bertie and William had joined Edward and Janet and were jumping impatiently up and down, demanding their supper. And then they all went home.

After supper – impossibly strained, with only Janet's cheerful, optimistic presence to ease it – the children went, protesting, up to bed, and Cassia said to Edward, 'May I talk to you?'

'What about?' he said, his face so angry, so bleak as he looked at her, that she was frightened.

'The future.'

'Oh, that,' he said.

'Yes. What we are going to do, whether you have made a decision about the practice yet—'

'Oh, well, that is easy at least. Of course you can't have it. I would no more dream of handing this practice over to you than to Bertie. In fact, I rather think he would make a better job of it.'

'What? Edward, what on earth are you talking about? You seemed so receptive to the idea before, I don't understand. Look, I'm sorry about my absence, but it was crucial. I will explain, of course, but I had to go—'

'To be with Moreton, I suppose. I don't think I want to have it explained.'

She stood there, staring at him, and felt as if she were falling, very fast, into some kind of deep swirling vacuum. Finally, she said, 'You know about that?'

'Yes, Cassia, I know about that. I was informed by his wife, as a matter of fact. Very neat, don't you think?'

Why on earth hadn't Harry warned her, told her they all knew? God, how she hated him. 'Edward, I'd like to explain.'

'Look,' he said, and his face was white, contorted with rage and a dreadful misery she could scarcely bear to confront, 'I don't really want any explanation. I don't care what you do now, Cassia. It is of little interest to me. You have lied, and lied to all of us, you have neglected your children, you have humiliated me beyond endurance. My dearest wish would be that I need never see you again. Sadly that cannot be, at least for the time being. We have the children to make arrangements for. But don't, please, insult me by pretending you can explain. It all seems very clear to me. You've been sharing his bed for months, years for all I know, all our marriage, while putting up your obscene front of self-righteousness, and I find it disgusting. Abhorrent.'

'Edward—'

'Be quiet!' he said, and she thought for a moment he was going to hit her. 'Be quiet. I don't want to hear from you. You've always been attracted to him, I knew that. You were in love with him when you were a schoolgirl even, certainly after you met me. I dare say it was part of your plan.'

'I didn't have a plan,' she said, hearing her own voice rising, cracking with rage, 'I did not have any kind of plan. I had nothing to do with Harry for years and years, all the time we were married—'

'How very virtuous of you!'

'Shut up!' she shouted, losing her own temper now. 'Shut up, I'm not trying to make excuses, I'm trying to tell you how wrong you are, I was not sleeping with Harry Moreton until—'

'Until when? When exactly? I'm so interested to know.'

'Until a few months ago,' she said, her voice very low, 'when I knew our marriage was over.'

'Oh, I see. Very commendable. Please forgive me for misjudging you.'

'But you do misjudge me!' she cried. 'You do, you do. I tried so hard for so long, while we were married, I tried to be good—' They were standing up, quite close to one another, confronting one another: oddly symbolic, drawing up sides in battle, two opposing armies.

'Oh, for Christ's sake!' he said. 'Please spare me this self-sanctification, Cassia. It is, of course, extraordinarily unusual and noble for a woman to be faithful to her husband, to try to be good, as you put it. Except in that hideous circle that your friends, like Harry Moreton, move in. And I'm sorry, incidentally, you should have had to try so hard. I imagined, foolishly that our marriage was happy, that there need not have been too much effort involved in it all. I was wrong, it seems. What a failure I have been, in every possible way.'

'Edward, please don't start that!'

'I don't have to start it,' he said, 'because it has always been so. I should never have had anything to do with you, Cassia, let alone married you. It was a disaster for me the day I met you. I hope you realise that.'

'And for me,' she cried, driven from patience finally, 'for me as well. You love to present yourself as the injured party, don't you, Edward, as the poor, oppressed husband, but it's unfair, utterly untrue. All those years you oppressed me. You wouldn't let me near this practice in any way, you kept me out of it, occasionally allowed me to mix up some glucose and water, or bandage a knee. You wanted it all for yourself, to be the great, the all-powerful doctor. You were afraid I'd show you up, be in some way your equal, not your superior even, but your equal. Are you really so surprised I went my own way, with my own friends, my own—'

'Your own lover, in your own bed, in your own house in London. You're little better than a whore, Cassia, a—'

'Stop it! Stop it, stop it!' A small violent presence had entered the room, pushed them forcibly apart: it was Bertie, his face ashen, with two spots of high colour on his cheeks, his eyes wide, horrified as he looked up at them. 'It's horrible, I hate you both. You promised, you promised you'd be friends, that you wouldn't get divorced. Why did you say that if it wasn't true?'

'Bertie, Bertie, darling.' Cassia reached down to him, tried to take him in her arms, to comfort him; he pushed her away, his small chest heaving.

'Don't do that. Don't. It's true what Daddy says, you're always going away, always leaving us here. William was crying last night because he thought you'd miss the concert.'

'Bertie, I—' She dropped her arms in despair.

'Bertie, come here.' Edward reached out to him now, but Bertie turned on him like a small fury.

'No. I hate you too. You're horrible, not letting Mummy help you. Why can't she look after the practice, why not? Just because Maureen said she couldn't—'

'What?' said Cassia. This pierced even her concern over Bertie. 'What was that about the practice?'

'Nothing,' said Edward, 'not now, for Christ's sake.'

She accepted it, tried again with Bertie, to reach him somehow, to comfort him. 'Bertie, come along, darling, let's go and sit down and talk about this.'

'No. I don't want to, there's nothing to talk about.' Bravado suddenly deserted him; he stood there between them, rather uncertain suddenly, looking down at the floor.

Edward put out his hand, tried to put it on Bertie's shoulders; he pushed it furiously away.

'Bertie.' A soft voice spoke from the doorway; it was Janet. 'Bertie, do you want to come upstairs with me?'

'No,' said Bertie sulkily, but he hesitated, then walked slowly towards the door.

Janet looked at them both as she ushered him through it, gave them a rather weak smile. 'I'm sorry, I thought he was in his room. He'll be all right with me for a bit.'

Cassia and Edward looked at one another silently across the vast yawning gulf that had been their marriage. And then she turned and went up to the room that had become hers and lay down on the bed, fully clothed, and wept until she could weep no more.

'Cassia! Cassia, wake up, for God's sake.' It was Edward: she struggled to sit up. It was still dark. 'Bertie's gone.'

'What do you mean he's gone? Where's he gone?'

'I don't know. That's the whole point. He's run away.'

'Run away! Oh, Edward, no, he can't have done, when, how—'

'I don't know,' he said. 'He was asleep when I went to bed, I checked on him.'

'Yes, and I did in the night. I got up to go to the lavatory, and checked on him then, I was afraid he'd still be crying.'

'What time was that?'

'Oh, about half past three.'

'What time is it now?'

'Just after six.'

They were to repeat these details many, many times over the next few days.

Janet had discovered Bertie's absence. She had got up at five thirty, hearing Delia crying, had settled her and then gone to check on Bertie herself. His bed had been empty, and she had assumed he was downstairs, making himself a hot drink, something he was allowed to do now. But he wasn't there; he wasn't anywhere in the house. After a few minutes she had woken Edward – Edward, thought Cassia, pain piercing her, why Edward, why not me, have I really become so much less of a parent? – and told him what had happened.

The three of them searched the house, the garden; Edward took out the car and drove down to the village, round the lanes, came back grim faced. It was still dark; that somehow seemed to make it worse.

'He can't have got far,' Cassia kept saying over and over again, 'not in the dark. There aren't any buses, nothing, and surely, surely ...' Her voice tailed off, she was afraid to finish the sentence.

'He wouldn't have taken a lift?' said Edward. 'God knows.'

'Oh, Edward, I've always told him not to, never, ever to get in a car with anyone, go off with anyone he doesn't know.'

'I know. But ...' But driven by misery, by desperation, children did anything.

'Oh God,' she said.

'We'd better tell the police.'

'Shouldn't we check with his friends first, just to make sure he hasn't gone there, or to Peggy's maybe, or Mrs Briggs?' Anyone would have told them, of course, if Bertie had arrived, unheralded, in the middle of the night; but it was something to grab at, a hopeful straw to clutch.

'I think, Dr Fallon, Mrs Fallon, we should tell the police,' said Janet. 'The sooner they know, the sooner they can start looking.' She was pale herself, clearly very shaken.

'Yes, of course,' said Cassia. 'We will. Janet, sit down, you look terrible.'

'I blame myself,' she said, 'I should have heard him, I don't understand it.'

'Janet,' said Edward firmly, 'you are the last person to feel any sense of blame. If it had not been for you, he would probably have gone sooner.'

Cassia looked at him, briefly angry again, thinking he was casting stones at her; but he was beyond such a thing, he was just staring in front of him, desperately shaken. 'Yes,' she said quickly, 'that's true. Don't blame yourself, Janet, for a moment. Come on, then, Edward, you'd better do it.'

It was a terrible phone call: it seemed to make the whole thing darker, official; Bertie had ceased to be a little boy who had run away, had become a missing child, possibly abducted.

Edward put the phone down, very gently. 'They're coming round straight away,' he said, 'to interview us.' He walked heavily into the study and shut the door; Cassia looked after him helplessly.

The police – or rather one constable – arived at about eight. William was awake now, very shaken, but excited by the drama, by Bertie's courage.

'He didn't say anything to you, William, did he?' said Cassia desperately. 'Anything at all?'

'No. I just heard him crying, when I was going to bed. I went in and he told me to go away. He wouldn't tell me what the matter was.'

Police Constable Allen was large, self-important, sternly kind. He took a painstaking description of Bertie, so painstaking, in fact, that Cassia thought she might scream. They managed to establish what he was wearing by a process of elimination: grey shorts, brown jersey, brown shoes, school raincoat.

It was comforting to find his sports kitbag: it seemed to indicate he might just have gone for a long walk, rather than planning to stay away. On the other hand his money box was empty: 'But he only had threepence,' said William, 'he'd bought Christmas presents with the rest.' That seemed almost more unbearably poignant than anything.

They searched the house, in every possible place, even absurd places like the garden shed; they looked in their own letterbox for a note, but there wasn't one.

'Is that a good sign, do you think?' said Cassia to PC Allen. 'I mean, does it mean he doesn't intend to stay away?'

PC Allen raised his thick eyebrows in the direction of the ceiling, shook his head. 'I really don't know, madam,' he said. 'You never can tell with youngsters.'

Cassia had been standing by the window, dredging up the courage to ask the terrible, the almost unspeakable question. 'PC Allen, there isn't – there hasn't been any kind of – of trouble recently, has there? With children? I mean, well, you know—' She stopped, unable to continue; she kept hearing Harry Moreton's voice saying 'he's a paedophile', kept seeing those children leaving Rollo Gresham's house, wondering how many such people there were in England, in its safe green country lanes and villages, rather than in hot, dusty, fly-ridden cities far away.

He looked at her in silence as if wondering exactly what to say to her, then, 'Well, madam, not as far as I know, not in this area, no. But we never can be sure, of course, we must always be watchful, and they're very cunning, these people, very cunning indeed. They get the children's trust, give them sweets, that sort of thing.'

'Oh,' said Cassia, 'oh, I see. Well, I don't think Bertie would fall for that. I have talked to him about it—' But often, she had heard, the people who abducted children were known to them, people they trusted, people they thought would never harm them.

'Now I'm sorry,' said PC Allen, 'but I must ask you both whether there's been any trouble at home, anything to upset the lad, an argument perhaps?'

'Yes,' said Edward finally, after a short silence, 'yes, there was an argument last night, I'm afraid, between my wife and me.'

An argument, thought Cassia, remembering the horror of it, that screaming, abusive, violent exchange: that hadn't been an argument, it had been domestic violence.

'I see, sir. And the lad witnessed this, heard you, did he?'

'I'm afraid he did, yes.'

'And he seemed upset, did he?'

'Yes. Yes, I'm afraid so.'

'Right. Well, that could explain why he went. It's often the way, I'm afraid. On the other hand, if it is the case, the children come home again, once they've had a chance to cool down a bit. So try not to blame yourselves too much. Resilient little things, children. Now then, I think that's everything for now. I wonder if you have a recent picture of the lad that we can circulate to the other stations in the vicinity?'

'Yes,' said Cassia, 'I have one, wait.'

She ran up to the spare room. There was a picture of Bertie by the bed, she had framed it when he went off to school, taken on the day last summer that Sir Richard had come down, the day she had heard about Miss Monkton visiting Leonora in Paris. Bertie was standing holding his cricket bat and laughing, his hair flopping over his face, his skinny legs and arms tensed, waiting for the ball; he had been all right then, she thought, it had been before any of these traumas – before school, before Collins, before any of it – just a normal happy little boy with a normal happy family.

If only she could turn the clock back, or rather the calendar, how differently she would have behave, how differently things would turn out, and Bertie would still be sitting here, at the breakfast table, eating his toast, making a mess, and she would be saying don't use your own knife, Bertie, use the butter knife with the butter. How could she ever have cared about such things, crumbs in the butter …

'Here you are,' she said, holding it out to PC Allen, 'this was taken in September, he hasn't changed very much since then.'

Not so that you could see it, perhaps.

The postman arrived, saw PC Allen leaving. 'Anything wrong, Mrs Fallon?'

'Yes,' she said, 'yes, there is. Bertie's missing, he's run away.'

'When was that, then?' said the postman.

'Oh, this morning. Early,' she said, and burst into tears.

'Oh, now, you don't want to upset yourself,' he said, patting her shoulder awkwardly. 'Boys will be boys, always running away. I was always running away myself, led my mum a fine dance. He'll come home when he's hungry, sure as anything. I bet you five bob he'll have turned up by six o'clock tonight.'

But six, and then seven and eight o'clock came, and the postman had lost his five bob.

Bertie approached the gates of St John's, the gates he had been driven through that last time by his mother, with feelings of such intense relief; the lights of the school were on, everyone must be having supper. He wasn't quite sure now why he had come, it seemed a bit stupid suddenly, but he had just felt that if he was here, if he could make himself remember exactly how unhappy he had been, how desperate, it might help, might make the new trouble seem less awful. He remembered vividly sitting on his mother's knee, warm and safe and comfortable for the first time for weeks, when she brought him home – and telling her he would rather come back here than she and his father were divorced. He'd thought he would just go in, wander round a bit, and try and think how bad it had been – and then he'd phone home and tell them where he was, ask them to collect him.

He was very cold now, though; very cold indeed. There was an icy wind blowing and he only had his short trousers on. Stupid, that, but then he hadn't thought about the cold when he'd got dressed. Where could he shelter just for a bit, while he thought, tried to decide what to do? Maybe the chapel: yes, that was an idea. He'd go in there, sit for a bit, and then – well, then maybe he'd just go home anyway. He didn't need reminding about the misery. He could see already that it had been worse than his parents quarrelling. Even worse.

Bertie slipped in through the door – it seemed almost warm inside – and sank into one of the pews. He was very tired, very, very tired; he'd been walking all day, except for that one bus ride he'd spent his last threepence on; it'd be nice to sit down, have a rest. He lay down, on his side, pulled his legs up on to the seat. Just for a few minutes, only a few minutes.

They had phoned everyone they knew in the area, everyone Mrs Briggs and Peggy knew, every parent of every child at the school; and then started on everyone they knew in London.

Rupert seemed a possibility; Bertie had adored him, it seemed quite likely he might have gone to find him, to talk to him. They asked Cecily, of course, Fanny and Bertie had become great friends, 'Fanny might have heard from him, even,' Cassia had said, frantically waiting to be put through to Cecily; but Fanny hadn't, she was upset when she learnt that Bertie was missing, said in her sweet middle-aged way that she would certainly keep an eye open for him. They even phoned Edwina, for Bertie had seemed to rather like Edwina at Laurence's christening, had pronounced her pretty – but all in vain. None of them had heard from or seen Bertie.

He wouldn't panic, Bertie had told himself, when he heard the key turning in the chapel door, when the caretaker had not seemed to heed his hammering and his cries; they would be back in the morning to unlock it for morning prayers, and then he could escape. It was cold, and very lonely, but it was all perfectly all right, he could pile the choirboys' cassocks on to him to keep warmer, and get through the night somehow. It was dark and a bit scary, of course, frightening shadows and funny noises, a sort of scuffling that made him jump and want to scream at first, until he realised it was the mice. There were lots of mice in the organ loft, it had been one of his few happier memories at the school: boys in the choir, Bertie among them, had taken bits of cheese down to feed them; nothing to be frightened of there.

And there was a tap in the little vestry, where the cassocks were kept, he could get a drink if he was thirsty: yes, he'd be absolutely fine till the morning. And then he could get out and ask if he could phone his parents. It would be all right. Of course it would.

Much later, after school supper, at which the headmaster had congratulated the boys on their singing at the end-of-term service, he went down to the caretaker's cottage to make sure he had locked the chapel and the other outbuildings.

'We won't be back till after Christmas, Worthington, want to make sure everything's safe and sound. Don't want any odd characters coming in.'

Worthington assured him he had locked it very carefully. 'And made sure the cat wasn't in there, sir, of course. We don't want her starving over Christmas, do we?'

'No,' said the headmaster, 'we don't.'

The police had begun to search for Bertie in earnest on Tuesday morning. The first day, they had simply been circulating his picture, showing it to stationmasters, guards, bus conductors, professing a certain confidence; now on the second they were clearly more worried, searching the woods, barns, the riverbank, were talking of diving in the local gravel pit. When they said that, Cassia only just got to the lavatory in time; she came out, green and shaking, to find Edward in the hall, looking for the first time since she had come back from Morocco almost friendly.

'Are you all right?' he said.

'Yes. No. Oh, I don't know. This is so dreadful, Edward, and I did it, it's my fault.'

'No,' he said, quite sharply, 'no, you mustn't say that, it's not your fault entirely, or mine. We both did it, we are both to blame. Come along, come and sit down, you look all in.'

Astonished, she followed him into the kitchen and let him make her a cup of tea.

★

By lunchtime on Tuesday, Bertie's fists were raw with beating on the great door of the chapel, and his voice hoarse with shouting. He was also extremely hungry.

He had woken when it was still dark, waited for the light to come, shaking with terror; his only companion, his only comfort, his watch, with its luminous dial and nice, comforting tick, given to him by Edward when he first went away to school. He stared at it, taking in the time, five o'clock, thinking how long it would be before it was time for prayers, when he would be released, and only stopped himself screaming with a huge effort. Later he wondered if screaming might have helped; someone might actually have heard him in the still darkness.

As light came, he felt better, calmer: told himself it was after all only a matter of hours now before they came. And later, much later, heard the cars arriving endlessly ... and then leaving again, and as the day wore on, a terrible, dreadful silence.

Cassia sat by the telephone all day, occasionally sleeping briefly. She had paced the house all night in a terrible restlessness, feeling somehow that if she sat down, was comfortable even for a moment, she would be betraying Bertie. Edward had his own restlessness, would take out the car every two or three hours, and drive round, in an ever increasing radius, simply looking for him. 'I know it's probably quite useless,' he said, 'but I feel I have to do something.'

Very late on Tuesday evening, as she woke from some fitful half-sleep, cold and unbearably stiff, the phone rang. She snatched it up; it was Harry.

'Cassia?'

'Yes. Yes, hallo, Harry.'

'Sorry, did I wake you?'

'No, what time is it?'

'Eleven. I just got back from Morocco. Edwina told me about Bertie. Have you found him yet?'

'No. No, we haven't.'

'I'm so sorry,' he said, 'so terribly sorry. Is there anything I can do?'

'Only find him,' she said, and burst into tears and put the phone down. She could feel no hostility towards him any more, nor anger, as she could not towards Edward; all the emotion in her had been absorbed, consumed by her misery and her fear.

Bertie was so cold now he could hardly think; he tried to keep warm, to do his best, he knew that was important; he remembered that Scott of the

Antarctic, whom he had read about recently, had stressed you must not get too cold, or you just fell asleep, and he kept stomping round the chapel, beating his hands against his sides at regular intervals all morning, determined to keep his spirits up as well as his temperature, but as it grew dark again, he began to despair and crawled into his pew, covering himself with his cassocks, so hungry it hurt, a terrible awful pain, and prayed, earnestly and for a long time, that someone would find him soon.

He realised now that it was possible that no one might come until after Christmas and that he would by then be quite dead; but he tried very hard not to think about it. He couldn't, he mustn't. If he did, he'd stop trying. He knew you could live for a long time just on water, that however hungry you were, you didn't die while you had water, but on the other hand, he thought he might die of the cold.

Prayer seemed the best thing, and God must surely listen more attentively to someone in a church than anywhere else. He couldn't think of many prayers, so he just said the Lord's Prayer over and over again, and in between, a more desperate 'Please, please, God, let someone find me soon'. He finally fell asleep, but he had forgotten to wind up his watch and had no idea what the time was when he woke again. And that did make him cry, and he really did feel alone.

On the Wednesday morning, there was a police message on the wireless, asking for information that might help them find a small boy called Bertram Fallon – answering to the name of Bertie – 'three foot nine inches, brown hair, brown eyes, last seen at his home at …'

Cassia sat there, listening to the description of this little boy, answering to the name of Bertie, who was her son, and began to feel herself going mad.

She was quite sure now he was dead; she saw his body, lying cold and still in some ditch or barn, had come to regard death indeed as the better option, better than the alternative, than abduction, sexual – what was the official phrase? – sexual interference. Her mind created and veered away from and then re-created hideous visions of small, trusting Bertie, lured into an alliance, subjected to some hideous abuse, from which even if he was rescued he would never recover.

William became very distraught that morning, and it was impossible to comfort him. He cried for hours, begging her to tell him where Bertie might be, what might have happened to him, and Delia had picked up the misery in the house and cried endlessly as well. It grated on Cassia's nerves so badly that she finally snapped and slapped Delia hard, on the leg; she looked at it, the red mark, the symbol of her bad mothering not only of Delia but of Bertie as well, and started to cry herself.

Janet came in, picked up Delia and soothed her and offered to make yet another pot of the tea they were all existing on. 'Don't feel badly about Delia, Mrs Fallon, she's fine, and I can see you're at breaking point. Look, why don't you go and lie down just for an hour or so? I'll wake you immediately if there's any news at all.'

She refused, but then lay down anyway, and then fell asleep, waking again to hear the phone ringing; it was the police, someone had seen a child answering Bertie's description in Birmingham.

'Birmingham! But how, why? Oh God, oh my God—'

The policeman was gentle with her. 'Don't take too much notice of it, madam, this happens with a radio appeal, it's doubled edged. That's why we postpone it for a while. People ring in all the time. The calls all have to be followed up, obviously, and nine times out of ten it's someone quite different, but yes, the Birmingham police will be alerted.'

It happened three more times: Bertie had been seen in Oxfordshire, hitching a lift on a farmyard lorry; in Glasgow, going into a bus shelter; in St Ives, running along the beach.

'It can't be him, it can't,' said Cassia. 'It's some kind of a vision, a ghost they're seeing—' and then stopped, realising that Bertie might indeed be dead, have become a ghost

For some reason, these calls broke Edward's spirit; Cassia went into the study halfway through the morning and found him weeping at his desk. She had no emotional reserves left to help him, and went out again quietly, closing the door behind her.

He came out after about an hour, tear stained and pale. 'You wouldn't come for a walk, would you?' he said. 'I feel I need some fresh air.'

'Edward, we can't both go out,' she said sharply.

Janet stood up and said, 'I agree with that, but would you like me to come with you, Dr Fallon? I would quite like some fresh air myself.'

'Yes,' he said, 'yes, that would be very nice, thank you.'

Watching them leave the house together, Cassia experienced, for the first time since Monday morning, an emotion that was nothing to do with Bertie. She wasn't sure, but it seemed to be hope; and why, she certainly could not imagine.

Bertie had more or less given up trying to keep warm now; he was so hungry it seemed easier just to lie still. If he kept absolutely still, he had discovered, he didn't feel the cold so much; and a rather nice feeling was beginning to take him over, a sort of dreaminess. He had done a bit more praying, but he was beginning to give up hope in God as well now.

Maureen was taking all the surgeries; she was clearly upset and glad to be able to do something to help. Cassia looked at her as she rushed off that day in the middle of a very snatched meal to visit a toddler whose mother had phoned up hysterically with reports that he had swallowed some bleach, and wondered why she had disliked her quite so much.

When Maureen came back, she said tentatively, 'Was the baby all right?'

'Oh, yes. It wasn't bleach, it turned out to be gin. And only a bit. I think she thought if she said that on the phone I wouldn't come. People are very strange.'

'Yes, they are. And that woman is notorious, a nightmare, always leaving stuff out where her children can get at it. It was some aspirin tablets once before, poor little thing had to be stomach-pumped. What did you give it, lots of milk?'

'Yes.' She looked at Cassia warily. 'I'm so sorry, Mrs Fallon, about Bertie. I haven't really said it to you before. Still no news?'

'No, no news.'

'It must be terrible for you.'

'Yes,' said Cassia briefly, 'yes, it is.'

'Mrs Fallon ...'

'Yes, Maureen?'

'There's something on my conscience. Something I feel very bad about. I shall say this to Dr Fallon as well, but I feel I must say it to you. Dr Fallon asked me if I thought he should let you have the practice, when he goes to do his membership. He just wanted another opinion, to help him make up his mind. It's very important, of course.'

'I'm aware of that,' said Cassia coldly. 'Do go on.'

'Well, I'm afraid I said I didn't think it was a very good idea.'

'Yes, I rather gathered that from Bertie. Why not, Maureen?'

'I was being very small minded, I'm afraid. And I'm sorry, very sorry. I think you'd be marvellous. I'll tell Dr Fallon so.'

'Thank you, but don't worry about it. I really can't care about anything at the moment.'

'Well, it's very nice of you to be so generous.'

As it began to grow dusk again, Bertie lost hope and stopped trying. He didn't even bother with the water any more, he didn't seem to be so hungry or thirsty, and the trip to the vestry to get it seemed long and exhausting. Better just to lie still, and let the dreaminess take over. He couldn't shout any more, he wasn't strong enough, nor could he beat on the door: the cuts and bruises on his hands were hurting quite a lot, and anyway, it wasn't worth it, nobody was going to hear. Nobody at all, he was going to die here, alone with God. God and the mice.

He lay, curled up on his pew, and thought about his mother, whom he loved so much, who was so warm and loving and so much fun, thought about sitting on her knee, curling up on her lap, although he was much too big to do that really, but sometimes he still did it, talking to her, telling her things; she always listened to him seriously, never dismissed his worries as foolish, his stories as boring. Even if she did go away a lot working, it seemed worth it when she came back. Perhaps he would never see her again. And the last things he had said to her had been so terrible: he had said he hated her, that she was horrible.

He didn't mean it, or about his father: he loved them both, he wanted to see them again more than anything in the world. It was very, very sad that they couldn't be together, but if they couldn't and if he could only see them separately, tell them he loved them both, that would do. Nothing was worse than the thought of dying here alone, and never seeing them again, never telling them he loved them both, that he was sorry he'd said such awful things. They were saying awful things too, to each other, but they could all say they were sorry, sort something out, start again. But you couldn't start again if you were dead.

There were three more sightings of Bertie that afternoon: then at about four the phone stopped ringing. The thought of another hideous night, with all its attendant visions, filled Cassia with horror. It was very cold and had started to sleet; surely no child could survive out in this, she thought, not for a third night, a child dressed only in school shorts and a raincoat. She sat staring out at the gathering darkness, listening to the wind shrieking, shrinking from it all, from what Bertie must be going through. She put her head down on her arms, as Edward had done earlier, and started to cry: and having started became hysterical, unable to stop. It was very quiet in the house; Edward had gone out on a call, to a desperate woman whose husband was having a heart attack, he said he must go, and she had said, yes, that he must.

Dimly through her sobbing, she heard the phone ringing, on and on, nobody answering it. Where were they all? What were they doing? Finally, she hauled herself on to shaking legs and dragged herself to it, fearing, knowing it was yet another useless call, another false sighting. She picked it up, unable to say anything, simply sobbing uselessly down the line.

'Cassia? Cassia, it's Harry. Listen, I've had an idea. Where was that school Bertie went to?'

She knew it was absurd, impossible, but it was an idea at least, something to pursue. Shaking, shuddering, she phoned the school, the headmaster's house. There was no reply. Well, they would have broken up, of course, there wouldn't be anyone there. So he couldn't be there. Could he?

But he might.

She could go down there. She might be able to get in, climb through the hedge or over the gates. There was the lodge, where the caretaker lived, that was worth a try. Yes, she would go.

It seemed a very long thirty miles, in the dark and the sleet. She only saw half a dozen other vehicles all the way; everyone was very sensibly staying at home. As she drove on, the sleet turned to snow; the road became slithery, dangerous. Surely it had never taken this long to get to the school before. She remembered the day they had first brought Bertie, a warm, golden September day, how she had kept looking at him, sitting quietly in the back seat, smiling his strained, polite smile: she seemed to remember that journey passing in minutes.

The school was on the further outskirts of Arundel. She had to make her way through the town, and she twice took a wrong turning, missed signposts in the dark; the second time she had to ask some people the way, and sat listening to them as they directed her, and they might have been speaking Chinese for all the sense it made, and she drove on blindly, still down the wrong road.

She had no idea why she was pursuing this rather wild idea so fervently: common sense told her it was almost certainly a wild goose chase, but there was a glimmer of logic in it that gave her hope. And anything was better than sitting by the telephone.

She found the school finally, passed a farm gate she remembered on what she knew was the wrong side of the road, swung round in mid-lane, skidded, hit a large log with her nearside wheel. Cursing, she got out, terrified of a puncture, but apart from a couple of heavy dents in the wheel, it was unscathed.

And then, wonderfully, she saw in front of her the lights of the caretaker's lodge. She slammed on her brakes, skidded on the icy ground, jumped out of her car and ran, shouting, towards the door.

'Well, I haven't seen a boy,' said Mr Richards, slightly crossly, as if such a thing would have been rather distasteful, 'not since they all went home.'

'And when was that?'

'Oh, yesterday morning. About midday. It's been very quiet since then, of course and—'

'Yes, I'm sure it has. Can we look, though? Can we go over to the school?'

'Oh, I don't know,' said Mr Richards. 'I'd have to get the headmaster's permission, of course, and—'

'Mr Richards, my little boy has been missing for three days. Anything is worth a try, now can we please go over to the school?'

Bertie had seen the car lights: they swung briefly through the darkness of the chapel. He had been asleep and had woken just before they came. He lay there, stupefied with cold, wondering if he should do some more shouting and screaming, as he had each time he had heard a car before, and decided he couldn't be bothered. It was such a struggle and his hands hurt so much, and they never heard him anyway. He pulled the cassocks back over his head, and tried to go to sleep again.

The headmaster had been out to a cocktail party, and was not pleased to see her on his return, associating her as he did with trouble and the confrontation of his school's shortcomings. He had heard about Bertie's disappearance, he told her, on the wireless, pointed it out with some kind of strange satisfaction, as if it confirmed his belief that Bertie had always been troublesome, that it had been him, not the school, at fault

It was quite impossible, he said, that Bertie was anywhere on the school premises, the cleaners would have found him, the school had been cleaned from top to bottom at the end of term.

'I don't care how clean it is, I want to go over it. Now.'

He looked at her and recognised his defeat; they toured classrooms dormitories, lavatories: no Bertie.

'You see, I did tell you,' he said, 'he couldn't have been here.'

'Outside, outbuildings?'

'Only the cricket pavilion.'

'Let's look there.'

'Mrs Fallon—'

'Let's look.'

The cricket pavilion was empty; so was the lavatory block by the playing fields, the scene of so much of Bertie's torment.

'You see, Mrs Fallon, he isn't here, it's really quite impossible.'

'Yes, well, thank you for looking.'

'I'll escort you back to your car.'

She felt he was doing it more to make sure she had left the premises than to be courteous. They walked back to the car in silence.

'Well,' he said, holding out his hand, 'I hope you find him. I'm sure you will, he's probably just being naughty.'

She had forgotten how much she disliked him until that moment; but she had no strength left to argue with him. 'I hope so,' she said, getting into the car, starting the engine.

'Happy Christmas, Mrs Fallon.' He hesitated, then clearly feeling he should say something pleasant, 'We missed Bertie at the carol service. He has a lovely voice.'

She smiled at him, unable to speak, swung the car away from the house, towards the gates.

Bertie heard the car leaving again, driving off, and burrowed deeper into the cassocks. He had been right not to try: whoever it was would never have come.

A quarter of a mile down the lane, Cassia suddenly heard the headmaster's voice again, took in his words. The carol service! The carol service. In the chapel. She had forgotten the chapel, set back, halfway up the drive, they all had. Was it worth trying there? Probably not. And it meant more arguments, more pitting her exhausted will against other people's strongly resistant ones, but ...

She felt shocked at herself. How could she possibly give up on Bertie, fail him, while there was the faintest drift of hope? She braked violently, turned the car in the road, and drove back.

'He couldn't be there,' said Mr Richards.

'Why not?'

'Well, I locked it up before the end of term,' he said, as if that made perfect sense, 'the night before.'

'I'm afraid,' said Cassia, 'that doesn't seem to me a reason at all. Come along, Mr Richards, let's go.'

'I'll have to ask,' he said, glaring at her, 'have to ask again, and it's late, tomorrow would be easier.'

'And tonight would be safer. Bertie might be starving in there. Do you

680

want to have his ...' she paused, brought the dreadful words out ... 'his death on your conscience?'

Mr Richards looked at her, reached for his keys.

Janet was just trying to persuade William to eat his supper when she heard the phone. She could hardly face it, hearing yet another futile message, or another person enquiring if Bertie had been found, was tempted to let it ring. Then she took a deep breath and went out to the hall and picked it up.

Edward, returning from his patient, walking heavily into the hall, saw Janet standing by the phone, saw her replace it very gently in its cradle, saw that she was crying, tears streaming down her face.

'He's dead, isn't he?' he said, after a long silence. 'Bertie's dead?'

'No,' she said, 'no, he isn't, he's alive, Mrs Fallon's got him, he's all right.'

'Oh God,' said Edward, and because it seemed the most natural, the most inevitable thing in the world, walked forward to where she stood and put his arms round her. 'Shush,' he said, 'don't cry, it's all right. Everything's going to be all right now.'

William had come out of the kitchen, had heard everything; he looked at them standing there, the two of them, and said, 'Where's Bertie? Where's Mummy?' adding, staring up at them interestedly, 'Why are you shagging?'

Edwina was working at the desk in her sitting room when the phone rang; she went down to Harry in his study, and said, her voice most unusually trembly, 'It's Cassia, she wants to speak to you. Bertie's been found.'

She heard Harry saying, 'I just went over and over in my head everything I knew about Bertie, and it seemed it might be possible,' and, 'I do listen to you, Cassia, you see, I do think ...' There was a silence, and then his voice, very quietly, 'I love you too,' before she closed the door.

EPILOGUE

12 May, 1937

Trafalgar Square did not look quite its staid self as dawn broke on the morning of 12 May, 1937; quite apart fom the flags flying proudly from all the large imposing buildings set around it, and the bunting draping every conceivable and drapable space, it was lined from edge to edge with people in sleeping bags, most of them already awake, many of them not having slept at all, drinking tea from Thermos flasks, waving Union Jacks at anyone who came past, and the more determinedly lively of them already singing. They were in one of the best possible places in the country that morning, those people, had the perfect view, for through Admiralty Arch, particularly proudly decked with flags, they could see right down The Mall, and would be able not only to watch the coronation procession as it came along Whitehall, but then to make their way towards the palace when the royal family returned and came out on to the balcony.

Peggy and Mr and Mrs Briggs were in that crowd, had travelled up the night before, since the family were all in London, and only Maureen Johnson remained, minding the practice. She was very sniffy about the coronation, Peggy remarked to Mrs Briggs, had said to Mrs Fallon, or rather Dr Fallon, she never could remember to call her that even now, that she had not the slightest interest in any of them, and would be pleased to be on call.

'She's got no fun in her, that one,' she said, and Mrs Briggs said she'd often thought the same herself, but she wouldn't be there much longer, and it had been very good of her to turn down her new job, in order to ease the new doctor in for six months or so.

'Not that I can think of her as the doctor, least of all the new one, but there you are, she seems to be making a wonderful job of it, everyone's very happy with her. I wouldn't have thought she'd want Dr Johnson there herself, but still, they seem to get on quite well most of the time.'

Edward Fallon, who had been up most of the night dealing with several emergencies, culminating in a rather dramatic tracheotomy and its attendant problems, decided he would go to bed and sleep through the coronation. Like Maureen Johnson, he felt no interest in any of the people concerned, linked as they were in his mind with a rather long and very painful personal chapter in his own life, but at nine o'clock the phone rang in his small room with a message to call a Miss Fraser as soon as possible.

Edward sighed, although fairly happily, and went to the nearest telephone, which was not really cleared for personal calls, but he felt, on account of having made rather a good job of the tracheotomy, he deserved it. He phoned Janet Fraser, who was sounding extremely cheerful and lively and told him that her new employers, a very nice family in The Boltons, had given her the day off, that she would really like to try and catch a glimpse of the procession, and was Edward free that day, as he had thought he might be, having completed a seventy-two-hour stint on Casualty.

Edward said that he was, but that he was very tired and really had very little interest in the procession, and Janet said she was sorry, but that neither of those excuses seemed very acceptable to her, and if Edward really wished their relationship to flourish, as he had indicated many times over the past few months, then he must try to be a little more positive about everything; and then added, laughing into his rather indignant silence, that she was only teasing, and she wanted to see him anyway, but if he was too tired then she'd have to find someone else to go with her.

'I'll come and watch the beastly thing,' Edward said, hastily, and Janet said she didn't want to hear him telling her how beastly it was all the way through, she wanted him to enjoy it, and as her father had always told her and as she always told all her charges, enjoying things was simply a matter of determination.

'All right, I'll come and enjoy the beastly thing,' said Edward, 'but can I have a couple of hours' sleep first?'

'As long as it's only a couple. Would you like me to come and wake you up? I think I can find that nasty little room of yours by now.'

Edward said he would like that very much indeed.

Cecily and the girls were going to watch the procession from a balcony in Whitehall, outside the office of an erstwhile colleague of Benedict's.

Cecily, who was not feeling very well that morning, was less enthusiastic about it than she had expected, but the girls were very excited, particularly at the prospect of seeing the little princesses riding in the coach.

'It'll be just like the end of the pantomime, won't it?' said Stephanie. 'Do you remember, when we went to see Rupert at Brighton, when he was Buttons?'

'I wish Justin could come with us,' said Fanny. 'He makes things so much more fun always.'

'Yes, he does,' said Stephanie, 'I love Justin. I wish you'd marry him, Mummy, then it would be fun all the time. Why won't you? Then we could be bridesmaids, we've never been bridesmaids ...'

'I'm not going to marry anybody just so you two can be bridesmaids,' said Cecily firmly.

'You don't have to marry anybody, you've got to marry Justin. Why won't you? I know he wants to marry you.'

'How do you know that?'

'Well, he's always kissing you and calling you his darling.'

'There's more to marriage than that,' said Cecily slightly primly.

Justin was setting up a rather difficult shot in the blissful peace of the studio in a Style House rendered utterly still and quiet by the national holiday, when Cecily phoned. He was surprised; he had thought she would already be on her balcony, as he called it.

'Hallo, my darling. Why aren't you helping the King and Queen to be crowned?'

'It's not time to go just yet.'

'I'm sorry I can't come,' he said.

'It's all right. Honestly. I'm sorry I was cross about it. I was being silly. Of course it's a good opportunity for you.'

'It is. And then I can enjoy you this evening with a clear conscience.'

'Yes. Justin?'

'Yes, Cecily?'

'Fanny and Stephanie were just telling me they want to be bridesmaids. At a wedding. Soon.'

'Oh, really?' he said, slightly absently. 'Whose?'

'Ours.'

There was a long silence, then he said. 'But, Cecily, you said—'

'I know what I said. But maybe I was wrong. And two years seems a rather long time suddenly. Also I've just got a feeling I might be bursting out of any frock I had to wear soon.'

'What? Darling, we're not back to the fat phobia again, are we? I thought we'd got that well and truly behind us.'

'Well,' said Cecily, 'there's fat and fat. And I've got something else to tell you, Justin. I was sick this morning. And yesterday.'

'Poor darling. I'm so sorry. Why do you think— Oh, Cecily. Oh, my God. Oh, heavens above. Look, just go and lie down immediately and wait for me, I'll find a taxi and come over, straight away.'

'You'll do no such thing,' said Cecily severely, 'you must finish your photographs. Otherwise I'll think they were an excuse, to get you out of watching the coronation. I'm perfectly all right now, honestly. I have experienced this sort of thing before. But a June wedding might be rather nice, don't you think?'

'Divine,' said Justin, 'absolutely divine.'

Edwina Moreton was watching the procession from another vantage point, an office in Trafalgar Square, in the company of Francis Stevenson-Cook and a few other close friends. Later that evening she was giving a dinner party at her very chic new house in Cheyne Walk; much of the *beau monde* of London would be there, all hoping that they, or their clothes or their houses, might find a mention in the dazzling new column she had launched in *Style* magazine called 'Talk About ...', a wonderful blend of gossip and fashion, a microcosm of the magazine itself, as she had explained it to Francis Stevenson-Cook when first proposing it. She had become very well known very quickly, on the strength of that column, photographed, quoted, in demand everywhere. That was not only an inevitable but a most fortunate result of it, supplying her as it did with an ongoing source of material. So much admired was the column, indeed, that there was talk of it being launched in American *Style* in the autumn, and she had been invited to New York to meet the social editor there.

'Edwina, darling, you look marvellous.' It was an old friend from her debutante days, rushing at her from across the room. 'Lovely to see you, haven't seen you since you became so frightfully famous. Is your gorgeous husband here?'

'Not really my husband any longer,' said Edwina cheerfully. 'We're getting divorced as soon as is humanly possible.'

'Oh, darling, I'm so sorry ...'

'No, no, don't be, it's the most amicable divorce ever, we're great friends still, see each other for lunch at least every two weeks, it's really much better all round, he's far nicer to me these days.'

'Oh, splendid,' said the woman, slightly uncertainly, 'I'm so glad.

Well, I've often thought James and I would get on much better if we weren't married, perhaps we should follow your example?'

'Yes, good idea,' said Edwina, slightly vaguely, 'only I do warn you, you need a frightfully good lawyer, you have to make sure you're going to get exactly what you want. Even Harry made a bit of a fuss about the house, it is rather large, but then I told him I needed a decent place if I wasn't going to regret the whole thing. I mean, we both needed it to be … right, after all. Now you must excuse me for a moment, I'm needed over there …'

In a large Victorian villa on the outskirts of Dorking, known as Maple House, about a dozen young women were sitting listening to a very graphic account of the coronation procession on the wireless, and toasting the King and Queen and the little princesses from the bottles of sherry that had been supplied by the Fallon Trust for the occasion. The two or three dozen children who were staying in the house, as their mothers enjoyed what the trust described as a respite, were playing in the garden under the watchful eye of three of the five girls employed to help the mothers get the most out of their respite.

Later there was to be a party in the garden, and the tables were already set up, red, white and blue bunting hanging between the trees, and a Union Jack from every window. The older children were engaged in blowing up red and blue balloons which the younger ones were in their turn popping rather determinedly, and two of the mothers who had tired of listening to the wireless were carrying out the big gramophone through the french windows to provide music for the party.

There was great excitement because the local paper had come to interview Mr and Mrs Douglas, who were in overall control and ran the house for the trust; it had attracted a great deal of attention, being the flagship in what was to be a series of similar establisments.

The official purpose of the charity, which was itself called Respite, was to provide what amounted to a holiday for exhausted young women, overburdened with children, their bodies worn out with too much childbearing, their spirits worn down with caring for their innumerable offspring and their demanding husbands. The women, who had usually heard about Respite through the Birth Control Association, could apply for a week or sometimes even a fortnight's break there, with their children; a panel for the trust, appointed by Dr Cassia Fallon, assessed each case on its merits. It had only been going for a few weeks and there was already a long waiting list; so far, despite the most gloomy prognostications from a great many people, most notably Mrs Ada Forbes

– who was nevertheless a most tireless chairlady of the charity committee of Maple House – only two of the hundred or so young women who had already been granted a stay there had taken advantage of the situation and helped themselves to more than the food, lodging, companionship and sensible advice which was offered to them. Most of them simply returned to their homes and their lives refreshed, although already a handful – to the great satisfaction of all those in charge, but especially Dr Fallon – had decided they would like to bring about some more dramatic change in their circumstances, and were doing such heady things as taking correspondence courses, looking into the possibilities of training as short-hand typists, or even nurses when their children were a little older.

The reporter, having finished his interview and taken some photo-graphs, was invited to stay for the party in the garden, but refused, explaining that he had several street parties to cover that afternoon; but as he told Mr and Mrs Douglas, having thanked them for giving him his interview, he had been pleasantly surprised to find the atmosphere of Maple House most impressively cheerful and calm.

'Oh, they all expect us to be somewhere between the workhouse and Bedlam,' said Mrs Douglas cheerfully, 'we're quite used to it,' and she went out into the garden to lead a patriotic singsong, commencing with 'Rule, Britannia'. It was that sort of day.

Rupert Cameron had not been watching the procession because he was rehearsing. Jasper Hamlyn and James Piggott had both decided that *Letters* should be brought up to date, made absolutely topical to incorporate and capitalise upon coronation fever, and Piggott had written two more letters which Hamlyn was now insisting went into that night's performance; it didn't *sound* very complicated, as Rupert said plaintively, but it meant other adjustments throughout the piece, final phrases moved along, and it was actually very complicated indeed.

'Rupert, darling, don't be difficult,' said Jasper Hamlyn.

Rupert wasn't often difficult, but he was very tired and beginning to feel the strain of doing *Letters* eight times a week for eight months. Moreover, ever since the night of the abdication, when he found himself so surprisingly holding her in his arms, he had found working with Eleanor an appalling strain. Unrequited love was a terrible thing in any case; sitting on the stage with her, speaking words to her of passion and regret, hearing her returning them, and then watching her hurrying off home to her own life as the curtain came down, her own emotions so clearly untouched, was a nightly torture.

He had regretted it so much, that moment; absolute madness. She had been so clearly embarrassed afterwards, had pulled away from him, said she must be getting home, had refused his offer of seeing her to her train even, and next day had been patently anxious to make it clear that she wished nothing more than that they should be friends again. He knew he was not the sort of man she was attracted to; she liked serious, intellectual people, not foolish, vapid ones given to extravagant chatter. Her husband had been a professor of botany, nothing to do with the theatre at all, and she had often told Rupert how she admired cleverness, the ability to think, to originate ideas above all things. Rupert could not remember an idea he had originated in his entire life.

And, of course, she must think him such a fool; chasing after young girls, indulging in endlessly unsuitable love affairs. He had even embarked on one such relationship since that night, in an endeavour to cure himself of the new aching, tender longing for Eleanor; more swiftly disastrous even than usual, and of course she had known, had teased him about it.

She had not yet arrived for the rehearsal, and he had to struggle through the first of the new letters with Jasper Hamlyn reading in for her; by the time she arrived, flushed with excitement, having seen the whole procession, without planning it at all, from the corner of Parliament Square, he was very irritated indeed.

'I was walking through, you know, just on the off-chance, and I saw the tiniest gap in the crowd and just worked my way forward, it was wonderful, I was overcome with patriotic zeal.'

'Really,' said Rupert severely, 'I thought you of all people would have regarded the whole thing as lot of hysterical nonsense.'

'So would I,' she said, looking at him rather seriously, 'but somehow, you know, seeing the wonderful coach and the pair of them in their crowns, and little princesses and the old Queen, so brave and imposing – suddenly you felt it was terribly important, a historic moment. Especially standing there, so near the Houses of Parliament. Sorry, Rupert.'

'Well, I'm very pleased for you,' he said, rather severely, feeling not pleased at all, 'but perhaps now we could get on with real life. We have a great deal to get through in very little time.'

'Yes, of course,' said Eleanor, coolly, taking off her coat, 'and then, when we break for lunch, I have some news for you all.'

She's getting married, thought Rupert; she's found some filthy intellectual to marry her and originate ideas, and felt extremely sick.

'You'd better tell us now,' he said, anxious to get it over, hearing his voice still irritable and hating himself for it, 'then we can get back to work. What is it?'

She looked at them slightly nervously, and then visibly took a deep breath. 'I'm leaving the play,' she said, quieter, less elated suddenly, 'just as soon as you can find someone else. Of course I will stay as long as I possibly can, and I hate the idea in some ways, but I've had an offer of a film, in Hollywood, and my agent says I must accept.'

There was a very long silence, then, 'What film?' said Jasper and Rupert in absolute unison, and an absolute unison of tone, outraged disbelief.

'It's a version of one of Somerset Maugham's stories, "The Letter". I am to play the lead. I can't tell you more now, but they are prepared to pay for me and Portia to go out there, and that will be wonderful for her, of course.'

'Darling, that is simply wonderful,' said Jasper, going over to her and kissing her. 'I don't know how we shall manage without you, but of course go you must. How thrilling, how very clever of you.'

'Thank you,' said said, smiling at him, returning the kiss. 'Yes, it is exciting, and Portia is beside herself and already planning to find Fred Astaire and offer her services to him.'

And Rupert then, in a performance which he knew would have won him an Oscar, smiled too, said, 'How marvellous, darling, I am so terribly proud of you.'

And then they stopped even pretending to rehearse and went to the pub, where Jasper managed to procure a bottle of rather inferior champagne, and they toasted her and her success, in between toasting Their Majesties, along with all the other occupants, and then went back to the theatre 'just for the briefest runthrough,' said Jasper, 'then you'll both have to improvise, oh, God, Rupert, how are we going to manage without her?' and Rupert, still doing his Oscar-winning, said he couldn't imagine, but it was so exciting, they couldn't begrudge it to her for a moment, and then finally at about half past three, she excused herself and went to her dressing room to find an aspirin, 'I've got a headache, too much champagne, so silly of me,' and was gone for rather a long time.

She came back looking rather pale, and fluffed the same line three times. Rupert, running out now of Oscar-winning qualities, snapped at her, and told her she should try to remember she wasn't quite a Hollywood star yet and retakes were unfortunately impossible in the theatre. She stood looking at him in silence for a moment, her face flushed, and then ran out off the stage.

'You bastard,' said Jasper, 'you unutterable bastard. Go and tell her you're sorry.'

Rupert made his way to Eleanor's dressing room; he knocked on the door. She didn't respond, and he knocked again and then again, and said,

'Eleanor, I'm sorry, so sorry, it was a dreadful thing to say, please forgive me.'

Still no answer: he tried the door but it was locked. Half exasperated, half anxious now, he went down to the stage doorman's office and took the dressing-room pass key from the hook.

It was still difficult to open the door, the other key being in the other side, but it finally worked. He opened it carefully, cautiously, half expecting to receive a stream of abuse, and found her sitting silently in front of the make-up mirror, tears pouring down her face. Her reaction seemed rather extreme to Rupert; his remark had not seemed to him so unpleasant as to quite justify this reaction. But a lifetime of working with women, falling in love with them, knowing them intimately, had taught him that logic seldom entered their emotional equations.

'I'm so sorry,' he said again, 'I shouldn't have said it, I ought to be put up against a wall and—'

He was unprepared for what happened next: a pot of make-up-removing cream flew through the air and struck him on the side of the head. 'Don't say it!' she shouted. 'Don't say you ought to be shot, or strung up, I can't stand it.'

He yelped with pain, sat down, clutching at his head where the cream had landed; it felt damp, and he felt something warm trickle down his face. 'It's blood,' he said, staring rather stupidly at his reddened hand. 'You've cut me.'

'Good,' she said, 'I'm glad. I hope it hurts. I hope it hurts you as much as you've hurt me,' and then, as if suddenly hearing herself, clapped her hand over her mouth, and said, 'Oh, Rupert, I'm so sorry. Really so very sorry.' She reached for some cotton wool, started rather ineffectually dabbing at his head with it.

'If you really want to hurt me, you're doing well,' he said. 'That's making it much worse.'

'Good,' she said. 'I mean – oh, God, I don't know what I mean.'

'Why are you so angry with me?' he said. 'I don't understand, it's so unlike you.'

'Yes, it is, isn't it?' she said. 'Utterly unlike me, Eleanor, sweet, gentle, patient Eleanor, never being difficult, never making a fuss, just listening to you quietly, all your bloody troubles. Well, I've had enough, enough of the whole bloody thing, I'm worn out with it, months and months of it—'

'What bloody thing?' he said. 'I don't understand. I was so pleased for you, I'm sorry I said what I did, but I was tired and my head ached and—'

'Are you really pleased I'm going?' she said. 'Really, really pleased?'

'Yes,' he said carefully, back on Oscar-winning form, 'yes, of course I am. I'm delighted,' and then she sat down in her chair and burst into tears again.

And then Rupert understood.

'You,' he said a great deal later, after he had kissed her a great many times, and told her how much he loved her, had been told how much she loved him, had allowed her to clean up the cut on his head and give him some medicinal brandy, had told her she was on no account to go to Hollywood on her own, that if she was intent on going, he would come too, and *Letters* could take care of itself, had heard that she dreaded going, she had hated Hollywood the one time she had been there, that all she wanted to do was stay in London, and probably give up acting altogether, that, yes, she would be quite happy keeping house for an actor, that would be absolutely fine …

'You, Eleanor Studely,' he said, 'you should be put up against a wall and shot. Fancy not telling me all this earlier. Emancipated woman like you.'

'So how did you find the procession?' said Harry Moreton. They were having dinner at the Connaught; the dining room was looking astonishingly cosmopolitan, full of visiting dignitaries from overseas for the coronation.

Cassia had taken the children and Tessa, the new nanny, to see the procession and had left them eating fish and chips (out of newspaper, their chosen treat) in the kitchen at Walton Street. It had been a rather uncomfortable evening; Harry was in a strange mood, awkward, truculent even, interspersed with an almost aggressive cheerfulness.

'Wonderful. The King embodied virtue and reliability, the Queen looked very beautiful, and the little princesses were enchanting.'

'Lucky King,' said Harry, scowling at her.

'What do you mean?'

'I mean he's managed to find a woman whose only ambition is to look after him and him alone, or him and his children, not hundreds of sick and depressing people. Aren't you tired of that practice of yours yet, Cassia?'

'No, Harry, I'm not, I'm blissfully happy. I'm sorry your plan has misfired so badly, but it's really very nice for me.'

'What on earth do you mean?'

'I mean that here I am, thanks to you and Leonora, running my own medical practice, and it's absolutely wonderful.'

'Yes, well, it might be wonderful for you. It's pretty hellish for me. I only get to see you about once a week, twice at the most, and then you're quite liable to rush off and deliver a baby or something. Will you come home with me tonight at least?'

'Harry, I can't. I have to be at Monks Ridge very early, to take morning surgery. I'm sorry.'

'So am I. Don't you want to come home with me, sleep with me?' His voice had risen slightly; the people at the next table looked at them interestedly.

'Yes,' she said quickly, 'yes, of course I do, but – well, I told you. I have to get back. We're driving down very early in the morning.'

'I really don't know how much longer I can stand this,' he said.

'Harry, I'm very sorry. I don't quite see what I can do about it, though.'

'No, so you keep saying. It seems very obvious what you can do about it to me. When I think of all the time you wasted, all those years we could have been together. Cassia, please, please will you marry me? Soon. Come and live with me. Please.'

'Live with you where?'

'In my house. Of course. Where else?'

'Harry, I keep telling you, I can't do that. I'm sorry. I can't give up the practice, and I certainly can't bring the children to London.'

'Well – ' he hesitated – 'suppose I moved to Sussex. Became a commuting man. God help me. Surely that would convince you, a sacrifice like that?' He heard her hesitation, pounced. 'That'd be all right, wouldn't it? You could still carry on looking after all those dreadful people. The children would like it. Bertie and William could have ponies. Bertie's dying to ride, we were talking about it the other day. I said I'd teach him to jump, take him hunting. We're great friends, you know, he and I, he's never got over the fact that it was me who thought of where he might be when he ran away.'

'Yes, I know you're friends,' she said.

'Well, then?'

She was silent; he sat watching her. She could feel him watching her. It was tempting, the thought of him being in Sussex. It might work. And she wanted it so much, to marry him, to be with him. But something still frightened her, held her back. And she knew what it was …

'What is it?' he said. 'I still don't understand why you won't give in, Cassia. What more can I do? I've— Yes, what is it?'

The waiter had appeared beside them. 'Coffee, Mr Moreton, sir? And any brandy, liqueurs?'

'Yes, coffee. And brandy. Cassia?'

She shook her head. The waiter went away.

'Right. How would that be? I can't tell you how the proposition horrifies me, but I'd do it. For you.'

She said nothing.

'Jesus. All right, then, how about this? I'll put some money into that bloody charity of yours. You can have a poorhouse in every town if you want to—'

'Don't call them poorhouses. And don't disparage it, Harry, my trust, it's so important to me, a way of putting the money to really proper use, you know that.'

'Sorry. I'm sorry. But surely you're impressed by the offer?'

'No, I'm not,' she said, her voice loud with desperation, 'I'm not, and that's exactly it: it's mine, the trust, not yours, you don't understand.'

'But I'm trying,' he said, 'I'm trying, for Christ's sake.' There was a silence, then he sat back in his chair and looked at her very seriously. 'You're making me very unhappy, you know,' he said. He looked unhappy: unhappy and very tired.

Go on, Cassia, tell him you'll change the situation, tell him you'll give up the practice, or at least some of it, tell him you'll marry him. But she wouldn't, couldn't; she actually opened her mouth to begin and then saw him again in the garden at the Mamounia, smiling complacently, telling her how he and Leonora had planned things for her, and the old rage and resentment rose in her and she sat silent, looking down at the table. It was too impossible to explain to him. She was still angry with him when she thought about it all dispassionately, thought about him plotting, playing with her life. And somehow, whatever he said, whatever he promised, she couldn't quite believe he'd changed.

'You can't believe I've changed, can you?' he said.

'No, Harry. I can't. I'm sorry.'

'Or that I'm trying to change?'

She was silent again, staring at him.

He sighed. 'I don't know that there is any future for us after all, you know,' he said suddenly. 'I can't wait for ever, Cassia, waiting for some revelation to strike you on your own tortuous road to Damascus. I've done as much as I can. I truly believe that.'

She sat there, panic suddenly hitting her, but still she didn't speak. She couldn't. She didn't dare.

'Suppose ...' he said suddenly, looking up at her. 'Suppose ... yes? What is it?'

The waiter had appeared again; he looked nervous. 'Mr Moreton, I'm so very sorry, but—'

'Yes. What is it, for God's sake? Is the place on fire or something?'

'Mr Moreton, owing to the enormous demand this evening – all the Americans, you know – we have only ...' He finally brought the words out rather slowly: 'We have none of your favourite brand of coffee. Tonight. I'm so sorry, Mr Moreton.'

Harry looked at him, an expression of absolute incredulity on his face. God, thought Cassia, now there's going to be a scene. One of the famous Moreton scenes that had taken place in virtually every restaurant in London. She smiled reassuringly up at the waiter, could see the *maître d'* hovering in the background, clearly *au fait* with the situation, clearly ready to move in if necessary. And then heard the words, the absolutely extraordinary words:

'I don't give a toss about the coffee,' said Harry Moreton. 'You can bring me coffee essence for all I care. I'm trying to have an important conversation here, and I most certainly don't want to be bothered about which bloody coffee I'm going to drink.'

'Yes, Mr Moreton. Sorry, Mr Moreton. Thank you.' He hurried away.

Cassia sat looking at Harry for a while in silence, and he looked back at her, scowling. Finally she smiled at him. He smiled rather uncertainly back.

'What did I say?' he said.

'Something very important,' she said, 'very important indeed.' Then she leaned across the table, took his face in her hands and kissed him on the mouth.

'I think perhaps I could work part-time, after all,' she said finally, 'and a house in Sussex would be simply lovely. Now let's go home to bed, shall we?'